OXFORD WORLD'S CLASSICS

THE ILIAD

THE ILIAD has its roots in an ancient tradition of oral poetry, which flourished in the 8th and 7th centuries BC. Nothing certain is known about Homer, who was depicted by the Greeks as a blind beggar and divine singer; they considered him to be the greatest poet that ever lived. To him are credited two astonishing works of genius, the *Iliad* and the *Odyssey*.

ANTHONY VERITY was Master of Dulwich College before his retirement. His previous translations include Theocritus, *The Idylls* (2002) and Pindar, *The Complete Odes* (2007).

BARBARA GRAZIOSI is Professor of Classics at Durham University. Her research focuses on ancient Greek literature and its readers—both ancient and modern. Her books include *Inventing Homer* (2002) and *Homer: The Resonance of Epic* (2005).

OXFORD WORLD'S CLASSICS

*For over 100 years Oxford World's Classics have brought
readers closer to the world's great literature. Now with over 700
titles—from the 4,000-year-old myths of Mesopotamia to the
twentieth century's greatest novels—the series makes available
lesser-known as well as celebrated writing.*

*The pocket-sized hardbacks of the early years contained
introductions by Virginia Woolf, T. S. Eliot, Graham Greene,
and other literary figures which enriched the experience of reading.
Today the series is recognized for its fine scholarship and
reliability in texts that span world literature, drama and poetry,
religion, philosophy, and politics. Each edition includes perceptive
commentary and essential background information to meet the
changing needs of readers.*

OXFORD WORLD'S CLASSICS

——

HOMER

The Iliad

——

Translated by
ANTHONY VERITY

With an Introduction and Notes by
BARBARA GRAZIOSI

OXFORD
UNIVERSITY PRESS

OXFORD
UNIVERSITY PRESS

Great Clarendon Street, Oxford OX2 6DP
United Kingdom

Oxford University Press is a department of the University of Oxford.
It furthers the University's objective of excellence in research, scholarship,
and education by publishing worldwide. Oxford is a registered trade mark of
Oxford University Press in the UK and in certain other countries

First published 2011
First published as an Oxford World's Classics paperback 2012
Impression:15

British Library Cataloguing in Publication Data

Data available

Library of Congress Cataloguing in Publication Data

Data available

ISBN 978–0–19–964521–3

**Printed in Great Britain by
Clays Ltd, Elcograf S.p.A.**

CONTENTS

Introduction   vii

Note on the Text and Explanatory Materials   xxvii

Note on the Translation   xxix

Select Bibliography   xxx

Maps   xxxiii

THE ILIAD

BOOK ONE	3
BOOK TWO	19
BOOK THREE	42
BOOK FOUR	54
BOOK FIVE	68
BOOK SIX	91
BOOK SEVEN	105
BOOK EIGHT	118
BOOK NINE	133
BOOK TEN	151
BOOK ELEVEN	166
BOOK TWELVE	188
BOOK THIRTEEN	200
BOOK FOURTEEN	222
BOOK FIFTEEN	236
BOOK SIXTEEN	255
BOOK SEVENTEEN	277

BOOK EIGHTEEN 297

BOOK NINETEEN 313

BOOK TWENTY 324

BOOK TWENTY-ONE 337

BOOK TWENTY-TWO 353

BOOK TWENTY-THREE 366

BOOK TWENTY-FOUR 389

Explanatory Notes 410

Index of Personal Names 451

INTRODUCTION

VIVID, painful, and direct, the *Iliad* is one of the most influential poems of all time. It has continuously featured in the school curriculum for two-and-a-half millennia; and, even before then, audiences regularly heard it performed at public festivals and in private houses. The success of the *Iliad* is astonishing, particularly because this poem is neither easy nor pleasant. Already in antiquity, listeners struggled to understand its language, and sometimes fell asleep during performances. And yet the difficulties posed by the diction and sheer length of the poem are insignificant when compared to the demands that the *Iliad* makes on our hearts and minds. This poem confronts, with unflinching clarity, many issues that we had rather forget altogether: the failures of leadership, the destructive power of beauty, the brutalizing impact of war, and—above all—our ultimate fate of death. That the *Iliad* has been so widely heard and read is not just a testament to its immense power. It also speaks of the commitment of its many readers, who have turned to it in order to understand something about their own life, death, and humanity.

The composition of Homeric epic

It is not at all clear when or how the *Iliad* was composed, or what purpose it might have served. If no literature from ancient Greece survived, we certainly would not expect it to start with a monumental poem about the anger of Achilles. We would rather assume that it began with shorter compositions destined for specific occasions (for example, wedding songs and funeral laments), and answering practical purposes such as courtship, party entertainment, and martial exhortation. We know that those kinds of compositions did exist, and indeed the *Iliad* makes reference to them. What it does not do is explain its own existence. Scholars have ferociously debated the origins of the *Iliad*, partly because the poem reveals so little about them. At a very general level, the poem shows awareness of material circumstances not found before the later eighth or early seventh century BCE, such as temples and cult statues, narrative art, and knowledge of the world extending from Thrace to Phoenicia and Egypt. This gives a *terminus post quem*: the poem cannot have been composed much before 700 BCE.

Some historians argue that the rapidly changing social and political circumstances of the early seventh century demanded an intense exploration of authority, and that the *Iliad* answers to that need. Even a brief summary of the plot shows that the poem is indeed much concerned with how authority is established, questioned, and maintained. It opens with a startling invocation to the Muse:

> Sing, goddess, the anger of Achilles, Peleus' son,
> the accursed anger which brought the Achaeans countless
>   agonies...

Achilles' anger inflicts countless agonies not on the enemy, the Trojans—but on his own side, the Greeks, or rather 'Achaeans' as Homer calls them.[1] The reason for his anger is quickly explained. The narrative is set sometime towards the end of the Trojan War, and starts with the arrival of a priest of Apollo at the Achaean camp: he has come to ransom his daughter Chryseïs, who was captured by the Achaeans in a raid, and assigned to Agamemnon as a slave. Agamemnon refuses to release her, claiming that he finds her more enjoyable than his own wife, and threatens her father. Outraged by Agamemnon's behaviour, Apollo sends a plague that devastates the Achaean army. Eventually, Agamemnon agrees to release Chryseïs to appease the god, but demands recompense for his loss—in the form of Achilles' own slave Briseïs. Achilles is so angry at this demand that he comes close to killing Agamemnon, though Athena restrains him, and he decides to withdraw from the war instead. The poem shows how, without him, the Achaeans suffer heavy losses on the battlefield, and the Trojans come close to burning their ships. In the face of imminent defeat, Agamemnon offers to return Briseïs and to add many more gifts besides, but Achilles rejects an embassy detailing Agamemnon's offers. It is only after the death of his closest friend Patroclus that Achilles returns to the fighting. He is determined to avenge him by killing Hector, best of the Trojans. His mother Thetis warns him that he will die soon after Hector, but Achilles returns to the battlefield regardless. He kills Hector, lashes his body to his chariot, and drags it to his hut. The poem ends when Priam, Hector's father, arrives at the

---

[1] The Achaean army is made from contingents from the whole of Greece, but is never called 'Greek' in the poem. That word has a much more specific application in Homeric epic: it describes people coming from Hellas, in northern Greece (see Map 1). When describing the whole army, Homer uses three different collective names: Achaeans, Danaans, or Argives.

Achaean camp and offers ransom to Achilles in return for Hector's body. Achilles is reminded of his own father, another old man who will never see his son again. He sends Priam back with Hector's body, and the women lead the funeral laments for him. As the last line in the poem says,

So they conducted the funeral rites for Hector, breaker of horses.

Clearly, the *Iliad* is deeply concerned with leaders and their people. The countless agonies of the Achaeans are told in painful detail: they die when Agamemnon offends the priest and Apollo sends the plague—and they die again when Achilles quarrels with Agamemnon and withdraws from the fighting. The Trojans die too, even more copiously. Hector's death is the most affecting in the whole poem, partly because its consequences for his wife, his baby son, and the entire Trojan community are made very clear. The death of Hector symbolizes the fall of the city itself. Historians point out that, in the palatial culture of the late Bronze Age, authority was diffuse, and that this might have inspired stories like the *Iliad*; they also argue that the rapid social and political changes of the seventh century—when we can trace expanding communities, new settlements, increased trade and travel—provide an appropriate context for a poetic exploration of authority.[2] This seems right, but the issues explored in the *Iliad* remain interesting and relevant in later times too. The common soldier Thersites is ridiculed and humiliated in the assembly; commander-in-chief Agamemnon is exposed, in the narrative, as authoritarian and weak; Achilles, in the extremity of his behaviour, seems inhuman even to the gods; and Hector, by his own admission, fails his people. Depending on how we read these characters, we can attach different political meanings to the *Iliad*. The main point is that no interpretation leads to a single original audience, or to a specific political agenda in support of which the poem must have been composed. Flawed leaders like Agamemnon are always interesting; and critics of authority, like Achilles and Thersites, are never entirely comfortable. The *Iliad* tells a story of universal appeal. This is something that the ancient Greeks themselves articulated in their earliest responses to the poem. The philosopher Xenophanes, writing in the sixth century BCE, described Homer as a universal teacher since time immemorial.[3]

    [2] For a good summary, see R. Osborne, 'Homer's Society', in R. Fowler (ed.), *The Cambridge Companion to Homer* (Cambridge, 2004), 206–19.
    [3] Fr. 10 in H. Diels and W. Kranz (eds.), *Die Fragmente der Vorsokratiker*, 3 vols., 6th edn. (Berlin, 1951–2).

However uncertain the exact context in which the *Iliad* was composed, it is clear that it was aimed at a broad and committed audience. The *Iliad* is more than 15,000 lines long, and it would have taken approximately three full days (or nights) to perform it in its entirety.[4] Performances of this kind must have required some infrastructure and organization—and we know that, from the sixth century onwards, they received institutional support. The Athenian tyrant Pisistratus, or one of his sons, decreed that the Homeric poems should be recited at the most important city festival, the Great Panathenaea.[5] Every four years, at a feast in honour of their patron goddess, the Athenians listened to the *Iliad*. We do not have as much information about Homeric performances in other cities, but we know they took place. Several sources describe professional epic reciters, known as 'rhapsodes', travelling from city to city and performing Homeric poetry at public festivals and private gatherings.[6] The earliest authors known to have discussed Homer come from opposite ends of the Greek-speaking world: Xenophanes came from Colophon in Asia Minor, and Theagenes, another early interpreter of Homer, came from Rhegium in southern Italy. The sixth-century poet Simonides of Ceos (an island in the Aegean Sea) explicitly praised and quoted Homer in his own poetry. The material record confirms the picture suggested by our written evidence: it preserves late archaic images inspired by the *Iliad* and originating from several different places.[7] All this evidence provides a *terminus ante quem* for the *Iliad*: by the late sixth century BCE the poem was well known.

Scholars continue to debate the exact date of the *Iliad*. Their disagreements stem, in part, from a difference in emphasis: some seek to pinpoint the original contribution of an early poet, others focus on the earliest documented context for Homeric recitation, which is the Panathenaea. Beyond these differences, all Homerists agree that sixth-century performances and texts must have captured something considerably older. An examination of the language and style of Homeric epic shows that it stems from a very long tradition of oral poetry. Homeric Greek is an artificial mixture of several different dialects.

---

[4] Many scholars have tried to reconstruct how the *Iliad* might have been performed, see e.g. O. Taplin, *Homeric Soundings: The Shaping of the 'Iliad'* (Oxford, 1995).

[5] See esp. [Plato], *Hipparchus* 228b and Lycurgus, *In Leocratem* 102.

[6] For a vivid, if rather hostile, portrait of a rhapsode, see Plato's *Ion*.

[7] The visual evidence for Iliadic scenes is collected in J. Burgess, *The Tradition of the Trojan War in Homer and the Epic Cycle* (Baltimore, 2001), 53–94.

It was never used by any real-life community, but rather developed, over several centuries, for the purpose of singing the deeds of gods and men.[8] The predominant dialect is Ionic, but there is also a strong Aeolic component. Linguists identify Euboean and Boeotian influences too, and point to several Attic elements, though many of these concern matters of spelling, and therefore testify to the influence of a written Athenian text, rather than to an early Attic contribution to epic diction. Compared to modern linguists, ancient Homeric scholars were even more wide-ranging in their characterization of Homeric diction: they claimed that Homer knew *all* the Greek dialects. This is an exaggeration that reflects, in part, the status of the *Iliad* as a poem that appealed to all the Greeks. It also captures the astounding linguistic richness and variety of Homeric epic: there are very many ways to say 'he was' or 'to be', for example. Some Homeric expressions and forms seem relatively recent, and some are very old: there may even be remnants of Mycenaean Greek, a language that was spoken in the second millennium BCE. At times, it seems that even the poet of the *Iliad* is unsure about the exact meaning of some of the inherited expressions he uses. They sound grand and heroic but—for the sake of clarity—he adds possible synonyms and etymologizing explanations inside the poem. These internal explanations are, of course, lost in translation: reading the *Iliad* in the original Greek gives a much better sense of the historic depth and richness of its language. References to material objects, in the poem, offer a good analogy for the effect of Homeric words: many artefacts fit a late eighth- or early seventh-century context, but some are much older. At 10.261–5, for example, Homer describes a boar's-tusk helmet that fell out of use after the fifteenth century BCE. Linguistic and archaeological evidence shows that the epic tradition developed in the course of many centuries, and went through very different linguistic environments, social contexts, and material cultures.

One of the most striking features of Homeric epic, and the tradition from which it stems, is its repetitiveness. Achilles is called 'swift-footed' again and again and again—even when he sulks, motionless, in his hut. Hector is 'Hector of the glittering helmet'. After a meal, Homeric characters always 'put away the desire for eating and drinking'. At daybreak, 'early-born Dawn with her rosy fingers appears'. Comparative studies have established that such repeated phrases,

[8] On Homeric Greek, see further G. Horrocks, 'Homer's Dialect', in I. Morris and B. Powell (eds.), *A New Companion to Homer* (Leiden, 1997), 193–217.

or 'formulae', help bards compose poetry in real time, as they perform in front of an audience. In the 1930s two American scholars—Milman Parry and Albert Lord—travelled to what was then Yugoslavia, and recorded the performances of illiterate Bosnian singers in local coffee-houses.[9] They showed that these singers were able to recite poems as long as the *Iliad*—not by remembering a fixed script, but by combining formulaic expressions, and by arranging them into well-established narrative patterns or 'themes'. Formulae and themes were, to a large extent, inherited: they had developed over generations, in order to enable singers to compose, or re-compose, their poems in the course of live performances. The singer had at his disposal a stock of different formulae that described the same character, situation, thing, or action, each of which had a specific metrical shape. He could choose the appropriate formula depending on how many beats he needed in order to reach the end of the line. Parry showed that, in Homeric epic, there is usually just one formula describing a particular character or action in any given number of beats. This formulaic economy enables singers to get to the end of the line, without having to take too long thinking about different options for describing an action or character. For example, depending on how many beats he needs to get to the end of the line, the poet can say 'Achilles', or 'glorious Achilles', or 'swift-footed Achilles', or 'swift-footed glorious Achilles'. Parry and Lord made a tremendous contribution to our understanding of Homeric epic, but their work also posed new problems and questions.

One problem concerns the meaning and interpretation of Homeric formulae. Parry himself reached rather discouraging conclusions on that issue: he argued that some traditional formulae have little meaning, that audiences feel indifferent towards them, and that they are perhaps best left untranslated. This sort of conclusion does not seem entirely satisfactory: formulaic expressions are not equivalent to an instrumental interlude, or a bit of humming, or some other wordless rhythmical 'filling' that enables singers to keep the performance going. They are words, and affect audiences through their meaning, as well as through their rhythmical qualities. It is true that formulae are not always sensitive to context, but that can in itself become a poetic resource. For example, 'swift-footed' Achilles refuses to leave his hut

---

[9] See M. Parry, *The Making of Homeric Verse: The Collected Papers of Milman Parry* (Oxford, 1991), and A. Lord, *The Singer of Tales*, 2nd rev. edn. (Cambridge, Mass., 2000).

for most of the *Iliad*: this tension between his traditional description and what he actually does draws attention to his problematic behaviour. Most of the time, traditional expressions unobtrusively shape the narrative, but sometimes the poet brings them into sharp focus. At 6.467–70, for example, baby Astyanax realizes that his father is indeed 'Hector of the gleaming helmet': he looks at the terrifying thing on top of his father's head, and screams. There is often a dynamic, expressive tension between the traditional formulations used by the poet, and the specific situations he describes. Formulae fasten characters and things to specific qualities, but the poet tells a far less stable story. Leaders, for example, are called 'shepherds of the people', but in the *Iliad* the people perish, inexorably.[10] It seems then that the tools of oral poetry, far from being a convenient but stilted aid to composition, enable the poet to tell his story powerfully and idiomatically.[11]

The second problem raised by the comparative study of oral poetry is that the *Iliad* is not, actually, an oral poem: what we have is a written text. Scholars have long debated the possible role of writing in the composition of Homeric epic; the German philologist Friedrich August Wolf famously tackled the issue in his *Prolegomena ad Homerum* (1795), a work that inaugurated modern classical scholarship. The earliest examples of Greek alphabetic writing date to the second half of the eighth century BCE. The most interesting piece of evidence, for Homerists, is a modest clay cup found in Ischia, an island off the coast of Naples. It bears an inscription which proudly announces in verse: 'I am the cup of Nestor . . .' There is no physical resemblance between this modest vessel and the gold cup of Nestor in the *Iliad*, but the inscription may well be a playful reference to some poem about the legendary Nestor and his cup. Some have argued that the extremely regular layout of the verse inscription may reflect the influence of epic texts written on papyrus or leather, though such texts (if they existed) need not have been our *Iliad*. It seems, then, that the *Iliad* harnesses the resources of a rich and ancient tradition of oral poetry, but also comes into existence at a time when writing was beginning to develop. Quite what influence this new technique had on the composition and

[10] See further J. Haubold, *Homer's People: Epic Poetry and Social Formation* (Cambridge, 2000).

[11] J. M. Foley makes this point very persuasively in *Homer's Traditional Art* (University Park, Pa., 1999); see further B. Graziosi and J. Haubold, *Homer: The Resonance of Epic* (London, 2005), and A. Kelly, *A Referential Commentary and Lexicon to Homer, 'Iliad VIII'* (Oxford, 2007).

preservation of the poem is something we will never know for sure. As Albio Cassio points out, in a balanced and judicious assessment of the evidence, our *Iliad* is 'likely to be the result of extremely complicated processes involving both orality and writing, which we can no longer reconstruct'.[12]

Our own interest in writing may ultimately lead to wrong assumptions about its role and importance in early Greece. In the *Iliad*, writing (or something close to it) is depicted as a nasty business: at 6.168–70 Proetus sends Bellerophon into exile, giving him a folded tablet in which he has inscribed the order to kill the bearer of the message. This is the only reference to writing in the whole poem: there is no hint, in Homeric epic, that writing may be used to record great deeds, or help singers compose their songs. This may simply be because the Homeric poems are set in a distant, heroic past, where writing did not yet exist or was just being invented by resourceful crooks like Proetus. The actual context of composition of the *Iliad* may have been quite different from the situation depicted inside the poem. What remains true beyond all speculation, however, is that the poet of the *Iliad* describes his own work in terms of singing, and expects future generations to hear about what happened at Troy by listening.

The poet's voice

From antiquity to the present, there has been much speculation about the author of the *Iliad*. The Greeks considered him the greatest poet that ever lived, but knew nothing certain about him: the earliest sources that mention his name are speculative and contradictory. They depict him as a blind beggar and a divine singer; someone who suffered many indignities in life, and composed the most beautiful poetry. These ancient portraits of Homer tell us something important about the early reception of epic, but say little about the actual composition of the *Iliad*.[13] In some ways, the situation today is rather similar: those who attempt to give a detailed portrait of Homer often reveal more about themselves than about Homeric epic. Albert Lord, for example, imagined Homer as an illiterate singer dictating his poems to a scribe. As many have noted, this Homer closely resembles a Bosnian singer

---

[12] A. Cassio, 'Early Editions of the Greek Epics and Homeric Textual Criticism', in F. Montanari (ed.), *Omero tremila anni dopo* (Rome, 2002), 114.

[13] See B. Graziosi, *Inventing Homer: The Early Reception of Epic* (Cambridge, 2002).

performing for Lord himself. Lord wrote under dictation, and also used audio recording. The situation in early Greece was different: writing was infrequent, slow, and expensive. We therefore do not know to what degree the circumstances of Bosnian singers and American scholars in the 1930s offer a fitting parallel for those in which the *Iliad* was actually composed and written down.

Rather than looking for the poet *of* the *Iliad*, then, it seems more fruitful to look for the poet *in* the *Iliad*, and listen to his voice. In the opening invocation to the Muse, the poet confidently asks the goddess to sing about the anger of Achilles, from the time when he quarrelled with Agamemnon. After the proem, the story begins precisely with the quarrel: from that moment onwards, the voice of the poet and that of the Muse blend together. It is only when the poet approaches a particularly difficult or important topic that he again puts some distance between himself and the goddess, and asks for help. This happens, for example, at the beginning of the Catalogue of Ships (2.484–93):

> Tell me now, Muses who have your homes on Olympus—
> for you are goddesses, and are present, and know everything,
> while we hear only rumour, and know nothing—
> who were the commanders and princes of the Danaans.
> As for the soldiery, I could not describe or name them,
> not even if I had ten tongues and ten mouths,
> an indestructible voice, and a bronze heart within me,
> unless the Muses of Olympus, daughters of aegis-wearing
> Zeus, were to recount all those who came to besiege Ilium.
> So I shall relate the ships' captains and the number of their ships.

The Muses alone 'are present, and know everything'. Without their help, the poet is in the same position as his audience: 'we hear only rumour, and know nothing.' This is a declaration of dependence, and a plea for knowledge. The Muses are close to the poet, and they help him perform his song. But they are also 'present' in a different sense: they know everything with the reliability of an eyewitness. The poet himself has no sure knowledge about those who fought at Troy, because—as he repeatedly points out—they lived long before him, and were far superior to 'men as mortals now are'. It is only with the help of the Muses that he can give a precise account of what happened at Troy, 'as if he had been there himself'.[14]

---

[14] These are the words Odysseus uses when complimenting the blind singer Demodocus on the accuracy of his song about Troy (*Odyssey* 8.489–91): 'You sing the

Many details in the narrative speak of the poet's direct access to his subject matter. For example, he occasionally addresses his own characters.[15] These apostrophes are so startling, that ancient and modern readers have thought they betray something about the poet—a special affection for some of his characters, for example. Not all direct addresses seem to express affection, but they all add to the immediacy of the story. The poet is, at times, so close to his characters that he even talks to them. By contrast, he never addresses his real audience. He never asks for attention, for example, or flatters his listeners. Rather than talking to or about his audience, the poet gives them a direct insight into what happened during the Trojan War.

In general, the *Iliad* conveys a clear sense of the poet's presence at Troy, and even of the specific vantage-point from which he observes the action: he views the battlefield from above, facing Troy and keeping his back to the sea. The curved coastline, with its beached Achaean ships, is arranged before him 'like a theatre'.[16] When he describes what happens 'on the left' or 'on the right' of the battlefield, he is always speaking from that specific viewpoint. He is, however, not confined to observing things from there: he can zoom in and describe, for example, how Polypoetes' spear breaks through Damasus' forehead, and makes pulp of the brain inside (12.181–7). He can observe at close quarters how a pair of horses trip over a branch, breaking free of their chariot— and then zoom out in order to show how the horses join a chaotic, general stampede towards Troy (6.38–41). Contemporary readers often comment on the cinematic qualities of Homer's poetry;[17] but there were no helicopters in antiquity from which to take aerial shots, and no cameras zooming in or out. For the ancient Greeks, Homer's powers were truly divine: they called him *theios aoidos*, 'the divine singer', and with good reason. Apart from the poet, only the gods could view things from above, or observe the fighting at close quarters, objectively, and without fear of death. The poet himself makes that point at 4.539–44, where he claims that someone who entered the battlefield under divine

fate of the Achaeans precisely, according to order; | what they did and endured and all they suffered, | as if you had been there yourself, or heard from someone who had.'

[15] See e.g. 7.104 (Menelaus), 15.582 (Melanippus), 16.787 (Patroclus), 20.2 (Achilles), 20.152 (Apollo).

[16] This is the description of the ancient Homeric scholar Aristarchus, see Explanatory Notes, note to lines 14.30–6.

[17] On Homer and the cinema, see esp. M. M. Winkler (ed.), *Troy: from Homer's 'Iliad' to Hollywood Epic* (Oxford, 2007).

protection, and could not be touched by missiles, would agree with his own assessment of how hard Trojans and Achaeans fought.

Divine inspiration, then, is not just a matter of conventional invocations to the Muses: it tells us something crucial about how the poet views things. The Catalogue of Ships, for example, is a dazzling display of the poet's knowledge, and of his powers of visualization. He starts in Aulis and spirals out, mentioning well over a hundred place-names, and organizing them in a way that shows he has a clear mental picture of the whole of Greece.[18] The poet's encyclopaedic command of his subject matter emerges from many other details. For example, he always mentions by name those who die on the battlefield, and often adds a unique detail about them: Protesilaus leaves behind a wife 'tearing her cheeks in grief | in a half-built house' (2.700–1). Axylus used to live by a main road, 'and he would entertain everyone' (6.13). These details suggest that the poet knows more about his characters than he chooses to tell. We would long to hear more about them: we perceive our loss—precisely at the moment when they die.[19]

The many similes that punctuate the narrative also tell us something important about the poet's knowledge. Some images occur in many variations and evoke the grandness of the epic world: lions and hunters, for example, feature prominently not just in the *Iliad*, but also more generally in early Greek and Near Eastern art and poetry. Other similes are more specific, and suggest a keen sense of observation. At 5.902–4, for example, Ares' blood coagulates as quickly 'as when fig-juice thickens white milk when . . . a man stirs it'. At 17.389–97 the Trojans and the Achaeans pull Patroclus' body in opposite directions, like leather-tanners stretching a skin. At 23.712–13 the Achaeans grasp each other's hands 'like crossing rafters that a renowned carpenter has | fitted in the roof of a high house'. At 23.760–3 Odysseus runs behind Ajax

> . . . as close as the weaving-rod of a fine-girdled
> woman is to her breast as she deftly draws it tight with her hands,
> pulling the spool along the warp, and holding it close to her
>   breast . . .

[18] See Explanatory Notes, note to line 2.493, which is based on G. Danek, 'Der Schiffskatalog der Ilias: Form und Funktion', in H. Heftner and K. Tomaschitz (eds.), *Ad Fontes! Festschrift für Gerhard Dobesch* (Vienna, 2004), 59–72.

[19] On minor characters in the *Iliad*, see further the excellent study by J. Griffin, *Homer on Life and Death* (Oxford, 1980), esp. ch. 4.

In this simile, in particular, there is a palpable sense that the woman is being observed as she works. She is intent on her weaving, and we can imagine someone looking at her—and noticing how close she pulls the weaving-rod to her breast. Just so, in the poet's vision, Odysseus pulls close to Ajax in the foot-race.

Often the poet of the *Iliad* describes things from the perspective of an implicit observer: narratologists call this technique 'focalization'. At times the same scene is focalized through different characters in close succession. At 6.401, for example, when Hector looks at his baby son Astyanax, the poet adopts the language of a doting parent, piling on words of endearment for the little boy. Only a little later, however, when it is Astyanax who looks at his father, the poet shares the bewildered, terrified perspective of the baby boy (6.468–70). Although the poet has great powers of empathy—even for characters so young they cannot speak—he never loses his overall control of the narrative. He always knows, for example, what the gods are doing and, even more importantly, what they are planning. The characters, by contrast, have a very limited understanding of the gods, and are often deluded about their own circumstances. We see them struggle, in their ignorance, with their hopes and fears—while the poet tells us exactly what is in store for them.

There is only one character in the poem who seems able to look at the situation with the same clarity and detachment as the poet: Helen, daughter of Zeus. This is how Homer first introduces the beautiful woman who caused the Trojan War. While her two husbands, Menelaus and Paris, prepare to face each other in single combat, the goddess Iris goes to look for her (3.125–8):

> She found Helen in her hall; she was weaving a great web,
> a red double cloak, and on it she was working the struggles
> of the horse-breaking Trojans and the bronze-shirted Achaeans
> that they were undergoing for her sake at the hands of Ares.

Like the poet, Helen weaves a picture of the Trojan War. She even sees herself as the subject of future poetry (6.357–8):

> Zeus has given us a wretched portion, so that in time hereafter
> we may become a theme for the songs of generations yet to come.

And yet, not even Helen shares the poet's full and objective knowledge of all things. At 3.234–42, for example, she scans the battlefield looking for her brothers among the Achaean troops, and wonders why she cannot see them. At that point the poet tells us that they died in Lacedaemon, before the Trojan War had even started.

The poet often draws attention to the ignorance of his own characters. Most famously, he describes Andromache making arrangements for Hector to have a bath, when he is already dead (22.440–6):

> She was at her loom in the tall house's innermost part, weaving
> a red double cloak, and working a pattern of flowers into it.
> She called out through the house to her lovely-haired servants
> to set a great tripod over the fire, so that Hector might have
> a warm bath when he returned from the fighting—poor
> innocent that she was, and did not know that grey-eyed Athena
> had beaten him down at Achilles' hands, far away from baths.

Even when the poet does not offer explicit comments of this kind, it is clear that he and his audience share an understanding that the characters inside the poem do not have. This understanding stems, in part, from a shared knowledge of the epic tradition: audiences of all times always knew that Troy was destined to fall, and that the Achaeans would suffer greatly on their return home.

The main effect of our knowledge, and of the characters' lack of it, is a sense of tragic irony—a realization that mortals have no sure understanding of the gods, or even of their own situation. For once, when listening to the poet, we share his divine perspective—but the spectacle is not simply entertaining, because the pain, suffering, and uncertainty of Homer's characters are ultimately our own.

Achilles' anger

The very first line of the *Iliad* announces a grand poem about a very specific issue: the anger of Achilles. The poem describes only a handful of days towards the end of the Trojan War: it does not include the fall of Troy, or even the death of Achilles. By leaving those events outside the remit of his narrative, the poet invites us to focus on his chosen theme. The first word in the original Greek text is *mēnin*, a rare term for anger which describes the vengeful wrath typical of the gods. Soon after the proem, the same word occurs again: at 1.75 it describes Apollo's angry reaction to Agamemnon's insults, and his decision to inflict a plague on the Achaeans. This verbal correspondence underlines a more general truth: at the beginning of the poem Achilles behaves very much like a god.[20] When Agamemnon insults him, he plans the extermination of the Achaeans. His asks his mother, the goddess Thetis, to enlist the help of Zeus, and the supreme god agrees to his plan: the Achaeans will perish as long as Achilles refuses to fight. No ordinary mortal could react to Agamemnon's arrogance by sending a personal envoy to Mount Olympus—but Achilles is the son of a goddess, and behaves accordingly. The problem is that Achilles is mortal: the fact that he must die complicates his relationship to Agamemnon, and ultimately compromises his plan.

When Agamemnon realizes that without Achilles he will lose his army, his honour, and the war, he offers to return Briseïs, together with countless other gifts. The women, cities, tripods, and other goods that Agamemnon promises to Achilles in book 9 betoken a transferral of honour on a quite unprecedented scale. And yet, Achilles refuses Agamemnon's offer, pointing out that no amount of wealth can compensate for the loss of his life (9.400–9):

> ... I do not think
> that anything is of equal worth to my life, not even all the wealth
> they say that Ilium, that well-populated city, once possessed
> in time of peace before the sons of the Achaeans came,
> nor all the wealth that the stone threshold of the archer
> Phoebus Apollo guards inside his temple in rocky Pytho.
> Cattle and flocks of sturdy sheep can be got by raiding, and
> tripods and herds of chestnut horses can be made one's own,
> but raiding and getting cannot bring back a man's life
> when once it has passed beyond the barrier of his teeth.

The god Apollo may be content with guarding his riches 'in rocky Pytho' (a rare reference to his sanctuary at Delphi); but the mortal Achilles must guard something far more precious to him: his life.

As the poem unfolds, Achilles' mortality is thrown into sharp relief, and it becomes increasingly clear that his fate is bound to that of other mortals. Already in book 11, soon after he has rejected Agamemnon's offer, Achilles notices the wounded Achaean leaders as they return to camp, and sends Patroclus to make enquiries. His friend returns with terrible news, and asks Achilles to let him, at least, return to the battlefield and lend his support. Achilles is worried about Patroclus' safety but agrees to his request, and gives him his own armour for protection.

---

[20] On Achilles and Apollo, see esp. G. Nagy, *The Best of the Achaeans: Concepts of the Hero in Archaic Greek Poetry*, 2nd edn. (Baltimore, 1999).

Soon after, Hector kills Patroclus and takes Achilles' armour as spoils. At that point Achilles enters the battlefield again, not because his attitude to Agamemnon has changed (several details in the narrative suggest that it has not), but because revenge now matters to him more than life itself. According to Apollo, Achilles' reaction to the death of Patroclus is excessive and inexcusable. This is what he says to the other gods at 24.44–54:

> '. . . Achilles has killed pity, and there is no respect in him,
> respect that both greatly harms and also benefits men.
> Any man, I suppose, is likely to have lost someone even dearer
> to him than this, a brother born of the same mother, or even a son,
> but in the end he gives up his weeping and lamentation,
> because the Fates have placed in men a heart that endures; but
> this Achilles first robs glorious Hector of his life and then ties him
> behind his chariot and drags him round the burial-mound of his
> dear companion. Yet he should know that there is nothing fine
> or good about this; let him beware of our anger, great man
> though he is, because in his fury he is outraging mute earth.'

In Apollo's view, Achilles must stop defiling Hector's body, and start to consider his pain in relation to that of other mortals. It may be that his suffering is not as great as that of a man who loses a brother, or a son. Later in book 24 Achilles comes precisely to that realization—when he sees Priam, and thinks about the imminent bereavement of his own father.

All this suggests that Achilles may not be so special after all. His anger is as devastating as that of the gods, but his confrontation with death is something we all recognize. There are, in fact, many parallels for the story of Achilles—some are embedded in the poem itself, and others belong to broader ancient traditions of poetry. For example, Phoenix tries to persuade Achilles to accept Agamemnon's gifts by telling him the story of Meleager—who refused to go to war out of anger, but who ultimately returned to the fighting in order to defend his wife and home (9.529–99). Here too a young man initially opts out, rejecting the social obligations placed upon him, but eventually must recognize the bonds of affection that link him to others, and which ultimately lead him to face death. Quite how hard Phoenix presses the details of Meleager's story in order to turn it into a fitting example for Achilles is something that scholars have long debated. What remains clear is that, just like Phoenix, the poet himself invites us to see the story of Achilles as an example of a wider truth. In the early Greek tradition other narratives echoed that of Achilles. For example, the early epic poem *Aethiopis*, now largely lost, told the story of Memnon, king of the Ethiopians. Memnon too was the son of a goddess, Dawn, and of a mortal man, Tithonus—and he too had to die. These echoes suggest that the story of Achilles' anger, though specific in the detail, has its roots in a wider ancient understanding of what it means to be mortal. This emerges with special clarity when we compare the *Iliad* with the *Epic of Gilgamesh*.

This extraordinary Babylonian poem resembles the *Iliad* not just in some striking details, but in overall conception.[21] Like Achilles, Gilgamesh is of mixed human and divine ancestry, and the greatest man that ever lived. When his closest friend Enkidu dies, he resolves to go in search of eternal life. He undertakes a long and difficult journey to meet Utnapishtim, the survivor of a great flood and the only man who has been granted immortality. In the Old Babylonian version of the poem he meets a wise ale-wife in the course of his journey, who tells him:

> 'You will not find the eternal life you seek.
> When the gods created mankind,
> they appointed death for mankind,
> kept eternal life in their own hands.
> So, Gilgamesh, let your stomach be full,
> day and night enjoy yourself in every way,
> every day arrange for pleasures.
> Day and night, dance and play,
> wear fresh clothes.
> Keep your head washed, bathe in water,
> appreciate the child who holds your hand,
> let your wife enjoy herself in your lap.'[22]

In the extremity of his pain, Gilgamesh does nothing of the sort. Immediately after Enkidu's death he tears out his hair, casts off his fine clothes, and roams in the wilderness wearing an animal skin. He continues to travel until he finds Utnapishtim—and it is only at that

---

[21] On the parallels between Greek and Near Eastern Epic, see M. L. West, *The East Face of Helicon: West Asiatic Elements in Greek Poetry and Myth* (Oxford, 1997).

[22] Quoted from S. Dalley, *Myths from Mesopotamia: Creation, The Flood, Gilgamesh, and Others*, 2nd edn. (Oxford, 2000), 150. For the *Epic of Gilgamesh*, see A. R. George, *The Babylonian Gilgamesh Epic: Introduction, Critical Edition and Cuneiform Texts*, 2 vols. (Oxford, 2003).

point that he learns a fundamental lesson. In the Standard Babylonian version, Utnapishtim tells him that he will never find the secret of eternal life, and then sends him home with a fresh set of clothes.

Achilles' physical reaction to bereavement closely resembles that of Gilgamesh. When Patroclus dies, he defiles himself. He refuses to eat, and cannot sleep (24.1–10):

> ... the assembly broke up and the people dispersed, each
> company to its swift ships, and all their thoughts were of food
> and the pleasure of sweet sleep; but Achilles wept ceaselessly
> as he remembered his dear companion, and sleep that subdues
> all took no hold of him. He tossed and turned, thinking with
> longing of Patroclus, of his manhood and his valiant strength, of
> all that he had accomplished with him and the trials he had endured,
> of wars of men undergone and the arduous crossing of seas.
> As he called all this to mind he let fall huge tears,
> lying at one time on his side and at another on his back,
> and then again on his face; then he would rise to his feet ...

Achilles' mother suggests to him that he should sleep with Briseïs, in an argument that, in essence, is the same as that of the ale-wife in the Old Babylonian version of *Gilgamesh*. This is what Thetis says at 24.130–2:

> It is indeed a good thing to lie with a woman,
> since your life will not be long and I shall lose you,
> and already death and your harsh destiny stand beside you.

Achilles seems inconsolable, but eventually does follow his mother's advice and sleeps with Briseïs. When Priam enters his hut, he is eating. Priam, by contrast, is still feeling the rawest pain at the loss of Hector: he has just covered himself in dung—and has not eaten or slept since the death of his son. Eventually, Achilles persuades him to eat, drink, and sleep, telling him the story of Niobe—a mythical mother who lost her twelve children and yet managed (according to Achilles) to have a meal after that. Again it seems that Achilles adapts the details of Niobe's story in order to make his point; and yet what he is trying to say is a general truth about human life. That truth emerges clearly after Achilles and Priam have eaten together (24.628–32):

> when they had put from themselves the desire for food and drink
> then Priam of Dardanus' line looked in amazement at Achilles,
> seeing how huge and handsome he was, for he seemed like the gods;

> and Achilles too was amazed at Priam of the line of Dardanus,
> seeing his noble appearance and hearing him speak.

The poet even says that Achilles and Priam took 'pleasure from look-ing at each other' (24.633). After their defilement, hunger, thirst, and sheer exhaustion, these two men share a meal and, in the calm that follows, reach beyond their own personal suffering. Their pleasure is an affirmation of life in the face of death.

The Trojan War

The *Iliad* tells the story of Achilles' anger, but also encompasses, within its narrow focus, the whole of the Trojan War. The title promises 'a poem about Ilium' (i.e. Troy), and the poem lives up to that description. The first books recapitulate the origins and early stages of the Trojan War. The quarrel over Briseïs mirrors the original cause of the war, for it too is a fight between two men over one woman. The Catalogue of Ships in book 2 acts as a reminder of the expedition; book 3 introduces Helen and her two husbands; book 4 dramatizes how a private quarrel over a woman can become a war; in book 5 the fighting escalates; and book 6 takes us into the city of Troy. The narrative now looks forward to the time when the Achaeans will capture the city: it anticipates the end of the poem, and of the war itself. The bulk of the *Iliad* is devoted to the fighting on the battlefield. It describes only a few days of war, but the sheer scale of the narrative, and its relentless succession of deaths, come to represent the whole war.[23]

The poet is specific about the horrors of the battlefield: wounds, for example, are described in precise and painful detail. At 13.567–9 Meriones pursues Adamas and stabs him 'between the genitals and navel, in the place | where battle-death comes most painfully to wretched mortals'. At 15.489–500 Peneleos thrusts his spear through Ilioneus' eye-socket, then cuts off his head and brandishes it aloft. At 20.469–1 Tros tries to touch Achilles' knees in supplication, but Achilles stabs him

> . . . in the liver with his sword,
> and the liver slid out of his body, and the dark blood from it
> filled his lap . . .

---

[23] For a more detailed, book-by-book summary of the *Iliad*, see the Explanatory Notes.

No Hollywood version of the *Iliad* is as graphic as the poem itself. Descriptions of the physical impact of war are matched by an unflinching psychological account of those who fight in it. Homer shows exactly what it takes to step forward in the first line of battle, towards the spear of the enemy. He describes the adrenaline, the social conditioning, the self-delusion required.[24] And the shame of failure, which is worse than death.[25]

The truth and vividness of the *Iliad* have struck many readers. In her towering exploration of violence, Simone Weil, for example, calls the *Iliad* 'the most flawless of mirrors', because it shows how war 'makes the human being a thing quite literally, that is, a dead body. The *Iliad* never tires of showing that tableau.'[26] Weil was writing in 1939: her *L'Iliade ou le poème de la force* did not just describe the Trojan War; it anticipated the Second World War, and prophesied how it would again turn people into things. Just like Weil, women inside the *Iliad* make powerful statements against violence—and even against the courage of their own men. Hector's wife Andromache, for example, tells him that his own prowess will kill him, and that he will make her a widow (6.431–2). When confronted with his wife's words, Hector claims he would rather die on the battlefield than witness her suffering (6.464–5). He then tries to console her in the only way he knows: by imagining more wars. He picks up his baby son and prays that he may be stronger than him and, one day, bring home the spoils of the enemy, so that his mother may rejoice (6.476–81). This is how the poet Michael Longley, in the context of the Troubles in Northern Ireland, paraphrases Hector's prayer: he 'kissed the babbie and dandled him in his arms and | prayed that his son might grow up bloodier than him'.[27]

The Trojan War, the Second World War, the Troubles: the *Iliad* is intertwined with all stories about all wars. Already in antiquity it was part of a wider tradition of poetry, which found its inspiration in the ruins of a Bronze Age city, well visible on the coast of Asia Minor.[28]

[24] On these issues see, among others, M. Clarke, *Flesh and Spirit in the Songs of Homer* (Oxford, 1999), and R. Scodel, *Epic Facework: Self-Presentation and Social Interaction in Homer* (Swansea, 2008).

[25] See D. Cairns, *Aidōs: The Psychology and Ethics of Honour and Shame in Ancient Greek Literature* (Oxford, 1993).

[26] The best English edition is by J. P. Holoka, *Simone Weil's 'The Iliad or The Poem of Force': A Critical Edition* (New York, 2003).

[27] M. Longley, *The Ghost Orchid* (London, 1995), 226.

[28] On the site of Troy, see J. Latacz, *Troy and Homer: Towards a Solution of an Old Mystery*, trans. K. Windle and R. Ireland (Oxford, 2004).

The *Iliad* often refers to that wider tradition. For example, when Hector picks up his baby and dandles him in his arms, his gesture recalls that of an enemy soldier who will soon pick up the little boy—and throw him off the walls of Troy. Other early poems described the death of Astyanax in a manner that clearly recalled his last meeting with his father. Some stories about the fall of Troy were known to the poet of the *Iliad* and his earliest audiences; others were inspired by it. As a result, the *Iliad* became more allusive and complex in the course of time.[29] This is how Zachary Mason describes the situation in a recent novel inspired by Homer:

It is not widely understood that the epics attributed to Homer were in fact written by the gods before the Trojan war—these divine books are the archetypes of that war rather than its history. In fact, there have been innumerable Trojan wars, each played out according to an evolving aesthetic, each representing a fresh attempt at bringing the terror of battle into line with the lucidity of the authorial intent. Inevitably, each particular war is a distortion of its antecedent, an image in a warped hall of mirrors.[30]

Mirrors and distorted mirrors: what readers ask of the *Iliad* is whether things can be different. Whether we must imagine wars and more wars, like Hector when he prays for his son, or whether there can perhaps be peace—and even a poetics of peace. This is, for example, the insistent question of the German post-war poet Peter Handke, in *Der Himmel über Berlin*.[31] The *Iliad* itself offers no clear answer, only fleeting images of peace in the form of distant memories, startling comparisons, and doomed aspirations. Hector runs past the place where the Trojan women used to wash their clothes before the war (22.153–9). Andromache wishes Hector had died in his own bed (24.743–5). Athena deflects an arrow like a mother brushing away a fly from her sleeping baby (4.129–33). On the shield of Achilles—which is a representation of the whole world—there is a city at war, but there is also a city at peace. There is a wedding, and the vintage, and a row of boys and girls dancing to music (18.478–608). These images are precious, because they are so very rare.

---

[29] See B. Graziosi and J. Haubold, *Homer. 'Iliad 6': A Commentary* (Cambridge, 2010).

[30] Z. Mason, *The Lost Books of the 'Odyssey'* (London, 2010), 54.

[31] The film, directed by Wim Wenders, scripted by Handke, and released in English as *Wings of Desire*, explores the divided city of Berlin and (as its German title indicates) the sky above it. It was released in 1987, only two years before the fall of the Berlin wall.

NOTE ON THE TEXT AND EXPLANATORY MATERIALS

EDITING the *Iliad* is a difficult task because—as the Introduction points out—there are some open questions about the composition and transmission of the poem. Those who believe that Homer created a master copy of the *Iliad* in the late eighth or early seventh century BCE privilege readings that look old, find it easier to justify interventions that aim at consistency, and tend to emend or expunge passages or features that seem recent relative to other aspects of the text. Those who believe that the *Iliad* may stem from a more drawn-out process of textual fixation are prepared to allow for a less consistent and early-sounding text. The present translation is based on the critical edition by H. van Thiel, published by Olms-Weidmann in 1996: it presents the transmitted text with cautious editorial interventions. One of its advantages, for the purposes of this translation, is that it includes in square brackets passages that circulated in antiquity, but which are not transmitted, or only weakly attested, in the medieval manuscripts. These passages are not considered authentic by the editor, but tell us something about the early textual history of the *Iliad*: they have been included in this translation—which helpfully follows the line numeration of the original text—and left in square brackets. This makes them available, for the first time, to readers of the Oxford World's Classics.

The Explanatory Notes include succinct book summaries: they are meant to help the reader appreciate the overall design and plot of the poem, and locate specific episodes in it. The notes clarify geographical and mythical references, offer brief accounts of ancient rituals and other practices to which the poem alludes, draw attention to echoes, allusions, and correspondences within the poem, and comment on some key passages and additional lines. They occasionally draw from ancient explanations and commentaries. Two maps offer minimal information on the geography of Greece and Asia Minor, and facilitate an appreciation of the Catalogue of Ships and the Catalogue of the Trojans and their Allies in the second book of the *Iliad*. Full, accurate, and up-to-date maps are available in the second volume of J. Latacz and A. Bierl, *Homers Ilias. Gesamtkommentar* (Munich and Leipzig, 2000–); this commentary is now the standard work of reference for any rigorous engagement with the *Iliad*. A short bibliography offers suggestions for further reading in English.

NOTE ON THE TRANSLATION

THE translation respects as far as possible the line numeration of Homer's Greek, which means that references to the original text can easily be matched to the line numbers in the margin of this version. It does not claim to be poetry: my aim has been to use a straightforward English register and to keep closely to the Greek, allowing Homer to speak for himself—for example, in the use of repeated epithets and descriptions of recurrent scenes. I have tried to avoid importing alien imagery, and have preserved variations in sentence length. Similarly, I have kept clear of 'poeticizing' Homer at one extreme and reducing the scale of his invention to the level of a modern adventure story at the other. Both approaches, not unknown to recent translators, tend to get in the way of the poem's directness and power.

I have benefited greatly from the criticism and encouragement of friends in preparing this version. John Taylor and Tessa Smith gave me sound advice; Michael Clarke steered me expertly through drafts of the early books; and Barbara Graziosi's scholarship and ear for a telling phrase lie behind most pages. As always, my editor Judith Luna has been a constant support. Any surviving inaccuracies and infelicities are entirely my own.

Anthony Verity

SELECT BIBLIOGRAPHY

ONLY works written in English and wholly or partially intelligible to readers who do not know Latin or Greek have been included.

Commentaries

Jones, P. V., *Homer's 'Iliad': A Commentary on Three Translations* (London, 2003).

Kirk, G. (ed.), *The 'Iliad': A Commentary*, 6 vols. (Cambridge, 1985–93).

Postlethwaite, N., *Homer's 'Iliad': A Commentary on the Translation of Richmond Lattimore* (Exeter, 2000).

Willcock, M., *A Commentary on Homer's 'Iliad'* (London, 1978–84).

Companions to Homer

Cairns, D. (ed.), *Oxford Readings in Homer's 'Iliad'* (Oxford, 2001).

Finkelberg, M. (ed.), *The Homer Encyclopaedia*, 3 vols. (Oxford, 2011).

Fowler, R. (ed.), *The Cambridge Companion to Homer* (Cambridge, 2004).

Jong, I. J. F. de (ed.), *Homer: Critical Assessments*, 4 vols. (London, 1999).

Morris, I., and Powell, B. (eds.), *A New Companion to Homer* (Leiden, 1997).

Stubbings, F. H., and Wace, A. J. (eds.), *Companion to Homer* (London, 1960).

Willcock, M. M., *A Companion to the 'Iliad', Based on the Translation by Richmond Lattimore* (Chicago, 1976).

Critical Studies

Adkins, A., *Merit and Responsibility: A Study in Greek Values* (Oxford, 1960).

Bakker, E., *Pointing at the Past: From Formula to Performance in Homeric Poetics* (Cambridge, Mass., 2005).

Boedeker, D. (ed.), *The World of Troy: Homer, Schliemann, and the Treasures of Priam* (Washington, DC, 1997).

Burgess, J., *The Tradition of the Trojan War in Homer and the Epic Cycle* (Baltimore, 2001).

Cassio, A. C., 'Early Editions of the Greek Epics and Homeric Textual Criticism', in F. Montanari (ed.), *Omero tremila anni dopo* (Rome, 2002), 105–36.

Clarke, M., *Flesh and Spirit in the Songs of Homer* (Oxford, 1999).

Dué, C., *Homeric Variations on a Lament by Briseis* (Lanham, Md., 2002).

Edwards, M. W., *Homer: Poet of the 'Iliad'* (Baltimore, 1987).

Finley, M. I., *The World of Odysseus*, 2nd edn. (London, 1977).

Foley, J. M., *Homer's Traditional Art* (University Park, Pa., 1999).

Ford, A., *Homer: The Poetry of the Past* (Ithaca, NY, 1992).

Graziosi, B., *Inventing Homer: The Early Reception of Epic* (Cambridge, 2002).

—— and Haubold, J., *Homer: The Resonance of Epic* (London, 2005).

—— and Haubold, J., *Homer: 'Iliad VI'* (Cambridge, 2010).

Griffin, J., *Homer on Life and Death* (Oxford, 1980).

—— *Homer: 'Iliad IX'* (Oxford, 1995).

Haubold, J., *Homer's People: Epic Poetry and Social Formation* (Cambridge, 2000).

Janko, R., *Homer, Hesiod and the Hymns: Diachronic Development in Epic Diction* (Cambridge, 1982).

Jones, P. V. (ed.), *Homer: German Scholarship in Translation*, trans. G. M. Wright and P. V. Jones (Oxford, 1997).

Jong, I. J. F. de, *Narrators and Focalizers: The Presentation of the Story in the 'Iliad'*, 2nd edn. (London, 2004).

Kelly, A., *A Referential Commentary and Lexicon to Homer, 'Iliad VIII'* (Oxford, 2007).

Latacz, J., *Homer: His Art and his World*, trans. J. P. Holoka (Ann Arbor, Mich., 1996).

—— *Troy and Homer: Towards a Solution of an Old Mystery*, trans. K. Windle and R. Ireland (Oxford, 2004).

Lord, A., *The Singer of Tales*, 2nd edn. with foreword and CD-rom ed. S. Mitchell and G. Nagy (Cambridge, Mass., 2000).

Lynn-George, M., *Epos: Word, Narrative and the 'Iliad'* (Basingstoke, 1988).

Mackie, H., *Talking Trojan: Speech and Community in the 'Iliad'* (Lanham, Md., 1996).

Macleod, C. W. (ed.), *Homer: 'Iliad XXIV'* (Cambridge, 1982).

Martin, R., *The Language of Heroes: Speech and Performance in the 'Iliad'* (Ithaca, NY, 1989).

Mueller, M., *The Iliad*, 2nd edn. (London, 2009).

Nagy, G., *Homeric Questions* (Cambridge, Mass., 1996).

—— *The Best of the Achaeans: Concepts of the Hero in Archaic Greek Poetry*, 2nd edn. (Baltimore, 1999).

—— *Homer's Text and Language* (Champaign, Ill., 2004).

Parry, M., *The Making of Homeric Verse: The Collected Papers of Milman Parry*, ed. A. Parry (Oxford, 1971).

Pulleyn, S., *Homer: 'Iliad I'* (Oxford, 2000).

Pucci, P., *Odysseus Polytropos: Intertextual Readings in the 'Odyssey' and the 'Iliad'* (Ithaca, NY, 1987).

Redfield, J., *Nature and Culture in the 'Iliad': The Tragedy of Hector*, 2nd edn. (Chicago, 1994).

Schein, S., *The Mortal Hero: An Introduction to Homer's 'Iliad'* (Berkeley and Los Angeles, 1984).

Scodel, R., *Listening to Homer: Tradition, Narrative, and Audience* (Ann Arbor, Mich., 2002).

Scodel, R., *Epic Facework: Self-Presentation and Social Interaction in Homer* (Swansea, 2008).

Scully, S., *Homer and the Sacred City* (Ithaca and London, 1990).

Slatkin, L., *The Power of Thetis: Allusion and Interpretation in the 'Iliad'* (Berkeley and Los Angeles, 1992).

Snodgrass, A., *Homer and the Artists: Text and Picture in Early Greek Art* (Cambridge, 1998).

Taplin, O., *Homeric Soundings: The Shaping of the 'Iliad'* (Oxford, 1992).

Wees, H. van, *Status Warriors: War, Violence and Society in Homer and History* (Amsterdam, 1992).

West, M. L., *The East Face of Helicon: West Asiatic Elements in Greek Poetry and Myth* (Oxford, 1997).

—— *The Making of the 'Iliad': Disquisition and Analytical Commentary* (Oxford, 2010).

Wilson, D., *Ransom, Revenge, and Heroic Identity in the 'Iliad'* (Cambridge, 2002).

Winkler, M. M. (ed.), *Troy: from Homer's 'Iliad' to Hollywood Epic* (Oxford, 2007).

Zanker, G., *The Heart of Achilles: Characterization and Personal Ethics in the 'Iliad'* (Ann Arbor, Mich., 1994).

Further Reading in Oxford World Classics

Greek Lyric Poetry, trans. M. L. West.

Hesiod, *Theogony and Works and Days*, trans. M. L. West.

Homer, *The Odyssey*, trans. Walter Shewring, introduction by G. S. Kirk.

—— *The Homeric Hymns*, trans. Michael Crudden.

Myths from Mesopotamia: Creation, The Flood, Gilgamesh, and Others, trans. Stephanie Dalley.

Virgil, *Aeneid*, trans. Frederick Ahl, introduction by Elaine Fantham.

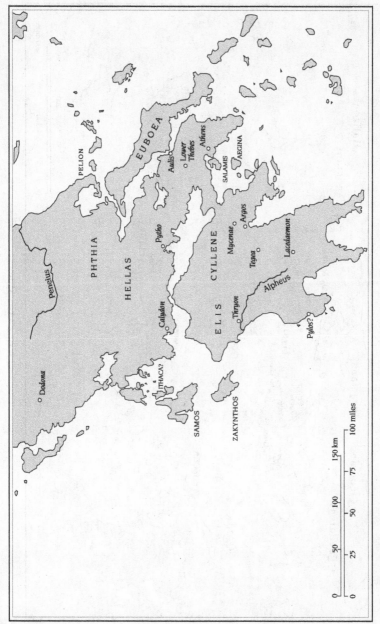

MAP 1. Greece

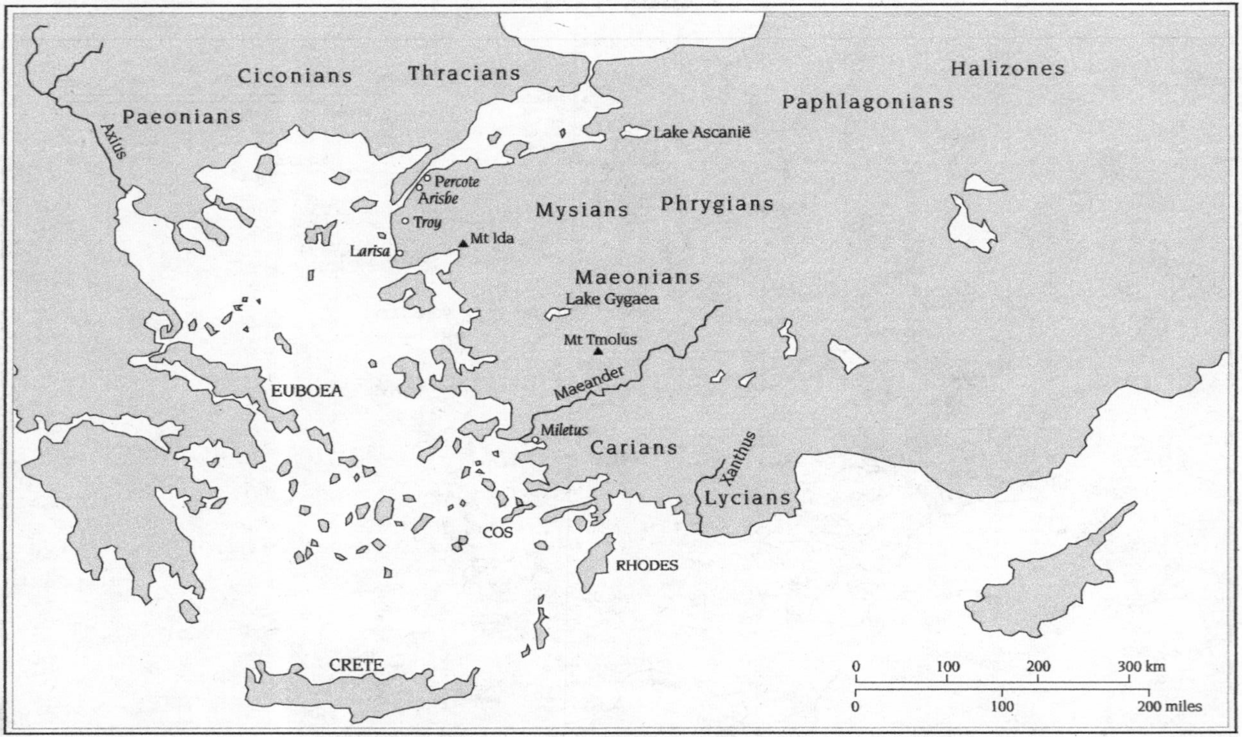

MAP 2. Asia Minor

THE ILIAD

BOOK ONE

SING, goddess, the anger* of Achilles, Peleus' son,
the accursed anger which brought the Achaeans countless
agonies and hurled many mighty shades of heroes into Hades,*
causing them to become the prey of dogs and
all kinds of birds; and the plan of Zeus was fulfilled.   5
Sing from the time the two men were first divided in strife—
Atreus' son,* lord of men, and glorious Achilles.
Which of the gods was it who set them to quarrel and fight?
The son of Zeus and Leto,* for he was bitter against the king, and
roused an evil plague through the camp, and the people went on
     dying,   10
because the son of Atreus had dishonoured his priest Chryses.
This man had come to the swift ships of the Achaeans to
redeem his daughter, bringing a boundless ransom and holding
in his hands the woollen bands of Apollo who shoots from afar,*
fixed to a golden staff. He entreated all the Achaeans, but   15
especially the two sons of Atreus, marshals of the people:
'You sons of Atreus, and you other well-greaved Achaeans,
may the gods who have their homes on Olympus grant
that you sack the city of Priam and return safely home.
Only release my dear child, and accept this ransom, and   20
show reverence to Zeus' son Apollo who shoots from afar.'

   Then all the rest of the Achaeans shouted their approval, that
they should be in awe of the priest and accept the splendid ransom,
but this found no favour in the heart of Atreus' son Agamemnon;
he sent Chryses roughly away, and added a harsh command: 25

   'Let me not discover you, old man, beside our hollow ships,
either dawdling here now or returning again later,
in case your staff and the god's bands prove no help to you.
I will not let the girl go; before I do, old age will find her
in my house in Argos, far from her fatherland, going   30
back and forth at the loom and serving me in my bed.
Go, do not provoke me; this way you will return unharmed.'

   So he spoke, and the old man was afraid and did as he said,
and silently made his way along the shore of the loud-roaring sea.
Then, going some way apart, the old man prayed at length   35

to lord Apollo, whom Leto of the beautiful hair bore:
'Hear me, lord of the silver bow, you who stand guard over
Chryse and sacred Cilla, and govern Tenedos* with your power,
Smintheus;* if ever I built a temple that pleased you
or if I ever burnt for you the fat-wrapped thigh-bones*   40
of bulls or goats, I beg you to fulfil this plea for me:
may the Danaans pay for my tears with your arrows.'
    So he spoke in prayer, and Phoebus Apollo heard him,
and came down from Olympus' heights furious in his heart,
his bow and lidded quiver hanging from his shoulders.   45
The arrows clattered against the angry god's shoulder
as he moved; and he came on like nightfall.
Then, sitting apart from the ships, he let fly an arrow,
and his silver bow sang out with a terrible noise.
First he went after the mules and the swift dogs, and then loosed   50
piercing arrows at the men themselves, shooting without cease;
and all the time the corpse-pyres burnt, crowded together.
    For nine days the god's shafts ranged throughout the camp,
and on the tenth Achilles summoned the people to an assembly;
the goddess Hera of the white arms had put this into his mind,   55
since she cared for the Danaans, because she saw them dying.
So when they had assembled and were gathered together,
swift-footed Achilles rose and spoke among them:
'Son of Atreus, I think we shall now be turned back from here
to wander home again—if, that is, we can avoid death—   60
if the Achaeans are to be beaten down by plague as well as war.
Come, let us interrogate some prophet or priest
or interpreter of dreams, for dreams too come from Zeus,
who may tell us why Phoebus Apollo is so bitter against us,
whether he finds fault with us over some vow or hecatomb,*   65
to see if he will accept the savour of lambs and unblemished
goats, and so be willing to turn the plague away from us.'
    So he spoke and took his seat again, and among them rose
Calchas, the son of Thestor, by far the best of bird-interpreters,
who understood the present, the future, and the past,   70
and had guided the ships of the Achaeans to Ilium
by the prophetic skill which Phoebus Apollo had given him.
With generous intent he spoke out and addressed them:
'Achilles, dear to Zeus, you command me to explain
the anger of Apollo, the lord who shoots from afar.   75

Well, I shall speak, but you must mark my words and swear
to come to my help willingly in both word and deed,
because I think I shall infuriate a man who has supreme
authority over the Argives, and whom the Achaeans obey.
A king is the more powerful when he is angry with a lesser man,   80
because even if he stifles his anger there and then
he feeds the resentment afterwards in his breast until
he brings it to fulfilment. Now tell me if you will protect me.'
    Then in answer swift-footed Achilles addressed him:
'Take courage, and speak out whatever divine truth you know.   85
I swear by Apollo, dear to Zeus, to whom you, Calchas,
pray when you expound divine revelations to the Danaans,
that while I live on earth and have the power of sight
no one will lay heavy hands on you by the hollow ships,
no man of all the Danaans, not even if you mean Agamemnon,   90
who now boasts that he is by far the best of all the Achaeans.'
    Then the blameless prophet took courage and spoke:
'It is not over a vow or hecatomb that he finds us at fault,
but because of his priest, whom Agamemnon dishonoured
and did not accept the ransom and release his daughter;   95
that is why the shooter from afar* torments us, and will do so again.
Nor will he drive the ugly, shameful plague from the Danaans
until the girl with darting eyes is returned to her father,
without ransom and without payment, and a holy hecatomb
is taken to Chryse; only then might we appease and persuade him.'   100
    So he spoke and took his seat again, and among them rose
the hero son of Atreus, wide-ruling Agamemnon,
full of distress; his dark heart was filled to the brim
with fury, and his two eyes were like flashing fire.
First of all he addressed Calchas, with a look of hate: 105
'Prophet of evil, never yet have you told me anything good;
it is always dear to your heart to prophesy calamities,
and you have never given us good news or brought it to fulfilment.
And so now you prophesy and speak publicly to the Danaans,
claiming that the one who shoots from afar is tormenting us   110
because I was not willing to accept the splendid ransom
for the girl, Chryses' daughter, even though it is my desire
to keep her in my house; and indeed I prefer her to Clytemnestra
my wedded wife, since she is in no way inferior to her in
stature or in beauty, nor in understanding or accomplishments.   115

Even so, I am prepared to give her back, if that is the better course;
I would wish the people to survive rather than to perish.
But you must at once get ready another prize for me, so that I
alone of the Argives am not without one, since that cannot be right;
you can all see that my prize is going elsewhere.'   120

   Then in answer glorious swift-footed Achilles addressed him:
'Most illustrious son of Atreus, rapacious beyond all other men,
how can the great-spirited Achaeans give you a prize?
We know of no great common store of possessions anywhere;
everything that we sacked from cities has been distributed,   125
and it is not fitting that the people should collect it together again.
No; you must now give the girl up to the god, and the Achaeans
will compensate you three- and fourfold, if ever Zeus
grants that we tear apart the strongly walled city of Troy.'
   Then in answer lord Agamemnon addressed him: 130
   'Godlike Achilles, great man though you may be, do not try to
deceive me in this, since you will not outwit nor get the better of me.
Are you telling me to give the girl back and to sit here meekly
with no reward, simply so that you may keep your prize?
Well, if the great-spirited Achaeans award me a prize,   135
suiting it to my desire, equal in status to the other, I will accept it;
but if they will not, then I shall myself come and take one,
either yours, or the prize belonging to Ajax or Odysseus,
and carry it away; and the man to whom I come will be angry.
However, we shall give thought to this at a later time;   140
as for now, come, let us drag a black ship down to the bright sea,
and gather some oarsmen for the purpose, and put on board
a hecatomb, and embark Chryses' fair-cheeked daughter
herself. And let there be one man, a counsellor, as captain,
either Ajax or Idomeneus or glorious Odysseus,   145
or you, son of Peleus, most outrageous of men, so that
you may make offerings and appease the far-worker* for us.'

   Looking at him darkly swift-footed Achilles addressed him:
'You wear shamelessness like a garment, and your mind is full of greed!
How can any of the Achaeans readily obey your orders, to   150
join an expedition or to try their strength with men in battle?
For my part, I did not come here to fight because of the Trojan
spearmen, since they have done me no wrong at all:
they have never driven off my cattle or my horses,
nor have they ever destroyed my crops in rich-soiled Phthia,*   155

nurturer of men, since between us lies a very great
distance, of shadowy mountains and the roaring sea.
It was you we followed, shameless brute, to please you, to win
honour for Menelaus and for you, you dog, from the Trojans.
But you care nothing for this, and pay it no heed.   160
And now you threaten to take my prize from me in person, for
which I laboured hard, and the sons of the Achaeans gave it to me.
I never receive a prize equal to yours whenever the Achaeans
sack some well-populated citadel of the Trojans;
it is always my hands that sustain the greater part of the   165
violent conflict, but when there is a sharing-out of booty
your prize is by far the greater, and I go back to my ships with
some small thing, yet dear to me, exhausted by the fighting.
So now I shall return to Phthia, since it is far and away better
to go home on my curved ships; I am not minded to stay here,   170
without honour, heaping up riches and wealth for you.'
    Then in answer Agamemnon, lord of men, addressed him:
'Run away, then, if your heart so urges you. I shall not beg you
to stay on my account, since there are many others near me
to give me honour, and especially Zeus the counsellor.   175
Of all the Zeus-nurtured kings you are the most hateful to me,
for strife and war and battles are always dear to your heart;
and even if you are very strong, that must be a gift from some god.
Go home with your ships and your companions and
lord it over the Myrmidons; I care nothing about you, and   180
your anger does not trouble me. But this is my threat to you:
Phoebus Apollo is taking Chryses' daughter from me,
and I shall send her back on my ship with my companions;
but I shall come myself to your hut and take away Briseus'
lovely-cheeked daughter, your prize, so that you may know well   185
how much more powerful I am than you, and so that others too
may fear to speak to me as an equal and match me face to face.'
    So he spoke, and grief rose up in the son of Peleus, and the heart
in his hairy chest was divided in two as he deliberated
whether to draw his sharp sword from beside his thigh and   190
drive the others away, and kill the son of Atreus,
or to suppress his bitter anger and subdue his heart.
He was pondering this in his heart and in his mind, and was
drawing his great sword from its scabbard, when Athena came
from the high sky; the goddess white-armed Hera had sent her,   195

since she loved and cared equally for both men in her heart.
She stood behind Peleus' son and grasped him by his fair hair,
appearing to him alone, and none of the others saw her.
Achilles was amazed, and turned round, and at once recognized
Pallas Athena, for her eyes shone with a terrible light;   200
and he addressed her, speaking with winged words:*
'What are you doing here, daughter of aegis-wearing Zeus?*
Is it to mark these arrogant insults from Atreus' son Agamemnon?
I tell you this plainly, and I believe it will be fulfilled:
one day soon his high-handedness will cause him to lose his life.'   205

    Then in answer the goddess grey-eyed Athena addressed him:
'I have come from the high sky to stop your fury, hoping that
you will obey me. The goddess Hera of the white arms sent me,
for she loves and cares equally for both of you in her heart.
Come, leave off your strife and take your hand from your sword,   210
though you may abuse him in words, and tell him how things will be.
For I tell you this plainly, and indeed it will be fulfilled:
one day you will have three times as many splendid gifts to
pay for these insults. Restrain yourself now, and do as we say.'

    Then in answer swift-footed Achilles addressed her: 215
'Goddess, a man must respect the words of you both,
however great the anger in his heart; for it is better this way.
If a man obeys the gods, they are more ready to listen to him.'

    So he spoke, and set his heavy hand on the silver hilt, and
thrust the great sword back into its scabbard, and did not disobey   220
the word of Athena; and she went away towards Olympus,
to the house of Zeus, wearer of the aegis, to join the rest of the gods.
Then the son of Peleus once again addressed the son of Atreus
with wounding words, and was not yet ready to give up his anger:
'Wine-sodden man, with the eyes of a dog and the heart of a deer!   225
Never yet have you been brave enough to arm with the people for war,
or to set out for an ambush with the best of the Achaeans,
for that course seems to you to be as dangerous as death.
No, it is much better to skulk in the broad camp of the Achaeans
and to take away the gifts of any man who speaks out against you.   230
You are a people-devouring king, for you rule over nonentities;
otherwise, son of Atreus, this would be the last outrage you caused.
But I tell you this plainly, and I swear a great oath with it:
by this staff, which will never again grow leaves and shoots
since it first left the trunk where it was cut in the mountains,   235

nor will it sprout again, for the bronze axe has stripped away
the leaves and bark all around it, and now in turn the judgment-
giving sons of the Achaeans hold it in their hands, upholding
the ordinances of Zeus; and this will be a mighty oath to you:
one day longing for Achilles will come upon the sons of the
    Achaeans,   240
every one of them; and then, for all your grief, you will have no power
to help them, when many fall and die at the hands of man-slaying
Hector; and you will tear apart the heart within you in anger,
because you denied all honour to the best of the Achaeans.'
   So the son of Peleus spoke and flung the staff, studded   245
with golden nails, to the ground, and sat down himself.
On the other side Atreus' son still raged; but among them Nestor
of the sweet words leapt up, the clear-voiced orator of the Pylians,*
from whose tongue flowed a voice sweeter than honey.
In his lifetime two generations of mortal men had already   250
died, those who had been raised with him and those born
afterwards in holy Pylos, and he was now ruling over the third.
With generous intent he spoke out and addressed them:
'Surely great distress is coming to the land of Achaea!
How Priam and the sons of Priam would be overjoyed,   255
and all the rest of the Trojans would be glad in their hearts,
if they were to hear of all this fighting between the pair of you,
you who excel among the Danaans in both counsel and battle.
Come, listen to me. You are both younger than me,
and I have in times past kept company with better men   260
than you, and never did they treat me with disdain.
I have never seen, nor shall I ever see, such men as
Peirithous and Dryas, shepherd of his people,
and Caeneus and Exadius and godlike Polyphemus,*
[and Theseus, son of Aegeus, who resembled the immortals.] *   265
They were the mightiest of all men on earth in their rearing;
they were the mightiest, and they fought with the mightiest,
with mountain-dwelling beasts, and they dealt them an appalling death.
These were my companions when I came from Pylos,
from a far distant land, because they had summoned me.   270
I gave a good account of myself in the fighting; and against them
no one of mortals who now live upon the earth could fight.
Moreover, they listened to my advice and obeyed my words.
So you too both should listen to me, since it is better to listen.

You, great man though you are, must not take the girl from this man,   275
but let her be, since the Achaeans' sons first gave him her as a prize.
As for you, son of Peleus, do not seek to rival a king by force,
since a staff-holding king to whom Zeus grants glory
enjoys a greater portion of honour than other men do.
Even if you are stronger, it is because your mother is a goddess;   280
but he is the greater, because he rules over more people.
Son of Atreus, give up your anger; it is I who entreat you
to renounce your bitterness against Achilles, who is
a mighty bulwark for all the Achaeans in ruinous war.'

Then in answer lord Agamemnon addressed him: 285
'Very well, old man; all that you say is according to due measure.
But this man desires to be above all other men,
desires to rule over all men, to lord it over everyone,
to give orders to all, though I think some will not obey him.
Even if the gods who live for ever have made him a spearman,   290
is this a reason for insulting words to burst from his mouth?'

Breaking in on him, glorious Achilles answered:
'I should certainly be called a coward and a man of no account
if I were to give way to you in everything you say.
Go and give these orders to others, but do not instruct me,   295
because I have no mind to listen to you any further.
But I tell you another thing, and you should store it in your mind:
I shall not fight you with my bare hands for the girl's sake, not you
or anyone else; you all gave her to me, and then you took her away.
But as for the rest of the possessions that I keep in my black ship,   300
you will not take any of them and carry them off against my will.
Come on now, put me to the test, so that these here also may see,
and quickly your black blood will gush out over my spear.'

So these two fought with violent words, one against the other,
and stood up, and broke up the assembly beside the Achaeans' ships.   305
Peleus' son went away to his huts and well-balanced ships
with the son of Menoetius* and his own companions,
and Atreus' son dragged a swift ship down to the sea, and
picked out twenty rowers to go in it, and loaded on to it a hecatomb
for the god, and brought Chryses' lovely-cheeked daughter and   310
set her on it; and much-scheming Odysseus went aboard as captain.

So they embarked and sailed along the watery pathways, and
the son of Atreus commanded the people to purify themselves.
When they had purified themselves and thrown the defilement

into the sea,* they sacrificed to Apollo unblemished hecatombs   315
of bulls and goats, beside the shore of the unresting sea, and
the savour reached the high sky, caught up in the whirling smoke.

So they busied themselves throughout the camp; but Agamemnon
did not give up the quarrel and the threat he had made to Achilles
before this, but spoke to Talthybius and Eurybates,   320
the two who were his heralds and diligent attendants:
'Go to the hut of Achilles, son of Peleus, and take Briseus'
lovely-cheeked daughter by the hand and bring her here.
If he does not give her to you, then I shall come in person
and get her, and with more men; and that will be the worse for him.'   325

So he spoke, and sent them away, and laid a harsh command on them.
Reluctantly they made their way along the shore of the unresting sea,
and came to the huts and ships of the Myrmidons.
They found Achilles beside his hut and his black ship,
sitting inactive; and when he saw them he was not glad.   330
The two men were terrified, and stood there, in awe of
the king, and did not address a word to him or ask him questions;
but he understood in his heart and spoke to them:
'Welcome, heralds, messengers of Zeus and of men.
Come closer; it is not you I blame, but Agamemnon,   335
who is sending you here for the girl, Briseus' daughter.
Come, Patroclus, sprung from Zeus,* bring the girl out and
give her to these men to take away. Let them be witnesses
in the sight of the blessed gods and of mortal men,
and of him, that ruthless king, if ever in future   340
a need arises for me to turn ugly destruction away
from the rest. His mind is surely hurtling towards ruin,
and he has not the sense to look before him and behind, to
ensure that the Achaeans survive, fighting beside their ships.'

So he spoke, and Patroclus obeyed his dear companion, and   345
brought Briseus' lovely-cheeked daughter out of the hut and
gave her to them to take away. They returned to the Achaeans' ships,
and the woman went with them, reluctantly. But Achilles wept,
and at once took himself apart from his companions and sat on
the shore of the grey sea, gazing out over the boundless expanse.   350
Stretching out his arms he prayed at length to his dear mother:
'Mother, you gave me birth to live for only a short while, so surely
the Olympian, Zeus the high-thunderer, ought to have bestowed
some honour on me; but as it is he has given me none, not even

a little. Atreus' son, wide-ruling Agamemnon, has dishonoured   355
me. He has taken away my prize in person, and keeps it for himself.'
   So he spoke, shedding tears, and his revered mother heard him
as she sat in the depths of the sea next to her aged father.
Quickly she rose up from the grey sea like a mist,
and took her seat in front of him as he wept his tears,   360
and stroking him with her hand she spoke to him, saying:
'Child, why are you weeping? What sorrow has entered your heart?
Tell me, do not hide it in your mind, so that we both may know.'
   With a heavy groan, swift-footed Achilles addressed her:
'You do know. Why should I tell you all this when you know it?   365
We went to Thebe, the sacred city of Eëtion,* and
sacked it and brought all the plunder here. This the
sons of the Achaeans distributed properly among themselves,
and picked out for Atreus' son Chryses' lovely-cheeked daughter.
But then Chryses, the priest of Apollo who shoots from afar,   370
came to the swift ships of the bronze-shirted Achaeans, intending
to redeem his daughter, bringing a boundless ransom, and
holding in his hands the woollen bands of Apollo the far-shooter,
fixed to a golden staff, and he entreated all the Achaeans,
but especially the two sons of Atreus, marshals of the people.   375
Then all the rest of the Achaeans shouted their approval,
that they should be in awe of the priest and accept the
     splendid ransom,
but this found no favour in the heart of Atreus' son Agamemnon,
and he sent him roughly away, and added a harsh command.
The old man went back in anger; and Apollo heard him   380
when he prayed, because he was very dear to him,
and let loose deadly shafts against the Argives; and the people
kept dying, one after another, and the god's arrows ranged
everywhere throughout the Achaeans' broad camp. Our prophet,
with sure knowledge, explained the far-worker's divine will to us,   385
and it was I who first urged that we should at once appease the god;
but at this anger took hold of Atreus' son, and instantly he rose
and made threats against me, which have indeed been fulfilled.
Now the darting-eyed Achaeans are sending the girl, Chryses' child,
with a swift ship to Chryse, and are taking gifts for the lord Apollo,   390
while heralds have lately come and taken from my hut that other girl,
Briseus' daughter, whom the sons of the Achaeans gave to me.
I beg you, if it is in your power, have care for your son;

go to Olympus and entreat Zeus, reminding him of any
service of word or deed that you have done to Zeus' heart.   395
Indeed, I often heard you boasting in the halls of my father,
when you said that you alone among the immortals
averted ugly destruction from Cronus' son of the dark clouds,
at the time when other Olympians, Hera and Poseidon
and Pallas Athena, were wishing to tie him down.   400
But you, goddess, came and released him from his bonds,
quickly summoning to high Olympus the hundred-handed one
called Briareus by the gods, but all men call him
Aegaeon;* and he is mightier than his father. He took
his seat next to the son of Cronus, exulting in his triumph, and   405
the blessed gods cowered in fright and did not try to bind him.
Sit beside Zeus now and take hold of his knees* and remind him
of this, to see if he will agree to help the Trojans by penning
the Achaeans in by their ships' sterns along the seashore and
killing them; so that they all may take delight in their king,   410
and that the son of Atreus, wide-ruling Agamemnon, may come to
know his delusion, in that he did not honour the best of the Achaeans.'
    Then Thetis answered him, shedding tears:
'Ah, my child, why did I bear you, giving birth to such suffering?
If only you could sit at ease by your ships without tears and grief,   415
since your portion of life is but short, and not at all long.
But you are doomed to a swift death, to be wretched beyond
all men; it was indeed to a cruel destiny that I bore you in my halls.
Still, I shall say these words for you to Zeus who delights in the
thunderbolt, going to snow-covered Olympus, to see if he will listen;   420
and as for you, sit now beside your swift-travelling ships and
rage against the Achaeans, and hold back altogether from the war.
Zeus went yesterday to Ocean to join the blameless Ethiopians*
and to take part in a feast, and all the other gods went with him;
on the twelfth day he will come again to Olympus,   425
and then I shall go to Zeus' house with its bronze floor
and I shall entreat him; and I believe I shall persuade him.'
    So she spoke and went away, leaving him there,
bitterly angry in his heart because of the well-girdled woman,
whom they were taking from him by force, against his will.   430
Now Odysseus was nearing Chryse with the holy hecatomb, and
when they had sailed into the harbour with its many deep bays
they furled the sail and stowed it in the black ship, and

then quickly slackened the forestays and laid the mast
in its crutch, and with oars rowed the ship on to an anchorage.   435
Out they threw the anchor-stones, and made the stern-cables fast,
out they themselves landed on to the shore of the sea,
out they brought the hecatomb for Apollo who shoots from afar,
out stepped Chryses' daughter from the sea-traversing ship.
Then much-scheming Odysseus escorted her to the altar   440
and gave her into her father's arms and said to him:
'Chryses, Agamemnon, lord of men, has sent me to
bring you your daughter and to offer a holy hecatomb to
Phoebus on the Danaans' behalf, that we may appease the lord
who has been bringing grief and lamentation on to the Argives.'   445
    So he spoke, and gave her into his arms, and with joy he received
his dear child. Quickly the others set out the holy hecatomb
for the god in due order around the well-built altar;
then they washed their hands and lifted up the barley grains.
And among them Chryses prayed in a loud voice, lifting up his
       hands: 450
'Hear me, god of the silver bow, you who stand guard over Chryse
and sacred Cilla, and rule over Tenedos with your power:
you listened to me when I prayed to you before, and
gave me honour, and bore heavily on the Achaean people;
so this time also bring this plea to fulfilment for me: 455
now turn aside the ugly plague from the Danaans.'
    So he spoke in prayer, and Phoebus Apollo heard him.
When they had prayed and sprinkled the barley grains, they first
pulled back the beasts' heads, then slit their throats and flayed them,
then cut away the thigh-bones and wrapped them in fat, covering   460
them above and below, and laid raw hunks of meat upon them.
These the old man burnt on billets of wood, and poured
       gleaming wine
over them; and young men held five-pronged forks in their hands.
When the thigh-bones were burnt up and they had tasted the entrails,
they chopped the rest of the meat small and threaded it on skewers,   465
and cooked it with great care, and then drew it all off.
When they had finished their work and made the meal ready
they feasted, and no one's heart lacked a fair share in the meal.*
When they had put from themselves the desire for food and drink,
young men filled mixing-jars to the brim with drink and   470
distributed it to all, after first pouring libations into the cups.

So all day long the young men of the Achaeans set about
appeasing the god with songs, chanting a beautiful paean,*
singing of the far-worker; and he heard it and was glad in his heart.

When the sun went down and darkness came over them,   475
they lay down to sleep beside the ship's stern-cables;
but when early-born Dawn with her rosy fingers appeared,
then they put out to sea for the broad camp of the Achaeans,
and Apollo who shoots from afar sent them a following wind.
The men set up the mast and spread the white sail aloft,   480
and the wind blew into the belly of the sail, and a dark
wave sang out loudly about the stem as the ship sailed on,
speeding over the waves and keeping close to its course.
When they reached the broad camp of the Achaeans
they dragged the black ship up on to the land,   485
high on the sands, and positioned long props under it,
and themselves dispersed to their huts and their ships.

But still he raged, sitting idle beside his swift-travelling ships,
the son of Peleus, sprung from Zeus,* swift-footed Achilles.
No longer did he frequent the assembly where men win glory,   490
nor ever go to the war, but wasted his dear heart away, staying
where he was, but yearning for the battle-cry and the fighting.

But when the twelfth dawn from that day appeared,
the gods who live for ever did indeed return to Olympus,
all together, and Zeus led the way. Thetis did not forget   495
her son's requests, but rose up through the waves of the sea,
and early in the morning flew up to the vast high sky and Olympus.
She found Cronus' wide-thundering son sitting apart from the rest
on the topmost peak of Olympus, mountain of many ridges.
Sitting in front of him, she caught him by the knees with her   500
left hand and with her right reached up and grasped his chin,*
and addressed Zeus, the son of Cronus, entreating him:
'Father Zeus, if ever I was of service to you among the immortals
in word or in deed, then bring this plea to fulfilment for me:
honour my son; he is fated to have the briefest life of all men,   505
and now Agamemnon, lord of men, has dishonoured him—
he has taken away his prize in person, and keeps it for himself.
I beg you, Olympian Zeus, counsellor, to honour him;
give victory to the Trojans, until such time as the Achaeans
make amends to my son and increase his honour.'   510

So she spoke; and Zeus the cloud-gatherer gave her no answer,

but sat for a long time in silence. Thetis had grasped his knees,
and kept tight hold of them, and asked him a second time:
'Promise me without fail, and nod your head in assent, or else
deny me (for you have nothing to fear), and so I will know well   515
how much I am the least honoured among all the gods.'

　Then, deeply angered, Zeus the cloud-gatherer addressed her:
'This will surely prove a bad business; you will cause me to
quarrel with Hera, and she will provoke and abuse me.
Even as it is, she is always arguing with me among the immortal   520
gods, saying that I take the Trojans' side in the fighting.
Go away now, in case Hera finds out that you are here.
I shall see to this matter, and bring it to fulfilment; look,
I shall nod my head in assent to you, so that you will trust me,
for this is the most important sign that comes from me to the   525
immortals; no word of mine can be revoked or beguiled
or denied, when once I have nodded my head in assent.'

　So the son of Cronus spoke, and nodded his dark brows in assent,
and the locks of the lord's deathless hair swung forward
on his immortal head, and he made great Olympus tremble.   530

　So these two left their plotting and went their separate ways;
Thetis leapt from shining Olympus into the deep sea,
and Zeus went to his house. All the gods stood up together
from their seats in the presence of their father, and no one dared
to stay seated as he approached, but they all stood facing him.   535
There he seated himself on his throne; but Hera knew well
when she saw him that Thetis had been scheming with him,
Thetis the silver-footed, daughter of the ancient of the sea.*
At once she addressed Zeus, the son of Cronus, in jeering words:
'Crafty schemer, which of the gods has been plotting with you now?   540
It is always your delight to keep away from me and ponder
in secret before deciding something. Never yet have you
brought yourself to tell me openly what you are brooding on.'

　Then the father of gods and men answered her:
'Hera, do not expect to know about all my thoughts;   545
they will turn out hard for you, even though you are my wife.
As for those that it is fitting for you to hear, no one
will know before you, either of gods or men; but when
I am minded to muse on something apart from the gods,
you must not seek to know it or to question me closely.'   550

　Then the ox-eyed lady Hera answered him:

'Most dread son of Cronus, what is this that you have said?
In the past I have not questioned you closely or sought to know,
but you have devised whatever you wished in complete peace;
but now I am terribly afraid in my mind that silver-footed Thetis,   555
daughter of the ancient of the sea, has contrived to beguile you.
Early in the morning she sat beside you and grasped your knees,
and I fancy you have nodded your head in assent, saying you will
honour Achilles, and kill many of the Achaeans beside their ships.'

    Then Zeus who gathers the clouds addressed her in answer: 560
'You are possessed,* and always fancying things; I cannot elude you.
Even so you will achieve nothing, and this will take you
further from my heart, and that will be the worse for you.
If this is how things are, it must be that I wish them to be so.
You should sit in silence and abide by my words; if not,   565
all the gods who are on Olympus will be unable to help you
when I come near and lay my irresistible hands upon you.'

    So he spoke, and the lady ox-eyed Hera was afraid,
and sat in silence, bending her heart to submission, and
in Zeus' house the gods of the high sky were troubled;   570
but among them Hephaestus the famed craftsman began to speak,
out of concern for his dear mother, Hera of the white arms:
'Well, this will indeed be a bad business, and not to be borne,
if you two give rise to strife in this way because of mortals,
and provoke brawling among the gods. There will be no pleasure   575
at all in the splendid feast, since ill feeling will prevail.
To my mother I give this advice, though she knows it herself:
to give in to our dear father Zeus, so that he will not again
reprimand her, and so throw our feast into disarray.
What if the Olympian god of the lightning had a mind to   580
hurl us bodily from our seats? He is much the most powerful here.
No, you must approach him with words that are gentle,
and then straightaway the Olympian will be merciful to us.'

    So he spoke, and leaping up he placed a two-handled cup
in his dear mother's hand, and addressed her: 585
'Be patient, my mother, and endure, troubled though you are,
or else I may see you, dear as you are to me, beaten
before my eyes; and then, though grieved, I would not be able
to help you, since it is a hard thing to defy the Olympian.
Indeed, once before when I was eager to come to your help   590
he seized me by the foot and flung me from the divine threshold:

all day long I dropped through the air, and with the sun's setting
fell upon Lemnos,* and there was little life left in me;
but straight after my fall the Sintian men* took care of me.'

So he spoke, and the goddess Hera of the white arms smiled,   595
and as she smiled took the cup from her son in her hand.
Then he, moving from left to right, poured out sweet nectar
for all the other gods, drawing it off from the mixing-bowl;
and unquenchable laughter broke out among the blessed gods,
when they saw Hephaestus shuffling* about the house.   600

And so the whole day long until the setting of the sun
they feasted, and no one's heart lacked a fair share in the feast,
nor were they denied the beautiful lyre which Apollo held,
nor the Muses, who sang antiphonally with their lovely voices.

But when the bright light of the sun had gone down   605
they went to prepare for sleep, each to their own house,
to where the far-famed bow-legged god Hephaestus
had in his cunning skill built a house for each of them.
And Zeus, the Olympian god of the lightning, went to his bed,
where he always rested when sweet sleep came upon him; there   610
he went up and slept, and beside him was Hera of the golden throne.

BOOK TWO

Now all other beings, gods and horse-marshalling men,
slept the night long, but sweet sleep did not keep hold of Zeus;
he was pondering in his mind how he might give honour to
Achilles, and kill many men beside the Achaeans' ships.
And this seemed to him in his heart to be the best plan,   5
to send a destructive Dream to Agamemnon, son of Atreus.
Addressing the Dream, he spoke with winged words:
'Away now, destructive Dream, to the Achaeans' swift ships;
go into the hut of Agamemnon, son of Atreus, and
repeat everything to him exactly as I instruct you.   10
Command him to arm the flowing-haired Achaeans with
all speed, because now he may take the Trojans' city with its
wide streets; the immortals dwelling on Olympus are no longer
divided in their purpose, for Hera has bent the wills of them all
by her pleading, and affliction has laid hold of the Trojans.'   15
   So he spoke, and when it had heard his words the Dream departed,
and came without delay to the swift ships of the Achaeans.
It made for Atreus' son Agamemnon, and found him
asleep in his hut, and deathless slumber was poured over him.
It stood above his head* in the likeness of Neleus' son   20
Nestor, whom Agamemnon valued most of the elders;
assuming this likeness, the god-sent Dream addressed him:
'You sleep, son of Atreus, war-minded breaker of horses;
but a man of counsel should not sleep the whole night through,
one to whom the people are entrusted and who has so many cares.   25
Now listen quickly to me; I am a messenger to you from Zeus,
who though far away is deeply concerned for you and pities you.
He commands you to arm the flowing-haired Achaeans
speedily, because now you may take the Trojans' city with its
wide streets. The immortals dwelling on Olympus are no longer   30
divided in their purpose, for Hera has bent the wills of them all
by her pleading, and affliction sent from Zeus has laid hold of
the Trojans. Store this then in your heart; do not let forgetfulness
possess you, when once mind-cheering sleep has released you.'
   So it spoke and departed, and left him there, pondering   35
these things in his heart, which would not be fulfilled;

he thought he would take the city of Priam on that same day,
fool that he was, and did not know what deeds Zeus was planning,
who was about to inflict even more anguish and lamentation on
both Trojans and Danaans in the course of the harsh conflict.   40
He woke from his sleep, and the divine voice was poured over him;
he started up, then stood and clothed himself in his soft tunic,
beautiful and not yet worn, and threw over it his great cloak.
Under his shining feet he bound his fine sandals,
and from his shoulders he slung his silver-riveted sword.   45
He picked up his ancestral, never-decaying staff, and holding it
made his way along the ships of the bronze-shirted Achaeans.

   Now the goddess Dawn had reached high Olympus,
to announce the daylight to Zeus and the other immortals,
when Agamemnon commanded the clear-voiced heralds   50
to summon the flowing-haired Achaeans to an assembly.
So they made the summons, and the men gathered with great speed.

   But first he held a council of the great-spirited elders
beside the ship of Nestor, the king who was born in Pylos.
When he had called them together he framed a subtle plan: 55
'Listen to me, friends. A god-sent Dream came to me in my sleep
through the deathless night, and it most closely resembled
glorious Nestor in appearance and stature and form.
It stood above my head and spoke these words to me:
"You sleep, son of Atreus, war-minded breaker of horses;   60
but a man of counsel should not sleep the whole night through,
one to whom the people are entrusted and who has so many cares.
Now listen quickly to me; I am a messenger to you from Zeus,
who though far away is deeply concerned for you and pities you.
He commands you to arm the flowing-haired Achaeans   65
speedily, because now you may take the Trojans' city with its
wide streets. The immortals dwelling on Olympus are no longer
divided in their purpose, for Hera has bent the wills of them all
by her pleading, and affliction sent from Zeus has laid hold of
the Trojans. Store this in your heart." So it spoke, and   70
flew away from my sight, and sweet sleep released me.
So come, let us see if we can arm the sons of the Achaeans for battle.
But first I shall test them with words, as is right, and
I shall urge them to flee in their many-benched ships, and
you must go among them and try to hold them back with words.'   75

   So he spoke and took his seat again, and among them

arose Nestor, who was king in sandy Pylos.
With generous intent he spoke out and addressed them:
'My friends, chieftains and rulers of the Argives,
if anyone else of the Achaeans had told us of this dream   80
we would say it was false, and would turn our backs on it;
but the man who saw it claims to be the best of the Achaeans.
So come, let us try to arm the sons of the Achaeans for battle.'

    So he spoke, and was the first to leave the assembly, and the rest,
all the staff-holding kings, stood up after him and obeyed   85
the shepherd of the people; and the people rushed to meet them.
As when troops of swarming bees stream out
from a hollow rock in bursts, one after another,
and settle in clusters on springtime flowers, and
then, massing together, fly off in different directions;   90
so the numerous tribes streamed out by companies
from their ships and huts along the wide sea shore
to the assembly place. And among them blazed Rumour,
Zeus' messenger, urging them ever onwards; and so they gathered.
And the assembly was in turmoil, and the earth groaned   95
under the men as they sat down, and there was an uproar. Nine
heralds set about holding them back, shouting, hoping to stop
their clamour and make them listen to the Zeus-nurtured kings.
So the people hastily sat down, and kept to their seats,
and stopped their shouting. Then lord Agamemnon arose,   100
holding the staff which Hephaestus had made by his craft.
Hephaestus had given it to lord Zeus, the son of Cronus,
and then Zeus had given it to the guide, slayer of Argus;*
lord Hermes gave it to Pelops, whipper of horses, and
Pelops in his turn gave it to Atreus, shepherd of the people.   105
Atreus as he died left it to Thyestes, rich in flocks,
and Thyestes in his turn left it to Agamemnon to wield,
to rule over many islands and the whole of Argos.*
Leaning on this staff, Agamemnon addressed the Argives:
'Friends, Danaan heroes, ministers of Ares! Zeus, the son of   110
Cronus, has mightily snared me in a cruel delusion,
hard god that he is, who once promised and assured me that I
should return home only after sacking strongly walled Ilium;
but now he has planned an evil deception, and tells me to
return to Argos without glory, after losing many of my people.   115
This must I suppose be pleasing to Zeus the all-powerful,

who has indeed destroyed the crowns of many cities,
and will do so again; for his might is the greatest of all.
But this will be a shameful thing for future men to hear,
that so fine and numerous a host of Achaeans fought   120
a vain and futile war, fighting against men who were
fewer in number, with no success to be shown at its end.
If we were minded, both Achaeans and Trojans, to make
a solemn truce and both sides to reckon their numbers,
the Trojans to count up those who have houses in the city,   125
and we Achaeans to arrange ourselves in groups of ten;
and if each group were to choose a Trojan to pour their wine,
then there would be many tens who lacked a wine-pourer—
so greatly, I say, do the sons of the Achaeans outnumber
the Trojans who dwell in the city. But they have allies   130
from many cities on their side, men who wield the spear,
who thwart me mightily and prevent me from sacking Ilium,
that well-populated city, for all my desire to do so.
Already nine years from great Zeus have passed, and, as we see,
the ships' timbers have rotted and their rigging has gone slack;   135
and our wives and our infant children must be sitting
in our halls longing for our return, while our enterprise,
the cause of our coming here, remains quite unaccomplished.
Come then, let us all be agreed, and do as I say:
let us go away in our ships to our dear native land,   140
because we shall never capture Troy of the wide streets.'

So he spoke, and roused the spirit in the breasts
of all those in the army who did not know his purpose.
The assembly was stirred like the tall waves of the sea,
the open sea by Icaria,* when the East and South Winds   145
churn it up, swooping down from the clouds of father Zeus.
As when the West Wind moves over a deep cornfield and stirs it,
and the ears of corn bend before its violent onset,
so the whole assembly was stirred, and the men rushed
shouting towards the ships, and underneath their feet the dust   150
rose and hung suspended in the air. They called to each other
to lay hold of the ships and drag them down to the bright sea,
and they began to rake out the slipways and pulled the props from
under the ships; in their longing for home their shouts reached the sky.

Then the Argives would have returned home, against their
    destiny,
                                                                       155

if Hera had not spoken to Athena with these words:
'Daughter of aegis-wearing Zeus, Atrytone,* this will not do!
It seems that the Argives are about to flee home to their
dear native land, over the broad back of the sea. If they do,
they will leave to Priam and the Trojans a reason to boast—　160
I mean Argive Helen, on whose account many of the Achaeans
have died at Troy, far from their dear native land.
Go now among the people of bronze-shirted Achaeans
and with coaxing words try to hold back every man, and
do not let them drag their well-balanced ships down to the sea.'　165

　So she spoke, and the goddess grey-eyed Athena did not disobey her,
but went swooping down from the peaks of Olympus,
and quickly came to the swift ships of the Achaeans.
There she found Odysseus, the equal of Zeus in scheming,
standing idle; he had not laid hold of his well-benched black ship,　170
because sadness had entered his heart and his spirit.
Standing nearby the goddess grey-eyed Athena addressed him:
'Son of Laertes, sprung from Zeus, Odysseus of many schemes,
are you really about to fall into your many-benched ships,
all of you, and to run home like this, to your dear native land?　175
If so, you will leave to Priam and the Trojans a reason to boast—
I mean Argive Helen, on whose account many of the Achaeans
have died at Troy, far from their dear native land.
Come now, do not delay, but go among the people of the Achaeans,
and with coaxing words try to hold back every man, and　180
do not let them drag their well-balanced ships down to the sea.'

　So she spoke, and he knew he had heard a goddess's voice,
and set off at a run, throwing away his cloak, which was retrieved
by the herald Eurybates, who came from Ithaca and served him.
He himself went to meet Agamemnon, son of Atreus, and　185
received from him the ancestral, never-decaying staff, and
holding it made his way along the ships of the bronze-shirted Achaeans.

　Whenever he came across a king or man of eminence,
he would stand beside him and try to restrain him with coaxing words:
'You are possessed! It is not right to threaten you as if you were　190
a coward; go, sit down again and make all your people sit as well.
You do not yet know clearly what the son of Atreus intends;
he is testing the Achaeans' sons now, but soon he will hit them hard.
Did we not all hear what he said in the council? I am afraid
that in his bitterness he may punish the sons of the Achaeans.　195

Great is the temper of kings who are nurtured by Zeus;
their honour comes from Zeus, and Zeus the counsellor loves them.'

    But whenever he saw a man of the common people yelling out,
he would belabour him with the staff and shout at him:
'You are possessed! Sit down quietly and listen to the words of others   200
who are better fighters than you; you are feeble and unwarlike,
not someone to be reckoned with either in war or in counsel.
There is no way that we Achaeans can all be kings here.
Many rulers are an evil thing; let there be a single commander,
one king, to whom the son of crooked-scheming Cronus has given   205
[a staff and the power to judge, to decide for his people].'

    So by his authority he brought them under control, and they streamed
back again from their ships and huts to the assembly place,
with the noise of a wave of the loud-bellowing sea when it
crashes on to a great beach, and the wide sea echoes its roar.   210

    So they all settled down and kept to their seats, except for
one man, Thersites, who kept whining on; his talk was full of chaos,
and he had a mind crammed with words, numerous and disorderly,
though he used them in a wild and unruly way, to argue with the kings;
and he would say what he thought would be amusing to the   215
Argives. He was the ugliest man who had come to besiege Ilium:
he was bandy-legged, and lame in one foot, and his shoulders
were hunched together, narrowing on to his chest, and his
head grew to a point, and sprouted a scanty crop of hair.
He was especially hated by Achilles and Odysseus, for it was   220
his way to provoke them; but now against glorious Agamemnon
he began to shout abuse, yelling and screaming. The Achaeans
were outraged in their hearts, and grew violently angry with him;
but still he harangued Agamemnon, shouting at the top of his voice:
'What is your complaint this time, Atreus' son? What more
        do you want?   225
Your huts are crammed full of bronze, and there are many
women in your huts, expressly chosen, whom the Achaeans
give to you before anyone else whenever we capture a city.
Is it more gold you hanker after, gold such as one of the horse-
breaking Trojans may bring from Ilium as ransom for his son,   230
whom I or another Achaean have captured and delivered here?
Or is it a young woman you want, to couple with in love,
and to keep her apart for yourself? It is not right for one
who is their leader to make trouble for the sons of the Achaeans.

Weak fools, wretched fools, women of Achaea, no longer men! 235
Let us make our way home in our ships and leave this one
here at Troy to brood on his winnings; he will soon find out
whether the rest of us will come to his help or not. And now
he has even dishonoured Achilles, a much better man than him,
taking his prize away in person and keeping it for himself. 240
But there is no rage in Achilles' heart, and he is slow to act—
otherwise, son of Atreus, this would be your last outrage.'

So Thersites spoke, provoking Agamemnon, shepherd of the people.
But glorious Odysseus quickly came up and stood beside him,
and looking at him darkly rebuked him with hard words: 245
'Thersites, you may be a clear-voiced speaker, but your words are wild.
Restrain yourself; do not hope to be the one man who argues with kings.
I do not believe there is any mortal less warlike than you,
out of all those who came with the sons of Atreus to besiege Ilium.
So—let's have no more bawling out the names of your kings, 250
trying to make sure of a voyage home by flinging abuse at them.
We do not yet know for sure how these things will be, whether
we sons of Achaeans will return home in triumph or in defeat;
yet here you sit and behave insolently towards Agamemnon,
shepherd of the people, because the Danaan heroes give him 255
a great many gifts; your speech is nothing but jeering abuse.
But I tell you this plainly, and it will certainly be fulfilled:
if ever I find you playing the fool again as you are now,
may the head of Odysseus no longer sit on his shoulders,
and may I no longer be called the father of Telemachus, 260
if I do not lay hands on you and strip you of your garments,
your cloak and your tunic, which cover up your shame,
and send you away weeping to the swift ships, when I have
thrashed you out of the assembly with shameful blows.'

So he spoke, and with the staff beat Thersites on his back 265
and shoulders; he doubled up, and a huge tear fell from his eyes,
and on his back a bloody weal swelled up, raised by
the blows of the golden staff. He sat down again, terrified
and in pain, and with a helpless look wiped the tear away.
But the rest, vexed though they were, laughed happily to see it, 270
and this is what they would say, each man looking at his neighbour:
'Well, we know that Odysseus has done countless fine things,
both leading us with good counsel and deploying us in battle,
but this is by far the best thing he has done among the Argives,

stopping this blustering and intemperate man speaking in the
     assembly.   275
I do not think Thersites' proud spirit will ever again urge him
to use such insulting words to pick fights with the kings.'

   So spoke the mass of men; and now Odysseus, sacker of cities,
stood up, holding the staff, and by his side grey-eyed Athena
in the likeness of a herald commanded the people to be silent,   280
so that the nearest and the furthest of the sons of the Achaeans
might hear what he said and reflect on his advice.
With generous intent he spoke out among them:
'Son of Atreus, lord, it seems now that the Achaeans are minded
to make you thoroughly disgraced among mortal men, and   285
they will not fulfil the promise that they made to you
on their voyage here from Argos,* rearer of horses: that you
would return home only after sacking Ilium of the strong walls.
They are behaving like young children or widowed women,
when they start wailing to each other about their return home—   290
clearly the battle-toil discourages them, and so they want to go back.
Even a man who spends one month apart from his wife
will brood impatiently beside his many-benched ship, which
winter storms and swelling seas keep confined to the shore;
but in our case this is now the ninth circling year that we have   295
remained here inactive. I do not therefore blame the Achaeans
for their brooding impatience beside the curved ships; yet it is
surely a shameful thing to wait so long and return empty-handed.
Be patient, my friends, and hold out for a time, and we will learn
whether Calchas prophesies truly to us or not. What I shall   300
now say we remember well in our minds, and you are all
witnesses, those whom the spectres of death have not carried off:
it seems like yesterday or the day before that the Achaeans' ships
assembled at Aulis,* bringing ruin to Priam and to the Trojans,
and we on sacred altars that surrounded a spring were   305
sacrificing unblemished hecatombs to the immortals,
under a beautiful plane tree from which bright water flowed,
when a momentous sign appeared: a snake with a blood-red back,
hideous, that the Olympian himself had dispatched into the light,
slithered out from under the altar and made for the plane-tree.   310
Now in this were some sparrow's fledglings, infant children,
on the topmost branch, cowering under the leaves,
eight of them, and the mother who bore them made nine.

The snake swallowed them down, all squeaking piteously, and
their mother fluttered about them, lamenting her dear brood, and   315
as she cried over them it coiled itself up and caught her by the wing.
But when it had devoured the sparrow's children and their mother,
the god who had caused it to appear made it into a clear sign:
the son of crooked-scheming Cronus turned it to stone,
and we stood there in amazement at what had happened.   320
When this dreadful prodigy had interrupted the gods' hecatombs,
Calchas straightaway interpreted it for us, and spoke out:
"Why have you fallen silent, flowing-haired Achaeans?
It is for us that Zeus the counsellor has revealed this great sign—
late appearing, and late in fulfilment, but its fame will never die.   325
As this creature has devoured the children and the sparrow herself,
eight of them, and the mother who bore them made nine,
so shall we make war at Troy for that number of years,
and in the tenth we shall take the city with its wide streets."
So he spoke out, and all this has now been fulfilled.   330
So come, stand firm where you are, all you well-greaved
Achaeans, until such time as we take the great city of Priam.'

    So he spoke, and the Argives gave a great yell, and the ships
resounded loudly around to the shouts of the Achaeans,
as they acclaimed the speech of godlike Odysseus.   335
Then among them the horseman Gerenian* Nestor spoke up:
'Come, come! Truly, your speeches are like children's,
infants, who know nothing of the business of war.
What is now to become of our oaths, and the agreements we made?
We may as well throw into the fire all men's counsels and
    stratagems,   340
those libations of unmixed wine, and the right hands we trusted in;
we are fighting with words, but to no purpose, and we cannot
find a remedy, even though we have been here for a long time.
Son of Atreus, you must hold your purpose unshaken, as before,
and command the Argives in the harsh conflict, and   345
leave these others to die, the one or two of the Achaeans
who are plotting in secret—though it will all come to nothing—
to go back to Argos before they find out about the promise
of Zeus who wears the aegis, whether it is false or not.
I believe that the son of Cronus, the all-powerful, nodded assent   350
to us on the day that the Argives boarded their swift-travelling
ships, bringing bloodshed and doom to the Trojans, when he

flashed lightning on our right, showing us an auspicious sign.
So let no one hurry to sail away towards his home
until each man of you has slept with the wife of a Trojan,   355
and has exacted vengeance for Helen's struggles and groans.
But if anyone has an overwhelming desire to leave for home,
let him merely touch his well-benched black ship, and
in the sight of all he will meet death and destruction.
Come, lord, consider well and listen to the advice of another;   360
whatever I say to you, you should not cast it aside.
Separate the army by tribes and by clans, Agamemnon,
so that clan may support clan and tribe may support tribe.
If you do this, and if the Achaeans follow your orders,
you will find out the cowards among the leaders and people,   365
and the brave men, because they will fight in their own companies.
You will find, too, if it is by divine will that you fail to destroy the city,
or because of men's cowardice and their ignorance of warfare.'
    Then in answer lord Agamemnon addressed him:
'Once again, old man, you far surpass the Achaeans' sons in debate.   370
Father Zeus and Athena and Apollo, how I wish that
I had ten counsellors such as this man among the Achaeans!
Then the city of lord Priam would soon reel before us,
when it has been captured and devastated by our hands.
But Zeus, Cronus' aegis-wearing son, has brought me anguish,   375
pitching me into disputes and quarrels that cannot be resolved.
We fought, I and Achilles, for the sake of a girl,
matching violent words, and I was the first to become angry;
but if ever we can agree on one course of action, no longer
will the Trojans' evil day be put off, not even for a short time.   380
So go now and make your meal, and prepare for Ares' warfare;
let each man take care to sharpen his spear and fettle his shield,
let each man take care to give their meal to his swift-footed horses,
let each man take care to inspect his chariot well and prepare for war,
so that all day long we may join in the judgement of hateful Ares.   385
There will certainly be no intervening respite, not even a little,
until the coming of night brings men's fury to judgement.
Sweat will cover the strap across his chest of each man's body-
protecting shield, and the hand on his spear will grow weary, and
sweat will cover each man's horse as it strains at the polished
    chariot.   390
And if I chance to see anyone attempting to hang back from

the battle by the beaked ships, there will be no sure way
for him thereafter to escape the dogs and vultures.'
    So he spoke, and the Argives gave a great roar, like a wave
churned up by the South Wind's onset, falling on to a steep shore 395
against a jutting rock that the breakers, driven by winds
from every quarter, never leave, but come at it from every side.
They rose quickly to their feet and scattered to their ships,
and lit fires, everyone in his own hut, and ate their meal.
Each man sacrificed to one of the gods who live for ever, 400
praying that he would escape death and the grind of Ares' warfare.
But Agamemnon, lord of men, sacrificed a bull,
a fat five-year-old, to the all-powerful son of Cronus, and
summoned the elders, chieftains of the whole Achaean force:
Nestor came first of all, and the lord Idomeneus, 405
then the pair called Ajax and the son of Tydeus,
then sixth came Odysseus, the equal of Zeus in scheming.
Uninvited came Menelaus, master of the war-cry,
for he knew in his heart how troubled his brother was.
They stood around the bull, and lifted up the barley grains, 410
and among them lord Agamemnon spoke in prayer:
'Mightiest, most glorious Zeus of the dark cloud, dwelling in the
upper air, grant that before the sun sets and darkness comes
I shall hurl the palace of Priam down headlong,
blackened in smoke, and burn its doors with ravaging fire, 415
and that I shall rip Hector's tunic into tatters on his chest,
slashed by the bronze; and may great numbers of his companions
fall face-forward on the earth, biting the ground with their teeth.'
    So he spoke, but the son of Cronus did not yet fulfil his prayer;
he accepted the sacrifice, but prolonged their miserable toil. 420
Now when they had prayed and sprinkled the barley grains,
first they pulled back the bull's head, slit its throat and flayed it,
then cut away the thigh-bones and wrapped them in fat, covering
them above and below, and laid raw hunks of meat on them.
These they laid on to billets of dead wood and burnt them, 425
then spitted the entrails and held them over Hephaestus' fire.
When the thigh-bones were burnt up, and they had tasted the entrails,
they chopped the rest of the meat small and threaded it on skewers,
and cooked it with great care and then drew it all off.
When they had finished their work, and made the meal ready, 430
they feasted, and no one's heart lacked a fair share in the meal.

But once they had put from themselves the desire for food and drink,
among them the horseman Gerenian Nestor began to speak:
'Most glorious son of Atreus, Agamemnon lord of men,
let us not spend more time conversing, nor any longer   435
postpone the work which a god is putting into our hands.
Come now, let the heralds of the bronze-shirted Achaeans
make a proclamation and assemble the people by ships,
and let us go together as we are throughout the broad camp
of the Achaeans, so that we may quickly stir up bitter Ares.'   440
    So he spoke, and Agamemnon lord of men did not disobey him.
Immediately he ordered the clear-voiced heralds to make
a proclamation, calling the flowing-haired Achaeans to war;
so they made their proclamation, and the men gathered very quickly.
Then Atreus' son and with him the kings, nurtured by Zeus,   445
busily mustered the army, and in their midst was grey-eyed Athena,
holding the precious aegis, ageless and immortal,
from which fluttered a hundred tassels, all golden,
all of them skilfully woven, each worth a hundred oxen.
Holding this she darted swiftly in and out of the Achaean people,   450
provoking them to action, and in each man she stirred up strength
in his heart to engage in the war and fight without ceasing;
and so then war became sweeter to them than a return
in their hollow ships to their dear native land.
    As when devastating fire blazes through an enormous forest   455
on a mountain peak, and its glare is seen from afar,
so as they marched the glitter from the stupendous mass of bronze
flashed all around through the upper air and reached the high sky.
    As the numerous companies of winged birds,
geese or cranes or swans with their long necks, gather   460
on the Asian water-meadow, by the streams of Caÿster,*
and soar this way and that, exulting in their wings, and
settle with a clamour, and the meadow resounds with their cries,
so the army's numerous companies poured out from ships
and huts on to the plain of Scamander;* and the ground under   465
the feet of men and horses gave back a terrifying sound.
They took their stand on the flowery plain of Scamander,
numberless as the leaves and flowers that appear in spring.
    As many as the numerous companies of swarming flies
that swarm about the sheepfold of a herdsman   470
in the season of spring, when pails brim with milk,

so many were the flowing-haired Achaeans facing the Trojans
and taking their stand on the plain, raging to break them utterly.
 And just as goatherds easily separate their far-wandering
flocks of goats, when they have become mixed up in the pasture, 475
so the commanders mustered their men on this side and on that,
ready for the conflict; and in their midst was lord Agamemnon,
his gaze and head like Zeus who delights in the thunderbolt,
in girth like Ares, and with the chest of Poseidon.
Just like an ox which far surpasses all the rest of a herd, 480
a bull, which stands out among the cattle gathered round it,
even so Zeus made the son of Atreus on that day,
conspicuous in the soldiery, pre-eminent among the heroes.
 Tell me now, Muses who have your homes on Olympus—
for you are goddesses, and are present, and know everything, 485
while we hear only rumour, and know nothing—
who were the commanders and princes of the Danaans.
As for the soldiery, I could not describe or name them,
not even if I had ten tongues and ten mouths,
an indestructible voice, and a bronze heart within me, 490
unless the Muses of Olympus, daughters of aegis-wearing
Zeus, were to recount all those who came to besiege Ilium.
So I shall relate the ships' captains and the number of their ships.*
 Of the Boeotians, Peneleos and Leïtus were their captains,
and Arcesilaus and Prothoënor and Clonius; 495
these were the men who lived in Hyria and rocky Aulis,
Schoenus and Scolus and Eteonus with its many peaks,
Thespeia, Graea, and Mycalessus of the wide dancing-places,
and who occupied Harma and Eilesium and Erythrae,
and those who possessed Eleon and Hyle and Peteon, 500
Ocalea and the well-built fortress of Medeon,
Copae, Eutresis, and Thisbe rich in doves, and
those who lived around Coronea and grassy Haliartus,
those who inhabited Plataea and who lived in Glisas,
those who possessed Lower Thebes,* that well-built fortress, 505
and sacred Onchestus, Poseidon's splendid grove,
and who inhabited Arne, rich in vines, and who held Mideia
and sacred Nisa and Anthedon on the far borders.
Of these people, fifty ships had come, and in each
one hundred and twenty young Boeotians had embarked. 510
 Those who lived in Aspledon and Minyan Orchomenus

were led by Ascalaphus and Ialmenus, sons of Ares,
whom Astyoche bore in the house of Actor, Azeus' son,
to mighty Ares; a modest virgin, she went up to her chamber
and there the powerful god lay with her in secret.   515
Under these was marshalled a fleet of thirty hollow ships.

The captains of the Phocians were Schedius and Epistrophus,
sons of Iphitus, the great-hearted son of Naubolus.
These were the men who held Cyparissus and rocky Pytho,
sacred Crisa and Daulis and Panopeus,   520
and those who occupied Anemoreia and Hyampolis,
and those whose homes were by the bright river Cephisus,
and those who inhabited Lilaea next to the springs of Cephisus.
They were accompanied by forty black ships.
Their captains ordered the ranks of the Phocians and   525
stationed them on the left flank, close to the Boeotians.

The Locrians were commanded by Oïleus' son, swift Ajax,
the lesser one, not as huge as Ajax, son of Telamon, but
much smaller. He was of slight build, and wore a linen jerkin,
but he far excelled all the Hellenes and Achaeans with the spear.   530
These were the men who lived in Cynus and Opous
and Calliarus, in Bessa and Scarphe and lovely Augeiae,
Tarphe and Thronion, and the land around Boagrius' waters.
Accompanying Ajax came forty black ships
of the Locrians who live opposite sacred Euboea.   535

As for the fury-breathing Abantes, who held Euboea,
Chalcis and Eiretria and Histiaea, rich in vines,
Cerinthus next to the sea and the steep fortress of Dius,
those who inhabited Carystus and those who lived in Styra—
these in their turn were commanded by Elephenor, a shoot of Ares,* 540
son of Chalcodon, captain of the great-hearted Abantes.
With him came the swift Abantes, their hair streaming behind them,
spearmen raging with their out-thrust ash shafts
to tear through the corslets on their enemies' chests.
Accompanying Elephenor came forty black ships.   545

Then there were those who lived in Athens, a well-built city,
the people of great-hearted Erechtheus, whom long ago Athena
Zeus' daughter nurtured, after the grain-giving earth had borne him,
and established him in Athens, in her own rich temple;
and there with an offering of bulls and rams the young men   550
of the Athenians appease him in each year's wheeling course.

These in their turn were commanded by Menestheus, Peteus' son.
No man had yet been born upon earth who was his equal
in the deployment of chariots and shield-bearing men;
only Nestor could rival him, since he was from an older time.   555
Accompanying Menestheus came fifty black ships.

Ajax brought twelve ships from Salamis, and
stationed them where the Athenians' troops were deployed.

As for those who inhabited Argos and fortified Tiryns,
Hermione and Asine which lie on the deep gulf,   560
Troezen and Eionae, and vine-bearing Epidaurus,
and those young Achaean men who held Aegina and Mases,
they in their turn were led by Diomedes, master of the war-cry,
and Sthenelus, dear son of far-famed Capaneus.
Third with them came Euryalus, a man resembling the gods,   565
son of Mecisteus the king, who was the son of Talaus.
Diomedes, master of the war-cry, commanded the whole force,
and accompanying them came eighty black ships.

As for those who inhabited the well-built city of Mycenae,
wealthy Corinth and well-built Cleonae,   570
and who lived in Orneiae and lovely Araethyrea,
and Sicyon, where Adrestus was the first king,
and those who inhabited Hyperesie and steep Gonoëssa
and Pellene, and had their home in Aegion
and all the coastal strip of Aegialus, and broad Helice—   575
the captain of their hundred ships was Agamemnon,
son of Atreus, and with him came by far the most numerous
and best men. He stood in their midst, armed in flashing bronze,
exulting, conspicuous among all the heroes because
he was the best, and brought by far the largest army.   580

As for those who lived in low-lying Lacedaemon, riven by
gorges, in Pharis and Sparta and Messe rich in doves,
and who lived in Bryseiae and lovely Augeiae,
and those who held Amyclae and the maritime fortress of Helus,
and who possessed Laas and lived around Oetylus,   585
these and their sixty ships were commanded by his brother,
Menelaus, master of the war-cry. They were stationed apart,
and he moved among them, drawing strength from his passion,
urging them on to battle; most of all he desired in his heart
to exact vengeance for Helen's struggles and groans.   590

As for those who lived in Pylos and lovely Arene,

Thryon where Alpheus is forded, and well-built Aepy,
and whose home was Cyparesseïs and Amphigeneia,
Pteleus and Helus and Dorion, where the Muses
met Thamyris the Thracian on his way from Oechalia,   595
from the house of Eurytus the Oechalian, and ended his singing,
because he boasted that he would win the prize, even if the
Muses themselves, daughters of aegis-wearing Zeus, were to sing;
in their anger they mutilated him, and took away his marvellous
gift of singing, and made him forget his lyre-playing art.   600
Of these the commander was the horseman, Gerenian Nestor,
and with him were mustered ninety hollow ships.

As for those who held Arcadia, under Cyllene's steep mountain,
near the tomb of Aepytus, where men fight hand to hand,
and those who lived in Pheneus and Orchomenus, rich in flocks,   605
Rhipe and Stratië and Enispe, swept by winds,
and those who possessed Tegea and lovely Mantinea,
and those who possessed Stymphelus, and who lived in
Parrhasië, these were commanded by the son of Ancaeus,
lord Agapenor, with sixty ships; and in each ship   610
many men of Arcadia skilled in warfare had embarked.
Atreus' son Agamemnon, lord of men, had himself given them
well-benched ships to cross the wine-faced open sea,
since they had no knowledge of seafaring matters.

As for those who lived in Buprasium and glorious Elis,   615
all the land that Hyrmine and Myrsinus on the far borders
and the rock of Olenus and Alesion enclose between them,
of these there were four captains, and each man was accompanied
by ten swift ships, and many Epeians had embarked on them.
Some were commanded by Amphimachus and Thalpius,   620
one a son of Cteatus and the other of Eurytus, both of Actor's family.
Diores, the mighty son of Amarynceus, was captain of the third,
and godlike Polyxeinus was captain of the fourth division,
the son of king Agasthenes, who was the son of Augeas.

As for those from Dulichium* and the sacred Echinean   625
Islands, who live across the sea opposite Elis,
these were commanded by Meges, the equal of Ares,
Phyleus' son, whom the horseman Phyleus, dear to Zeus, fathered;
he had long ago quarrelled with his father and migrated
to Dulichium. Accompanying him came forty black ships.   630

Odysseus led the great-spirited Cephallenians,

who held Ithaca and Neritum with its trembling leaves,
and lived in Crocyleia and rugged Aegilips,
and those who possessed Zakynthos and inhabited Samos,
and those who possessed the mainland and the coast opposite.   635
Of these the captain was Odysseus, the equal of Zeus in scheming.
Accompanying him came twelve ships with red-painted prows.

   Thoas, son of Andraemon, commanded the Aetolians
who occupied Pleuron and Olenus and Pylene,
Chalcis that lies on the coast, and rocky Calydon;   640
the sons of great-hearted Oeneus were no longer alive,
nor Oeneus himself, and fair-haired Meleager was dead,*
to whom all power had been entrusted to rule over the Aetolians.
Accompanying him came forty black ships.

   The Cretans' commander was Idomeneus, famed with the spear.   645
They possessed Cnossus and fortified Gortyn,
Lyctus and Miletus, and Lycastus with its chalk cliffs,
and Phaestus and Rhytion, well-populated cities; and
there were other men, who lived in Crete of the hundred cities.
Of all these Idomeneus, famed with the spear, was commander,   650
and with him Meriones, the equal of Enyalius, killer of men.
Accompanying them came eighty black ships.

   Tlepolemus, the valiant and mighty son of Heracles,
brought from Rhodes nine ships of proud Rhodians,
who lived on Rhodes in three separate settlements,   655
Lindos and Ialysus and Cameirus with its chalk cliffs.
Their commander was Tlepolemus, famed with the spear,
whom Astyocheia bore to mighty Heracles, when he had
carried her off from Ephyre, from the river Selleïs, after
sacking many cities of strong young men, nurtured by Zeus.   660
Now when Tlepolemus had grown up in their well-built house
he soon afterwards killed his father's maternal uncle,
Licyminus, a shoot of Ares, who was now an old man.
At once he built some ships, and assembling a great company
fled away across the sea, because the other sons and   665
grandsons of mighty Heracles had threatened him.
After many wanderings and hardships he came to Rhodes,
and his men settled there by tribes in a threefold division,
and were loved by Zeus, who rules over both gods and men,
and the son of Cronus showered them with astounding wealth.   670

   Nireus brought three well-balanced ships from Syme,

Nireus, the son of Aglaea and lord Charopus,
Nireus, who was the handsomest man of all the Danaans who
came to besiege Ilium, excepting the blameless son of Peleus;
but he was a feeble man, and few people came with him.   675

    As for those who possessed Nisyros, Crapathos, and Casos,
and Cos, city of Eurypylus, and the Calydnian Islands,
these men were commanded by Pheidippus and Antiphus,
the two sons of King Thessalus, the son of Heracles,
and with them were mustered thirty hollow ships.   680

    Now all those whose home was Pelasgian Argos,
and those who lived in Alus and Alope, and those from Trachis,
and those who possessed Phthia and Hellas of beautiful women,
and were called Myrmidons and Hellenes and Achaeans,
the captain of their fifty ships was Achilles.   685
But they had no thought for war's hideous clamour,
because there was no one to lead them in the battle line;
glorious swift-footed Achilles was lying among the ships,
angry over the girl, Briseus' daughter of the beautiful hair,
whom he had chosen from Lyrnessus' spoils after much labour,   690
when he had sacked Lyrnessus and the walls of Thebe, and
had struck down Mynes and Epistrophus, famous spearmen,
who were the sons of King Euenus, son of Selepus. And so
he lay there, grieving for her; but he was soon to rise again.

    As for those who possessed Phylace and flowery Pyrasus,   695
the precinct of Demeter, and Iton mother of flocks,
Antron by the sea and Pteleus with its beds of grass,
these were commanded by warlike Protesilaus
while he was alive, but now the black earth held him below.
His wife was left behind in Phylace, tearing her cheeks in grief, 700
in a half-built house. One of Dardanus' people killed him
as he leapt from his ship, the very first of the Achaeans. Even so
they were not leaderless, though they yearned for their captain;
Podarces, a shoot of Ares, was their marshal, Iphicles'
son, who was himself the son of Phylacus rich in flocks,   705
and he was full brother to great-hearted Protesilaus,
and older than him in years; but the hero warlike Protesilaus
was the better man, and more skilled in war. His people
did not lack a leader, though they longed for this fine man.
Accompanying Podarces came forty black ships.   710

    As for those who lived around Pherae beside Lake Boebaïs,

in Boebe and Glaphyrae and well-built Iolcus,
the captain of their eleven ships was Admetus' dear son,
Eumelus, borne to him by Alcestis, bright among women,
the most beautiful of the daughters of Pelias.   715

   As for those who lived in Methone and Thaumacië
and possessed Meliboea and rugged Olizon,
their captain was the skilled archer Philoctetes,
in charge of seven ships; in each of them fifty rowers
had embarked, well skilled in fighting strongly with their bows.   720
But he was lying on an island, enduring cruel agonies,
on sacred Lemnos, where the Achaeans' sons had left him,
suffering from the foul wound of a deadly water-snake.
There he lay in torment; but the Argives would soon
turn their minds to lord Philoctetes beside their ships.* Even so   725
his men were not leaderless, though they longed for their captain;
Medon, the bastard son of Oïleus, was their marshal,
he whom Rhene had borne to Oïleus, sacker of cities.

   As for those who possessed Tricce and craggy Ithome,
and those who held Oechalia, city of Oechalian Eurytus,   730
these men were commanded by the two sons of Asclepius,
excellent healers both, Podaleirius and Machaon;
and with them were mustered thirty hollow ships.

   Those who possessed Ormenion and the spring Hypereia,
and those who possessed Asterion and Titanus' white peaks   735
were led by Eurypylus the splendid son of Euaemon.
Accompanying him came forty black ships.

   As for those who possessed Argissa and lived in Gyrtone,
in Orthe, and the city of Elone and white Oloösson,
they were commanded by Polypoetes, steadfast in war,   740
the son of Peirithous, who was fathered by immortal Zeus;
renowned Hippodameia had borne him to Peirithous
on the day that he took his revenge on the hairy Centaurs*
and expelled them from Pelion as far as the Aethices' land;
he was not alone, but with him came Leonteus, a shoot of Ares,   745
son of high-hearted Coronus, himself the son of Caeneus.
Accompanying them came forty black ships.

   Gouneus brought twenty-two ships from Cyphus.
Following him were the Enienes and the Peraebi, steadfast in war,
who made their homes around Dodona, where winters are harsh,   750
and by those who worked the land around lovely Titaressus,

which pours out its beautiful waters into the Peneius,
though it does not mingle with silver-eddying Peneius,
but flows along on its surface like olive oil; it is a
branch of the waters of Styx, dreadful river of oaths.*   755

Prothous, son of Tenthredon, was captain of the Magnetes,
who lived around Peneius and Pelion with its quivering
leaves. The swift Prothous was their commander,
and accompanying him came forty black ships.

These then were the leaders and commanders of the Danaans.   760
Now tell me, Muse, who was the most outstanding of those
who followed Atreus' sons, both themselves and their horses.

The finest horses belonged to the son of Pheres,
now driven by Eumelus; they were swift as birds, and were alike
in coats and age, their backs dead level measured by the rule.   765
Apollo of the silver bow had raised them in Pereia,
both mares, and they carried in them the terror of Ares.
Of men, by far the best was Ajax, Telamon's son, so long as
Achilles kept up his anger; but Achilles was much the strongest,
as were the horses which carried Peleus' blameless son;   770
but he was lying beside his curved sea-traversing ships,
full of anger against Agamemnon, shepherd of the people,
the son of Atreus; and his people were amusing themselves
on the seashore by throwing the discus and javelin,
and shooting with the bow; and each man's horses stood beside   775
his chariot, cropping clover and wild, marsh-growing parsley,
doing nothing. The chieftains' chariots stood well covered near
their huts, while the men, yearning for their captain, loved by Ares,
wandered up and down through the camp and did not fight.

So the Achaeans marched on as if the whole earth were
        grazed by fire,   780
and the ground under their feet groaned as if thunder-delighting Zeus
was angry, as when he lashes the earth around Typhoeus
in the land of the Arimi, where men say is Typhoeus' bed.*
Just so the earth groaned loudly under their feet
as they marched; and very quickly they crossed the plain.   785

Now to the Trojans a messenger came, wind-footed swift Iris,
with a message for them, full of pain from aegis-wearing Zeus.
They were holding an assembly at Priam's gates,
all gathered together, both the young and the old; and
swift-footed Iris stood close to Priam and addressed him,   790

likening her voice to that of Priam's son Polites, who was
the Trojans' lookout, and, trusting in his feet's speed, used to sit
on top of the burial-mound of ancient Aesyetes,* watching
for when the Achaeans would attack from their ships.
Assuming this man's likeness, swift-footed Iris addressed Priam: 795
'Old man, it is always your way to delight in endless speeches,
just as before in times of peace; but now relentless war has arisen.
I tell you, I have taken part in many battles of men, but
never before have I seen such a host, nor one so numerous.
More than anything, they are like leaves or grains of sand   800
as they march, ready to fight, over the plain towards the city.
Hector, to you especially I give this command, and you must carry it out:
there are many allies throughout the great city of Priam, speaking
different tongues, for they come from peoples spread over the earth;
let each one of these give orders to those he rules over,   805
and let him marshal his countrymen and then lead them out.'

So she spoke, and Hector did not fail to recognize a goddess' voice,
and quickly broke up the assembly. The Trojans rushed to arms,
all the gates were opened, and the peoples streamed out,
on foot and in chariots, and a great clamour arose.   810

There is in front of the city a steep mound, set at
some distance from it on the plain, with clear space
around it, to which men give the name of Batieia, but
the immortals call it the burial-mound of the dancer Myrine.*
There now the Trojans and their allies marshalled themselves.*   815

The Trojans' commander was great Hector of the glittering helmet,
Priam's son; and with him were armed by far the best and
most numerous people, raging to fight with their spears.

The captain of Dardanus' people was the valiant son of Anchises,
Aeneas, whom the goddess Aphrodite bore to Anchises,   820
a goddess lying with a mortal on the slopes of Ida.
He was not alone, but with him were the two sons of Antenor,
Archelochus and Acamas, well skilled in all the arts of battle.

Those who inhabited Zeleia, under the lowest shoulder of Ida,
wealthy men, who drank the black waters of Aesepus,   825
called Troes—these were led by the splendid son of Lycaon,
Pandarus, to whom Apollo himself had given his bow.

As for those who held Adresteia and the land of Apaesus,
and possessed Pityeia and the steep mountain of Tereia,
their captains were Adrestus and Amphius of the linen jerkin,   830

the two sons of Merops from Percote, who above all men
was skilled in seercraft; he tried to prevent his sons
from going to man-destroying war, but they would not listen
to him, for the spectres of black death were leading them on.

As for those who occupied Percote and Practius,   835
and possessed Sestus and Abydus and bright Arisbe,
their captain was Asius, son of Hyrtacus, marshal of the army—
Asius, son of Hyrtacus, whom huge gleaming horses
had brought from Arisbe, which is near the river Selleïs.

Hippothous led the tribes of Pelasgians, famous spearmen,   840
who had their home in Larisa of the rich soil.
Their captains were Hippothous and Pylaeus, shoots of Ares,
two sons of Pelasgian Lethus, who was himself the son of Teutamus.

Acamas and the hero Peirous were leaders of the Thracians,
all those whose lands the strong-flowing Hellespont encloses.   845

Captain of the Ciconian spearmen was Euphemus, son of
Troezenus, who was himself the son of Ceas, nurtured by Zeus.

Pyraechmes led the Paeonians with their curved bows
from far-off Amydon, by the broad-flowing Axius,
whose water is the most beautiful that flows over the earth.   850

The Paphlagonians were led by hairy-chested Pylaemenes,
from the land of the Eneti, home of a strain of wild mules;
they possessed Cytorus and inhabited Sesamon,
living in splendid houses around the river Parthenius
and Cromne and Aegialus and lofty Erythini.   855

The Halizones' captains were Odius and Epistrophus
from far-off Alybe, which is the birthplace of silver.

The Mysians' leaders were Chromis, and Ennomus the bird-seer—
though bird-lore could not save him from black doom;
he was beaten down by the hands of Aeacus' swift-footed
      grandson   860
in the river, along with the other Trojans he cut down there.

Phorcys and godlike Ascanius were leaders of the Phrygians
from far off Ascanië; and they were raging to fight in the
      crush of battle.

The Maeonians were commanded by Mesthles and Antiphus,
two sons of Talaemenes, whom the lake Gygaea bore;   865
they led the Maeonians, whose homeland was under Tmolus.

Nastes commanded the Carians, who spoke a foreign tongue;
they held Miletus and the thickly wooded Mount Phthires,

and the waters of Maeander and Mycale's steep peaks.
Their leaders were Amphimachus and Nastes,   870
Nastes and Amphimachus, splendid sons of Nomion.
Amphimachus came to the war wearing gold ornaments, like a girl,
the fool; they gave him no protection against miserable death
when beaten down by the hands of Aeacus' swift-footed grandson,
in the river; and war-minded Achilles carried off his gold.   875
   Sarpedon and blameless Glaucus were captains of the Lycians,
who came from far-off Lycia, beside the rolling Xanthus.

BOOK THREE

Now when both sides had been marshalled with their leaders,
the Trojans advanced, screeching and shouting like birds;
as when the screech of cranes is heard in the high sky,
when they have fled from winter's onset and prodigious rain,
and screaming fly towards the streams of Ocean,*   5
bringing death and destruction to the Pygmy men,*
challenging them through the air to deadly conflict.
But the Achaeans went on in silence, breathing fury,
raging in their hearts to fight on each other's behalf.

As when the South Wind sheds a mist over mountain peaks—   10
no friend to shepherds but for the thief better than night—
when a man can see only as far as he can throw a stone,
so under their feet a dense cloud of dust arose from the men
as they marched; and very quickly they crossed the plain.

When they had advanced to within close range of each other,   15
from the Trojans Alexander,* handsome as a god, came out to fight,
wearing over his shoulder a leopard-skin and a curved bow
and a sword; shaking his two spears, tipped with bronze,
he issued a challenge to all the best men of the Argives
to fight with him in grim conflict, matching strength to strength. 20

When Menelaus, dear to Ares,* caught sight of Alexander
advancing with great strides in front of the soldiery,
just as a lion exults when it lights upon a great corpse,
discovering an antlered stag or a wild goat—the lion is
starving, and devours it quickly, in case swift hounds   25
and strong young men are on its trail—so Menelaus
exulted when his eyes fell on Alexander, handsome as a god,
and, thinking to avenge himself on the wrongdoer,
he quickly leapt fully armed from his chariot to the ground.

Now when Alexander, handsome as a god, saw him appear   30
in the front ranks, his dear heart was shattered, and he
withdrew into his companions' ranks, to avoid the death-spectre.
As when a man who has seen a snake in a mountain glen
starts back, and a trembling seizes hold of his legs,
and he jumps backwards and pallor grips his cheeks,   35
so Alexander, handsome as a god, shrank back into the

mass of proud Trojans, terrified by the son of Atreus.

But when Hector saw him he rebuked him with shaming words:
'Paris, Disaster-Paris, superbly beautiful, woman-crazy seducer!
I wish you had never been born, or had else died unmarried.   40
Indeed I would have preferred this, and it would have been far better
for you than to be thus mocked and despised by others.
How the flowing-haired Achaeans must laugh out loud, thinking
that with us a chieftain becomes a champion only because he is
handsome to look at, even if there is no strength or courage in his
    heart.   45
Was this how you were when you sailed over the sea
in your sea-traversing ships with a band of trusty companions,
and lived among foreigners and carried off a beautiful woman
from a distant land, kin of spear-fighters as she was,
to be a great affliction to your father, the city, and all the people,   50
but a delight to your enemies and a disgrace to yourself?
Can you really not stand up against Menelaus, dear to Ares?
You would find out what kind of man he is whose lovely wife you keep;
and then your lyre would be of no help to you, nor Aphrodite's gifts,
nor your hair and beauty, when you roll in the dust's embrace.   55
But the Trojans are great cowards; otherwise by now you would be
wearing a stone garment,* in return for all the misery you
    have caused.'

Then Alexander, handsome as a god, addressed him in turn:
'Hector, you reproach me deservedly, and not beyond my deserts—
always your heart is like an axe which keeps its edge, and   60
which cuts through a plank in the hands of a man who shapes
ship-timber with his skill, and it adds power to his stroke;
just so is the never-wavering heart in your breast.
But do not throw the sensual gifts of golden Aphrodite in my face;
indeed, men should never spurn the gods' splendid gifts,   65
that they alone can bestow, and no man can have them by choice.
But now, if you want me to engage in the battle and fight,
make all the rest of the Trojans and Achaeans sit down, and
set me in the middle ground against Menelaus, dear to Ares,
to do battle for the sake of Helen and all her possessions;   70
and whichever of us is victorious and proves the stronger, let him
fairly take all the possessions and the woman, and carry them home.
And let everyone else make a solemn truce and pledge friendship;
so may you all live on in rich-soiled Troy, and may they return

to horse-rearing Argos and Achaea, home of beautiful women.'   75
    So he spoke, and hearing his words Hector was greatly pleased,
and went into the middle ground and forced back the Trojans'
companies, gripping his spear in the middle; and they all sat down.
But the flowing-haired Achaeans began to shoot at him, making
him their mark and trying to hit him with arrows and stones.   80
Then the lord of men, Agamemnon, gave a great shout:
'Hold back, Argives; sons of the Achaeans, do not shoot!
Hector of the glittering helmet is impatient to tell us something.'
    So he spoke, and they held back from the fighting and quickly
fell silent. Then Hector addressed both the armies: 85
'Listen to me, Trojans and well-greaved Achaeans, and hear
the words of Alexander, on whose account this quarrel has arisen.
His command is that all the rest of the Trojans and Achaeans
should lay their fine armour on the earth that nourishes many,
and that he and Menelaus, dear to Ares, should fight alone   90
in the middle ground for the sake of Helen and all her possessions.
Whichever of them is victorious and proves the stronger, let him
fairly take all the possessions and the woman and carry them home.
Let the rest of us make a solemn truce and pledge friendship.'
    So he spoke, and they all remained silent and still.   95
Then Menelaus, master of the war-cry, addressed them:
'Listen now to me too, for it is my heart that chiefly feels
this pain; I am minded that today the Argives and Trojans
should go their separate ways, since you have suffered much
because of my quarrel, and because of Alexander, who began it.   100
Whichever one of us has death and his destiny in store for him,
let him die, and the rest of you may quickly go your separate ways.
Now bring two lambs, one white and the other black, to be
offered to Earth and Sun, and let us bring a third for Zeus.
Bring mighty Priam out here, so that he can make a solemn truce   105
in person; his sons are arrogant and unreliable, and he will make sure
no one oversteps the mark and so wrecks the oaths sworn by Zeus.
Young men's minds are for ever floating high in the air,
but when an old man takes a hand he looks to the future and the past,
and so the matter may be best concluded for both sides.'   110
    So he spoke, and both Achaeans and Trojans were glad,
since they hoped to put an end to the miseries of war.
They held back their chariots in the ranks and jumped down
from them, and took off their armour and laid it on the ground,

close to one another, and there was little space between them.　115
Hector sent two heralds off to the city, with orders
to bring the lambs quickly and to summon Priam,
and lord Agamemnon sent Talthybius to go off to
the hollow ships, and ordered him to fetch two
lambs; and he did not disobey glorious Agamemnon.　120

　Now Iris came with a message to white-armed Helen,
in the likeness of her husband's sister, the wife of Antenor's son,
whom the lord Helicaon, the son of Antenor, had as his wife—
Laodice, the most beautiful of the daughters of Priam.
She found Helen in her hall; she was weaving a great web,　125
a red double cloak, and on it she was working the struggles
of the horse-breaking Trojans and the bronze-shirted Achaeans
that they were undergoing for her sake at the hands of Ares.
Standing close to her swift-footed Iris addressed her:
'Come with me, dear bride, and witness the extraordinary deeds　130
of the horse-breaking Trojans and the bronze-shirted Achaeans:
those who before were waging tear-laden war on each other
on the plain, and lusting after the deadly conflict,
are now, look, seated in silence, and the fighting has stopped;
they are leaning on their shields, and their long spears are stuck　135
in the ground beside them. Alexander and Menelaus, dear to Ares,
are about to fight over you with their long spears, and
you will be famed as the dear wife of the one who wins.'

　So the goddess spoke, and thrust into Helen's heart sweet longing
for her former husband and her city and her parents.　140
At once she wrapped a white linen scarf round her head
and hurried from her chamber, shedding a soft tear,
not alone, but two women servants accompanied her:
Aethre daughter of Pittheus, and ox-eyed Clymene.
Quickly they reached the place where the Scaean gates* were.　145

　Those who attended Priam—Panthous and Thymoetes,
Lampus, Clytius and Hicetaon, shoot of Ares, and
Ucalegon and Antenor, both men of sound judgement, all elders
of the people—these were sitting with him at the Scaean gates.
Because of old age they had given up warfare, but they were　150
excellent speakers, like cicadas which perch on trees
in a wood, singing away in their lily-like voices;
such were the leaders of the Trojans, as they sat on the tower.
When they saw Helen making her way to the tower,

they spoke softly to one another, in winged words: 155
'It is not a matter of blame that the Trojans and well-greaved
Achaeans should suffer agonies for so long over such a woman;
she is terribly like the immortal goddesses to look on.
But for all her beauty, it is better for her to go away in their ships,
and not stay here as a future affliction for us and our children.'   160
     So they spoke, but Priam raised his voice and called to Helen:
'Come here, dear child, and sit beside me, so that you can see
your former husband, your kinsmen and your friends—
you are not to blame in my eyes, but the gods are to blame,
who have stirred up tear-laden war for me with the Achaeans—   165
and so that you can give a name to that monstrous man,
that valiant and mighty Achaean, and tell me who he is.
There are certainly others who are taller in stature, but
I have never yet cast eyes on anyone as handsome as him,
nor one so full of dignity. He looks like a kingly man.'   170
     Then Helen, bright among women, answered him and said:
'Dear father-in-law, you deserve my respect and awe;
evil death should have been my choice when I came here
with your son, leaving my home and my family,
my late-born daughter and the pleasant company of my friends.   175
But that is not how it happened, and so I waste away in tears.
Now I will tell you what you ask and question me about:
that man is the son of Atreus, wide-ruling Agamemnon,
both a noble king and a mighty spearman, and he was also my
husband's brother, bitch-faced that I am—if this ever really
      happened.'   180
     So she spoke, and the old man marvelled at him, and said:
'Fortunate son of Atreus, child of good fortune, blessed by the gods,
you have indeed many sons of the Achaeans under your sway.
In time past I travelled to Phrygia, rich in vines, and there
I saw a great many Phrygians, men with nimble horses,   185
the peoples of Otreus and of godlike Mygdon,* who
at that time were encamped along the banks of Sangarius.*
I was their ally, you see, and was numbered among them
on the day that the Amazons* came, who are a match for men.
But not even they were as many as the darting-eyed Achaeans.'   190
     Next the old man's eyes fell on Odysseus, and he asked her:
'Come, tell me about this man too, dear child; who is he?
He is shorter in stature than Agamemnon, son of Atreus,

but broader in the shoulders and chest to look upon.
His armour is lying on the earth that nourishes many,   195
but he is prowling along the ranks of men like a ram;
I would say he was like a thick-fleeced ram
that roams in and out of a huge flock of white sheep.'

Then in answer Helen, daughter of Zeus, said to him:
'Now that one is the son of Laertes, much-scheming Odysseus,   200
who was reared in the land of Ithaca, rugged though it is, and
who is skilled in all kinds of trickery and cunning schemes.'

Then in his turn sagacious Antenor addressed her:
'Lady, what you have said is indeed quite true.
Glorious Odysseus has been here before, some time ago   205
with Menelaus, dear to Ares, on a mission concerning you.*
I received them as guest-friends and welcomed them in my halls,
and I came to know the appearance of both, and their clever schemes.
When they mingled with the Trojans in their assembly and
all were standing, broad-shouldered Menelaus was the taller,   210
and when both were sitting Odysseus was the more dignified.
But when they began to weave their cunning speeches before us all,
Menelaus for his part spoke with a rapid fluency,
briefly but very clearly, not being a man of many words,
nor stumbling in speech; and indeed he was the younger man.   215
But whenever much-scheming Odysseus leapt to his feet
he would stand there and look down, eyes fixed on the ground,
not waving the staff backwards and forwards, but
holding it stiffly, like a man who did not know what to do;
you would take him for a surly person, a genuine fool.   220
But when he released his great voice from inside his chest,
speaking words like flakes of snow falling in winter,
then no other mortal could compete with Odysseus,
and we were no longer so surprised at the sight of him.'

The third man whom the old man saw was Ajax, and he asked: 225
'Who is that other Achaean, a valiant and mighty man,
whose head and broad shoulders stand out above the Argives?'

Then long-robed Helen, bright among women, answered:
'That is the massive Ajax, bulwark of the Achaeans.
And on the other side, among the Cretans, stands Idomeneus,   230
like a god, and around him are gathered the Cretan captains.
Many times Menelaus, dear to Ares, entertained him
in our house, whenever Idomeneus came from Crete.

And now I can see all the other darting-eyed Achaeans,
whom I could easily recognize and name for you,   235
but there are two marshals of the peoples I cannot see:
horse-breaking Castor and Polydeuces the skilful boxer,
full brothers of mine, born to the same mother as me.
Either they did not accompany the army from lovely Lacedaemon,
or they did come here in their sea-traversing ships   240
but are now reluctant to enter the battle of men, made
uneasy by my disgrace and the many insults against me.'
     So she spoke; but the life-giving earth already held them
back home in Lacedaemon, in their dear native land.
     Now heralds were bringing offerings to the gods throughout
          the city,   245
to ratify the treaty—two lambs and cheering wine, fruit of the earth,
in a goatskin bag; and Idaeus the herald brought a
shining mixing-bowl and wine-cups, made of gold,
and standing next to the old man Priam he roused him, saying:
'Up now, son of Laomedon;* the chieftains of the Trojan   250
horse-breakers and the bronze-shirted Achaeans are calling you
to go down on to the plain, to make a solemn truce.
Alexander and Menelaus, dear to Ares, are about
to fight for the woman's sake with their long spears;
the woman and her possessions will go to the one who wins,   255
and the rest of us will make a solemn truce and pledge friendship—
we to live on in rich-soiled Troy, and they to return to
horse-rearing Argos and Achaea, home of beautiful women.'
So he spoke, and the old man shuddered, and told his companions
to yoke the horses, and they quickly obeyed his order.   260
Priam mounted the chariot and pulled back on the reins, and
Antenor climbed into the finely made chariot beside him, and
they drove the swift horses through the Scaean gates on to the plain.
     When they reached the assembled Trojans and Achaeans,
they got down from the chariot to the earth that nourishes many   265
and strode to the middle ground between the Trojans and Achaeans.
Immediately Agamemnon, lord of men, rose to his feet,
and with him much-scheming Odysseus. Excellent heralds
drove the solemn truce offerings together, and mixed wine
in a bowl, and poured water over the kings' hands.   270
Then the son of Atreus with his hand drew the knife
that always hung next to his sword's great scabbard,

and cut hairs from the lambs' heads, and the heralds
distributed these among the Trojan and Achaean chieftains.
Then Atreus' son prayed in a loud voice, holding up his hands: 275
'Father Zeus, ruling from Mount Ida,* greatest and most glorious,
and you, Sun, who sees all things and hears all things!
Rivers and Earth, and you two who below the earth punish
men who have died, if any have sworn false oaths*—
be witnesses, and see that these solemn oaths are kept.   280
If it should happen that Alexander kills Menelaus, then
let him keep Helen for himself, and all her possessions,
and let us return home in our sea-traversing ships.
But if fair-haired Menelaus should kill Alexander, then
the Trojans must give back Helen and all her possessions,   285
and must pay the Argives the compensation that is proper
and recognized as such, even by generations in time to come.
But if Priam and the sons of Priam are unwilling to pay me
compensation when Alexander has fallen, then
I shall fight on after that to secure reparation,   290
and I shall stay here until I reach the end of the war.'
    So he spoke, and slit the lambs' throats with the pitiless bronze.
He laid them on the ground, gasping as their life ebbed
away, for the bronze had taken away their strength.
Then they drew the wine from the mixing-bowl into cups   295
and poured it out, and prayed to the gods who live for ever.
And this is what one of the Trojans or Achaeans would say:
'Zeus, greatest and most glorious, and all you other gods;
whichever side is the first to violate these oaths, may their
brains be poured out on the ground as this wine is, theirs and   300
their children's; and may their wives be mastered by strangers.'
    So they spoke, but the son of Cronus did not yet fulfil their prayers.
And among them Priam of the line of Dardanus spoke, saying:
'Listen to me, Trojans and well-greaved Achaeans;
I am now going back to Troy that is swept by the winds,   305
since I cannot bring myself to see my dear son
doing battle before my eyes with Menelaus, dear to Ares.
Zeus doubtless knows, as do the other immortal gods,
for which of the two the end of death has been appointed.'
    So the godlike man spoke, and laid the lambs in his chariot,   310
then mounted himself, and pulled back on the reins,
and Antenor climbed into the finely made chariot beside him.

So the two of them went on their way, back towards Ilium;
but Hector, the son of Priam, and glorious Odysseus
first measured out the ground, and after that   315
took two lots and shook them in a bronze helmet,
to see which man should throw his bronze-tipped spear first.
And the peoples prayed, and held up their hands to the gods,
and this is what one of the Achaeans or Trojans would say:
'Father Zeus, ruling from Mount Ida, greatest and most glorious; 320
whoever it was who brought these troubles on to both sides,
grant that he may die and go below into the house of Hades,
but grant too that we may enjoy friendship and a solemn truce.'

So they spoke, and great Hector of the glittering helmet shook
the lots, looking away; and the lot of Paris quickly leapt out.   325
Then they all sat down in ranks, in the place where each one's
high-stepping horses and finely worked armour lay.
Then that man put his fine armour on over his shoulders—
glorious Alexander, husband of Helen of the beautiful hair.
First of all he fastened greaves around his shins,   330
splendid ones, fitted with silver ankle-pieces;
then over his chest he put on a corslet which belonged
to his brother Lycaon; and it fitted him equally as well.
Around his shoulders he threw his silver-riveted sword,
made of bronze, and after that his huge, massive shield.   335
On his powerful head he set a well-made helmet with a
horse-tail crest; and the plume nodded terribly above him.
Then he chose a stout spear, which fitted his grasp.
And in the same way Menelaus, dear to Ares, put on his armour.

So when they were armed among the soldiery on either side,   340
they strode into the middle ground between Trojans and Achaeans,
glaring grimly at each other; and amazement gripped the onlookers,
both horse-breaking Trojans and well-greaved Achaeans.
They took their stand near each other on the measured ground,
shaking their spears and full of rage at each other.   345
Alexander was the first to throw his far-shadowing spear,
and it hit the perfectly balanced shield of Atreus' son, but
the spear did not shatter it, for its bronze point was bent back
on the mighty shield. Then Menelaus, Atreus' son, stood up
ready to throw the bronze, and made a prayer to father Zeus: 350
'Lord Zeus, grant me revenge on the man who wronged me at the start,
glorious Alexander, and beat him down under my hands,

so that among later generations too a man may shudder to
think of wronging the host who has offered him friendship.'

So he spoke, and poised his long-shadowing spear and threw it,　355
and it hit the perfectly balanced shield of Priam's son;
the massive spear passed through the shining shield
and drove through the intricately worked corslet,
going straight on to cut through the tunic next to his ribs;
but Paris leaned aside and avoided the black death-spectre.　360
Then the son of Atreus drew his silver-riveted sword and
swinging his arm high struck the other's helmet plate, but there
the sword shattered into three or four pieces, and fell from his hand.
Atreus' son gazed up at the broad high sky and cried out:
'Father Zeus, there is no one who causes more mischief than you!　365
Truly, I thought I had taken revenge on Alexander for his villainy,
but instead my sword has broken in my hands, and my spear
sped uselessly from my hand, and I did not strike him down.'

So he spoke, and sprang and seized Paris by the horsehair-crested
　　helmet,
and swinging him round began to drag him towards the well-greaved
　　Achaeans.　370
Paris was being choked by the embroidered strap at his soft throat,
which was drawn tight under his chin to secure his helmet; and
now Menelaus would have dragged him away, winning immense glory,
had not Aphrodite, daughter of Zeus, been sharp enough to see it,
and broken the strap that was made from a slaughtered ox's hide.　375
The helmet came away empty in Menelaus' brawny hand,
and the hero whirled it round his head and flung it among
the well-greaved Achaeans, and his trusty companions retrieved it;
then he leapt back towards Paris, raging to kill him with his
bronze-tipped spear; but Aphrodite snatched Paris away　380
very easily, as a god will do, wrapping him in a dense mist,
and set him down in his fragrantly perfumed chamber.

She herself went off to summon Helen, and found her on the
high tower, with a large group of Trojan women around her.
Grasping Helen's nectar-scented veil in her hand she pulled it　385
and spoke to her, likening herself to a woman of many years,
a wool-comber, who when Helen lived in Lacedaemon
used to work fine wool; and Helen loved her very much.
In the likeness of this woman bright Aphrodite addressed her:
'Come with me; Alexander is calling for you to return home.　390

There he is in his chamber, on the spiral-decorated bed,
glowing in his beauty and clothing. You would not think
he had come from fighting with someone, but was going to
the dance, or had just returned and was sitting down to rest.'

So she spoke, and quickened Helen's heart within her breast;   395
and when she recognized the goddess's beautiful neck,
her desirable breasts and her bright-sparkling eyes,
she was amazed, and spoke to her, saying:
'Lady, why are you so anxious to lead me astray like this?
Are you intending to take me away to some well-populated city,   400
to somewhere in Phrygia or lovely Maeonia, where
there is perhaps some other mortal man who is dear to you?
Or is it because Menelaus has overcome glorious Alexander,
and wishes to take me, loathed woman, to his home,
that you now stand beside me here with guile in your heart?   405
Well, go and sit beside him yourself, and forsake the path
of the gods, and never set your feet again on Olympus,
but all the time suffer on his behalf and wait on him,
until such time as he makes you his wife, or even his slave.
As for me, I will not go there to serve that man's bed,   410
for that would bring blame on me; all future Trojan women
will despise me, and I already have grief enough in my heart.'

At this bright Aphrodite became enraged and addressed her:
'Do not provoke me, obstinate woman, or I may grow angry and
desert you, and come to hate you as violently as now I love you;   415
I may well plan some fatal enmity between the two sides,
Trojans and Danaans, and then you will die a wretched death.'

So she spoke, and Helen, daughter of Zeus, was afraid,
and went away, covering her face with her shining white veil,
in silence, and no Trojan woman saw her; a divinity guided her.   420

When they reached the splendid house of Alexander,
the women servants at once turned to their tasks, while she,
bright among women, went to her high-roofed chamber.
Then the goddess Aphrodite who loves to smile brought
a chair and placed it for her opposite Alexander; and   425
Helen, daughter of Zeus the aegis-wearer, took her seat on it,
and turning her eyes away from him spoke sharply to her husband:
'So you have returned from the fighting! I wish you had died there,
beaten down by the mighty man who was my husband before you.
There was a time when you would boast that you were a better man   430

than Menelaus, dear to Ares, in strength of arm and with the spear;
so go now, make your challenge to Menelaus, dear to Ares,
to fight you once again, face to face. But no—I advise you
to hold back, and not to match your strength recklessly
with fair-haired Menelaus in battle or in the fighting,   435
because you may be quickly beaten down by his spear.'

Then Paris answered and addressed her with these words:
'Wife, do not attack my heart with these harsh taunts.
Yes, this time Menelaus defeated me, with Athena's help,
but another time I shall defeat him; we too have gods on our side.   440
Come now, let us go to bed and find delight in love;
never before has desire enveloped my senses like this,
not even when I first stole you away from lovely Lacedaemon
and sailed away in my sea-traversing ships, and on the island
Cranaë* I took you to bed and made love to you—that is how   445
I now desire you, and sweet longing takes hold of me.'

So he spoke, and led the way to the bed, and his wife went with him.
And so the two of them lay together on the fretted bed;
but Atreus' son prowled among the soldiery like a wild beast,
hoping to catch sight of Alexander, handsome as a god.   450
But no man of the Trojans or of their far-famed allies
could point Alexander out to Menelaus, dear to Ares; certainly
they would not have hidden him out of love, if anyone had
seen him, since they all hated him like the black death-spectre.
Then Agamemnon lord of men spoke among them: 455
'Listen to me, Trojans and Dardanians and allies:
since the victory clearly belongs to Menelaus, dear to Ares,
you must give back Argive Helen, and her possessions
along with her, and must pay the compensation that is proper
and recognized as such, even by generations in time to come.'   460

So spoke Atreus' son, and the rest of the Achaeans applauded him.

BOOK FOUR

Now the gods were sitting beside Zeus, gathered in
assembly on a golden floor, and in their midst lady Hebe
served them with nectar, and they pledged each other in
golden cups, looking out towards the city of the Trojans.
Then the son of Cronus tried to provoke Hera with   5
taunting words, speaking out with a hidden purpose:
'Menelaus has a pair of goddesses to support him,
Hera of Argos and Athena of Alalcomenae;* and yet
they are sitting here as onlookers, leaving him alone and
enjoying the spectacle, while Aphrodite who loves to smile   10
stands always beside Paris, keeping away death's spectres;
and just now she saved him when he thought he would die.
Even so, the victory clearly belongs to Menelaus, dear to Ares,
so let us consider how these things should be done:
whether we should again stir up destructive war and   15
grim conflict, or bring both sides together in friendship.
If this second way proves pleasing and welcome to all,
then the city of lord Priam could continue to thrive,
and Menelaus could take Argive Helen home again.'

So he spoke, and Athena and Hera muttered to each other;   20
they were sitting close together, plotting misery for the Trojans.
Athena was silent, and did not say a word, feeling resentful
towards father Zeus, and harsh bitterness gripped her;
but Hera's breast could not contain her anger, and she addressed him:
'Most dread son of Cronus, what is this that you have said?   25
How can you expect my toil to count for nothing, unfulfilled—
the sweat that I poured painfully out, and my horses' weariness
as I was gathering a force to bring misery to Priam and his sons?
Do as you will—but, I tell you, we other gods will not all approve.'

Then, deeply angered, Zeus the cloud-gatherer answered her: 30
'You are possessed! How have Priam and the sons of Priam
done you such great wrong that you rage so relentlessly
to tear Ilium apart, that well-built city?
Only if you were to enter its gates and long walls yourself,
and to eat the raw flesh of Priam and the sons of Priam and   35
the rest of the Trojans, would you perhaps satisfy your anger.

Do as you will. I would not want this quarrel to become
a great conflict between the two of us in time to come—
but I tell you another thing, and you should store it in your mind:
whenever it is my passionate desire to destroy a city and 40
I choose one inhabited by men who are dear to you,
do not try to thwart my anger, but leave me to do as I will.
I give way to you in this willingly, though with an unwilling heart,
because of all the cities under the sun and the starry high sky
that are inhabited by men who live on the earth, 45
the most prized in my heart was always sacred Ilium,
and Priam and the people of Priam of the fine ash spear.
Never has my altar lacked a fair share of the feast, of drink-
offerings and the savour of burnt flesh, which is our privilege.'
  Then the lady ox-eyed Hera answered him: 50
'There are three cities which are by far the dearest to me,
Argos and Sparta and Mycenae of the wide streets,
and these you may sack, whenever they incur your heart's hatred.
I shall certainly not stand in your way, nor grudge them to you,
for if I was resentful and stopped you destroying them 55
I would gain nothing by it, since you are far stronger than me.
But you must not allow my labour to come to nothing,
since I too am divine and my ancestry is the same as yours, and
I am the most honoured of crooked-scheming Cronus' children,
in two ways: through my birth, and because I am renowned 60
as your wife, and you are lord of all the immortals.
So—let us give way to each other in this matter,
I to you and you to me; and the rest of the immortal gods
will follow us. Command Athena immediately to enter
the grim conflict between Trojans and Achaeans; tell her 65
to try to ensure that the Trojans are the first to give offence
to the far-famed Achaeans, by breaking their oaths.'
  So she spoke, and the father of gods and men did not disobey her,
but immediately addressed Athena with winged words:
'Go as fast as you can to the Trojan and Achaean camps, 70
and try to ensure that the Trojans are the first to give
offence to the far-famed Achaeans, by breaking their oaths.'
  So speaking he roused Athena, who was already eager to go,
and she went swooping down from the peaks of Olympus.
Just as a meteor that the son of crooked-scheming Cronus 75
sends as a portent to sailors or to a people's broad encampment,

a bright star, and a shower of sparks shoots out from it;
so Pallas Athena swooped down to earth, and sprang into
the middle ground; and amazement gripped the onlookers,
horse-breaking Trojans and well-greaved Achaeans alike.   80
And this is what they would say, each man looking at his neighbour:
'Surely evil war and grim fighting will break out again,
or else Zeus will bring about friendship between both sides,
Zeus who is the dispenser of war to mankind.'
    That is what the Trojans and Achaeans were saying; and   85
Athena stole into the mass of Trojans in the likeness of a man,
Laodocus, the son of Antenor, the mighty spearman,
and looked for godlike Pandarus, in the hope of finding him.
And she found him, the blameless and mighty son of Lycaon,
standing idle, and around him were strong ranks of shield-bearing   90
men, who had come with him from the waters of Aesepus.*
Standing beside him she addressed him with winged words:
'War-minded son of Lycaon, will you perhaps do as I tell you,
and have the courage to let fly a swift arrow at Menelaus,
and so win gratitude and glory before all the Trojans,   95
but most of all in the sight of the prince Alexander?
From him especially you would be sure to receive splendid gifts,
if he were to see Menelaus, the warlike son of Atreus,
struck down by your shaft and laid on the painful pyre.
So come, shoot an arrow at splendid Menelaus,   100
and vow to sacrifice to Lycian-born Apollo,* renowned
with the bow, a splendid hecatomb of first-born lambs
when you return to your home in Zeleia, the sacred city.'
    So Athena spoke, and swayed the thoughts of a thoughtless man.
At once he took out his well-polished bow, made from the horns   105
of a full-grown wild goat that he himself had once shot in the chest
as it emerged from a rocky place while he waited in a hide,
and he hit it in the chest; and it fell backwards on to the rock.
On its head grew horns of sixteen palms' length, and
these a craftsman who worked in horn had fitted together,   110
smoothing the whole bow skilfully, and adding a tip of gold.
Pandarus braced the bow's point firmly against the ground,
and bent it back and strung it, and his excellent companions held
their shields in front of him, in case the warlike sons of the Achaeans
charged him before Menelaus, Atreus' warlike son, was
        shot down.   115

Then he opened the lid of his quiver, and from it took an arrow,
feathered, not yet released, and a bearer of black agony.
Quickly he fitted the bitter shaft to the bowstring and
vowed to sacrifice to Lycian-born Apollo, renowned
with the bow, a splendid hecatomb of first-born lambs   120
when he returned to his home in Zeleia, the sacred city.
Then, gripping the notches and ox-gut string together, he pulled,
bringing the string back to his chest and the iron tip to the bow.
When he had bent the great bow so that it made an arc
it sang out, the string gave a loud cry, and the sharp arrow   125
leapt forth, raging to fly into the enemy soldiery.

But, Menelaus, the blessed immortal gods had not forgotten you,
and the first to your aid was Zeus' daughter who gathers the spoils.*
She stood before you and fended off the sharp-pointed arrow,
turning it away from your flesh just like a mother brushing   130
a fly from her child who is lying in sweet sleep, and with
her own hand she guided it instead to where its gold buckles
held his belt together and overlapped the double corslet.
The bitter arrow struck the close-fitting belt, and driving
through the elaborately decorated belt forced its way   135
through the finely worked corslet and the loin-plate,
a defence against missiles, that he wore to shield his flesh;
this was his best protection, but the arrow flew straight
through it too, just grazing the surface of the hero's flesh;
and at once dark blood began to flow from the wound.   140

As when a woman stains ivory with purple dye,
a woman of Maeonia or Caria,* to be a cheek-piece for horses;
it lies in the store chamber, and many horsemen pray
that their horse might wear it, but it lies there, a king's delight,
both an adornment for his horse and a glory for his charioteer;   145
just so, Menelaus, were your shapely thighs stained
with blood, and your shins and handsome ankles below.

At this Agamemnon, lord of men, shuddered,
when he saw the black blood flowing down from the wound,
and Menelaus himself, dear to Ares, shuddered too;   150
but when he saw that the barbs and binding were still
outside his flesh the spirit was gathered back into his breast.
With a deep groan lord Agamemnon spoke to his companions,
holding Menelaus by the hand, and they groaned with him:
'Dear brother, so it was for your death that I swore those oaths, 155

setting you alone in front of the Achaeans to fight the Trojans;
now they have shot you, and trampled on the solemn oaths.
But an oath cannot count for nothing, nor the blood of lambs,
nor unmixed wine libations, nor our right hands that confirmed the pact.
Even if the Olympian does not bring fulfilment immediately,   160
he will do so in full, however late, and men will pay a high price,
with their own lives and with their wives' and children's lives as well:
for I know this very well in my mind and in my heart,
that there will come a day when sacred Troy will be destroyed,
and Priam and the people of Priam of the fine ash spear, and   165
Zeus, the son of Cronus, seated on high, dwelling in the upper air,
will himself shake the dark aegis in the face of all men,
in anger at their oath-breaking. So this will not be unfulfilled;
but terrible grief will come on me because of you, Menelaus,
if you die here and complete your life's allotted portion.   170
And then I will return to thirsty Argos covered in contempt,
for the Achaeans will immediately think of their homeland,
and we will abandon Argive Helen* here, for Priam and the
Trojans to boast over; and the ploughland will rot your bones
as you lie here in Troy with your mission unaccomplished.   175
And this is what one of the arrogant Trojans will say as he
leaps up and down on the grave-mound of splendid Menelaus:
"This is how Agamemnon's anger should always turn out!
He brought an army of Achaeans here on a useless errand,
and look, he has gone back home to his dear native land   180
with empty ships, leaving the brave Menelaus behind."
So they will say; and then I hope the wide earth will gape before me.'

    Then fair-haired Menelaus spoke, minded to give him courage:
'Do not despair, and do not alarm the people of the Achaeans;
the sharp arrow did not lodge in a fatal place; before it could,   185
my bright gleaming belt protected me, and underneath it
my body-shield and the loin-plate that bronze-smiths forged.'

    Then in answer lord Agamemnon addressed him:
'Dear Menelaus, I pray that it is as you say.
But a healer will attend to your wound and will spread   190
ointments on it to deliver you from your black pain.'

    So he spoke, and addressed Talthybius, the godlike herald:
'Talthybius, go as fast as you can and summon here Machaon,
the worthy son of Asclepius* the excellent healer,
so that he can examine Menelaus, Atreus' warlike son,   195

whom some man skilled in archery has shot at and wounded—
some Trojan or Lycian, bringing glory to himself but grief to us.'

So he spoke, and the herald heard and did not disobey him,
but set off for the people of bronze-shirted Achaeans,
looking out keenly for the hero Machaon. He found him   200
standing idle, and around him were strong ranks of shield-bearing
men, who had come with him from horse-rearing Tricce.
Standing close, he addressed him with winged words:
'Quickly, son of Asclepius! Lord Agamemnon summons you
to examine Menelaus, the warlike captain of the Achaeans,   205
whom some man skilled in archery has shot at and wounded—
some Trojan or Lycian, bringing glory to himself but grief to us.'

So he spoke, and quickened the spirit in Machaon's breast,
and they set off through the soldiery along the wide Achaean camp.
When they reached the place where fair-haired Menelaus   210
lay wounded, and around him all the best men were gathered
in a circle, he went and stood in their midst, a man like a god,
and at once pulled the arrow out from the close-fitting belt;
and as it was pulled out the sharp barbs were broken backwards.
Then he loosened the gleaming belt, and underneath it the   215
body-shield and loin-plate that bronze-smiths had forged.
When he saw the wound, where the bitter arrow had struck,
he sucked the blood from it and skilfully applied soothing ointments
that Cheiron had long ago given his father as a token of friendship.

While they were attending to Menelaus, master of the war-cry,   220
the ranks of shield-bearing Trojans came on at them, and
the Achaeans armed again, and called up their desire for battle.

Then you would not have seen glorious Agamemnon drowsing,
nor shrinking in fear, nor hanging back from the fighting,
but fervently eager for the battle where men win glory.   225
He left his horses behind, and his chariot, inlaid with bronze;
his attendant kept the snorting horses in reserve—he was
Eurymedon, the son of Ptolemaeus, who was Peiraeus' son—
and gave him strict orders to hold them nearby until weariness
should overtake his limbs while he marshalled his many troops;   230
and so on foot he roamed up and down the ranks of men.
If he saw any of the swift-horsed Danaans busying themselves
he would stand nearby and try to strengthen their courage:
'Argives, do not let your surging courage ebb away;
men who swear falsely will get no help from father Zeus, and   235

those who were the first offenders, by breaking their oaths,
will have their tender flesh devoured by vultures, while
we in our turn will carry off their dear wives and infant
children in our ships, when we have sacked their city.'

But whenever he saw men holding back from hateful war   240
he would rebuke them severely with angry words:
'Contemptible Argive braggarts, have you no shame?
Why are you standing there in a daze, just like fawns
that are exhausted after running a long way over a plain,
and stop still, and there is no courage in their hearts?   245
That is how you are standing, in a daze, and not fighting.
Are you waiting for the Trojans to reach the place where your ships
with their fine sterns are drawn up on the shore of the grey sea,
to see if the son of Cronus will hold his protecting hand above you?'

So he ranged through the ranks of men as their commander,   250
and as he went among the mass of men he came upon the Cretans,
who were arming themselves under war-minded Idomeneus.
Idomeneus was in the front rank, like a wild boar in his courage,
and Meriones was urging on the rearmost companies.
When he saw them Agamemnon lord of men was delighted,   255
and he immediately addressed Idomeneus with gentle words:
'Idomeneus, I esteem you above all the swift-horsed Danaäns,
whether it is in war or in any other kind of enterprise,
or in feasting, whenever the best men of the Argives
mix gleaming wine in a bowl for a meeting of elders.   260
While the other flowing-haired Achaeans may drink up
only their fixed portion, your cup always stands full,
just as mine does, for you to drink when the spirit moves you.
Up, then, for battle! Be the man you have always claimed to be!'

Then in answer to him Idomeneus, leader of Cretans, spoke: 265
'Son of Atreus, I will surely be your faithful companion,
just as I promised and undertook at the outset of this war.
But you must stir up all the other flowing-haired Achaeans,
to fight as soon as we may, because the Trojans have undone
their oaths. Now death and calamity are in store for them,   270
since they were the first to offend, by breaking their oaths.'

So he spoke, and the son of Atreus passed on, glad in his heart.
As he went through the mass of men he found the two called Ajax;
they were arming, and a cloud of foot-soldiers came with them.
As when a goatherd on his lookout sees a cloud   275

approaching over the open sea, driven by the West Wind,
and because he is far away it seems to him blacker than pitch
as it advances over the sea and brings a great whirlwind with it,
and he shudders when he sees it, and drives his flock into a cave;
so the close-packed companies of Zeus-nurtured strong young men   280
advanced towards the deadly battle under the two called Ajax,
dark-coloured, and bristling with shields and spears.
When he saw them the lord Agamemnon was delighted,
and he addressed them, speaking with winged words:
'You two named Ajax, commanders of bronze-shirted Argives,   285
I give you no orders, since it is not fitting to urge you on,
and you yourselves are driving your people to fight with vigour.
Father Zeus and Athena and Apollo, how I wish that
there was a spirit like this in the breasts of everyone!
Then the city of lord Priam would quickly reel before us,   290
captured and devastated by our hands.'

     So he spoke and left them, and went on in search of others.
Next he found Nestor, the clear-voiced speaker of the Pylians,
preparing his companions and urging them on to fight,
and they were led by huge Pelagon, and Alastor and Chromius,   295
and lord Haemon, and Bias, shepherd of the people. He had
deployed the charioteers in front, with their horses and chariots,
and behind them large numbers of excellent foot-soldiers,
to be a bulwark in war. The weakest he drove into the middle,
so that even the reluctant would be compelled to fight.   300
First he gave orders to the charioteers, instructing them to
hold their horses back and not to cause disorder among the soldiery:
'Let no one, relying on his own chariot-skill and bravery,
be in a rage to fight the Trojans alone, in front of the rest,
nor let him retreat, for this way you will be the less effective.   305
But if a man in his chariot comes within reach of an enemy's,
let him thrust with his spear, since that is much the better way.
This is how men in times past would storm cities and their walls,
keeping this strategy and resolution firmly in their hearts.'

     So the old man urged them on, for he knew the wars of long ago;   310
and when he saw him lord Agamemnon was delighted,
and addressed him, speaking with winged words:
'Old man, I could wish that your knees' vigour was equal to
the spirit in your breast, and your strength was unimpaired; but
old age that comes to all wears you down. How I wish that another   315

man could take on your age, and you could join the younger men!'
    Then Nestor the Gerenian horseman answered him:
'Son of Atreus, I too could fervently wish myself to be
the man I was when I killed glorious Ereuthalion.*
But the gods do not grant everything to men at once;   320
I was a young man then, but now old age presses hard on me.
Nonetheless, I shall go with my charioteers and direct them
with counsel and in words, for that is the privilege of old men.
The spear-fighting will be done by younger men, who are
later-born than me, and have confidence in their strength.'   325
    So he spoke, and Atreus' son passed on, glad in his heart.
He found the son of Peteos, Menestheus, whipper of horses,
standing idle, and with him were Athenians, raisers of the war-cry.
Close by them stood much-scheming Odysseus, and
around him the ranks of Cephallenians, no weaklings,   330
were standing idle, for their people had not yet heard the war-cry,
since the companies of horse-breaking Trojans and Achaeans
had but recently roused themselves to action. So they waited,
standing there, waiting until another Achaean band should advance
and make an attack on the Trojans, and so begin the fighting.   335
When he saw them Agamemnon, lord of men, rebuked them,
and he addressed them, speaking with winged words:
'Son of Peteos, who was a king nurtured by Zeus—
and you too, you expert in low cunning, obsessed with gain—
why are you cowering here out of the way, waiting for others?   340
You two ought to be taking your stand among the front ranks
and going to face the searing heat of the battle.
You are the first to be invited to any feast of mine,
whenever we Achaeans prepare a feast for the elders,
where it is your pleasure to eat roast meat and drink   345
cups of honey-sweet wine for as long as you wish; but now
you would happily look on even if ten Achaean squadrons were
fighting with the pitiless bronze, before you stirred yourselves.'
    Then much-scheming Odysseus looked at him darkly and replied:
'Son of Atreus, what words are these that cross your teeth's barrier? 350
How can you say that I hang back from the battle, whenever
we Achaeans stir up bitter war against the horse-breaking Trojans?
If this is your concern and your desire, you will soon see Telemachus'
dear father fighting in the thick of the front ranks of horse-breaking
Trojans. But as for you, your words are nothing but empty wind.'   355

At this lord Agamemnon smiled, when he saw that Odysseus
was angry, and taking back his words answered him:
'Son of Laertes, sprung from Zeus, Odysseus of many schemes,
I have no great need to rebuke you, nor am I giving you orders,
because I know that the spirit which you keep in your breast   360
is kindly disposed; and your thoughts are my thoughts.
So come; if hard words have been spoken, we shall later
make things right—and may the gods throw all this to the winds.'
    So he spoke and left them, and went in search of others.
He found the son of Tydeus, high-spirited Diomedes, standing   365
inactive surrounded by his horses and close-jointed chariots,
and next to him was standing Sthenelus, son of Capaneus.*
When he saw Diomedes lord Agamemnon rebuked him,
and addressed him, speaking with winged words:
'Son of war-minded Tydeus the horse-breaker, what is this?   370
Why are you cowering here, eyeing the battle-lines?
Tydeus would not have been content to skulk like this,
but would engage the enemy far in front of his companions;
that is what those who saw him in action used to say. I myself
never met or saw him, but they say he excelled all other men.   375
He did once come to Mycenae, not with hostile intent
but as a guest, with godlike Polyneices, trying to raise an army;
they were planning a campaign against Thebes' sacred walls,*
and earnestly begged my people to give them illustrious allies—
and they were ready to give them, and agreed to their request.   380
But Zeus sent us ill-omened signs, and dissuaded us;
and so when they had set out and were some way on the road,
and had come to Asopus' grassy meadows, thick with reeds,
the Achaeans appointed Tydeus to be their envoy.
So he set off, and came upon a large number of Cadmeians*   385
holding a feast in the house of powerful Eteocles.
Though he came as a stranger, alone among many Cadmeians,
the horse-driver Tydeus was not afraid, but challenged them
to athletic contests, and beat them in every event,
easily; that was the kind of support that Athena gave him.   390
At this the Cadmeians, whippers of horses, grew angry,
and on his way back they laid a strong ambush, gathering
fifty young men together; and there were two captains,
Maeon, son of Haemon, a man resembling the immortals,
and Autophonus' son Polyphontes, steadfast in war.*   395

On these men too Tydeus let loose an ugly death,
for he killed them all, sending only one back to his home;
it was Maeon he sent, persuaded by signs from the gods.
Such a man was Tydeus the Aetolian; but he fathered a son
inferior to him in battle, though one better at making speeches.'   400

   So he spoke, and mighty Diomedes gave him no answer,
put to shame by the rebuke of his respected king;
but the son of splendid Capaneus answered:
'Son of Atreus, do not tell lies when you know the truth.
We can claim to be much better than our fathers,   405
since we actually captured the city of seven-gated Thebes,*
though we led a smaller force, and against stronger walls,
trusting in signs from the gods and in the help from Zeus,
while they perished as a result of their own recklessness.
So do not rank our fathers' honour equal to ours.'   410

   But mighty Diomedes looked at Sthenelus darkly and said:
'Friend, be silent, sit down and listen to what I say.
I am not angry with Agamemnon, shepherd of the peoples,
because he is urging the well-greaved Achaeans to fight;
it is him that the glory will attach to if the Achaeans   415
cut down the Trojans and capture sacred Ilium, and his
will be the greater grief if the Achaeans are cut down.
So come, let us two also call up our surging courage.'

   So he spoke, and jumped from his chariot to the ground, fully armed,
and the bronze rang out terribly on the lord's chest as he   420
leapt; and then even the most steadfast would have felt some fear.

   As when waves of the sea beat on an echoing shore,
in quick succession under the West Wind's driving force;
they first raise themselves up on the open sea, and then
break with a great roar on the dry land, and, arching high,   425
rear to a crest on both sides of headlands and spew salt spray;
so then the companies of Danaans moved in quick succession
relentlessly towards the battle; each one's leader gave the orders,
and the rest came on in silence, and you would not think
that so large an army had a voice in their breasts as they followed,   430
so silent they were, in fear of their leaders. Around them all
gleamed the finely worked armour that they wore in their ranks.
But as for the Trojans, just like sheep who stand in great numbers
in the courtyard of a wealthy man, waiting to yield their white milk,
bleating incessantly because they can hear their lambs' cries,   435

so a confused clamour arose throughout their broad camp;
they did not all use the same speech or language, but their
tongues were mixed, summoned as they were from many lands.
Ares urged them on, and grey-eyed Athena urged the Achaeans,
and there were Terror and Panic, and endlessly raging Strife,   440
sister and companion of man-slaughtering Ares,
who at first raises herself to only a lowly height but later,
though she walks on the earth, rears her head to reach the high sky.
She now cast the poised conflict into the middle ground,
striding through the soldiery and swelling the agonized cries of men.   445

When the sides had met in a single place and come to grips,
then there was a clash of leather shields and spears and
the fury of bronze-armoured warriors. Bossed shields
smashed against each other, and a tremendous clamour arose,
made up of the groans of dying men and the exultant   450
cries of their killers; and the earth ran with blood.
As when two torrents in winter sweep down from the mountains
and, fed by great springs, unite their floods in spate at a
place where watercourses meet in some deep ravine,
and a shepherd far away in the mountains hears their roar;   455
such was the uproar and commotion of the armies as they clashed.

Antilochus was the first to kill a Trojan chieftain,
a fine man fighting in the front rank, Echepolus, Thalysius' son.
Throwing first, he hit the plate of his horsehair-crested helmet;
the bronze spear-point struck him on the forehead and pierced   460
right through the bone, and darkness covered his eyes,
and he toppled like a tower in the fierce conflict.
When he fell lord Elephenor seized him by the feet, Elephenor
Chalcodon's son, captain of the great-hearted Abantes,
and dragged him out of missiles' way, eager to strip him quickly   465
of his armour; but his eagerness was short-lived, because
as he dragged the dead man away great-spirited Agenor saw him,
and, as he stooped, stabbed him with his bronze-tipped spear
in the side where his shield left him exposed, and loosened his limbs.
So his breath left him, and over him a grim tussle began   470
as Trojans and Achaeans fought each other; like wolves
they leapt upon each other, and man struggled with man.

Next Ajax, son of Telamon, felled the son of Anthemion,
Simoeisius, a man in the prime of youth, whom his mother
had borne by the banks of Simoeis on her way down from Ida,   475

when she had been there with her parents to inspect their flocks.
And so they called him Simoeisius, but he did not repay
his dear parents for his upbringing; his life-span was brief,
for he was beaten down by the spear of great-spirited Ajax.
As he advanced among the front ranks, Ajax struck him   480
on the right nipple, and the bronze tip passed clean through
the shoulder, and he fell to earth in the dust like a poplar
that has grown tall in a wide, low-lying water-meadow;
it is trimmed below, but from the very top branches sprout,
and then a chariot-maker fells it with the flashing iron,   485
meaning to bend it into a wheel-rim for a handsome chariot,
and it lies drying beside the banks of a river.
Such was Simoeisius, son of Anthemion, slain by Ajax sprung
from Zeus. Then Antiphus of the bright corslet, Priam's son,
threw his sharp spear at Ajax from among the soldiery.   490
He missed him, but hit Leucus, Odysseus' excellent companion,
in the groin as he was dragging the dead man to one side,
and he collapsed over it and the body dropped from his hand.
Odysseus' spirit was deeply angered at Leucus' death, and
he strode through the front-fighters helmeted in gleaming
    bronze;   495
taking his stand very close to Leucus he looked keenly around
and then threw his shining spear. The Trojans retreated
when they saw him throw, and he did not let it fly in vain,
but hit Democoön, one of Priam's bastard sons, who
had come from Abydus, where he kept swift mares.   500
Odysseus, enraged for his companion, hit him with his spear
on the temple, and the bronze spear-point passed through
and out the other side; darkness covered his eyes,
and he fell with a thud, and his armour clattered about him.
The front-fighters retreated, and glorious Hector with them,   505
and the Argives gave a great yell, and dragged the dead men back,
and pressed on even further. But Apollo, looking down
from Pergamus,* grew indignant and shouted to the Trojans:
'Up with you, horse-breaking Trojans—do not yield the battle
to the Argives! Their flesh is not made of stone or iron, able 510
to withstand the flesh-tearing bronze when they are hit.
Moreover Achilles, lovely-haired Thetis' son, is not fighting,
but is brooding over his heart-sore bitterness beside his ships.'
  So spoke the terrible god from the city, while the daughter

of Zeus, splendid Tritogeneia,* urged on any of the Achaeans 515
she saw holding back as she went among the soldiery.

Next, his due destiny shackled Diores, son of Amarynceus:
he was struck by a jagged stone on the right leg,
close to his ankle; a captain of the Thracians threw it,
Peirous, the son of Imbrasus, who had come from Aenus. 520
The pitiless stone smashed the two tendons to nothing,
and his bones as well, and he fell backwards in the dust,
stretching out both hands towards his dear companions,
gasping out his life. Peirous, the man who threw the stone,
rushed up and thrust his spear in by the navel; Diores' bowels 525
all spilled out on to the ground, and darkness covered his eyes.

But as Peirous ran back Thoas the Aetolian hit him with his spear
in the chest above his nipple, and the bronze point stuck fast
in his lung. Thoas came up close and wrenched the massive spear
out of his chest; then, drawing his sharp sword, he drove it 530
into the middle of Peirous' belly, and robbed him of his life.
Yet he did not strip his armour; Peirous' companions surrounded him,
Thracians with hair piled high, and with long spears in their hands,
and though Thoas was huge and powerful and splendid
they drove him back; and he was shaken, and gave ground. 535
So the two warriors lay stretched in the dust next to each other,
one a Thracian and the other a man of the bronze-shirted Epeians,
both leaders; and around them many others were being killed.

Then no longer could any man have faulted their war-work as he
entered the action—anyone who, as yet uninjured and unstabbed by 540
piercing bronze, was roaming in the thick of battle, with Pallas Athena
taking him by the hand and holding off the missiles' onset;
for on that day many men of the Trojans and Achaeans
lay sprawled next to each other, face down in the dust.

BOOK FIVE

Next, to Diomedes, the son of Tydeus, Pallas Athena gave
fury and daring, so that he might distinguish himself
among all the Argives, and also win illustrious fame.
From his helmet and shield she caused unwearied fire to blaze,
like the star* that in late summer rises to shine with especial   5
brightness after it has bathed in the waters of Ocean. Such
was the fire she made blaze from his head and shoulders, and
she thrust him into the battle's midst, where the turmoil was greatest.
    There was among the Trojans a man called Dares, a
blameless, rich man, a priest of Hephaestus. He had two sons,   10
Phegeus and Idaeus, both skilled in every art of battle.
These separated themselves from the rest and rushed out to face
Diomedes from their chariot, while he was on the ground, on foot.
When they had advanced to within close range of each other,
Phegeus was the first to fling his far-shadowing spear, but   15
the spear-point passed over the left shoulder of Tydeus' son
and did not hit him. Then Tydeus' son threw his bronze-tipped spear,
and the weapon did not fly in vain from his hand, but
hit Phegeus in mid-chest, and toppled him from the chariot.
Idaeus sprang back, leaving his beautifully made chariot,   20
and did not have the courage to stand over his slain brother;
nor indeed would he himself have escaped death's black spectre,
had not Hephaestus rescued him, shrouding him in night, unharmed,
so that his old priest might not be utterly overwhelmed by grief.
The son of great-spirited Tydeus drove off their horses   25
and gave them to his companions to take back to the hollow ships.
When the great-spirited Trojans saw the two sons of Dares,
that one had fled and the other was lying dead by his chariot,
anger swelled up in them all; but grey-eyed Athena took
impetuous Ares by the hand and addressed him in these words: 30
'Ares, doom of mortals Ares, bloodstained sacker of walled cities,
shall we not leave the Trojans and Achaeans alone to struggle
together, and see to which side father Zeus grants the glory?
Let us withdraw, and in this way avoid the anger of Zeus.'
    So she spoke, and led impetuous Ares away from the battle,   35
and made him sit beside the high banks of Scamander,

and the Danaans began to drive the Trojans back. Each of
their leaders killed his man: first, Agamemnon, lord of men,
toppled huge Odius, captain of the Halizones, from his chariot;
he was the first to turn away, and Agamemnon planted his spear　40
in his back between the shoulders, and drove it out through his chest.
He fell with a thud, and his armour clattered about him.

　　Then Idomeneus killed Phaestus, the son of Borus,
the Maeonian, who had come from rich-soiled Tarne.
Spear-famed Idomeneus pierced him with his long lance　　45
in the right shoulder as he was about to climb into his chariot;
he tumbled from the chariot, and hateful darkness took him.

　　Idomeneus' attendants stripped him of his armour, and
then Menelaus, Atreus' son, with his sharp spear killed
Scamandrius, the son of Strophius, a man skilled in the chase,　50
a fine hunter, whom Artemis herself had taught to
shoot down all kinds of wild beasts that live in mountain forests.
But this time Artemis shooter of arrows could not help him,
nor could the marksmanship in which he formerly excelled,
because Atreus' son Menelaus, famed with the spear,　　55
struck him with a spear in the back as he fled before him,
between the shoulders, and drove it through his chest.
He collapsed on to his face, and his armour clattered about him.

　　Meriones struck down Phereclus, son of Tecton who was
Harmon's son, who had the skill in his hands to fashion all kinds　60
of intricate work, for Pallas Athena loved him above all others.
It was he who had built for Alexander the well-balanced ships
which began the trouble, and brought misery to all the Trojans
and to himself, since he knew nothing of the gods' ordinances.
Meriones went after him, and when he caught up with him　　65
struck him in the right buttock, and the spear-point
passed clean through under the bone into his bladder.
Phereclus screamed and fell to his knees, and death enveloped him.

　　Meges killed Pedaeus, son of Antenor—a bastard son, but
glorious Theano had brought him up with the same faithful care　70
that she gave to her own dear children, out of regard for her husband.
The spear-famed son of Phyleus came close to him and
struck with his sharp spear at the muscle in his neck; the bronze
passed clean through his teeth, severing the tongue's root, and
he collapsed in the dust, the cold bronze clenched in his teeth.　75

　　Eurypylus, son of Euaemon, killed glorious Hypsenor,

the son of proud-spirited Dolopion, who was the priest of
Scamander and was honoured by the people as if he were a god.
As he fled before him Eurypylus, Euaemon's splendid son,
ran him down and lunging forward drove his sword through   80
Hypsenor's shoulder, and sheared off his heavy arm.
The bloody arm fell to the ground, and dark death and
his cruel destiny came down and fastened on his eyes.

So they laboured on in the fierce conflict. As for the son
of Tydeus, you could not tell whose side he was on,   85
whether he was allied with the Trojans or with the Achaeans.*
He stormed over the plain like a river in spate, a winter
torrent that quickly sweeps dykes away in its surging course;
close-built embankments cannot hold it back, nor can
walls raised to defend flourishing orchards resist its   90
sudden onslaught, when the heavy rain from Zeus has fallen,
and far and wide destroys the fruits of strong men's toil.
So the close-packed ranks of Trojans were thrown by Tydeus' son
into confusion, nor for all their numbers could they withstand him.

Now when Pandarus, the splendid son of Lycaon, saw him   95
storming over the plain, scattering the companies before him,
he quickly aimed his curved bow at the son of Tydeus,
and hit him in the right shoulder as he charged forward,
on a plate of his corslet. The bitter arrow flew through it,
holding a straight course, and his corslet was spattered with blood.   100
Then Lycaon's splendid son let out a great shout over him:
'Up with you, great-spirited Trojans, whippers of horses!
The best of the Achaeans has been wounded, and I do not think
he will long hold out against my mighty arrow, if it truly was
the lord son of Zeus* who sent me here when I left Lycia.'   105

So he spoke, boasting, but the swift arrow did not fell Diomedes,
and he turned back and stood in front of his horses and
chariot and spoke to Sthenelus, son of Capaneus:
'Quick, dear son of Capaneus, get down from the chariot,
so that you can pull the bitter arrow from my shoulder for me.'   110

So he spoke, and Sthenelus jumped from the chariot to the ground,
and standing by him pulled the swift arrow out from behind his shoulder,
and the blood speared up through the closely woven tunic.
Then Diomedes, master of the war-cry, spoke in prayer:
'Hear me, daughter of Zeus who wears the aegis, Atrytone: 115
if ever you stood beside my father with kindly intent

in deadly war, this time be a friend to me too, Athena.
Let me kill this man; grant that he may come within my spear-cast,
this man who shot me before I saw him, and who claims that
I do not have long to look upon the bright light of the sun.' 120
    So he spoke in prayer, and Pallas Athena heard him,
and brought lightness to his legs and his arms again.
Standing nearby she addressed him with winged words:
'Take courage now, Diomedes, to fight against the Trojans;
I have thrust into your breast the fury of your father, 125
fearless fury, such as the shield-wielding horseman Tydeus had.
And I have taken from your eyes the mist that was there before,
so that you can easily distinguish between god and man.
So if some god now comes down here to test you,
you must not fight face to face with any of the immortal gods— 130
except only that if Aphrodite, daughter of Zeus, enters
the battle, you may wound her with the sharp bronze.'
    So grey-eyed Athena spoke, and went away, and the son
of Tydeus at once set off and joined the front-fighters.
Though even before he was raging in his heart to fight the Trojans, 135
yet now three times that fury seized him, like a lion that a
shepherd watching over thick-fleeced sheep in open country
has wounded but not killed when it leapt over his sheepfold's fence;
he has provoked its strength, but he cannot then defend his flock,
and the lion gets into the enclosures, and the helpless sheep 140
run about in panic. They fall in heaps, piled one on another,
and the lion, still raging, leaps away over the fold's high fence.
So did mighty Diomedes plunge raging in among the Trojans.
    Next he killed Astynous and Hypeiron, shepherd of the people;
one he pierced above the nipple with his bronze-tipped spear, 145
and struck the other's collarbone with his great sword
next to the shoulder, and sheared it away from his back and neck.
He left them where they were, and went after Abas and Polyidus,
the sons of Eurydamas, the aged expounder of dreams.
He had interpreted no dreams for them when they left for Troy, 150
and now mighty Diomedes stripped them of their armour.
Next he went after Xanthus and Thoön, two sons of Phaenops,
both late-born; their father was now worn out by grim old age,
and had fathered no other son to inherit his possessions.
Diomedes killed them, depriving them of their dear lives, 155
both of them, and bequeathed lamentation and cruel grief

to their father, since he could not welcome them back alive
from the war. Distant cousins shared out his wealth.

Next he caught two sons of Priam of the line of Dardanus,
Echemmon and Chromius, as they rode out in one chariot.   160
As a lion springs on a herd of cattle and breaks the neck
of a calf or cow as they graze in a wooded place,
so the son of Tydeus thrust them both brutally from their chariot,
though they resisted, and stripped them of their arms.
He gave the horses to his companions, to drive back to the ships.   165

While he was spreading havoc among the ranks of men, Aeneas
saw him and set off through the battle and the confusion of spears,
seeking godlike Pandarus, in the hope of finding him.
And he came upon the blameless and mighty son of Lycaon,
and standing before him spoke directly to him: 170
'Pandarus, where now are your bow and your winged arrows,
and your fame? No man here can compete with you in archery,
nor does any man in Lycia boast that he is better than you.
Come now, lift your hands to Zeus and let fly an arrow at this man,
the one who stands supreme here, who is inflicting great hurt   175
on the Trojans, loosening the knees of many fine men—
unless he is some god who has a grudge against the Trojans,
being angry over a missed offering; a god's anger is hard to bear.'

Then in answer the splendid son of Lycaon addressed him:
'Aeneas, counsellor of the bronze-shirted Trojans,   180
this man seems to me exactly like Tydeus' war-minded son,
for I recognize him by his shield and his vizored helmet,
and the look of his horses; but I do not know for sure if it is a god.
If this is the man I think it is, Tydeus' war-minded son, this
crazed assault cannot happen without a god, and some immortal   185
must be standing close to him, his shoulders shrouded in mist,
who has turned aside the swift arrow that was on course to hit him;
I have already let fly an arrow at him, and it hit his right
shoulder, passing right through the plate of his corslet, and
I believed that I was on the point of sending him to Hades, but   190
even so I did not fell him. So some resentful god must be here.
Here I do not have horses, or a chariot that I can mount;
yet in Lycaon's halls you must know that I have eleven chariots,
fine ones, freshly built, brand new. Over them cloths
are spread, and next to each of them pairs of horses   195
stand, champing on white barley and emmer wheat.

And indeed as I left, my father, the old spear-fighter
Lycaon, gave me much advice in his well-built house,
telling me I should take my stand in a horse-drawn chariot
and lead the Trojans into the harsh conflict of battle.   200
I did not listen to him—and it would have been much better if
I had—wanting to spare my horses, in case they ran short of fodder in
places where men are crowded together, and they used to plentiful food.
So I left them behind, and I came to Ilium on foot,
relying on my bow, but that was to turn out no use to me: 205
already I have let fly an arrow at two of their champions,
the son of Tydeus and Atreus' son, and in both I have
made the blood flow with a clear hit, but it only provoked them
the more. So it was for a miserable destiny that I took down my
curved bow from its peg, on the day that I came leading my   210
Trojans to beautiful Ilium, doing a service to glorious Hector.
But if I ever go back home and cast eyes on my native land,
on my wife and on my great high-roofed house,
may some stranger cut off my head, there and then,
if I do not smash this bow with my hands and throw it   215
into the blazing fire; it was useless gear to bring with me.'

  Then Aeneas, captain of the Trojans, answered him:
'Do not talk like that, I beg you! Nothing will change until
you and I go to meet this man with chariot and horses,
to match our strength and bring him to the test in full armour.   220
So come, climb into my chariot, and you will see the
worth of the horses of Tros,* which have the skill to range
swiftly over all the plain, whether in pursuit or retreat.
They will carry us safely back to the city, if Zeus continues
to give the glory to Diomedes, the son of Tydeus.   225
Come now, take the whip and the shining reins, and
I will get down from the chariot, and enter the fighting—
or you can go to meet this man, while I take care of the horses.'

  Then the splendid son of Lycaon addressed him:
'Aeneas, you must take care of the reins and the horses yourself;   230
they are more likely to pull the curved chariot under the hands of
their accustomed driver, if we have to flee from Tydeus' son.
I am afraid that if they cannot hear your voice they will grow
restive and take fright, and refuse to carry us out of the battle,
and then the son of great-spirited Tydeus could attack   235
and kill us and drive away your single-hoofed horses.

No, you must drive the chariot and horses yourself,
and I will face his onslaught with my sharp spear.'
    So they spoke, and mounted the finely worked chariot,
and, raging, guided the swift horses towards Tydeus' son.   240
Sthenelus, the splendid son of Capaneus, saw them coming,
and quickly addressed Tydeus' son with winged words:
'Diomedes, son of Tydeus, delight of my heart, I can
see two mighty men coming at you, raging for the fight,
filled with immense strength; one is the skilled bowman,   245
Pandarus, who boasts that he is the son of Lycaon,
while the other boasts that he was born the son of
blameless Anchises, and that his mother was Aphrodite.
Come, let us retreat in our chariot, and do not, I beg you, storm
like this through the front-fighters, or you may lose your dear life.'   250
    But mighty Diomedes looked at him darkly and addressed him:
'Do not talk to me of flight; I do not think you will persuade me.
I am not the kind of man to hang back from the fight,
nor to cower in fear; my fury is still firmly fixed within me.
But I am loath to mount my chariot, and will go to meet them   255
just as I am; Pallas Athena does not allow me to be afraid.
As for those two, their swift horses will not carry them home,
away from me, even if one or the other of them escapes.
And I tell you another thing, and you should store it in your mind:
if Athena of many counsels grants me the glory of   260
killing these two, you must leave these swift horses
of ours here, tying their reins to the chariot-rail, and
turn your mind to Aeneas' horses; make a dash for him
and drive them from the Trojans to the well-greaved Achaeans.
You must know, they are of the same stock that Zeus the wide-   265
thunderer gave to Tros as compensation for his son Ganymedes,
for they were the best of all horses under the dawn and the sun.
Anchises, lord of men, bred from this bloodstock by deceit,
by putting mares to the stallions without Laomedon's knowledge.*
From them six foals were born in his halls, and of these   270
he kept four for himself, and raised them at his manger,
and he gave two, provokers of panic, to Aeneas.
If we were to capture these we would win glorious fame.'
    As they were speaking to one another in this way,
the other two quickly closed on them, driving their swift horses.   275
Then the splendid son of Lycaon was the first to speak:

'Steadfast-hearted, war-minded son of proud Tydeus!
So my swift shot, my bitter arrow, did not fell you; but this time
I will test you with my spear, and perhaps I will strike you down.'
So he spoke, and poised his long-shadowing spear and threw it,   280
and hit the shield of Tydeus' son; and the bronze point
flew clean through it and reached Diomedes' corslet.
At this Lycaon's splendid son gave a great shout:
'You are hit, deep in your side! I do not think you will
hold out much longer; you have given me great glory.'   285
    Fearlessly, mighty Diomedes addressed him:
'You missed—you did not hit me! I think that before
you are finished with all this one or other of you will fall and
with his blood glut Ares, the fighter with the oxhide shield.'
    So he spoke and hurled his spear, and Athena guided it on to   290
Pandarus' nose by his eye, and it went through his white teeth.
The relentless bronze cut his tongue away at the root,
and the point then came out underneath his chin.
He tumbled from the chariot, and his bright-glittering armour
clattered about him, and the swift-footed horses   295
started in fear; and there his life and fury ebbed away.
    Now Aeneas jumped down, holding his shield and long spear,
fearing that the Achaeans would drag the dead man away from him.
He stood astride him like a lion, trusting in his strength,
holding before him his spear and perfectly balanced shield,   300
raging to kill anyone who might come to challenge him,
and yelling terribly. But the son of Tydeus picked up a rock
in his hand, a mighty feat, which not even two men such as
mortals now are could hold up, but he easily lifted it on his own.
With this he hit Aeneas on the hip-joint, where the thigh-bone   305
revolves in the hip socket, and men call it the cup.
He smashed Aeneas' cup, and severed both sinews as well,
and the rough rock stripped away his skin. The hero sank to
his knees and stayed there, propping himself on the ground
with his brawny hand; and black night covered his eyes.   310
    Then indeed Aeneas lord of men would have died,
had not Aphrodite, daughter of Zeus, been quick to see him—
his mother, who had borne him to Anchises, herdsman of cattle.
Around her dear son she wrapped her white arms, and
held before him a concealing fold of her white dress as a   315
defence against missiles, in case any of the swift-horsed Danaans

should hurl a spear into his chest and take away his life.
    So she set about rescuing her dear son from the fighting by
stealth; but the son of Capaneus did not forget the agreement
that Diomedes, master of the war-cry, had made with him.   320
He held back his own single-hoofed horses, keeping them
from the battle's confusion, and tied their reins to the chariot-rail,
and made a dash for the fine-maned horses of Aeneas, and
drove them away from the Trojans to the well-greaved Achaeans.
He gave them to Deipylus, his dear companion, whom he
        esteemed   325
above all his peers, because their minds thought alike,
telling him to drive them to the hollow ships. Then the hero
mounted his own chariot and took up the shining reins,
and at once drove the strong-hoofed horses towards Tydeus' son,
raging. Diomedes was pursuing Cypris* with the pitiless bronze,   330
knowing what an unwarlike goddess she was, and not one
of those reckoned to take command when men are at war—
she was certainly no Athena, nor Enyo,* sacker of cities.
When the son of great-spirited Tydeus caught up with her,
after pursuing her through the dense soldiery, he sprang forward 335
and, lunging, stabbed her with his sharp spear on the wrist,
where it was soft. The spear passed clean through the deathless
garment which the Graces had woven for her, piercing the flesh
above the palm's base, and the goddess' deathless blood flowed;
this was ichor, the kind of blood that flows in the blessed gods, 340
for they eat no bread, and do not drink gleaming wine,
and so are without blood, and men call them immortals.
She gave a loud scream, and let her son fall from her,
but Phoebus Apollo caught him up in his arms, protecting him
in a dark cloud, in case any of the swift-horsed Danaans   345
should hurl a bronze spear into his chest and take away his life.
Then Diomedes, master of the war-cry, shouted aloud over her:
'Daughter of Zeus, stay away from warfare and fighting!
Is it not enough that you lead feeble women astray?
If you keep joining the battle, I think you will come to be   350
terrified of war, even when you only hear others speak of it.'
    So he spoke, and she went away, distraught and in great pain.
Wind-footed Iris lifted her up and led her out of the mass of men,
exhausted with pain, and her lovely skin was darkening.
On the left of the battlefield she found impetuous Ares   355

sitting alone, his spear and swift horses resting against a cloud.
Falling to her knees she urgently entreated her dear brother,
begging him for his horses with their headbands of gold:
'Dear brother, help me to escape. Give me your horses, so that
I may reach Olympus, where the immortal gods have their seat.   360
I am sorely troubled with a wound, which a mortal man gave me—
Tydeus' son, who would now fight even against father Zeus.'
    So she spoke, and Ares gave her the horses with golden headbands,
and she mounted the chariot, suffering in her dear heart,
and Iris mounted beside her and took up the reins in her hand,   365
and whipped the pair to make them go; and they flew willingly on.
Soon they arrived at steep Olympus, seat of the gods,
and there swift wind-footed Iris pulled up the horses, unyoked
them from the chariot, and threw immortal fodder before them.
Bright Aphrodite collapsed on to the knees of Dione   370
her mother, who took her daughter in her arms, and
stroking her with her hand addressed her, saying:
'Dear child, which of the Uranian* gods has done this to you
so thoughtlessly, as if you had committed some public mischief?'
    Then Aphrodite who loves to smile answered her: 375
'It was the son of Tydeus, arrogant Diomedes, who wounded me,
because I rescued my dear son from the fighting by stealth—
Aeneas, who is by far the dearest of all men to me.
This grim conflict is no longer between Trojans and Achaeans,
but now the Danaans are fighting against immortals as well.'   380
    Then Dione, bright among goddesses, answered her:
'Endure, my child, and bear this, distressed though you are;
many of us who have our homes on Olympus have suffered
at men's hands, when we tried to inflict harsh pain on each other.
Ares for one suffered, when Otus and mighty Ephialtes,   385
the sons of Aloeus, bound him in strong chains;
for thirteen months he was imprisoned in a bronze jar,
and then even Ares, insatiable in war, would have died
had not their stepmother, the beautiful Eëriboea, taken
the news to Hermes; he stole Ares out of the jar—and he was   390
now in a weak state, for the cruel chains were wearing him down.*
Again, Hera suffered when the mighty son of Amphitryon*
wounded her in her right breast with a three-barbed
arrow, and incurable anguish seized hold of her.
Monstrous Hades suffered too with the rest,* hit by a swift arrow 395

when that same man, the son of Zeus who wears the aegis,
shot him at Pylos among the dead men and gave him over to pain.
He went away to the house of Zeus on high Olympus, grieving
in his heart and pierced through with agony, for the arrow
had driven into his massive shoulder, and was vexing his heart.   400
But Paeëon* spread pain-killing ointments on his wound
and healed him, since he was not made to suffer death.
Heracles was a hard and violent man, not troubled by the outrages
he committed with his bow on the gods who hold Olympus.
As for you, the goddess grey-eyed Athena set this man against you,   405
fool that he is, since Tydeus' son does not know in his heart
that the man who fights with immortals is not at all long-lived;
such a man has no homecoming from war and grim conflict*
to find his children crying 'Daddy' as they climb on to his knees.
So let the son of Tydeus, even if he is very mighty, now   410
take care that no god more warlike than you fights against him;
or else Aegialeia, the prudent daughter of Adrestus
and the steadfast wife of Diomedes, breaker of horses, may
one day rouse her household from sleep with mourning cries,
longing in vain for her wedded husband, the best of the Achaeans.' 415
    So she spoke, and with her hands wiped away the ichor from
Aphrodite's wrist; it was healed, and the harsh pain was soothed.
Now the others had been watching this, Athena and Hera,
and they began to tease Cronus' son Zeus with mocking words;
and the first to speak was the goddess grey-eyed Athena: 420
'Father Zeus, will you be angry at what I am going to say?
I do believe that Cypris has been persuading some Achaean woman
into following the Trojans, whom she now loves to excess,
and while she was caressing this lovely robed Achaean woman
she scratched her delicate hand on a golden pin.'   425
    So she spoke, and the father of gods and men smiled,
and calling golden Aphrodite to him spoke to her:
'Warfare's business, my child, is not for you; your task is
to occupy yourself with matters of desire and marriage,
leaving all this to be the concern of swift Ares and Athena.'   430
    As they were talking to each other in this way,
Diomedes, master of the war-cry, sprang forward at Aeneas.
He knew that Apollo himself had spread his arms over him,
but even so he was not in awe of the great god, and kept rushing at
Aeneas, to kill him and to strip him of his famous armour.   435

Three times he sprang at him, raging for the kill, and
three times Apollo battered his shining shield back;
but when he charged for the fourth time, like some divine being,
Apollo who shoots from afar gave a terrible shout and addressed him:
'Think, son of Tydeus, and shrink back, and do not hope to   440
match yourself with gods! The races of immortal gods and
of men who walk upon the earth can never be the same.'
   So he spoke, and Tydeus' son drew back a little space,
avoiding the anger of Apollo who shoots from afar.
As for Aeneas, Apollo set him apart from the mass of men   445
in the holy shrine on Pergamus where his temple stood.*
There Leto and Artemis,* shooter of arrows,
nursed him in the spacious sanctuary and renewed his glory;
and Apollo of the silver bow fashioned a phantom in the
exact likeness of Aeneas and with the same armour,   450
and around this phantom the Trojans and glorious Achaeans
hewed at each other's oxhide shields, held before their chests,
both round shields and those made from stretched shaggy hides.
Then indeed Phoebus Apollo addressed impetuous Ares:
'Ares, doom of mortals, bloodstained Ares, sacker of walled cities,   455
will you not go after this man and take him from the battle?
I mean Tydeus' son, who would now fight even against father Zeus.
First he grappled with Cypris and wounded her on the wrist,
and after that he came at me like some divine being.'
   So he spoke, and settled down on the heights of Pergamus,   460
while murderous Ares went among the Trojan ranks and urged them
on, in the likeness of Acamas, swift commander of the Thracians,
and gave instructions to the Zeus-nurtured sons of Priam:
'You sons of Priam, a king nurtured by Zeus, how long
will you allow your people to be killed by the Achaeans?   465
Will you wait until they are fighting about your strongly made gates?
Lying there is a man whom we honour as much as glorious Hector—
Aeneas, the son of great-hearted Anchises. Come, let us
rescue our fine companion from the roaring tumult of battle.'
   So he spoke, and quickened the fury and spirit in each man.   470
Then Sarpedon too rebuked glorious Hector with hard words:
'Hector, tell me, where has that fury gone that you had before?
You used to say, I recall, that you could hold the city on your own,
without men or allies, just you and your brothers and brothers-in-law.
And yet I cannot see or make out a single one of them now,   475

but they are cowering like hounds around a lion,
while we, who are only here as your allies, do the fighting.
I indeed have come a very great distance to be your ally:
Lycia is far away, beside the Xanthus with its swirling waters,
where I left my dear wife and my infant son, and   480
a great store of treasure, such as a poor man would envy;
but for all that I urge on the Lycians, and am myself raging
to fight man to man, even though I have no possessions here
that the Achaeans would want to plunder and carry off.
Meanwhile, you stand idle, and do not even order your people   485
to stand their ground and fight to protect their wives.
Take care that you are not caught in the all-embracing meshes
of a corded net, and so become the prey and spoil of your enemies,
because they will very soon sack your well-populated city.
And yet all this should be your concern day and night—   490
to entreat the captains of your far-famed allies to hold unceasingly
to their task; this way you may shake off their harsh rebuke.'

    So Sarpedon spoke, and his words bit into Hector's thoughts;
at once he leapt fully armed from his chariot to the ground,
and ranged through the whole camp, shaking two spears,   495
urging the Trojans to fight, and rousing up the grim conflict.
They turned and rallied, and stood facing the Achaeans,
but the Argives massed and stood their ground, and did not run.
As when on a sacred threshing-floor a wind carries the chaff away
when men are winnowing, at the time when fair-haired Demeter*   500
separates grain and chaff under the hurrying winds, and
the heaps of chaff grow white; so then did the Achaeans
turn white under the fall of dust which the horses' hoofs
kicked up through their ranks, and sent up to the high brazen sky,
as the men closed again in battle, and the charioteers kept
        wheeling back.   505
So they drove their hands' fury forward; and impetuous Ares,
roaming everywhere, drew a veil of night over the battle
to help the Trojans. He was carrying out the commands of
Phoebus Apollo of the golden sword, who had ordered him
to wake the spirit of the Trojans, when he saw Pallas Athena   510
leaving the field; for she was the Danaans' champion.
Then he sent Aeneas out from his richly endowed sanctuary,
and thrust fury into the breast of the shepherd of the people.
Aeneas took his place among his companions, and they were glad

when they saw him coming back alive and restored to health,   515
and full of noble fury; but they did not question him at all, for the toil
before them, stirred up by the god of the silver bow and by Ares,
doom of mortals, and by endlessly raging Strife, would not let them.

    As for the Danaans, the two called Ajax, with Odysseus and Diomedes,
were driving them on to fight; but even without their urging   520
the men had no fear of the Trojans' violent onslaught,
but stood their ground like clouds that the son of Cronus
holds motionless over the peaks of mountains on a windless day,
while the fury of the North Wind and of the other
blustering winds which scatter the shadowing clouds with   525
their shrill blasts is asleep; so the Danaans stood unmoved,
waiting for the Trojans, and refused to turn in flight.
Atreus' son roamed through the ranks, with constant exhortations:
'My friends, be men, and put courage in your hearts,
and feel shame before each other in the fierce crush of battle!   530
Men who feel shame are more often saved than killed,
while those who run away find neither glory nor courage.'

    So he spoke, and quickly threw his spear and hit a leading man,
a companion of great-spirited Aeneas, Deicoön, who was
the son of Pergasus, and whom the Trojans honoured as much as   535
Priam's sons, since he was always quick to fight in the front ranks.
Lord Agamemnon hit him with his spear on the shield,
which could not stop it, and the bronze flew right through,
driving beyond the belt into the base of his belly.
He fell with a thud, and his armour clattered about him.   540

    Then in his turn Aeneas killed two of the best men of the Danaans,
Crethon and Orsilochus, the sons of Diocles,
whose father's home was in well-built Pherae;* he was a
man of great wealth, and was descended from a river,
Alpheus, which flows in a broad stream through the Pylians' land,   545
and he fathered Ortilochus to be king over many men.
Ortilochus in turn was father to great-spirited Diocles,
and to Diocles there were born two sons, twins,
Crethon and Orsilochus, who were skilled in all battle's arts.
When they reached youth's fullness they accompanied   550
the Argives in their black ships to Ilium rich in horses,
to win compensation for Atreus' sons, Agamemnon and
Menelaus; but there the end of death covered them both.
They were like a pair of lions raised by their mother

in deep wooded thickets high in the mountains, lions   555
that pillage the enclosures of men's farms, and carry off
their cattle and sturdy sheep, until they in their turn
fall into men's hands and are killed with the sharp bronze;
just so were they overcome at the hands of Aeneas
and crashed to the ground like lofty pine trees.   560

    When they had fallen the warrior Menelaus felt pity for them,
and strode through the front-fighters helmeted in gleaming bronze,
shaking his spear. Ares stirred up the fury in him, intending
that he should be beaten down by the hands of Aeneas.
But Antilochus, great-spirited Nestor's son, saw him, and   565
strode up through the front-fighters; he was greatly afraid that
the people's shepherd might be hurt and bring all their toil to nothing.
The two men were poising their sharp spears ready in their hands,
facing each other and in a frenzy to fight, when Antilochus came
and stood very close to the shepherd of the people, and   570
Aeneas, swift fighter though he was, did not stand his ground
when he saw the two men standing firm, side by side.
So these dragged the dead men back into the Achaean people,
and laid the wretched pair in the arms of their companions,
and turned back and began to fight again in the front ranks.   575

    There they killed Pylaemenes, who was the equal of Ares,
captain of the great-spirited shield-bearing Paphlagonians.
He was standing still when Menelaus, son of Atreus, famed
with the spear, pierced him with his spear, hitting his collarbone.
Antilochus struck down Mydon, his attendant and charioteer,   580
Atymnius' fine son, as he wheeled his single-hoofed horses,
hitting him with a rock full on his elbow; and the reins with their
white ivory decoration fell from his hands and dropped into the dust.
Antilochus sprang at him and drove his sword into Mydon's temples,
and he fell from the well-made chariot, gasping for breath,   585
head-first in the dust, buried up to his head and shoulders.
For some time he stuck there—for the sand was deep—until
his horses kicked him and laid him flat on the dusty ground.
Antilochus whipped them up, and drove them back to the Achaean camp.

    But Hector noticed them across the ranks, and sprang after them   590
with a yell; and companies of the Trojans followed him
in all their strength. They were led by Ares and lady Enyo,
she bringing with her Confusion, reckless in war,
while Ares held a spear of prodigious size in his hands,

roaming now in front of Hector and now behind him.   595
    When he saw him Diomedes, master of the war-cry, shuddered.
As when a man who is crossing a great plain stands
helpless before a swift-moving river that flows towards the sea,
and seeing it churned into foam runs back a little way;
so then Tydeus' son drew back, and spoke to his people: 600
'My friends, in the past we have been filled with amazement at
glorious Hector, as a spearman and a brave fighter, but there is
always one of the gods at his side, to save him from ruin,
as now Ares stands there next to him, in the likeness of a mortal.
Come, keep your faces towards the Trojans, and retreat   605
steadily, and do not rage to pit your strength in battle against gods.'
    So he spoke, and the Trojans came up very close to them.
Then Hector killed two men who were skilled in warfare,
Menesthes and Anchialus, who were both in one chariot.
When they fell huge Ajax, Telamon's son, felt pity for them;   610
he went forward, and standing nearby let fly with his shining spear,
and hit Amphius, the son of Selagus, who lived in Paesus,
a man of much property and rich in corn-land; but his destiny
had brought him to come to the help of Priam and his sons.
Ajax, son of Telamon, hit him on his belt, and   615
the far-shadowing spear lodged at the base of his belly,
and he fell with a thud. Illustrious Ajax ran up to strip him
of his armour, but the Trojans rained their spears on him,
sharp and gleaming, and he caught many of them on his shield.
Setting his heel on the dead man he pulled the bronze-tipped spear   620
out of him; but he could not then strip the fine armour
from Amphius' shoulders, since he was hard pressed by missiles,
and was also frightened by the proud Trojans' steadfast defence,
who confronted him bravely in numbers, grasping their spears,
and who, for all his size and strength and splendour,   625
forced him back from them; and he was shaken and withdrew.
    So they laboured away in the fierce crush of battle.
Then Tlepolemus, the great and valiant son of Heracles,
was roused by his harsh destiny to attack godlike Sarpedon.
When they had advanced to within close range of each other,   630
one a son and the other a grandson of Zeus the cloud-gatherer,
Tlepolemus was the first to speak to the other man:
'Sarpedon, counsellor of the Lycians, what compulsion
is forcing you, a man unskilled in fighting, to cower here?

Men lie when they say that you are the offspring of Zeus   635
who wears the aegis, since you fall far short of those men
who in former generations were fathered by Zeus—
such men as they say the mighty Heracles was.
He was my steadfast-spirited, lion-hearted father, and
long ago came here in search of the mares of Laomedon,*   640
with no more than six ships and a smaller force of men,
but he sacked the city of Ilium and made widows of its streets.
But you have a coward's heart, and your people are dying.
I do not think that your coming here from Lycia will prove
to be a defence to the Trojans, not even if you are very strong;   645
no, you will pass through Hades' gates, beaten down at my hands.'
      In answer to him Sarpedon, the captain of the Lycians, said:
'Tlepolemus, Heracles did indeed destroy sacred Ilium,
but only through the folly of a man, splendid Laomedon,
who rewarded his good deeds with words of abuse and   650
refused him the mares, on whose account he had come so far.
As for you, I say that you will here meet death and the
black spectre at my hands; beaten down under my spear, you will
give the glory to me and your life to Hades, master of famous horses.'
      So spoke Sarpedon, and Tlepolemus lifted his ash spear,   655
and both the long spears flew from their hands at the same
time. Sarpedon hit the other in the middle of his neck,
and the pain-loaded point passed clean through it,
and dark night came down and covered his eyes.
But Tlepolemus hit Sarpedon on the left thigh with his   660
long spear, and the point sped furiously through, grazing
the bone; but as yet his father kept destruction from him.
      The glorious companions of godlike Sarpedon began
to carry him from the fighting; the long spear dragged
and weighed him down, but in their haste no one noticed   665
or thought to pull the ash spear from his thigh so that
he could stand, such was the trouble they had in protecting him.
      On the other side the well-greaved Achaeans began to carry
Tlepolemus from the fighting. Glorious Odysseus of the enduring
spirit saw him, and his dear heart within him was raging: 670
he pondered then in his heart and in his spirit
whether to pursue the son of loud-thundering Zeus further
or to take away the lives of more of the Lycians.
But it was not great-hearted Odysseus' destiny to

kill the mighty son of Zeus with the sharp bronze, and so   675
Athena turned his thoughts towards the mass of Lycians.
He killed Coeranus and Alastor and Chromius,
Alcandrus and Halius and Noëmon and Prytanis; and then
glorious Odysseus would have slain yet more Lycians,
had not great Hector of the glittering helmet been quick to notice.   680
He strode through the front-fighters, helmeted in gleaming bronze,
bringing terror to the Danaans; and at his coming Sarpedon,
the son of Zeus, was glad, and addressed him plaintively:
'Son of Priam, do not let me lie here, to become the prey
of the Danaans, but help me; and after this may my life leave me   685
in your city of Troy, since it seems I was not after all
destined to return to my home in my dear native land,
to bring gladness to my dear wife and my infant son.'
    So he spoke, but Hector of the glittering helmet did not reply,
and rushed past him, impatient to thrust back the Argives   690
as quickly as possible, and to take away the lives of many.
Then his glorious companions made godlike Sarpedon
sit beneath a handsome oak, sacred to Zeus who wears the aegis;
and the ash spear was wrenched out of his thigh
by mighty Pelagon, who was his dear companion.   695
His life's breath left him, and a mist spread over his eyes,
but then he recovered, and a gust of the North Wind
blew on him and revived his feebly breathing spirit.
    Now the Argives, faced by Ares and bronze-helmeted Hector,
at no time turned in flight towards the black ships   700
nor made a counter-attack, but retreated steadily to the
rear when they realized that Ares was helping the Trojans.
    Who was the first, and who the last to be slaughtered
by Hector, son of Priam, and by brazen Ares?
Teuthras first, and then Orestes, whipper of horses,   705
Trechus the spearman from Aetolia, and Oenomaus,
Helenus, son of Oenops, and Oresbius with his glittering loin-plate,
who lived in Hyle, carefully husbanding his wealth,
on the shore of the Cephisian lake; and near him
lived other Boeotians, possessors of a richly fertile land.   710
    When the goddess white-armed Hera saw the Argives
being slaughtered in the fierce crush of battle,
she straightaway addressed Athena in winged words:
'Daughter of Zeus the aegis-wearer, Atrytone, this will not do!

Worthless indeed was the undertaking we gave to Menelaus—   715
that he would sack strongly walled Ilium before returning home—
if we allow murderous Ares to rage in this way.
Come now, let us two also call up our surging courage.'
    So she spoke, and the goddess grey-eyed Athena did not disobey her.
Hera set about harnessing her horses with golden headbands,   720
Hera, elder goddess, daughter of great Cronus,
and Hebe quickly fitted the curved wheels to the chariot.
These are bronze, with eight spokes, on the ends of the iron axle;
their rims are made of gold, imperishable, and on them
are fitted tyres of bronze, a wonder to look on, and   725
the hubs are made of silver, revolving on both sides.
The car is woven of tightly plaited gold and silver straps,
and there are double rails running right round it;
from it extends a silver pole, and on to its end Hera
lashed a fine golden yoke, and to this she fastened   730
the golden yoke-straps. Then she led her swift-footed horses
under the yoke, impatient for strife and the battle-cry.
    And Athena, the daughter of Zeus who wears the aegis,
let fall on to her father's threshold the soft embroidered
robe which she herself had laboured over with her own hands,   735
and put on the tunic of Zeus who gathers the clouds,
and clothed herself in armour for war, the bringer of tears.
Around her shoulders she threw the tasselled aegis,
a terrifying sight, around which is set in a circle Panic,
and with it Strife and Courage, and with it chilling Rout,   740
and with it the head of the hideous monster Gorgon,
terrifying and grim, a portent of Zeus who wears the aegis.
On her head she placed a twin-crested helmet with four plates,
golden, decorated with foot-soldiers from a hundred cities.
She stepped on to the brightly blazing chariot, and gripped the spear,   745
heavy, thick, and massive, with which she beats down ranks of men,
of heroes with whom she, child of a mighty father, is enraged.
Then Hera quickly lashed the horses with her whip, and
of their own accord the gates of the high sky groaned open, gates held
by the Seasons,* who have charge of the great sky and Olympus,   750
either to push aside the dense cloud or to close it up together.
Through these gates they steered the horses, driven on by the whip,
and they found the son of Cronus sitting apart from the
other gods on the topmost peak of many-ridged Olympus.

There the goddess white-armed Hera reined in the horses   755
and put a question to Zeus, the supreme son of Cronus, saying:
'Father Zeus, are you not angry with Ares for these cruel deeds,
the great numbers of fine Achaean people he has killed,
pointlessly and recklessly—a cause of grief to me, while Cypris
and Apollo of the silver bow take their ease, delighted to have   760
unleashed this madman, who has no notion of divine order?'
Father Zeus, will you be at all angry with me if I give Ares
a painful thrashing and drive him from the battlefield?'

    Then in answer Zeus who gathers the clouds addressed her:
'I will not; stir up Athena who gathers the spoils against him,   765
for she is the one most used to dealing out harsh pain to him.'

    So he spoke, and the goddess white-armed Hera did not disobey him,
and whipped the horses; and they flew willingly onward
between the earth and the high sky, set with stars.
As far as a man can see with his eyes into the misty distance   770
as he sits on a lookout, gazing out over the wine-faced sea,
so far is the leap of the loud-whinnying horses of the gods.
When they came to Troy and the streams of the two rivers,
to the place where Simoeis and Scamander unite their waters,*
there the goddess white-armed Hera reined in the horses and   775
freed them from the chariot, and poured a thick mist around them;
and Simoeis thrust up ambrosia for them to graze on.

    But the two goddesses set out, stepping like wild pigeons,
full of rage to come to the help of the Argives.
When they came to where the most numerous and the best men   780
were standing, crowding around the mighty horse-breaker
Diomedes, in the likeness of flesh-devouring lions
or wild boars whose strength is in no way feeble, there
the goddess white-armed Hera stopped and cried aloud,
taking the appearance of great-hearted Stentor the brazen-voiced,   785
whose shout was as loud as that of fifty other men:
'Shame, Argives, you things of disgrace, admired only for your
handsome looks! As long as glorious Achilles came into the battle
the Trojans never marched out in front of the Dardanian
gates,* because they were in terror of his massive spear.   790
But now they are fighting far from their city, by our hollow ships.'

    So speaking she quickened the fury and spirit in each man.
Then the goddess grey-eyed Athena made quickly for the son
of Tydeus, and she found the lord beside his horses and chariot,

cooling the wound which Pandarus had dealt him with his arrow,   795
for sweat was causing the broad strap of his round shield
to chafe it. It was troubling him, and his hand was growing
weary as he held up the strap and wiped away the dark blood.
The goddess laid her hand on the horses' yoke and spoke to him:
'Truly Tydeus fathered a son who bears him little resemblance: 800
Tydeus was short in stature, but he was a fighter!
Even at the time when I would not allow him to fight or
push himself forward—when alone of the Achaeans he came
as an envoy to Thebes,* alone among a crowd of Cadmeians,
and I told him to restrain himself as he feasted in their halls—   805
even then, with the same audacious spirit as in former times
he challenged the young Cadmeians and beat them in every event,
easily; that was the kind of supporter I was to him.
And now here I stand beside you and keep you from harm,
and with all my heart urge you to do battle with the Trojans;   810
but either weariness from your many assaults has sunk into your limbs,
or perhaps it is heart-sapping fear that has gripped you. If so,
you are no offspring of Tydeus, the son of war-minded Oeneus.'
    Then in answer mighty Diomedes addressed her:
'I know you, goddess, daughter of Zeus who wears the aegis;   815
so I shall speak openly and hide nothing from you.
It is not heart-sapping fear that grips me, nor irresolution;
I am still holding in my mind the commands that you gave me:
you would not allow me to fight the blessed gods face to face,
except only that if Aphrodite, daughter of Zeus, should enter   820
the battle I was allowed to wound her with the sharp bronze.
For that reason I am now falling back, and I have ordered
all the rest of the Argives to gather around me here;
I can see that it is Ares who is lording it on the battlefield.'
    Then in answer the goddess grey-eyed Athena addressed him: 825
'Diomedes, son of Tydeus, delight of my heart,
you should not on this account be afraid of Ares or any other
of the immortals; that is the kind of support I give to you.
So come now, direct your single-hoofed horses first against Ares,
go close and strike him; do not be in awe of impetuous Ares,   830
this crazed god, this shape formed of evil, this two-faced scoundrel,
who not long ago spoke with Hera and me and undertook
to fight against the Trojans and bring aid to the Argives, but
now stands alongside the Trojans, and has forgotten his promise.'

So speaking she pulled Sthenelus back with her hand and
    shoved   835
him from the chariot towards the ground, and he quickly leapt down.
She mounted the chariot and stood beside glorious Diomedes,
a raging goddess; and the oaken axle groaned aloud at its
load, for it carried a fearsome goddess and the best of men.
Pallas Athena laid hold of the whip and reins, and   840
at once directed the single-hoofed horses straight at Ares,
who was stripping the armour from huge Periphas,
Ochesius' illustrious son, by far the best man of the Aetolians.
Bloodstained Ares was busy stripping him, but Athena put on
the helmet of Hades, so that the towering god should not see her.   845

When Ares, doom of mortals, saw glorious Diomedes,
he left monstrous Periphas to lie there, in the place
where he had killed him and robbed him of his life,
and made straight for Diomedes, breaker of horses.
When they had advanced to within close range of each other,   850
Ares first lunged over the yoke and the horses' reins
with his bronze-tipped spear, raging to take the life from him;
but the goddess grey-eyed Athena caught it with her hand
and forced it up and out of the chariot, so that it flew aimlessly by.
Then Diomedes, master of the war-cry, lunged in his turn   855
with his bronze-tipped spear, and Pallas Athena drove it
at the base of Ares' belly, where his loin-plate was belted;
here Diomedes hit and wounded him, biting through his fine flesh,
and pulled the spear out again; brazen Ares bellowed,
as loud as the yells of nine- or ten-thousand men grappling   860
with each other on a battlefield in the war-god's strife.
At this, fear and trembling seized both Achaeans and Trojans,
so loud was the bellowing of Ares, insatiable in war.

Like a dark mass of air that appears out of the clouds
when a violent wind springs up after burning heat,   865
so brazen Ares appeared before Tydeus' son Diomedes,
rising with the clouds right up to the wide high sky.
Quickly he came to the seat of the gods, steep Olympus,
and took his seat next to Zeus, Cronus' son, grieving in his heart,
and showed him the immortal blood flowing from the wound;   870
full of complaint he addressed Zeus with winged words:
'Father Zeus, are you not angry when you see cruel deeds like this?
We gods always have to endure the most appalling sufferings

through each other's scheming when we do favours to men.
We are all at war with you, because you fathered this witless girl,   875
this cursed goddess, whose mind is always set on deeds of malice.
All of the other gods who live on Olympus obey
your will, and we are each of us subject to you; but her
you do not reproach in word or deed, but let her run free,
just because you yourself are the father of this murderous child.   880
Now she has let loose Tydeus' son, arrogant Diomedes,
in crazed assault against the immortal gods.
First he closed with Cypris and wounded her on the wrist,
then hurled himself at me, Ares himself, like some divine being.
But my swift feet carried me away, or I would now be suffering   885
long-lasting anguish there among the ghastly piles of dead,
or would live on enfeebled by the blows of his bronze.'

Zeus who gathers the clouds looked at him darkly and said:
'You two-faced scoundrel, do not sit here and whine to me!
Of all the gods who live on Olympus you are the most hateful to me: 890
strife and war and fighting are always dear to your heart.
Your mother's spirit too is ungovernable, one that does not yield—
Hera, whom I find it hard to control with my words;
so I think it is at her prompting that you are suffering like this.
Even so, I shall not allow you to be in pain any longer,   895
for you are my offspring, and your mother bore you to me;
but if any other god had fathered you, to cause such carnage,
you would long ago have been lower than the offspring of Uranus.'

So he spoke, and summoned Paeëon to cure him,
and Paeëon spread pain-killing ointments over his wound   900
and healed it; for Ares was not made to suffer death.
As when fig-juice thickens white milk when it is
liquid but very quickly becomes clotted when a man
stirs it,* so swiftly did Paeëon heal impetuous Ares.
Then Hebe bathed him, and dressed him in fine clothes, and   905
he took his seat beside Cronus' son Zeus, exulting in his glory.

Then the two goddesses returned to the house of great Zeus,
Argive Hera and Athena of Alalcomenae, when they had
halted the man-slaying exploits of Ares, doom of mortals.

BOOK SIX

So the grim fighting of Trojans and Achaeans was left to itself,
and the battle ranged widely, this way and that over the plain,
each side aiming their bronze-tipped spears at the other
in the ground between the waters of Simoeis and Xanthus.

Ajax, son of Telamon, bulwark of the Achaeans, was the first   5
to break through the Trojan line, bringing hope to his companions,
by striking down a man who was the best of the Thracians,
Acamas, son of Eussorus, a valiant and mighty man.
Throwing first, Ajax hit him on the ridge of his horsehair-crested
helmet, and the bronze point lodged in his forehead, piercing   10
through to the bone; and darkness covered his eyes.

Then Diomedes, master of the war-cry, killed Axylus
the son of Teuthras, who lived in well-built Arisbe;
he was rich in possessions and hospitable towards men, for
his house was by the roadside, and he would entertain everyone.   15
But not one of these could now save him from miserable death
by standing before him to face his enemy; Diomedes robbed
two men of their lives, Axylus and his attendant Calesius, who was
his charioteer at this time, and both sank below the earth.

Euryalus killed first Dresus and then Opheltius,   20
and went after Aesepus and Pedasus, whom long ago
the river nymph Abarbareë had borne to blameless Bucolion;*
Bucolion was the son of splendid Laomedon, his first
to be born, but his mother gave birth to him in secret.
Bucolion lay in love with this nymph while tending his sheep,   25
and she conceived and gave birth to twin sons;
but Mecisteus' son loosened their fury and shining limbs,
and he stripped the armour from their shoulders.

Next Polypoetes, steadfast in war, killed Astyalus,
and Odysseus with his bronze-tipped spear slew Pidytes,   30
who came from Percote, and Teucer killed brilliant Aretaon.
Ablerus was killed by the shining spear of Antilochus,
Nestor's son, and Agamemnon, lord of men, slew Elatus,
who lived beside the banks of broad-flowing Satnioeis,
in steep Pedasus.* The hero Leïtus overtook Phylacus   35
as he was running away, and Eurypylus slew Melanthius.

Next Menelaus, master of the war-cry, captured Adrestus
alive. His horses, bolting in panic over the plain, had tripped over
a tamarisk branch and broken the pole away where it was joined
to the curved chariot, and had run off by themselves towards   40
the city, where the rest of the Trojans were fleeing in terror.
Adrestus was whirled out of the chariot next to the wheel,
head-first on to his face in the dust. Menelaus, Atreus' son,
stood over him, holding his far-shadowing spear,
and Adrestus grasped him by the knees, entreating him: 45
'Son of Atreus, take me alive, and accept a fitting ransom;
there is much treasure stored up in my rich father's house,
bronze and gold and elaborately worked iron, from which
my father would gladly give you a boundless ransom,
if he learnt that I was alive by the ships of the Achaeans.'   50
So he spoke, and would have persuaded the heart in Menelaus' breast;
he was about to hand him over to his attendant to escort
to the swift ships of the Achaeans, but Agamemnon
ran up and stood before him, and berated him loudly:
'My dear brother Menelaus, why so concerned for other men?   55
Can it be that you were so generously treated by Trojans
back in your own home?* Let not one of them escape sheer ruin
at our hands, not even the man-child which a mother
carries in her womb, not even him, but let them all
be obliterated from Troy, to vanish unremembered.'   60
So speaking the hero turned his brother's purpose,
urging destiny's decree; and Menelaus thrust the hero
Adrestus from him with his hand, and lord Agamemnon
stabbed him in the side. Adrestus fell back, and Atreus' son
set his heel on his chest and pulled out the ash spear.   65
Next Nestor called out to the Argives with a great shout:
'Friends, Danaan heroes, attendants of Ares,
let no one hang back here, greedy for spoils,
hoping to carry the biggest portion back to his ships!
Killing men is our task; afterwards you may take booty   70
when you will, stripping the bodies that lie about the plain.'
So he spoke, and quickened the fury and spirit in each man.
And then the Trojans, dear to Ares, would have been forced back
into Ilium by the Achaeans, overcome by feebleness of spirit,
had not a man stood next to Aeneas and Hector—Priam's son   75
Helenus, by far the best of bird-interpreters, who said to them:

'Aeneas and Hector! On you, above all Trojans and Lycians,
rests the labour of war, since you are the best at
both fighting and planning, whatever the enterprise.
Make a stand here, go up and down among the people and   80
rally them in front of the gates before they run away and fall
into their women's arms, and become a joy to our enemies.
Then, when you have stirred all the companies to action,
we shall make our stand here and fight with the Danaans,
even though we are very weary; for necessity bears hard on us.   85
But you, Hector, must go into the city, and speak there to
your mother and mine. Tell her to gather the matrons
at the temple of grey-eyed Athena on the city's heights,
and to unlock the doors of the sacred house, and tell her
to choose the robe which she judges to be the loveliest   90
and largest in her hall, and which is most precious to her,
and to lay it on the knees of Athena of the beautiful hair,
and to promise to sacrifice twelve heifers in her temple, yearlings
untouched by the goad, in the hope that Athena will pity
the city and the Trojans' wives and their infant children.   95
So she may keep the son of Tydeus away from sacred Ilium,
that savage spearman, ruthless deviser of panic rout,
the one I reckon to be the mightiest of the Achaeans.
Not even Achilles, leader of men, caused us so much terror,
and they say he is the son of a goddess. But this man's rage   100
goes too far, and no man can match him in fury.'

So he spoke, and Hector did not disobey his brother.
At once he leapt fully armed from his chariot to the ground,
and ranged through the whole army, shaking his two sharp spears,
stirring them to fight and rousing up the grim conflict.   105
They rallied and took their stand facing the Achaeans;
and the Argives gave ground and left off the slaughter,
thinking some immortal had come from the starry high sky
to give help to the Trojans, seeing how they had rallied.
Then Hector gave a great shout and called out to the Trojans: 110
'High-hearted Trojans, and you allies of far renown!
Be men, my friends, and call up your surging courage,
while I go back into Ilium to talk to the elders, who are
our counsellors, and tell our wives to pray to the gods
and to promise to make them an offering of hecatombs.'   115

So Hector of the glittering helmet spoke, and went on his way;

and the dark hide kept knocking at his ankles and neck,
the hide which ran as an outer rim around his bossed shield.

    Now Glaucus, Hippolochus' son, and the son of Tydeus
came together in the ground between the sides, in a rage to fight.   120
When they had advanced to within close range of each other
Diomedes, master of the war-cry, was the first to speak:
'Who among men doomed to die are you, my lord?
I have never seen you in the battle where men win glory
before; and yet now you have gone far beyond everyone else   125
in daring, since you stand up against my far-shadowing spear.
Unhappy are the parents whose sons oppose my fury!
But if you are some immortal, come down from the high sky,
I am not the kind of man to fight against sky-dwelling gods.
Not even the son of Dryas, mighty Lycurgus,* not even he   130
lived for long after quarrelling with the gods of the high sky:
long ago he pursued the nurses of frenzied Dionysus
throughout the sacred land of Nysa;* they all threw their
Bacchic staffs to the ground, wounded by the ox-goad
of man-slaying Lycurgus, and Dionysus fled, plunging below   135
the sea's waves, and Thetis took him, terrified, to her bosom,
for cruel trembling had seized him at the man's threats.
But then the gods who live at their ease were angry with Lycurgus,
and Cronus' son blinded him; and indeed he did not have long
to live, since he was hated by all the immortal gods.*   140
So I too am unwilling to fight against the blessed gods.
But if you are one of mortals who eat the fruit of the tilled earth,
come closer, so that you may sooner be caught in the snares of death.'

    Then the illustrious son of Hippolochus addressed him:
'Great-spirited son of Tydeus, why do you ask about my family?   145
As is the family of leaves, so it is also with men:
the wind scatters the leaves on the ground, but the forest breaks
into bud and makes more when the spring season comes round.
So with the family of men, one generation grows and another ceases.
But if you really want to know for certain, to find out exactly   150
about my family, it is one which many people know.
There is a city, Ephyre,* in a corner of horse-rearing Argos,
and here lived Sisyphus, who more than any man loved gain—
Sisyphus, son of Aeolus.* He fathered a son, Glaucus,
and Glaucus had a son, blameless Bellerophon,* to whom   155
the gods gave beauty and manhood fit to win lovers;

but Proetus* planned mischief for him in his heart, and
since he was much stronger drove him out of the land of
Argos—for Zeus had made him subject to Proetus' staff of power.
Proetus' wife, glorious Anteia, was mad with desire for him,   160
and longed to make secret love with him, but she could not sway
sagacious Bellerophon, because he was a right-thinking man.
Accordingly the queen spoke deceitfully to Proetus:
"Proetus, you must kill Bellerophon, or else be killed
yourself; he wanted to make love with me against my will."   165
So she spoke, and anger seized her lord at what he had heard,
but he held back from killing, for he felt awe at this in his heart;
instead he sent Bellerophon to Lycia, and gave him some deadly signs,
many life-destroying things, marked by him in a folded tablet,
and told him to show these to his father-in-law, so ensuring his death.   170
So Bellerophon set off for Lycia under the gods' blameless guidance;
but when he reached Lycia and the flowing Xanthus,
the king of broad Lycia treated him with honour and generosity:
for nine days he entertained him, and sacrificed nine oxen,
but when rosy-fingered Dawn appeared on the tenth day   175
he questioned Bellerophon, and asked to see the message
that he had brought for him from his son-in-law Proetus.
When he was given the deadly message from his son-in-law
he first of all ordered Bellerophon to kill the ferocious Chimera;
this was a being sprung from the gods, not from men,   180
a lion in front, a serpent behind, and in her middle a goat,
and she breathed out a terrible fury of blazing fire.
Bellerophon, guided by portents from the gods, killed her.
For his second task he fought with the far-famed Solymi,*
and this, he said, was the hardest battle with men he had endured.   185
Then for his third task he slew the Amazons,* who are a match for men.
But on his return the king wove another cunning plot against him:
after choosing the best fighters from broad Lycia
he set them in an ambush; but they did not return home,
because blameless Bellerophon slaughtered them to a man.   190
When the king realized that he was of noble, divine descent,
he kept him in Lycia, and offered him his own daughter,
and gave him half of all the honours of his kingship; and
the Lycians cut out for him an estate of their very best land,
fine country of vineyards and ploughland, for him to cultivate.   195
War-minded Bellerophon's wife bore him three children,

Isandrus and Hippolochus and Laodameia.
Zeus the counsellor lay with Laodameia, and she gave
birth to godlike Sarpedon, whose helmet is made of bronze.
But even Bellerophon came to be hated by all the gods,   200
and he wandered on his own over the Aleian plain,*
gnawing at his spirit and avoiding the trodden ways of men.
His son Isandrus was killed by Ares, insatiable in war,
while fighting against the far-famed Solymi, and Artemis
of the golden reins became angry with Laodameia and killed her.   205
Hippolochus was my father, and I declare myself his son;
he sent me to Troy, and would often give me instructions—
always to be the best and to stand out above other men, and
not to bring disgrace on my father's family, who were
by far the most distinguished in Ephyre and in broad Lycia.   210
This, then, is the family and bloodline which I boast is mine.'
    So he spoke, and Diomedes, master of the war-cry, was glad.
He planted his spear in the earth that nourishes many,
and addressed the shepherd of the people in affectionate words:
'You must then be a guest-friend of my family from ancient times!   215
Long ago glorious Oeneus* entertained blameless Bellerophon
in his halls and kept him there for twenty days, and
they gave each other fine gifts of guest-friendship:
Oeneus gave Bellerophon a belt, shining with purple dye,
and Bellerophon gave Oeneus a gold two-handled cup,   220
which I left behind in my palace when I came here.
Tydeus I do not remember, as I was still small when he
left me, at the time when the Achaean force perished at Thebes.
Therefore I am your dear guest-friend in the heart of Argos,
and you are mine in Lycia whenever I go to that land.   225
Let us then avoid each other's spears, even in the thick of battle;
there are many Trojans and their far-famed allies for me
to kill, whoever a god sends me and my legs can overtake, and
there are many Achaeans from whom you may slay those you can.
Let us exchange our armour, so that these men too may know   230
that we claim to be guest-friends from our grandfathers' time.'
    So they spoke together, and jumped down from their chariots,
and clasped each other's hands and made their friendship firm.
But then Zeus the son of Cronus took away Glaucus' wits,
since he exchanged armour with Diomedes, Tydeus' son,   235
gold in return for bronze, a hundred oxen's worth for nine.

Now when Hector had reached the Scaean gates and the oak tree,
the Trojans' wives and daughters ran up and surrounded him,
asking about their sons and brothers and relations
and husbands. But he told them all to pray to the gods,   240
each in turn; for misery was already in store for many of them.

When he arrived at Priam's splendid house, which was
constructed with polished stone porticoes—in it
there were fifty chambers made of polished stone,
built so as to be close to each other; and there the sons   245
of Priam used to sleep next to their wedded wives;
and opposite, for his daughters, opening off the courtyard,
there were twelve roofed chambers made of polished stone,
built so as to be close to each other, and there the sons-in-law
of Priam used to sleep next to their respected wives—   250
there his mother, the gently dowered lady, came to meet him,
bringing with her Laodice, the most beautiful of her daughters.
She gripped his hand tightly in hers, and addressed him, saying:
'My child, why ever have you left the daring battle, to come here?
The sons of the Achaeans—evil name!—must be pressing hard on   255
you as they wage war around the city; and your heart has sent you
to come here and hold your hands up to Zeus from the city's height.
Wait, I beg you, so that I can bring you honey-sweet wine,
for you to pour libations to father Zeus and the other immortals
first; and after that you may enjoy it, if you will drink.   260
When a man is weary, wine greatly increases his fury,
even as you are weary, fighting to defend your kinsmen.'

Then in answer to her Hector of the glittering helmet spoke:
'My revered mother, do not offer me mind-cheering wine,
for fear that you sap my limbs' fury, and I forget my courage.   265
And awe restrains me from pouring gleaming wine to Zeus
with unwashed hands; nor is it right to pray to Cronus' son
of the dark clouds when one is spattered with blood and gore.
No; you must go to the temple of Athena who gathers the spoils,
with offerings, once you have gathered the matrons together;   270
then choose the robe which you judge to be the loveliest
and largest in your hall, and which is most precious to you,
and place it on the knees of Athena of the beautiful hair,
and promise that you will sacrifice twelve heifers in her temple,
yearlings, untouched by the goad, if only she will pity   275
the city and the Trojans' wives and infant children.

So may she keep the son of Tydeus away from sacred Ilium,
that savage spearman, ruthless deviser of panic rout.
Go now to the temple of Athena who gathers the spoils,
and I shall go in search of Paris, to summon him,   280
to see if he is willing to listen to my words. How I wish
that the earth would gape beneath him! The Olympian raised him
to be a sore affliction to the Trojans and to great-hearted Priam
and his sons. If I could see him going down to Hades' house
I could say that my heart had forgotten its joyless grief.'   285
    So he spoke, and she went away into her house and summoned
her servants, and they went through the city to gather the matrons.
She herself went down into a sweet-smelling chamber
where her robes were stored: richly embroidered work of
Sidonian women whom Alexander himself, who looked like a god,   290
had brought from Sidon, when he sailed over the wide sea
on the voyage which brought well-born Helen to his home.
Lifting out one of these Hecuba took it as a gift for Athena,
the one that was the most intricately worked, and the largest,
and it shone like a star, and lay stored under all the rest.   295
Then she set off, and many matrons hurried after her.
    When they reached the temple of Athena on the city's heights
Theano of the beautiful cheeks opened the doors for them—
Theano, Cisseus' daughter, wife of Antenor, breaker of horses,
whom the Trojans had made the priestess of Athena.   300
Then they all with loud cries held up their hands to Athena,
and Theano of the beautiful cheeks took the robe
and laid it on the knees of Athena of the lovely hair,
and called out in prayer to the daughter of great Zeus:
'Lady Athena, city's defender, bright among goddesses,   305
shatter the spear of Diomedes, and grant that he may fall
face-down in front of the Scaean gates, and we will
straightaway sacrifice twelve heifers to you in your temple,
yearlings untouched by the goad, if only you will pity
the city and the Trojans' wives and their infant children.'   310
    So she spoke in prayer, but Pallas Athena lifted her head in denial.
Now while they were praying in this way to great Zeus' daughter,
Hector had set off for the splendid house of Alexander,
which Paris himself had built with the help of those
who then were the finest craftsmen in rich-soiled Troy;   315
they had made for him a chamber and a hall and a courtyard

next to the houses of Priam and Hector, on the city's heights.
There Hector, loved by Zeus, went in, and in his hand
was a spear eleven cubits long; the shaft's bronze point
gleamed before him, and round it ran a golden neck-ring.   320
He found Paris in his chamber, looking after his magnificent armour,
his shield and corslet, and turning his curved bow over in his hands.
Argive Helen was sitting there with her serving-women,
instructing her maidservants over their far-famed handiwork.
Seeing him Hector rebuked him with shaming words: 325
'You are possessed! It is not good to nurse this anger in your heart.
Our peoples are dying, fighting around the city and its steep walls,
and it is on your account that war and the battle-cry blaze
about this city; and you would be quick to quarrel with
anyone else you saw holding back in the face of hateful war.   330
So get to your feet, or the city will soon be destroyed by deadly fire.'
    Then in answer Alexander who looked like a god addressed him:
'Hector, you rebuke me rightly, and not beyond the proper limit,
so I shall answer likewise, and you must listen and mark my words.
It is not so much through anger or resentment at the Trojans   335
that I sit in my chamber, but wanting to give way to my misery.
But now my wife has persuaded me with beguiling words,
urging me to return to battle; and I too think that this would be
the better course, since victory shifts from one man to another.
But come, wait here a while, and let me put on Ares' armour—   340
or else go first, and I shall follow; I think I shall overtake you.'
    So he spoke; and Hector of the glittering helmet did not answer;
but Helen addressed him with honey-sweet words:
'Brother-in-law, I am a bitch and a cold-hearted mischief-maker;
I wish that on that first day when my mother bore me   345
an evil storm-wind had carried me away to some mountain
or into the surge of the loud-roaring sea, where the waves
would have swept me away, before these things could happen.
But since the gods have ordained that these dire things shall be,
then I wish that I was the wife of a better man, one who knew   350
the meaning of disgrace, and the outrage that men can feel.
As for this man, his wits are not firmly fixed, nor will they ever
be so; and I think he will receive his reward for that.
But come, enter, and sit down on this chair, brother-in-law,
since it is your mind that war's toil especially besets, because   355
of me, bitch that I am, and because of Alexander's delusion.

Zeus has given us a wretched portion, so that in time hereafter
we may become a theme for the songs of generations yet to come.'
   Then in answer great Hector of the glittering helmet said:
'Do not make me sit, Helen; loving as you are, you will not win me   360
over, for my heart is already urging me to go to the Trojans' help,
since they long for me while I stay away from them.
Your task is to rouse this man—and he should stir himself to action,
and so be able to catch me up while I am still in the city.
Now I will go to my own house, in order to see the people   365
of my house and my dear wife and my infant son,
since I do not know if I shall ever come back to them again,
or if the gods will soon beat me down under the Achaeans' hands.'
   So Hector of the glittering helmet spoke and departed,
and quickly came to his well-appointed house,   370
but he did not find white-armed Andromache in his halls;
she had left with their son and a finely robed woman servant,
and was standing on the tower, crying and lamenting.
When Hector could not find his blameless wife at home
he went and stood at the threshold and said to the serving-women: 375
'Come, serving-women, and tell me this truthfully:
where has white-armed Andromache gone from the hall?
To my sisters' houses, or those of my brothers' finely robed wives?
Or has she gone to Athena's temple, where all the other lovely-haired
Trojan women are seeking to appease the dread goddess?'   380
   Then in answer his trustworthy housekeeper addressed him:
'Hector, you order me to speak the truth; she has not gone
to your sisters' houses or those of your brothers' finely robed wives,
nor has she gone to Athena's temple, where all the other lovely-haired
Trojan women are seeking to appease the dread goddess, but   385
she has gone to the great tower of Ilium, because she has heard
that the Trojans are hard pressed, and the Achaeans are triumphant.
She went in a great hurry, making towards the wall,
like a frenzied woman; and a nurse has taken the child with her.'
   So the housekeeper spoke, and Hector hurried from the house,   390
back by the way he had come, along the well-built streets.
When he had passed through the great city, and had reached
the Scaean gates, from where he would go out on to the plain,
his richly dowered wife came rushing to meet him,
Andromache, the daughter of great-hearted Eëtion*—   395
Eëtion, who had lived under wooded Placus, in Thebe

under Placus,* and had ruled over the Cilician people;
and his daughter was married to bronze-helmeted Hector.
She came now to meet him, and the nurse came with her,
carrying at her breast the child of tender mind, only a baby, 400
Hector's cherished son, who resembled a beautiful star,
and whom he called Scamandrius, but all the rest called
Astyanax, because Hector on his own defended Ilium.*
When he saw the child Hector smiled without speaking,
but Andromache wept tears as she stood beside him, 405
and gripping his hand tightly in hers she spoke to him:
'Man possessed, your fury will destroy you! You have no pity
for your infant son or for me, ill-fated woman, I who will
soon be your widow; for soon the Achaeans will all set on you
and kill you. And when I lose you, it will be better for me 410
to sink down below the earth, because when you have gone
to meet your death there will be no comfort for me,
but only misery. I have no father or revered mother—
my father was killed by glorious Achilles when
he sacked the well-populated city of the Cilicians, Thebe 415
of the high gates; though he killed Eëtion, he did not strip him
of his armour, for he was held back by awe in his heart, but
cremated him with his finely worked armour and heaped up
a burial-mound over him. And the mountain nymphs,
daughters of Zeus the aegis-wearer, planted elm trees round it. 420
And as for the seven brothers who lived with me in my halls,
they all went down on the same day to the house of Hades;
swift-footed glorious Achilles slew them, every one,
as they tended their shambling oxen and white-fleeced sheep.
As for my mother, who was queen under wooded Placus, 425
he carried her off here with the rest of the plunder,
but then set her free in return for a boundless ransom, and
Artemis the arrow-shooter shot her down in her father's halls.
Hector, you are my father and my revered mother
and my brother, and you are my tender husband; 430
come, show me pity, and stay here on this tower, and
do not make your son an orphan and your wife a widow.
Station the people beside the fig tree, where the city
is most easily scaled and the wall is open to assault—
three times their best men have made an attempt there, 435
under the two called Ajax and far-famed Idomeneus,

and under the sons of Atreus and Tydeus' stalwart son;*
perhaps some man skilled in divine revelations has told them,
or it is their own hearts that instruct them, and urge them on.'
   Then in answer great Hector of the glittering helmet addressed
      her: 440
'Wife, all this concerns me too; but I would feel terrible shame
before the Trojans and the Trojan women with their trailing robes
if I were to hang back from the battle, like a coward.
Nor does my heart order me to do this, since I have learnt
always to be brave and to fight among the foremost Trojans,   445
winning great glory for my father and for myself.
For I know full well in my mind and in my heart
that the day will come when sacred Troy will be destroyed,
and Priam and the people of Priam of the fine ash spear.
Yet I am not as troubled by the Trojans' future pain,   450
or by what Hecuba herself will endure, or lord Priam,
or my brothers, the many and brave men who will
fall in the dust, overcome by our enemies, as much as
by your pain, when some bronze-shirted Achaean
leads you weeping away, robbing you of the day of freedom;   455
to be in Argos, weaving at the loom at another woman's command,
and carrying water from the spring Messeïs or Hypereia,*
much against your will; and a harsh necessity will lie upon you.
And some man when he sees you shedding a tear will say:
"That is the wife of Hector, who was always the greatest   460
of the horse-breaking Trojans, when they fought around Ilium."
That is what they will say; and it will be a fresh grief for you,
widowed of a man who might have saved you from the day of slavery.
May I be dead, and hidden under a mound of the heaped earth,
before I hear your cries as you are dragged captive away.'   465
   So speaking illustrious Hector stretched out his arms to his son;
but the boy shrank back crying into the bosom of his
finely girdled nurse, terrified at the sight of his dear father
and frightened by the bronze and the horsehair crest,
seeing how it nodded on top of his helmet, a terrifying thing.   470
His dear father and his revered mother laughed out loud,
and at once illustrious Hector took the helmet from his head
and laid it, gleaming brightly, on the ground.
He kissed his dear son and dandled him in his arms,
and spoke in prayer to Zeus and all the other gods: 475

'Zeus, and all you other gods, grant that this son of mine
may be marked out above the Trojans, as I am, and be
strong and brave as me, and may he rule Ilium by might;
and may men one day say as he returns from battle, "This man
is far better than his father." May he kill his enemy and   480
bring home bloody spoils, and may his mother's heart be glad.'

So he spoke, and laid his son in his dear wife's arms,
and she took him to her sweet-smelling bosom,
laughing through her tears. Seeing this, her husband pitied her,
and stroked her with his hand, and spoke to her, saying: 485
'Woman possessed! Do not grieve too much for me in your heart.
No man is going to dispatch me to Hades before my due time;
and as for that time, no man, I say, can ever escape it,
whether coward or brave, when once he has been born.
Go back to the house and take charge of your own tasks,   490
the loom and the distaff, and tell your women servants
to go about their work. War must be the concern of men,
of all those who were born in Ilium, and mine more than any.'

So speaking illustrious Hector picked up his helmet
with its horsehair crest, and his dear wife set off for home,   495
often turning round to look at him, and weeping huge tears.
Very soon she came to the well-appointed house of
man-slaying Hector, and inside it she found many
women servants, and roused up lamentation in them all.
So they wept for Hector in his house while he was still alive,   500
for they did not believe he would come back again from
the war, escaping the fury and hands of the Achaeans.

Nor had Paris delayed long in his lofty house, but when
he had put on his fine armour, intricately worked with bronze,
he hurried through the city, confident in his swift feet.   505
As when a horse that is kept at the manger and fed full with barley
breaks its tether and gallops exultantly, hoofs drumming,
over the plain, since its habit is to bathe in the waters
of a sweet-flowing river; it holds its head high, and its mane
flows about its shoulders, and confident in its splendour   510
its legs carry it easily to the haunts and pastures of horses;
so Paris, Priam's son, strode down from high Pergamus,
shining brightly in his armour like the beaming sun, and laughing
aloud as his swift feet carried him along. Very soon he
caught up with his brother, glorious Hector, as he was about   515

to turn away from the private conversation with his wife.
Then Alexander who looked like a god was the first to speak:
'Dear brother, surely I have detained you in your haste,
by dawdling and not coming at the right time, as you told me.'

Then in answer Hector of the glittering helmet addressed him: 520
'You are possessed! No one whose judgement is rightly ordered
could deny your battle-work its due, since you are a stalwart man;
but you hang back wilfully and refuse to fight, and at that
the heart in my breast is pained, when I hear shameful reports
about you from the Trojans, who endure great toil on your behalf.   525
Still, let us go on. Later we shall set all this right, if ever Zeus
allows us to set up the wine-bowl of freedom in our halls,
in honour of the gods of the high sky, who live for ever,
after we have driven the well-greaved Achaeans out of Troy.'

BOOK SEVEN

So illustrious Hector spoke, and rushed out of the gates,
and with him went his brother Alexander, both raging
in their hearts to join the battle and the fighting.
As when a god sends a breeze to eager sailors,
when they are weary from sweeping the sea with their oars   5
of polished pine, and exhaustion has loosened their limbs,
so these two appeared before the desperate Trojans.

Then they began the killing. Paris slew King Areïthous' son,
Menesthius who lived in Arne,* and he was the son of
Areïthous the club-wielder and ox-eyed Phylomedusa.   10
Hector struck Eïoneus in the neck with his sharp spear,
underneath his fine bronze helmet, and loosened his limbs.
Glaucus son of Hippolochus, captain of the Lycians,
hit Iphinous, Dexius' son, in the shoulder with his spear
in the crush of battle as he leapt up behind his swift mares,   15
and he fell from his chariot to the ground, his limbs slackened.

When the goddess grey-eyed Athena saw that these two
were cutting down the Argives in the crush of battle,
she set off and swept down from the heights of Olympus
to sacred Ilium. Apollo, looking down from Pergamus,   20
came to meet her, since he was plotting victory for the Trojans.
These two encountered each other by the oak tree,*
and lord Apollo, son of Zeus, addressed her first:
'Daughter of great Zeus, why have you come yet again
raging from Olympus, urged on by your great heart?   25
Is it to grant the battle's victory in turn to the Danaans,
because you have no pity for the Trojans as they die?
Come now, listen to me, and it will be much better for us:
let us now put an end to the fighting and the conflict,
for this day; and after this they will fight again, until they reach   30
their goal in Ilium, since it is the desire of you immortal
goddesses that this city should be utterly destroyed.'
Then in answer the goddess grey-eyed Athena addressed him:
'Let it be so, shooter from afar; indeed I too had this in mind
when I came from Olympus to join the Trojans and Achaeans.   35
So tell me, how do you mean to put an end to this war of men?'

Then in answer lord Apollo, son of Zeus, addressed her:
'Let us arouse savage fury in Hector, breaker of horses,
to challenge one of the Danaans to fight, man against man,
matching strength to strength in the grim conflict;   40
then perhaps the bronze-greaved Achaeans will be alarmed,
and will send someone out to fight alone against glorious Hector.'

So he spoke, and the goddess grey-eyed Athena did not disobey him.
Now Helenus, Priam's dear son, understood in his heart
the plan which the designing gods had decided upon;   45
he went and stood next to Hector, and spoke to him:
'Hector, son of Priam, the equal of Zeus in scheming,
I beg you to listen to me, since I am your brother:
make all the other Trojans and Achaeans sit down, but
yourself challenge whoever is the best of the Achaeans   50
to fight with you in grim conflict, matching strength to strength.
I do not think it is your destiny yet to die and meet death—
that is how I hear the voice of the gods who live for ever.'

So he spoke, and Hector was mightily glad when he heard his words,
and strode into the middle ground, grasping the middle of his spear,   55
and held back the Trojan companies; and they all settled down.
And Agamemnon made the well-greaved Achaeans sit down too,
and Athena and Apollo of the silver bow settled themselves too,
taking on the likeness of vultures, and perching on a tall
oak tree that was sacred to father Zeus who wears the aegis,   60
taking pleasure in the sight of the men, whose ranks sat
close-packed, bristling with shields and helmets and spears.
As when the West Wind suddenly springs up, and ripples
unfurl over the open sea, and the sea grows black beneath it,
so were the ranks of Achaeans and Trojans as they settled   65
on the plain. Then Hector spoke out to both sides:
'Listen to me, Trojans and well-greaved Achaeans,
and I will tell you what the spirit in my breast urges me.
Cronus' son who sits on high has left our oaths unfulfilled,
and has misery in mind for both of us in his plans,   70
until the day that you take Troy with its fine fortifications
or are yourselves beaten down beside your sea-traversing ships.
In your midst are the champions of all the Achaeans;
if the spirit of any one of them impels him to fight with me,
let him come before all as a champion against glorious Hector.   75
This I declare, and may Zeus be a witness for us:

if this man should take me down with the sharp-bladed bronze,
let him strip my armour and carry it off to his hollow ships;
but he should return my body to its home, so that in death
the Trojans and their wives may grant me the due rite of fire.   80
But if I overcome him, and Apollo grants me my prayer,
I shall strip his armour and take it back to sacred Ilium,
and hang it in the temple of Apollo who shoots from afar,
but him I shall return after death to his well-benched ships,
so that the flowing-haired Achaeans may bury him and   85
heap up a grave-mound for him beside the broad Hellespont.*
And one day a man may say, even one of generations to come,
as he sails past in his many-benched ship over the wine-faced sea:
"That is the burial-mound of a man who died long ago;
he fought as a champion once, and illustrious Hector killed him."   90
This is what someone will say; and my fame will never die.'
   So he spoke, and they all remained silent and still;
they were ashamed to refuse his challenge, yet afraid to accept it.
Finally Menelaus stood up and spoke out among them,
rebuking them bitterly, and groaning deeply in his heart: 95
'Oh, you are full of brave words—Achaean women, no longer men!
This will indeed bring contempt on us, beyond endurance,
if not a single Danaan man will go to meet Hector.
May you all turn into water and earth, each one of you,
sitting here bereft of spirit, utterly lacking desire for glory;   100
I myself will put on armour to fight this man; as for the snares
of victory, they are held above us by the immortal gods.'
   So he spoke, and put on his splendid armour.
Then, Menelaus, the end of your life would have come
at the hands of Hector, for he was by far the stronger man,   105
had not the kings of the Achaeans leapt up and seized you,
and if Atreus' son himself, wide-ruling Agamemnon, had not
gripped you by the right hand and spoken directly to you, saying:
'Zeus-nurtured Menelaus, you are out of your mind! There is
no need for this madness. Restrain yourself, troubled though you are,   110
and do not out of rivalry hope to fight a better man than you—
Hector, son of Priam, whom other men shrink to face.
Even Achilles shuddered to confront him on the battlefield
where men win glory, and he is a far better man than you.
No, go now and sit with the band of your companions, and   115
the Achaeans will put forward another champion against this man.

Hector may be without fear and unable to get his fill of fighting,
but I think that even he will gladly bend his knee in rest, if he
can escape from the fierce fighting and the grim conflict.'
   So speaking the hero turned his brother's thoughts aside,   120
urging what destiny had decreed, and Menelaus was persuaded.
His attendants then gladly took the armour from his shoulders;
but Nestor rose to his feet and spoke out among the Argives:
'This is not good! Great sorrow is coming to the land of Achaea!
Surely Peleus, the aged driver of horses, would groan aloud—   125
Peleus, that excellent counsellor and speaker of the Myrmidons,
who once took great delight in questioning me in his house,*
asking me about the ancestry and birth of all the Argives.
If he now heard that they were all cowering before Hector
he would raise his hands repeatedly to the immortal gods,   130
praying for his life to leave his body and go down to Hades' house.
Father Zeus and Athena and Apollo, if only I were as young
as I was when men fought beside the fast-flowing Celadon—
men of Pylos gathered together against spear-wielding Arcadians
by the walls of Pheia, along the waters of Iardanus.*   135
Among them Ereuthalion* stood up as a champion, a man like a god,
wearing on his shoulders the armour of lord Areïthous—
glorious Areïthous, to whom men and fine-girdled women
gave the name of Club-Wielder, because he used to fight
not with the bow and arrows nor with the long spear,   140
but would smash enemy companies down with an iron club.*
Lycurgus killed him by cunning, not by force, on a narrow
road, where his iron club could not save him from death;
before he could use it Lycurgus skewered him through the middle
with his spear, and he sprawled on his back on the ground.   145
He stripped Areïthous of the armour that brazen Ares had given him
and from this time forward always wore it in the grind of Ares' war;
but when Lycurgus was growing old in his halls
he gave it to his dear attendant Ereuthalion to wear, and
he was wearing it when he challenged all our best men.   150
They began to tremble, and were terrified, and no one dared stand;
but my much-enduring spirit released in me the courage
to enter the battle—and I was the youngest-born of them all.
So I fought with him, and Athena fulfilled my boast,
and he was the tallest and mightiest man that I ever killed,   155
and there he lay, his bulk spreadeagled this way and that.

If only I were as young again, with my strength unimpaired!
Then Hector of the glittering helmet would soon meet his match.
But not one of you, who are champions of all the Achaeans,
has the desire and passion to meet Hector face to face.'　　　　160
　So the old man provoked them, and nine men in all stood up.
Easily the first to rise was Agamemnon, lord of men,
and next after him rose mighty Diomedes, Tydeus' son,
and after them the pair called Ajax, clothed in impetuous courage,
and after them Idomeneus and Idomeneus' attendant　　　　165
Meriones, who was the equal of man-slaying Enyalius,*
and after them Eurypylus, the splendid son of Euaemon,
and then rose Thoas, Andraemon's son, and glorious Odysseus,
all of them eager to do battle with glorious Hector.
Then among them Nestor, the Gerenian horseman, spoke again:　170
'Now shake lots thoroughly, to see who will be chosen;
that man will surely gladden the well-greaved Achaeans,
and will himself be gladdened in his heart, if only he can
escape from the fierce fighting and the grim conflict.'
　So he spoke, and they marked their lots, each man his own,　175
and threw them into the helmet of Atreus' son Agamemnon.
And the people prayed, holding their hands up to the gods,
and this is what they would say, each looking up to the wide high sky:
'Father Zeus, let it be the lot of Ajax, or that of Tydeus' son,
or even that of the king himself of Mycenae, rich in gold.'　180
　So they spoke; Nestor, the Gerenian horseman, shook the helmet,
and out leapt the lot that they had indeed wished for,
that of Ajax. A herald carried it round the whole group
from left to right, showing it to all the Achaean champions,
and each man disclaimed it when he did not see his own mark.　185
But when, carrying it round the whole group, he came to the man
who had marked and thrown it into the helmet, illustrious Ajax
held out his hand, and the herald stood by him and handed it to him,
and Ajax saw and recognized his mark, and was glad in his heart;
he threw the lot on to the ground at his feet, and spoke:　190
'My friends, this is indeed my lot! And I am glad
in my heart, because I think I shall defeat glorious Hector.
So come; while I am putting on my armour for the battle,
you must pray to the lord Zeus, son of Cronus, silently
to yourselves, so that the Trojans do not overhear you—　195
or no, pray out loud, since we have no fear of any man;

no one can pit his will against mine and force me back
by force or by craft, since I do not think I was born
and bred on Salamis to be so utterly lacking in skill.'

So he spoke, and they prayed to lord Zeus, son of Cronus,   200
and this is what they would say, each looking up to the wide high sky:
'Father Zeus, you who rule from Ida,* mightiest and most glorious,
grant that Ajax may be victorious and win bright glory;
but if Hector also is dear to you, and you care for him,
give both men equal strength, and make their glory equal.'   205

So they spoke, and Ajax began to arm himself in flashing bronze.
When he had put all his armour about his body he then
strode out, looking like monstrous Ares advancing
when he goes to war and looks for men whom Cronus' son
has brought together to fight in the fury of life-devouring strife.   210
Just so Ajax, bulwark of the Achaeans, rose up towering,
with a smile on his terrible face, his legs beneath him
making great strides while he shook his far-shadowing spear.
The Argives were glad when they saw him, but
a dreadful trembling stole over the limbs of every Trojan,   215
and even Hector's heart began to knock against his chest;
but he could not retreat or turn back into the mass of people,
since it was through his own battle-lust that he had challenged Ajax.
Ajax drew close to him, carrying his tower-like shield, bronze
with seven oxhide layers, made for him by the craftsman Tychius,   220
by far the best of leather-workers, whose home was in Hyle;*
he had made the flashing seven-oxhide shield for Ajax from
well-nourished bulls, and had laid on top an eighth layer of bronze.
Holding this in front of his chest, Ajax son of Telamon
stood very close to Hector, and threateningly addressed him: 225
'Now, Hector, you will find out for certain, one against one,
what kind of champions the Danaans also have among them,
even apart from Achilles the lion-hearted breaker of ranks.
He is now lying by his curved sea-traversing ships,
deeply angry against Agamemnon, shepherd of the people;   230
but we have the kind of men who can stand up against you,
and there are many of us; so begin the battle and the fighting.'

Then in answer great Hector of the glittering helmet spoke:
'Ajax son of Telamon, sprung from Zeus, ruler of the people;
do not put me to the test as if I were some feeble child,   235
or a woman who knows nothing of war's business.

No, I know well enough about battles and the killing of men;
I know how to handle my toughened shield to the right
and the left—which for me is what real shield-work means.
I know how to storm into the battle of swift chariots, and   240
I know in close combat how to step to deadly Ares' dance.
Prepare! I have no wish to look for a chance to catch a man like you
unawares with my cast; I will throw openly, to see if I can hit you.'

  So he spoke, and poised his long-shadowing spear and threw it,
and hit the terrible seven-oxhide shield of Ajax on its   245
outer covering of bronze, which was the eighth layer upon it.
The relentless bronze tore its way through six folds,
but was stopped by the seventh hide. Then in his turn
Ajax, sprung from Zeus, let fly his far-shadowing spear
and hit the perfectly balanced shield of Priam's son.   250
The massive spear passed through the shining shield,
and forced its way through his intricately worked corslet;
it cut clean through Hector's tunic, next to his ribs,
but he leaned to one side and avoided death's black spectre.
Then both together grasped their spears and pulled them out   255
and fell upon each other like flesh-devouring lions,
or like wild boars whose strength is far from feeble.
Priam's son jabbed his spear at the middle of Ajax's shield,
but the bronze did not break through, and its tip was bent back.
Ajax sprang at Hector and pierced his shield; straight through   260
went the spear, and smashed back his raging advance;
driving on, it cut his neck, and the black blood spurted out.
Even so Hector of the glittering helmet did not stop fighting,
but fell back, and in his brawny hand picked up a rock
which was lying on the plain, black, jagged, and huge.   265
Hurling this he hit Ajax's terrible shield of seven hides
on its centre, on the boss, and the bronze rang out all around;
but Ajax in his turn picked up a much bigger stone and
whirling round flung it, forcing enormous strength into it,
and the millstone-like rock smashed the shield inwards,   270
and Hector's knees crumpled, and he fell on to his back, splayed
out, crushed under his shield; but Apollo soon set him upright.
Then they surely would have hewed at each other with swords
at close quarters, had not the heralds, messengers of Zeus and men,
come forward, one a Trojan and the other a bronze-shirted Achaean,   275
Talthybius and Idaeus, both men of good judgement,

and held up their staffs in the middle ground between both;
and Idaeus the herald, a man skilled in wise counsel, spoke out:
'Dear sons, put an end to this battle and do not fight any more;
Zeus who gathers the clouds holds you both dear,   280
and you are both excellent spearmen; this we all know.
But now night is upon us, and it is good to give way to night.'
    Then in answer Ajax, son of Telamon, addressed him:
'Idaeus, you two must tell Hector to say these words; it was
through his own battle-lust that he challenged all our champions.   285
Let him be the first to stop, and I will certainly follow his lead.'
    Then in answer to him huge Hector of the glittering helmet said:
'Ajax, some god has given you stature and might and sound
judgement, and you are by far the best Achaean spear-fighter;
so let us now put an end to fighting and conflict,   290
for today. After this we shall fight again, until some deity
decides between us, and gives the victory to one or the other.
But now night is upon us, and it is good to give way to night,
and then you will bring joy to all the Achaeans beside their ships,
and especially whatever kinsmen and companions you have.   295
I for my part shall go through the great city of lord Priam, and
gladden the Trojans and the Trojan women with their trailing robes,
who are about to go into the sacred assembly to pray on my account.
But come, let us give each other gifts that bring glory with them,
so that men from among Achaeans and Trojans may say: 300
"Truly these two fought each other in heart-devouring strife,
but then they parted and were joined in friendship." '
    So speaking he fetched a silver-riveted sword and gave it
to Ajax, together with its scabbard and skilfully cut belt,
while Ajax gave him a sword-belt, bright with purple dye.   305
So they parted; one went back to the Achaean host
and the other left for the gathering of Trojans; and these
were glad when they saw him coming, alive and unharmed,
having escaped the fury and irresistible hands of Ajax;
they escorted him to the city, scarcely believing he was safe.   310
And on the other side the well-greaved Achaeans escorted
Ajax, exulting in his victory, to glorious Agamemnon.
    When they reached the huts of lord Agamemnon,
the son of Atreus sacrificed an ox on their behalf,
a male beast, five years old, to the all-powerful son of Cronus.   315
This they flayed and prepared, and divided into joints,

and chopped the meat skilfully and threaded it on to skewers,
and cooked it with great care and then drew it all off.
When they had finished their work and made the meal ready
they feasted, and no one's heart lacked a fair share in the meal;   320
and the hero son of Atreus, wide-ruling Agamemnon,
honoured Ajax with the whole length of the chine.
When they had put from themselves the desire for food and drink,
then first of all the old man began to weave a scheme—
Nestor, whose counsel even before this had proved to be the best.   325
With generous intent he spoke and addressed them:
'Son of Atreus, and you other champions of all the Achaeans!
Seeing that many flowing-haired Achaeans have been killed,
and violent Ares has now spilled their dark blood along Scamander's
clear waters, and their shades have gone down to Hades,   330
at dawn you must hold the Achaeans back from fighting.
Let us assemble then and bring the dead men back here on wagons
hauled by oxen and mules. After that let us burn them
a little way from the ships, so that each may take a man's bones
home to his children, when we return to our native land.*   335
Let us then pile up one single grave-mound around the pyre,
throwing it up in a heap from the ground, and up against it let us
quickly build a high-towered wall,* to protect both ships and men.
In this wall let us construct some well-fitting gates,
so that there shall be a way through them to drive chariots;   340
and close to it on the outside let us dig a deep ditch,
which with its circuit may protect chariots and men, in case
we should one day be pressed hard by the proud Trojans' onslaught.'
  So he spoke, and all the kings gave their approval.
The Trojans also held an assembly on Ilium's city heights,   345
next to Priam's gates;* they were full of fear and confusion,
and among them sagacious Antenor was the first to speak:
'Listen to me, Trojans and Dardanians* and allies,
and I shall tell you what the heart in my breast urges.
Come now—let us give Argive Helen and her possessions with her   350
back to Atreus' sons to carry away. We are fighting now because
we have broken our solemn oaths; I do not therefore suppose
that any advantage will come to us, unless we do as I say.'
  So speaking he sat down again; and among them there
stood up glorious Alexander, husband of Helen of the lovely hair,   355
who answered and addressed winged words to him:

'Antenor, what you now advise does not please me; you know
that you could have thought of some better speech than this.
But if you really are in earnest when you say this openly,
then surely the gods themselves must have destroyed your wits.   360
So I shall speak out among the Trojans, breakers of horses:
I declare outright that I will not give the woman back, though
as for the possessions that I brought from Argos to my house, I am
willing to give them all back, and to add more from my own store.'

  So speaking he sat down again; and among them there stood up   365
Priam of Dardanus' line, the equal of the gods in counsel,
who with generous intent spoke and addressed them:
'Listen to me, Trojans and Dardanians and allies,
and I shall tell you what the heart in my breast urges.
Prepare and eat your supper now throughout the city, as always,   370
and be sure to set sentries, and let each man be vigilant.
And when dawn comes, let Idaeus go to the hollow ships
and report to Atreus' sons, Agamemnon and Menelaus,
the words of Alexander, on whose account this quarrel has arisen.
And let him add this shrewd proposal: ask if they are willing   375
to hold back from war's hideous clamour until we burn
our dead. After this we will fight again, until some deity
decides between us, and gives the victory to one side or the other.'

  So he spoke, and they listened carefully and did as he said.
Then they ate their supper in ranks throughout the army,   380
and when dawn came Idaeus made his way to the hollow ships;
there he found the Danaans, attendants of Ares, at assembly,
beside the stern of Agamemnon's ship. Taking his stand
in their midst the loud-voiced herald addressed them:
'Sons of Atreus and you other princes of all the Achaeans,   385
Priam and the other splendid Trojans instruct me to report to you—
in the hope that it may be acceptable and pleasing to you—
the words of Alexander, on whose account this quarrel has arisen:
as for the possessions which Alexander brought to Troy in his
hollow ships—if only he had died before he did—all these   390
he is willing to give back, and to add more from his own store;
but as for the wedded wife of glorious Menelaus, he says
he will not give her up, though the Trojans strongly urge him to.
Furthermore they told me to invite you, if you are willing, to
hold back from war's hideous clamour until we have burnt   395
our dead; and after that we shall fight again until some deity

decides between us, and gives the victory to one side or the other.'
  So he spoke, and they all remained silent and still;
but at last Diomedes, master of the war-cry, spoke among them:
'Let no man now accept the possessions of Alexander,   400
nor Helen; even a very foolish man can see that the snares
of death are already fastened tight around the Trojans.'
So he spoke, and all the sons of the Achaeans shouted their
approval, amazed at the words of Diomedes, breaker of horses.
Then lord Agamemnon addressed Idaeus: 405
'Idaeus, you have yourself heard the Achaeans' words,
how they answer you; and I too am pleased with what they say.
But as for burning your dead, I do not at all begrudge it you;
when there are dead men there can be no reason to hold back
from appeasing them swiftly with fire, now that they have died. 410
May Zeus, Hera's loud-thundering husband, witness these oaths.'
  So speaking he held his staff up in the sight of all the gods,
and Idaeus went back towards sacred Ilium.
Now the Trojans and Dardanians were sitting in assembly,
all gathered together, waiting for when Idaeus should come.   415
And he came, and standing in their midst reported
his message. Then with great haste they busied themselves
with two tasks, some to collect the dead and others to look for wood.
And on their side the Argives hurried from their well-benched ships,
some to collect the dead and others to look for wood.   420
  The sun was rising through the high sky from the deep
waters of peacefully flowing Ocean, its light beginning
to strike the tilled land, when the two sides met. It was
a hard matter to distinguish one dead man from another,
but when they had washed the bloody gore from them with water, 425
weeping warm tears, they lifted them on to wagons.
Great Priam forbade them to cry out,* and so they piled
their dead on to a pyre in silence, grieving in their hearts;
then after burning them in the fire they returned to sacred Ilium.
In the same way, the well-greaved Achaeans on their side   430
piled their dead on to a pyre, grieving in their hearts; and
after burning them in the fire they set off for the hollow ships.
  When it was not yet dawn, but still the night that is half-light,
a troop of Achaeans, specially chosen, gathered around the pyre
and piled up a single grave-mound around it, throwing it up   435
in a heap from the ground, and up against it they built

a wall with high towers, to protect both ships and men.
In this wall they constructed well-fitting gates, so that
there should be a way through them to drive chariots,
and close to it on the outside they dug a deep ditch,   440
great and wide, and inside it they planted stakes.

    The flowing-haired Achaeans were busying themselves with this
and the gods, sitting with Zeus the lightning-sender in their midst,
marvelled at the great work of the bronze-shirted Achaeans.
Among them Poseidon the earthshaker was the first to speak: 445
'Father Zeus, is there any mortal left on the boundless earth
who will tell the immortals of his thoughts and purposes?
Can you not see? Here are the flowing-haired Achaeans again—
they have built a wall in front of their ships, and have driven a ditch
around it, but they have not offered splendid hecatombs to the gods.   450
Doubtless its fame will extend as far as the dawn spreads its light,
and then men will forget the wall which Phoebus Apollo and I
once laboured hard together to build for the hero Laomedon.'*

    Then, deeply angered, Zeus who gathers the clouds addressed him:
'Come, come, earthshaker of wide power—what a thing to say!   455
Some other god might well shudder at this invention, one who
was far inferior to you in his hand's strength and his fury,
but your fame will surely extend as far as the dawn spreads its light.
Consider now; when the flowing-haired Achaeans have after this
gone away with their ships to their dear native land,   460
you may tear this wall down and scatter it all over the salt sea;
you may cover the great seashore once again with sand, and so,
you may be sure, the Achaeans' great wall will be blotted out.'

    So they spoke, one to another, in this way. And the sun
went down, and the Achaeans' work was finished, and   465
they slaughtered oxen, hut by hut, and ate their supper.
Some ships had arrived from Lemnos, carrying wine,
many of them, sent by Euneus who was the son of Jason,
he whom Hypsipyle had borne to Jason,* shepherd of the people;
and as a special gift to Atreus' sons Agamemnon and Menelaus   470
Jason's son gave them a cargo of sweet wine, a thousand measures.
From these ships the flowing-haired Achaeans bought their wine,
some in exchange for bronze, some in exchange for flashing iron,
some in exchange for hides, some in exchange for living cattle,
and some in exchange for slaves; and they prepared a splendid feast.   475
Then all night long the flowing-haired Achaeans feasted,

and in the city the Trojans and their allies did the same; but
all night long Zeus the counsellor planned misery for the Achaeans,
and kept up a terrifying thunder. Pale fear began to grip them,
and they spilled the wine from their cups on to the ground, and
no one   480
dared drink until he had made a libation to Cronus' all-powerful son.
Then they lay down to rest, and received the gift of sleep.

BOOK EIGHT

Now saffron-robed Dawn was spreading over the whole earth,
and Zeus who delights in thunder called an assembly of gods
on the topmost peak of many-ridged Olympus.
He himself addressed them, and the gods all listened with care:
'Hear me, all you gods and goddesses, and I shall   5
tell you what the heart in my breast commands me;
and let no one, whether female divinity or male, try to
frustrate my plan; you must all approve it here
so that I may quickly bring these matters to an end.
If I see anyone turning his back on the other gods and   10
wanting to go and help the Trojans or to the Danaans,
he will be struck down and have a painful return to Olympus;
or else I shall seize and hurl him into murky Tartarus,
far, far away, where there is the deepest pit under the earth,
and there are gates of iron and a threshold of bronze,   15
as far below Hades as the high sky is above the earth.*
Then he will learn how far I am the strongest of all the gods.
So come now, gods, and test me, so that you all may find out:
let down a rope of gold from the high sky,* and
all of you, gods and goddesses, take hold of it; even so,   20
however hard you toil at it, you will not be able to drag me,
Zeus the supreme counsellor, from the high sky down to earth.
But if ever I were to turn my mind to hauling on the rope,
I could pull you up, and the earth and the sea with you;
and then I would fasten the rope around a crag of Olympus,   25
and everything would then be left hanging, high in the air.
That is how much stronger I am than both gods and men.'

So he spoke, and they all remained silent and still,
amazed at his words, for he had spoken with great force.
At last the goddess grey-eyed Athena spoke among them: 30
'Our father, son of Cronus, supreme among rulers,
we do know well that your strength is irresistible;
but for all that we feel pity towards the Danaan spearmen,
who will surely bring their lives to a miserable end, and perish.
Still, we shall hold back from the warfare, as you command,   35
and will offer to the Argives such counsel as will benefit them,

so that they do not all perish as a result of your anger.'

Then Zeus who gathers the clouds smiled at her and said:
'Be comforted, my dear child, Tritogeneia; I did not speak
with serious intent; and towards you I am minded to be gentle.'   40

So he spoke, and harnessed under the yoke his two horses,
brazen-footed swift flyers who had flowing manes of gold,
and himself put on clothes of gold, and took up his whip,
golden and skilfully made, and mounted his chariot.
Then he whipped the horses into motion, and they eagerly   45
flew on between the earth and the starry high sky.
He came to Ida with its many springs, mother of wild beasts,
to Gargarus, where he has a precinct and a smoking altar.
There the father of gods and men reined in his horses and
untied them from the chariot, and poured a thick mist about them.   50
He himself sat down on the mountain peaks, exulting in his glory,
watching the city of the Trojans and the ships of the Achaeans.

Now the long-haired Achaeans took their meal in haste,
each in his own hut, and at once began to arm themselves, and
on their side, in the city, the Trojans too were arming themselves—   55
fewer in number, but still raging to join the battle's mêlée, through
hard necessity, since they were fighting for their wives and children.
All the gates were opened, and the people streamed out,
soldiers on foot and in chariots; and a huge clamour went up.

When the ranks had met in one place and come to grips,   60
then there was a clash of leather shields and spears and
the fury of bronze-armoured warriors. Bossed shields
smashed against each other, and a tremendous clamour arose,
made up of the groans of dying men and the exultant
cries of their killers; and the earth ran with blood.   65

Now as long as it was still morning and the sacred day was growing,
both sides' missiles struck home, and the people kept falling;
but when the sun stood astride the midpoint of the high sky,
then indeed father Zeus held up his golden scales,* and in them
he put two spectres of death, the bringer of long misery, one for   70
the horse-breaking Trojans and one for the bronze-shirted Achaeans.
Taking the bar by the centre he lifted it up, and the Achaeans'
destined day sank down; their spectres settled on the earth that
nourishes many, while the Trojans' leapt up to the broad high sky.
Zeus himself thundered loudly from Ida, and let fly   75
a blazing flash into the Achaean host; and when they saw it

they were stunned, and pale fear took hold of them all.
     Then neither Idomeneus nor Agamemnon had the will
          to stand firm,
nor did the two called Ajax, attendants of Ares, stand firm.
Only Gerenian Nestor, protector of the Achaeans, stood his ground—   80
not that he willed it, but his horse was exhausted, hit by an arrow
from glorious Alexander, the husband of lovely-haired Helen;
it was hit on the top of its head, where a horse's mane starts
to grow upon its skull, and it is a most vulnerable point.
The arrow sank into its brain, and it reared up at the pain,   85
and reeling from the bronze it stampeded the other horses.
While the old man was trying to cut the horse's trace-reins,
slashing at them with his sword, Hector's swift horses
came up through the mêlée, carrying their daring charioteer
Hector; and then the old man would have lost his life,   90
had not Diomedes, master of the war-cry, been quick to notice.
He gave a terrible cry, and urged Odysseus to help him:
'Son of Laertes, sprung from Zeus, Odysseus of many schemes,
where are you running, turning back into the crowd like a coward?
Take care! Someone may plant a spear in your back as you flee;   95
stand firm, and let us drive this cruel warrior away from the old man.'
     So he spoke, but much-enduring glorious Odysseus did not
hear him, and ran past to the hollow ships of the Achaeans.
Tydeus' son, though on his own, plunged into the front-fighters
and took his stand in front of the chariot of the old man,   100
Neleus' son, and addressed him, speaking with winged words:
'Old man, it seems that the young fighters are wearing you down;
your power has gone to nothing, painful old age presses hard on you,
your attendant is exhausted, and your horses are slowing down.
Come now, get up on to my chariot, and you will see   105
what the horses of Tros can do in pursuit and retreat,
galloping this way and that across the plain, these
inspirers of panic rout, that I captured from Aeneas.*
Let our two attendants see to your horses, and let us steer mine
straight at the horse-breaking Trojans, so that Hector   110
may know whether the spear in my hands too is full of rage.'
     So he spoke, and Nestor the Gerenian horseman did not disobey him.
Then the two powerful attendants, Sthenelus and
courteous Eurymedon, saw to Nestor's horses, and
the two others got up into the chariot of Diomedes.   115

Then Nestor took the shining reins into his hands, and
lashed the horses, and they quickly drew close to Hector,
who charged straight at them, raging; Tydeus' son threw his spear,
but missed Hector, and hit his attendant and charioteer,
who was Eniopeus, the son of arrogant Thebaeus,   120
on his chest next to the nipple, as he held the horses' reins.
He toppled from the chariot, and his swift-footed horses
started back; and there his life and fury were loosened.
Bitter grief for his charioteer crowded thick into Hector's heart,
but he left him, distressed though he was for his companion,   125
to lie there, and went in search of another bold charioteer; and
not for long did his horses lack a master, since he quickly found
daring Archeptolemus, Iphitus' son, and made him mount
behind his swift-footed horses, and gave the reins into his hands.

Then dreadful deeds, impossible to bear, would have been done,   130
and they would have been penned inside Troy like lambs,
had not the father of gods and men been quick to notice.
He thundered terribly, and launched a shining bolt, and
made it fall to the ground in front of Diomedes' horses;
a terrifying flame of burning sulphur shot up from it,   135
and the horses took fright and cowered under the chariot;
the shining reins slipped from Nestor's hands, and
he was afraid in his heart and spoke to Diomedes:
'Quick, Tydeus' son, turn your single-hoofed horses back in flight;
can you not see that there is no courage to be had from Zeus?   140
Now Zeus, the son of Cronus, is granting glory to Hector—
for today, though tomorrow it will be our turn, if he so wishes.
There is no man, however powerful, who can thrust aside
the will of Zeus, since Zeus is much stronger than we are.'

Then Diomedes, master of the war-cry, answered him: 145
'Old man, all that you have said is according to due measure;
but this is a bitter grief that comes over my heart and spirit,
because one day Hector will speak among the Trojans and say,
"Tydeus' son ran before me and went back to his ships."
So one day he will taunt me; then may the wide earth gape
    before me.'   150

Then Nestor, the Gerenian horseman, answered him and said:
'Ah, son of war-minded Tydeus, what a thing to say!
Even if Hector calls you a coward and a weakling,
the Trojans and Dardanians will not believe him, nor

the wives of the great-spirited Trojan shield-bearers,   155
when you have hurled their tender bedfellows into the dust.'
   So he spoke, and wheeled the single-hoofed horses round in flight,
back through the mêlée, and the Trojans and Hector gave an
astonishing shout and showered them with whirring missiles.
Great Hector of the glittering helmet shouted loudly after Diomedes: 160
'Son of Tydeus, the swift-horsed Danaans used to honour you
above others, with the best place, the best meat and full cups of wine,
but now they will despise you; you have turned out to be a woman.
Well, away with you, feeble doll! It will not be because of
my yielding that you will climb our walls, or carry off our women 165
in your ships; before that happens I shall give you your destiny.'
   So he spoke, and Tydeus' son's mind was divided, whether
to wheel his horses round and fight, matching strength to strength.
Three times he pondered in his mind and in his heart, and
three times Zeus the counsellor thundered from Mount Ida,   170
sending the Trojans a sign that the battle was veering to one side.
Then Hector gave a loud shout and called out to the Trojans:
'Trojans and Lycians and Dardanian hand-to-hand fighters,
be men, my friends, and call up your surging courage!
I see that the son of Cronus favours us, and promises victory   175
and great glory to me, but affliction for the Danaans—
those fools, who have devised the fortifications you can see,
feeble and futile as they are. They will not hold back my fury;
horses can easily jump across the ditch that they have dug.
As soon as I find myself among their hollow ships,   180
then let men turn their thoughts to destructive fire, so that
I can set their ships ablaze with flames, and kill the Argives
next to their ships, panic-stricken amidst the smoke.'
   So he spoke, and summoned his horses, and said to them:
'Xanthus and you, Podargus, Aethon and bright Lampus,   185
now is the time when you must repay me for the lavish care
that Andromache, daughter of great-hearted Eëtion,
gave you, serving you mind-cheering wheat, and mixing it
with wine, to drink when the spirit urged you, before she
served me, I who am proud to be her tender husband.   190
So come, press on as fast as you can, and we shall seize
the shield of Nestor, whose fame reaches the high sky—
they say it is all made of gold, both itself and its cross-struts—
and strip from the shoulders of horse-breaking Diomedes

his finely worked corslet, which Hephaestus laboured to make. 195
If we can capture these two things, I could hope that
the Achaeans will this very night embark on their swift ships.'

So he spoke, boastfully, and lady Hera was angry with him,
and stirred on her throne, and caused high Olympus to shake.
She spoke to the huge god Poseidon, face to face: 200
'Do you see this, earthshaker of far-reaching power?
Not even the heart in your breast has pity for the Danaans
as they die—yet they bring you many pleasing offerings to Helice
and Aegae,* and you have always desired them to be victorious.
Suppose that we who side with the Danaans were minded 205
to beat the Trojans back, and so frustrate wide-thundering Zeus,
he would surely feel distressed, sitting there alone on Ida.'

At this the lord earthshaker was deeply angered and answered her:
'Hera, your words are reckless; what a thing to say!
I certainly would not wish the rest of us to fight against Zeus 210
the son of Cronus, since he is very much stronger than we are.'

So they spoke, one to another, in this way. Meanwhile
the space beyond the ships that was bounded by wall and ditch
was filled with both horses and shield-bearing men, close
packed together; it was Hector, Priam's son, equal of swift Ares, 215
who penned them in, since Zeus had given him the glory.
And he would have burnt the well-balanced ships with blazing fire,
had not the lady Hera put it into Agamemnon's mind to take it
on himself to set about urging the Achaeans to swift action.
He made his way along the huts and ships of the Achaeans 220
holding his great purple cloak in his brawny hand,
and stopped by the deep-bellied black ship of Odysseus,
which was in the middle, so that a shout could carry both ways,
both towards the huts of Ajax, Telamon's son, and towards Achilles';
for these had dragged up their well-balanced ships at the furthest
        points, 225
trusting in their courage and in the strength of their hands.

Agamemnon called out to the Danaans in a far-carrying shout:
'Shame, Argives, you things of disgrace, admired only for your
handsome looks! We claim to be the best men—but where are our
boasts now, those empty, loud boasts that you made on Lemnos* 230
as you ate your fill of the meat of straight-horned oxen
and drank from bowls that brimmed with wine? You claimed
that each man could stand up to one- or two-hundred Trojans

in battle; yet now we are not even good enough to face one man,
Hector, who will soon burn our ships with destructive fire.   235
Father Zeus, did you ever ruin a powerful king like this before,
driving delusion into him and robbing him of great glory?
And yet I say that I never passed by any splendid altar of yours
on my unlucky voyage here in my many-benched ship
without burning on all of them the fat and thigh-bones of oxen,   240
impatient as I was to sack the strongly walled city of Troy.
So, Zeus, I beg you, fulfil this plea at least for me:
grant that we may get away safely and escape, and do not allow
the Achaeans to be beaten down like this by the Trojans.'

   So he spoke, and the father pitied him as he wept tears, and   245
nodded his assent that his people should survive and not perish.
Straightaway he sent an eagle, the best omen among winged things,
holding in its claws a fawn, the offspring of a swift hind;
it dropped the fawn beside the splendid altar of Zeus, where
the Achaeans used to sacrifice to Zeus, source of all omens.   250
And when they saw that the bird had come from Zeus, they sprang
more vigorously at the Trojans, and called up their battle-lust.

   Then no man of the Danaans, numerous though they were,
could boast that he drove his swift horses in front of Tydeus' son,
urging them across the ditch, matching his strength in the close
          fight.   255
Diomedes was easily the first to kill a Trojan chieftain,
Agelaus, son of Phradmon; he had wheeled his horses in flight,
and as he turned Diomedes skewered him in the back with his spear,
right between the shoulders, and drove it through his chest.
Agelaus fell from his chariot, and his armour clattered about him.   260

   After him came the sons of Atreus, Agamemnon and Menelaus,
and behind them the two called Ajax, clothed in impetuous courage,
and after him Idomeneus, accompanied by his attendant
Meriones, the equal of Enyalius, slayer of men,
and after them came Eurypylus, Euaemon's splendid son.   265
The ninth to come was Teucer, tensing his curved bow,
and he took his stand behind the shield of Ajax, Telamon's son.
Ajax would lift the shield a little way, and then Teucer
would peer out and let fly an arrow, shooting someone down
in the mêlée; and the man would fall there and give up his life,   270
and Teucer would turn and shelter with Ajax, like a child running
to its mother, and Ajax would cover him with his shining shield.

Which man of the Trojans did blameless Teucer first kill?
The first were Orsilochus and Ormenus and Ophelistes,
Daetor and Chromius and godlike Lycophontes,   275
and Amopaon the son of Polyaemon, and Melanippus;
all of these he laid in quick succession on the all-nourishing earth.
Agamemnon, lord of men, was glad to see him slaying
whole companies of the Trojans with his powerful bow,
and he came and stood beside him and addressed him: 280
'Teucer, dear man, son of Telamon, captain of the people,
shoot on like this, and perhaps you will prove to be the Danaans'
salvation, and Telamon's, who nurtured you as a child
and cared for you in his house, though you were his bastard;
now bring him closer to glory, even though he is far away.   285
And I tell you this plainly, and it will surely be fulfilled:
if ever Zeus who wears the aegis and Athena grant
that I may tear Ilium apart, that well-built city, it will be
in your hands—after myself—that I shall first place the prize
of honour, either a tripod, or a pair of horses with their chariot,   290
or a woman, who will go up to your bed and share it with you.'
    Then in answer blameless Teucer addressed him:
'Atreus' glorious son, why do you urge me on when I am eager
on my own account? Be sure that while the strength is in me
I will not stop; ever since we forced them back towards Ilium   295
I have been looking for a chance to kill men with my bow.
Eight arrows with long barbs I have let fly, and they have
all stuck fast in the flesh of war-swift strong young men;
but this maddened dog I am not able to strike down.'
    So he spoke, and let fly another arrow from his bowstring,   300
straight at Hector, and his heart longed to shoot him down.
But he missed Hector, and with his arrow struck
blameless Gorgythion, Priam's brave son, in the chest;
his mother had come in marriage from Aesyme,*
beautiful Castianeira, who was in stature like a goddess.   305
As when in a garden a poppy droops its head to one side,
heavy with the weight of its seed and with spring showers,
so his head, weighed down by his helmet, slumped to one side.
    Then Teucer let fly another arrow from his bowstring,
straight at Hector, and his heart longed to shoot him down.   310
But he failed a second time, for Apollo made him miss his mark,
and he hit Archeptolemus, Hector's daring charioteer, in his

chest next to the nipple as he launched himself into battle.
He toppled from the chariot, and his swift-footed horses
started back, and there his life and fury were loosened.   315
Bitter grief for his charioteer crowded thick into Hector's heart,
but he left him there, grieved though he was for his companion,
and called to his brother Cebriones, who happened to be nearby,
to pick up the horses' reins; and Cebriones heard and obeyed him.
Hector himself jumped to the ground from the gleaming chariot,   320
with a terrible yell; he picked up a large rock in his hand and made
straight for Teucer, his heart driving him on to knock him down.
Teucer had pulled a bitter arrow from his quiver and fitted it
to the bowstring; as he drew the string back to his shoulder,
raging to shoot at him, Hector of the glittering helmet hit him   325
with the jagged rock at the point where the collarbone marks off
the neck and chest, and it is a most vulnerable spot, and
broke his bowstring. Teucer's hand went numb at the wrist and
he sank to his knees, motionless, and the bow fell from his hand.
Ajax did not desert his brother when he fell, but ran up   330
and stood over him and sheltered him with his shield.
Then two trusty companions lifted him on to their shoulders,
Mecisteus, the son of Echius, and glorious Alastor,
and carried him, groaning deeply, back to the hollow ships.
    Then once again the Olympian stirred up fury in the Trojans,   335
and they drove the Achaeans straight back towards the deep ditch;
Hector strode among the front-fighters, exulting in his strength:
as when a hound snaps at a wild boar or a lion from
behind, biting its flanks and hindquarters and running it down
on swift feet, and keenly watches the lion's twists and turns,   340
so Hector pressed hard on the flowing-haired Achaeans,
all the time killing the hindmost; and they turned in flight.
When they had passed the stakes and crossed the ditch
in their flight, and many had been beaten down by Trojan hands,
they halted beside the ships and made a stand there,   345
calling out to each other and holding up their hands,
each man praying in a loud voice to all the gods, while
Hector was wheeling his fine-maned horses this way and that,
glaring with the eyes of Gorgo* or of Ares, doom of mortals.
    When the goddess white-armed Hera saw them she felt pity,   350
and straightaway she addressed Athena with winged words:
'Daughter of Zeus the aegis-wearer, look at this! Shall we two

give up caring about the Danaans as they die? It is our last chance.
They will surely bring their lives to a miserable end, dying
under the onslaught of one man, Hector, Priam's son; his fury　　355
is now irresistible—you can see what terrible things he has done.'

　　Then in answer to her the goddess grey-eyed Athena said:
'If only this man could utterly lose his fury and his life,
slain in his native land at the hands of the Argives!
But my father is crazed, and his mind is set on no good—　　360
hard god, always opposing me and frustrating my schemes.
He has not the smallest memory of the many times I saved
his son, when exhausted by the labours that Eurystheus set him.
Heracles had only to cry out to the high sky, and Zeus
would send me down from the high sky to bring him help.　　365
Had I been shrewd enough to know all this in my mind when
he was sent down to the house of Hades the gate-guardian,
to bring the hound of hateful Hades back from Erebus,
he would not have escaped over the fast-flowing streams of Styx.*
But now Zeus hates me, and has carried out Thetis' designs,　　370
that one who kissed his knees and took his chin in her hand,
and entreated him to honour Achilles, sacker of cities;
but the day will come when he calls me his dear grey-eyes again.
Now, you must harness your single-hoofed horses for us,
while I go into the palace of Zeus who wears the aegis　　375
and clothe myself in armour for war, to see whether
Hector of the glittering helmet, Priam's son, will be glad
when we two show ourselves along the battle-lines of war,
or whether the Trojans too will glut the dogs and vultures
with their fat and flesh, when they fall beside the Achaeans' ships.'　　380

　　So she spoke, and the goddess white-armed Hera did not disobey her;
she set about harnessing her horses with their golden headbands—
Hera, elder goddess, daughter of great Cronus.
But Athena, daughter of Zeus who wears the aegis,
let fall on to her father's threshold the soft embroidered　　385
robe which she herself had laboured over with her own hands,
and put on the tunic of Zeus the gatherer of clouds,
and clothed herself in armour for war, the bringer of tears.
She stepped on to the brightly blazing chariot and gripped the spear,
heavy, thick, and massive, with which she beats down ranks of men,　　390
of heroes with whom she, child of a mighty father, is enraged.
Then Hera quickly lashed the horses with her whip; and

of their own accord the gates of the high sky groaned open, gates
held by the Seasons,* who have charge of the great sky and Olympus,
either to push aside the dense cloud or to close it up together.   395
Through these gates they steered their horses, driven on by the whip.

   But when father Zeus saw them from Ida he was terribly angry,
and dispatched Iris the golden-winged with a message:
'Away now, swift Iris, and turn them back, and do not let them
come up against me; it is not good that we should meet in battle.   400
For I tell you this plainly, and it will surely be fulfilled:
I shall lame these swift horses in their harness, and I shall
fling them both out of the chariot and shatter it to pieces.
And not even in the circle of ten returning years will they be healed
of the wounds which my thunderbolt will inflict on them;   405
so the grey-eyed one may learn what it is to fight with her father.
With Hera I am not so much angry or so incensed,
since it is always her custom to thwart me in everything I say.'

   So he spoke, and storm-footed Iris arose to take her message,
and set off from the mountains of Ida for far Olympus.   410
Just outside the gates of many-valleyed Olympus she met the pair
and tried to stop them, and reported Zeus' words to them:
'Where is your fury taking you? Why does the heart in you rage so?
The son of Cronus will not allow you to help the Argives.
The son of Cronus has threatened—and it will be fulfilled—   415
to lame these swift horses of yours in their harness, and to
fling you both out of the chariot and shatter it to pieces,
and not even in the circle of ten returning years will you be healed
of the wounds which his thunderbolt will inflict on you;
so you may learn, grey-eyed one, what it is to fight with your father.   420
With Hera he is not so much angry or so incensed,
since it is always her custom to thwart him in everything he says.
But you are indeed most wretched, and a shameless bitch,
if you are really bold enough to raise your huge spear against Zeus.'

   So Iris of the swift feet spoke, and departed from them,   425
and then Hera addressed Athena with these words:
'Daughter of Zeus who wears the aegis, I can no longer
agree to our fighting against Zeus just for mortals' sake!
Let some of them die and let the others live, as chance has it,
and let Zeus make judgements on the Trojans and the Danaans   430
according to the thoughts in his heart, as is right.'

   So she spoke, and turned the single-hoofed horses back;

and the Seasons unyoked the fine-maned horses
and tethered them at their immortal mangers, and
leaned the chariot body against the shining courtyard wall.   435
Then the goddesses took their seats on golden chairs
among the rest of the gods, troubled in their hearts.

    Now father Zeus had driven his fine-wheeled chariot and horses
from Ida to Olympus, and had come to the seat of the gods.
The renowned earthshaker unyoked his horses for him, and   440
set the chariot body on its base, and spread a cloth over it.
Wide-thundering Zeus took his seat on a golden throne,
and great Olympus trembled underneath his feet.
Only Athena and Hera took their seats apart from Zeus,
and said nothing to him nor asked him any questions;   445
but he understood in his mind and addressed them:
'Athena and Hera, why are you so troubled?
Surely you are not weary from the battle where men win glory,
from slaying Trojans, for whom you have a terrible hatred?
It is not possible, such is my fury and my invincible hands,   450
for all the gods on Olympus to turn me from my purpose;
but as for you two, trembling seized your bright limbs
before you even saw war and the cruel deeds of war.
I tell you this plainly, and it would surely have been fulfilled:
if my thunderbolt had struck you, you would never have returned   455
in your chariot to Olympus, where the immortals have their seat.'

    So he spoke, and Athena and Hera muttered to each other,
sitting close together and planning misery for the Trojans.
Athena was silent, saying not a word, being full of resentment
towards father Zeus, and savage bitterness gripped her;   460
but Hera could not contain the anger in her breast, and said:
'Most dread son of Cronus, what is this that you have said?
We know very well that your strength is not negligible,
but for all that we feel pity for the Danaan spearmen,
who will surely bring their lives to a wretched end, and die.   465
Still, we will certainly hold back from war, if you command us,
and will offer to the Argives such counsel as will benefit them,
so that they do not all perish as a result of your anger.'

    Then in answer to her Zeus who gathers the clouds said:
'In the morning, ox-eyed lady Hera, if you wish it,   470
you will see the son of Cronus in even greater fury,
destroying great numbers of the Argive spearmen's army;

for towering Hector will not cease from the fighting
until swift-footed Achilles is roused up beside his ship,
on the day when they will fight by their ships' sterns   475
in a dreadful narrow space, for the sake of the dead Patroclus;
so it is ordained. As for your anger, it does not concern me,
not even if you roam as far as the lowest limits of
the earth and the sea, where Iapetus and Cronus sit,*
taking no delight in the rays of Hyperion the sun or in   480
the winds, and deep Tartarus surrounds them. Even if
your wanderings take you there, your ill-temper will not
concern me; there is no more shameless a bitch than you.'
   So he spoke, and white-armed Hera made no reply.
Now the bright light of the sun dropped into Ocean,   485
drawing black night over the grain-giving earth. The Trojans
were not glad when the light sank down, but for the Achaeans
dark night's coming was welcome, an answer to many prayers.
   Now illustrious Hector led the Trojans away from the ships,
and held an assembly, beside the swirling river,   490
in an open place where the ground was clear of dead men.
They jumped to the ground from their chariots and began to listen
to the speech which Hector, dear to Zeus, made. In his hand
he held a spear eleven cubits long, and the shaft's bronze point
gleamed before him, and round it ran a golden neck-ring.   495
Leaning on this he made his speech to the Trojans:
'Listen to me, Trojans, Dardanians and allies; I had thought
that we would destroy all the Achaeans and their ships,
and would then make our way back to windswept Ilium,
but darkness has come and prevented us, and that above all   500
has saved the Argives and their ships along the seashore.
So let us now give way to black night's persuasion,
and prepare our supper; unyoke your fine-maned horses
from their chariots, and throw fodder before them;
bring oxen and sturdy sheep from the city, quickly,   505
and supply yourselves with mind-cheering wine and
bread from your halls, and collect a great quantity of wood,
so that all night long until early-born dawn we may keep
many fires alight, and their brightness may reach the high sky,
in case during the night the flowing-haired Achaeans   510
stir themselves to escape over the broad back of the sea.
They must not board their ships when they wish, without a fight;

no, when they reach home, many of them must have a wound
to tend, one inflicted by an arrow or a sharp spear as they
leapt on to their ships, so that others too may hesitate before   515
waging tear-laden war against the horse-breaking Trojans.
Let the heralds, dear to Zeus, proclaim throughout the city
that boys in their early youth and grey-haired old men
should bivouac on the god-built walls around the city,
and that the womenfolk should each light a great fire   520
in their halls; and let there be a trustworthy guard set, so that
no enemy band may enter the city while its people are absent.
Let this be done, great-hearted Trojans, as I declare.
Let these sound orders of mine suffice for the present, and
I shall make announcements tomorrow to the horse-breaking
       Trojans: 525
I pray in hope to Zeus and all the other gods that I shall drive
these dogs, brought here by death-spectres, away from here,
[those whom the spectres carry upon their black ships.]
So for this night we must keep watch at our stations,
and tomorrow, at break of day, let us put on our armour   530
and wake fierce Ares beside the hollow ships,
and then I shall know if mighty Diomedes, Tydeus' son,
will drive me back from the ships towards the wall, or if I
will cut him down with the bronze and carry off his bloody arms.
Tomorrow he will discover if he has the courage to withstand   535
the onslaught of my spear; but I rather think that when the sun
rises for tomorrow he will lie, speared through, in the front ranks,
and many of his companions around him. If only I
could be immortal and ageless for all my days,
and honoured as Athena and Apollo are honoured,   540
as surely as this coming day will bring ruin to the Argives!'
    So Hector spoke, and the Trojans shouted their approval.
They set free their sweating horses from the yoke,
and tethered them with leather thongs, each beside his chariot;
and from the city they brought oxen and sturdy sheep,   545
quickly, and they supplied themselves with mind-cheering wine
and bread from their halls, and collected a great quantity of wood;
[and they sacrificed perfect hecatombs for the immortals,]*
and the winds carried the savour from the plain up to the high sky.
[But sweet though it was the blessed gods did not feast on it,   550
and had no wish to, for sacred Ilium was deeply hateful to them,

and Priam and the people of Priam of the fine ash spear.]

   So they sat for the whole night, along the battle-lines of war,
with great thoughts in mind, and their fires burnt in great numbers.
As when in the high sky stars shine out in their brilliance   555
around the shining moon, when the upper air is windless,
and every crag and jutting peak and mountain glen is clear
to see; boundless bright air breaks down from the high sky,
and all the stars are visible, and the shepherd is glad in his heart;
so many were the fires that the Trojans kindled in front of Ilium,   560
shining out between the ships and the streams of Xanthus.
A thousand fires were burning on the plain, and beside each
sat fifty men in the brightness of the blazing fire.
Their horses stood champing on white barley and emmer wheat
beside their chariots, waiting for Dawn on her lovely throne.   565

BOOK NINE

So the Trojans kept their watch; but the Achaeans were gripped
by awesome Rout, the companion of chilling Panic, and
all their best men were struck down by unbearable grief.
As when two winds churn up the fish-rich sea,
the North Wind and the West, blowing from Thrace;   5
suddenly they start up, and the dark waves mass and rise
to a crest, and spew out heaps of seaweed along the shore;
so were the hearts of the Achaeans torn in their breasts.
    The son of Atreus was struck to his heart with huge grief,
and went among the clear-voiced heralds, ordering them   10
to summon each man to an assembly, calling him by name,
but not to shout aloud; and he was busy himself with the foremost.
They took their seats in the assembly, in despair; and
Agamemnon stood up, weeping tears like a spring of black
water which pours its dark stream down over a sheer cliff;   15
so Agamemnon addressed the Argives, groaning deeply:
'My friends, chieftains and rulers of the Argives! Zeus
the son of Cronus has snared me in a cruel delusion,
hard god that he is, who before this promised and assured me
that I should return home only after sacking strongly walled Ilium; 20
but now he has planned an evil deception, and orders me
to go back to Argos without glory, after losing many people.
This must I suppose be pleasing to Zeus the all-powerful,
who has indeed destroyed the crowns of many cities,
and will do so again; for his might is the greatest of all.   25
But come, let us all be agreed, and do as I say:
let us flee with our ships, back to our dear native land,
because we shall never take Troy with its wide streets.'
    So he spoke, and they all remained silent and still.
For a long time the Achaeans' sons were speechless with despair,   30
but at last Diomedes of the mighty voice spoke among them:
'Son of Atreus, I will begin by challenging your folly, here,
lord, in the assembly, where it is proper; so do not be angry.
You have already insulted my courage in front of the Danaans,*
saying that I was no fighter, and a coward; and all this   35
is known to the Argives, both young men and old.

The son of crooked-scheming Cronus gave you gifts by halves:
along with your staff he granted you honour beyond all men,
but courage, which confers most authority, he did not give you.
Man possessed, do you really think the sons of the Achaeans   40
are no fighters and cowards, as you tell us they are?
If your own heart especially is urging you to go home,
then go. The way lies before you, and your ships are stood to
by the sea, the many ships that came with you from Mycenae;
but the rest of the flowing-haired Achaeans will stay here   45
until such time as we sack Troy—or no, rather let them also
take flight in their ships to their dear native land, and
we two, I and Sthenelus, will fight on until we reach
our goal in Ilium; for it was with a god that we came here.'

So he spoke, and the sons of the Achaeans all shouted in approval,   50
amazed at the words of horse-breaking Diomedes.
Then the horseman Nestor stood up and spoke among them:
'Son of Tydeus, in warfare your might is beyond others',
and in counsel you are the best of all men of your age.
No one of the Achaeans could treat your words with contempt,   55
or argue against them, but your speech did not reach its end—
but then, you are a young man, and you could be my son,
my latest-born. Still, there was good sense in your words
to the Argive kings, since you spoke according to due measure.
But come; because I declare proudly that I am senior to you,   60
let me speak out and make everything plain, and no one
will treat my words with scorn, not even lord Agamemnon;
since shut out from brotherhood, from law and from hearth
is the man who falls in love with bitter civil discord.
Now, for the moment, let us surrender to black night and   65
prepare our meal, and let sentries be posted outside the wall,
along the ditch we have dug, each in their place.
These are the orders I give to the younger men; after that,
Atreus' son, you must take the lead, for you are the most kingly.
Give your elders a feast—the right thing to do, causing you no shame,   70
since your huts are full of wine, which the Achaeans' ships
bring in every day from Thrace over the broad open sea.
All hospitality is your duty, for you rule over many people.
When many are gathered together you must listen to the man
who offers the best advice; the Achaeans are all in urgent need   75
of good and shrewd advice, because our enemies are lighting

many fires near the ships, and what man could be glad at that?
This night will either break the army in pieces or save it.'

So he spoke, and they listened carefully and did as he said.
Out hurried the sentries wearing their armour,   80
led by Thrasymedes, Nestor's son, shepherd of the people,
and by Ascalaphus and Ialmenus, sons of Ares,
and by Meriones and Aphareus and Deïpyrus,
and by glorious Lycomedes, the son of Creion.
There were seven captains of the guards, and with each went   85
one hundred young men, holding long spears in their hands.
They filed out and took their posts between the ditch and the wall,
and there they lit fires, and each man prepared his meal.

Then Atreus' son gathered the elders of the Achaeans together
in his hut, and set before them a feast to satisfy their hearts.   90
They reached out for the food that lay ready before them,
and when they had put away the desire for eating and drinking,
the very first to begin weaving his counsel was the old man
Nestor, whose advice in time past too had proved to be the best.
With generous intent he spoke and addressed them: 95
'Most glorious son of Atreus, Agamemnon, lord of men,
with you I shall begin, and with you I shall end, because
you are lord over many peoples, and Zeus has entrusted to you
a staff and ordinances, for you to give counsel on their behalf.
Therefore you must above all men give and take advice,   100
and must carry out another's proposal, if his heart urges him
to speak for the good; he will depend on you, whatever he begins.
Now I shall speak as it seems to me to be best,
because there is no one who will think of a better plan
than that which I have long held in my mind, and still hold,   105
since the time when, Zeus-born, you went to Achilles' hut
and took away the girl, Briseus' daughter, despite his anger,
entirely against our judgement; and indeed I did my utmost
to dissuade you, but you gave in to your great-hearted spirit
and dishonoured a mighty man, whom even the immortals   110
have honoured—you took his prize and kept it. Still, let us
even now consider how we may appease and persuade him
with acceptable gifts and with flattering words.'

Then in answer Agamemnon, lord of men, addressed him:
'Old man, you are not wrong when you describe my delusion.   115
I was deluded, and I myself do not deny it. The man whom

Zeus loves in his heart is worth many people—as he has now
honoured that man, and has beaten down the Achaean people.
But because I was deluded and yielded to base feelings
I am willing to make amends, and to pay him a boundless ransom.   120
In the presence of you all let me name the splendid gifts:
seven tripods untouched by fire, and ten talents of gold,
twenty gleaming cauldrons, and twelve powerful horses,
race-victors, prize-winners with the speed of their feet.
The man who came to own all that my single-hoofed horses   125
have brought me in prizes would not be lacking in booty,
nor would he be without possession of precious gold.
And I will give him seven women, skilled in fine handiwork,
Lesbians, whom I chose when he himself took Lesbos,
the well-built city, and they surpassed all womankind in beauty.   130
These I will give him, and with them the one I then took away,
Briseus' daughter; and moreover I will swear a great oath
that I have never gone up to her bed nor lain with her,
as is the usual way of mankind between men and women.
All these will be put before him immediately; but if some day   135
the gods grant us to sack the great city of Priam, let him enter it
at the time when we Achaeans are sharing out the booty
and pile his ship high with gold and bronze, all that he wants,
and let him choose for himself twenty Trojan women,
those who are the most beautiful after Argive Helen.   140
And if we reach Achaean Argos, that most fertile of lands,
he can be my son-in-law, and I will treat him like Orestes,*
my last-born, who is raised amidst great abundance.
And I have three daughters in my well-constructed hall,
Chrysothemis and Laodice and Iphianassa;* of these he may   145
take the one he chooses to be his own, without bride-gifts,*
to Peleus' house. And I will give him dowry-gifts as well,
in plenty, such as no man has ever given with his daughter:
I will give him seven well-populated cities,
Cardamyle and Enope and Hire with its grassy pastures,   150
sacred Pherae, and Antheia with its deep meadows,
beautiful Aepeia, and Pedasus, country of vines.*
All these are near the sea, on the borders of sandy Pylos,
and in them live men who are rich in sheep and rich in cattle,
and they will honour him with gifts, as if he were a god,   155
and under his staff's rule they will live in obedient prosperity.

All this will I do for him, if only he gives up his anger.
Let him give way—only Hades is implacable and inflexible,
and that is why of all gods he is the most hated by mortals—
and let him take his place below me, since I am the more kingly,   160
and because I declare that I am older than him by birth.'
    Then the Gerenian horseman Nestor answered him, and said:
'Most glorious son of Atreus, Agamemnon, lord of men,
the gifts that you now offer lord Achilles are not to be despised;
so come, let us select men and dispatch them to go   165
without delay to the hut of Achilles, son of Peleus.
Come now, let those on whom my eye falls accept this duty:
first of all Phoenix, dear to Zeus, should be the leader,
and with him should go huge Ajax and glorious Odysseus,
and of the heralds let Odius and Eurybates accompany them.   170
Bring water for our hands, and command holy silence,
for us to pray to Cronus' son Zeus, to see if he will pity us.'
    So he spoke, and his words were pleasing to them all.
Straightaway heralds poured water over their hands,
and young men filled mixing-jars to the brim with wine   175
and distributed it to all, after first pouring libations into the cups.
When they had made libations and drunk to their hearts' desire,
they set out from the hut of Atreus' son Agamemnon;
and the horseman Gerenian Nestor kept giving them instructions,
looking sharply at each man, but especially at Odysseus,   180
as to how they should try to persuade Peleus' blameless son.
    So they* went along the shore of the loud-roaring sea,
praying earnestly to the earth-holder, shaker of the earth,
that they would easily persuade the great heart of Aeacus' grandson.*
And so they came to the huts and ships of the Myrmidons,   185
and they found him delighting his heart with a clear-voiced lyre,
fine and intricately worked, and on it was a silver cross-piece;
he had chosen it from the spoils when he sacked Eëtion's city.*
With this he was delighting his heart, singing the glorious deeds of men,
and only Patroclus was with him, sitting opposite him in silence,   190
watching for the time when Achilles should end his singing.
So they came forward, and glorious Odysseus led them,
and stopped in front of him. Achilles leapt up in amazement,
still holding his lyre, and left the seat where he had been sitting;
and likewise Patroclus, when he saw the men, stood up.   195
Swift-footed Achilles greeted and addressed them:

'Welcome, my true friends! Some pressing need must bring
you here, the Achaeans I love the most, even in my anger.'

So speaking glorious Achilles led them into his hut,
and sat them down on seats spread with bright purple cloths,   200
and at once spoke to Patroclus, who was standing nearby:
'Son of Menoetius, quick, bring out a larger mixing-bowl
and make the mixture stronger, and set out a cup for each man;
these men who have come under my roof are my dearest friends.'

So he spoke, and Patroclus obeyed his dear companion.   205
In the light of the fire he set down a great butcher's block,
and laid on it the backs of a sheep and a fat goat,
and also the chine of a full-grown hog, rich with fat.
Automedon held them for him, while glorious Achilles jointed them.
He chopped the meat carefully and threaded it on to skewers,   210
and Menoetius' son, a man equal to the gods, built up the fire.
When the fire had burned down and the flame had faded
he spread the embers out and laid the skewers above them,
resting them on props, and sprinkled sacred salt over them.
Then, when he had cooked the meat and piled it on to platters,   215
Patroclus fetched bread and set it out on the table
in fine baskets; but Achilles apportioned the meat.
He then took his seat facing godlike Odysseus, against
the opposite wall, and ordered his companion Patroclus to
sacrifice to the gods; and he threw the first pieces into the fire.   220
They reached out for the good things that lay ready before them,
and when they had put from themselves the desire for food and drink
Ajax nodded to Phoenix. But glorious Odysseus noticed this,
and filling a cup with wine he drank a toast to Achilles:
'Greetings, Achilles! We have not lacked our fair share   225
in the feasting, either in the hut of Agamemnon, Atreus' son,
or indeed here now, for there is much food here to satisfy
our hearts. But pleasant feasts are not now our concern,
Zeus-nurtured man; we see great suffering, too great, and
we are afraid. It is in the balance whether we save or lose   230
our well-benched ships—unless you put on courage's garment.
The high-hearted Trojans and their far-famed allies
have pitched their camp up against the wall and the ships,
and have lit many fires throughout their camp, and they think
they will no longer be held back, but will fall on our black ships.   235
Zeus, the son of Cronus, reveals signs favourable to them by his

lightning on the right; and Hector exults greatly in his strength,
raging prodigiously, trusting in Zeus, and respecting
neither men nor gods; a cruel frenzy has entered him.
He prays for the bright Dawn to appear as soon as possible, and   240
vows that he will hack the tops of the stern-posts from our ships,
and burn the ships themselves with ravaging fire, and cut down
the Achaeans beside them, panic-stricken amidst the smoke.
And I have a terrible fear in my heart that the gods will
fulfil his threatening words, that it will indeed be our fate   245
to perish here at Troy, far from Argos, rearer of horses.
Up, then, if you are determined, late though it is, to rescue
the weary Achaeans' sons from the Trojans' war-clamour.
You will certainly suffer if you delay, for once evil is done
there is no cure to be found; long before that happens, consider   250
how you may keep the day of disaster away from the Danaans.
My dear friend, your father Peleus, surely impressed this on you
on the day that he sent you from Phthia to join Agamemnon:
"My son, as for strength, Athena and Hera will give it to you
if they so wish it; but you must curb the great-hearted spirit in   255
your breast, since it is a better thing to preserve good fellowship.
Avoid the strife that leads to destruction, and the Argives,
both young and old, will show you the more respect."
That is what the old man told you, but you are forgetting it.
Give way, even now, and leave off your heart-sore bitterness;   260
if you quit your anger Agamemnon will give you worthy gifts.
Come now, listen to me, and I shall describe to you all the
gifts which Agamemnon has promised to you from his huts:
seven tripods untouched by fire, and ten talents of gold,
twenty gleaming cauldrons, and twelve powerful horses,   265
race-victors, prize-winners with the speed of their feet.
The man who came to own all that his single-hoofed horses
have brought him in prizes would not be lacking in booty,
nor would he be without possession of precious gold.
He will give you seven women, skilled in fine handiwork,   270
Lesbians, whom he chose when you yourself took Lesbos,
the well-built city, and they surpassed all womankind in beauty.
These he will give you, and with them the one he then took away,
Briseus' daughter; and moreover he will swear a great oath
that he has never gone up to her bed nor lain with her,   275
as is the usual way of mankind between men and women.

All these will be put before you immediately; but if some day
the gods grant us to sack the great city of Priam, you may
go into it when we Achaeans are sharing out the booty,
and pile your ship high with gold and bronze, all that you want,   280
and you may choose for yourself twenty Trojan women,
those who are the most beautiful after Argive Helen.
And if we reach Achaean Argos, that most fertile of lands,
you can be his son-in-law, and he will treat you like Orestes,
his last-born, who is raised amidst great abundance.   285
And he has three daughters in his well-constructed hall,
Chrysothemis and Laodice and Iphianassa; of these you may
take the one you choose to be your own, without bride-gifts,
to Peleus' house. And he will give you dowry-gifts in addition,
in plenty, such as no man has ever given with his daughter: 290
he will give you seven well-populated cities,
Cardamyle and Enope and Hire with its grassy pastures,
sacred Pherae, and Antheia with its deep meadows,
beautiful Aepeia, and Pedasus, country of vines.
All these are near the sea, on the borders of sandy Pylos,   295
and in them live men who are rich in sheep and rich in cattle,
and they will honour you with gifts as if you were a god,
and under your staff's rule they will live in obedient prosperity.
All this will he do for you, if only you give up your bitterness.
But if the hatred in your heart for Atreus' son is now too great,   300
both for the man and his gifts, at any rate have pity on all the rest
of the Achaeans, suffering in the camp, and they will honour you
as a god; and you could well win vast glory in their eyes,
for now you could kill Hector, since his murderous madness
will bring him very close to you; he reckons he has no equal   305
among the Danaans who have been brought here in their ships.'
        Then in answer swift-footed Achilles addressed him:
'Son of Laertes, sprung from Zeus, Odysseus of many schemes,
I must say what I say with frankness, and tell you bluntly
what thoughts are in my mind and how they will be fulfilled,   310
so that you do not sit there trying to coax me, each in his way;
for that man is as hateful to me as the gates of Hades
who hides one thing in his mind but says another.
I shall tell you, then, what seems best to me:
I do not think that Atreus' son Agamemnon will persuade me,   315
or the other Danaans, since I now see that battling with

the enemy, on and on without ceasing, earns no gratitude.
The man who just stands there and the man who fights bravely
get the same share; coward and brave are equally honoured;
a man dies just the same, whether he has done much or nothing.   320
I have endured pain in my heart, always risking my life in battle,
but I get no more of a share than others, not even a little.
Like a bird which brings all the morsels she can find
to her unfledged young, and suffers herself because of it,
so I too have passed many nights without sleeping, and   325
have come through days that were bloodstained with fighting,
struggling against men, fighting for the sake of their wives.*
Twelve cities of men have I sacked from my ships,
and on land I claim eleven such around rich-soiled Troy.
From all of these I took much splendid treasure, and   330
always I brought it back and gave it all to Agamemnon,
son of Atreus; and he would stay behind by the swift ships
and take it, sharing it out in small lots, keeping most for himself.
All that he gave as prizes to the chieftains and kings is
stored safely in their keeping; from me alone of the Achaeans   335
he took my prize, and keeps the wife who warmed my heart. Well,
let him sleep beside her and take his pleasure. Why must Argives
make war against Trojans? Why did Atreus' son assemble an army
and bring it here? Was it not for lovely-haired Helen's sake?
Are then Atreus' sons the only ones among mortal men   340
who love their wives? Surely every good man of sound mind
loves his own and cherishes her, just as I for my part
loved mine from my heart, though she was won by my spear.
But now that he has cheated me, taking my prize from my arms,
let him not test me—I know him too well; he will not persuade me.   345
No, Odysseus, let him take thought with you and the other kings
as to how you may keep destructive fire away from the ships.
He has certainly laboured very hard while I was absent;
he has built a wall, look, and dug a ditch alongside it,
a great wide one, and he has planted stakes in it;   350
but for all that he cannot contain the might of Hector,
killer of men. So long as I was fighting with the Achaeans
Hector was unwilling to do battle away from his walls,
but came only as far as the Scaean gates and the oak tree;
there once he waited for me alone,* and scarcely escaped my attack.   355
But now, since I have no wish to fight against glorious Hector,

tomorrow I shall make a sacrifice to Zeus and all the other gods,
and I shall drag my ships down to the sea and pile them full;
then you will see, if you have a mind to and if it matters to you,
my ships sailing at break of day over the Hellespont   360
rich in fish, and my men in them straining at their oars.
And if the famed earthshaker grants me a good voyage,
on the third day we should reach rich-soiled Phthia. I have
much wealth there, which I left when I came here—to my cost.
And from here I shall take more—gold and red bronze,   365
and women with fine girdles, and grey iron—everything,
at any rate, that fell to my lot; but my prize, the one he gave me,
lord Agamemnon, Atreus' son, has taken back, violently
insulting me. Tell him everything that I am telling you,
quite openly, so that the rest of the Achaeans may be angry too,   370
in case he is hoping to cheat some other man of the Danaans,
clothed as he always is in shamelessness. But as for me,
he would not dare to look me in the face, the dog.
I will not join him in his counsels, or in his actions;
he has cheated and wronged me. Let him not try to deceive me   375
again with words—once is enough; let him ruin himself
as he pleases; Zeus the counsellor has robbed him of his wits.
I abominate his gifts, and I value him no more than a splinter.
Not even if he were to offer me ten or twenty times
all that he now possesses, and anything else he may acquire,   380
or all the wealth that flows into Orchomenus or into Thebes
in Egypt,* where the houses are crammed full with treasure,
and which has one-hundred gates, and two-hundred men
can ride out through every one, with chariots and horses;
not even if he gave me gifts as numerous as the sand or dust—   385
not even then would Agamemnon win over my heart, until
he has paid me back in full for this heart-wounding outrage.
I will not marry a daughter of Atreus' son Agamemnon,
not even if she rivals golden Aphrodite in her beauty,
and is a match for grey-eyed Athena in the work of her hands—   390
not even then will I marry her; let him choose another Achaean,
whose rank is equal to his, and who is more kingly than I am.
If the gods preserve me, and if I reach my home, then
surely Peleus himself will search out a wife for me:
there are many Achaean women throughout Hellas and Phthia,   395
daughters of chieftains who defend their cities, and

whichever of these I want I shall make my dear wife.
Indeed, my proud spirit has many times moved me
to take a wedded wife there, a well-matched partner,
to enjoy the treasures that aged Peleus has amassed; I do not think   400
that anything is of equal worth to my life, not even all the wealth
they say that Ilium, that well-populated city, once possessed
in time of peace before the sons of the Achaeans came,
nor all the wealth that the stone threshold of the archer
Phoebus Apollo guards inside his temple in rocky Pytho.*   405
Cattle and flocks of sturdy sheep can be got by raiding, and
tripods and herds of chestnut horses can be made one's own,
but raiding and getting cannot bring back a man's life
when once it has passed beyond the barrier of his teeth.
My mother, Thetis of the silver feet, tells me that there are   410
two spectres carrying me towards the end of death:*
if I remain here and fight around the city of the Trojans,
I shall lose my homecoming, but my fame will never die,
while if I go back home to my dear native land,
my noble fame will be lost, but my life will be long,   415
and the end of death will not come quickly upon me.
As for the rest of you, I would advise you all to
sail home, because you will never reach your goal
of taking sheer Ilium, since Zeus the wide-thunderer has
stretched his hand over it, and its people have taken heart.   420
So go back now and report my answer plainly to the
Achaeans' chieftains—for that is the office of elders—
so that they can devise another, better plan in their minds,
such as will safeguard their ships and the Achaean people
beside the hollow ships, since this plan that they have invented   425
as a result of my stubborn anger will not work out for them.
But let Phoenix stay behind and spend the night with us,
so that he may sail with me on my ships to our dear native land
tomorrow, if he so wishes; I will not compel him to come.'

So he spoke, and they all remained silent and still,   430
amazed at his words, so forcibly had he refused them.
But at last Phoenix, the old horse-driver, spoke out, bursting
into tears, because he feared greatly for the Achaeans' ships:
'Illustrious Achilles, if returning is really in your thoughts,
and you have no mind at all to keep destructive fire   435
from the swift ships, because bitterness has entered your heart,

how can I be left behind here, dear child, without you,
alone? Your father, the old horse-driver Peleus, sent me to you
on the day that he dispatched you from Phthia to Agamemnon,
a mere lad, not yet skilled in warfare that touches all men alike,   440
nor yet in debate, where men grow into distinction.
For this reason he sent me to teach you all these things,
to be both a speaker of words and a doer of deeds.
So, dear child, I have no wish to be left alone after this
without you, not even if a god himself were to promise   445
to scrape away my old age and make me young and vigorous,
as I was when I first left Hellas of the beautiful women,
escaping from a quarrel with my father Amyntor, Ormenus' son,
who was furious with me because of a lovely-haired concubine;
he was infatuated with her, and dishonoured his wife,   450
my mother; and she would take me by the knees, entreating me
to lie with the concubine first, to make her loathe the old man.
I listened to her and did the deed; but my father quickly found out
and cursed me at length, and called on the hateful Furies
to make sure that he would never set on his knees a dear son   455
who was born to me. And the gods fulfilled his curses—
Zeus of the world below* and dread Persephone.
[I planned to kill him with the sharp bronze, but one
of the immortals stayed my anger, putting into my mind
the talk of my people and how men would censure me,   460
so that I should not be called a father-slayer among the Achaeans.]*
After this the spirit in my breast could no longer be confined,
to continue living in my father's halls while he was so angry.
Even so, my cousins and kinsmen who lived round about
earnestly entreated me and tried to keep me there in his halls,   465
and sacrificed many sturdy sheep and shambling
crook-horned cattle; and many a hog, rich with fat,
was stretched out over Hephaestus' flame to be singed,
and much wine was drunk from the old man's jars.
Nine nights they passed sleeping close around me,   470
keeping watch by turns, and the fires never went out—
one in the portico of the well-walled courtyard, and
another in the entrance, in front of the doors of my room.
But when the tenth dark night came upon me,
I broke down the close-fitting doors of my room   475
and escaped, and leapt over the courtyard wall, easily,

unseen by the men on guard and the women servants.
So I became a fugitive through Hellas of the wide dancing-floors,
and came to rich-soiled Phthia, mother of flocks,
to lord Peleus; and he received me with kindness,   480
and loved me as a father loves his own dear son,
a last-born only son, heir to many possessions, and he
enriched me, and made over a numerous people to me,
and I lived on the frontier of Phthia, ruling over the Dolopians.*
And, godlike Achilles, I made you into the great man you are,   485
loving you with all my heart; you never wanted to go to a feast
with anyone else, or to eat a meal in your own halls
until I had set you on my knees and given you your fill,
first cutting your meat and holding the wine to your lips;
many times have you soaked the tunic on my chest,   490
dribbling wine down it in your childish helplessness.
So, I have endured much on your account, and toiled hard,
knowing that the gods were not going to bring into being
any offspring of mine; I made you my son, godlike Achilles,
so that one day you could protect me from ugly destruction.   495
So come, Achilles, master your great spirit; you should not
have a pitiless heart—even the gods can be made to bend,
though their greatness and honour and power exceed our own.
Men can sway them with sacrifices and propitiating prayers,
petitioning them with drink-offerings and the smoke of burnt
          offerings,   500
whenever a man has overstepped the mark and done wrong.
Indeed, there are Pleas for Forgiveness, daughters of great Zeus,
who are lame and wrinkled, and their eyes are squinting,
and their office is to follow in pursuit of Delusion.
Now Delusion is strong and swift-footed, and therefore   505
far outruns them all, and gets in first, bringing hurt to men
all over the world; but the Pleas follow and heal them.
If a man respects these daughters of Zeus when they approach,
they give him great blessings and listen to his prayers;
but if anyone denies and stubbornly rejects them, they go   510
to Cronus' son Zeus and entreat him, asking for Delusion
to go along with him, so that he will be hurt, and pay the price.
So come, Achilles; you too must grant the daughters of Zeus
the respect that bends the minds of others, fine men though they are.
If Atreus' son was not offering you gifts, and promising   515

more to come, but was persisting in his furious rage,
I would not be telling you to cast your anger aside and
to defend the Argives, however much they have need of you;
but as it is, he is offering you much now, and has promised more,
and he has sent the best men on a mission to entreat you,   520
choosing them from the Achaean people—and they are also
the Argives you love most. Do not scorn their words or their
coming here, though before this your anger could not be blamed.
So it was in former times too—the famous tales we have heard
of heroes, of when violent anger came over one of them; but   525
they were open to gifts, and could be won over by speeches.
There is a story I recall from long ago, just as it happened, though it
was not a recent event; we are all friends here, so I will tell it to you.

The Curetes and Aetolians, steadfast in battle, were fighting
around the city of Calydon, and were slaughtering each other: 530
the Aetolians were defending lovely Calydon, while
the Curetes were raging to sack it in the war of Ares. Artemis
of the golden throne had sent the Aetolians an evil thing, being
angry because Oeneus had not offered her the first-fruits from
his hillside orchard. The other gods were feasting on hecatombs,   535
and it was only to great Zeus' daughter that he offered nothing;
either he forgot, or he did not intend to do it; but his mind was
mightily deluded. Furious, the archer-goddess, that divine being,
sent against him a fierce wild boar, a white-tusked creature,
which kept causing great damage by ravaging Oeneus' orchard: 540
it ripped out many tall trees and threw them to the ground,
roots, fruits, and blossom all at the same time.
This boar was killed by Meleager, the son of Oeneus,
after he had gathered together huntsmen and hounds
from many cities, for it could not be overcome by a few,   545
so huge it was, and had set many men upon the painful pyre.
The goddess stirred up a great clamour and uproar over it
between the Curetes and the great-spirited Aetolians,
as to who should win the prize of its head and shaggy hide.
Now so long as Meleager, dear to Ares, kept fighting,   550
matters went badly for the Curetes, and they were not able
to stand their ground outside the wall, many as they were;
but when anger entered Meleager—such as swells the heart
in the breasts of other men too, even the sound of mind—
because he was angry with his own mother Althaea,   555

he lay beside his wedded wife, beautiful Cleopatra,
child of Euenus' daughter Marpessa of the lovely ankles,
and of Idas, who was the strongest among earth-dwelling men
at that time—he it was who took up his bow to challenge
lord Phoebus Apollo over the girl with lovely ankles;　　560
later Cleopatra's father and revered mother gave her the name
Alcyone in their halls, because Marpessa had endured the fate of
the mournful kingfisher, the halcyon; she would weep because
Phoebus Apollo, the shooter from afar, had stolen her away—
it was beside this Cleopatra that Meleager lay, brooding on his　　565
heart-wounding anger, furious at his mother's curses, who was
grieving for her brother's killing, and she prayed often to the gods,
and many times beat with her hands on the earth that feeds many,
sitting hunched forward and soaking her lap with tears,
as she called upon Hades and dread Persephone to　　570
bring death to her son; and the Fury, the drinker of blood,
whose heart cannot be placated, heard her from Erebus.
And soon the noise and din of the Curetes rose about the gates,
as they battered the walls; and the elders of the Aetolians
kept sending the best priests of the gods to Meleager, entreating　　575
him to come out and fight, and promising him a huge gift:
they told him he could choose a magnificent estate in
the place where the lovely plain of Calydon was richest—
a tract of fifty acres, half of it vine-producing country
and half cleared ploughland, to be carved out for himself.　　580
And many times the aged horse-driver Oeneus entreated him,
standing on the threshold of his high-roofed chamber and
rattling its close-jointed doors as he implored his son;
many times his sisters and his revered mother entreated him,
but he refused them all the more; many times his companions　　585
tried, those who were closest to him and dearest of all.
But for all that they could not win over the heart in his breast,
until missiles rained thick on his chamber, and the Curetes
began to climb on the walls and to set fire to the great city.
Then indeed his finely girdled wife entreated Meleager　　590
with lamentation, and described in full all the miseries
that happen to people when their city is captured—
the enemy kill the men, fire levels the city with the ground,
and strangers carry off their children and deep-girdled women.
When he heard this dreadful tale Meleager's spirit was quickened,　　595

and he set off and put on his brightly gleaming armour.
And so, though he had yielded to his anger, he kept the evil day
from the Aetolians; but they did not give him the many fine gifts
they had promised, and he saved them from disaster for nothing.*
Do not, I beg you, have thoughts like his, dear boy, and do not   600
let some god turn you on to that course; it will be harder to defend
the ships when they are already ablaze. There are the gifts—
take them, and the Achaeans will honour you like a god.
But if you enter the man-destroying conflict without gifts,
you will not have the same honour, even if you drive the war away.'   605

    Then in answer swift-footed Achilles addressed him:
'Phoenix, aged father, nurtured by Zeus, this is an honour*
I do not need; it is by Zeus' will, I believe, that I am honoured,
and this will stay with me beside my curved ships, as long as
the breath remains in my breast and my own knees can lift me.   610
But I tell you another thing, and you should store in your mind:
do not break my resolve with your grieving and lamentation,
hoping to win favour with the hero son of Atreus; do not
take his side, or I, who love you, may come to hate you.
For you, the honourable course is to hurt the man who hurts me;   615
this way you may have half my kingdom and enjoy half my honour.
These men can take my answer back; you must stay here
and sleep on a soft bed, and then as soon as dawn appears
we shall decide whether to go home or to stay here.'

    So he spoke, and signalled silently to Patroclus with his eyebrows, 620
to make up a thick bed for Phoenix, so that the others might
think the sooner of leaving the hut for home. Then Ajax,
the godlike son of Telamon, spoke out among them:
'Son of Laertes, sprung from Zeus, Odysseus of many schemes,
let us go; I do not think our embassy's purpose will be fulfilled,   625
on this journey at any rate; we must quickly report
his reply to the Danaans, even though it is not good,
for they will surely now be sitting waiting for it. Achilles
has turned the great-hearted spirit in his breast to cruelty,
hard man, and he has no regard for his companions' love,   630
we who used to honour him above all others beside the ships.
He is without pity. And yet, a man will accept compensation
for his dead brother or his own son from the man who killed him;
the murderer pays a great price and stays among his people,
and the other's heart and proud spirit are restrained,   635

now that he has accepted amends.* But as for you, the gods
have given you a harsh and implacable heart in your breast—
and all for one girl. Now we are offering you seven, the very best,
and many other gifts besides; so make your heart gracious, and
respect your obligations as a host—we are here under your roof   640
on behalf of the whole Danaan army, and we are eager to remain
your nearest and dearest friends among all the Achaeans.'
      Then in answer swift-footed Achilles addressed him:
'Ajax, son of Telamon, sprung from Zeus, ruler of the people,
all that you have said seems much in keeping with my mind;   645
but my heart swells with bitterness whenever I think of
what happened, of how contemptuously Atreus' son treated me
before the Argives, like some wandering migrant who has lost
his rights. No; go back now and report my answer, in public:
I shall not think of entering the bloodstained war   650
until glorious Hector, the son of wise Priam,
reaches as far as the huts and ships of the Myrmidons,
killing the Argives and consuming the ships with fire.
But I think that when he reaches my hut and black ship
Hector will be held back, raging though he is for battle.'   655
      So he spoke, and they each picked up a two-handled cup,
made a libation, and returned along the row of ships, and Odysseus
led the way. But Patroclus ordered his companions and maids
to make up a thick bed for Phoenix as quickly as they could.
The women obeyed, and made up the bed as he had told them,   660
with fleeces and a rug and the softest of linen cloths; and there
the old man lay down and waited for the bright Dawn.
But Achilles went to sleep in the inmost part of his well-built hut,
and beside him lay a woman whom he had brought from Lesbos,
Diomede of the beautiful cheeks, the daughter of Phorbas.   665
Patroclus lay on the other side, and beside him too was a woman,
Iphis of the lovely girdle, whom glorious Achilles had given him
when he captured sheer Skyros,* the citadel of Enyeus.
      Now when the others reached the huts of Atreus' son,
the sons of the Achaeans stood up and drank their health,   670
one here, one there, in golden cups, and began to question them;
and the first to ask a question was Agamemnon, lord of men:
'Odysseus of many tales, great glory of the Achaeans, tell me:
is he willing to keep destructive fire away from our ships, or
did he refuse, and does anger still grip his great-hearted spirit?' 675

Then in answer much-enduring glorious Odysseus addressed him:
'Most glorious son of Atreus, Agamemnon, lord of men,
the man has no mind to quench his anger, but is even more
filled with fury, and he repudiates you and your gifts.
He tells you to take thought among the Argives as to   680
how you may save both the ships and the Achaean people;
as for himself, he threatened that as soon as dawn breaks
he will drag his well-benched, balanced ships down to the sea.
Moreover, he said that he advises all the rest of you to
sail for home, because you will never reach your goal   685
of taking sheer Ilium, because Zeus the wide-thunderer has
stretched his hand over it, and its peoples have taken heart.
So he spoke; and these who went with me will say the same,
Ajax and the two heralds, both men of sound judgement.
But the old man Phoenix is sleeping there, urged by Achilles,   690
so that he can sail with him on his ships to his dear native land
tomorrow, if he wishes; but he will not compel him to come.'

So he spoke, and they all remained silent and still,
amazed at his words, so forcibly had he spoken. For a long time
the sons of the Achaeans were speechless with despair, but   695
at last Diomedes, master of the war-cry, spoke out among them:
'Most glorious son of Atreus, Agamemnon, lord of men:
I wish that you had never entreated the blameless son of Peleus
and offered him countless gifts; he is a proud man at any time,
but now you have driven him to even greater arrogance.   700
Let us leave him alone, to decide whether he goes or
stays; later he will fight again, whenever the heart
in his breast prompts him to and a god stirs him up.
So come, let us all accept what I say: for the present,
all should go to bed, now that you have had your hearts'   705
fill of food and wine, for that is our fury and courage;
and when lovely Dawn with her rosy fingers appears, you
must quickly marshal the people and chariots before the ships,
and urge them on, and fight yourself among the front-warriors.'

So he spoke, and all the kings assented to what he said,   710
amazed at the words of Diomedes, breaker of horses.
Then they made libations, and went each to his own hut,
and there they lay down to rest, and received the gift of sleep.

BOOK TEN

Now all the other chieftains of the Achaean people
slept through the night by their ships, overcome by soft sleep;
but sweet sleep did not take hold of Atreus' son Agamemnon,
shepherd of the people, as he pondered much in his mind.
As when the husband of lovely-haired Hera flashes his lightning,   5
foretelling a heavy fall of rain or a prodigious hailstorm
or a blizzard, when snow covers the ploughed fields,
or somewhere opens the great jaws of harrowing war,
so Agamemnon kept groaning aloud, from the depths
of the heart in his breast, and the spirit within him trembled.   10
Whenever he looked towards the plain of Troy
he marvelled at the many fires burning before Ilium,
and at the noise of pipes and flutes and the clamour of men.
But when he looked at the ships and army of the Achaeans
he would tear the hair from his head by the roots, praying to   15
Zeus who sits on high; and his noble heart groaned aloud.
And this seemed to him in his heart to be the best plan,
to go before all others to Nestor, the son of Neleus,
to see if he could with him devise some excellent counsel
that would keep disaster away from all the Danaans.   20
So he rose, and put a tunic about his chest,
and bound fine sandals under his shining feet,
then slung round himself the hide of a great tawny lion,
blood-dark and reaching to his feet, and picked up his spear.

In the same way trembling gripped Menelaus, for with him too   25
sleep would not sit on his eyelids; he was afraid that some harm
would befall the Argives, who for his sake had crossed a wide
expanse of water to Troy, determined on audacious war.
First he covered his broad back with a leopard's
dappled skin, then lifted up a bronze helmet and placed it   30
on his head, and with his brawny hand picked up a spear.
He set off to rouse his brother, who was the supreme ruler
over all the Argives, and was honoured by the people like a god.
He found him by the stern of his ship, putting his fine armour
around his shoulders; and he was glad to see his brother come.   35
Menelaus, master of the war-cry, was the first to speak:

'Brother, why are you arming like this? Are you sending
one of your companions to spy on the Trojans? I am terribly
afraid that no one will undertake this mission for you,
to go out and spy on the enemy forces, alone in the   40
immortal night; he will have to be a man of very bold heart.'
      Then in answer lord Agamemnon addressed him:
'Zeus-nurtured Menelaus, we have need of a plan, you and I,
a shrewd one, that will protect and save the Argives
and their ships, since Zeus' mind has turned away from us.   45
Clearly, he has heeded Hector's offerings more than ours;
I have never seen, nor have I heard anyone tell of,
a single man devising as much destruction in one day as
Hector, dear to Zeus, has inflicted on the sons of the Achaeans—
and on his own, for he is no dear son of a god or goddess.   50
I think that the things he has done will trouble the Argives for
many, many years, such is the harm he has dealt the Achaeans.
But go now, run swiftly along the row of ships and summon
Ajax and Idomeneus; and I will go in search of glorious
Nestor, and will urge him to rise, to see if he is willing   55
to go out and give orders to the devoted company of the sentries.
They are most likely to listen to him, for it is his son
who is in charge of the sentries, he and Idomeneus' attendant
Meriones; to them especially we entrusted this duty.'
      Then Menelaus, master of the war-cry, answered him: 60
'I will; but what do you mean by these orders and instructions?
Am I to remain there with them, waiting for you to come,
or shall I run back to you when I have given them their orders?'
      Then in answer Agamemnon, lord of men, addressed him:
'Stay there, in case we somehow miss one another   65
as we go, for there are many footpaths through the camp.
Wherever you go, shout aloud to the men to stay awake,
reminding each of his ancestry and his father's name, and
addressing all with respect. And do not show a haughty spirit;
we too must toil, on our own account—for this, it seems, is the   70
heavy affliction that Zeus gave us when we were born.'
      So he spoke, and sent his brother on his way with clear orders.
He himself set off to look for Nestor, shepherd of the people,
and found him beside his hut and his black ship, lying on
his soft bed. Next to him lay his intricately worked armour,   75
a shield and a pair of spears and a shining helmet, and

by him too lay his bright-gleaming belt, which the old man
wore round him when he armed for man-destroying war,
leading his people, for he would not give in to painful old age.
Nestor lifted his head and raised himself on his elbow,   80
and addressed the son of Atreus with a question:
'Who are you, going alone about the camp and along the ships
through the dark night, when other mortals are asleep?
Are you looking for one of your mules, or some companion?
Speak; do not creep silently up on me. What do you want here?'   85
    Then in answer Agamemnon, lord of men, addressed him:
'Nestor, son of Neleus, great glory of the Achaeans,
you should recognize Agamemnon, Atreus' son, the one
whom Zeus has set amidst endless labours, beyond all men,
while there is breath in my breast and my knees can lift me.   90
I am wandering like this because sweet sleep does not sit
on my eyes, and the war and the Achaeans' troubles vex me,
and I am terribly afraid for the Danaans, and my heart
will not stay still, and I am distraught, and my heart leaps
out of my breast, and my bright limbs shake beneath me.   95
If you are minded to act—since sleep does not visit you either—
let us go out there to the sentries, to inspect them,
in case they are exhausted by toil and sleeplessness
and have fallen asleep, and have quite forgotten to keep watch.
The enemy are encamped close by, and we do not know   100
what they intend; they might even attack us by night.'
    Then Nestor the Gerenian horseman answered him:
'Most glorious son of Atreus, Agamemnon, lord of men,
Zeus the counsellor will surely not fulfil all Hector's designs,
everything that he now hopes for; no, I believe that   105
he will have more troubles to struggle with, if only Achilles
can turn his dear heart away from his destructive anger.
I shall certainly go with you; but let us also wake some others,
Tydeus' son the renowned spearman, and Odysseus,
swift-footed Ajax and Meges, the stalwart son of Phyleus.   110
And someone should go in search of other men too, and
summon them: I mean godlike Ajax and lord Idomeneus,
for their ships are furthest away on either side, and not close by.
As for Menelaus, though I love and respect him, I must quarrel
with him—and I will not hide it, even if you are angry with me—   115
because he is asleep, and has left you to toil on your own.

I could wish that he was working now among all the chieftains,
entreating them, because an intolerable need has come upon us.'
    Then in answer Agamemnon, lord of men, addressed him:
'Old man, at other times I might even urge you to blame him,   120
since he is often remiss and unwilling to take his part in the toil;
not because he gives way to cowardice or thoughtlessness,
but because he always looks to me and waits for my lead.
But this time he woke well before me, and came after me,
and I sent him forward to summon the men you are asking about.   125
Come then, let us go; we shall find them with the sentries,
in front of the gates, which is where I told them to gather.'
    Then Nestor the Gerenian horseman answered him:
'If that is so, none of the Argives will be angry with him
or disregard him, when he gives orders and urges men on.'   130
    So he spoke, and put a tunic on over his chest, and
bound fine sandals under his shining feet, and with a
clasp fastened about himself a bright purple cloak,
long and double folded, and it had a thick wool nap on it.
He picked up his stout spear, pointed with sharp bronze,   135
and set off along the ships of the bronze-shirted Achaeans.
The first man whom the Gerenian horseman Nestor roused
from sleep was Odysseus, the equal of Zeus in scheming;
he called to him, and the sound flowed quickly around his mind,
and he came out of his hut and addressed them, saying: 140
'Why are you wandering alone like this about the camp, along
the ships, through the immortal night? Has some great need arisen?'
    Then Nestor the Gerenian horseman answered him:
'Son of Laertes, sprung from Zeus, Odysseus of many schemes,
do not be angry; a great grief has indeed crushed the Achaeans.   145
Come, follow me, and we will wake others too, those who
should rightly offer their advice as to whether we flee or fight.'
    So he spoke, and Odysseus of many schemes went into his hut
and slung a finely worked shield over his shoulders, and followed them.
They went in search of Tydeus' son Diomedes, and found him   150
outside his hut, with his armour. Around him his companions
were sleeping, their heads on their shields; and their spears
had been driven into the ground, upright on their butt-ends,
and the bronze shone like the lightning of father Zeus. The hero
was asleep, and under him was spread the hide of a field ox,   155
and a bright rug was pulled up underneath his head.

Nestor the Gerenian horseman stood close to wake him;
stirring him with his foot, he rebuked him to his face:
'Wake up, son of Tydeus! Why sleep all night? Have you
not heard that the Trojans are camped on the rising plain, 160
close by the ships, and only a narrow space now separates us?'

So he spoke, and Diomedes woke and sprang up very quickly,
and addressed Nestor, speaking with winged words:
'You are hard, old man, and you never rest from toil.
Are there not other sons of the Achaeans, younger men, 165
who might better go up and down the camp, rousing
each of the kings? Old man, you are impossible to control!'

Then in answer Nestor the Gerenian horseman addressed him:
'All that you say, my friend, is according to due measure;
I do have blameless sons, and I have men, many of them, 170
any of whom could go up and down the camp and summon people.
But a very great need has overwhelmed the Achaeans,
and matters now stand upon a razor's edge for all of us
Achaeans: either survival, or an exceedingly miserable death.
So come; if you have any pity for me, go and rouse swift Ajax 175
and Meges, Phyleus' son—you are a younger man than I am.'

So he spoke, and Diomedes slung over his shoulders the hide
of a great tawny lion, reaching to his feet, and picked up his spear;
he set off, and woke the two men, and brought them back with him.

When they joined the sentries at the place where they 180
were gathered, they did not find their leaders asleep,
but they were all sitting there, armed and wide awake.
As dogs who keep restive watch over sheep in a fold,
having heard some ferocious wild beast coming down
the mountains and through the woods, and a great clamour arises 185
from the men and hounds pursuing it, and their sleep is lost;
so sweet sleep was lost to the sentries' eyelids too as they
kept watch through the uneasy night, since all the time
they were facing the plain, waiting to hear the Trojans coming.
The old man was glad when he saw them, and rallied them 190
with his speech, [and addressed them, speaking with winged words]:
'This is the way, dear children, to keep watch! Do not let sleep
catch anyone unawares, in case we become a delight to our enemies.'

So he spoke, and strode over the ditch, and the other
Argive kings followed him, all who had been called to the council. 195
And with them went Meriones and Nestor's splendid son,

since they had been invited by the others to join their debate.
When they had crossed over the deep-dug ditch they sat down
in an open space where the ground was clear of the dead men
who had fallen, the place where towering Hector had turned back   200
from slaughtering the Argives, when night covered the earth.
Sitting there they began to converse with each other,
and the first to speak was Nestor the Gerenian horseman:
'My friends, could not some man put his trust in his
audacious spirit, to go among the great-spirited Trojans   205
and see if he could capture some enemy straggler,
or perhaps hear some rumour among the Trojans,
and so find out their plans, whether they are bent on
remaining here by the ships, away from their homes, or if,
having crushed the Achaeans, they will return to their city?   210
He could find all this out, and then come back to us
unscathed, and great would be his fame under the high sky,
among all men, and he will receive a noble reward:
all the chieftains who have command over ships
will each and every one give him a black sheep,   215
a ewe with its suckling lamb, a possession without equal;
and he will always be invited to their feasts and banquets.'
    So he spoke, and they all remained silent and still, but
Diomedes, master of the war-cry, spoke out among them:
'Nestor, my heart and my proud spirit prompt me   220
to steal into the camp of our enemies the Trojans, who lie
close by—but if some other man were to come with me,
I would find more encouragement and confidence.
When two go together, one can discern before the other
what is best for them; and even if one on his own can see this,   225
his mind has a shorter reach, and his resource is weaker.'
    So he spoke, and many men wanted to go with Diomedes.
The two called Ajax, attendants of Ares, wanted to go,
Meriones wanted to go, Nestor's son wanted fervently to go,
Atreus' son Menelaus, famed with the spear, wanted to go,   230
and stalwart Odysseus wanted to steal in among the Trojan
soldiery, for the heart in his breast was always daring.
Then Agamemnon, lord of men, spoke among them:
'Diomedes, son of Tydeus, delight of my heart,
you shall choose whichever companion you want, the best   235
of those who have come forward, for many are raging to go.

But do not, out of respect in your heart, leave the better man
and take the worse with you, yielding to your esteem for him
and looking to his ancestry—not even if he is more kingly.'
        So he spoke, and he was terrified for fair-haired Menelaus.   240
Diomedes, master of the war-cry, spoke out among them again:
'If you are really telling me to choose a companion myself,
how could I then forget godlike Odysseus,
whose heart and proud spirit are ready beyond others'
for all kinds of labours, and Pallas Athena loves him.   245
If he comes with me, we could even pass through blazing fire
and return safe together, because his mind has no equal.'
        Then in turn much-enduring glorious Odysseus addressed him:
'Son of Tydeus, do not over-praise me, or dwell on my faults;
you are speaking among Argives, who surely know me.   250
Come, let us go; night is almost at an end, and dawn is near,
the stars' course is advanced, and most of the night has gone;
two-thirds of it are spent, and only the third part is left.'
        So speaking they both put on their terrifying armour.
Thrasymedes, steadfast in war, gave the son of Tydeus   255
a two-edged sword—because he had left his own by the ship—
and a shield, and placed on his head a helmet made of
oxhide, without a horn or a crest, the kind that is called a
skullcap, and it protects the heads of strong young men.
Meriones gave Odysseus a bow and a quiver and   260
a sword, and placed on his head a helmet of leather,
carefully made: on the inside it was stretched tight
by many straps, and on the outside close-set pieces
of a shiny-toothed boar's white tusks ran this way and that,
very cunningly made; and inside it was fitted a felt cap.*   265
Autolycus had once stolen this from Amyntor, Ormenus' son,
when he broke into his strongly built house in Eleon, and
he gave it to Amphidamas of Cythera to take to Scandeia;
Amphidamas gave it to Molus as a mark of guest-friendship,
and Molus gave it to his son Meriones for him to wear;   270
and now it was set for his protection on the head of Odysseus.*
        So when the two of them had put on their terrifying armour
they set off, leaving all the chief men where they were.
And Pallas Athena sent them an omen on the right, a heron
close to their path; they could not see it with their eyes   275
through the dark night, but they heard its piercing cry.

Odysseus was glad of the bird-omen, and prayed to Athena:
'Hear me, child of Zeus who wears the aegis, you who stand
by me in all my labours, and who do not forget me when I am
stirred to action; now especially show me favour, Athena,   280
and grant that we may return to the ships in glory,
having done some great deed that will disquiet the Trojans.'

    Next, Diomedes, master of the war-cry, prayed in his turn:
'Hear me too, daughter of Zeus, Atrytone;* go with me
as once you went with my father, glorious Tydeus,   285
into Thebes, when he went as an envoy from the Achaeans.*
He had left the bronze-shirted Achaeans beside the Asopus,
and was taking beguiling words to the Cadmeians in
that place; but on his way back he devised terrible deeds,
with your help, bright goddess, and you readily stood beside him.   290
So now again be willing to stand beside me and protect me,
and I will in turn sacrifice to you a yearling heifer, broad of brow,
not yet broken, one that no man has yet led under the yoke;
I will sacrifice her to you, and I will cover her horns with gold.'

    So they spoke in prayer, and Pallas Athena heard them.   295
And when they had prayed to great Zeus' daughter,
they went on their way like two lions through the black night,
amidst the carnage, the dead men, the war-gear, and the black blood.

    Nor indeed did Hector allow the proud Trojans to sleep,
but he called together all their chief men to an assembly,   300
all those who were leaders and captains of the Trojans;
and when he had summoned them he put forward a shrewd plan:
'Is there anyone who will undertake to perform a task for me,
in return for a great reward? The recompense will be ample:
I will give him a chariot and two horses with powerful necks,   305
the best that there are beside the swift ships of the Achaeans,
to whoever dares—and he will also win glory for himself—
to go up close to their swift-travelling ships, and to find out
whether the swift ships are being guarded as before,
or whether, having now been beaten down at our hands,   310
they are thinking among themselves of flight, and, worn out
by sheer weariness, do not care to watch through the night.'

    So he spoke, and they all remained silent and still.
Now there was among the Trojans a son of the sacred herald
Eumedes called Dolon,* who was rich in gold and bronze—   315
a man of most ugly appearance, but swift-footed;

Eumedes had five daughters, and he was the only son.
This man then spoke out to the Trojans and to Hector:
'Hector, my heart and my proud spirit urge me to draw close
to the swift-travelling ships and find out about them.   320
So come, hold up the staff there, and swear to me that you
will truly give me the horses and chariot, intricately worked
with bronze, that now carry the blameless son of Peleus, and
I shall prove no useless spy for you, nor frustrate your hopes:
I shall go straight through the camp, until I reach the ship   325
of Agamemnon, where their chieftains will doubtless
be deliberating in council, whether to flee or to fight.'

So he spoke, and Hector put his hand to the staff and swore to him:
'Let Zeus himself, the deep-thundering husband of Hera, witness
that no other Trojan shall ride behind those horses except you,   330
and you, I declare, will take your delight in them for ever.'

So he uttered an oath that would come to nothing; but it made
Dolon bold. At once he slung a curved bow over his shoulders,
and over everything threw the pelt of a grey wolf, and
on his head a ferret-skin cap, and he took up a sharp spear   335
and started off from the camp for the ships; but he was not
destined to return from the ships and bring word to Hector.

He had left the mass of men and horses behind him and was
on his way, full of fierce intent, when Odysseus, sprung
from Zeus, saw him approaching, and addressed Diomedes: 340
'Look, Diomedes! Here is a man coming from their camp;
I do not know whether he means to spy on our ships,
or intends to strip the armour from one of the dead men.
Let us first allow him to pass by us on his way to the plain,
a little way, and after that we can rush out and capture him   345
quickly; and if he chances to outrun us on swift feet,
keep forcing him towards the ships, away from their camp,
darting at him with your spear, so that he cannot escape to the city.'

So they spoke, and turned off the path and lay down among
the dead men; and Dolon, in his ignorance, quickly ran past.   350
But when he was as far ahead as the width of a day's
mule-ploughing—and mules are better than oxen
at dragging the jointed plough through deep fallow land—
the pair ran after him; and he, hearing the sound, stopped still,
thinking in his heart that they were his Trojan companions   355
come to turn him back, because Hector had ordered him to return.

But when they were separated by a spear-cast or even less,
he realized that they were enemies, and quickened his limbs
into swift flight; and they quickly roused themselves in pursuit.
As when two sharp-toothed hounds, skilled in the chase,   360
press in never-relenting pursuit on a young deer or a hare,
through a wooded land, and it runs screaming before them,
so the son of Tydeus and Odysseus, sacker of cities,
in never-relenting pursuit cut Dolon off from his own people.
Now when in his flight towards the ships he was about to   365
fall in with the sentries, then indeed Athena cast fury
into Tydeus' son, so that none of the bronze-shirted Achaeans
might boast that he hit Dolon first and Diomedes was second.
Threatening him with his spear, mighty Diomedes addressed him:
'Stop there, or my spear will find you; and then I do not think   370
you will long escape sheer destruction at my hand.'
     So he spoke, and let fly the spear, but deliberately missed the man;
the point of the polished spear passed over his right shoulder
and stuck fast in the ground. Dolon stood motionless, terrified
and stammering, the teeth in his mouth chattering, and he was   375
pale with fear. The two caught up with him, panting, and
seized him by the arms, and he burst into tears and spoke:
'Take me alive, and I will ransom myself; in my house
there is bronze and gold and elaborately worked iron,
from which my father would gladly give you a boundless ransom,   380
if he learnt that I was alive by the ships of the Achaeans.'
     Then in answer Odysseus of many schemes addressed him:
'Do not despair, and do not let death cast your spirit down;
but come, tell me this, and give me an exact account:
where are you going all alone, away from your camp to the ships,   385
through the dark night, when all other mortals are asleep?
Do you mean to strip the armour from one of the dead men?
Or has Hector sent you out towards our hollow ships, to spy
on everything there? Or did your own heart impel you?'
     Then Dolon answered him, and his legs beneath him were
          trembling: 390
'Hector has greatly deluded me, driving me out of my mind,
promising to give me the single-hoofed horses of splendid
Peleus' son, and his chariot, intricately worked with bronze;
he has ordered me to go through the swift dark night
and come close to our enemies' ships, and to find out   395

whether the swift ships are being guarded as before,
or whether, having now been beaten down at our hands,
they are thinking among themselves of flight, and, worn out
by sheer weariness, do not care to watch through the night.'

At this Odysseus of many schemes smiled and addressed him: 400
'These were indeed great rewards that your heart longed for,
the horses of Aeacus' war-minded grandson; but they are
hard to master and to drive, at least for mortal men,
except for Achilles, whom an immortal mother bore. But
come, tell me this, and give me an exact account: when you   405
came here where did you leave Hector, shepherd of the people?
Where is his armour of war lying, and where are his horses?
How are the other Trojans' pickets placed, and where do they sleep?
What plans have they made among themselves—are they resolved
to stay where they are, near the ships and far from their city, or   410
will they return to the city, having now beaten down the Achaeans?'

Then in answer Dolon, son of Eumedes, addressed him:
'Very well, I will give you an exact account of all this:
Hector, in company with all those who are his advisors,
is holding a council beside the grave-mound of godlike Ilus,*   415
away from all the hubbub. As to the pickets you ask about,
hero, none has been appointed to defend or guard the camp.
At every watch-fire there are Trojan men under orders to
stay wide awake and encourage each other to keep guard;
but as for our allies, who are summoned from many lands,   420
they are asleep, and leave it to the Trojans to keep watch,
not having their children and wives lying near at hand.'

Then in answer Odysseus of many schemes addressed him:
'I see; but where are they sleeping—among the horse-breaking
Trojans, or apart from them? Tell me clearly, so that I may know.'   425

Then Dolon, the son of Eumedes, answered him:
'Very well, I will give you an exact account of all this:
by the sea are the Carians and Paeonians with their curved bows,
and the Leleges and the Caucones and the glorious Pelasgi;
the proud Mysians were assigned a place towards Thymbre, with   430
the Phrygians, fighters from horses, and the Maeonian horse-marshals.*
But why are you asking me to describe all this in detail?
If you two are raging to steal into the Trojan soldiery, over there
at the furthest point, away from the rest, are the Thracians,
newly arrived, and with them is their king Rhesus, Eïoneus' son.*   435

His horses are the finest and the biggest I have ever seen:
they are whiter than snow, and they run like the winds.
His chariot is finely decorated with gold and silver,
and he has brought with him massive armour of gold,
a wonder to look at; it is not right for mortal men   440
to wear such things, but only for the immortal gods.
But take me now to your swift-travelling ships,
or else tie me up and leave me here, tightly bound,
and you can both go and test my account, to find out
if I have spoken to you according to the truth, or not.'   445

      Mighty Diomedes looked at him darkly, and addressed him:
'I warn you, Dolon; do not put thought of escape in your heart;
your news may be good, but you have fallen into our hands,
and if we now accept a ransom or let you go free,
you will surely return some day to the Achaeans' swift ships,   450
either to spy on us or to fight us, matching strength to strength.
But if you are beaten down by my hands and lose your life,
you will never after this be an affliction to the Argives.'

      So he spoke. Dolon was about to touch his chin in entreaty
with his brawny hand, but Diomedes lunged with his sword and   455
drove it through the middle of his neck, severing both tendons;
and his head rolled in the dust while he was still speaking.
They stripped the ferret-skin cap from his head, and
his wolf's pelt and curved-back bow and long spear;
and glorious Odysseus held them aloft in his hand   460
to Athena who gathers the spoils, and spoke in prayer:
'Be glad with these, goddess; of all the immortals on Olympus
you will be the first we shall call on for help. Now help us again,
and bring us to the horses and sleeping-places of the Thracians.'

      So he spoke, and lifted the spoils high above him and   465
hung them on a tamarisk bush; above it he set a clear marker,
pulling together a bundle of reeds and sturdy tamarisk branches,
so that they should not miss it, returning through the swift dark night.
So the pair went onward through the war-gear and the black blood,
and as they went came quickly to the company of the Thracians.   470
These were sleeping, worn out by weariness, and their fine
weapons were piled neatly beside them on the ground,
in three rows; and by each man stood a pair of horses.
Rhesus was sleeping in the midst, and next to him his swift horses
were tethered with leather straps to the end of his chariot's rail.   475

Odysseus saw him first, and pointed him out to Diomedes:
'This must be the man, Diomedes, and these must be the horses
that Dolon, the man whom we have killed, told us about.
So come, and bring your strong fury into play; this is no time
to stand idle here with your weapons. Untie the horses—or   480
rather I will take care of the horses while you kill the men.'

   So he spoke, and grey-eyed Athena breathed fury into Diomedes,
and he began to kill, laying about him with his sword; and a shameful
groaning arose from the men he felled, and the ground grew red
with blood. As a lion comes upon flocks which have no herdsman,   485
either sheep or goats, and it leaps on them with havoc in its heart,
so the son of Tydeus kept at the men of Thrace, until he had killed
twelve of them. Whenever Tydeus' son stood over a man and
struck with his sword, Odysseus of many schemes would come
from behind and seize him by the foot and drag him out of
   the way—   490
with this plan in his mind, that the fine-maned horses might
pass easily through the camp and not tremble in their hearts
as they trod on dead men; for they were still unused to them.
When the son of Tydeus came upon the Thracian king,
he was the thirteenth whose sweet life he plundered as he lay   495
there gasping; for by Athena's contrivance an evil dream—
Diomedes, Oeneus' grandson—had that night stood over his head.*
Meanwhile steadfast Odysseus released the single-hoofed
horses and tied them together with thongs, and drove them
out of the camp, beating them with his bow, since he had not   500
thought to pick up the shining whip from the finely worked chariot.
Then he whistled a signal to glorious Diomedes who, however,
hung back, thinking of the most audacious thing that he could do,
either to seize the chariot where the finely worked armour lay and
drag it off by its pole, or else to lift it aloft and carry it away; 505
or whether he should rob even more Thracians of their lives.
As he was pondering this in his mind, Athena came and
stood next to him, and addressed glorious Diomedes:
'Son of great-spirited Tydeus, think now about your return to
your hollow ships; you will not want to reach them in panic flight, 510
for it may be that some other god will wake the Trojans.'

   So she spoke, and he knew he had heard a goddess' voice,
and quickly mounted; and Odysseus struck the horses with
his bow, and they flew towards the swift ships of the Achaeans.

But Apollo of the silver bow was not keeping blind watch:　　515
he could see Athena looking after the son of Tydeus, and,
enraged with her, went down among the massed soldiery of the
Trojans and roused Hippocoön, a counsellor of the Thracians
and Rhesus' excellent cousin. He started up from sleep, and
when he saw the empty place where the swift horses had stood,　　520
and the men gasping their last amidst the ghastly carnage,
he groaned aloud and called on his dear companion by name.
An enormous noise of shouting arose from the Trojans
as they flocked to the place; they were amazed at the terrible deeds
that the men had done before returning to their hollow ships.　　525

　　When the pair reached the place where they had killed Hector's spy,
Odysseus, loved by Zeus, reined in the swift horses, and
Tydeus' son leapt to the ground and placed the bloody spoils
in Odysseus' hands, and then mounted once again.
He whipped up the horses, and they flew willingly on　　530
towards the hollow ships, for their hearts were set on it.
The first to hear the hoofbeats was Nestor, and he spoke:
'My friends, chieftains and rulers of the Argives, my heart
urges me to speak; will it turn out that I am deceived or right?
The beat of swift-hoofed horses strikes on my ears;　　535
may this mean that Odysseus and mighty Diomedes are
driving single-hoofed horses here, straight from the Trojans!
But I am terribly afraid in my heart that the Argives' chieftains
have suffered some setback, and the Trojans are in full cry after them.'

　　He had not yet finished speaking when the pair arrived.　　540
They jumped down to the ground, and the others gladly
welcomed them with clasped right hands and cordial words;
and the first to question them was Nestor the Gerenian horseman:
'Come now, Odysseus of many tales, great glory of the Achaeans,
tell me how you two won these horses. Did you steal into the　　545
Trojan soldiery, or did some god meet you and give them to you?
They are amazing, and look to me like the rays of the sun.
I am always meeting Trojans in battle—I can claim that
I do not hang back by the ships, aged warrior though I am—
but I have never yet seen or clapped my eyes on such horses.　　550
No, I think some god met you and made you a present of them,
for both of you are dear to Zeus who gathers the clouds, and
to grey-eyed Athena, daughter of Zeus who wears the aegis.'

　　Then in answer Odysseus of many schemes addressed him:

'Nestor, son of Neleus, great glory of the Achaeans,   555
it would be easy for a god, if he wished it, to give us even finer
horses than these, since the gods are far stronger than we are.
No, these horses that you ask about, old man, have just come
here from Thrace. Courageous Diomedes killed their lord,
and twelve companions with him, all of them chieftains.   560
The thirteenth man was a scout we caught near the ships,
one whom Hector and the other splendid Trojans
had sent out to be a spy on us in our camp.'

    So he spoke, and drove the single-hoofed horses across the ditch,
laughing aloud, and the other Achaeans went happily with him.   565
When they reached the well-built hut of Tydeus' son
they tied the horses up with finely cut leather straps,
at the manger where Diomedes' own swift-footed
horses were standing and munching honey-sweet wheat.
And Odysseus laid the bloodstained spoils of Dolon in   570
his ship's stern, until they could make an offering to Athena.
Then they waded into the sea and began to wash off
the abundant sweat from their legs and necks and thighs.
When the waves of the sea had washed away the abundant
sweat from their skin, and their dear hearts were refreshed,   575
they stepped into polished baths and soaked themselves;
and having bathed and anointed themselves richly with oil,
the pair sat down to supper, and from the full mixing-bowl
they drew off honey-sweet wine and made an offering to Athena.

BOOK ELEVEN

Now Dawn arose from her bed beside splendid Tithonus,
to bring light to immortals and to mortals, and Zeus
dispatched Strife to the swift ships of the Achaeans—
a goddess of pain, holding in her hands a portent of war.
She stood on Odysseus' deep-bellied black ship, which was   5
in the middle of the line, so that a shout could reach both ends,
both to the hut of Ajax Telamon's son, and to Achilles' hut;
these had dragged up their balanced ships at the furthest points,
trusting in their courage and in the strength of their hands.
Standing there the goddess gave out a great, terrifying shout,   10
in a piercing voice, and cast into the heart of each Achaean
great strength to take up arms and fight without ceasing;
and at once war became a sweeter thing to them than
a return in their hollow ships to their dear native land.

   Then Atreus' son shouted to the Argives, ordering them   15
to arm; and among them he himself put on the shining bronze.
First of all he fastened greaves around his shins,
splendid ones, fitted with silver ankle-pieces;
then over his chest he put on a corslet, one that Cinyras
had once given him as a mark of guest-friendship.   20
Cinyras had heard in Cyprus the momentous news
that the Achaeans were to sail in their ships for Troy, and
for that reason sent him this gift, to find favour with the king.
On it there were ten bands of dark-blue enamel,
and twelve bands of gold and twenty of tin;   25
dark enamel snakes reached up towards the neck,
three on either side, like the rainbows that Cronus' son
imprints on a cloud as a portent for mortal men.
Around his shoulders he slung his sword; on it there were
rivets of gold, shining brightly, and the scabbard holding it   30
was silver, fitted with golden shoulder-straps.
He lifted up the body-covering shield, intricately worked
and beautiful and strong; round it ran ten bronze circles,
and on them there were twenty bosses of white tin,
and in the middle there was one of dark-blue enamel.   35
On the centre was set like a circlet a grim-faced Gorgon,

staring hideously, and about her were Terror and Panic.
From this shield hung a silver shield-strap, and on it
writhed an enamel snake with three heads that twisted
this way and that but grew from a single neck.   40
On his head he set a twin-ridged helmet with four plates
and a horsetail crest; and the plume nodded terribly above him.
He chose for himself two stout spears, tipped with bronze
and sharp, and the gleam of their bronze reached
to the high sky. Athena and Hera thundered over him,   45
to show honour to the king of Mycenae, rich in gold.

   Then each man instructed his charioteer to
rein in his horses in good order there by the ditch,
while they themselves, fully armed, streamed over on foot;
and their shouts rose unquenchable in the early morning.   50
They formed up at the ditch well before the charioteers,
who arrived soon after them. Cronus' son aroused
a dreadful uproar among them, and from the clear air
rained down drops heavy with blood, because he
intended to hurl many mighty heads down to Hades.   55

   On their side the Trojans formed up on rising ground
in the plain, around huge Hector and blameless Polydamas
and Aeneas, who was honoured by the Trojan people like a god,
and around the three sons of Antenor—Polybus, glorious Agenor,
and the unmarried Acamas, who looked like the immortals.   60
Among the front ranks Hector carried a perfectly balanced shield;
like the death-bringing star that appears rising out of the clouds,*
shining brightly, and then sinks again into the shadowing clouds,
so Hector would at one time appear among the front ranks,
and at another at the rear, urging them on. And all in bronze   65
he shone like the lightning of father Zeus who wears the aegis.

   Just like reapers who start from opposite ends of the field
of a powerful man, and drive their path through
wheat or barley, and the handfuls fall thick and fast;
so the Trojans and Achaeans surged forward and began   70
to cut each other down, and neither side thought of fatal flight;
the battle kept them head to head, and they stormed in
like wolves. Strife the bringer of groans was glad at the sight,
for she alone of the gods attended their fighting;
the other gods were not present, but were sitting   75
peacefully in their own halls, where each one's

fine palace had been built along Olympus' upland glens,
and they were all at odds with Cronus' son of the dark
clouds, because he wished to give glory to the Trojans.
But the father paid them no attention; he had slipped away   80
from the others, and was sitting alone, exulting in his glory,
looking out towards the Trojans' city and the Achaeans' ships,
at the lightning-flash of bronze, at the slayers and the slain.

As long as it was morning, and the sacred day was growing,
both side's missiles struck home, and the people kept falling;   85
but at the time when a woodcutter prepares his meal
in the mountain glens, because he has worn out his arms
with felling tall trees, and weariness comes over his spirit,
and the desire for pleasant food takes hold of his mind,
then the Danaans called out to their companions along the lines,   90
and by their courage broke through the enemy ranks. Agamemnon
was the first to charge; he killed Bienor, shepherd of the people—
first the man, and then his companion, Oïleus whipper of horses,
who had leapt down from the chariot and stood facing him,
and as he came raging on Agamemnon pierced his forehead   95
with his sharp spear. The heavy bronze helmet could not stop it,
and it passed through both it and the bone, and his brain inside
was all turned into pulp; and the man was beaten down in his rage.
Agamemnon, lord of men, left them both where they were,
their chests gleaming, for he had stripped them of their tunics,   100
and he pressed on, looking to kill and strip Isus and Antiphus,
two sons of Priam, one a bastard and one born in wedlock,
both standing in one chariot; the bastard was holding the reins,
while far-famed Antiphus stood beside him. Achilles had once
captured them on Ida's ridges as they tended their sheep and   105
bound them with pliant osiers, and set them free for a ransom;
but this time Atreus' son, wide-ruling Agamemnon, hit Isus
on the chest with his spear, above the nipple, and struck Antiphus
with his sword beside the ear, and threw him from the chariot.
He hastened to strip the pair of them of their fine armour,   110
recognizing them, for he had seen them before by the swift ships,
when swift-footed Achilles had brought them down from Ida.
As a lion easily crushes the bones of a swift hind's
young fawns, when it has come upon their lair and seized
them in its mighty teeth, and rips out their tender hearts;   115
and the mother, even if she chances to be nearby, cannot

help them, because fearful trembling overcomes her limbs,
and at once she darts away through dense thickets and woodland,
in a sweating fervour to escape the powerful beast's attack;
so not one of the Trojans could keep death from these two,   120
but were themselves driven in panic before the Argives.

Next he caught Peisander and Hippolochus, steadfast in battle,
the sons of war-minded Antimachus, who more than anyone
had taken the gold of Alexander, a splendid gift, and would
never allow Helen to be returned to fair-haired Menelaus;   125
it was his two sons that lord Agamemnon caught, both in
one chariot, and both were trying to hold the swift horses,
but the shining reins had fallen from their hands, and
their horses were in confusion; Atreus' son rose like a
lion before them, and from the chariot they entreated him: 130
'Take us alive, Atreus' son, and you will receive a worthy ransom:
many treasures lie stored in the house of Antimachus,
bronze and gold and elaborately worked iron, from which
our father would gladly give you a boundless ransom,
if he learnt that we were alive by the ships of the Achaeans.'   135

So these two, weeping, addressed the king with
soft words, but they received a hard answer:
'If you are truly the sons of war-minded Antimachus,
he who once in the Trojans' assembly advised that Menelaus,
who had come on an embassy with godlike Odysseus,* should be   140
killed there and then and not be allowed back to the Achaeans,
then now you will surely pay for your father's ugly act.'

So he spoke, and with a spear-cast to his chest knocked Peisander
out of his chariot, and he lay flat on his back on the earth.
Hippolochus leapt down, but Agamemnon killed him on the
    ground,   145
slicing his arms away and cutting off his head with his sword,
and sending the trunk rolling like a log away through the soldiery.
He left them there, and sped on to where the fighting in the ranks
was thickest, and with him went other well-greaved Achaeans.
Foot-soldiers killed foot-soldiers, and charioteers slew charioteers,   150
slashing at them with the bronze and driving them into flight;
and on the plain a dust-cloud rose under the chariots, kicked up
by the horses' thundering hoofs. Lord Agamemnon kept up
the pursuit, killing all the time and urging the Argives forward.
As when destructive fire falls on a forest full of dry wood,   155

and a swirling wind carries it everywhere, and bushes are
uprooted and topple down, driven by the fire's onrush;
so the routed Trojans kept falling before Agamemnon,
son of Atreus, and many strong-necked horses
rattled their empty chariots along the battle-lines of war,   160
missing their blameless charioteers, who were now lying
on the earth, far more appealing to vultures than to their wives.

   Now Zeus withdrew Hector from the dust and flying weapons,
from the slaughter of men and the blood and the uproar,
and Atreus' son pressed on, shouting urgently to the Danaans.   165
The Trojans kept pouring back, past the burial-mound of old Ilus,*
son of Dardanus, across the mid-plain and past the wild fig tree,*
straining to reach the city; and Atreus' son kept up his pursuit,
screaming, and his irresistible hands were spattered with gore.
When the Trojans reached the Scaean gates and the oak tree,*   170
there they halted and stood, waiting for one another;
many were still fleeing in panic over the mid-plain, like cattle
stampeded by a lion that has come on them in the dead of night;
the rest have scattered, and one alone faces sheer death, and
first the lion seizes the neck in its powerful jaws and breaks it,   175
and then greedily gulps down its blood and all its entrails.
So lord Agamemnon, son of Atreus, pursued the Trojans,
all the time killing the hindmost; and they fled in panic.
Many men fell from their chariots, head-first or on to their backs,
at the hands of Atreus' son, such was the driving fury of his spear.   180
But when he was about to pull up below the city and its steep wall
then indeed the father of gods and men came down
from the high sky and took his seat on the peaks of Ida of
many springs; and he was holding a thunderbolt in his hands.
Quickly he sent Iris of the golden wings away with a message: 185
'Away now, swift Iris, and give this message to Hector:
as long as he can see Agamemnon, shepherd of the people,
rampaging among the front-fighters and killing the ranks of men,
so long let him hold back, but order the rest of the people
to keep grappling with the enemy in the fierce crush of battle.   190
But when Agamemnon is struck by a spear or hit by an arrow
and leaps back into his chariot, then I will promise him the strength
to kill, right up to when he reaches their well-benched ships,
and the sun goes down and sacred darkness comes on.'

   So he spoke, and wind-footed swift Iris did not disobey him,   195

but flew down from the heights of Ida to sacred Troy,
and she found glorious Hector, son of wise Priam,
standing behind his horses in his close-jointed chariot.
Swift-footed Iris stood next to him and addressed him:
'Hector, son of Priam, the equal of Zeus in scheming,   200
father Zeus has sent me to bring you this message:
as long as you can see Agamemnon, shepherd of the people,
rampaging among the front-fighters and killing the ranks of men,
so long hold back from the fighting, but order the rest of the people
to keep grappling with the enemy in the fierce crush of battle.   205
But when Agamemnon is struck by a spear or hit by an arrow and
leaps back into his chariot, then Zeus will promise you the strength
to kill, right up to when you reach their well-benched ships,
and the sun goes down and sacred darkness comes on.'

So swift-footed Iris spoke, and left him, and Hector   210
leapt, fully armoured, from his chariot to the ground, and
hefting his sharp spears he ranged through the whole army,
urging the men to fight and rousing them for the grim conflict.
They rallied, and took their stand facing the Achaeans,
while the Argives on their side strengthened their companies.   215
So the battle-order was set, and they stood facing each other, and
Agamemnon was the first to leap out, eager to fight in front of all.

Tell me now, Muses, who have your homes on Olympus,
who was the first to come out and oppose Agamemnon,
whether of the Trojans themselves or of their far-famed allies.   220

It was Iphidamas, the son of Antenor, a valiant and mighty man,
who was raised in rich-soiled Thrace, mother of flocks;
his mother's father raised him in his house when he was a
little child—Cisses, who fathered Theano of the lovely cheeks.
When he reached the time of manhood, when men long for glory,   225
Cisses tried to keep him there, and offered him his daughter's hand;
but straight after his marriage he left the bridal room, hearing news
of the Achaeans' coming, and went to Troy with an escort of
twelve curved ships. He had left these balanced ships at Percote,
and had continued on his journey on foot to Ilium, by himself.   230
He it was who then came out to face Atreus' son Agamemnon.
When they had advanced to within close range of each other,
Atreus' son threw and missed, and his spear was deflected,
and Iphidamas stabbed him on the belt, below his corslet,
putting his weight behind the blow and trusting in his brawny hand;   235

but he could not pierce the gleaming belt, and long before that
happened his point met the silver and was bent back like lead.
Wide-ruling Agamemnon grasped the spear with his hand
and pulled it towards himself, raging like a lion, wrenching it
from Iphidamas' hand, and struck him in the neck with his sword   240
and loosened his limbs. There he fell, and slept the sleep of bronze,
pitiable man, helping his countrymen and far from his wedded wife,
his bride, from whom he had no joy, though he had given much:*
first he gave a hundred cattle, and promised a thousand more,
goats and sheep mixed, from the countless flocks he owned.   245
And now Agamemnon, son of Atreus, stripped him of his gear,
and went back with the fine armour through the Achaean soldiery.

     When Coön saw him—Coön, a man distinguished among men,
who was the eldest son of Antenor—a powerful grief
for the death of his brother covered his eyes. He came up   250
unnoticed with his spear at glorious Agamemnon's side and
stabbed him on the middle of his forearm, below the elbow,
and the point of the shining spear passed clean through.
At this Agamemnon, lord of men, shuddered,
but even so he did not give up the battle and the fighting,   255
but sprang at Coön with his wind-hardened spear. At this
Coön, raging, seized the foot of his brother, his father's son,
and began to drag him away, calling out to all the leading men;
but as he dragged him through the mass, Agamemnon stabbed him below
his bossed shield with a bronze-tipped spear, and loosened his limbs,   260
and coming up to him cut his head off, over the dead Iphidamas.
So there Antenor's sons filled up the measure of their lives at the hands
of the king, Atreus's son, and went down into the house of Hades.

     Now the son of Atreus, so long as the blood welled up warm
from his wound, went up and down the Trojan ranks,   265
attacking them with spear and sword and great stones;
but when the wound began to dry, and the blood stopped flowing,
then sharp pains began to assail the fury of Atreus' son.
As when a sharp spasm seizes a woman in labour, a piercing
pang, sent by the Eilythyiae, goddesses of painful birth,   270
bringers of bitter suffering and daughters of Hera,
so sharp pains began to assail the fury of Atreus' son.
He leapt up into his chariot, and ordered the charioteer
to drive towards the hollow ships, for his heart was in anguish.
He called out in a penetrating voice, shouting to the Danaans: 275

'My friends, chieftains and rulers of the Argives,
now it is your task to keep the wearisome conflict away
from our sea-traversing ships, since Zeus the counsellor
has not allowed me to fight all day against the Trojans.'

So he spoke, and his charioteer whipped the fine-maned horses   280
towards the hollow ships, and they flew willingly on;
their chests were covered in foam and spattered beneath with dust,
as they carried the wounded king away from the battle.

When Hector saw that Agamemnon was falling back,
he called to the Trojans and Lycians with a far-carrying shout: 285
'Trojans and Lycians, and Dardanian hand-to-hand fighters,
be men, my friends, and call up your surging courage!
Their best man has gone, and Cronus' son Zeus has given me
great glory. Now drive your single-hoofed horses straight
at the mighty Danaans, and so win even greater glory!'   290

So he spoke, and quickened the fury and spirit in each man.
As when a huntsman sets on his white-toothed hounds
in pursuit of some boar in the wilds, or a lion,
so Hector, Priam's son, the equal of Ares, doom of mortals,
set the great-spirited Trojans on in pursuit of the Achaeans.   295
He himself strode with high confidence among the front-fighters,
and rushed into the fighting like a violent squall that sweeps
down and churns the violet-coloured sea into swelling motion.

Who then was the first, and who the last, to be killed
by Hector, Priam's son, when Zeus had granted him glory?   300
They were Asaeus first, and Autonous and Opites,
Dolops, son of Clytius, and Opheltius and Agelaus,
Aesymnus and Orus and Hipponous, steadfast in battle.
These were leaders of the Danaans, and after them he killed
a mass of men. As when the West Wind pounds clouds that are   305
blown up by the clearing South Wind, beating them with its
violent blast, and the waves swell hugely and roll onward,
and the spray is scattered by the veering wind's assault;
so the people were beaten down in their multitudes by Hector.

Then dreadful deeds, impossible to bear, would have been done,   310
and indeed the Achaeans would have fled and fallen by their ships,
had not Odysseus called out to Diomedes, son of Tydeus:
'Tydeus' son, what has made us forget our surging courage?
Come here, my friend, and stand by me; we will surely be
blamed if Hector of the glittering helmet captures the ships.'   315

Then in answer mighty Diomedes addressed him:
'Certainly I will stay and hold off their attack; but our relief
will be short-lived, since it is clear that Zeus the cloud-gatherer
wishes to give victory to the Trojans and not to us.'
So he spoke, and toppled Thymbraeus from his chariot to the
    ground,   320
hitting him with a spear on the left nipple; and Odysseus
felled godlike Molion, who was lord Thymbraeus' attendant.
They left them there, having put an end to their fighting,
and rushed into the soldiery, spreading confusion, as when
two boars fall with fearless intent on a pack of hunting hounds;   325
like them they turned and charged, killing Trojans, and the Achaeans
were glad to catch their breath as they fled before glorious Hector.
Next they took a chariot with two men, chieftains of their people,
the two sons of Merops from Percote, who above all men
was skilled in seercraft; he had tried to prevent his sons   330
from going to man-destroying war, but they would not listen
to him, for the spectres of black death were leading them on.
It was these whom Diomedes, the spear-famed son of Tydeus,
robbed of their life and breath, and took away their glorious arms.
And Odysseus slew and stripped Hippodamus and Hypeirochus.   335
Then the son of Cronus, looking down from Ida, pulled the conflict
taut, making it on equal terms; and both sides kept killing one another.
Tydeus' son hit and wounded Agastrophus, the hero son of Paeon,
on the hip-joint with his spear. His chariot and team were not at hand
for him to escape—he was mightily deluded in his mind,   340
for his attendant was holding them some way apart, while he
stormed through the front-fighters on foot, until he lost his dear life.
Hector was quick to see this along the ranks, and ran at them
screaming, and with him went companies of the Trojans.
Seeing Hector, Diomedes, master of the war-cry, shuddered,   345
and at once addressed Odysseus, who was close by:
'Look, here is a great affliction rolling in on us—towering Hector;
come, let us stand firm, wait for him and then drive him off.'
So he spoke, and poising his long-shadowing spear threw it,
aiming at the head, and he did not miss, and hit Hector on   350
his helmet's crest; but bronze rebounded from bronze, and
did not reach the handsome flesh, stopped by the vizored
three-layered helmet which Phoebus Apollo had given him.
At once Hector ran a long way back, joining the soldiery, then

dropped to his knees and paused, propping himself on the ground　355
with his brawny hand; and dark night covered his eyes.
But while the son of Tydeus was following his spear-cast
far through the front-fighters to where it had fallen on the earth,
Hector recovered his breath, and leaping into his chariot
drove off into the mass of men, and avoided the black death-spectre.　360
Mighty Diomedes darted after him with his spear, and addressed him:
'Dog, this time you have escaped death again, though disaster
came very near you. Once again Phoebus Apollo has saved you,
the god you doubtless pray to when you enter the thudding of spears.
Be sure that I shall make an end of you when I next meet you,　365
if I too can discover a god somewhere to come to my aid.
But now I shall go after the rest, and hope to overtake them.'
　　So he spoke, and began to strip the arms of Paeon's spear-famed son.
But Alexander, the husband of lovely-haired Helen,
aimed his bow at the son of Tydeus, shepherd of the people,　370
leaning against a pillar of the grave-mound that men had
made for Ilus, Dardanus' son, elder of the people in time past.
Diomedes was stripping the bright-shining corslet from
mighty Agastrophus' chest, and the shield from his shoulders
and his strong helmet, when Paris pulled against his bow's grip　375
and shot; and the arrow did not fly vainly from his hand,
but hit the flat part of Diomedes' right foot, and the arrow
went clean through and stuck in the earth. Paris laughed happily
and leapt from his hiding-place and spoke, boasting:
'You are hit, and my arrow did not fly in vain! How I wish　380
I had hit you in the base of your belly and taken your life away,
for then the Trojans would have had some relief from their misery,
they who shudder at you as bleating goats before a lion.'
　　Then mighty Diomedes answered him, in no way alarmed:
'You archer*——braggart, hair-curled dandy, ogler of girls!　385
If you were to face me in a trial of strength, in full armour,
you would get no help from your bow and your showers of arrows;
and now you have but scratched the flat of my foot, and yet you boast.
I am no more troubled than if a woman or a careless child had hit me,
for the arrow of a cowardly, worthless man is a feeble thing.　390
Quite different is the sharp spear that I throw, which takes
a man's life there and then, even if it only grazes him;
his wife tears her cheeks in grief, his children are made orphans,
and he reddens the ground with his blood and rots away,

and there are more vultures gathered round him than women.'   395
    So he spoke, and Odysseus the renowned spearman came near
and stood in front of him. Diomedes sat behind him, and pulled
the sharp arrow from his foot, and a painful spasm ran through his flesh.
He leapt up into his chariot, and ordered the charioteer
to drive towards the hollow ships, for his heart was in anguish.   400
    Odysseus, the renowned spearman, was left on his own, and not one
of the Argives stayed with him, for fear had gripped them all.
Deeply troubled, he spoke to his great-hearted spirit:
'What is to become of me now? A great disgrace if I flee,
in fear of their massed men; but even worse to be captured   405
alone, for Cronus' son has put the rest of the Danaans to flight.
But why does my dear heart debate with me in this way?
I know well that those who run from the battle are cowards,
while those who fight bravely in war must take their stand
unyieldingly, either to kill others or be killed themselves.'   410
    While he was considering this in his mind and in his heart,
the ranks of shield-bearing Trojans came up on him, and penned
him in their midst—but they brought suffering on themselves.
As when hounds and strong young men close eagerly
in on a boar, and it breaks out of a dense coppice,   415
whetting its white fangs in its crooked jaws, and they
rush to surround it; the noise of gnashing teeth rises up, but
they bravely stand their ground before it, terrible though it is;
so the Trojans closed around Odysseus, dear to Zeus.
And first he wounded blameless Deïopites on the shoulder,   420
leaping forward and aiming high with his sharp spear,
and after them he cut down Thoön and Ennomus.
Next, when Chersidamas had jumped down from his chariot,
he stabbed him with his spear in the groin, under his bossed
shield; he fell in the dust, clawing the earth with his hand.   425
Odysseus left them there, and with his spear wounded
Charops, Hippasus' son, full brother of wealthy Socus.
Socus, a man like a god, ran up to protect him, and
standing very close to him addressed Odysseus:
'Odysseus of many tales, insatiate of trickery and toil,   430
today you will either boast over two sons of Hippasus,
when you have killed two fine men and stripped their armour,
or else you will lose your own life, struck down by my spear.'
    So speaking he lunged at Odysseus' perfectly balanced shield,

and the massive spear passed through the shining shield,   435
and forced its way through his intricately worked corslet,
and tore the flesh right away from his flank; but Pallas Athena
did not allow it to drive through into the hero's guts.
Odysseus realized that the spear had not hit a fatal place,
and giving ground he addressed Socus: 'Miserable man,   440
now sheer destruction is surely catching up with you!
You have indeed stopped me doing battle with the Trojans,
but I tell you here and now that death and its black spectre
will be with you on this day, when beaten down by my spear you give
the glory to me and your shade to Hades, master of famous horses.'   445

   So he spoke, and Socus turned and began to run away, but
as he twisted round Odysseus planted his spear in his back,
between the shoulders, and he drove the point through his chest,
and Socus fell with a thud. Glorious Odysseus boasted over him:
'Socus, son of war-minded Hippasus, breaker of horses,   450
the end of death has come to you before you could escape it.
Luckless man, neither your father nor your revered mother
will close your eyes in death, but flesh-eating vultures
will tear at you, flapping their fast-beating wings about you.
But if I die, the glorious Achaeans will bury me with due rites.'   455

   So he spoke, and began to pull war-minded Socus' massive
spear out from his flesh and from his bossed shield. As he
wrenched it out the blood spurted up, and his heart was distressed.
When the great-spirited Trojans saw Odysseus' blood,
they called to each other down the ranks and made for him   460
all together; and he gave ground, and shouted to his companions.
Three times he shouted in a voice as large as a man's head can hold,
and three times Menelaus, dear to Ares, heard his cry,
and quickly spoke to Ajax, who was standing nearby:
'Ajax, son of Telamon, sprung from Zeus, ruler of the people,   465
I can hear the shouts of stout-hearted Odysseus ringing round me,
and they sound as if the Trojans have cut him off in the harsh
conflict; they have isolated him and are pressing him hard.
Come, let us go through the soldiery; rescue is the best course.
I am afraid that left alone like this something may happen to him,   470
brave though he is; and that will be a great loss to the Danaans.'

   So he spoke and led the way, and the other, a godlike man, followed,
and they found Odysseus, dear to Zeus; and around him
the Trojans were swarming like blood-red mountain jackals

around a stricken horned stag that a man has shot with an   475
arrow from his bowstring. The stag evades him on swift
feet, as long as its blood is warm and its knees can lift it;
but when the swift arrow overcomes it the flesh-eating
jackals tear it apart on the mountains, in a dark wood;
and then some divine power leads a lion there, a ravening   480
beast, and the jackals scatter in fright, and the lion eats the stag.
So the Trojans, many and courageous, crowded round
war-minded Odysseus of the cunning wiles, but the hero
kept the pitiless day from himself, lunging at them with his spear.
Then Ajax drew near, carrying his shield that was like a tower, and 485
stood by him, and the Trojans scattered in fright, this way and that;
and then warlike Menelaus took him by the hand and led him away
from the mass of fighters, while his attendant drove up his chariot.
     Next, Ajax sprang at the Trojans and killed Doryclus,
a bastard son of Priam, and after that wounded Pandocus,   490
and also wounded Lysandrus and Pyrasus and Pylartes.
As when a brimming river in winter spate, swollen by rain
from Zeus, sweeps down from the mountains to the plain,
and carries along with it dead oaks and pines in abundance,
and flings a mass of driftwood out into the sea,   495
so then glorious Ajax drove them in confusion over the plain,
cutting down both horses and men. As yet Hector knew
nothing of this, since he was fighting on the battle's far left,
by the banks of the river Scamander, where men's heads
were falling thickest, and an unquenchable clamour was rising   500
around huge Nestor and around warlike Idomeneus.
Among these Hector was fighting, causing terrible havoc
with spear and chariot-skill, crushing the ranks of young fighters.
But even so the glorious Achaeans would not have given ground,
had not Alexander, husband of Helen of the lovely hair,   505
checked the great deeds of Machaon, shepherd of the people,
hitting him with a three-barbed arrow on his right shoulder.
At this the Achaeans, breathing fury, were greatly afraid that
as the battle shifted towards the Trojans he might be captured.
At once Idomeneus addressed glorious Nestor: 510
'Nestor, son of Neleus, great glory of the Achaeans,
come, mount your chariot and let Machaon mount beside you,
and drive your single-hoofed horses with all speed to the ships;
a healer who has the skill to cut out arrows and apply

soothing ointments is worth a great number of other men.'   515
So he spoke, and Nestor the Gerenian horseman did not disobey him;
straightaway he mounted his own chariot, and Machaon,
son of the blameless healer Asclepius, got up beside him.
He lashed the horses, and they flew eagerly onward
towards the hollow ships, for that is where they wished to be.   520

Now Cebriones, standing beside Hector in his chariot,
saw that the Trojans were in confusion, and addressed him:
'Hector, while we two are engaged with the Danaans here
on the furthest flank of war and its hideous clamour, the rest
of the Trojans are in wild confusion, both horses and men.   525
It is Telamon's son Ajax who is causing the rout; I know him well,
from the broad shield he wears across his shoulders. Let us too
direct our horses and chariot straight there, where especially
men in chariots and on foot are clashing in fierce strife,
killing each other, and an unquenchable clamour goes up.'   530

So he spoke, and lashed the fine-maned horses with his
loud whip; and they, hearing the whip's crack, carried the
swift chariot at speed in among the Trojans and Achaeans,
trampling dead men and shields alike. The axle beneath it and
the rails round the platform were splashed all over with the blood 535
that was thrown up in showers by the horses' hoofs and
by the wheel-tyres. Hector was impatient to enter the mass
of men, to leap in and break through them; he caused
dreadful confusion among the Danaans, and gave his spear
little rest. Up and down the ranks of the fighters he went,   540
doing battle with spear and sword and huge stones,
but kept away from engaging with Ajax, son of Telamon,
[for Zeus was angry with him when he fought with a better man.]*

But now father Zeus, seated on high, aroused terror in Ajax: he stood
dumbfounded, and slung his shield of seven oxhides behind him,   545
and looking keenly around him like a wild beast, turned in flight
towards his own men, moving slowly step by step and many times
wheeling round. As when country people and their dogs drive
a tawny lion away from the yard where they keep their cattle,
and keeping watch all night will not allow it to take   550
a fat beast from among the cattle; it is desperate for meat,
and keeps coming at them, but without success, for spears
and burning bundles of sticks fly thick from bold hands
against it, and terrify it for all its impatience,

and at daybreak it goes away, grieved at heart. So then   555
Ajax withdrew before the Trojans, grieved at heart, with
deep reluctance; for he was greatly afraid for the Achaeans' ships.
As when a stubborn donkey, passing a cornfield, defies the boys
driving it, and though many sticks have been broken on its sides
it goes into the field and causes havoc in its deep crop, and   560
the boys beat it with sticks, but their strength is weak, and they
drive it out with difficulty, only when it has had its fill of food;
so then the high-hearted Trojans and their allies, assembled
from many lands, kept attacking great Ajax, Telamon's son,
thrusting at the centre of his shield with their polished spears.   565
At one time Ajax would recollect his surging courage and
wheel round, keeping the companies of horse-breaking
Trojans at bay, and then again he would turn in flight.
So he prevented them all from marching on the swift ships,
standing alone in battle-fury on the ground between Trojans   570
and Achaeans. Spears were flung at him from bold hands;
some, as they flew towards him, stuck in his great shield,
and many, before they could reach his white body, came
to rest in the ground between, yearning to taste his flesh.

     When Eurypylus, the splendid son of Euaemon, saw that   575
Ajax was being overwhelmed by dense showers of missiles,
he went and stood beside him and let fly with his shining spear,
and hit Apisaon, son of Phausius, shepherd of the people,
in the liver below his midriff, and quickly loosened his knees.
He leapt forward, and began to strip the armour from his shoulders;   580
but when Alexander, who looked like a god, saw Eurypylus
stripping the armour from Apisaon, he immediately drew
his bow against him, and hit him with an arrow in his
right thigh; and the shaft broke, and weighed his leg down.
At once he withdrew into his companions' band, avoiding the   585
death-spectre, and with a piercing cry shouted to the Danaans:
'My friends, chieftains and rulers of the Argives,
rally now and make a stand, and keep the pitiless day away
from Ajax, who is overwhelmed by missiles, and I do not think
he will escape war's hideous clamour. Come now, stand fast   590
around huge Ajax, son of Telamon, and confront the enemy!'

     So the wounded Eurypylus spoke, and they stood close
beside him, leaning their shields against their shoulders
and levelling their spears before them; Ajax came to meet them,

and turned and stood when he had reached his companions' band. 595
    So they fought on in the likeness of blazing fire.
Meanwhile Neleus' mares, sweating, were carrying Nestor
out of the battle, and with him Machaon, shepherd of the people.
Glorious swift-footed Achilles was aware of this and saw him;
he was standing on the stern of his deep-bellied ship, 600
watching the grim toil of war and the miserable rout.
At once he addressed his companion Patroclus, calling
to him from the ship, and Patroclus heard from the hut
and came out, looking like Ares; and this was to be the start
of his downfall. Menoetius' stalwart son spoke first: 605
'Why do you call me, Achilles? What need have you of me?'
Then in answer swift-footed Achilles addressed him:
'Glorious son of Menoetius, delight of my heart,
now I think that the Achaeans will gather about my knees
and entreat me, for an intolerable need has come upon them. 610
But go now, Patroclus, dear to Zeus, and ask Nestor
who this is that he is bringing wounded from the battle.
From behind he looks in every way like Machaon,
the son of Asclepius; but I did not see the man's eyes,
since the horses passed me by as they bolted onward.' 615
    So he spoke, and Patroclus obeyed his dear companion,
and set off at a run for the huts and ships of the Achaeans.
    When the others reached the hut of Nestor, Neleus' son,
they got down from their chariot on to the earth that nourishes many,
and Eurymedon his attendant unyoked the old man's horses 620
from the chariot. The two then dried the sweat from their shirts,
standing in the wind beside the seashore, and then
went into the hut and took their seats on the chairs there.
Hecamede of the lovely hair prepared a brew for them, the girl
whom the old man had won at Tenedos when Achilles sacked it,* 625
and she was the daughter of great-hearted Arsinous; the Achaeans
had picked her out for him because he was the best of all in counsel.
First she pushed up a table before them, a beautiful
thing, well-polished and with dark-enamel feet, and on it
set a bronze bowl with an onion, as a side-dish for the drink, 630
and yellow honey and beside it bread made of sacred barley, and
next to these a very beautiful cup,* which the old man had brought
from his home; it was studded with golden rivets, and had
four handles; on each handle were two golden doves, feeding,

one on either side; and underneath it rested on two feet.*   635
Other men would find it hard to raise the cup from the table
when it was full, but the old man Nestor could lift it easily.
In this cup the woman who looked like a goddess made them
a brew of Pramnian wine, grating goat's cheese into it
with a bronze grater, and sprinkling white barley on top;   640
and when she had prepared the brew she invited them to drink.
When they had drunk and driven away their parching thirst
and were engaging each other in pleasant conversation,
Patroclus, a man like a god, appeared standing at the door.
When the old man saw him he jumped up from his shining chair,   645
took him by the hand, led him in, and told him to be seated.
But Patroclus refused, staying where he was, and addressed him:
'No chair for me, Zeus-nurtured old man, nor will you persuade me;
he is easily offended and quick to anger, the man who sent me
to find out who the wounded man is that you are bringing back—
          but I   650
know him myself, for I recognize Machaon, shepherd of the people.
So now I shall go back on my errand and report to Achilles;
you know well, Zeus-nurtured old man, how terrifying a man
he is, likely to find fault even with one who is blameless.'

Then in answer Nestor the Gerenian horseman addressed him: 655
'Why is Achilles now so touched with pity for the Achaeans' sons,
all those who have been wounded by spears? He knows nothing
of the great grief that has arisen in the camp, now that the best men
are lying in their ships, wounded by thrown and stabbing weapons.
Mighty Diomedes, son of Tydeus, has been wounded by a spear,   660
while spear-famed Odysseus and Agamemnon have been stabbed;
Eurypylus has been shot in the thigh by an arrow,
and just now I brought this other man out of the battle,
pierced by an arrow from the bowstring. Yet the brave Achilles
cares nothing for the Danaans, and feels no pity for them.   665
Is he waiting until our swift ships burn with destructive fire
on the seashore, despite all the efforts of the Argives,
and until we are killed one after another—since my strength
is no longer as it used to be when my limbs were supple?
I wish I was as young and healthy,* and my strength as secure,   670
as I was when a dispute arose between us and the Eleians*
over the matter of a cattle raid, and I killed Itymoneus,
the fine son of Hypeirochus, whose home was in Elis.* I was

driving off his herds in reprisal, and while he was defending
his cattle in the front-fighters a spear from my hand struck him,   675
and he fell dead, and his rustic people fled in panic.
We drove off a huge amount of booty from the plain:
fifty herds of oxen, and as many flocks of sheep, as many
herds of swine, and as many wandering flocks of goats,
and one hundred and fifty head of chestnut horses,   680
all mares, many of them with their suckling foals.
All these we drove into Pylos, city of Neleus, into the city
by night; and Neleus was delighted in his heart, because
such success had come my way as a young man going to war.
When dawn appeared heralds proclaimed in a clear voice   685
that all who had a debt owing in bright Elis should come forward;
and those who were chieftains of the Pylians rounded up and
shared out the booty, for the Epeians owed a debt to many,
since we in Pylos had become enfeebled and few in number:
in the years before this Heracles, that violent being, had attacked   690
and weakened us, and all our best men had been killed.
We sons of blameless Neleus had been twelve in all, but
of these I alone was left, and all the others had perished.
As a result of this the bronze-shirted Epeians grew arrogant, and
in their reckless machinations committed acts of violence
      against us.   695
Out of the booty aged Neleus chose a herd of cattle and a great flock
of sheep, selecting three hundred, and their shepherds with them,
because he had a huge debt owing to him in bright Elis:
four prize-winning horses, together with their chariot, had been
on their way to the games, intending to race for the prize   700
of a tripod; but Augeias,* lord of men, had kept them in his house
and had sent the charioteer away, grieving for his horses.
The old man was enraged at these words and deeds, and so chose
for himself a huge amount of booty. The rest he gave to the people
to share out, so that no one to his knowledge should leave without   705
a fair share. So we were busy with all this, and making offerings
to the gods around the city, and on the third day the Epeians
arrived all together, many men and single-hoofed horses
in great haste, and with them the two Moliones in armour,
still boys, with no experience yet of surging courage.   710
Now there is a city called Thryoessa, set on a steep hill,
far off beside the Alpheus, on the borders of sandy Pylos,

and to this the Epeians laid siege, raging to destroy it utterly.
But when they had scoured the whole plain, Athena came to us
by night, in haste from Olympus, telling us to arm ourselves,   715
and she assembled an army in Pylos—men by no means unwilling,
but eagerly impatient to go to war. Now Neleus would not
allow me to wear armour, and he hid my horses from me,
because he said that I knew nothing as yet of war's work.
But all the same I surpassed even our own chariot-fighters,   720
though I was on foot; such was the way Athena framed the battle.
There is a river called Minyeïus* that empties into the sea
near Arene,* and there we Pylian chariot-fighters waited for
the bright dawn, and the foot-soldiers' bands came streaming up.
Hastily we armed ourselves in our gear, and set out and   725
came at midday to the sacred waters of Alpheus.
There we sacrificed fine victims to all-powerful Zeus,
and a bull to Alpheus, and a bull to Poseidon,
but to grey-eyed Athena a cow from the herd; and
then we took our supper in ranks throughout the camp,   730
and lay down to sleep, each man in his armour,
by the banks of the river. Now the great-spirited Epeians
were camped around the city, raging to destroy it utterly,
but before they could, Ares' mighty handiwork was revealed
to them: when the sun rose bright above the earth we prayed   735
to Zeus and to Athena and joined together in battle.
When the conflict between Pylians and Epeians began, I was
the first to kill a man, and I seized his single-hoofed horses—
he was Mulius the spearman, the son-in-law of Augeias,
whose eldest daughter he had married, fair-haired Agamede,   740
and she knew all the drugs that the wide earth nourishes.
As he charged at me I hit him with my bronze-tipped spear,
and he fell in the dust; then I leapt into his chariot and took
my place among the front-fighters. The great-spirited Epeians
fled in panic this way and that when they saw the leader   745
of their chariot-fighters fall, a man who excelled in battle.
But I sprang at them in the likeness of a black tempest,
and I captured fifty chariots, and in each of them two men
fastened their teeth on the earth, beaten down by my spear.
And indeed I would have cut down the two Moliones, the sons of   750
Actor, had not their father, the wide-ruling earthshaker, carried
them safe from the battle, covering them with a dense mist.*

So there Zeus granted a great victory to the Pylians,
for we went after them over the wide rolling plain,
killing the men and gathering up their fine armour, 755
until we brought our chariots to Buprasium, rich in wheat,
and to the Olenian rock and the place that is called the hill
of Alesium;* and there Athena turned our people back.
There I killed my last man and left him there, and the Achaeans
drove their swift horses back from Buprasium to Pylos, 760
and all praised Zeus among gods and Neleus among men.
Such a man I was among men—if I ever was. But Achilles is
the only one who will benefit from his valour—though I think
he will weep much when it is too late and the people have died.
My dear friend, I will tell you the advice that Menoetius gave you 765
on the day that he sent you from Phthia to join Agamemnon;
we two were in the house, I and glorious Odysseus,
and we easily heard all the advice he gave you in his halls.
We had come to the well-appointed palace of Peleus while we
were assembling an army throughout Achaea that nourishes many. 770
And we found the hero Menoetius there in the house, and you,
and with you Achilles. The aged horse-driver Peleus was burning
an ox's fat-wrapped thigh-bones for Zeus who delights in the thunder,
in an enclosed space of his court; he was holding a golden cup,
and pouring gleaming wine over the burning offerings. 775
You two were occupied with the ox-meat, when we appeared,
standing in the doorway; Achilles jumped up, amazed,
and taking us by the hand led us in and invited us to sit,
and put before us the food that is right for strangers to receive.
When we had satisfied our desire for food and drink, 780
I spoke first, saying that both of you should come with us.
You readily agreed, and your fathers both gave you much advice:
the old man Peleus exhorted his son Achilles
always to be the best, and to stand out above others;
but this was the advice that Actor's son Menoetius gave you: 785
"My son, Achilles is more distinguished than you in birth,
but you are the older. He is far stronger than you, but it is
for you to speak shrewdly to him, and give him advice
and guidance; and he will obey you, to his benefit."
So the old man advised you, but you have forgotten. Even now 790
you could speak like this to war-minded Achilles, and you might
win him over; who knows if you might with a god's help arouse

his spirit by persuasion? A friend's persuasion is a good thing.
But if in his heart he is trying to avoid some divine revelation,
and his revered mother has brought him a message from Zeus,   795
let him at least send you out, and the rest of the Myrmidon people
with you, and perhaps you will prove to be the Danaans' saving light.
Let him give you his fine armour to wear into battle, and
perhaps the Trojans will mistake you for him and hold back
from the battle, and the Achaeans' warlike sons will breathe again,   800
worn down though they are; there is little breathing-space in war.
Being unwearied, you might easily drive men who are exhausted
in the battle's uproar back to the city from the ships and huts.'

   So he spoke, and roused the spirit in the other's breast, and
he set off running past the ships towards Achilles, grandson   805
of Aeacus. But when as he ran Patroclus reached the ships
of glorious Odysseus, where they held their assembly and
public tribunal, and where they had built altars to the gods,
there he was met by Eurypylus, son of Euaemon,
a man sprung from Zeus, limping out of the battle,   810
wounded in the thigh by an arrow. Sweat was streaming
from his shoulders and head, and from his painful wound
black blood was oozing; but even so his mind was unshaken.
Seeing this the stalwart son of Menoetius took pity on him,
and, groaning, he addressed him with winged words: 815
'Oh you poor wretches, leaders and rulers of the Danaans—
so after all it seems you will glut the swift dogs in Troy
with your white fat, far from your friends and native land!
But come, tell me, hero Eurypylus, sprung from Zeus,
is there any way that the Achaeans can restrain huge Hector,   820
or are they now to perish, beaten down by his spear?'

   Then in turn the wounded Eurypylus addressed him:
'Patroclus, sprung from Zeus, there can be no more defence
for the Achaeans; they will fall beside their black ships.
All those who were before the best men among us now   825
lie in their ships, wounded by thrown or stabbing weapons
at the Trojans' hands, whose strength is always increasing.
But come, help me, and take me to my black ship;
cut the arrow from my thigh and wash away the dark blood
with warm water, and spread soothing ointments over it—   830
those excellent medicines that they say you learnt from Achilles,
who was taught by Cheiron, most just of the Centaurs.*

We do have healers, Podaleirius and Machaon, but I think
that one of them is lying in his hut nursing a wound,
himself in need of a blameless healer, while the other   835
is out on the plain, facing the Trojans and ferocious Ares.'
    Then in turn the stalwart son of Menoetius addressed him:
'How can these things be? What are we to do, hero Eurypylus?
I am on my way to deliver to war-minded Achilles the words
that Gerenian Nestor, protector of the Achaeans, spoke;   840
but even so I shall not abandon you, exhausted as you are.'
    So he spoke, and gripping the people's shepherd round the waist
he led him to his hut. An attendant saw them and spread oxhides
on the ground, and there Patroclus laid him down and with a knife
cut the sharp, piercing arrow out of his thigh, and with
    warm water   845
washed the dark blood away. Then with his hands he crushed a bitter
root, a killer of pain, and applied it, and wholly relieved his agony;
and the wound began to dry, and the blood stopped flowing.

BOOK TWELVE

So Menoetius' stalwart son attended to the wounded Eurypylus
in the huts. Meanwhile the Argives and Trojans fought on
in massed conflict, and it seemed that the Danaans' ditch
would no longer hold out, nor the wide wall behind it.
They had built this to shelter their ships, and had driven the ditch   5
alongside it, to protect their swift ships and the vast booty
within its bounds; but they had not offered splendid hecatombs
to the gods, and it was built without the immortal gods'
sanction, and therefore did not remain standing for long.
As long as Hector lived, and Achilles kept his anger alive,   10
and the city of Priam the king remained unsacked,
so long the great wall of the Achaeans also endured;
but when all the best men of the Trojans were dead, and
many of the Argives had been killed, though some were left,
and in the tenth year the city of Priam had been sacked, and   15
the Argives had sailed in their ships to their dear native land,
then indeed Poseidon and Apollo devised a plan to
sweep the wall away, channelling the fury of rivers on to it,
all those that flow from the mountain range of Ida to the sea:
Rhesus and Heptaporus and Caresus and Rhodius,   20
Granicus and Aesepus, and bright Scamander and Simoeis,*
where many oxhide shields and helmets and a generation
of the half-divine had fallen in the dust. Phoebus Apollo
diverted all these rivers' mouths to disgorge in the same place,
and for nine days he flung their waters at the wall; and Zeus rained   25
without ceasing, to sweep the wall more rapidly out to sea.
The earthshaker, holding his trident in his hands, himself
took the lead, and carried away on his waves all the footings
of logs and rocks which the Achaeans had laboured to lay,
and levelled the beach beside the strong-flowing Hellespont;   30
and when he had swept the wall away he covered the great shore
again with sand, and diverted the rivers back to stream in
the channels where their lovely-flowing water had run before.*

This is what Poseidon and Apollo would do in the future;
but now war and its clamour were blazing around the   35
well-built wall, and the timbers of its towers reverberated

as missiles struck it. The Argives, subdued by Zeus' lash,
were penned in and confined next to their hollow ships,
terrified by Hector, the ruthless deviser of panic rout.
He, as before, was fighting in the likeness of a whirlwind;   40
as when a boar or a lion is surrounded by hounds
and huntsmen and twists about, exulting in its strength,
while they form themselves into a close-knit wall
and confront it, and hurl their spears thick and fast
from their hands; but its superb heart is not daunted   45
or driven away in fear, and it is its courage that kills it;
again and again it wheels about, testing the ranks of men,
and wherever it charges the ranks of men retreat.
So Hector went wheeling about among the soldiery,
urging his companions to cross the ditch; but not even   50
his swift-footed horses would attempt it for him, but stood
whinnying loudly at its very edge: the wide ditch
terrified them, and it was not easy to jump or to
cross, since its banks along the whole length
were overhanging, and at the top it was planted   55
with great sharp stakes set close together, fixed there
by the sons of the Achaeans as a defence against the enemy.
No horse drawing a well-wheeled chariot could easily
get over it, and so the Trojans were thinking to try on foot.
Then Polydamas stood next to daring Hector, and spoke: 60
'Hector, and all you leaders of Trojans and allies,
it is madness to try driving our swift horses over the ditch.
It is extremely hard to cross; there are sharp stakes set
upright in it, and behind them is the Achaeans' wall.
And there is no room for chariot-fighters to dismount there   65
and fight; it is a narrow place, and I think we shall come to grief.
If high-thundering Zeus in his hatred for them means to
destroy them utterly, and is intent on helping the Trojans,
I for my part would wish this to happen here and now, that
the Achaeans should die here far from Argos, their names
        forgotten;   70
but if they should rally and make a counter-attack from the ships,
and we become encumbered in the ditch that they have dug,
I do not think that even one man would then get back
to the city with the news, once the Achaeans have turned
to face us. So come, let us all do what I propose: 75

let our attendants hold the horses back by the ditch,
and let us arm ourselves in our gear as foot-soldiers
and all accompany Hector in a body; the Achaeans will not
resist us, if indeed they are caught fast in the snares of death.'

So Polydamas spoke, and his prudent advice pleased Hector,   80
and at once he leapt, fully armed, from his chariot to the ground.
Nor did the other Trojans stay massed together in their chariots,
but when they saw glorious Hector they all jumped down.
Each man then instructed his own charioteer
to hold his horses in good order, there by the ditch,   85
while they separated and formed themselves up, and,
marshalled into five sections, marched off behind their leaders.

Those who went forward with Hector and blameless Polydamas
were the best and the most numerous, raging beyond the rest
to break through the wall and fight by the hollow ships;   90
Cebriones made a third with these—Hector had left behind
another man, weaker than Cebriones, with his chariot.
Paris led the second company, with Alcathous and Agenor;
Helenus and godlike Deïphobus, two sons of Priam,
were in charge of the third, and with them went the hero Asius—   95
Asius, son of Hyrtacus, whom huge gleaming horses
had brought from Arisbe, which is near the river Selleïs.*
The fourth company was led by the valiant son of Anchises,
Aeneas, and with him were the two sons of Antenor,
Archelochus and Acamas, well skilled in all battle's arts.   100
The commander of the far-famed allies was Sarpedon, and
he chose Glaucus and warlike Asteropaeus to go with him,
for they seemed to him to be without doubt the best of
all men, after himself; but he stood out above everyone.
When they had formed up, oxhide shields overlapping,   105
they eagerly made straight for the Danaans, thinking that no one
could now resist them, and that they would fall on the black ships.

The rest of the Trojans and their far-famed allies
followed the advice given by excellent Polydamas;
but Asius, son of Hyrtacus, captain of men, was unwilling   110
to leave his horses there with his attendant charioteer,
and drove up close to the swift ships, chariot and all,
fool that he was; he would not escape death's evil spectres
and make his way back from the ships to windswept Troy,
taking delight in his horses and his chariot. Before   115

he could, his accursed destiny overwhelmed him, in the
spear of Idomeneus, the splendid son of Deucalion.*
Asius charged towards the left of the ships, where the Achaeans
were returning with their horses and chariots from the plain;
here he drove his horses and chariot across, and at the gates   120
he did not find the doors shut, nor the long crossbar in place,
since men were keeping them wide open, hoping to save
any of their companions fleeing from the battle to the ships.
Asius aimed straight with his chariot for this point, and his men
followed with shrill screams, thinking that the Achaeans   125
could resist no longer, but would fall beside their black ships—
fools, for in the gateway they found two of the best fighters,
the high-hearted sons of Lapith spear-fighters;
one was mighty Polypoetes, the son of Peirithous, and
the other was Leonteus, the equal of Ares, doom of mortals.   130
Now these two took their stand in front of the high gateway,
looking like high-crested oak trees on the mountains
that day after day stand up to wind and rain,
securely fixed there by their great long roots;
so these two, trusting in the strength of their hands,   135
stood up to the charge of huge Asius, and did not take flight.
The Trojans, with a mighty shout, made straight for
the well-built wall, holding up their shields of dried oxhide,
grouped around lord Asius and Iamenus and Orestes,
Adamas, the son of Asius, and Thoön and Oenomaus.   140
For a time the Lapiths remained behind the wall, trying to
rouse the well-greaved Achaeans to fight in the ships' defence;
but when they saw that the Trojans were making a rush at
the wall, while the Danaans gave rise to shouting and panic,
they charged out and began to fight in front of the gateway,   145
looking like two wild boars on the mountains that confront
a noisy rabble of men and dogs coming at them; with
slanting forays they smash the underbrush about them,
ripping it up by the roots, and the noise of their clashing teeth
rises up, until some man with a spear-cast robs them of their lives.   150
So the shining bronze clashed on these two men's chests,
battered by enemy missiles, so fiercely did they fight,
trusting in the men above them and in their own strength.
Those above kept hurling stones from the well-built
towers, in defence of themselves and their huts and their   155

swift-travelling ships; and these fell to the ground like flakes of
snow that a fierce blizzard, driving the dark clouds onwards,
heaps up in drifts on the earth that nourishes many;
just so the missiles streamed from the hands of Achaeans
and Trojans alike, and helmets and bossed shields   160
rang harshly, as rocks huge as millstones struck them.
Then indeed Asius, son of Hyrtacus, groaned aloud,
and striking both thighs spoke out in impotent rage:
'Father Zeus, so you too have turned out to be a complete
and utter liar! I did not think that the Achaean heroes   165
would withstand our fury and our irresistible hands;
but they are like flickering-bodied wasps or bees
that have made their habitation by a rocky road, and
will not abandon their hollow house, but face the men
who are tracking them, and fight to defend their children.   170
Just so these men, though they are only two, will not
fall back from the gates until they kill or are killed.'
    So he spoke, but his speech did not persuade the mind of Zeus,
whose heart wished rather to give the glory to Hector.
    Now other men were fighting about other gates, but it would   175
be hard for me to describe this in full, as if I were a god:
everywhere around the wall of stone there arose awesome
fire, and the Argives, for all their exhaustion, were compelled
to keep fighting for their ships; and all the gods who supported
the Danaans in battle were grieved in their hearts.   180
    But at this point the two Lapiths rushed into the war and
conflict, and the son of Peirithous, mighty Polypoetes,
hit Damasus with his spear, through his bronze-cheeked helmet;
the brazen helmet could not keep it out, and the bronze
point passed clean through and smashed the bone, and his brain   185
inside was all turned to pulp; so he crushed the man in his
frenzied charge, and after this he killed Pylon and Ormenus.
Leonteus, a shoot of Ares, hit Hippomachus, son of
Antilochus, with a spear-cast that went through his belt.
Next he drew his sharp sword from its scabbard and   190
darting through the soldiery first struck down Antiphates
from close quarters, who sprawled on his back on the ground.
Then he brought down Menon and Iamenus and Orestes,
all of them, one after another, on to the earth that nourishes many.
    While they were stripping the shining armour from these men,   195

the young men who accompanied Hector and Polydamas,
who were the best and most numerous warriors, and were raging
more than the rest to break through the wall and set the ships ablaze,
were still standing along the ditch, uncertain what they should do;
for though they were raging to cross it a bird-omen had appeared   200
to them, an eagle, skirting the army and flying high from right to left,
and carrying in its talons the portent of a blood-red snake,
still alive and struggling; this had not forgotten its battle-lust,
but, twisting backwards, bit its captor on the breast beside
its neck, and the bird, smarting with the pain, let it fall   205
to the earth, dropping it in the midst of the soldiery,
and with a scream flew away on the gusts of the wind.
The Trojans shuddered when they saw the writhing snake
lying among them, a sign from Zeus who wears the aegis.
Then indeed Polydamas stood beside bold Hector and spoke: 210
'Hector, it seems you are always rebuking me in assemblies,
though I give you good advice; it is of course not fitting
for one of the people to speak out against you, in council
or in war, but we must always promote your authority.
Now, however, I shall speak publicly as seems to me best.   215
Let us not press on to fight against the Danaans over their ships;
I will tell you how I think it will end, if indeed it was for
the Trojans that this omen came as they raged to cross the ditch—
an eagle, skirting the host and flying high from right to left,
and carrying in its talons the portent of a blood-red snake,   220
still alive; and then it let it fall before reaching its dear home,
and did not succeed in carrying it off to give to its children.
So we, even if with our mighty strength we break down the
Achaeans' gates and wall, and the Achaeans give ground,
we shall not return from the ships by the same way in good order,   225
since we shall leave many Trojans behind, whom the Achaeans,
as they defend their ships, will cut down with the bronze.
This is how a prophet would interpret this sign, one whom the people
trusted, and who had sure knowledge of portents in his heart.'
    Then Hector of the glittering helmet looked at him darkly,
        and said: 230
'Polydamas, what you advise does not now please me; you know
that you could have thought of some better speech than this.
But if you are serious in giving this public advice,
then the gods themselves must have destroyed your wits.

You say I should forget the plans of loud-thundering Zeus,   235
the promises that he gave me, and his confirming nod, and
you presume to tell me to put my trust in long-winged birds,
for which I have not the slightest regard or concern,
whether they fly to the right, towards the dawn and the sun,
or fly to the left, and towards the murky darkness.   240
No, let us put our trust in the plans of great Zeus,
who holds sway over all mortals and immortals. There is
one omen that is best of all—to fight for one's fatherland.
Why should you be so afraid of war and conflict?
Even if all the rest of us are killed beside the ships   245
of the Argives, you need have no fear of dying,
since your heart is not the kind to fight or to face the enemy.
However, if you do hold back from the slaughter, or persuade
some other man with your words to turn from the conflict,
you will instantly lose your life, struck down by my spear.'   250
     So he spoke, and led them on, and the others followed him
with an astonishing clamour; and Zeus who delights in the
thunder raised a storm-wind from the mountains of Ida
which blew dust straight against the ships, bewildering the
Achaeans' minds but giving glory to the Trojans and Hector.   255
Trusting in signs from Zeus and in their own strength, they
kept trying to breach the great wall of the Achaeans, striving to
tear out the towers' abutments and to pull down its battlements,
and to lever out the jutting buttresses that the Achaeans
had first sunk in the ground to be supports for the towers.   260
By uprooting these they hoped to breach the Achaeans' wall,
but the Danaans would not give way; closing the gaps in
the battlements with oxhide shields they kept throwing missiles
from behind them at the enemy as they advanced up to the wall.
     The two called Ajax were ranging everywhere on the towers,   265
all the time giving orders and stirring up the Achaeans' fury,
addressing one man with soft words, and rebuking another with
hard ones, if they saw anyone holding far back from fighting:
'Argive friends—exceptional warriors, or mediocre ones,
or those who are weaker, since men are by no means   270
all equal in war—now there is work for everyone to do.
But of course you know this for yourselves; let no one turn
back to the ships now that you have heard the call for battle,
but press forward and encourage one another, in the hope

that Olympian Zeus who sends the lightning will grant us to   275
fend off the enemy's assault and drive them back to the city.'

So they, with cheering shouts, roused the Achaeans for battle.
As the flakes of snow that fall thick and fast
on a day in winter, when Zeus the counsellor begins
to send the snow, revealing his shafts to men—   280
he lulls the winds, and keeps the snow falling until
he has covered high mountain peaks and jutting crags,
the fields of clover and the rich tillage of men,
and it settles thickly on the grey sea's bays and beaches,
and melts on the waves as they break on the shore; everything   285
is blanketed from above, when Zeus' heavy snowstorm falls—
so from both sides the stones flew thick and fast,
hurled both at the Trojans and by them at the Achaeans,
without ceasing; and over the whole wall the din rose up.

Even so the Trojans and illustrious Hector would never   290
have broken through the wall's gates and their long crossbar,
had not Zeus the counsellor roused his own son Sarpedon
against the Argives, like a lion against crook-horned cattle.
At once he held before him his perfectly balanced shield,
a fine work of beaten bronze, which a bronze-smith had   295
hammered out, and had stitched inside many layers of hide,
attached with golden fastenings all the way around its rim.
Holding this before him, and poising his two spears,
Sarpedon set out like a mountain-nurtured lion that has been
a long time without meat, and its noble spirit drives it on to   300
attack a strongly built farmyard and go after the sheep there;
and even if it finds herdsmen in that very place,
keeping watch over their flocks with dogs and spears,
it refuses to be driven from the sheepfold before attacking it,
and either pounces on a sheep and drags it away, or is itself   305
struck down in its onslaught by a spear from a quick hand.
So now godlike Sarpedon's spirit impelled him to
make a rush at the wall and break through its battlements.
At once he addressed Glaucus, son of Hippolochus:
'Glaucus, why are we two especially honoured in Lycia   310
with the best seats and cuts of meat, and ever-full wine-cups,
and all men look on us as if we were gods; and we
enjoy a huge estate, cut out beside Xanthus' banks,
fine land, of orchards and wheat-bearing ploughland?

That is why we must now take our stand in the first rank   315
of the Lycians, and confront the scorching heat of battle,
so that among the close-armoured Lycians men may say:
"Certainly those who rule us in Lycia are not without glory,
these kings of ours, who eat fattened sheep and drink
choice honey-sweet wine. There is also noble valour in them,   320
it seems, because they fight in the first ranks of the Lycians."
My dear friend, if we two could escape from this war
and were certain to live for ever, ageless and immortal,
I would not myself fight in the first ranks, nor
would I send you into the battle where men win glory;   325
but now, since, come what may, death's spectres stand over us
in their thousands, which no mortal can flee from or escape,
let us go forward, and give the glory to another man, or he to us.'

So he spoke, and Glaucus did not turn away, or disobey him,
and they strode straight ahead, leading a great company of Lycians.   330
When Menestheus, son of Peteus, saw them he shuddered,
for they were making for his tower, bringing destruction with them.
He peered along the Achaeans' tower, in the hope of seeing one
of the leaders, who might keep ruin away from his companions;
and he saw the pair called Ajax, insatiate of war, standing there,   335
and also Teucer, who had recently come up from his hut,
next to them. But he could not shout loud enough to be heard,
so great was the noise and the clamour that reached the high sky
as blows rained on shields and horsehair-crested helmets,
and on the gates; these had all been shut, and the Trojans   340
were standing at them, trying to shatter them and force a way in.
At once Menestheus dispatched the herald Thoötes to Ajax:
'Go, glorious Thoötes, run to Ajax and summon him—
or rather both the Ajaxes, for that would be the best course by far,
since sheer destruction will soon be done here,   345
so heavily do the Lycian leaders press us, they who before
have showed themselves formidable in the fierce crush of battle.
But if toil and fighting are springing up about them there as well,
at least let Ajax, the stalwart son of Telamon, come alone,
and let Teucer, a man skilled in archery, come with him.'   350

So he spoke, and the herald heard and did not disobey him,
but set off at a run along the wall of the bronze-shirted Achaeans,
and came and stood by the two called Ajax, and at once addressed them:
'You two named Ajax, leaders of the bronze-shirted Argives;

the dear son of Peteus, who was sprung from Zeus, directs you   355
to go to him, to face the toil of battle, if only for a short time—
better both of you, for that would be the best course by far,
since sheer destruction will soon be done there,
so heavily do the Lycian leaders press them, they who before
have showed themselves formidable in the fierce crush of battle;   360
but if toil and fighting are springing up about you here as well,
at least let Ajax, the brave son of Telamon, come alone,
and let Teucer, a man skilled in archery, come with him.'

So he spoke, and huge Ajax, Telamon's son, did not disobey him,
but at once addressed the son of Oïleus with winged words: 365
'Ajax, you and mighty Lycomedes stand here together, both of you,
and urge the Danaans to fight as strongly as they can;
I shall go over there and meet the enemy's attack, face to face,
and will quickly return once I have come to their rescue.'

So Ajax, the son of Telamon, spoke, and went on his way,   370
and Teucer, his brother by the same father, went with him,
and along with them Pandion carried Teucer's curved bow.
They went along inside the wall, and came to the tower
of great-spirited Menestheus, and found men hard pressed,
since the powerful leaders and commanders of the Lycians   375
were climbing up the ramparts like a black tempest; and so
they crashed together in battle, and the clamour rose up.

Ajax, the son of Telamon, was the first to kill a man,
great-spirited Epicles, one of Sarpedon's companions,
hitting him with a huge jagged rock which was lying   380
inside the wall on top of a heap, next to the ramparts. No man
among mortals who live now, even one in the prime of youth,
could easily lift it with both hands; but Ajax heaved it high
and flung it, and shattered his four-plated helmet, smashing all
the bones inside to pieces. Epicles plunged from the high tower   385
like an acrobat, and the breath abandoned his bones.
Then, as Glaucus, Hippolochus' mighty son, rushed forward
at the high wall, Teucer hit him with an arrow at the point where
he saw that his arm was exposed, and put an end to his battle-lust.
He sprang back from the wall, unobtrusively, so that no Achaean   390
should see that he was wounded and shout boastfully over him.
Grief rose in Sarpedon as soon as he realized that Glaucus
had left the fighting, but he did not forget his battle-lust;
he struck at Alcmaon, Thestor's son, with his spear and stabbed him,

and wrenched the spear out; Alcmaon followed it and fell forward, 395
and his armour, intricately worked with bronze, clattered about him.
Sarpedon seized the battlement with his massive hands
and pulled, and it fell away in one piece, and the wall
above was laid bare; and so he made a path for many men.

    Then Ajax and Teucer set upon him together; Teucer hit him 400
with an arrow on the shining belt that held his man-protecting
shield across his chest, but Zeus kept the death-spectres from
his son, unwilling for him be beaten down at the ships' sterns.
Then Ajax leapt at him and stabbed at his shield, but the spear
did not pass right through, though it flung back his frenzied
        attack.   405
Sarpedon gave ground a little way from the rampart, but did not
fall back completely, since his heart was hoping to win glory.
Wheeling round he called out to the godlike Lycians:
'Lycians, why abandon your surging courage
in this way? It is hard for me, powerful as I am, to   410
break through on my own and make a path to the ships.
Forward! The more men, the quicker the work is done!'

    So he spoke, and they trembled at their lord's loud rebuke,
and pressed on all the harder around their king, the counsellor.
On the other side the Argives strengthened their ranks   415
behind the wall, for an enormous task appeared before them:
the powerful Lycians were not able to break through
the Danaans' wall and make themselves a path to the ships,
but neither could the Danaan spearmen ever drive back
the Lycians from the wall when once they had reached it.   420
Like two men who are in dispute over boundary-stones,
on common ploughland, holding measuring-rods in their hands,
and quarrelling over the fair division of a narrow patch of earth,
so the battlements separated these men; and over them both sides
kept hewing at the oxhide shields held before the others' chests, 425
shields both round and made from stretched, fringed hides.
The flesh of many men was gashed by the pitiless bronze,
both when fighters exposed their backs as they turned,
and when they were stabbed clean through the shield itself.
Everywhere the towers and battlements were spattered   430
with the blood of men from both sides, Trojan and Achaean.
But for all that the Trojans could not put the Achaeans to flight;
they held out, just as when an honest wool-working woman holds

her scales, lifting up the wool and weight together and
balancing them, to earn some mean pittance for her children;   435
so the battle and the conflict was pulled taut on equal terms,
until the moment when Zeus gave the greater glory to Hector,
Priam's son, who was the first to leap inside the Achaeans' wall.
With a far-carrying shout he called out to the Trojans:
'Up with you, Trojan breakers of horses! Break down   440
the Argive wall, and hurl awesome fire on to their ships.'

  So he spoke, driving them on, and every ear caught his voice,
and they made straight for the wall in a body; then, gripping
their sharpened spears, they began to scale the abutments.
Hector had seized and was carrying a boulder that was lying   445
in front of the gates, broad at its base but pointed above;
not even the two best men in any city, among mortals
who live now, could easily lever it from the ground
on to a wagon, but he lifted it easily, even on his own;
the son of crooked-scheming Cronus made it light for him.   450
As when a shepherd easily carries the fleece of a ram
in one hand, and its weight sits but lightly on him,
so Hector picked up the boulder and made straight
for the planks that made up the tall double gates,
close-fitted and strong; two bars held them on the inside,   455
crossing over from each side, and one bolt kept them shut.
He came up and stood close, and putting his weight behind it
and with legs planted well apart, to give the rock extra force,
he flung it at the gate's middle and smashed it out of both pivots;
the rock's weight carried it inside, and the gates groaned loudly,   460
and the crossbars could not hold, and the planks were shattered
in all directions under the stone's impact. Illustrious Hector
sprang in, his face like swift night, shining in the terrible
bronze armour that he wore on his body, gripping two spears
in his hands. No one but a god could have faced and held
     him back   465
when he leapt inside the gates; and his eyes blazed with fire.
Whirling round towards the soldiery he called to the Trojans
to climb over the wall, and they obeyed his command;
at once some scaled the wall, while others streamed in through
the well-made gate itself. The Danaans scattered in panic   470
among their hollow ships, and the clamour rose unceasing.

BOOK THIRTEEN

N ow when Zeus had brought the Trojans and Hector to the ships,
he left the fighters beside them to endure toil and misery
without ceasing, while he himself turned his shining eyes away,
looking far off to the land of the horse-breeding Thracians, and
the Mysians, hand-to-hand fighters, and the splendid Hippemolgi,   5
drinkers of mares' milk, and the Abii, most upright of men.*
But towards Troy he did not turn his shining eyes at all,
since he did not expect in his heart that any immortal
would come to the help of either Trojans or Danaans.

But the lord earthshaker was not keeping blind watch: 10
he was sitting, gazing with awe at the war and strife,
high on the topmost peak of wooded Samothrace,*
from where the whole of Ida's mountain could be seen,
and the city of Priam and the ships of the Achaeans.
He had gone up there from the sea, and sat pitying the Achaeans,   15
beaten down by the Trojans; and he was mightily angry with Zeus.

Straightaway he came down from the rugged mountain,
striding on swift feet; and the high mountains and woods
trembled under the immortal feet of Poseidon as he came.
Three strides he made, and with the fourth reached his goal—   20
Aegae,* where his famous palace is built in the depths
of the sea, golden and gleaming, imperishable for ever.
There he went, and yoked his bronze-hoofed horses to his chariot,
swift-flying horses, their manes flowing with gold,
and armed himself in gold, and picked up his whip,   25
golden and finely made, and mounted the chariot and drove off
over the waves. Everywhere sea-monsters rose from their lairs
and sported as he came, for they recognized their lord,
and the sea was split apart in joy. The horses flew lightly on,
and the bronze axle beneath the chariot was not wetted;   30
and the springing horses carried him to the Achaean ships.

There is a wide cavern at the bottom of the deep sea,*
halfway between Tenedos and rugged Imbros, and
there Poseidon the earthshaker reined in his horses and
unyoked them, and threw immortal fodder before them,   35
for them to eat; around their hoofs he fastened golden tethers,

that could not be slipped or broken, so that they would wait there
securely for their lord's return. Then he made for the Achaean camp.
   Now the Trojans were following Hector, Priam's son, in a mass,
like flame or a storm-wind, raging without cease and   40
shouting and yelling loudly, hoping to capture the ships
of the Achaeans, and to kill all their best men beside them.
But Poseidon, the shaker and encircler of the earth,
rose from the depths of the salt sea and urged on the Argives,
taking the shape and tireless voice of Calchas. First he addressed   45
the two called Ajax, who were themselves raging to fight:
'You two named Ajax, it is for you now to save the Achaean
people, turning your minds to courage and not to chilling panic.
Elsewhere I do not fear the invincible hands of the Trojans—
they have climbed over our great wall in their masses,   50
but the well-greaved Achaeans will hold them all in check—
yet here I am terrified that we shall suffer some grim disaster,
here where that madman is leading them like a flame—
Hector, who boasts that he is the son of all-powerful Zeus.
May some god plant it in the minds of you both to stand   55
resolutely here yourselves, and urge others to do the same, and
then you might drive him back from the swift-travelling ships
despite his onslaught, even if the Olympian himself drives him on.'
   So the shaker and encircler of the earth spoke, and struck
both men with his rod and filled them with mighty fury,   60
and made their limbs quick, both their legs and their arms above.
Then, like a swift-winged hawk that springs up in flight
and hovers high up close to a beetling rock-face, and
then swoops to chase some other bird across the plain,
so Poseidon the earthshaker shot swiftly away from them.   65
Ajax, Oïleus' swift son, was the first to recognize the god,
and at once addressed Ajax, the son of Telamon:
'Ajax, this is one of the gods who live on Olympus, taking
the form of the seer and telling us to fight beside the ships;
it was certainly not Calchas, prophet and observer of birds;   70
I easily knew him from behind by the signs of his feet and
legs as he left—gods are recognizable, though they are gods.
And for my part, my own heart in my dear breast
now rouses me all the more to fight and do battle, and
my legs beneath and my hands above are raging to begin.'   75
   Then in answer Ajax, son of Telamon, addressed him:

'So too my invincible hands are raging as I grip my spear,
and fury rises up in me, and I am swept along by my legs
beneath me. Hector, Priam's son, may rage without ceasing,
but I am full of fervour to fight him, even all alone.'   80

While they spoke one to another in this way, delighting in
the battle-joy which the god had thrust into their heart,
the earth-encircler roused the Achaeans behind them
who were trying to refresh their spirits beside the swift ships.
Their limbs were slackened by cruel weariness, and   85
grief filled their hearts when they saw the Trojans,
who had climbed over the high wall in great numbers;
as they looked at them their eyes began to shed tears, since
they did not think they would escape disaster; but the earthshaker
moved easily among them and urged on the strong companies.   90
First he came to Teucer and roused him, and Leïtus
and the hero Peneleos, and Thoas and Deïpyrus,
Meriones and Antilochus, raisers of the battle-cry.
Urging these men on he addressed them in winged words:
'Shame, Argives, young fighters! It is in you that   95
I had trusted to keep our ships safe by your fighting;
if you are now holding back from war's misery, the day
has surely dawned for us to be beaten down by the Trojans.
This is indeed a great marvel for my eyes to see,
a terrible thing, which I never thought would come to pass: 100
the Trojans advancing on our ships, those men who before
were like frightened does, that are the food of jackals
and leopards and wolves in the woods, aimlessly
wandering without spirit, and there is no battle-joy in them.
So the Trojans before now were unwilling to stand and face   105
the hands and fury of the Achaeans, even for a little while;
but now they are fighting by our hollow ships, far from their city,
because of our leader's bungling and the people's negligence,
who are at loggerheads with him and have no desire to defend
their swift ships; and now they are being killed beside them. 110
If it really is the whole truth that the cause of this
is the hero son of Atreus, wide-ruling Agamemnon,
because he did not honour the swift-footed son of Peleus,
still there is no cause at all for us to hold back from the war.
No, let us quickly heal ourselves; good men's minds can be healed. 115
It is not good for you to give up your surging courage now,

you who are the best men in the camp. I myself would not
pick a fight with a man who held back from the battle
if he was a sorry creature, but with you I am angry in my heart.
My friends, your heedlessness will surely soon make this   120
calamity worse; come, set shame and men's censure in your hearts,
every one of you. A great conflict has arisen: you can see that
powerful Hector, master of the war-cry, has broken down the gates
and their long crossbar, and is fighting beside our ships.'

So the earth-encircler called to the Achaeans and urged them on.   125
Around the two called Ajax powerful companies took their stand,
men whom Ares would not treat with scorn if he met them, nor
would Athena, who drives the people on; the pick of their
best men were ready to face the Trojans and glorious Hector,
spear on spear fencing them in, and shield overlapping shield.   130
Shield pressed on shield, helmet on helmet, man on man,
and the horsehair crests on their bright helmet-plates touched
as they moved their heads, so close to each other did they stand.
Spears shaken by bold hands formed an interwoven mass,
and they faced straight ahead, raging to join the battle.   135

Now the Trojans charged in a body, and Hector led them,
raging straight ahead, like a boulder rolling down a cliff
that a river in winter flood has dislodged from its peak,
loosening the ruthless rock's footing with its huge flood;
it bounds high, flying onward, and the woods crash beneath it,   140
but still it keeps running on, uncurbed, until it reaches
the level plain and stops rolling, for all its eager haste.
Just so Hector threatened for a while to pass with ease
through the huts and ships of the Achaeans as far as the sea,
killing as he went; but when he met the close-packed companies   145
he came to a stop, right up against them; and the Achaeans' sons
facing him lunged with their swords and double-edged spears,
and drove him back, and he was sent reeling and gave ground.
Then he shouted to the Trojans in a far-carrying voice:
'Trojans and Lycians and Dardanian hand-to-hand fighters,   150
stand by me! The Achaeans will not fend me off for long, even
though they have ranged themselves in close order like a wall.
No, I think they will give way before my spear, if indeed it was
the chief of the gods who drove me on, Hera's loud-thundering husband.'

So he spoke, and quickened the fury and spirit in each man.   155
And among them Deïphobus, Priam's son, came striding on,

in high confidence, holding his perfectly balanced shield before him,
stepping lightly and advancing foot by foot under the shield's cover.
Meriones aimed at him with his shining spear, and did not
miss; he hit him on his perfectly balanced shield, which was   160
made of oxhide, but did not pierce it, for long before it could
the long spear snapped at its socket. Deïphobus held
the oxhide shield away from him, fearing in his heart
the spear of war-minded Meriones; but that hero turned
back into the mass of his companions, bitterly angry   165
at losing his victory and the spear that he had broken.
He set off for the huts and ships of the Achaeans, meaning
to fetch the long spear which he had left behind in his hut.

    The rest fought on furiously, and an unquenchable clamour arose.
Teucer, son of Telamon, was the first to kill a man,   170
the spearman Imbrius, son of Mentor rich in horses;
he used to live in Pedaeon* before the sons of the Achaeans came,
and had as wife Medesicaste, a bastard daughter of Priam;
but when the well-balanced ships of the Danaans came
he went back to Ilium, and excelled among the Trojans, and   175
lived with Priam, who honoured him like his own children.
This was the man Telamon's son stabbed with his long spear,
below the ear; he wrenched the spear out, and Imbrius toppled
like an ash tree that is felled by the bronze on a far-seen
mountain peak and brings its tender leaves down to the ground.   180
So Imbrius fell, and his intricate bronze-work armour rang about him.
Teucer sprang forward, in a rage to strip the armour from him,
and as he sprang Hector let fly his shining spear at him; but
Teucer was looking ahead, and avoided the bronze-tipped spear
by just a little, and Hector hit Amphimachus, son of Cteatus,   185
who was Actor's son, in the chest with the spear as he returned
to the battle; he fell with a thud, and his armour clattered about him.
Hector leapt forward to tear from the head of great-hearted
Amphimachus the helmet which fitted close to his temples;
Ajax thrust at him with his shining spear as he came on,   190
but no part of his body was exposed, for he was completely
covered in terrifying bronze. Ajax pierced the shield's boss,
and using his huge strength forced him back; Hector retreated
behind the two bodies, and the Achaeans dragged them away.
Glorious Stichius and Menestheus, captains of the Athenians,   195
carried Amphimachus back to the Achaean people, while the pair

called Ajax, raging with surging courage, seized Imbrius.
As two lions that have seized a goat from sharp-toothed
dogs and carry it away through dense undergrowth,
holding it in their jaws high above the earth,   200
so the two commanders called Ajax held Imbrius aloft
and stripped the armour from him. Oïleus' son, angry at
Amphimachus' death, cut the head from Imbrius' delicate neck,
and with a swing of his arm flung it like a ball through the soldiery;
and it came to rest in the dust in front of Hector's feet.   205

    Then indeed Poseidon was angry in his heart, because
Amphimachus,* his grandson, had fallen in the grim conflict,
and he set off along the huts and ships of the Achaeans,
to urge the Danaans on; and he was devising misery for the Trojans.
He was met by Idomeneus, famed with the spear, on his way   210
from tending a companion who had just retired from the fighting
and had been wounded by the sharp bronze behind his knee.
His companions had carried him back, and Idomeneus had given
the healers orders and was going to his hut, for he was still raging
to face the fighting, when the lord earthshaker addressed him,   215
likening his voice to that of Thoas, son of Andraemon,
who was ruler over the Aetolians in all Pleuron and in
steep Calydon,* and was honoured by the people like a god:
'Idomeneus, counsellor of the Cretans, where now are the threats
that the sons of the Achaeans used to utter against the Trojans?'   220

    Then in answer Idomeneus, leader of the Cretans, spoke to him:
'Thoas, there is no one man who is to blame now, at least
as far as I know; we are all skilled in the craft of warfare,
and no one has lost heart, gripped by fear, or has given way
to cowardice and is holding back from the dreadful fighting. No,   225
it must somehow be pleasing to the all-powerful son of Cronus that
the Achaeans should die here, their names forgotten, far from Argos.
Come, Thoas, you have always been a man to face the enemy,
and to urge on another when you see him giving up;
so do not stop now, but keep encouraging every man.'   230

    Then in answer Poseidon the earthshaker addressed him:
'Idomeneus, let the man who on this day deliberately
shirks the battle never return to his home from Troy,
but let him remain here and become the plaything of dogs.
Come now, fetch your armour and go with me; we must deal with   235
this matter together, if, though only two, we are to be of any help;

when men combine even poor fighters can show courage—
and we two have the skill to fight even with the best.'

So the god spoke, and went back into the struggle of men.
And Idomeneus, as soon as he reached his well-built hut,   240
put his fine armour on about his body, picked up two spears,
and set off, looking like the lightning that the son of Cronus
takes in his hand and hurls from bright Olympus, to
show mortals a sign; and its flash is seen far and wide.
Just so the bronze flashed about Idomeneus' breast as he ran.   245
When he was still close to his hut his attendant
valiant Meriones met him—he was on his way to fetch
a bronze-tipped spear—and mighty Idomeneus addressed him:
'Meriones, Molus' son, swift-footed, dearest of my companions,
why have you left the fighting and conflict to come here?   250
Are you wounded somewhere? Is a spear-point troubling you?
Or are you coming to look for me with some message? I for one
have no desire to sit idle in my hut, but am impatient to fight.'

Then in turn Meriones, a sagacious man, spoke to him:
'Idomeneus, counsellor of the bronze-shirted Cretans,   255
I have come to fetch a spear, to see if there is one left
in your hut, since I shattered the one I was carrying before
when I threw it at the shield of arrogant Deïphobus.'*

Then in turn Idomeneus, leader of the Cretans, spoke to him:
'If it is spears you want, you will find one, or even twenty,   260
standing against the shining outer wall of my hut,
Trojan spears that I took from men I killed. It is not my way
to stand at a distance in order to fight my enemies,
and that is why I have spears and shields with bosses,
and helmets and gleaming polished corslets.'   265

Then in turn Meriones, a sagacious man, spoke to him:
'I too have many spoils in my hut, taken from the Trojans,
and in my black ship, but they are not nearby for me to fetch.
And indeed I too can claim not to have forgotten my fighting spirit;
I take my stand among the front-fighters in the battle   270
where men win glory, whenever war's conflict arises.
It may be that some other bronze-shirted Achaean is unaware
of my fighting prowess, but you, I think, know it for yourself.'

Then in turn Idomeneus, leader of the Cretans, spoke to him:
'I know what your courage is like; what need to rehearse it?   275
If all our best men were now to be chosen by the ships

for an ambush, where men's courage can best be discerned,
and both the coward and the brave man reveal themselves—
for the coward's skin keeps changing colour, and
his spirit cannot be restrained to sit quietly within him,　　280
but he changes position, shifting his weight from one leg
to another, and the heart within his breast throbs noisily
as he imagines death's spectres, and his teeth begin to chatter;
but the brave man's skin does not alter, and he is not greatly
afraid, when once he has taken his place in the ambush of men,　　285
but prays to enter into the grim conflict as soon as he can—
even there, no man would disparage your fury and hands' strength.
If you were to be hit from afar or in close fight in battle's toil
the weapon would not fall from behind on to your neck or back,
but would meet you in the breast or belly as you press forward　　290
to take your place in the courtship of front-fighters.
But come, let us not stand here and talk of these things
like little boys, or people may become extremely angry;
go to my hut and choose a massive spear for yourself.'

So he spoke, and Meriones, the equal of swift Ares,　　295
quickly picked out a bronze-tipped spear from the hut
and went to join Idomeneus, full of longing for the battle.
Just as Ares, doom of mortals, goes into battle, and
with him goes his dear son Panic,* mighty and fearless,
who drives even the stout-hearted fighter to run in terror;　　300
and these two leave Thrace and arm themselves to join the
Ephyri or the great-hearted Phlegyans,* though they pay no
heed to the prayers of both, but give glory to one side or other;
so like them Meriones and Idomeneus, leaders of men,
marched out to war helmeted in gleaming bronze.　　305
Meriones was the first to address the other man:
'Son of Deucalion, where are you eager to join the soldiery?
On the right wing of the whole army, or in the centre,
or on the left wing, where more than anywhere I think
the flowing-haired Achaeans will prove unequal to the fight?'　　310

Then in turn Idomeneus, leader of the Cretans, spoke to him:
'In the centre of the ships there are others to defend them—
the two called Ajax, and Teucer, the best among the Achaeans
at archery, and a good man too in standing close combat.
These will compel Hector, Priam's son, to tire of the war,　　315
however ardent he is, and even though he is mightily strong.

It will be a very hard thing for him, raging though he is to fight,
to overcome their fury and their invincible hands
and to fire the ships, unless the son of Cronus himself
should hurl a blazing firebrand into the swift ships.   320
Huge Ajax, son of Telamon, will never yield to any man
who is mortal and who eats the grain of Demeter,
and who can be broken by bronze or by huge stones.
Not even to Achilles, breaker of ranks, would he give way in
standing close combat, though no one can rival him in running.   325
Let us make for the army's left, so that we may quickly learn
whether we are to give the glory to others, or they to us.'

So he spoke, and Meriones, swift Ares' equal, led the way, until
they reached the army at the place where Idomeneus had advised him.

When the Trojans saw Idomeneus, his courage like a flame,   330
and his attendant with him, in their finely crafted armour,
they shouted along the soldiery and all made towards him;
and a massed battle began at the sterns of the ships.
As when blasts of air blow furiously, driven by shrill winds,
on a day when the dust lies thickest on the roads,   335
and the winds raise a great turbulent cloud of dust;
so they crashed together in battle, raging in their hearts
to kill each other in the turmoil with the sharp bronze.
The battle that brings death to mortals bristled with the long
flesh-slicing spears that they flourished, and the brazen gleam 340
from glittering helmets and newly polished corslets and
shining shields blinded men's eyes as they charged together
in the mêlée; it would indeed be a hard-hearted man
who took pleasure in seeing this toil, and did not feel grief.

So the two mighty sons of Cronus,* their wills opposed,   345
brought about cruel anguish for the warrior heroes.
Zeus willed victory for the Trojans and for Hector,
to give honour to swift-footed Achilles; he did not want
the Achaean people to perish utterly before Troy, but
was bringing glory to Thetis and her strong-spirited son.   350
And Poseidon rose up from the grey sea and went secretly
among the Argives, urging them on; he was grieved to see them
beaten down by the Trojans, and was mightily angry with Zeus.
Both were indeed of the same ancestry and parentage, but
Zeus was the elder by birth, and had the greater knowledge;   355
and for that reason Poseidon avoided giving help openly,

and kept rousing them in the camp in the likeness of a man.
These two, one after the other, stretched tight the rope of
cruel strife and equal-balanced warfare over both sides; it was
unbreakable, not to be untied, and it loosened many men's knees.　360

　　Then Idomeneus, for all his grizzled hair, urged the Danaans on,
and leaping at the Trojans spread panic among them.
He killed Othryoneus from Cabesus, who now lived in Troy;
he had recently come there, drawn by news of the war,
and had asked for the most beautiful of Priam's daughters,　365
Cassandra, without bride-gifts, promising instead a mighty deed—
to drive the Achaeans' sons from Troy, resist though they might.
The old man Priam had agreed, and had promised to give him
the girl; and it was trusting in these promises that he was fighting.*
Idomeneus aimed at him with a cast of his shining spear,　370
and hit him as he strutted forward; the bronze body-armour
he wore was not strong enough, and the spear lodged in mid-belly.
He fell with a thud, and Idomeneus spoke triumphantly over him:
'Othryoneus, I must compliment you above all mortal men,
if indeed you are going to fulfil all that you promised to　375
Dardanus' son Priam, who pledged you his daughter;
we too could certainly make such a promise, and fulfil it—
we could give you the loveliest of the daughters of Atreus' son,
bringing her here from Argos, for you to marry, if only
you would help us sack Ilium, that well-populated city. So come　380
with us to our sea-traversing ships, so that we can agree marriage
terms; you will not find us hard dealers over a bride-price.'

　　So the hero Idomeneus spoke, and dragged him by the foot
through the harsh conflict, but Asius came up to protect him;
he was on foot in front of his horses, held ready by his charioteer,　385
and could feel their breath on his shoulders. He longed in his heart
to strike Idomeneus, but the other got in first with a spear
in the throat under his chin, and drove the bronze clean through.
Asius toppled as an oak topples, or a poplar, or a soaring
pine that woodsmen have cut down on a mountain　390
with their newly whetted axes, to become ship-timber;
so Asius lay sprawled in front of his chariot and horses,
roaring, and scrabbling at the blood-soaked dust.
His charioteer, unexpectedly stunned out of his wits,
was not bold enough to wheel his horses and so escape　395
the hands of his enemies, and Antilochus, steadfast in battle,

struck him with his spear, pinning him through the middle;
the bronze corslet that he always wore was no help to him,
and the spear stuck fast in mid-belly. Gasping, he fell from the
well-made chariot, and Antilochus, great-spirited Nestor's son,   400
drove his horses from the Trojans to join the well-greaved Achaeans.

   Then Deïphobus, grieving at Asius' death, came up very close
to Idomeneus, and let fly with his shining spear, but he
was looking ahead, and avoided the bronze-tipped spear;
he was protected behind his perfectly balanced shield,   405
the shield that he always carried, faced with oxhide and
gleaming bronze; and it was fitted with two cross-grips.
Behind this he crouched, quite hidden, and the bronze-tipped spear
flew over him, and as it grazed the shield it made a grating
sound; but it did not fly in vain from Deïphobus' heavy hand,   410
but hit Hypsenor, the son of Hippasus, shepherd of the people,
in the liver below his midriff, and at once loosened his knees.
Deïphobus gave a great shout, and boasted terribly over him:
'Now, surely, Asius does not lie unavenged! I think that even
as he travels to the house of Hades, the mighty gate-guardian,   415
he will rejoice in his heart, because I have sent him an escort.'

   So he spoke, and grief came over the Argives at his boasting,
and most of all he stirred war-minded Antilochus' heart,
who, grieved though he was, did not desert his companion,
and ran up and stood over him and sheltered him with his shield.   420
Then two trusty companions, Mecisteus, the son of Echius, and
glorious Alastor, lifted Hypsenor on to their shoulders and
carried him, groaning deeply, back to the hollow ships.

   Idomeneus did not slacken his great fury, but strove all the time
either to wrap some man of the Trojans in black night or to   425
crash to the ground himself, keeping ruin away from the Achaeans.
Next he killed the hero Alcathous, the dear son of Aesyetes,
nurtured by Zeus; he was the son-in-law of Anchises,
and had married the eldest of his daughters, Hippodameia,*
loved by her father and revered mother with all their hearts   430
in their halls, since she excelled all girls of her age
in beauty, in handiwork, and in good sense; and so it was
the best man in broad Troy who had gained her in marriage.
He it was whom Poseidon beat down by Idomeneus' hand,
bewitching his shining eyes and shackling his bright limbs;   435
he was unable either to run back or to swerve aside, but

stood motionless like a grave-pillar or a high-leafed tree,
while the hero Idomeneus stabbed him with his spear
in the middle of his chest, and broke through the bronze tunic
that had up to then kept death away from his body; but   440
this time the spear tore through it with a loud grating noise.
He fell with a thud, and the spear stuck fast in his heart,
whose beating caused the spear to quiver, even to its butt-end;
but then towering Ares took away the heart's fury, and
Idomeneus gave a great shout, and boasted terribly over him: 445
'Deïphobus, do we judge it fair that three men have been killed
in exchange for your one? That indeed was how you liked to boast.
You are possessed! Now you too should stand up against me, so that
you can see what kind of a visitor I, Zeus' offspring, am to
your land. In the beginning Zeus fathered Minos, Crete's guardian,   450
then Minos in his turn fathered a son, blameless Deucalion,
and Deucalion fathered me, to be lord over many men
in broad Crete; and now my ships have brought me here,
to be an affliction to you and your father and the other Trojans.'*

So he spoke, and Deïphobus' mind was divided in two,   455
whether to draw back and find some companion among
the great-spirited Trojans, or to make trial of Idomeneus alone.
And as he pondered it seemed to him the better course to go
in search of Aeneas. He found him at the very rear of the soldiery,
standing idle; he was all the time angry with glorious Priam,   460
because he paid him no honour, though he was a fine man among men.
Standing close, Deïphobus addressed him with winged words:
'Aeneas, counsellor of the Trojans, now surely is the time for you
to help your brother-in-law, if indeed grief for him touches you.
So come, let us go and save Alcathous; he was your sister's
        husband,   465
and used to look after you in his house, when you were but a child;
look, spear-famed Idomeneus has stripped his armour from him.'

So he spoke, and quickened the spirit in Aeneas' breast,
who made straight for Idomeneus, full of longing for battle.
But Idomeneus was not seized by panic, like some little boy;   470
he stood firm, like a wild boar that trusts in its strength
and stands firm against a great rabble of men attacking it
in a lonely place in the mountains; the bristles stick up
along its back, its eyes flash with fire, and it whets its
tusks, raging to defend itself against both men and dogs.   475

So spear-famed Idomeneus stood firm and would not give ground
to Aeneas as he came up to challenge him. He called out to
his companions, looking to Ascalaphus and Aphareus and Deïpyrus,
and Meriones and Antilochus, raisers of the battle-cry;
trying to rouse them, he addressed them in winged words: 480
'This way, friends, and help me—I am alone! I am terribly afraid
of the assault of swift-footed Aeneas, who is coming after me,
and who is a mighty man at killing men in battle, and is
in the flower of youth, when the strength of a man is greatest.
If we were matched in age, our spirit is such that he   485
would soon win a great victory, or it would be mine.'
    So he spoke, and they all had one purpose in their hearts, and
came and stood by him, resting their shields on their shoulders.
And on the other side Aeneas called out to his companions,
looking especially to Deïphobus and Paris and glorious Agenor,   490
who were with him leaders of the Trojans; and the people
followed them as sheep follow a ram from the pasture
to a drinking-place, and the shepherd is glad in his heart.
Just so the heart in the breast of Aeneas was glad,
when he saw that the mass of men were following him.   495
    So they rushed forward to fight with their long spears over
Alcathous, man to man, and on their chests the bronze armour
rang terribly as they aimed their weapons at each other
in the mêlée; and two warlike men above the rest,
Aeneas and Idomeneus, both the equal of Ares, were   500
straining to slash the other's flesh with the pitiless bronze.
The first to throw his spear was Aeneas, but Idomeneus
was looking ahead and avoided the bronze-tipped spear,
and Aeneas' point passed by and stuck quivering
in the earth, flying to no effect from his massive hand.   505
Then Idomeneus hit Oenomaus in the middle of his belly,
breaking through his corslet's plate, and his innards gushed out
round the bronze; he fell in the dust, clawing the earth with his hand.
Idomeneus tore his far-shadowing spear from the dead man,
but was not then able to strip the rest of the fine armour   510
from his shoulders, for he was pressed hard by missiles;
his feet were not steady enough to support him in a charge,
or to dart forward after his own weapon or to avoid another's.
So in standing combat he kept the pitiless day from himself, since
his feet could no longer carry him in swift flight from the battle.   515

As he retreated, step by step, Deïphobus threw his shining spear
at him, for he harboured a constant, enduring grudge against him.
But once again he missed, and hit Ascalaphus, Enyalius' son,*
with his spear; the massive spear passed through his shoulder,
and he fell in the dust, clawing the earth with his hand.   520
Towering Ares of the mighty voice had not yet found out
that his own son had fallen in the fierce crush of battle;
he was sitting on a peak of Olympus, under golden clouds,
confined by the will of Zeus to the place where the other
immortal gods also were sitting, banned from the war.   525

   Now men rushed to fight over Ascalaphus, man to man;
Deïphobus tore the shining helmet from him, but
Meriones, the equal of swift Ares, leapt at him and
struck him with his spear on the arm, and the vizored
helmet dropped from his hand clanging to the ground.   530
Meriones leapt at Deïphobus a second time, like a vulture,
and wrenched the massive spear from his upper arm,
and then retreated into the mass of his companions. Polites,
Deïphobus' full brother, put his arms around his waist
and led him away from war's hideous clamour, until he reached   535
his swift horses, which were waiting for him behind the battle,
together with their charioteer and finely worked chariot.
These carried him towards the city, in pain and groaning
deeply; and the blood poured from his newly wounded arm.

   But the rest fought on, and the clamour rose unquenchable.   540
Next, Aeneas sprang at Aphareus, son of Caletor, who had
turned to face him, and hit him in the throat with a sharp spear;
his head tilted backwards, and his shield and helmet
fell in on him, and life-breaking death poured over him.
Antilochus was watching Thoön closely, and as he turned away   545
leapt and stabbed him, and completely sheared away the vein
which runs all the way up the back until it reaches the neck;*
this he sheared away completely, and Thoön fell on his back
in the dust, stretching out both hands to his dear companions.
Antilochus sprang forward, and began to strip the armour   550
from his shoulders, looking keenly about him; the Trojans
massed around him and lunged at his bright-gleaming shield,
but could not get past it, even to graze Antilochus' soft flesh
with the pitiless bronze, for Poseidon the earthshaker
was protecting Nestor's son, even under the hail of spears.   555

He was never clear of enemies, but kept twisting about
to face them; nor was his spear ever at rest, but all the time
shook as he flourished it, and kept aiming, determined
either to hurl it at an enemy or to attack him at close range.

As he kept aiming at the soldiery he was seen by Adamas,   560
Asius' son, who, charging at him from close quarters, stabbed at
the middle of his shield with the sharp bronze; but Poseidon of
the dark-blue hair disabled his spear and denied him Antilochus' life;
half of it stuck where it was in Antiochus' shield like a
charred stake, while the other half dragged on the ground,   565
and Adamas retreated into the mass of his companions, avoiding
death's spectres; but as he went Meriones pursued and hit him
with his spear between the genitals and navel, in the place
where battle-death comes most painfully to wretched mortals.
There he planted the spear, and Adamas fell forward, impaled   570
on it, writhing like a bull that herdsmen on the mountains
bind with a rope of withies and forcibly drag it, resisting, away;
so the wounded man writhed—for a short time, not for very long,
until the hero Meriones came up close to him and wrenched
the spear from his flesh; and darkness covered his eyes.   575

Helenus drew close to Deïpyrus and struck him on the temple
with his huge Thracian sword, shattering his helmet, which,
knocked from his head, lay on the ground, and one of
the Achaean fighters picked it up as it rolled between his feet.
As for Deïpyrus, black night dropped down and covered his eyes.   580

Then grief seized Atreus' son, Menelaus, master of the war-cry,
and he made menacingly for the hero, lord Helenus,
shaking his sharp spear; Helenus drew his bow, pulling
the string back to the grip, and so both at once prepared to let fly,
one with a sharp spear, the other with an arrow from the
     bowstring.   585
The son of Priam hit Menelaus on the chest with his arrow,
on a plate of his corslet, but the bitter shaft sprang back from it;
as when on a great threshing-floor black-skinned beans
or chickpeas fly off a wide-bladed grain-shovel,
propelled by a shrill wind and the winnower's swing,*   590
so the bitter shaft flew far off from the corslet of
famed Menelaus, deflected a long way from its course.
Then Atreus' son, Menelaus, master of the war-cry, struck
Helenus' hand where he was holding the polished bow, and

the bronze-tipped spear drove clean through his hand into the bow.   595
He retreated into the mass of his companions, avoiding death's
     spectres,
his hand hanging at his side, trailing the ash spear after him.
Great-spirited Agenor, shepherd of the people, pulled it
out of his hand, and bound the hand up in a well-twisted
strip of sheep's wool, a sling, which his attendant was holding.   600
    Then Peisander made straight for renowned Menelaus;
but his evil allotted portion led him on to death's end,
to be beaten down by you, Menelaus, in the grim conflict.
When they had advanced to within close range of each other
Atreus' son missed his mark, and his spear was turned aside,   605
while Peisander jabbed at renowned Menelaus' shield,
but could not drive the bronze straight through it;
the wide shield stopped it, and the spear snapped at its socket,
though Peisander was glad in his heart, and hoped for victory.
Then Atreus' son drew his sword with the silver rivets   610
and leapt at Peisander, who raised from behind his shield
a fine axe of good bronze, fitted on to an olive-wood shaft,
long and well-polished; and they set upon each other.
Peisander struck the plate of the other's horsehair-crested helmet,
at the base of the plume itself, but as he attacked Menelaus   615
hit him on the brow, above the base of his nose; the bones cracked,
and his eyes, awash with blood, fell in the dust before his feet.
He collapsed and fell, and Menelaus set his heel on his chest
and stripped the armour from him, and boasting spoke to him:
'This is how you will retreat from the swift-horsed Danaans' ships,   620
you arrogant Trojans, still greedy for war's terrible clamour!
You are not slow to inflict insult and disgrace on others—
as you insulted me, you foul dogs, and had no fear in
your hearts of the harsh anger of Zeus the loud thunderer,
god of hosts and guests, who will one day destroy your steep city.   625
You carried away my wedded wife and many possessions,
unprovoked, after you had been warmly welcomed by her,
and now you are resolved to throw deadly fire into
our sea-traversing ships, and to kill the Achaean heroes.
One day you will be stopped, despite your desire for Ares' war.   630
Father Zeus, they say that you surpass all others in wisdom,
both men and gods; yet it is from you that all this comes,
your favour towards these wantonly violent men,

these Trojans, whose fury is intolerable, who cannot ever
get their fill of the fighting in equal-balanced warfare!   635
In all things there is a fullness, even of sleep and of love
and of sweet singing and pleasurable dancing; all these
are things where a man will want to have his fill, though not
in war; but these Trojans cannot get enough of fighting.'

So spoke blameless Menelaus, and stripped the bloody armour   640
from Peisander's body and gave it to his companions; then
he himself turned back again and joined the front-fighters.

Next Harpalion, son of the king Pylaemenes,* sprang at
Menelaus; this man had followed his dear father to Troy
to join the war, but did not return again to his native land.   645
He jabbed at the middle of Atreus' son's shield with his spear,
from close quarters, but could not drive the bronze straight through,
and retreated into the mass of his companions, avoiding death's spectres,
looking keenly about him, in case anyone's bronze should find his flesh.
As he retreated Meriones let fly a bronze-tipped arrow at him,   650
and hit him in the right buttock; the arrow passed
clean through his bladder and came out under the pubic bone.
Harpalion collapsed on the spot and breathed out his spirit
in the arms of his companions, lying stretched out on the earth
like a worm; and the dark blood flowed out, and soaked the ground. 655
The great-hearted Paphlagonians* busied themselves about him,
and setting him in a chariot carried him to sacred Ilium,
grieving, and with them went his father, weeping tears.
There was no compensation for the death of his son.

Paris was greatly angry in his heart at Harpalion's death,   660
for among the many Paphlagonians he had been his guest-friend;
enraged on his account, he let fly a bronze-tipped arrow.
Now there was a man called Euchenor, son of Polyidus the seer,
a rich man of noble birth, whose home was in Corinth. He had
boarded his ship knowing well that it would be his ruin and death, 665
because the old man, noble Polyidus, had often told him
that he would either waste away in his halls from a painful sickness
or go with the Achaean ships and be beaten down by the Trojans.
So he chose to go, avoiding both the Achaeans' heavy war-fine*
and a hateful sickness, and the agony his heart would suffer.   670
Paris hit him under the jaw, by his ear, and swiftly his life's breath
abandoned his limbs, and hateful darkness seized him.

So all the rest fought on in the likeness of blazing fire;

but Hector, loved by Zeus, had neither heard nor knew
that on the left of the ships his people were being overcome   675
by the Argives; and soon the glory would have gone to the
Achaeans, so strongly did the encircler and shaker of the earth
urge on the Argives, and also defended them with his strength.
So Hector held on where he had at first leapt inside the wall
and the gate, and broken the close-packed ranks of shield-bearing   680
Danaans, in the place where the ships of Ajax and Protesilaus were,
drawn up on the shore of the grey sea. The wall protecting these
had been built very low, and it was there that the Achaeans
were fighting at their fiercest, both they and their horses.

There were the Boeotians and Ionians with their trailing tunics,   685
and the Locrians and Phthians and splendid Epeians, but they
were hard put to resist glorious Hector's assault on their ships,
nor could they drive him back; he was like a flame.
Picked men of the Athenians were there, and among them
their leader was Menestheus, Peteus' son, and with him came   690
Pheidas and Stichius and valiant Bias. The Epeians' leaders
were Meges, son of Phyleus, and Amphion and Draceus,
and the Phthians' were Medon and Podarces, steadfast in war.
Now this Medon was a bastard son of godlike Oïleus,
and so half-brother to Ajax; but his home was in Phylace,   695
far from his native land, because he had killed a man,*
a brother of his stepmother Eriopis, wife of Oïleus; and
the other, Podarces, was the son of Iphicles, Phylacus' son.
These then were armed at the head of the great-spirited Phthians,
defending the ships and fighting alongside the Boeotians.   700
Ajax, the swift son of Oïleus, would never take his stand
far from Ajax, Telamon's son, not even for a short time;
just as a pair of dark-faced oxen on fallow land strain
with matched spirit at the close-jointed plough, and
around the base of their horns quantities of sweat spring up;   705
and only the well-polished yoke keeps them apart as they toil
along the furrow, and the plough reaches the field's headland;
so these two fighters stood close to each other, side by side.
The son of Telamon was accompanied by many excellent
companions from his people, who would take his shield   710
from him whenever weariness and sweat came over his limbs;
but Oïleus' great-hearted son had no Locrians with him,
since their hearts were not stalwart enough for standing combat;

they did not own bronze horsehair-crested helmets,
nor did they possess round shields and ash spears, but   715
they had come with him to Troy trusting in bows and slings
of twisted sheep's wool, with which they shot at the Trojans,
thick and fast, and broke down their companies.
So the former, in their finely worked armour, fought in front
against the Trojans and Hector of the bronze helmet, while the   720
Locrians, hidden, kept shooting from behind; and the Trojans
forgot their battle-lust, for the arrows bewildered them.

     Then the Trojans would have retreated in a sorry state
from the ships and the huts towards windswept Troy,
had not Polydamas stood next to bold Hector and spoken to him: 725
'Hector, you are a hard man to persuade with words of advice.
A god has given you prowess in war beyond other men,
and therefore you want to excel others in counsel too;
but you cannot choose to have everything as you want it.
A god gives prowess in war to one man, and to another   730
skill in the dance, and to a third the lyre and song,
and in another's breast wide-thundering Zeus sets an excellent
understanding, and many men derive benefit from it;
he is the salvation of many, and he himself knows this best.
Even so, I shall speak as it seems best to me,   735
seeing that the circlet of war is blazing all around you.
The great-spirited Trojans have crossed the wall, but
some of them are standing idle with their arms, while others
are fighting, few against many, scattered among the ships.
So come, withdraw, and summon all the best men to us,   740
and after that we shall carefully consider every plan,
whether we should fall on their many-benched ships,
in the hope that a god will want to give us the victory, or if
instead we should fall back from them unharmed. As for me,
I am afraid that the Achaeans will repay yesterday's debt,   745
since by their ships there waits a man insatiable in war,
and I do not think he will hold back from the battle for ever.'

     So spoke Polydamas, and his prudent advice pleased Hector,
and at once he leapt, fully armed, from his chariot to the ground,
and addressed Polydamas, speaking with winged words: 750
'Polydamas, hold back all the best men here, and
I will go over there and take charge of the fighting;
I shall then return quickly, when I have given them clear orders.'

So he spoke, and set off, looking like a snow-clad mountain;
shouting orders he flew through the lines of Trojans and their allies; 755
and they all rushed up to join the hospitable Polydamas,
the son of Panthous, when they had heard Hector's voice.
But Hector went up and down the front-fighters, looking for
Deïphobus and mighty lord Helenus, and Adamas, Asius' son,
and Asius, Hyrtacus' son, in the hope of finding them. 760
He found them, but they had not all escaped injury or death:
some were lying by the sterns of the Achaeans' ships,
having lost their life's breath at the hands of the Argives, while
others were back inside the city walls, wounded by cast or thrust.
But one he soon found, on the left of the battle, bringer of tears, 765
glorious Alexander, the husband of lovely-haired Helen,
encouraging his companions and urging them on to fight.
Standing next to him he addressed him in shaming words:
'Paris, Disaster-Paris, superbly beautiful, woman-crazed seducer!
Tell me, where are Deïphobus and mighty lord Helenus, 770
Adamas, Asius' son, and Asius, the son of Hyrtacus?
And where is Othryoneus? Now steep Ilium must be utterly
ruined, from top to bottom; this is surely the bitter end for you.'

Then Alexander who looked like a god answered him:
'Hector, your mind is always to blame one who is blameless; 775
at other times I may well have held back from the war,
but my mother did not bear me to be a complete coward:
ever since you roused your companions to fight by the ships*
we have been here, engaging the Danaans without
ceasing. The companions you ask after have been killed, 780
and only Deïphobus and the mighty lord Helenus*
have left the battlefield, both wounded in the hand by
long spears, though the son of Cronus kept death from them.
But now lead on, to wherever your heart and spirit tell you,
and we will go with you, raging for the fight; I do not think 785
we shall lack courage, as far as there is strength left in us—and
beyond his strength no man can fight, however spirited he is.'

So the hero spoke, and won over his brother's heart.
They set off for where the battle and conflict were fiercest,
around Cebriones and blameless Polydamas, and 790
around Phalces and Orthaeus and godlike Polyphetes, and
Palmys, and Ascanius and Morys, the two sons of Hippotion,
who had come as reliefs from Ascanië* of the rich soil

on the morning before; and now Zeus urged them to fight.
These came on like a squall of violent winds that   795
sweeps to earth, driven by the thunder of father Zeus,
and with a stupendous noise dives into the salt sea, and
in the loud-roaring sea countless waves swell up and crash,
arched over and white with foam, rank succeeding rank;
just so the Trojans came on in battle array, rank succeeding rank,   800
gleaming in bronze and following behind their leaders.
Hector, son of Priam, the equal of Ares, doom of mortals,
led them, holding in front of him his perfectly balanced shield,
deftly crafted with hides and covered with a thick layer of bronze;
and about his temples his shining helmet waved to and fro.   805
Edging forward, he tested the enemy companies from every side,
to see if they would yield to him as he moved up behind his shield;
but he could not weaken the spirit in the Achaeans' breasts.
Ajax strode hugely up, and was the first to challenge him:
'You are possessed! Come closer; why try to frighten the Argives   810
in this way? We are by no means unused to war, and it is
only by Zeus' vicious lash that we Achaeans are beaten down.
No doubt your heart is hoping to destroy our ships utterly,
but we too have hands ready to defend them in a moment.
Long before that happens, your well-populated city   815
will be captured and sacked by our hands.
But for you, I say that the time is near at hand when in flight
you will pray to father Zeus and the other immortals
to make your fine-maned horses swifter than hawks
as they carry you to your city, kicking up the dust on the plain.'   820

    And for him, as he spoke, a bird flew over from right to left,
a high-soaring eagle, and the Achaean army yelled for joy,
encouraged by the omen; but illustrious Hector answered:
'Ajax, you incoherent, oafish ox, what nonsense is this?
I wish I could be for all my days as surely a son of Zeus,   825
wearer of the aegis, and lady Hera could be my mother,
and I was held in the same honour as Athena and Apollo,
as certainly as this day will bring utter ruin on the Argives,
every one of them; and you will be killed with them, if you dare
to resist my long spear, which is going to tear your delicate skin.   830
You will fall by the Achaeans' ships, and you will glut
the dogs and vultures of the Trojans with your flesh and fat.'

    So he spoke, and took the lead, and the rest followed with

a stupendous clamour, and the people were yelling behind him.
The Argives on their side yelled in response, and did not forget　　835
their courage, but held out as the best of the Trojans attacked.
From both sides the clamour reached the upper air, even to the rays
　of Zeus.

BOOK FOURTEEN

N ow though Nestor was drinking in his hut he heard the shouting,
and he addressed the son of Asclepius with winged words:
'Consider, glorious Machaon, what is to be done now, for
the shouts of the strong young men by the ships are growing louder.
You must sit here and continue to drink gleaming wine,   5
until Hecamede of the lovely hair has heated water for a
warm bath and washed away the clotted blood, and I shall
go to a lookout place, and quickly find out what is happening.'
    So speaking he picked up the well-made shield of his son,
horse-breaking Thrasymedes, which was lying in the hut,   10
made of brightly shining bronze; for the son had his father's shield.
And he took up a stout spear, with a point of sharp bronze,
and stood outside the hut; and at once he saw an ugly sight—
the Achaeans in disorder, and the high-hearted Trojans behind
driving them into confusion; and the Achaean wall had fallen.   15
As when the great open sea heaves with a soundless swell,
foreboding the rushing onslaught of shrill-sounding winds,
and the waves cannot break, or roll on one way or another,
until some decisive wind comes down from Zeus;
so the old man pondered, his mind torn this way and that,   20
whether to go and join the soldiery of swift-horsed Danaans
or to make for Atreus' son Agamemnon, shepherd of the people.
And as he pondered it seemed to him the better course to look
for Atreus' son. Meanwhile the rest of them kept up the battle,
killing each other, and the relentless bronze rang about their bodies   25
as they jabbed at each other with swords and double-edged spears.
    As Nestor went, those Zeus-nurtured kings who had been wounded
by the bronze—the son of Tydeus and Odysseus and Atreus' son
Agamemnon—fell in with him on their way up from the ships.
Their ships had been drawn up a long way from the fighting,   30
on the shore of the grey sea, for the first ships had been hauled up
on to the plain, and the Achaeans had built a wall around their sterns.
But the beach, wide though it was, did not have space for
all the ships, and the people were cramped for room; and
for that reason they had drawn them up in rows, and had filled   35
all the space between the headlands along the coastline's wide bay.*

These men were coming up together, leaning on their spears,
wishing to see the battle and its clamour, and the hearts in their
breasts were grieving. When the old man Nestor met them,
the hearts in the breasts of these Achaeans were struck   40
with alarm, and lord Agamemnon spoke, and addressed him:
'Nestor, son of Neleus, great glory of the Achaeans,
why have you left the man-destroying war and come here?
I am fearful that towering Hector will fulfil the threat
he once made when speaking in the Trojan assembly,   45
that he would not turn back to Ilium from the ships
until he had set them ablaze and killed the men as well.
That was what he declared, and now it is all being fulfilled.
This is a disaster! The other well-greaved Achaeans must also
harbour bitterness against me in their hearts, as Achilles does,   50
if they are now refusing to fight beside the sterns of their ships.'
    Then the Gerenian horseman Nestor answered him:
'Indeed these things have been fulfilled, and not even Zeus
the high-thunderer himself could order them differently.
Certainly the wall has been destroyed, the wall that we trusted   55
would be an indestructible barrier for our ships and ourselves,
and our men by the swift ships are engaged in unceasing
and relentless battle. Nor could you tell, however hard you looked,
from which direction the Achaeans are being driven in disorder,
so confused is the killing; and the clamour reaches the high sky.   60
But let us consider what is to be done here, if thought
can achieve anything—I do not advise us to enter the
battle, since there is no way that a wounded man can fight.'
    Then in turn Agamemnon, lord of men, addressed him:
'Nestor, our men are now fighting by the sterns of their ships,   65
and neither the wall that we built has proved of use, nor the ditch
over which the Danaans toiled so hard, hoping in their hearts
that it would be an indestructible barrier for the ships and themselves;
so, I suppose, it must be pleasing to all-powerful Zeus, that the
Achaeans should die here, their names forgotten, far from Argos.   70
I knew it in the past when he willingly helped the Danaans,
and I know it now when he exalts the Trojans to the height
of the blessed gods, and has tied down our hands and our fury.
Come then, let us all be agreed, and do as I say:
let us drag down the ships that were drawn up first, near   75
the sea, and let us launch them all into the bright salt sea,

mooring them far out with anchor-stones, until the immortal
night comes—if the Trojans will leave off fighting even then;
and after that we may haul down all the rest of the ships.
There can be no blame in fleeing from ruin, even at night;   80
it is better for a man to flee and escape ruin than to be captured.'

   Much-scheming Odysseus looked at him darkly and addressed him:
'Son of Atreus, what words are these that cross your teeth's barrier?
Accursed man, I wish you commanded some other, spiritless,
army and did not rule over us, to whom Zeus has seemingly   85
given the charge of winding the thread of cruel wars from youth
right up to old age, until we perish, each and every one of us.
Can it really be that you are raging to abandon the city of Troy
with its wide streets, over which we have endured such misery?
Be silent, or some other of the Achaeans may hear your words,   90
words which no other man would even let pass through his mouth—
one, that is, who knew in his mind how to speak to good purpose,
and was a staff-holding king, and had as many people
subservient to him as the Argives over whom you rule.
From what you say, I think you have completely lost your wits,   95
when you tell us, surrounded as we are by war and clamour,
to drag our well-benched ships down to the sea; this will answer
still more of the Trojans' prayers—though even now they have
the mastery—and sheer destruction's scales will tip against us.
The Achaeans will not keep up the fight if the ships are dragged   100
seaward, but will keep looking about them, and lose their battle-lust.
And then, marshal of the people, your plan will end in disaster!'

   Then Agamemnon, lord of men, answered him:
'Odysseus, your harsh rebuke has gone straight to my heart.
I agree: I shall not order the sons of the Achaeans to drag   105
their well-benched ships down to the sea against their will.
Now, if there is someone who has better advice than this,
young or old, let him give it; and I would welcome it.'

   Then Diomedes, master of the war-cry, spoke out among them:
'That man is nearby, and we shall not have long to seek him—   110
if you are willing to listen to me, and none of you feels indignant
or resentful because I am the youngest in years among you.
Yet I too can boast that my birth was from a good father,
Tydeus, whom a heaped mound of earth now covers in Thebes.
Portheus had three blameless sons born to him, and   115
they lived in Pleuron and in steep Calydon: they were

Agrius and Melas, and the third was the horseman Oeneus,
father of my father, and he surpassed them all in courage.
Oeneus stayed there, but my father wandered away and settled
in Argos; such, it seems, was the will of Zeus and the other gods.*   120
There he married a daughter of Adrestus, and he lived
in a house of great wealth, and had abundant corn-bearing
ploughland, and many enclosures of trees round about,
and flocks in plenty; and he excelled all the Achaeans in
spear-craft. You will have heard all this, and know if it is true.   125
You cannot then say that I am a coward and a weakling by descent,
and so reject the advice I put before you, if it is good.
Let us go to the battlefield, wounded as we are—we are forced to—
and there let us keep ourselves away from the fighting, out of
missiles' range, so that no one receives wound upon wound;   130
but we shall rouse and send the rest into battle, those who before
were loyal in heart but now hang back and refuse to fight.'

So he spoke, and they listened carefully and did as he said;
and they set off, and Agamemnon lord of men led them.

But the renowned earthshaker was not keeping blind watch,   135
and went to meet them in the likeness of an old man,
and grasped Atreus' son Agamemnon by the right hand,
and addressed him, speaking with winged words:
'Son of Atreus, the deadly heart of Achilles must surely now
be glad in his breast, as he looks on the slaughter and rout   140
of the Achaeans; there is no sense in him, not even a little.
May he die, then; may a god cripple his strength.
But against you the blessed gods are not yet completely hostile;
the Trojan leaders and rulers will some day raise the dust
across the wide plain, and you yourself will see them   145
fleeing towards their city, away from the ships and huts.'

So he spoke, and sped away over the plain with a great shout,
as loud as the shouts of nine- or ten-thousand men as they
grapple with each other on a battlefield in Ares' strife;
so loud was the cry which the lord earthshaker let fly   150
from his chest, and he cast great strength into the heart
of every Achaean, to go to war and fight without ceasing.

Now Hera of the golden throne saw this happening before her eyes
from where she stood on a peak of Olympus; and at once
she recognized her brother and husband's brother bustling about   155
the battle where men win glory, and she was glad in her heart;

but then she saw Zeus sitting on the topmost crest of Ida
with its many springs, and he was hateful to her heart.
Then ox-eyed lady Hera deliberated as to how she
might deceive the mind of Zeus who wears the aegis;   160
and this seemed to her in her heart to be the best plan:
to make herself exceptionally beautiful and to go down to Ida,
in the hope that he would feel the desire to sleep beside
her and make love to her, and she would pour a soft,
forgetful sleep over his eyelids and his crafty mind.   165
She set off for the chamber that her dear son Hephaestus
had made for her, and had set the close-fitting doors on their posts
and made them fast with a secret bolt, that no other god could pull back;
and there she went in and closed the shining doors.
First she washed every smudge from her desirable body   170
with deathless balm, and anointed her clothing* richly with
deathless olive oil; this was her perfumed garment, and it
only had to be shaken in the bronze-floored house of Zeus
for its fragrance to be spread over the earth and the high sky.
She smoothed this oil also over her beautiful body and hair,   175
and with her hands plaited the shining hair that fell
in its undying beauty from her immortal head.
Then she put on the deathless dress, which Athena had woven
for her to a smooth finish and had embroidered with many designs,
and pinned it over her breast with golden clasps.   180
Round her waist she fastened a girdle with a hundred tassels,
and set earrings with three drops like mulberries in the
pierced lobes of her ears, and they shone with great allure.
Then the bright goddess covered her hair with a veil,
beautiful and not yet worn, and it was as bright as the sun;   185
and under her gleaming feet she bound fine sandals.
When she had adorned her body with all her finery
she made her way from the chamber and called Aphrodite
aside from the other gods and addressed her:
'Tell me, dear child—will you do something for me that I ask,   190
or will you refuse, holding a grudge in your heart
because I help the Danaans and you help the Trojans?'

     Then in answer Aphrodite, daughter of Zeus, said:
'Hera, elder goddess, daughter of great Cronus,
say what is in your mind; my heart tells me to fulfil it,   195
if I am able, and it is something that may be accomplished.'

Lady Hera addressed her, with guile in her heart:
'Give me now that love and desire, with which you
overcome everyone, both immortals and mortal men.
I am going to the limits of the earth that feeds many, to visit   200
Oceanus, first father of the gods, and their mother Tethys,
who raised me kindly and brought me up in their own house
when they received me from Rhea, when wide-thundering Zeus
imprisoned Cronus under the earth and the unresting sea.
These I am going to visit, and I shall dispel their unresolved strife;   205
for a long time now, since anger invaded their hearts, they have
kept apart from each other, from love and from the marriage-bed.
If I could win both their hearts round with my words
and bring them back to loving union in the marriage-bed,
I should earn their friendship and respect for ever.'*   210

Then Aphrodite who loves to smile answered her:
'It is not possible for me to refuse your request, nor is it right,
since you sleep in the arms of Zeus, highest of the gods.'
So she spoke, and untied from her breasts a stitched and
embroidered band, on which all her enchantments were crafted;*   215
on it was love, on it was desire, and on it was seductive
dalliance, which steals away the wits even of men of good sense.
This she thrust into Hera's hands and spoke to her, saying:
'There! Take this embroidered band, and tie it to your
breast; all things are crafted on it, and I do not think   220
you will come back without achieving your heart's desire.'
So she spoke, and the lady ox-eyed Hera smiled,
and smiling tied the band to her breast.

So Aphrodite, daughter of Zeus, went to her house,
and Hera darted away, leaving the peak of Olympus,   225
and alighted on Pieria and lovely Emathia; she sped on
to the snowy mountains of the Thracian horse-breeders,
over their highest peaks, and her feet did not touch the ground;
from Athos she continued over the swelling open sea,
and came to Lemnos, the city of godlike Thoas.*   230
There she fell in with Sleep, the brother of Death,
and grasping his hand in hers she spoke to him, saying:
'Sleep, you who are lord over all gods and all men,
as you have listened to my requests before, so now again
do as I say; and I shall be grateful to you for ever.   235
Lull Zeus' shining eyes to sleep under his brows for me,

as soon as I have lain down in love next to him, and
I shall give you as gifts a fine throne, imperishable for ever,
made of gold; my son, bow-legged Hephaestus, will make it
with his craft, and will set below it a stool for your feet,   240
where you may rest your gleaming feet when you are feasting.'
      Then in answer sweet Sleep addressed her:
'Hera, elder goddess, daughter of great Cronus,
any other of the gods who live for ever I might
lightly lull to sleep, even the waters of Ocean   245
himself, who is the first father of all the immortals.
But as for Zeus, Cronus' son, I would not approach him,
nor would I lull him to sleep, unless he himself ordered it.
I have learnt wisdom from a task you set me once before,
on the day when Heracles, that arrogant son of Zeus,   250
sailed from Ilium, after he had sacked the Trojans' city.
Then indeed I stilled the mind of Zeus, wearer of the aegis,
softly pouring myself around him; and you devised ruin
against Heracles in your heart, rousing blasts of violent winds
over the sea, and carried him off to well-populated Cos,   255
far from all his friends. When Zeus awoke he became angry and
began to fling gods about his house, and looked especially for me;
and he would have hurled me from the high sky into the sea,
into oblivion, had not Night, who subdues gods and men, saved me;
I had fled to her as a suppliant, and though Zeus was angry he
    stopped,   260
for he was in awe of doing anything displeasing to swift Night.
Now, once again, you are telling me to do something impossible.'*
      Then the goddess ox-eyed lady Hera addressed him:
'Sleep, why do you brood on these things in your mind?
Do you think wide-thundering Zeus will be as angry when he   265
helps the Trojans as he was on behalf of his own son Heracles?
Come now, agree and I will give you one of the younger
Graces for you to marry, so that she shall be called your wife—
[Pasitheë, whom you will desire for all your days.']*
      So she spoke, and Sleep was gladdened, and said in answer: 270
'Come then, and swear to me by the inviolable water of Styx,*
and with one hand take hold of the earth that nourishes many,
and with the other the glittering sea, so that all the gods
who are below the earth with Cronus may be our witnesses,
that you will on oath give me one of the younger Graces—   275

I mean Pasitheë, whom I myself have desired all my days.'

So he spoke, and the goddess white-armed Hera did not disobey him,
and she swore as he had ordered her, naming all the gods
who are under Tartarus, and are called Titans.*
When she had sworn and brought her oath to an end,　　280
they left the cities of Lemnos and Imbros behind and continued,
clothed in mist, and quickly passed on their journey.
They reached Ida with its many springs, mother of wild beasts,
at Lecton; here they first left the sea, and went on above the
dry land, and the tops of the trees shook under their feet.*　　285
There Sleep halted before the eyes of Zeus could see him,
and climbed up into a tall fir tree, the loftiest then growing
on Ida, which stretched up through the mist into the high sky.
On this he sat, hidden by the branches of the fir tree,
in the likeness of a shrill-voiced mountain bird that　　290
the gods call 'chalcis' and men call the hawk-owl.*

But Hera went quickly on to Gargarus, the summit
of lofty Ida, and Zeus who gathers the clouds saw her.
The moment he saw her, desire enveloped his crafty mind,
just as it used to when they would first go to their bed and　　295
make love together, without their dear parents' knowledge.
Zeus stood in front of her and spoke to her, saying:
'Hera, what has driven you to come down here from Olympus?
And where are the horses and chariot that you ride in?'

Then with guile in her heart lady Hera addressed him:　　300
'I am going to visit the limits of the earth that feeds many,
to see Ocean, first father of the gods, and their mother Tethys,
who raised me kindly and brought me up in their own house.
I shall visit them, and dispel their never-ending strife:
for a long time now, since anger invaded their hearts, they have　　305
kept apart from each other, from love and from the marriage-bed.
My horses are standing at the foot of Ida of the many springs,
my horses that will carry me over the dry land and water;
but I have come down here now from Olympus because of you,
in case you become angry with me afterwards, if I go off　　310
to the house of deep-flowing Ocean without telling you.'

Then in answer Zeus who gathers the clouds addressed her:
'Hera, you can set out for that place at any time in future;
but now, let us go to bed and turn our thoughts to love.
Never before has desire for a goddess or for a woman　　315

so flooded around and subdued the heart in my breast,
not even when I fell in love with the wife of Ixion,
who bore me Peirithous, equal of the gods in counsel,
nor with Danaë of the lovely ankles, Acrisius' daughter,
who bore me Perseus, renowned among all men,   320
nor when I desired the daughter of far-famed Phoenix,
who bore me Minos and godlike Rhadamanthys,
nor when I desired Semele or Alcmene in Thebes—
Alcmene gave birth to Heracles, a child of mighty spirit,
while Semele bore me Dionysus, the joy of mortals—   325
nor when I desired lady Demeter of the lovely hair,
nor when I desired splendid Leto, nor you yourself—
never has such desire for you or sweet longing seized me.'*

   Then with guile in her heart lady Hera addressed him:
'Most dread son of Cronus, what is this that you have said?   330
If you are longing now to lie with me and make love
on the peaks of Ida, where everything can easily be seen,
how would it be if one of the gods who live for ever
were to see us two sleeping, and then go and report it to
all the other gods? I could not then rise from this bed and   335
go back to your house; it would be a most shameful thing.
But if this is what you really want, and your heart is set on it,
you have a chamber that your dear son Hephaestus built
for you, and made fast the close-fitting doors on their posts;
let us go there and lie down, since bed is your desire.'   340

   Then in answer Zeus who gathers the clouds addressed her:
'Hera, do not be afraid on that account, that some god or man
will see us; I shall wrap a golden cloud around us,
such that not even the Sun could see us through it,
he whose light gives him the keenest sight of all.'   345

   So the son of Cronus spoke, and clasped his wife in his arms;
and beneath them the bright earth put forth fresh-growing grass
and dew-drenched clover and crocus and hyacinth,
thick and soft, which kept them raised above the ground.
On this the two of them lay, wrapped in a beautiful   350
golden cloud; and from it fell drops of glistening dew.

   So the father slept, motionless on the height of Gargarus,
overcome by sleep and love, clasping his wife in his arms;
but sweet Sleep set off at a run for the ships of the Achaeans,
to carry his message to the shaker and encircler of the earth,   355

and standing next to him he addressed him with winged words:
'Poseidon, you may now put your heart into helping the Danaans
and giving them the glory—for a short time only, while Zeus
is still asleep, for I have wrapped soft slumber about him;
Hera beguiled him into going to bed to make love.'   360

So he spoke, and left to join the renowned tribes of men,
setting Poseidon free to help the Danaans even further; and he,
with a great leap forward among the front-fighters, called out:
'Argives, are we once again going to yield the victory to Hector
Priam's son, for him to capture our ships and win glory?   365
That is what he says and boasts he will do, because Achilles
is staying idle by the hollow ships, his heart full of bitterness;
but we will not miss him overmuch, if only the rest
of us can bestir ourselves to come to each other's help.
So come, let us all be agreed, and do as I say: 370
let us arm ourselves with the best and biggest shields
there are in the camp, and cover our heads with blazing-bright
helmets, and take the longest spears in our hands, and
march out. I shall lead the way, and I do not think that Hector,
Priam's son, will yet resist us, for all his great frenzy.   375
And let every man who is resolute in battle, and shoulders
a small shield, give it to a lesser man and arm himself with a larger.'

So he spoke, and they listened carefully and did as he said;
and even the kings, wounded though they were, armed themselves—
Tydeus' son and Odysseus and Atreus' son Agamemnon.   380
They went through the soldiery exchanging weapons of war:
the good man put on good armour, and gave worse to the worse.
When they had equipped themselves in gleaming bronze,
they made ready to go, and Poseidon the earthshaker led them,
gripping in his brawny hand his terrible long-bladed sword,   385
which is like a lightning-flash; no one may engage
with him in cruel warfare, but fear holds men back.

On the other side illustrious Hector was marshalling the Trojans.
Then indeed the grim contest of war was stretched tight
by Poseidon of the dark-blue hair and glorious Hector,   390
one fighting on the Argives' side, the other on the Trojans'.
As the two sides crashed together with a mighty clamour
the sea surged up to the huts and ships of the Argives; but
neither the sea's waves thundering on to the land, when they
are stirred up from the deep by the North Wind's fierce blast,   395

nor the roaring of a blazing fire that springs up in the
clearings of a mountain, ready to burn down the forest,
nor the howling of the wind in high-leaved oak trees
when its bellowing rage is at its very loudest,
are as loud as were the shouts of Trojans and Achaeans,   400
when with terrifying yells they rushed upon each other.

     First illustrious Hector let fly his spear at Ajax,
who had turned to face him directly, and he did not miss,
but hit him where two straps were stretched across his chest,
one supporting his shield and the other his silver-riveted sword,   405
and these two protected his soft flesh. Hector was enraged
that his swift weapon had flown from his hand in vain,
and he fell back among the band of his companions, avoiding
the death-spectre. As he retreated, huge Ajax, Telamon's son,
picked up a stone, one of many that served as props for   410
the swift ships, and which were rolling about the fighters' feet,
and hit Hector on the chest, above his shield-rim and near his neck,
sending him spinning like a top with the blow, staggering
this way and that. As when an oak tree falls, uprooted by a strike
from father Zeus, and a fearful stench of sulphur rises from it,   415
and courage deserts those who come close to look at it,
because the thunderbolt of Zeus is a hard thing to endure;
so Hector's fury quickly collapsed to the ground in the dust.
The spear dropped from his hand, and his shield and helmet fell in
on him, and his armour, intricately worked with bronze, clattered
     about him.   420
The sons of the Achaeans gave a loud shout and ran up,
hoping to drag him away, and began to hurl their spears,
thick and fast, but no one could stab or hit the shepherd of the
people; before they could, chieftains came and stood over him,
Polydamas and Aeneas and glorious Agenor and   425
Sarpedon, captain of the Lycians, and blameless Glaucus.
And none of the rest deserted him, but held their round shields
in front of him; and his companions lifted him in their arms
and carried him from the battle's toil to his swift horses,
which were standing waiting for him at the rear of the battle   430
and the fighting, with their charioteer and finely crafted chariot.
They set off to carry him, groaning heavily, towards the city.

     But when they came to the crossing of the clear-flowing river,
swirling Xanthus, whose father was immortal Zeus, there

they lifted him from the chariot to the ground, and splashed   435
water over him; and he revived and looked upwards,
and getting to his knees spewed up a cloud of dark blood.
Then he sank back on to the ground, and black night
covered his eyes, for the blow was still crushing his spirit.

When the Argives saw Hector withdrawing, they sprang   440
the more eagerly at the Trojans, and called up their battle-lust.
Well before all the rest swift Ajax, son of Oïleus, leapt at
Satnius, Enops' son, and wounded him with his sharp spear—
Satnius, whom a blameless water-nymph had borne to
Enops as he tended his cattle by the banks of Satnioeis.   445
He it was that Oïleus' son, famed with the spear, came up to
and stabbed in the side; he fell on to his back, and over him
Trojans and Danaans grappled in the fierce crush of battle.
Polydamas, son of Panthous, wielder of the spear, came up
to protect him, and hit Prothoënor, the son of Areïlycus,   450
on the right shoulder, and the massive spear drove through
his shoulder, and he fell in the dust, clawing the earth with his hand.
Polydamas gave a great shout, and boasted loudly over him:
'Once again, I reckon, a spear has not leapt aimlessly
from the massive hand of Panthous' great-spirited son!   455
An Argive has given it a home in his flesh, and I think he will
use it as a staff when he goes down into the house of Hades.'

So he spoke, and grief entered the Argives at his boast;
most of all he stung the heart of Telamon's war-minded son
Ajax to anger, because Prothoënor had fallen very near him.   460
As Polydamas retreated he threw a shining spear at him,
but Polydamas avoided the black death-spectre with a
sideways leap, and the man who received it was Antenor's son
Archelochus, for the gods had planned that he should die.
The spear hit him at the joining-point of head and neck,   465
on the topmost vertebra, and sheared through both tendons;
and as he fell his head and his mouth and nose
hit the ground long before his legs and knees.
Ajax in his turn shouted to blameless Polydamas:
'Think on this, Polydamas, and give me a true answer: 470
is it not fair that this man was killed in exchange for
Prothoënor? He does not seem a low-born man to me, nor of
low-born stock—more like horse-breaking Antenor's brother,
or his son; there is a close family likeness about him.'

He said this knowing the truth; and grief seized the Trojans'
     hearts.   475
Then, standing over his brother, Acamas stabbed Promachus,
a Boeotian, with his spear, as he tried to drag the dead man off by his feet.
Acamas gave a great shout, boasting loudly over him:
'Argive braggarts—you can never have your fill of making threats!
I tell you, we are not the only ones to whom hardship and misery   480
will come, but one day you too will be cut down like this man.
See there how your companion Promachus sleeps, beaten down
by my spear; repayment for my brother's death has not been
slow in coming. This is why a man will pray to leave a
kinsman behind in his halls—someone to ward off harm.'   485
     So he spoke, and grief came over the Argives at his boast;
but most of all he stung war-minded Peneleos' heart;
he leapt at Acamas, and Acamas could not withstand
the onslaught of lord Peneleos. Next he stabbed Ilioneus,
son of Phorbas, rich in flocks, whom Hermes loved   490
most of all the Trojans, and had given him riches; and
Ilioneus was the only son his mother bore to Phorbas.
Peneleos stabbed him below the brow, at the eye's base,
and forced out his eyeball; the spear passed straight through
the eye-socket and the tendons of his neck, and he collapsed,   495
stretching out both hands. Peneleos drew his sharp sword
and drove it at the middle of his neck, and struck off his head,
helmet and all, and it fell to the ground. The massive spear stayed
stuck in his eye; Peneleos lifted up the head, like a poppy-head
on its stem, and displayed it to the Trojans, and spoke boastingly: 500
'Trojans, take my words and tell the dear father and mother
of splendid Ilioneus to set up lamentation in their halls; nor will
the wife of Promachus, son of Alegenor, have any joy
at the return of her beloved husband, whenever it is that
we sons of the Achaeans sail with our ships from Troy.'   505
     So he spoke, and trembling stole into all their limbs, and
each man looked about to find some escape from sheer ruin.
     Tell me now, Muses, who have your homes on Olympus,
who was the first of the Achaeans to take the bloody spoils
from a man killed, after the famed earthshaker turned the battle.   510
It was Ajax first, the son of Telamon, who stabbed Hyrtius,
son of Gyrtias, captain of the stout-hearted Mysians.*
Antilochus stripped the spoils from Phalces and Mermerus,

and Meriones killed Morys and Hippotion,
and Teucer slew Prothoön and Periphetes.   515
Atreus' son then stabbed Hyperenor, shepherd of the people,
in the side, and the bronze tore into him and let out
a stream of innards; his life rushed hastily through the
gaping wound, and darkness covered his eyes.
But it was Ajax, Oïleus' swift son, who killed the most;   520
no one was his equal at pursuing on foot when men fled
in panic, after Zeus had stirred up the rout among them.

BOOK FIFTEEN

Now when the retreating Trojans had crossed the stakes and the
ditch, and many had been beaten down at the Danaans' hands,
they came to a stand beside their chariots and waited there,
pale with fear and thrown into confusion; and Zeus awoke
on the peaks of Ida at the side of Hera of the golden throne, and   5
sprang up and stood there, and saw the Trojans and Achaeans—
the Trojans in disorder and the Argives driving them on
from behind, and among them was the lord Poseidon.
He saw Hector lying on the plain, and around him were sitting
his companions; he was gasping painfully, dazed, and   10
vomiting blood, for it was not the feeblest of the Achaeans
who had felled him. As he watched, the father of gods and men
felt pity for him, and looking darkly at Hera addressed her:
'Hera, you are impossible to control! It is surely your evil plotting
that has taken glorious Hector from the battle and routed his
        people.   15
I wonder: shall I take the lash to you, and will you once again
be the first to reap the benefit of your mischievous scheming?
Or do you not remember when you were hung on high, and I tied
two anvils on your feet, and twisted a golden, unbreakable chain
around your hands? You hung there in the upper air, in among   20
the clouds, and the gods on high Olympus stood around you
distraught, but could not release you; whoever I came upon
I would seize and hurl from the threshold, and when they reached
the earth there was little life in them.* Even so, my ceaseless
anguish for godlike Heracles would not let my heart rest;   25
you had won over the North Wind's storm-blasts, and he helped you
in your wicked scheme to send Heracles over the unresting sea,
and then you brought him to Cos, that well-populated island.*
But I rescued him from there, and brought him back to
horse-rearing Argos, after he had suffered many hardships.   30
I will remind you of this to force you to give up your trickery,
so that you may know if your love-making in bed will profit you—
this abandoning the gods and lying with and deceiving me.'
    So he spoke, and the lady ox-eyed Hera shuddered,
and addressed him, speaking with winged words: 35

'May my witnesses be earth and the wide high sky above,
and the water of Styx that flows downwards,* which is
the greatest and most terrible oath among the blessed gods,
and also your sacred head and our shared bridal bed,
a thing by which I would never swear falsely: 40
it is not through my desire that Poseidon the earthshaker
is afflicting the Trojans and Hector, and aiding their enemies.
It must be that his own heart urges and commands him,
for he pitied the Achaeans when he saw them hard pressed
by their ships. But I would certainly advise him too to follow   45
wherever you, lord of the dark cloud, may lead him.'
    So she spoke, and the father of gods and men smiled,
and he answered her, speaking with winged words:
'Lady ox-eyed Hera, if in future you were truly to be
of the same mind as me when you sit with the immortal gods,   50
then Poseidon would quickly change his mind and follow
your and my wishes, however much he wanted his own way.
However, if what you are saying really is the exact truth,
go now to the assembly of the gods and summon Iris
and Apollo, renowned with the bow, to come here: 55
Iris must go among the people of bronze-shirted Achaeans
and instruct the lord Poseidon to abandon the fighting
and return to his own house, and Phoebus Apollo
must stir Hector up to enter the battle, and
breathe fury into him again, to make him forget   60
the pain that now oppresses his heart; he must instil a
spiritless panic in the Achaeans and drive them back again,
so that they fall back in flight on the many-benched ships of
Peleus' son Achilles. He will then send his companion Patroclus
into battle. Illustrious Hector will kill him with his spear   65
in front of Ilium, after Patroclus has slain many young
men, and among them my own son, glorious Sarpedon.*
In bitter rage at his death, glorious Achilles will then kill Hector.
From that time on I shall bring about a counter-attack
from the ships, keeping it up unremittingly, until the Achaeans   70
capture steep Ilium, through the designs of Athena.
But until then I shall not give up my anger, nor shall I allow
any other of the immortals to help the Danaans down there,
until I bring to fulfilment the plea of Peleus' son, just as
I promised him at the beginning, and nodded my head in assent,   75

on the day that the goddess Thetis clasped my knees,
entreating me to give honour to Achilles, sacker of cities.'
    So he spoke, and the goddess white-armed Hera did not disobey him,
but set off from the mountains of Ida for high Olympus.
As swiftly as the astute mind of a man who has travelled   80
through many lands darts among the many thoughts he keeps,
saying to himself, 'I wish I was in this place, or in that place,'
so speedily did the lady Hera fly away in urgent haste;
and she reached steep Olympus and joined the gathering
of the immortal gods in Zeus' house, and when they saw her   85
they all rose quickly and held out their cups in welcome.
She ignored the others, but accepted a cup from Themis*
of the lovely cheeks; she was the first to meet Hera,
and addressed her, speaking with winged words:
'Hera, what brings you here? You seem distraught; it must be   90
that the son of Cronus, your husband, has made you afraid.'
    Then in answer the white-armed goddess Hera addressed her:
'Goddess Themis, do not ask me about that; you yourself know
how overbearing and unbending his spirit is. Now
make the fairly apportioned feast ready in the gods' house,   95
and you will hear, in company with all the other immortals,
what dreadful deeds Zeus is about to reveal; and in case some are
hoping to enjoy the feast, I do not think that they will all be
glad in their hearts to hear the news, neither mortals nor gods.'
    So the lady Hera spoke and took her seat, and   100
the gods in the house of Zeus were troubled; she smiled
with her lips, but the forehead above her dark brows
showed no softening. Angrily she addressed them all:
'What fools we are to rage witlessly against Zeus!
We are still determined to approach him and stop his schemes   105
by argument or by force, but he sits apart and pays no attention,
and has no regard for us; he says that his power and strength
make him beyond doubt supreme among the immortal gods.
So you must each accept whatever troubles he sends you—
as now, I believe, suffering has been laid up for Ares: 110
his son has been killed in the fighting—Ascalaphus,
dearest of men, whom huge Ares acknowledges his own.'*
    So she spoke, and Ares struck his powerful thighs
with the flat of his hands, and spoke in sorrow:
'Do not now blame me, you who have your homes on Olympus,   115

if I go to the Achaeans' ships and avenge my son's slaughter,
even if it is my destiny too to be struck down by Zeus' thunderbolt
and to lie among the dead men, in the blood and dust.'

    So he spoke, and ordered Terror and Panic to yoke
his horses, and himself put on his brightly shining armour.   120
Then an even greater, more painful bitterness and anger
would have arisen between Zeus and the immortal gods,
had not Athena, terrified on all the gods' behalf, leapt up from
the throne where she was seated and run through the doorway, and
pulled the helmet from his head and the shield from his shoulders,   125
and seized the bronze spear from his massive hand and set
it aside. She rounded on impetuous Ares with these words:
'Madman, your wits are wandering! You are ruined! Your ears hear,
but to no avail; your mind and your sense of shame have gone!
Did you not hear what the goddess white-armed Hera said—   130
she who only now has come from Olympian Zeus?
Do you really want to take your full measure of punishment,
and then be forced to come back, chastened, to Olympus,
and sow the seeds of great suffering for the rest of us?
Because Zeus will quickly abandon the high-hearted Trojans and   135
Achaeans, and will make for us on Olympus with violence in mind,
and will lay hands on us, one after another, guilty and innocent alike.
So I tell you now to give up your bitterness over your son;
many a man, better than him in his hands' strength, has been killed
before now, and will be killed again. It would be a hard thing   140
to keep safe the children and offspring of every mortal man there is.'

    So she spoke, and made impetuous Ares sit back on his throne.
Then Hera summoned Apollo to come out of the house,
and Iris, she who carries messages between the gods,
and addressed them, speaking with winged words: 145
'Zeus orders you both to go to him on Ida as quickly as you can;
when you have arrived and looked upon the face of Zeus,
you must do whatever he orders and instructs you.'

    So the lady Hera spoke, and went back into the house and
sat down on her throne; and the two gods darted off in flight,   150
and came to Ida of the many springs, mother of wild beasts,
and found wide-thundering Zeus sitting on the height of
Gargarus, and a fragrant cloud encircled him like a crown.
The two gods came and stood before Zeus who gathers the clouds;
and when he saw them he was not angry in his heart,   155

because they had quickly obeyed the words of his dear wife.
He addressed Iris first, speaking with winged words:
'Away now, swift Iris, and go to the lord Poseidon,
and report to him all that I say, and do not be a false messenger:
tell him to leave the battle and the fighting alone and to   160
join the assembly of gods, or else to go back into the bright sea.
If he does not obey my orders, and makes light of them,
then let him reflect in his mind and in his heart that,
mighty though he is, he may not have the endurance to
resist my onset, since I reckon myself much stronger than him,   165
and older by birth; but his heart does not baulk at thinking himself
my equal, even though the other gods live in dread of me.'

So he spoke, and wind-footed swift Iris did not disobey him,
but dived down from the mountains of Ida to sacred Ilium.
As when snow or freezing hail drops from the clouds at the onset   170
of a blast from the North Wind, whose birth is in the upper air,
so rapidly swift Iris dropped down, impatient to be off,
and standing nearby addressed the famed shaker of the earth:
'Dark-haired encircler of the earth, I have come here
bringing a message to you from Zeus who wears the aegis.   175
He orders you to leave the battle and the fighting alone and to
join the assembly of gods, or else to go back into the bright sea.
If you do not obey his orders, and make light of them,
he threatens to come here in person and fight you, matching
strength to strength; he warns you to keep out of the reach   180
of his hands, since he reckons himself much stronger than you,
and older by birth; but your heart does not baulk at thinking
yourself his equal, even though the other gods live in dread of him.'

Then, deeply angered, the renowned earthshaker answered:
'This is too much! Great though he is, he has spoken arrogantly,   185
if he wants to restrain me by force against my will, when I am
his equal in honour. We are three brothers, borne by Rhea to Cronus,
Zeus and myself, and the third is Hades, who rules over the dead.
The world was divided into three, and each was given his portion:
when the lots were shaken I was awarded the grey salt sea,   190
to live in it for ever; Hades drew the murky darkness, and
Zeus the wide high sky, among the clouds and upper air,
but the earth and high Olympus were left common to all three.*
So I shall not live according to Zeus' will, not at all. Let him
live at his ease in his third portion, powerful though he is,   195

and let him not try to frighten me with his hands' strength,
as if I were some abject coward; it would be better for him to
use his violent threats on his sons and daughters, his own children,
who are under compulsion to listen to the orders that he gives.'

Then in answer wind-footed swift Iris spoke to him: 200
'Dark-haired encircler of the earth, is this then the grim and
unyielding message that I am to take back to Zeus? Will you not
change your mind, just a little? Good men's minds can be swayed.
You know how the Furies always side with the firstborn.'*

Then in answer Poseidon the earthshaker addressed her: 205
'Goddess Iris, what you say is surely according to due measure;
and it is an excellent thing when a messenger is right-thinking.
But this is a bitter grief that comes over my heart and spirit,
when Zeus is minded to rebuke with harsh words one who
has an equal share, and has been allotted a like portion.   210
Still, though I am indignant, I will give way for now; but
I will tell you another thing, and it is a threat straight from my heart:
if against my will, and the will of Athena who gathers the spoil,
and against the will of Hera and Hermes and lord Hephaestus—
if he spares steep Ilium and is unwilling to sack it, and   215
refuses to give a great victory to the Argives, he should
know that the bitterness between us will be without remedy.'

So speaking the shaker of the earth left the Achaean army
and dived into the sea; and the Achaean heroes felt his absence.
Then Zeus who gathers the clouds addressed Apollo: 220
'Go now, dear Phoebus, and look for bronze-helmeted Hector;
the encircler and shaker of the earth has by now
gone away into the sacred sea, avoiding my sheer anger—
or else others too would certainly have heard of our quarrel,
even the gods who live with Cronus below the earth.*   225
But this course was a far better thing for me and for him, that
though he was angry before he should avoid my hands,
since the matter would not have been settled without sweat.
Come now, take the tasselled aegis* in your hands and
shake it fiercely to put the Achaean heroes to flight, and,   230
shooter from afar, let illustrious Hector be your special care:
stir up great fury in him until such time as the Achaeans
in their flight come to their ships and the Hellespont;
from that moment on I myself will plan in word and deed
how the Achaeans may in turn gain a breathing-space from their toil.'   235

So he spoke, and Apollo was not deaf to his father's words,
but set off down from Ida's mountains like a hawk,
a swift killer of doves, the fastest of all flying creatures.
He found glorious Hector, wise Priam's son, no longer lying
down, but sitting up; he had just recovered his senses, and could now   240
recognize his companions around him. His gasping and sweating
ceased, once the mind of Zeus the aegis-wearer had roused him.
Standing close, Apollo who shoots from afar addressed him:
'Hector, son of Priam, why do you sit here apart from the rest,
with little life in you? Has some disaster overtaken you?'   245

Exhausted, Hector of the glittering helmet answered him:
'Which of the gods are you, lord, who ask me this, face to face?
Did you not hear how, as I was killing his companions
by the sterns of the Achaean ships, Ajax, master of the war-cry,
hit me in the chest with a rock, and stopped my surging courage?   250
Indeed, I had thought that on this day I would breathe out
my dear life and pass down to the dead and the house of Hades.'

Then in answer lord Apollo who shoots from afar addressed him:
'Take courage now; such is the helper whom the son of Cronus
has sent to you from Ida, to stand by and defend you—   255
I, Phoebus Apollo of the golden sword, am protecting you
as I have done before, both you yourself and your steep citadel.
So come now, command your many charioteers to
drive their swift horses up against the hollow ships;
I shall go ahead of them and make the whole way smooth   260
for the horses; and I shall put the Achaean heroes to flight.'

So he spoke and breathed great fury into the shepherd of the people.
As when a horse that is kept in a stall and fed full with barley
breaks its tether and gallops exultantly, hoofs drumming,
over the plain, since its habit is to bathe in the waters   265
of a sweet-flowing river; it holds its head high, and its mane
flows about its shoulders, and confident in its splendour
its legs carry it easily to the haunts and pastures of horses;
so swiftly did Hector move his knees and legs, and urge
on his charioteers, when he had heard the voice of the god.   270
As when men who live in the country set out with their
dogs in swift pursuit of a horned stag or a wild goat,
but it is saved by a sheer rock-face and a shady wood,
and it was not after all their due destiny to catch it;
but hearing the shouts a bearded lion appears in their way,   275

and at once sends them running back, despite their resolve;
so the Danaans for a while kept up the pursuit in a body,
jabbing at the enemy with swords and double-edged spears;
but when they saw Hector ranging up and down the ranks of men
they were all terrified, and their spirits dropped beside their feet.   280

Then Thoas, the son of Andraemon, spoke among them; he was
by far the best of the Aetolians, both skilled in spear-throwing and
a fine man in standing combat, and few Achaeans could defeat him
in the assembly, whenever the young men competed in debate.
With generous intent he spoke out and addressed them: 285
'This is indeed a great marvel that I see before my eyes!
Here he is once again, escaping death's spectres and rising up—
Hector I mean! The heart of each one of us surely hoped
that he had died at the hands of Ajax, son of Telamon;
but now some god has rescued him and kept him alive,   290
Hector, who has indeed loosened the knees of many Danaans,
and will, I think, do so again—for it is not without the will
of loud-thundering Zeus that he stands raging in the front ranks.
So come, let us all be agreed, and do as I say:
let us order the mass of soldiery to turn back to the ships,   295
while those of us who claim to be the best fighters in the army
make a stand with spears held before us, in the hope that we can
meet and hold off his first assault; I think that he, for all his
heart's raging, will be afraid to plunge into the mass of Danaans.'

So he spoke, and they listened carefully and did as he said.   300
And those who were led by Ajax and lord Idomeneus,
and by Teucer and Meriones, and by Meges, the equal of Ares,
called on the best men and formed a close-set battle-line,
intending to face Hector and the Trojans; and behind them
the mass of soldiery retreated towards the Achaeans' ships.   305

Now the Trojans pressed forward in a body, and Hector led them
with long strides; and in front of him went Phoebus Apollo,
his shoulders wrapped in a cloud, and holding the surging aegis,
terrible with its shaggy fringe, and shining brightly, that Hephaestus
the bronze-smith had given to Zeus to carry, to make men flee in
     terror;   310
holding this in his hands Apollo led the people forward.

The Argives massed and resisted them, and a piercing clamour
arose from both sides. Arrows sprang from bowstrings,
and spears in great numbers flew from bold hands;

some pierced the bodies of young men, swift in the fight,   315
but many fell in the middle ground before reaching white flesh
and stuck in the earth, longing to glut themselves on flesh.
As long as Phoebus Apollo held the aegis steady in his hands,
both sides' missiles struck home, and the people kept falling;
but when he looked full in the faces of the swift-horsed Danaans   320
and shook it, and himself gave a great loud shout, he stupefied
the hearts in their breasts, and they forgot their surging courage.
As two wild beasts drive a herd of cattle or a great flock of sheep
into turmoil, coming on them suddenly in the depth of
black night, when there is no herdsman at hand, so the   325
Achaeans fled in terror, spiritless; for Apollo let confusion
loose among them, and gave the glory to Hector and the Trojans.

Then, when they had broken the battle-front, man killed man.
Hector slew Stichius and Arcesilaus,
one the leader of the bronze-shirted Boeotians, and   330
the other the trusty companion of great-spirited Menestheus,
and Aeneas killed and stripped Medon and Iasus.
Now Medon was the bastard son of godlike Oïleus
and so half-brother to Ajax, but his home was in Phylace,*
far from his native land, because he had killed a man,*   335
the brother of his stepmother Eriopis, wife of Oïleus;
and Iasus was one of the captains of the Athenians,
and was called the son of Sphelus, who was Boucolus' son.
Polydamas slew Mecisteus, and Polites killed Echius
in the battle's forefront, and glorious Agenor killed Clonius.   340
As Deïochus fled with the front-fighters Paris hit him at
the base of his shoulder, and drove the bronze clean through.

While the Trojans were stripping these men's armour, the Achaeans
rushed frantically this way and that, entangled in the stakes and
ditch that they had dug, and were forced to fall back behind the wall.   345
Then Hector called out to the Trojans with a great shout:
'Leave these bloodstained spoils, and press on to the ships!
If I see anyone going to any other place, and not to the ships,
I shall make sure he dies there on the spot, and the men and
women of his family will not give him the due rite of burning,   350
but dogs will tear him to pieces in front of our city.'

So he spoke, and with a downward swing of his shoulders whipped
his horses, and called out along the Trojan ranks; and they all went
with him, raising a stupendous clamour, driving their chariot-hauling

horses onward. And in front of them Phoebus Apollo   355
kicked down the banks of the deep ditch with ease,
making a heap out of them in its midst, and built up
a long, broad causeway, as wide as the cast of a spear
when a man throws it to make trial of his strength.
Over this the Trojans poured in massed order, and in front   360
Apollo held out the precious aegis; and with great ease
he broke down the Achaean wall, just as a boy builds
sandcastles on the seashore, in the way that children have, and
then delights in knocking them over again with hands and feet.
So you, lord Apollo, shattered the immense toil and labour   365
of the Achaeans, and provoked them to panic-stricken flight.

So the Achaeans halted beside the ships and stopped there,
calling out to each other and holding up their hands
to all the gods, and praying fervently, each and every man;
and Nestor the Gerenian, protector of the Achaeans, prayed   370
hardest of all, lifting his hands up to the starry high sky:
'Father Zeus, if ever one of us back in Argos, rich in wheat,
burnt for you the thigh-bones of ox or sheep, wrapped in fat,
and prayed for his return, and you assented and promised it,
remember that now, Olympian, and keep the pitiless day from us,   375
and do not let the Trojans beat the Achaeans down in this way.'
So he spoke in prayer, and Zeus the counsellor thundered loudly,
when he heard the prayers of the old man, son of Neleus.

But when the Trojans heard the thunder of Zeus the aegis-wearer
they called up their battle-lust and charged harder at the Argives.   380
Just as when on the wide ways of the sea a huge wave,
driven on by the wind's violence—for this is what chiefly
causes the waves to swell—sweeps over the gunwales of a ship,
so the Trojans swept over the wall with a loud yell,
driving their chariots on, and began a close-combat fight   385
by the sterns: the Trojans from chariots, with double-edged spears,
and the Achaeans, after climbing high on to their black ships,
with the long jointed pikes that they had lying in the ships
for fighting at sea,* clothed at their point in bronze.

Now Patroclus, as long as the Achaeans and Trojans were   390
fighting around the wall, some way from the swift ships,
was sitting in the hut of kindly Eurypylus, and
cheering him with talk, and spreading ointments
over his aching wound to soothe his black pains;*

but when he saw that the Trojans were charging at the wall,   395
and that shouting and panic were spreading among the Danaans,
he groaned aloud, and striking both thighs with the flat
of his hands spoke in lamentation to Eurypylus:
'Eurypylus, I can no longer stay here with you, however
much you need me, for a great conflict has now arisen.   400
Let your attendant look after you now, and I shall
go quickly to Achilles, to persuade him into the fighting.
Who knows if, with some god's help, I may arouse his spirit
by my persuasion? A friend's persuasion is a potent thing.'
    So he spoke, and left on quick feet. Meanwhile the Achaeans   405
were stoutly holding off the Trojans' attack, but they could not
drive them from the ships, though they were fewer in number;
nor could the Trojans ever break the companies of the Danaans,
and so make their way in among their huts and ships.
As a carpenter's cord in the hands of a skilful craftsman,   410
a man who is proficient in every kind of craft through
Athena's guidance, makes a straight line along a ship's timber,
so the fierce fighting was stretched taut between them.
Some were fighting round one ship, and some round another;
but Hector made straight for splendid Ajax, to engage him,   415
and the pair of them toiled in battle around a single ship; but
neither could Hector drive Ajax away and hurl fire into the ship,
nor could Ajax force him back, since a god was urging him on.
Then glorious Ajax hit Caletor, the son of Clytius, in the chest
with a spear as he was bringing fire up to the ship, and   420
he fell with a thud, and the torch dropped from his hand.
When Hector saw that his cousin had fallen in the dust
before his eyes, in front of the black ship,
he called out to the Trojans and Lycians with a great shout:
'Trojans and Lycians and Dardanian hand-to-hand fighters,   425
do not back away from the battle in this narrow space,
but rescue Clytius' son, so that the Achaeans do not strip
his armour, now that he has fallen in the assembly of the ships.'
    So Hector spoke, and let fly a shining spear at Ajax,
but missed him, and hit Lycophron, son of Mastor,   430
an attendant of Ajax from Cythera, who lived with him
because he had killed a man in sacred Cythera;
the sharp bronze struck him on the head above his ear
as he stood next to Ajax, and he fell from the ship's stern

on to his back in the dust, and his limbs were loosened. 435
Ajax shuddered, and addressed his brother:
'Dear Teucer, look, our trusty companion has been killed—
Mastor's son from Cythera, whom we honoured at home
in our halls as much as we did our own dear parents.
Great-spirited Hector has killed him; where now are your swift 440
death-bearing arrows, and the bow that Phoebus Apollo gave you?'
    So he spoke, and Teucer understood, and ran up to stand beside him,
carrying in his hand his curved bow and the quiver that held
his arrows, and at once began to shoot his arrows at the Trojans.
And he hit Cleitus, the splendid son of Peisenor, the companion 445
of Polydamas, who was the splendid son of Panthous,
as he held the reins in his hands, for he was busy with his horses,
driving them to where the companies' confusion was thickest,
hoping to please Hector and the Trojans; but disaster soon
overtook him, and no one could ward it off, though they longed to. 450
The grief-bearing arrow lodged in the back of his neck,
and he toppled from the chariot, and his horses shied away,
making the empty chariot rattle. Lord Polydamas quickly saw
this, and came up before anyone else to head the horses off;
he then gave them to Astynous, son of Protiaon, urging him 455
strongly to keep him in sight and hold them nearby.
Then he himself went back and joined the front-fighters.
    Next, Teucer aimed another arrow at bronze-helmeted Hector,
and he would have ended the battle by the Achaean ships
if he had hit him and taken away his life in his time of triumph; 460
but he did not catch the crafty mind of Zeus unawares, who
was protecting Hector, and even as Teucer drew the well-twisted
string on his blameless bow at Hector, Zeus broke it, and robbed
Telamon's son of his glory; the bronze-weighted shaft
swerved off its target, and the bow dropped from his hand. 465
At this Teucer shuddered, and addressed his brother:
'Some divine being must be cutting all our battle-plans short!
He has knocked the bow from my hand, and broken
the newly twisted string that I tied this morning,
so that it would stand up to the volleys of my leaping arrows.' 470
    Then in answer huge Ajax, son of Telamon, spoke:
'Dear brother, leave your bow and quick-flying arrows to lie
here; some god has a grudge against the Danaans and has
made them useless. Take a long spear in your hand and a shield

on your shoulder, and do battle with the Trojans, and stir up the rest   475
of the people. Even if they defeat us, let them not capture our
well-benched ships without a struggle; let us call up our battle-lust!'

   So he spoke, and Teucer laid his bow down in his hut,
and slung about his shoulders a shield with four hide layers,
and set on his mighty head a well-made helmet with a   480
horsehair crest; and the plume nodded terribly above it.
He picked up a stout spear, tipped with sharp bronze,
and set off running quickly, and took his stand by Ajax's side.

   Now when Hector saw that Teucer's weapons were useless,
he called out to the Trojans and Lycians with a great shout: 485
'Trojans and Lycians and Dardanian hand-to-hand fighters,
now be men, my friends, and call up your surging courage,
here by the hollow ships; I have seen with my own eyes
how Zeus has ruined one of their best men's weapons.
Courage that comes from Zeus can easily be discerned by men,   490
both by those to whom he pledges the glory of victory,
and by those whom he makes weak and has no wish to defend—
just as now he is weakening the Argives' fury, and helping us.
So mass together and fight by the ships, and if any of you
meets his due death, whether struck from afar or in close fight,   495
let him die, for it is no ugly thing if a man dies fighting for
his country; his wife and children will be safe in the future,
and his house and plot of land will be unharmed, if one day
the Achaeans sail away in their ships to their dear native land.'

   So he spoke, and quickened the fury and spirit in every man.   500
On the other side, Ajax called out to his companions:
'Shame, Argives! It is now certain that we shall either die,
or be saved and drive this danger away from our ships.
Do you really think that, if Hector of the glittering helmet takes
the ships, you can all get back to your native land on foot?   505
Can you not hear Hector urging on all his people?
You can see how great his rage is to set the ships on fire;
it is not a dance he is inviting you to, but a fight.
For us, there can be no better plan or stratagem than
to match hands and fury with them in close combat;   510
better to decide things once and for all, to die or to survive,
than to be slowly crushed like this in a grim struggle
beside the ships, at the hands of men worse than us.'

   So he spoke, and quickened the fury and spirit in every man.

Then Hector killed Schedius, the son of Perimedes,   515
a captain of the Phocians, and Ajax killed Laodamas,
Antenor's splendid son, a leader of foot-soldiers.
Polydamas slew Otus, a man from Cyllene, companion
of Phyleus' son Meges, captain of the great-spirited Epeians.
When Meges saw this he leapt at him, but Polydamas swayed   520
out of his reach, and Meges missed him—Apollo would not
let Panthous' son be beaten down in the front-fighters—
and stabbed Croesmus in the middle of his chest with his spear.
Croesmus fell with a thud, and Meges began to strip the gear
from his shoulders, but as he did so Dolops sprang at him—   525
an expert spearman, who was Laomedon's grandson, and
the mightiest of Lampus' sons, well skilled in surging courage;
he now closed with Meges and leapt at him, jabbing his spear
at the middle of his shield, but the close-set corslet he wore
protected him with its fitted plates. Meges' father Phyleus   530
had once brought this from Ephyre,* from the river Selleïs;
a guest-friend there, Euphetes, lord of men, had given it to him
to wear in war as a defence against men of the enemy,
and now it kept destruction away from his son's flesh.
Meges thrust with his ash spear at the topmost plate   535
of Dolops' bronze helmet with its horsehair plume, and
broke off the plume of horsehair, and it fell in one piece,
bright with fresh sea-purple dye, to the dusty ground.
For a time Dolops stood his ground and fought, hoping for victory,
but then warlike Menelaus came up to help Meges,   540
and stood with a spear at his side, unnoticed, and hit Dolops
in the shoulder from behind; the eager spear, speeding forward,
came out through his chest, and he crumpled and fell headlong.
Meges and Menelaus came up to strip the bronze armour
from his shoulders, but Hector called out to his kinsmen,   545
every one of them, and the first he rebuked was Hicetaon's son,
mighty Melanippus. For a while, before the enemy came,
this man used to pasture his shambling cattle in Percote,*
but when the well-balanced ships of the Danaans arrived
he returned to Ilium, and excelled among the Trojans,   550
and lived near Priam, who honoured him like his own children.
It was he whom Hector rebuked; he spoke, calling him by name:
'Melanippus, are we to give up like this? Is your dear heart
not moved at all at your cousin's killing? Can you not see

how they are busying themselves with stripping Dolops' gear?   555
Come with me; we can no longer stand off from the Argives,
but must fight with them until either we kill them, or they
destroy steep Ilium from top to bottom, and slaughter her citizens.'

So he spoke, and led the way, and the godlike man went with him.
But huge Ajax, son of Telamon, urged on the Argives: 560
'Be men, my friends, and put shame in your hearts, and in
the harsh crush of battle have regard for what other men think;
when men fear disgrace in others' sight, more escape than are killed,
but there can be no strength or glory in panic-stricken flight.'

So he spoke, and they too raged to drive the enemy back,   565
and lodged his words in their hearts, and fenced the ships
with a wall of bronze; and Zeus roused the Trojans against them.
Then Menelaus, master of the war-cry, prompted Antilochus:
'Antilochus, there is no one among the young Achaeans
who is swifter of foot or braver than you in the fight;   570
see if you can leap out and strike down some man of the Trojans.'

So he spoke, and hurried back; he had roused Antilochus,
who leapt forward from among the front-fighters, looked keenly
around him, and threw his shining spear. As he let the spear go
the Trojans gave ground, and the weapon did not fly in vain,   575
but hit Hicetaon's son, the arrogant Melanippus,
on the breast next to his nipple as he entered the battle;
he fell with a thud, and darkness covered his eyes.
Antilochus sprang at him like a hound pouncing on
a wounded fawn that a hunter shoots at and hits   580
as it leaps up from its den, and unlooses its limbs;
so Antilochus, steadfast in battle, leapt on you, Melannipus,
intent on stripping your armour. But glorious Hector saw him,
and came running up through the fighting to meet him.
Antilochus, swift fighter though he was, could not withstand him,   585
and fled like a wild beast that has done some hideous thing,
killing either a dog or a herdsman tending his cattle,
and flees before a body of men can be assembled;
so the son of Nestor fled, and the Trojans and Hector
showered him with whirring missiles, making an astonishing
     noise;   590
he reached the mass of his companions, and turned and stood.

Now the Trojans, in the likeness of flesh-eating lions,
kept charging at the ships, fulfilling the commands of Zeus,

who all the time woke great fury in them, but beguiled the hearts
of the Argives and took away their glory, and roused the Trojans;   595
in his heart he wished to give the glory to Hector, son of
Priam, so that he might hurl awesome, unwearying fire
on to the curved ships, and so fulfil all of the immoderate
prayer of Thetis. And so Zeus the counsellor was waiting
for his eyes to catch sight of the glare of a ship on fire,   600
since he intended the Trojans from that very moment to be
driven back from the ships, and to give glory to the Danaans.
With this in mind, he was urging Hector, Priam's son, to attack
the hollow ships, though Hector himself was now raging to do so;
he was mad like Ares, wielder of the spear, or like deadly fire   605
that rages over mountains, in the thickets of a deep wood;
there was foam around his mouth, and his eyes
flashed beneath his fierce brows, and about his temples
the helmet shook terrifyingly as Hector fought—
for Zeus himself in the high sky was his ally,   610
Zeus who gave him honour and glory, choosing him to be
one man out of a great many, since he was to be short-lived;
and already Pallas Athena was bringing on the day of
his due destiny, at the hands of the violent son of Peleus.
And indeed he was longing to test the ranks of men and break them,   615
wherever he saw the greatest numbers and the finest armour;
but even so he could not break them, raging wildly though he was,
since they stood tower-like in close formation, like a
huge sheer cliff that stands on the edge of the grey sea,
and holds out against the shrill winds' scurrying paths   620
and the waves that roll in and break against it.
So the Danaans stubbornly withstood the Trojans, and did not run.
But Hector, blazing all around like fire, leapt into their mass,
falling upon them like a violent wave, wind-nurtured
by storm-clouds, that crashes on to a swift ship; it is covered   625
all over in foam, and the wind's fearful blast
roars in its sail, and the sailors tremble in their hearts
in terror, only just being carried out of the way of death;
just so the spirits in the Achaeans' breasts were torn apart.
But Hector came on like a murderous lion falling on cattle   630
that are grazing in the low-lying land of a great water-meadow
in their thousands, and the herdsman with them does not know
how to fight off a beast from the carcass of a crook-horned cow,

and so all the time walks alongside the cattle at the front
or at the rear; and the lion leaps into the middle of the herd and   635
devours a cow, and all the rest cower in fear. So then the Achaeans
were panicked into amazing flight by Hector and father Zeus,
all of them; but Hector killed only one man, Periphetes from
Mycenae, the dear son of Copreus, who used to carry
messages from lord Eurystheus to the mighty hero Heracles.   640
This inferior man had fathered a son much better than him
in every kind of excellence, in speed of foot and in fighting,
who was in understanding among the finest in Mycenae.
It was he who now bestowed greater glory on Hector:
as he turned to retreat he tripped on the rim of the shield that   645
he carried, one that reached to his feet, a rampart against spears;
stumbling against this he fell on his back, and as he fell
to the ground his helmet rang mightily about his temples.
Hector was quick to see him, and ran up and stood close by,
and planted a spear in his chest, killing him in front of his   650
dear companions; despite their distress they could not help their
companion, for they themselves were terrified of glorious Hector.

　　The Argives were now in amongst their ships, and the topmost
line that had been hauled up first was protecting them; but the
Trojans poured in after them, and they were forced to retreat   655
from the nearer ships, and rallied by the huts in close formation,
and did not scatter throughout the camp, for shame and fear
restrained them; and they kept shouting encouragement to each other.
Now Nestor the Gerenian, protector of the Achaeans, more than
anyone entreated them and appealed to each in his parents' name: 660
'Be men, my friends, and put shame in your hearts, shame
before other men; and each one of you must call to mind
his wife and children, his possessions and his parents,
whether his parents are living or dead; though they
are not here, it is on their account that I beg you to   665
stand your ground resolutely, and not to be turned to flight.'

　　So he spoke, and quickened the fury and spirit in each man.
And Athena drove an amazing cloud of mist from their eyes,*
and the bright light of day shone out for them on both sides,
both from the ships and from the equally balanced battlefield, and   670
they could make out Hector, master of the war-cry, and his companions,
both those who were holding back in the rear and not fighting,
and those who were fighting in the battle by the swift ships.

Now great-hearted Ajax was not content in spirit to take his stand
in the place where the other sons of the Achaeans had retreated,   675
but kept ranging up and down the ships' half-decks* with huge strides,
wielding in his hands a huge pike that was used for sea-fighting,
firmly jointed with dowels, and twenty-two cubits long.
As a man well skilled in horsemanship, who from many horses
has harnessed together four and drives them at speed   680
from the plain towards a great city, along the public way,
and many people marvel at him, both men and women,
as he leaps from horse to horse, changing his stance but
all the time keeping secure on his feet, while the horses fly along;*
so Ajax kept ranging from deck to deck of the swift ships,   685
taking huge strides, and his voice reached the high sky
in constant terrible shouts, as he called to the Danaans
to defend their ships and huts. Nor did Hector
stay behind among the mass of close-armoured Trojans,
but just as a tawny eagle swoops down on a flock   690
of winged birds that are feeding beside a river—
geese or cranes, or swans with long necks—
so Hector made straight for a dark-prowed ship,
dashing right up to it; and from behind Zeus pushed him
with his huge hand, and urged his people to go with him.   695

Now once again bitter fighting broke out beside the ships;
you would think that the men felt no weariness or fatigue
as they grappled with each other, so fiercely did they fight.
And as they struggled these were the thoughts of each side:
the Achaeans did not think they could avoid disaster, but   700
would die, while the heart in the breast of each Trojan hoped
to set the ships on fire and to kill the Achaean heroes; these were
the thoughts in their minds as they stood up to face each other.
Then Hector laid hold of the stern of a sea-traversing ship,
a fine ship, swift over the sea, which had brought Protesilaus   705
to Troy, but did not take him back again to his native land.*
It was around his ship that the Achaeans and Trojans
were now cutting each other down, hand to hand; no longer
did they wait at a distance for volleys of arrows or spears,
but stood up at close quarters, both sides being of one mind,   710
and fought with sharpened axes and hatchets,
and with great swords and double-edged spears.
Many fine swords with black hilts fell to the ground,

some from hands, some cut from the shoulders of
men as they fought; and the earth ran dark with blood.   715
Once Hector had laid hold of the stern he did not let it go, but
gripping the sternpost with his hands called out to the Trojans:
'Bring fire! Mass all together, and renew the battle!
Now Zeus has given us a day to make up for all the rest—
a chance to capture the ships that came here against the gods' will,   720
and caused us great suffering, through the cowardice of old men,
who though I was eager to fight by the ships' sterns
persisted in holding me back and restraining my men.
But if wide-thundering Zeus was then wrecking our wits,
now he is himself encouraging and directing us onward.'   725

So he spoke, and they charged more fiercely at the Argives.
Ajax, overwhelmed by missiles, could no longer withstand them;
thinking he was about to die, he fell back a little way, leaving
the well-balanced ship's decks, on to a seven-foot thwart.
There he stood, alert, constantly thrusting the Trojans back from   730
the ships with his pike, whenever one brought up unwearying fire;
and all the time he called out orders to the Danaans, shouting terribly:
'Friends, heroes of the Danaans, attendants of Ares—
now be men, my friends, and call up your surging courage!
Do we suppose that there are men behind to help us, or that   735
there is a better wall, one that can keep ruin away from men?
There is certainly no tower-surrounded city nearby, where we could
find a force to turn the battle's tide and so save ourselves.
No, we are here on the plain of the close-armoured Trojans,
with our backs to the sea and far from our native land;   740
salvation lies in our arms, not in some slackening of war!'

So he spoke, and dashed forward, raging with his sharp spear;
and whenever any Trojan rushed up to the hollow ships
with blazing fire, in obedience to Hector's commands,
Ajax was waiting with his long spear and jabbed at him;   745
twelve men he wounded, at close quarters in front of the ships.

BOOK SIXTEEN

So they continued fighting around the well-benched ship;
but Patroclus stood beside Achilles, shepherd of the people,
weeping warm tears, like a spring of black water
that pours its dark stream down a sheer rock-face.
Swift-footed glorious Achilles felt pity when he saw him,   5
and addressed him, speaking with winged words:
'Patroclus, why are you weeping like a little girl who
runs at her mother's side and demands to be carried,
clutching at her dress, tugging her back as she tries to hurry,
and tearfully looking up at her until she is picked up?   10
That is what you are like, Patroclus, weeping soft tears.
Have you something to say to the Myrmidons, or to me, or
have you heard some message from Phthia, touching you alone?
Yet men say that Menoetius, son of Actor, is still living,
and Peleus, son of Aeacus, still lives among the Myrmidons—   15
these are two whose death we would be grieved to hear about.
Or perhaps you are weeping for the way that the Argives
are dying by the hollow ships, as a result of their own arrogance?
Tell me, do not hide it in your heart, so that we may both know.'
    Then, charioteer Patroclus, you groaned heavily and
            addressed him: 20
'Achilles, son of Peleus, by far the greatest of the Achaeans,
do not be angry. Yes, great distress has crushed the Achaeans:
all those who before this were the best of us are lying
in their ships, wounded by thrown or stabbing weapons.
Diomedes, the mighty son of Tydeus, has been hit, Odysseus   25
the renowned spearman and Agamemnon have been stabbed,
and Eurypylus has been hit by an arrow in the thigh.
Healers skilled in medicines are now busy about these men,
treating their wounds—but you, Achilles, cannot be moved.
O valiant man! May bitterness such as you store inside yourself   30
never grip me; how will you benefit men yet unborn
if you do not now protect the Argives from ugly ruin?
You are without pity—your father was not the horseman Peleus,
nor Thetis your mother, but it was the grey sea and sheer cliffs
that bore you, so unbending is your spirit. If in your heart   35

you are seeking to avoid some divine pronouncement, and
your revered mother has brought you a message from Zeus,
at least send me out, and send the rest of the Myrmidon people
with me, and perhaps I shall prove the salvation of the Danaans.
Give me your armour to wear around my shoulders, and   40
then the Trojans may mistake me for you, and hold back
from the fighting, and the Achaeans' warlike sons will breathe again
in their weariness; there is little enough breathing-space in war.
Those who are unwearied may easily drive men exhausted
in the conflict away from the ships and huts, back to their city.'   45

    So he spoke, entreating, great fool that he was, for it was to be
his own dreadful death and its spectre that he was praying for.
Deeply angered, swift-footed Achilles addressed him:
'O Patroclus, sprung from Zeus, what are you saying?
I know of no divine pronouncement that should concern me,   50
nor has my revered mother brought me a message from Zeus;
no, this is a bitter grief that has come over my heart and spirit,
when a man is ready to dispossess his equal and to
take back a prize, because he is the greater in power;
that is my bitter grief, after all the pains my heart has endured.   55
The girl whom the sons of the Achaeans chose as a prize for me,
whom I won with my spear when I sacked a strongly walled city—
lord Agamemnon, Atreus' son, has taken her back from my hands,
as if I were some wandering migrant who has lost his rights.
Still, all that is past and done; we should let it go. It is after all   60
impossible to keep bitterness alive in one's heart for ever,
though I did think that I would not give up my anger
until war and its clamour reached as far as my ships.
Here, put my famous armour around your shoulders
and lead the Myrmidons who love war into the battle,   65
now that a dark menacing cloud of Trojans is surrounding
our ships, and the Argives are hemmed in on the shore
of the sea, and hold on to only a narrow strip of land,
and the whole Trojan city has come out against them, full of
daring, because they cannot see my helmet's frontal   70
gleaming close to them. They would soon flee and fill up
the watercourses with their dead, if only lord Agamemnon had
used me kindly; as it is, they are fighting all around our camp.
The spear of Diomedes, Tydeus' son, rages no more
in his hands to keep destruction away from the Danaans,   75

nor have I yet heard the voice of Atreus' son shouting
from his hated mouth; it is man-slaying Hector's voice that
bursts around us as he urges on the Trojans, while they fill
the whole plain with their war-shout and defeat us in the battle.
Despite all this, Patroclus, you must attack them with vigour   80
and keep destruction from the ships, so that they do not
burn them with blazing fire, and rob us of our longed-for return.
Now listen, and I shall put the purpose of my instructions in your mind:
you must win great honour and glory for me in the sight of
all the Danaans, so that they will send the beautiful girl   85
back to me, and give me splendid gifts in addition. When
you have driven the Trojans from the ships, come back; and if
Hera's loud-thundering husband grants you the winning of glory,
do not set your heart on fighting against the war-loving
Trojans without me, because then you will diminish my honour.   90
And do not, as you take delight in the war and conflict,
killing Trojans as you go, lead your troops on to Ilium,
in case one of the ever-living gods of Olympus enters the battle
against you; Apollo who shoots from afar loves them dearly.
Instead, turn back again once you have brought salvation's   95
light to the ships, and leave the others to fight on the plain.
O father Zeus and Athena and Apollo, how I wish that
of all the Trojans there are, none could escape death, nor
any of the Argives, and that we two could avoid destruction,
so that we alone could tear down the sacred headdress of Troy!'*   100

So they spoke, one to another, in this way; but Ajax, overwhelmed
by flying weapons, could no longer stand his ground—
both the will of Zeus and the splendid Trojans' spear-casts
were beating him down, and his shining helmet rang terribly
about his temples as it was struck, battered again and again   105
on its well-made cheek-plates. His left shoulder was tiring
from constantly holding his glittering shield steady; but though
they kept throwing at him they could not knock it from his grasp.
All the time he was gripped by a painful gasping, and sweat
was running down in streams from all his limbs, and he had no   110
chance to draw breath; everywhere disaster was piled on disaster.

Tell me now, Muses who have your homes on Olympus,
how fire first fell upon the ships of the Achaeans.

Hector drew close to Ajax and struck his ash pike with
his great sword, hitting it at the socket below the point,   115

and sheared the tip clean away; Telamon's son Ajax kept
shaking the docked pole in his hand, uselessly, and far away
from him the bronze head fell with a clang to the ground.
Ajax shuddered, realizing in his blameless heart that this
was the work of gods, that Zeus the high-thunderer was   120
cutting their plans short, and plotting victory for the Trojans.
He gave way before the missiles, and the Trojans threw unwearying
fire on to the swift ship, and unquenchable flames quickly spread
over it. So fire swirled round the stern; but Achilles
struck both his thighs and addressed Patroclus: 125
'Up with you Patroclus, sprung from Zeus, driver of horses!
I can see the blaze of destructive fire, there, by the ships;
I am afraid they will take our ships, and then there will be no way
to escape; so put your armour on, quickly, while I gather the people.'
   So he spoke, and Patroclus began to arm himself in flashing
      bronze.   130
First he fastened greaves around his legs,
fine ones, fitted with silver ankle-clasps;
next he put on round his chest the elaborately crafted,
star-decorated corslet of swift-footed Aeacus' grandson.
Over his shoulders he threw a silver-riveted sword,   135
made of bronze, and after that a huge, massive shield.
On his powerful head he set a well-fashioned helmet
with a horse-tail crest; and the plume nodded terribly above him.
Then he chose two stout spears, which fitted his grasp.
The only weapon of Aeacus' blameless grandson he did not take   140
was his spear, heavy, thick, and massive; none of the Achaeans
could brandish it, but only Achilles knew how to handle it—the
Pelian ash spear, which Cheiron had long ago given to his dear father,
cut from a peak on Pelion,* to be the death of heroes.
Patroclus ordered Automedon to yoke the horses without delay,   145
Automedon, whom he honoured most after Achilles, breaker
of ranks, and could trust most of all to wait for his call in battle.
So Automedon led the swift horses under the yoke for him—
Xanthus and Balius, a pair who flew with the winds' blast,
whom Podarge the storm-mare had borne to the West Wind   150
as she grazed in a meadow beside the waters of Ocean.
In the trace-reins he harnessed the blameless Pedasus,
the horse that Achilles carried off when he took Eëtion's city;
though it was mortal, it could keep up with immortal horses.*

Meanwhile Achilles went up and down his huts and armed   155
all the Myrmidons in their gear; and they were like wolves, eaters
of raw flesh, whose hearts are full of unbelievable strength,
and who have killed a great horned stag on the mountains
and now tear it apart, and all their jowls are red with blood;
and they go in a pack to lap with their thin tongues   160
at the surface of the dark water of some murky spring,
belching forth clots of blood; and the spirit in their breasts
is without fear, and their bellies are crammed full.
Such were the chieftains and captains of the Myrmidons,
swarming to join the noble attendant of swift-footed Aeacus'   165
grandson; and in their midst stood warlike Achilles,
urging on the horses and the shield-bearing men.

There were fifty swift ships* that Achilles, loved by Zeus,
had brought to Troy, and in each of them there were
fifty men, his companions, seated at the benches;   170
he had appointed five captains, whom he trusted to
give orders, while he himself had high command over them.
The first line was led by Menesthius of the glittering corslet;
he was the son of Spercheius, a river fed by rain from Zeus,
and beautiful Polydore, daughter of Peleus, had borne him   175
to unwearying Spercheius, a woman sleeping with a god,
though in name he was the son of Borus, Perieres' son,
who publicly married her, after giving a huge bride-price.
In charge of the second line was warlike Eudorus,
born out of wedlock to Polymele, beautiful in the dance,   180
daughter of Phylas. The mighty slayer of Argus fell in love
with her when his eyes fell on her among singing girls,
in the chorus who danced for Artemis of the golden distaff,
goddess of the hunting-cry. At once Hermes the kindly god
went up into her chamber and lay with her in secret, and gave her   185
a glorious son, Eudorus, a peerless swift runner and fighter.
When Eileithyia, the goddess who attends painful birth,
had brought him into the light, and he saw the sun's rays,
then Echecles, Actor's son, a man of mighty strength, took her
as wife to his home, after giving an immense bride-price;   190
but the old man Phylas raised him kindly and brought him up,
showing him affection as if he had been his own son.
In charge of the third line was warlike Peisander,
the son of Maemalus, who was the best of all the Myrmidons

at fighting with the spear, after the companion of Peleus' son.   195
The fourth line was led by the old horse-driver Phoenix,
and the fifth by Alcimedon, the blameless son of Laerces.
When Achilles had drawn them all up in order and posted them
with their leaders, he laid a harsh command on them:
'Myrmidons, let me not find any of you forgetful of the threats   200
that you used to make against the Trojans beside the swift ships,
in all the time of my anger. Each one would blame me, saying:
"Hard son of Peleus, we see now that your mother raised you on bile—
pitiless man, holding your unwilling companions back by the ships.
Let us go back again in our sea-traversing ships to our homes,   205
since it is clear that ruinous bile has entered your heart."
That is what you often said against me when you met together; but now
you are faced with a great work of war, such as you desired before;
so let every man keep a brave heart, and fight against the Trojans.'

    So he spoke, and quickened the fury and spirit in each man;   210
and when they heard their king their lines closed more tightly.
As when a man fits together close-set stones to build the wall
of a tall house, as protection against the winds' violence,
so their helmets and bossed shields fitted tight together,
shield pressing on shield, helmet on helmet, man on man;   215
helmets with their horsehair crests and bright plates touched
when they moved their heads, so close they stood to each other.
And in front of everyone two men stood in their armour,
Patroclus and Automedon, with one intention in their minds,
to enter the battle in front of the Myrmidons. But Achilles   220
set off for his hut, and raised the lid of a chest,
fine and intricately worked, which silver-footed Thetis
had put on his ship to take with him, filling it full with tunics
and cloaks and woollen rugs, to protect him against the wind.
In it he had a finely worked cup; no other man ever   225
drank the gleaming wine from it, nor did Achilles ever
pour libations from it to any god except to father Zeus.
Taking this cup from the chest he first purified it with
sulphur,* and then rinsed it in a stream of clear water,
and washed his hands, and drew off some gleaming wine.   230
Then, standing in mid-court, he prayed and poured out the wine,
looking up to the high sky; and thunder-delighting Zeus heard him:
'Lord Zeus, god of Dodona, Pelasgian, you who live far away,
ruling over wintry Dodona; and around you live your interpreters

the Selli, who sleep on the ground and whose feet are unwashed;* 235
when I prayed to you in the past you heard my words, and
gave me honour, and dealt the Achaean people a heavy blow,
so this time also fulfil this plea for me:
I myself shall remain here in the ships' gathering-place,
but I am sending out my companion with many Myrmidons, 240
to do battle; grant him glory, wide-thundering Zeus,
and embolden the heart within him, so that Hector
may come to know whether my attendant has the skill
to fight on his own, or whether his hands rage irresistibly
only when I go into the grind of Ares' warfare. 245
But when he has driven the clamorous fighting from the ships,
let him come back unharmed to me by the swift ships, with
all his gear, and with his hand-to-hand-fighting companions.'

    So he spoke in prayer, and Zeus the counsellor heard him,
and the father granted him one request, but refused the other: 250
he granted that Patroclus should drive war and fighting from the ships,
but refused him a safe and sound return from the battle.
So when Achilles had poured a libation and prayed to father Zeus
he went back into his hut, and put the cup back in the chest,
and went out and stood in front of the hut; still he wished 255
in his heart to see the terrible conflict of Trojans and Achaeans.

    Meanwhile the men who had armed with great-hearted Patroclus
marched onward until with high thoughts they charged at the Trojans.
They came pouring out like wasps at a road's side,
whom boys love to provoke, forever in their childish folly 260
tormenting them in their nests beside the way;
and so they make a common nuisance for many people,
and if some traveller passing that way unwittingly
stirs them up, they fly out with courage in their hearts,
one and all, and do battle on their young ones' behalf. 265
With hearts and spirits like theirs the Myrmidons then
poured out from the ships, and an unquenchable shout rose up.
Patroclus called out to his companions with a great shout:
'Myrmidons, companions of Achilles son of Peleus!
Be men, my friends, and call up your surging courage, to honour 270
Peleus' son, who is far the best of the Argives by the ships,
and whose close-fighting attendants are also the best; so that
Atreus' son, wide-ruling Agamemnon, may come to know
his delusion, in that he did not honour the best of the Achaeans.'

So he spoke, and quickened the fury and spirit in each man,   275
and they fell in a mass upon the Trojans; and about them
the ships echoed terrifyingly to the shouts of the Achaeans.

When the Trojans saw the stalwart son of Menoetius,
the man himself and his attendant, gleaming in their armour,
all their hearts were perturbed, and their ranks wavered,   280
since they supposed that the swift-footed son of Peleus
had thrown off his anger and had chosen reconciliation; and
each man looked about for escape from sheer destruction.

Patroclus was the first to let fly with a shining spear,
right into the midst, where the confusion of men was thickest,   285
beside the stern of the ship of great-spirited Protesilaus,*
and he hit Pyraechmes, who had brought his horse-marshalling
Paeonians from Amydon, from the broad-flowing Axius;*
he struck him on the right shoulder, and he fell on his back
    in the dust,
groaning, and his Paeonian companions around him were   290
panic-stricken, for Patroclus had let loose terror among them all
by killing their leader, who was always their champion in battle.
Then he drove them away from the ships, and doused the blazing fire;
the half-burnt ship was left there, and the Trojans fled in terror
with an astounding clamour, and the Danaans poured out   295
between the hollow ships, and the shouts rose without ceasing.
As when Zeus who gathers the lightning drives a dense cloud
away from the lofty pinnacle of a huge mountain, and
all the crags and jutting peaks and mountain glens stand out,
and boundless bright air breaks down from the high sky;   300
so the Danaans drove the ravening fire from their ships and
breathed briefly again—though there was no pause in the fighting,
for the Trojans had not yet been forced back in headlong flight
from the black ships by the Achaeans, dear to Ares, but still
held out, retreating from the ships only in the face of greater
    force.   305

Then as the fighting spread further man killed man among
the chieftains. First, the stalwart son of Menoetius hit Areïlycus
in the thigh with his sharp spear just at the moment when
he was turning to run, and drove the bronze clean through;
his spear shattered the bone, and Areïlycus fell headlong   310
on the earth. Then warlike Menelaus stabbed Thoas in the chest
where it was unprotected next to his shield, and loosened his limbs.

Phyleus' son Meges watched Amphiclus as he charged at him,
and was too quick for him, lunging at the top of his leg
where a man's muscle is thickest; the tendons were ripped apart　　315
around the point of the spear, and darkness covered his eyes.
Of Nestor's two sons, Antilochus stabbed Atymnius with his
sharp spear; the bronze-tipped spear went clean through his side,
and he toppled forward. Maris, incensed on his brother's behalf,
sprang at Antilochus from close quarters, and took his stand　　320
over the dead man; but godlike Thrasymedes was too quick
for him, and before Maris could wound him lunged at his
shoulder, and did not miss; the spear's point tore the base of
his arm away from the muscles, and split it as far as the bone.
He fell with a thud, and darkness came down over his eyes.　　325
So these two were beaten down by the two brothers and
went down to Erebus; they were noble companions of Sarpedon,
spear-throwing sons of Amisodarus, who had reared
the ferocious Chimaera that brought ruin to many men.
Ajax, son of Oïleus, sprang at Cleobulus and took him　　330
alive, entangled in the confusion; there and then he struck him
in the neck with his hilted sword and loosened his fury—
the whole sword grew warm with his blood, and purple death
and his cruel destiny came down and fastened on to his eyes.
Peneleos and Lycon charged at each other, for they had missed　　335
with their spears; both throws had been in vain, and so they
ran at each other with their swords. Lycon swung at the
plate of the other's horsehair-crested helmet, but his sword
shattered at the hilt; then Peneleos struck him in the neck
below his ear, and the blade sank right in; only the skin held　　340
his head, and it slumped to one side, and his limbs were loosened.
Meriones overtook Acamas on swift feet and stabbed him
on the right shoulder as he was about to mount his chariot;
he toppled from the chariot, and a mist spread over his eyes.
Idomeneus stabbed Erymas in the mouth with the pitiless　　345
bronze, and the bronze-tipped spear passed clean through,
underneath his brain, and smashed the white bones;
his teeth were shaken out, and both eyes were filled
with blood; gaping, he blew blood up through his mouth
and nostrils, and a black cloud of death enveloped him.　　350
　　And so these Danaan leaders each killed his man.
As ravening wolves fall on lambs or kids, taking them

from herds that have become separated on the mountains
through their herdsman's folly, and the wolves see this,
and quickly carry the beasts off, since they have a timid spirit;   355
so the Danaans fell on the Trojans, whose minds turned to
clamorous flight, and they forgot their surging courage.

    Now huge Ajax was forever impatient to throw his spear at
Hector of the bronze helmet, but he in his battle-knowledge
kept his broad shoulders concealed behind his oxhide shield,   360
watching out for the whistle of arrows and the thud of spears.
He knew well that the battle had turned through his enemies' valour,
but still he stood his ground, trying to save his trusty companions.

    As when, after clear bright air, a cloud breaks into the high sky
from Olympus, when Zeus is unfurling a tempest,   365
so from the ships there arose shouting and the sounds of rout,
as the Trojans crossed the ditch again, but not in good order. Hector
was carried off by his swift-footed horses, arms and all, and abandoned
the Trojan people who were trapped, involuntarily, by the deep ditch;
and in the ditch many swift chariot-hauling horses   370
broke their pole at its end and left their lords' chariots behind.
Patroclus pursued them, incessantly urging on the Danaans,
with ruin in his mind for the Trojans, now that they were scattered,
and filling all the ways with shouts and the noise of rout; high above,
a dust storm spread up to the clouds as the single-hoofed horses   375
strained to escape from the ships and huts back to the city.
Patroclus, shouting, aimed straight for wherever he saw that
the people were in the greatest confusion; men fell headlong from
chariots under his axles, and their chariots turned upside-down.
The immortal swift horses that the gods had given to Peleus*   380
as a glorious gift pressed onward and cleared the ditch with one
bound; Patroclus' heart called to him to go after Hector, and he
longed to fell him, but Hector's swift horses carried him away.
As when the whole of the black land is oppressed by a storm
on a day in autumn, when Zeus pours down great torrents of rain;   385
he is full of rancour towards men and is furious with them,
because they give violent, crooked judgements in their assembly,
and drive out justice, with no concern for the gods' gaze,
and all the rivers in their land are flowing in full spate,
and everywhere torrents are tearing the hillsides away,   390
rushing with a mighty roar down from the mountains
headlong into the purple sea, sweeping away the works of men—

so great was the roar of the Trojan chariots as they fled.

When Patroclus had cut off the nearest companies he drove them
back again, penning them by the ships, and would not let them   395
make for the city, for all their striving, but charged in
among them between the ships, the river, and the high wall, and
began the killing, exacting payment for the deaths of many men.
First he hit Pronous with his shining spear, where his chest
was unprotected next to his shield, and loosened his limbs,   400
and he fell with a thud. Next, Patroclus leapt at Thestor,
the son of Enops; he had been knocked out of his senses, and
was sitting hunched in his well-polished chariot, and the reins
had slipped from his hands; Patroclus stood close and stabbed him
with his spear on his jaw's right side, driving it through his teeth,   405
then hoisted him with the spear, and dragged him over
        the chariot-rail,
like a man who sits on a jutting rock and drags a sacred fish out
of the sea with line and glittering bronze hook. So Patroclus
dragged Thestor, gaping, from his chariot on his shining spear,
and thrust him down on his face; and his life left him where
        he fell.   410
Next, as Erylaus charged at him, he struck him with a rock
on the middle of his head, and split it completely in two
inside his heavy helmet; and the man fell face-forward
to the ground, and life-breaking death poured round him.
Next he brought down Erymas and Amphoterus and Epaltes,   415
Tlepolemus, the son of Damastor, and Echius and Pyris,
Ipheus and Euippus and Polymelus, son of Argeas, all of them,
one after another, down to the earth that nourishes many.

When Sarpedon saw his companions with unbelted shirts
being beaten down at the hands of Menoetius' son Patroclus,   420
he called out in reproach to the godlike Lycians:
'Shame, Lycians! Where are you running? Be quick now!
I am going out to confront this man, to find out who it is
that prevails here, and has indeed inflicted great hurt on
the Trojans, unloosing the limbs of many noble men.'   425

So he spoke, and leapt fully armed to the ground from his chariot.
And on the other side Patroclus, when he saw him, jumped down
from his chariot. Like hook-taloned vultures with curved beaks
that fight, shrieking loudly, on some lofty peak,
so these two charged screaming against each other.   430

When the son of crooked-scheming Cronus saw them
he pitied them, and spoke to Hera, his sister and wife:
'This is a great sorrow for me, that it is the fate of Sarpedon,
dearest of men, to be beaten down by Patroclus, Menoetius' son.
As I ponder in my mind my heart is divided two ways,   435
whether I should pluck him up alive out of the battle,
bringer of tears, and set him down in the rich land of Lycia,*
or if I should now beat him down at the hands of Menoetius' son.'
    Then in answer the lady ox-eyed Hera said:
'Most dread son of Cronus, what is this that you have said?   440
This is a mortal man, whose due destiny was fixed long ago;
is it really your desire to release him from death's gloomy lament?
Go, do it; but all we other gods will not approve it.
And I tell you another thing, and you should store it in your mind:
if you send Sarpedon back to his own home, alive,   445
consider whether in the future some other god also will want
to send his own dear son away from the harsh crush of battle.
There are many sons of immortals fighting around the great city
of Priam, and you will cause terrible resentment among them.
No; if he really is dear to you, and your heart mourns for him,   450
allow him to be beaten down in the harsh crush of battle
at the hands of Patroclus, son of Menoetius;
but when his breath and life have gone from him,
send Death and sweet Sleep to carry him away
until they come to the land of broad Lycia, and there   455
his brothers and kinsmen will give him proper funeral rites,
with grave-mound and pillar, which is the privilege of the dead.'
    So she spoke, and the father of gods and men did not disobey her,
but began to rain a shower of bloody raindrops upon the earth,*
honouring his own dear son, whom Patroclus was about   460
to kill in rich-soiled Troy, far from his native land.
    When they had advanced to within close range of each other,
then Patroclus hit far-famed Thrasymelus,
who was the valiant attendant of lord Sarpedon,
in the base of his belly and loosened his limbs.   465
Sarpedon threw second at him with his shining spear and
missed Patroclus, but hit the horse Pedasus with the spear
on its right shoulder; it screamed as it gasped its life away,
and fell bellowing in the dust, and the life flew from it.
The other horses sprang sideways, the yoke creaked, and the reins   470

became tangled in them, since their trace-horse lay in the dust,
but Automedon, famed with the spear, found a remedy for that:
drawing his long-bladed sword from beside his sturdy thigh,
he lunged forward and skilfully cut the trace-horse free.
The other two straightened themselves and pulled at the reins,   475
and the two men came together again in heart-devouring war.

   Then Sarpedon missed again with his shining spear,
and its point passed over Patroclus' left shoulder,
and did not strike him; Patroclus in turn aimed his
bronze-tipped spear, and it did not fly from his hand in vain,   480
but hit Sarpedon where the midriff closes round the beating heart.
He toppled as an oak tree topples, or a poplar, or a
soaring pine that woodsmen have cut down on the
mountains with their newly whetted axes, to be ship-timber;
so Sarpedon lay sprawled in front of his horses and chariot,   485
roaring, and scrabbling at the blood-soaked dust.
As when a lion gets in among a herd and kills a bull,
a great-spirited, gleaming beast among shambling cattle,
and it dies bellowing under the lion's jaws,
so the captain of the shield-bearing Lycians   490
died raging, and called out to his dear companion:
'Glaucus, my friend, fighter among men, now you must
more than ever be a spearman and a daring fighter;
now, if you are swift, let ruinous war be your desire.
First, go everywhere up and down those who are leaders   495
of the Lycians and exhort them to do battle over Sarpedon;
and after that fight yourself with the bronze for my sake;
I shall in future time be a disgrace and a reproach to you,
for ever, for all your days, if the Achaeans strip me of
my armour, here where I fell at the gathering of the ships.   500
So be strong and hold firm, and urge on the people.'

   As Sarpedon spoke, the end of death covered his eyes
and nostrils; Patroclus planted his foot on his chest, and
wrenched the spear from his flesh, and the midriff came with it—
he had pulled out the spear's point and Sarpedon's life together.   505
There the Myrmidons held on to his snorting horses, anxious
to take flight, now that they were free of their lords' chariot.

   Terrible grief came over Glaucus when he heard Sarpedon's voice;
his heart was in turmoil, because he could not come to his aid.
With his hand he gripped his arm and squeezed it, for he was hurt   510

by the wound that Teucer, staving off ruin from his companions,
had caused with an arrow when Glaucus charged at the high wall.*
He spoke in prayer to Apollo who shoots from afar:
'Hear me, lord, you who are somewhere in the rich land
of Lycia, or in Troy! Wherever you are, you are able to hear   515
a man in torment, as now torment has come over me;
this wound I have is severe, and my whole arm is shot
through with piercing agony, and my blood will not dry,
and my shoulder is numb and useless because of it;
I cannot hold my spear firmly, nor am I able to go   520
into battle against the enemy. The best of men is dead,
Sarpedon, the son of Zeus—who will not help even his own son.
Lord, I beg you, heal this grave wound for me,
soothe the agony, and give me strength, so that I can
call out to my Lycian companions and urge them into battle,   525
and can myself fight over the body of the dead man.'

So he spoke in prayer, and Phoebus Apollo heard him,
and immediately stopped the pain, and dried the dark blood
in his agonizing wound, and cast fury into his heart.
Glaucus knew in his heart what had happened, and was glad   530
that the great god had listened to him when he prayed.
First he went everywhere among the leaders of the Lycians
and exhorted them to do battle over Sarpedon, and then
made his way with great strides among the Trojans,
to Polydamas, son of Panthous, and to glorious Agenor,   535
and then went to find Aeneas and bronze-helmeted Hector;
standing nearby he addressed them in winged words:
'Hector, you must now have completely forgotten your allies,
who for your sake are wasting their lives away far from
their friends and native land, while you refuse to help them.   540
Sarpedon, captain of the shield-bearing Lycians, lies dead,
who used to defend Lycia with his judgements and his strength;
brazen Ares has beaten him down under Patroclus' spear.
Come, my friends, take your stand beside me, and set anger
in your hearts, so that the Myrmidons do not strip his arms   545
and mutilate the dead man, being angry for all the Danaans
who have died, killed with our spears beside their swift ships.'

So he spoke, and overwhelming grief took hold of the Trojans,
uncontrollable and not to be endured, for Sarpedon was always
a rampart of their city, though from a foreign land; a great army 550

had come with him, and among them he was always their finest fighter.
They made straight for the Danaans, full of passion, and Hector
led them, enraged for Sarpedon's sake. But the Achaeans
were stirred up by the shaggy heart of Menoetius' son Patroclus;
first he addressed the two called Ajax, who were already raging to
    fight: 555
'You two called Ajax, now it must be your desire to defend yourselves,
to be as you have been before among men, or even better.
The man lying dead was the first to leap on to the Achaean wall*—
Sarpedon; let us see if we can capture and mutilate him,
and strip the armour from his shoulders, and beat down with   560
the pitiless bronze any of his companions who defend him.'
   So he spoke, and they themselves were raging to aid him in the fight.
On both sides then the armies strengthened their companies,
Trojans and Lycians, and Myrmidons and Achaeans,
and they crashed together, to fight over the dead man,   565
shouting terrifyingly; and the men's armour rang out loud.
Zeus spread a deadly darkness over the fierce crush of battle,
so that there should be deadly toil of battle over his dear son.
   At first the Trojans drove the darting-eyed Achaeans back;
by no means the worst man of the Myrmidons was struck down,   570
glorious Epeigeus, the son of great-spirited Agacles,
who used to rule over Boudeion, a well-populated city,
in former times; but he had killed a noble kinsman, and
came as a suppliant to Peleus and silver-footed Thetis, and
they had sent him to accompany Achilles, breaker of ranks,   575
to Ilium rich in horses, in order to fight against the Trojans.*
As this man laid hands on the dead Sarpedon, illustrious Hector
hit him on the head with a rock, and split it completely in two
inside his heavy helmet, and the man fell face-forward
over the body, and life-breaking death poured round him.   580
Grief came over Patroclus at the death of his companion,
and he charged straight through the front-fighters like a swift
hawk, which causes panic among doves and starlings;
just so, Patroclus, driver of chariots, you rushed straight for
the Lycians and Trojans, angry in your heart for your companion. 585
Next he hit Sthenelaus, the dear son of Ithaemenes,
on his neck with a rock, and tore the sinews away from it.
The front-fighters retreated before him, and illustrious Hector
with them; as far as is the carry of a long, light javelin

thrown by a man trying his strength in a competition or   590
in war, when he is hard pressed by life-breaking enemies,
so far the Trojans retreated, and the Achaeans drove them back.
The first to turn and face them was Glaucus, captain of the
shield-bearing Lycians, and he killed great-spirited Bathycles,
the dear son of Chalcon, whose home was in Hellas, and he was   595
conspicuous among the Myrmidons for wealth and prosperity.
As Bathycles pursued and was about to catch him, Glaucus suddenly
turned and stabbed him with his spear in the middle of his chest;
he fell with a thud, and thick grief seized the Achaeans,
because a fine man had fallen. The Trojans were hugely exultant,   600
and came up and stood round Glaucus in a mass; but the Achaeans
did not forget their valour, and their fury carried them straight at him.
There in his turn Meriones killed a helmeted man of the Trojans—
Laogonus, the daring son of Onetor, who was a priest of
Idaean Zeus, and was honoured by the people like a god.   605
Meriones hit him under his jaw and ear, and the life quickly
deserted his limbs, and hateful darkness took hold of him.
Aeneas let fly a bronze-tipped spear at Meriones,
hoping to hit him under the shield as he advanced; but
Meriones looked ahead, and avoided the bronze-tipped spear—   610
he crouched forward, and behind him the long spear
stuck fast in the ground, making its butt-end quiver,
and then towering Ares took the fury away from it.
[Aeneas' spear passed quivering into the earth,
since it had flown in vain from his powerful hand.]*   615
Aeneas grew angry in his heart, and spoke to him:
'Meriones, you may well be a good dancer, but my spear would
soon have stopped you once and for all, if only I had hit you.'

    Then in turn Meriones, famed with the spear, addressed him:
'Aeneas, it is hard for you, strong though you are, to   620
quench the fury of every man who comes face to face
with you in the fighting. You too were born a mortal, and
if I were to throw and hit you in the belly with the sharp bronze,
though mighty and confident in your hands you would soon give
the glory to me, and your shade to Hades, master of famous horses.'   625

    So he spoke, but the stalwart son of Menoetius rebuked him:
'Meriones, you are a fine man; but why use words like this?
My friend, insulting words will not make the Trojans turn back
from the dead man; the earth will hold many a man before that.

War's outcome hangs on the work of hands; the place for talk is   630
the council. It is not our task to heap words on words, but to fight.'
    So he spoke, and led off, and Meriones, a godlike man, followed.
As when the crashing caused by woodcutters rises up from
the clearings of a mountain, and the sound is heard far away,
so there rose up from the earth of wide ways the thudding   635
of bronze and of leather and of well-made oxhide shields,
as men jabbed at each other with swords and double-edged spears.
And now not even an observant man would have recognized glorious
Sarpedon, since he was covered by spears and blood and dust
from his head right down to the toes of his feet. And all   640
the time men were swarming over the dead man, like flies
in a farmyard that buzz around overflowing pails,
in the spring season when buckets are awash with milk;
just so they swarmed over the dead man, and Zeus never
turned his shining eyes from the harsh crush of battle, but   645
all the time kept looking down at them and musing in his heart,
debating at great length about the death of Patroclus,
whether illustrious Hector should now cut him down as well
with the bronze, there and then in the harsh crush of battle
over godlike Sarpedon, and strip the armour from his shoulders,   650
or if he should pile up war's arduous toil for even more men.
And as he pondered this seemed to him to be the better course,
that the valiant attendant of Achilles, son of Peleus,
should drive the Trojans and bronze-helmeted Hector
back again to the city, and should rob many of their lives.   655
First of all he put a spiritless temper into Hector, who
mounted his chariot and turned in flight, and called to the
other Trojans to flee, for he saw the work of Zeus' sacred scales.
Then not even the powerful Lycians stood firm, but they all
fled in terror when they saw their king struck in the heart,   660
lying in a heap of dead men—for many men had fallen over him
after the son of Cronus had prolonged the fierce strife.
The Achaeans stripped his gleaming bronze armour from
Sarpedon's shoulders, and the stalwart son of Menoetius
gave it to his companions to take to the hollow ships.   665
Then Zeus who gathers the clouds addressed Apollo:
'Come now, dear Phoebus; go and take Sarpedon out of
the spears' range, and wash away his dark blood, and then
carry him far away and bathe him in a river's waters and

anoint him with ambrosia and clothe him in immortal garments;   670
send him to be carried away by swift escorts,
the twin brothers Sleep and Death, who will quickly
set him down in the rich land of broad Lycia, where
his brothers and kinsmen will give him proper funeral rites,
with grave-mound and pillar, which is the privilege of the dead.'   675
    So he spoke, and Apollo did not fail to listen to his father.
He set off down from the mountain of Ida to the grim conflict,
and quickly lifted glorious Sarpedon out of the spears' range and
carried him far away and bathed him in a river's waters and
anointed him with ambrosia and clothed him in immortal garments;   680
then he sent him to be carried away by swift escorts,
the twin brothers Sleep and Death, who quickly
set him down in the rich land of broad Lycia.
    Now Patroclus shouted instructions to Automedon in his chariot
and went in pursuit of the Trojans and Lycians, and he was
        mightily   685
deluded, fool that he was. Had he marked the words of Peleus' son
he would surely have escaped the evil spectre of black death,
but the mind of Zeus is always more powerful than that of men:
he turns even the brave man to flight and takes away his victory,
easily, and yet at another time can himself rouse men to fight,   690
as now he caused resolve to enter the breast of Patroclus.
    Then who was it you first slew, Patroclus, and who last,
when the gods had summoned you to your death?
Adrestus was the first, and Autonous and Echeclus,
and Perimus, the son of Megas, and Epistor and Melanippus,   695
and after them Elasus and Mulius and Pylartes.
These he killed, and all the rest turned their minds to flight.
    Then the sons of the Achaeans would have taken high-gated Troy
at the hands of Patroclus, for he was storming ahead with his spear,
had not Phoebus Apollo taken his stand on the well-built wall   700
with thoughts of death for Patroclus, and minded to help the Trojans.
Three times Patroclus climbed a corner of the high wall,
and three times Apollo smashed him back, shoving
the shining shield away with his immortal hands;
but when he launched himself for the fourth time, like a god,   705
Apollo gave a terrible shout and spoke winged words to him:
'Go back, Patroclus, sprung from Zeus! It is not your destiny
that the city of the lordly Trojans should be sacked by your spear,

nor at the hands of Achilles, who is a far better man than you.'
So he spoke, and Patroclus fell back a long way,   710
avoiding the anger of Apollo who shoots from afar.
Meanwhile Hector was holding back his single-hoofed horses
by the Scaean gates, unsure whether to drive into the mêlée again
and fight, or to call out to the people to gather by the wall.
As he was musing on this Phoebus Apollo came and stood by him,   715
in the likeness of a vigorous and strong young man,
Asius, who was horse-breaking Hector's uncle on his mother's
side, a full brother of Hecuba, and the son of Dymas,
whose home was in Phrygia by the waters of Sangarius;
taking his likeness, Apollo, son of Zeus, addressed him: 720
'Hector, why have you stopped fighting? You should not do so.
I wish I were as much stronger than you as you are than me—
you would soon find it painful to withdraw from the fighting.
Come now, drive your strong-hoofed horses at Patroclus
to see if you can kill him, and if Apollo will give you glory.'   725
So he spoke, and went away, a god joining the toil of men;
and illustrious Hector ordered war-minded Cebriones
to lash the horses into the fighting. Apollo left them
and joined the mass of men, and let loose ruinous confusion
among the Argives, but gave glory to the Trojans and Hector.   730
Hector left the other Danaans alone, killing none of them,
but drove his strong-hoofed horses towards Patroclus;
Patroclus on the other side leapt to the ground from his chariot,
holding a spear in his left hand and in his right he held a stone,
jagged and shining, and his hand covered it completely.   735
He flung it with his weight behind it; the sharp stone did not
miss its man, nor fly in vain, but hit Hector's charioteer,
Cebriones, a bastard son of splendid Priam,
on the forehead as he was holding the reins.
The rock crushed both his brows together, and the bone   740
could not hold, and his eyes fell to the ground in the dust,
there before his feet; he dropped like a diver from
the well-made chariot, and the life left his bones.
Then, charioteer Patroclus, you addressed him jeeringly:
'Well, this is a very nimble fellow, and an agile diver!   745
Doubtless if he were on the fish-rich sea this man
could leap from a ship and satisfy the hunger of many
by looking for oysters, even in very stormy weather—

so agilely does he now dive from his chariot on to the plain.
So, it seems, there are acrobats even among the Trojans!'   750
    So speaking he made for the hero Cebriones with the spring
of a lion, that while causing a shambles in cattle-folds
is hit in the chest, and is killed by its own courage;
just so, Patroclus, you sprang at Cebriones, full of rage.
On the other side Hector jumped to the ground from his chariot,   755
and the two of them struggled over Cebriones like lions
on mountain peaks fighting with fearless spirits,
both of them hungry, over a hind that has been killed;
so these two raisers of the battle-cry, Patroclus, Menoetius' son,
and illustrious Hector, strained over Cebriones to   760
hack at each other's flesh with the pitiless bronze.
Hector seized him by the head, and would not let go, while
Patroclus on his side caught him by the foot; and the rest of
the Trojans and Danaans joined in the fierce crush of battle.
    As when the East and South Winds struggle with each other   765
in the clearings of a mountain to make a deep wood shake—
beech, ash, and smooth-barked oak tree, which dash their
long branches against each other with an astounding clamour—
and the noise of their cracking goes up as they break,
so the Trojans and the Achaeans leapt upon each other,   770
cutting men down, and neither side thought of fatal flight.
Around Cebriones many sharp spears were driven home,
and winged arrows too, springing from bowstrings, and
many great rocks were smashed into men's shields as they
struggled over him. And all this time he was lying in the whirling   775
dust, mightily in his might, his chariot-skill all forgotten.
As long as the sun bestrode the midpoint of the high sky
both sides' missiles struck home, and the men kept falling;
but when the sun sloped towards the time when oxen are unyoked,
then the Achaeans proved stronger, beyond what was fated.   780
They dragged the hero Cebriones out of the missiles' range, away
from the Trojans' shouts, and stripped the armour from his shoulders,
and Patroclus sprang at the Trojans with destruction in his heart.
Three times he leapt forward, the equal of swift Ares, yelling
terribly, and three times he killed nine men. But when he was   785
about to charge for the fourth time like some divine being,
then, Patroclus, the end of your life became clear to see;
in the fierce crush of battle Phoebus came to oppose you,

terrible god. Patroclus did not see him coming through the mêlée,
because he came to confront him concealed in a thick mist;   790
he stood behind Patroclus and struck his back and broad
shoulders with the flat of his hand, and his eyes whirled round.
Then Phoebus Apollo struck the helmet from his head,
and the vizored helmet rolled clanging away
under the feet of the horses, its plumes defiled   795
with blood and dust. Before this it had not been allowed
for this horsehair-crested helmet to be defiled with dust,
when it protected the head and handsome face of the
godlike man, Achilles; but this time Zeus gave it to Hector
to wear on his head—though his own death was near at hand.   800
Patroclus' long-shadowing spear, heavy, thick, and massive and
bronze-pointed, shattered completely in his hands, and his fringed
shield fell from his shoulders to the ground, together with its strap,
and lord Apollo, the son of Zeus, unfastened his corslet;
fatal delusion seized his wits, his glorious limbs were unloosed,   805
and he stood there in a daze. Then a Dardanian hit him from close
behind with his sharp spear, in the back, between the shoulders;
this was Euphorbus, the son of Panthous, who excelled all men
of his age in spear-throwing and chariot-skill and speed of foot,
and had already brought down twenty men from their chariots,   810
though it was the first time he had come in his chariot to learn about war;
it was this man who first threw a spear at you, charioteer Patroclus,
but he did not kill you; after pulling the ash spear from your flesh
he ran back and mingled with the soldiery, and would not wait
to face Patroclus in the battle, unarmed though he was.   815
He, beaten down by the god's blow and by the spear, began
to retreat to his companions' people, avoiding the death-spectre;
but when Hector saw that great-spirited Patroclus had been
wounded with the sharp bronze and was falling back,
he came up along the ranks and from close by thrust his spear   820
into the base of his belly, and drove the bronze clean through.
He fell with a thud, and brought great grief to the Achaean army.
As when a lion overpowers a tireless boar in battle—
the two of them fighting with fearless spirits on some
mountain's peaks over a little spring, where both want to drink—   825
and the lion violently beats it down as it struggles for breath;
so, after Menoetius' stalwart son had killed many men, Hector,
Priam's son, came close and with a spear robbed him of his life,

and boasting over him he addressed him with winged words:
'Patroclus, doubtless you thought you would sack our city,   830
and would rob the Trojan women of their day of freedom,
and would carry them off in ships to your dear native land.
Fool! To protect them, the horses of Hector were straining
on swift feet to join the fighting, and here am I, the finest
spear-fighter of the war-loving Trojans, to defend them from   835
the day of necessity. As for you, vultures will devour you here.
Poor wretch, not even Achilles, for all his greatness, could help you;
when you left and he stayed he doubtless said to you many times:
"Patroclus, driver of horses, do not come back to me here
at the hollow ships, until you have slashed the shirt of Hector,   840
slayer of men, around his chest, and covered it with his blood."
So, I think, he spoke to you, and persuaded your witless wits.'*
     Then, charioteer Patroclus, with little strength left you addressed him:
'Boast loudly while you can, Hector; Cronus' son Zeus and Apollo
have given you the victory, they who have beaten me down   845
easily—for it was they who stripped the armour from my shoulders.
But if twenty men such as you are had come to confront me
they would have died here and now, beaten down by my spear.
No, it was my fatal destiny and Leto's son that killed me,
and among men, Euphorbus; and you are the third to slay me.   850
But I tell you another thing, and you should store it in your mind:
you yourself have not long to live, and already death and
your own harsh destiny are standing close to you, beaten
down by the hands of Aeacus' grandson, blameless Achilles.'
     As he said this the end of death enveloped him, and his shade   855
winged its way from his limbs and went down to Hades,
lamenting its doom and leaving behind its manliness and youth.
Then illustrious Hector addressed him, though he was now dead:
'Patroclus, why do you prophesy a grim death for me?
Who knows if Achilles, the son of Thetis of the lovely hair,   860
may yet be struck down by my spear and lose his life before I do?'
     So speaking he set his foot on Patroclus and pulled the
          bronze-tipped spear
from the wound, and kicked him away from it to lie on his back;
then with his spear he immediately went in pursuit of Automedon,
the godlike attendant of swift-footed Achilles, since he was eager   865
to strike him down; but the swift-footed horses were carrying him off,
the immortal horses that the gods had given Peleus as a splendid gift.

BOOK SEVENTEEN

ATREUS' son Menelaus, dear to Ares, was not unaware that
Patroclus had been beaten down by the Trojans in the fighting.
He set off through the front-fighters, helmeted in gleaming bronze,
and stood over him, as a mother-cow that before this
has not given birth stands lowing over her firstborn calf;   5
just so fair-haired Menelaus stood over Patroclus.
In front of him he held his spear and perfectly balanced shield,
raging to kill any man who came up to confront him.
Nor did the fall of excellent Patroclus pass unnoticed by
Panthous' son Euphorbus of the blameless ash spear; he took   10
his stand close to warlike Menelaus and addressed him:
'Menelaus, Atreus' son, marshal of the people, nurtured by Zeus—
get back, leave the dead man, and let the bloodstained spoils lie;
no man of the Trojans or of their famous allies struck
Patroclus with his spear in the harsh battle-crush before I did;   15
so leave me alone to win splendid glory among the Trojans,
before I strike you down and rob you of your honey-sweet life.'

   Deeply angered, fair-haired Menelaus addressed him:
'Father Zeus, it is not a good thing to boast so insolently!
Not the fury of the panther, nor the fury of the lion,   20
nor the fury of the deadly wild boar, whose spirit in its breast
is the greatest of all as it glories in its might, is seemingly as great
as is the proud fury of Panthous' sons of the fine ash spear.
Yet the mighty Hyperenor, breaker of horses, did not go on
to take delight in his youth once he had faced and   25
insulted me.* He said I was the most contemptible fighter
among the Danaans; but I do not think it was on his own feet that
he returned, to bring happiness to his dear wife and wise parents.
So it is with you; if you challenge me I shall assuredly undo
your fury. I tell you: give way and go back into the mass   30
of men, and do not take your stand against me, or some
calamity may befall you; even a fool understands after the event.'

   So he spoke, but did not persuade Euphorbus, who answered him:
'Now, Menelaus, nurtured by Zeus, you will surely pay for
my brother whom you killed and spoke boastfully over, and   35
made his wife a widow, deep in her new marriage-chamber,

and brought unspeakable grief and lamentation to his parents.
I could bring some respite to these wretched people's lamenting
if I could take your head and your armour to them and
lay them in the hands of Panthous and bright Phrontis.   40
But now—our business must not remain longer without test
or fighting, whether it ends in victory or in flight.'
    So speaking he jabbed at Menelaus' perfectly balanced shield,
but the bronze did not break through it, and the spear-point
was bent back in the tough shield. Then Atreus' son Menelaus   45
stood up holding his bronze spear, and prayed to father Zeus,
and as Euphorbus fell back he stabbed him in the base of
his throat, throwing his weight behind his brawny hand's thrust;
the point passed clean through Euphorbus' tender neck,
and he fell with a thud, and his armour clattered about him.   50
His hair that was lovely as the Graces', his curls twisted and
pinned with silver and gold, were drenched with blood.
As when a man grows the healthy shoot of an olive tree
in a lonely place, a fine, flourishing shoot that has been
soaked by abundant water; light winds from every quarter   55
set it trembling, and it bursts into white blossom,
but then a wind suddenly arises and with a great gust
uproots it from its trench and lays it flat on the earth;
so lay Panthous' son, Euphorbus of the fine ash spear, when
Menelaus, Atreus' son, killed him and stripped his armour.   60
    As when some mountain-nurtured lion, trusting in its valour,
seizes on the cow that is the best in a herd at pasture,
and first takes the neck in its powerful jaws and breaks it,
and then greedily gulps down its blood and all its entrails,
tearing it apart; and around the lion dogs and shepherds   65
clamour loud and long, but from a distance, and are unwilling
to come up and confront it, because pale fear grips them;
so no Trojan's heart in his breast had the courage
to come up and confront splendid Menelaus.
Then Atreus' son would easily have stolen the famous armour   70
of Panthous' son, had not Phoebus Apollo grudged it him,
and roused Hector, the equal of swift Ares, against him,
likening himself to a man, Mentes, leader of the Cicones;*
and he addressed Hector, speaking with winged words:
'Hector, you are now running after what you cannot reach,   75
pursuing the horses of Aeacus' war-minded grandson;

they are troublesome for mortal men to subdue and drive,
except for Achilles, and he was born to an immortal mother.*
Meanwhile here is Menelaus, the warlike son of Atreus,
standing over Patroclus; and he has killed the best of the Trojans,   80
Euphorbus, Panthous' son, putting an end to his surging valour.'

So the god spoke and went back into the toil of men,
and bitter grief flooded into Hector's dark inner heart;
he looked keenly along the ranks, and immediately saw
one man stripping the famous armour, and the other lying   85
on the ground; and blood was flowing around the stab-wound.
He set off through the front-fighters, helmeted in gleaming bronze,
with a piercing shout, in the likeness of the unquenchable flame
of Hephaestus. Atreus' son was not unaware of his piercing cry,
and, deeply troubled, he spoke to his great-hearted spirit: 90
'What is to be done? If I leave the fine armour behind me,
with Patroclus, who lies here because he tried to avenge me,
I am afraid that any Danaan who sees it will be angry with me.
But if I confront Hector and the Trojans alone, and so avoid
disgrace, I fear that they will surround me, many against one;   95
Hector of the glittering helmet is bringing all the Trojans here.
But why does my dear heart debate with me in this way?
When a man aspires, against a god's will, to fight with another
whom the gods love, great suffering soon floods over him.
No man of the Danaans, then, will be angry with me, if he sees   100
me giving way before Hector, who fights with the help of the gods.
If only I could somewhere find Ajax, master of the war-cry,
then we could go together and call up our battle-lust, even
against a god's will, to see if we could drag the dead man away,
for Peleus' son Achilles; that would be the least bad of our troubles.'   105

While Menelaus was pondering all this in his heart and spirit,
the Trojan ranks advanced, and Hector led them.
Menelaus left the dead man, and gave way and retreated,
continually twisting round like a thick-maned lion
that dogs and men are chasing away from a farmyard   110
with spears and shouts; a chill invades the stalwart heart
within it and it retreats from the yard only with reluctance;
just so fair-haired Menelaus retreated from Patroclus.
When he reached the band of his companions he turned and
stood, looking about him keenly for huge Ajax, Telamon's son;   115
and very soon he saw him, on the left of the whole battle,

cheering on his companions and encouraging them to fight,
for Phoebus Apollo had cast astonishing terror into them.
Menelaus ran up towards him, and stood by him and said:
'Ajax, my friend, come this way! Patroclus is dead—let us hurry,   120
and we may at least be able to carry his body back to Achilles,
stripped though it is; Hector of the glittering helmet has his armour.'

So he spoke, and roused the spirit in war-minded Ajax, who strode
through the front-fighters, and with him went fair-haired Menelaus.
Now when Hector had stripped Patroclus' famous armour, he began   125
to pull at him, meaning to cut the head from his shoulders with the
sharp bronze, and to drag the body away and give it to the Trojan dogs.
But Ajax drew near, carrying his great shield that was like a tower,
and Hector gave ground, back into the mass of his companions,
and jumped into his chariot; and he gave the famous armour   130
to the Trojans to carry into the city, to be a great glory for him.
Then Ajax covered Menelaus with his broad shield, and
stood there, like some lioness standing in front of its young cubs;
it has led them through a forest and it falls in with some men
who are hunting and, exulting in its strength, it hoods its eyes,   135
drawing down the folds of skin that cover its brows.
In the same way Ajax stood over the hero Patroclus;
and on the other side of him Atreus' son, warlike Menelaus,
stood firm, while great grief swelled in his breast.

Then Glaucus, Hippolochus' son, captain of the men of Lycia,   140
looked darkly at Hector and rebuked him with rough words:
'Hector, you are handsome to look at, but you are unequal to the
fight; now we know that your fine reputation hides a cowardly girl.
Think now how you may save your town and its citadel
on your own, with only those warriors who were born in Ilium,   145
because not one of the Lycians will go out to fight the Danaans
on the city's behalf, since I now see that doing battle with the
enemy fighters, on and on without respite, earns no gratitude.
How could you ever rescue a lesser man among your massed troops,
hard man, now you have abandoned Sarpedon, your guest-friend   150
and companion, to the Argives, to be their prey and prize*—
Sarpedon, who served you loyally, both you and the city, while he
lived? Yet now you are not brave enough to save him from the dogs.
So now, if any of the men of Lycia will listen to me,
we shall go home, and sheer ruin will surely fall upon Troy.   155
If now the Trojans had dauntless, indomitable fury in them,

such as comes into men who for their native land's sake
will undergo toil and armed conflict with their enemies,
then we could quickly drag Patroclus back into Ilium;
and if we were to haul him out of the battle, and he came,   160
a dead man, into the great city of lord Priam, the Argives
would at once give up Sarpedon's fine armour, and we
could bring Sarpedon himself into Ilium.* Such is the man
whose attendant has been killed, by far the best of the Argives
among their ships, both he himself and his close-fighting
     followers.   165
But you had not the courage to stand and face great-spirited Ajax,
looking him in the eyes amidst the shouts of the enemy, nor
to charge straight at him, because he is a better man than you.'

     Then Hector of the glittering helmet looked darkly at him, and said:
'Glaucus, how can a man such as you speak so haughtily?   170
I am amazed; I had thought that you were the wisest man
among all those who live in Lycia of the fertile soil;
but now I scorn your wisdom utterly, as I hear you speak,
telling me that I could not stand up against towering Ajax.
I tell you, I am not one to shudder at battle or the din of chariots; 175
but the mind of Zeus the aegis-wearer always prevails, he who
turns even the brave man to flight, and takes away his victory,
easily, and yet at another time can himself rouse men to fight.
No, my friend; come here, stand by me and watch my handiwork,
and see if I shall show myself a coward all day long, as you say,   180
or whether I shall stop some Danaan, however great his desire
for brave deeds, from fighting to defend the dead Patroclus.'

     So he spoke, and gave a great shout and called out to the Trojans:
'Trojans and Lycians and Dardanian hand-to-hand fighters!
Be men, my friends, and call up your surging courage,   185
until I put on the fine armour of blameless Achilles,
which I stripped from mighty Patroclus after I killed him.'

     So Hector of the glittering helmet spoke, and left the deadly
warfare, and set off at a run, pursuing his companions on swift
feet, and quickly overtook them, for they were not yet far off,   190
carrying the famous armour of Peleus' son towards the city.
Standing apart from the tear-laden battle he changed his armour;
he gave his own gear to the Trojans who delight in war to
carry to sacred Ilium, while he put on the immortal armour
of Achilles, son of Peleus, which the gods of the high sky   195

had given to his father,* and he had presented it to his son when
he grew old; but the son did not grow old in his father's armour.

When Zeus who gathers the clouds saw from afar Hector
arraying himself in the armour of the son of Peleus,
he shook his head and spoke to his own heart: 200
'Wretched man! There is no thought of death in your heart,
yet it is close to you; you are putting on the immortal armour
of one who is the best of men, before whom other men quail.
It was his companion you killed, a gentle and mighty man, and
you were wrong to strip the armour from his head and shoulders;   205
but as compensation I will now put great power into your hands,
because you will not return from the battle, and Andromache
will not receive the famous armour of Peleus' son from you.'

So Cronus' son spoke, and nodded assent with his dark brows.
The armour fitted Hector's body, and Ares, the terrible   210
Enyalius, entered him, and his limbs were filled with
courage and strength. With a great yell he set off, looking
for his famed allies, and appeared before all of them
resplendent in the armour of Peleus' great-spirited son.
Going up and down the ranks he spoke to and roused each man: 215
Mesthles and Glaucus and Medon and Thersilochus,
Asteropaeus and Deisenor and Hippothous,
Phorcys and Chromius and Ennomus the bird-seer;
all these he encouraged, addressing them with winged words:
'Listen to me, you countless tribes of allies who live around us!   220
It was not because I was seeking or desiring a huge army
that I assembled each of you here from your cities, but
that you might of your own free will defend the Trojans' wives
and infant children for me against the war-loving Achaeans.
That is my purpose when I wear my people out, demanding gifts   225
and food for you—to make strong the spirit in each one of you.
Therefore let everyone turn and charge straight for the enemy,
either to die or to live; for that is the courtship of war.
And whoever makes Ajax give way to him, and drags Patroclus,
dead man though he is, in among the horse-breaking Trojans,   230
I shall award him half of the spoils, and half I shall keep
for myself; and so his glory will be as great as mine.'

So he spoke, and they lifted their spears and threw their weight
behind the charge, straight at the Danaans, for their hearts yearned
to drag the dead man from under Ajax, the son of Telamon—   235

fools, for he robbed many of their lives fighting over Patroclus.
Then indeed Ajax spoke to Menelaus, master of the war-cry:
'My friend, Menelaus, nurtured by Zeus, I do not now think
that even we two will return home from the war.
My great fear is not so much that the dead Patroclus   240
will soon glut the dogs and vultures of the Trojans, rather that
I am much afraid that some calamity will fall on my life, and
yours, since there is a cloud of war—Hector—enveloping
everything around us, and sheer destruction appears clear before us.
Come now, call out to the Danaans' chieftains; someone may hear.' 245

So he spoke, and Menelaus, master of the war-cry, did not
disobey him, and shouted to the Danaans with a piercing cry:
'My friends, leaders and rulers of the Argives—those who
drink at the public cost with Atreus' sons, Agamemnon and
Menelaus, and who each have a share in commanding the people, 250
and their honour and glory is bestowed on them by Zeus!
It is a hard matter for me to tell each of the leaders apart
when the strife of war blazes so fiercely round us, so let each
advance without being named, and feel outrage in his heart
that Patroclus should become a plaything for the dogs of Troy!' 255

So he spoke, and Ajax, the swift son of Oïleus, heard him clearly,
and was the first to come running through the fighting to meet him,
and after him came Idomeneus, and Idomeneus' attendant
Meriones, the equal of Enyalius, killer of men;
as for the rest, what man could recall and tell the names   260
of all those who after them roused the Achaeans to battle?

Now the Trojans pressed forward in a mass, and Hector led them.
As when, at the outpouring mouth of a river that is fed by Zeus,
a great wave roars against the current, and the seashore's
headlands round about bellow as the salt water washes back,   265
so loud were the Trojans' shouts as they came on. But the Achaeans
stood firm around Menoetius' son, with one purpose in their hearts,
fenced in as they were by their bronze shields; and over their
bright helmets the son of Cronus poured a thick mist,*
because even before this he had not hated Menoetius' son,   270
while he was alive and was the attendant of Aeacus' grandson.
He shrank from letting him become the prey of his enemies' dogs
in Troy, and so he roused his companions to fight over him.

At first the Trojans drove the darting-eyed Achaeans back, and
they abandoned the dead man and fled in fear; the arrogant   275

Trojans did not kill any with their spears, though they longed to,
but they did begin to drag the dead man away. But the Achaeans
were not likely to stay away for long; Ajax quickly rallied them,
Ajax, who after the blameless son of Peleus surpassed all
the other Danaans both in handsomeness and in deeds of hand.   280
He charged straight through the front-fighters, in courage
like a wild boar that on the mountains easily scatters dogs
and vigorous young men as it twists and turns through the glens;
just so glorious Ajax, the son of splendid Telamon,
rushed in among and easily scattered the Trojan companies   285
who were standing astride Patroclus with high hopes of
dragging him away to their city and so winning glory.

Hippothous, the illustrious son of Lethus the Pelasgian,*
had tied his sword-belt around the tendons of Patroclus' ankle
and was dragging him by the foot through the fierce crush of battle,   290
to ingratiate himself with Hector and the Trojans; but ruin quickly
came upon him, and none of his companions could save him, though
they longed to. Telamon's son sprang at him through the soldiery
and struck him at close quarters through his bronze-cheeked helmet;
the helmet of horsehair plumes split about the spear's point,   295
smashed by the great spear and Ajax's brawny hand, and
his brain, drenched in blood, spurted out of the wound along
the spear's socket, and there his fury was loosened; he let
great-hearted Patroclus' foot fall from his hands to the ground,
to lie there, and he fell beside it, on his face over the dead man,   300
a long way from Larisa of the rich soil; he could not repay
his dear parents for his upbringing, for his life-span was brief,
beaten down as he was by the spear of great-spirited Ajax.

Hector in his turn let fly at Ajax with his shining spear, but
Ajax was looking ahead and avoided the bronze-tipped spear,   305
narrowly; and Schedius, the son of great-spirited Iphitus,
by far the best of the Phocians, who had his home in splendid
Panopeus, and who ruled over many men, was the man whom
Hector hit, under the middle of his collarbone; the bronze
spear-point passed right through and came out under
           his shoulder,   310
and he fell with a thud, and his armour clattered about him.

Ajax in his turn hit Phorcys, the war-minded son of Phaenops,
in the middle of his belly while he was standing over Hippothous,
breaking through the plate of his corslet; the bronze let out a stream

of innards, and he fell in the dust, clawing the earth with his hand.   315
The front-fighters gave ground, as did illustrious Hector, and
the Argives gave a loud shout, and dragged the dead men back,
Phorcys and Hippothous, and peeled the armour from their shoulders.
    Then the Trojans would once again have retreated before the
        Achaeans,
dear to Ares, and gone up into Ilium, beaten down by their lack of
        spirit,   320
and the Argives would by their strength and power have won glory
even beyond their destiny allotted by Zeus; but Apollo in person
roused Aeneas, taking on the form of the herald Periphas,
son of Epytus, who had grown old with Aeneas' aged father,
practising his herald's craft, and was well disposed towards him;   325
it was in his likeness that Zeus' son Apollo addressed Aeneas:
'Aeneas, how could your people save steep Ilium if it is against
the will of a god? I have indeed seen other men save their cities,
trusting only in their strength and power, and in their courage
and numbers, even though their people were very few; but now   330
Zeus wills the victory for us, far more than for the Danaans,
and yet you are all in an amazing panic, and will not fight.'
    So he spoke; and Aeneas recognized Apollo who shoots from afar
when he looked him full in the face, and shouted loudly to Hector:
'Hector, and all you other captains of Trojans and allies, this is   335
now a cause of shame for us, to retreat before the Achaeans,
dear to Ares, and to go up into Ilium beaten down by our lack of spirit!
Even now one of the gods came and stood beside me, saying
that Zeus, the all-powerful schemer, is on our side in the battle.
So let us go straight at the Danaans, so that they do not find it   340
an effortless task to take the dead Patroclus back to their ships.'
    So he spoke, and sprang far beyond the front-fighters and stood there;
and the Trojans rallied and took their stand facing the Achaeans.
Then Aeneas with his spear wounded Leiocritus, who was
the son of Arisbas, the excellent companion of Lycomedes;   345
as he fell Lycomedes, dear to Ares, took pity on him, and
went and stood very close to him, and threw his bright spear,
and hit Apisaön, shepherd of the peoples, son of Hippasus,
in the liver below his midriff, and at once loosened his knees;
Apisaön had come from Paeonia where the soil is rich,   350
and after Asteropaeus was their best man in the fighting.
    As he fell, warlike Asteropaeus took pity on him, and

rushed straight forward, eager to grapple with the Danaans;
but he could not now do so, since they stood around Patroclus,
fenced on all sides by their shields, holding their spears before them.   355
Ajax ranged back and forth among them all, continually directing them,
ordering that none of them should fall back from the dead man,
nor should anyone fight far in front of the other Achaeans, but they
should all stand very close to Patroclus and fight hand to hand.
So towering Ajax gave his orders, and the earth was drenched   360
with crimson blood; dead men fell one on top of another,
Trojans and their allies who were filled with fury and Danaans
all together—for they too did not fight without shedding blood,
though far fewer of them perished, since all the time they were
mindful to keep sheer death from each other in the mass of men.   365
    So these men fought like fire, and you could not have said
whether the sun and the moon were still in their place,
since they were enveloped in mist, all the champions
who took their stand around the dead son of Menoetius.
All the rest of the Trojans and well-greaved Achaeans   370
were fighting untroubled under a clear sky; the sun's vivid
brightness was spread about them, and over all the earth
and the mountains there was no cloud to be seen. They fought
in bursts, standing far back and avoiding each other's whirring
missiles; but all the champions in the middle ground,   375
worn down by the pitiless bronze, were suffering terribly
from both the mist and the fighting.* Two splendid men,
Thrasymedes and Antilochus, had not yet discovered
that blameless Patroclus was dead; they thought he was still
alive, and fighting the Trojans in the forward clash of men.   380
These two, watching anxiously for their companions' death or flight,
were fighting apart from the rest, as Nestor had instructed them
when he roused them to leave the black ships and enter the battle.
    So all day long the huge struggle of their grim strife went on;
and all the while every man's knees and legs and feet   385
beneath him, and their arms and eyes, were soaking wet
with unremitting sweat and weariness, as they fought over
the noble attendant of Aeacus' swift-footed grandson.
As when a man gives the hide of a great ox, a bull,
one that has been soaked in fat, to his people to stretch out, and   390
they take it, and, standing round it in a circle, begin to stretch it,
and the moisture goes out of it and the fat sinks in while

many men pull, and the whole hide is stretched right through;*
so both sides kept pulling the dead man this way and that
in this narrow space, for their hearts had great hopes of   395
dragging him away, the Trojans to Ilium, and the Achaeans
to their hollow ships. So a savage struggle arose over him,
and neither Ares who drives the soldiery on nor Athena
could have made light of it as they watched, not even if they
were deeply angry, such was the ruinous toil of men and horses   400
that Zeus extended over Patroclus on that day. But glorious
Achilles did not yet know that Patroclus was dead,
because they were fighting a long way from the swift ships,
under the Trojans' walls; and so he never imagined in his heart
that he was dead, but thought he would go right up to the gates   405
and then return alive. He had no thought at all that Patroclus
would storm the citadel without him, nor even with him—
many times he had heard his mother telling him this would not be,
secretly, for she used to report the intentions of great Zeus to him.
But this time his mother had not told him of the great disaster   410
that had happened, that the companion he loved the most was dead.

    Meanwhile the others, wielding sharp spears in their hands,
were fighting unceasingly, hand to hand, over the dead man, killing
each other. And this is what one of the bronze-shirted Achaeans
would say: 'My friends, it will bring us no glory to go back to   415
the hollow ships; rather let the black earth gape open here
before us all, which would surely be a far better thing for us
if we are going to allow the Trojans, breakers of horses, to drag
this man back to their city and so win glory for themselves.'

    And this is what one of the great-spirited Trojans would say: 420
'My friends, if it is our destiny to be beaten down near this man,
all of us together, let no man draw back from the fighting.'

    This is what they were saying, seeking to quicken each man's fury.
So they fought on, and the clangour of iron rose up
to the brazen high sky, through the echoing upper air.   425
But the horses of Aeacus' grandson,* far from the battle,
had been weeping ever since they heard that their charioteer
had fallen in the dust at the hands of man-slaughtering Hector.
Automedon, the stalwart son of Diores, kept lashing them
with repeated blows of the swift whip, and many times   430
he spoke to them with soft words, and many times with threats;
but they had no wish either to go back to the ships by the broad

Hellespont, or to join the Achaeans in the fighting,
but as a grave-pillar that stands over the burial-mound
of a dead man or woman stays in place, firmly fixed,   435
so they stayed motionless, harnessed to the beautiful chariot,
their heads drooping to the earth; and hot tears
flowed from their eyes to the ground, as they mourned
in longing for their charioteer; and their thick manes were soiled,
hanging from the yoke-pad along both sides of the yoke.   440

   As they mourned, the son of Cronus noticed and took pity on them,
and shaking his head he addressed his own heart:
'Poor wretches! Why did we give you two to lord Peleus,
a mortal man, you who are both ageless and immortal?
Was it so that you might suffer pain along with luckless men?   445
Truly, among all things that breathe and creep over the earth
there is nowhere anything more pitiable than man.
But it cannot be that Hector, son of Priam, will ride in the
intricately made chariot behind you; I shall not permit it.
Is it not enough that he holds the armour and boasts idly over it?   450
No, I shall thrust fury into your knees and your hearts, so that
you can at any rate bring Automedon safe out of the fighting
to the hollow ships, for still I shall give the Trojans glory,
to keep killing until they reach the well-benched ships,
and the sun goes down and sacred darkness comes on.'   455

   So speaking he breathed valiant fury into the horses, and
they shook the dust from their manes to the ground, and
lightly carried the swift chariot in among the Trojans and Achaeans.
Behind them Automedon fought on, though he grieved for his
companion, swooping down in the chariot like a vulture after geese;   460
with ease he would elude the Trojans' noisy mêlée, and then
with ease swoop down, pursuing them through the crowded soldiery.
But as he sped along in pursuit he did not kill anyone,
because being alone in the sacred chariot he was not able
both to strike with his spear and to hold back his swift horses.   465
At last one of his companions caught sight of him—
Alcimedon, the son of Laerces, who was Haemon's son;
he stood behind the chariot and addressed Automedon:
'Automedon, which of the gods has put this profitless notion
into your heart, and has taken away your excellent wits?   470
You fight against the Trojans in the forefront of the soldiery,
alone, and yet your companion has been killed, and Hector is

preening himself, wearing Achilles' armour on his own shoulders.'
   Then in turn Automedon, son of Diores, addressed him:
'Alcimedon, what other Achaean man could control these   475
immortal horses as well as you and hold back their fury,
except for Patroclus, the equal of the gods in counsel, while
he lived? But now death and his destiny have overtaken him.
Come, take the whip and shining reins for yourself, and
I will dismount from the chariot and join the fighting.'   480
   So he spoke, and Alcimedon leapt into the chariot, swift to
the rescue; quickly he took the whip and reins into his hands,
and Automedon jumped down. Illustrious Hector noticed him,
and immediately addressed Aeneas, who was standing nearby:
'Aeneas, counsellor of the bronze-shirted Trojans,   485
look there; I see the horses of Aeacus' swift-footed grandson
coming plainly out to battle, driven by feeble charioteers.
Now I could hope to capture them—if, that is, you are willing
in your heart to help—since they would not be strong enough
to stand and match their battle-strength against the two of us.'   490
   So he spoke, and the valiant son of Anchises did not disobey him;
and they advanced together, their shoulders protected by shields
of dried and toughened oxhide, covered with a thick layer of bronze.
Together with them went Chromius and godlike Aretus,
and both in their hearts hoped fervently to kill   495
the two men and to drive off the strong-necked horses—
fools that they were, for they would not make their way back
from Automedon without bloodshed. He was praying to father Zeus,
and his dark inner heart was filled with courage and strength,
and straightaway he addressed Alcimedon, his loyal companion: 500
'Alcimedon, do not, I beg you, hold the horses far from me,
but keep them breathing close on my back, for I do not think
that Hector, son of Priam, will cease from his fury until
he has killed the two of us and mounted behind Achilles'
fine-maned horses, and has put the ranks of the Argive men   505
to flight, or else has himself been killed among the front-fighters.'
   So speaking he called out to the two called Ajax and to Menelaus:
'You two called Ajax, leaders of the Argives, and Menelaus!
As for the dead man, entrust him to the best men that there are,
to stand resolutely over him and fend off the enemy ranks;   510
but we here are alive—come, keep the pitiless day from us both,
for here in the tear-laden warfare Hector and Aeneas,

the best men among the Trojans, are pressing us hard.
Still, all this lies on the knees of the gods; I shall
throw my spear, and the rest will be Zeus' concern.'   515
  So he spoke, and poised his long-shadowing spear and threw it,
and hit the perfectly balanced shield of Aretus, which could not
keep the spear out, and the bronze passed clean through,
and drove through the man's belt into the base of his belly.
As when a strong man takes a sharpened axe, and   520
striking behind the horns of an ox from the fields cuts
clean through the tendon, and it starts forward and collapses,
so Aretus started forward and then fell on his back; the sharp
spear stuck quivering in his belly, and loosened his limbs.
Then Hector let fly at Automedon with his shining spear, but   525
he was looking ahead and avoided the bronze-tipped spear;
he crouched forward, and the long spear stuck fast
in the ground behind him, making its butt-end quiver,
and then towering Ares took the fury away from it.
Then they would have gone at each other with swords, hand to hand,   530
had not the two called Ajax, who had come up through the soldiery
at their companion's call, separated them, raging though they were;
struck with terror at the sight of them, Hector and Aeneas
and Chromius who looked like a god fell back once again,
and left Aretus where he was, his life torn out,   535
lying there. Automedon, the equal of swift Ares,
stripped him of his armour and spoke boastfully over him:
'Truly, I have relieved my heart a little of its grief at the death
of Menoetius' son, though it is a lesser man that I have killed.'
  So speaking he picked up the bloodstained spoils and laid them   540
in the chariot, and mounted himself, his feet and hands
covered in gore like a lion that has devoured a bull.
  Once again the grim struggle, cruel and tear-laden, was extended
over Patroclus; Athena had come down from the high sky and
wakened the strife, for Zeus the wide-thunderer had sent her   545
to stir up the Danaans, since now his mind had changed.
As when Zeus extends a dark-shimmering rainbow over mortals
in the high sky, to be a portent to them either of war or
to foretell a wintry storm, and it causes men to cease from
their labours on the land, and it is a vexation to flocks,   550
so Athena, wrapping herself closely in a dark-shimmering cloud,
descended on the Achaean people, and stirred up every man.

The first she addressed, urging him on, was Atreus' son,
mighty Menelaus—for he was standing close to her—
taking on the likeness of Phoenix, in form and tireless voice: 555
'Menelaus, it will surely be a disgrace and a reproach
to you if under the wall of the Trojans swift dogs
tear apart the loyal companion of splendid Achilles.
So be strong and steadfast, and urge on the whole army.'
    Then in answer Menelaus, master of the war-cry,
      addressed her: 560
'Phoenix, venerable father, long in years; how I wish that
Athena could grant me strength and fend off the spears' onrush,
and then I would be willing to stand by Patroclus and
defend him, for his death has touched my heart closely.
But Hector has the terrible fury of fire, and does not cease from   565
cutting men down with the bronze, for Zeus is granting him glory.'
    So he spoke, and the goddess owl-eyed Athena was glad,
because he had prayed to her before all the other gods.
She put force into his shoulders and into his knees,
and into his breast she implanted the daring of a fly,   570
that, however often it is brushed away from a man's skin,
persists in biting him, so delicious does it find human blood;
with daring like this the goddess filled his dark inner heart,
and he went and stood over Patroclus, and threw his shining spear.
Now there was among the Trojans a certain Podes, son of Eëtion,   575
a rich and noble man, and Hector honoured him above all
the people, since he was a friend and shared his feasts.
As this man darted back in flight, fair-haired Menelaus hit him
on the belt, and drove the bronze right through; he fell
with a thud, and Atreus' son Menelaus dragged him, dead,   580
away from the Trojans' side and back into his companions' band.
    But now Apollo came and stood next to Hector and stirred him on,
taking on the likeness of Phaenops, son of Asius, who of all his
guest-friends was dearest to him, and his home was in Abydus;
in his likeness Apollo who shoots from afar addressed Hector: 585
'Hector, what other man of the Achaeans will now fear you,
if you tremble like this at Menelaus, who in former times
was but a soft spearman? Now he has gone off, carrying on his own
a dead man from the Trojans' side; he has killed Podes, Eëtion's
son, your loyal companion, and a fine man in the front-fighters.'   590
    So he spoke, and a black cloud of grief enveloped Hector, and

he set off through the front-fighters, helmeted in gleaming bronze.
Then indeed the son of Cronus took up the tasselled,
shining aegis, and concealed Ida in clouds, and sent forth
a lightning-flash and a loud thunderclap, and shook the aegis,   595
and gave victory to the Trojans, causing panic among the Achaeans.

The first man to flee in panic was Peneleos, a Boeotian,
struck on the shoulder by a spear, as he kept his body facing
the enemy; it was a surface scratch, but Polydamas' spear
grazed the bone, since it had been thrown from close quarters.   600
Then Hector closed with Leïtus, son of great-spirited Alectryon,
and wounded him on the wrist, putting an end to his battle-lust;
he gazed around him and trembled, since he no longer thought
he could hold a spear in his hand and fight against the Trojans.
As Hector launched himself after Leïtus, Idomeneus   605
hit him on the corslet covering his chest, next to the nipple;
the long spear snapped at the socket, and the Trojans shouted.
Hector then aimed his spear at Idomeneus, Deucalion's son,
as he stood in his chariot, and missed him by only a little,
but hit Coeranus, Meriones' attendant and charioteer, who had   610
come with him from Lyctus, a well-built city. Idomeneus
had earlier come up on foot after leaving the well-balanced
ships, and he would have handed a great victory to the Trojans,
had not Coeranus quickly driven up his swift-footed horses; so
he proved to be Idomeneus' salvation, fending off the pitiless day,   615
but himself lost his life at the hands of man-slaying Hector.
He it was whom Hector hit under the jaw and ear, and the spear
tore his teeth out by the roots and cut his tongue in half.
He toppled from the chariot, letting the reins drop from his hands,
but Meriones stooped and picked them up from the ground   620
in his own hands, and addressed Idomeneus:
'Come, lash the horses now until you reach the swift ships;
you know yourself that the Achaeans are no longer victorious.'

So he spoke, and Idomeneus lashed the fine-maned horses
towards the hollow ships, for panic had fallen upon his heart.   625

Great-hearted Ajax and Menelaus were not unaware
that Zeus was handing victory in their turn to the Trojans.
The first of them to speak was huge Ajax, Telamon's son:
'What are we to do? Even a man who is a great fool
can see that father Zeus himself is helping the Trojans.   630
Every one of them who lets fly a spear, good fighter or bad,

hits his mark, since Zeus guides them all alike; but
all of ours fall to the ground, useless and ineffectual.
Come, let us devise the best plan we can on our own,
both how we may drag the body back, and also bring delight   635
to our dear companions by returning home ourselves;
doubtless they are looking this way full of grief, and do not think
that the fury and irresistible hands of man-slaying Hector
can yet be contained, but that they will fall upon our black ships.
I wish there were some companion to take a message quickly   640
back to Peleus' son, since I do not think he has even heard
the cruel news that his dear companion has been killed;
but I cannot see such a man anywhere among the Achaeans,
for they themselves and their horses are alike covered in mist.
Father Zeus, rescue the sons of the Achaeans from the mist,   645
I beg you, make the sky clear, give our eyes power to see!
Kill us in broad daylight if you wish, since this is your pleasure!'

So he spoke, and the father took pity on him as he wept;
immediately he scattered the darkness and drove the mist away,
and the sun burst out, and the battle was all made plain.*   650
Then indeed Ajax spoke to Menelaus, master of the war-cry:
'Look now, Zeus-nurtured Menelaus, to see if you can find
if Antilochus, the son of great-spirited Nestor, is still alive,
and urge him to go quickly to war-minded Achilles, and
tell him that the companion he loves beyond others is dead.'   655

So he spoke, and Menelaus, master of the war-cry, did not
disobey him, but set off like a lion that leaves a farmyard
when it has tired of plaguing the dogs and men
that keep watch all night and will not let it take a
fat beast from the cattle; it is desperate for meat,   660
and keeps coming at them, but without success, for spears
and burning bundles of sticks fly thick from bold hands
against it, and terrify it for all its impatience,
and at daybreak it goes away, troubled at heart.
Just so Menelaus, master of the war-cry, left Patroclus,   665
much against his will, for he was sorely afraid that the Achaeans
would flee in panic and abandon him as prey to the enemy.
He gave full instructions to Meriones and the two called Ajax:
'You two called Ajax, leaders of the Argives, and you, Meriones,
now is the time for men to call to mind the gentleness of   670
luckless Patroclus; it was his way to show kindliness to all

while he lived, and now death and his destiny have overtaken him.'

So speaking fair-haired Menelaus went on his way,
looking keenly around him like an eagle, which men say
has the sharpest sight of all winged creatures under the high sky;   675
even when it hovers on high it can detect the swift-footed hare
cowering under a thick-leaved bush, and swoops down
on it, quickly seizes it, and robs it of its life.
Just so, Zeus-nurtured Menelaus, your shining eyes whirled
everywhere among the numerous company of your companions,   680
to see if the son of Nestor was anywhere still alive.
Very quickly he noticed him on the left of the whole battle,
putting heart into his companions and urging them to fight;
standing close by, fair-haired Menelaus addressed him:
'Zeus-nurtured Antilochus, come here and learn the   685
cruel news—but how I wish it had never happened!
I think that you have already seen for yourself, and know that
a god is rolling affliction on to the Danaans, and that victory
lies with the Trojans. The best of the Achaeans has been killed,
Patroclus, and a great loss has come to pass for the Danaans.   690
You must run at once to Achilles by the Achaeans' ships and tell him,
to see if he can quickly bring the dead man back safe to his ship—
though stripped, since Hector of the glittering helmet has the armour.'

So he spoke, and hearing him Antilochus was struck with horror;
for a long time speechlessness gripped him, and his eyes   695
filled with tears, and his hearty voice was choked; but
he did not ignore the command of Menelaus, and set off
at a run, having given his armour to his blameless companion,
Laodocus, who was wheeling his single-hoofed horses round nearby.

So Antilochus' feet carried him, weeping, from the battlefield,   700
on his way to bring a painful message to Peleus' son Achilles.
But your heart, Zeus-nurtured Menelaus, had no wish to
help the hard-pressed Pylian companions whom Antilochus
had left behind him, though they greatly missed him.
Menelaus put glorious Thrasymedes in charge over them,   705
and himself went to stand again over the hero Patroclus. He ran
and stood by the two called Ajax, and at once addressed them:
'I have sent the man you spoke of back to the swift ships,
to go to Achilles of the swift feet; but I do not think he will
come now, hugely angry though he is with glorious Hector,   710
since he cannot fight against the Trojans without armour.

No, let us devise the best plan we can on our own,
both how we can drag the dead man back, and also ourselves
escape death and its spectres, away from the Trojans' war-clamour.'

Then huge Ajax, son of Telamon, answered him: 715
'Far-famed Menelaus, all that you say is according to due measure.
Now go, you and Meriones, and quickly lift the dead man
on to your shoulders, and carry him out of the conflict, while we two
stay and carry on the fight against the Trojans and glorious Hector—
one in name and one in spirit as we are, who in times past also   720
have taken our stand side by side and faced violent Ares.'

So he spoke, and with a tremendous heave they raised the dead man
in their arms and held him high. Behind them the Trojan army
gave a yell when they saw the Achaeans hoisting the dead man,
and they made straight for them like dogs that speed after   725
a wounded wild boar, running in front of young huntsmen;
for a while they race along, raging to tear it to pieces, but
when, trusting in its courage, it wheels round on them,
they back away and scatter in flight, this way and that.
So the Trojans, massed together, for a while kept pursuing,   730
jabbing at them with their swords and double-edged spears;
but when the two called Ajax wheeled round and took their stand
against them, their skin changed colour, and no one dared
dart forward and fight for possession of the dead man.

So those two, raging, carried the dead man from the battlefield, 735
towards the hollow ships, and round them the battle spread,
fierce as fire that suddenly bursts into a blaze and sweeps
through a city of men, and their houses are destroyed
in a great conflagration, fanned by a mighty roaring wind.
Just so the incessant uproar of horses and spear-carrying men   740
followed Menelaus and Meriones as they went on their way.
Like mules that devote their mighty fury to dragging a
beam or some huge ship-timber down from a mountain
along a rocky path, and the spirit in them is worn down
by weariness and sweat alike as they strain at their task;   745
so they with fierce energy carried the dead man; and behind them
the two called Ajax kept the enemy back, as a wooded ridge,
stretching in a continuous line across a plain, holds back a flood,
withstanding even the ravaging torrents of mighty rivers and
diverting all their waters so that they spread over the plain,   750
and the torrents' strength is not enough to break through;

so the two called Ajax kept fending off the Trojans' onslaught
behind them. But the Trojans continued the pursuit, two men
above all, Aeneas, the son of Anchises, and illustrious Hector.
As a flock of starlings or jackdaws flies in screaming turmoil   755
when they see a hawk coming after them, because it is a
bringer of death to their small fledglings, so the young men
of the Achaeans, pursued by Aeneas and Hector, fell back
in screaming turmoil and forgot their battle-lust.
Splendid gear fell in quantities about and around the ditch as   760
the Danaans fled in panic; and there was no stay in the fighting.

BOOK EIGHTEEN

S o they fought on in the likeness of blazing fire, and
Antilochus, swift-footed messenger, came to Achilles,
and found him in front of his ships with their tall sterns,
brooding in his heart on the things that were indeed being fulfilled.
Deeply troubled, he spoke to his great-hearted spirit: 5
'This is bad! Why are the flowing-haired Achaeans again
being driven in confusion and panic over the plain to the ships?
May it not be that the gods have brought about the painful
grief for my heart that my mother once foretold to me, saying
that while I still lived the best of the Myrmidons would   10
leave the sun's light, overpowered by Trojan hands.*
It must be that the stalwart son of Menoetius is dead—
stubborn man! I told him to drive the enemy's fire away and
to return to the ships, and not to pit his strength against Hector's.'*

    While he was pondering this in his mind and in his heart   15
Antilochus, the son of splendid Nestor, came up close to him,
weeping warm tears, and gave him the cruel message:
'Ah, son of war-minded Peleus, this is most painful news
for you to hear; how I wish it had never happened!
Patroclus lies dead, and they are even now fighting over his   20
stripped body; Hector of the glittering helmet has the armour.'

    So he spoke, and a black cloud of grief covered Achilles;
with both hands he gathered up the sooty dust and
poured it over his head, disfiguring his handsome face,
and the black ashes settled all over his fragrant tunic.   25
Mightily in his might, he lay stretched out in the dust,
and with his own hands tore and disfigured his hair.
The maidservants captured by Achilles and Patroclus
cried aloud in agony of heart and all rushed out of doors
to stand around war-minded Achilles, and with their hands   30
they beat their breasts, and each one's limbs were loosened.
On his other side Antilochus grieved, weeping tears and
holding Achilles' hands and groaning in his noble heart,
terrified that he might cut his throat with the iron.
Achilles gave a terrible cry, and his revered mother heard him,   35
sitting in the depths of the salt sea near her father the ancient,

and in turn screamed in grief, and the goddesses gathered round,
all the daughters of Nereus who lived in the deeps of the sea.
Around her gathered Glauce and Thaleia and Cymodoce,
Nesaeë and Speio and Thoë and ox-eyed Halië,   40
Cymothoë and Actaeë and Limnoreia,
Melite and Iaera and Amphithoë and Agauë,
Doto and Proto and Pherousa and Dynamene,
Dexamene and Amphinome and Callianeira,
Doris and Panope and far-famed Galateia,   45
Nemertes and Apseudes and Callianassa,
and there too were Clymene and Ianeira and Ianassa,
Maera and Oreithyia and Amatheia of the lovely hair, and
the other daughters of Nereus who lived in the deeps of the sea.
The shining white cave was filled with these nymphs, and they all   50
together beat their breasts, and the keening was led by Thetis:
'Listen to me sisters, daughters of Nereus, that you may all
hear and know well the great grief that is in my heart.
How wretched I am, unhappy in bearing the best of men!
I gave birth to a son who is blameless and mighty,   55
supreme among heroes. He shot up tall like a sapling,
and I nursed him like a young tree in a hill-orchard,
and I sent him away in his curved ships to Ilium,
to fight against the Trojans; but I shall never again
welcome him back home to the house of Peleus.   60
I know that while he is alive and looks on the sun's light
he is deeply troubled, and that going to him will bring no help.
But go I will, to see my dear child and to hear of the sorrow
that has come over him while he keeps away from the war.'

    So she spoke and left the cave, and the nymphs went with her,   65
weeping, and around them the waves of the sea were
split apart. When they reached rich-soiled Troy they came
ashore one by one, on the beach where the Myrmidons' ships
were drawn up close to each other around swift-footed Achilles.
He groaned heavily, and his revered mother stood next to him,   70
and with a shrill cry of grief took her son's head in her hands,
and in lamentation addressed him with winged words:
'My child, why do you weep? What grief has come over your heart?
Tell me, do not hide it. You can see that Zeus has fulfilled
what you prayed for before, when you held up your hands
    to him—   75

that the sons of the Achaeans should all be penned in by their ships,
feeling the want of you, and should suffer shameful treatment.'

With a heavy groan, swift-footed Achilles addressed her:
'Mother, the Olympian has indeed fulfilled that prayer for me;
but what pleasure can it bring me when my dear companion is dead,   80
Patroclus, whom I honoured above all my companions,
as much as my own life? I have killed him; Hector has
cut him down and stripped the huge armour from him, that
fine armour, a wonder to see, which the gods gave as a splendid gift
to Peleus on the day that they laid you in the bed of a mortal man.   85
How I wish that you had stayed with the immortal sea-goddesses,
and that Peleus had brought a mortal woman to his house as wife!
But as it is, you too must suffer countless sorrows in your heart:
your son will die, and you will never again welcome him
as he returns home, because my own heart tells me to   90
abandon the company of men and live no more—unless Hector
is first struck by my spear and gives up his life, and pays
the blood-price for the death of Patroclus, Menoetius' son.'

Then in answer Thetis addressed him, weeping tears:
'Then, my child, from what you say, you are indeed short-lived,   95
since straight after Hector's death your own is soon to come.'

Then, deeply troubled, swift-footed Achilles addressed her:
'Let me then die immediately, since it is clear I was not meant
to come to my companion's rescue at his killing; he died far from
his country, when he needed me to defend him from harm.   100
But now, since I shall not return to my dear native land, and
since I proved to be no saviour to Patroclus or to my other
companions, beaten down in numbers by glorious Hector,
while I sit here by the ships, a useless burden on the earth,
a man whose war-skill is beyond that of all the bronze-shirted   105
Achaeans—though there are others better in the assembly—
I wish that strife itself could perish from among gods and men,
and bitterness too, which causes even the wisest to become angry
and which spreads far sweeter than the dripping of honey
and swells like smoke in the breasts of men—even as   110
Agamemnon, lord of men, lately provoked me to anger.
Still, that is past and done; we must let it go, grieved though we are,
and must keep the spirit in our breast subdued by necessity.
Now I shall go out, to track down Hector, the destroyer of that
dear life, and after that I shall accept the death-spectre, whenever   115

Zeus and the other immortal gods wish to bring it on.
Not even the mighty Heracles could escape the death-spectre,
he who was loved above all by lord Zeus, the son of Cronus,
but his due destiny and Hera's cruel anger beat him down;*
and I too, if indeed a destiny like his has been shaped for me,   120
will one day lie in death. But for now, let me win splendid glory,
let me force some Trojan woman or deep-bosomed daughter
of Dardanus to wail in lamentation as with both hands she wipes
the flooding tears from her tender cheeks;* let them know that
I have stayed too long away from the warfare. Though you love me,   125
do not hold me back from the battle; you will not persuade me.'

Then the goddess Thetis of the silver feet answered him:
'All this is good and true, my child: it is no bad thing to
save one's hard-pressed companions from sheer destruction.
But your splendid gleaming armour of bronze is held by   130
the Trojans, and Hector himself of the glittering helmet
wears it triumphantly on his shoulders—though I do not think
he will glory in it for long, since death is close to him.
So do not go down yet into the dour struggle of Ares,
not until you see with your own eyes that I have returned;   135
because in the morning, at the rising of the sun, I shall come,
bringing you handsome armour from lord Hephaestus.'

So she spoke, and turned away from her son and left him,
and moving to face her sisters of the sea she addressed them:
'You must now go down into the broad gulf of the sea,   140
to visit the ancient of the sea and our father's house,
and tell him everything; I am going to high Olympus,
to find Hephaestus the renowned smith, to see if he is willing
to give me famous and far-shining armour for my son.'

So she spoke, and at once they dived below the sea's waves,   145
while she, the goddess Thetis of the silver feet, made her way
to Olympus, to fetch famous armour for her dear son.

So her feet carried her towards Olympus; meanwhile the Achaeans,
with inhuman shrieks, were fleeing in panic before man-slaying
Hector, and had reached the ships and the Hellespont. Nor could   150
the well-greaved Achaeans manage to drag the body of Patroclus,
Achilles' attendant, out of range of their missiles, for
once again the Trojans in their chariots caught up with it, and
with them was Hector, son of Priam, his courage like a flame.
Three times illustrious Hector caught hold of his feet from behind,   155

raging to drag him away, and calling loudly on the Trojans, and
three times the two called Ajax, clothed in impetuous courage,
smashed him back from the dead man; but Hector, trusting resolutely
in his fighting spirit, would now dash into the mêlée, and now
stand firm, yelling loudly; and not one step did he retreat.   160
As shepherds in open country are unable drive a tawny lion
that is racked by hunger away from a beast's carcass,
so the two fighters called Ajax could not frighten
Hector, son of Priam, away from the dead man.
And he would have dragged it away and won immense glory,   165
had not wind-footed swift Iris come running from Olympus
with a message to the son of Peleus to arm himself, without
the knowledge of Zeus and the other gods, for Hera had sent her.
Standing next to him she addressed him with winged words:
'Up with you, son of Peleus, most outrageous of men!   170
Go to Patroclus' help, for whose sake grim conflict has
broken out in front of the ships; men are killing each other,
some trying to keep harm from the dead man's body
while others, the Trojans, are straining to drag him towards
windswept Ilium—and more than anyone illustrious Hector   175
is raging to haul him away, for his heart is telling him to cut
the head from his soft neck and set it on the wall's palisade.
Get up—do not stay lying there! Put respect into your heart,
do not let Patroclus become a plaything for the dogs of Troy.
It will be your disgrace if he goes disfigured down to the dead.'   180
     Then glorious swift-footed Achilles answered her:
'Goddess Iris, which of the gods sent you as a messenger to me?'
     Then in turn wind-footed swift Iris addressed him:
'It was Hera, the honoured wife of Zeus, who sent me.
Cronus' son on his lofty seat does not know I have come, nor   185
any of the other immortals who live on snow-swept Olympus.'
     Then swift-footed Achilles spoke to her in answer:
'How am I to go into the fighting? The Trojans have my armour,
and my dear mother has said that I must not arm myself
until I see with my own eyes that she has come back here,   190
for she promised to bring me splendid armour from Hephaestus.
I do not know of any man whose armour I could put on,
unless it were the shield of Ajax, son of Telamon; but
he, I suppose, is now in the thick of the front-fighters,
causing havoc with his spear over the dead Patroclus.'   195

Then in turn wind-footed swift Iris addressed him:
'We too know well that your splendid armour is held over there;
but go to the ditch as you are, and show yourself to the Trojans,
and perhaps they will be frightened at the sight and hold back
from the fighting, and the Achaeans' warlike sons will breathe   200
again in their weariness; there is little breathing-space in war.'
    So swift-footed Iris spoke and departed from him;
and Achilles, loved by Zeus, arose, and around his
powerful shoulders Athena threw the tasselled aegis,
and around his head the bright goddess set a crown, a cloud of   205
gold, and from it she made a bright shining flame blaze out.
As when smoke rises from a city and reaches the upper air,
on some far distant island that enemies are besieging, and
all day long the defenders contest the issue from their city
in hateful Ares' war—but at the setting of the sun   210
beacons blaze out one after another, and their brightness
leaps aloft for those who live around to see, and the citizens
hope that these men will come to the rescue in their ships;
so the gleaming flash from Achilles' head reached the upper air.
He went out and stood in front of the wall, but did not join   215
the Achaeans, since he respected his mother's wise warning.
There he stood and shouted, and far away Pallas Athena
gave voice, and roused unspeakable confusion in the Trojans.
As loud as the sound that rings out from a trumpet
when a city is surrounded by life-breaking enemies,   220
so loud then rang out the shout of Aeacus' grandson.
When the Trojans heard Achilles' brazen voice, the hearts
of all were confused, and their fine-maned horses began
to wheel the chariots round, for their hearts sensed pain to come;
and when they saw the terrible, unwearying fire that the goddess   225
grey-eyed Athena had kindled blazing above the head of
Peleus' great-hearted son, the charioteers were stunned.
Three times glorious Achilles shouted loud across the ditch, and
three times the Trojans and their far-famed allies were thrown
into turmoil; then and there twelve of their best men perished,   230
entangled in their own chariots and spears. The Achaeans
were delighted, and dragged Patroclus out of missiles' range and
laid him on a litter, and his dear companions stood around him,
weeping; and swift-footed Achilles went with them,
letting fall hot tears, when he saw his faithful companion   235

lying on a bier, disfigured by the sharp bronze—
the man he had sent out to the battle with his horses
and chariot, but never welcomed him home again.

And now the lady ox-eyed Hera sent the unwearied sun
to return, unwillingly, into the streams of Ocean;   240
and the sun went down, and the glorious Achaeans
rested from the cruel conflict and the equally balanced war.

On their side, the Trojans retreated from the harsh crush
of battle, and unyoked their swift horses from the chariots
and, before thinking of their supper, gathered in an assembly.   245
They held this assembly standing on their feet, and no one dared
sit, for trembling had gripped them all, because Achilles had
appeared after a long time away from the painful fighting.
Among them the sagacious Polydamas was the first to speak,
Panthous' son, who alone of them could see the future and the past;   250
he was Hector's companion, and they were born in the same night,
though one was far better with words, and the other with the spear.
With generous intent he spoke out and addressed them:
'Think hard on both sides, my friends. For my part, I advise you
to go now to the city, and not to wait for the bright dawn   255
on the plain beside the ships; we are a long way from our wall.
As long as this man raged against glorious Agamemnon,
so long it was easier for us to fight against the Achaeans, and
I for one was happy to camp at night by the swift ships,
in the hope that we would capture their well-balanced ships.   260
But now I am terribly afraid of the swift-footed son of Peleus;
so over-violent is his spirit that he will not be content
to remain on the plain, where Trojans and Achaeans
share Ares' fury between them in the middle ground,
but he will fight to possess our city and its women.   265
Let us then return to the city; believe me, this is how it will be:
for now, immortal night has restrained the swift-footed
son of Peleus, but if tomorrow he charges out fully armed
and finds us here still, everyone will recognize him; and
the man who runs from him will be glad to reach sacred Ilium,   270
and many will be the Trojans who are devoured by dogs and
vultures—though may my words be as if they had not been said!
If, despite our misgivings, we are persuaded by my words,
we shall keep our forces safe tonight in the assembly-place,
and the towers and high gateways, and the tall polished doors   275

that are set close-fitting into them, will protect the city.
And tomorrow, at break of day, we shall put on our armour
and take our stand on the walls; and it will be the worse for anyone
who tries to come up from his ships and fight us round our walls;
he will be off back to his ships, when he has given his
    strong-necked   280
horses their fill of aimless running up and down below the city.
As for breaking into it, however great his anger he will not succeed,
nor will he ever sack it; before that happens, swift dogs will eat him.'

   Then Hector of the glittering helmet looked at him darkly, and said:
'Polydamas, what you say does not now please me—telling me   285
that we should go back and shut ourselves up in the city.
Have you not yet had your fill of being caged behind towers?
In times gone by all mortal men would tell tales of the city of
Priam, how it was rich in gold and rich in bronze; but now
these fine treasures have been spent and have left its houses,   290
and most of its wealth has gone as payment to Phrygia and
lovely Maeonia,* ever since great Zeus became angry with us.
Now, when the son of crooked-scheming Cronus has granted me
to win glory by the ships, and to pen the Achaeans in by the sea,
do not, foolish man, put thoughts like these in front of the people.   295
None of the Trojans will listen to you; I shall not allow it.
So come, let us all be agreed, and do as I say:
take your supper now in your ranks throughout the camp,
and be sure to set sentries, and let each man be vigilant;
and if any Trojan is troubled overmuch about his possessions,   300
let him collect them and give them to the people to devour as
commonly held goods, for it is better that they and not the Achaeans
should enjoy them. Then tomorrow, at daybreak, let us put on
our armour, and wake violent Ares beside the hollow ships.
If glorious Achilles really has risen up beside the ships,   305
it will be the worse for him, if that is what he wants; I shall not
run from war's hideous clamour, but will stand fast and face him,
and we shall see if it is he or I who wins the great victory.
Enyalius is an impartial god, and often kills the would-be killer.'

   So Hector spoke, and the Trojans shouted their approval,   310
fools that they were, for Pallas Athena had taken away their wits;
they gave their approval to Hector's disastrous counsel,
and not to Polydamas, who had framed excellent advice.
Then they ate their supper throughout the camp, while the

Achaeans all night long wailed in mourning for Patroclus.   315
Among them the son of Peleus began the unbroken lament,
laying his man-slaying hands on his companion's chest,
groaning loud and long like some thickly bearded lion
whose cubs a hunter of deer has secretly stolen away
in a dense wood; it returns too late and is struck by grief,   320
and ranges up and down the glens, tracking the man's trail,
hoping to find him, because bitter anger has gripped it—
so Achilles, groaning heavily, addressed the Myrmidons:
'Ah, truly it was a vain word that I spoke on that day
when I tried to reassure the hero Menoetius in his halls!   325
I said I would bring his son back to Opous, famed for his
sack of Ilium and bringing his fair share of the spoils.
But Zeus does not bring all men's schemes to fulfilment:
it is our destiny that we two will make the same earth red
here in Troy, since I too will not return home, and my father,   330
the aged horse-driver Peleus, will not welcome me in his halls,
nor Thetis my mother, but the earth will cover me here.
So now, Patroclus, since I am to follow you below the ground,
I shall not hold your burial rites until I have brought here
the armour and head of Hector, your great-spirited killer;   335
and in front of your pyre I shall cut the throats of twelve
noble sons of the Trojans,* because of my anger at your death.
Until then, you shall lie as you are beside my curved ships,
and around you deep-bosomed Trojan women and daughters
of Dardanus will mourn for you, day and night weeping tears,   340
women whom we toiled to capture by force and the long spear,
when we two sacked the prosperous cities of mortal men.'

    So glorious Achilles spoke, and called to his companions
to set a huge tripod over the fire, so that they might quickly
wash away the bloody gore from Patroclus. So they set a   345
three-legged cauldron for bath-water over the blazing fire,
and poured water into it and put wood beneath it for burning;
the fire began to spread round the cauldron's belly, and the water
grew hot, and when it was boiling in the flashing bronze
they washed Patroclus and anointed him richly with oil,   350
and filled his wounds with oil that was nine years old.
Then they laid him on a bier, and covered him with a linen cloth
from head to foot, and over this they spread a white robe.
Then, all night long, the Myrmidons gathered round Achilles

the swift-footed, and lamented and mourned for Patroclus.   355
    Then Zeus addressed Hera, his wife and sister:
'So, ox-eyed lady Hera, you have succeeded again,
and aroused swift-footed Achilles. It would seem that
the flowing-haired Achaeans must be your own children.'
    Then the lady ox-eyed Hera answered him, saying: 360
'Most dread son of Cronus, what is this that you have said?
Any man who is mortal and does not possess wisdom like ours
is allowed, I suppose, to do what he can for another man;
how then should I, who claim to be the best of goddesses,
in two ways, by my birth, and because I am famed as   365
your wife, and you are lord of all the immortals—how
should I not in my anger stitch together trouble for the Trojans?'
    So they spoke, one to another, in this way; meanwhile
Thetis of the silver feet came to Hephaestus' house, a house
imperishable, starry, and conspicuous among the gods' homes;   370
it was made of bronze, and the crook-footed god had built it himself.
She found him bustling about, sweating, and busying himself
with his bellows, for he was forging tripods, twenty in all,
that were to stand around the wall of his well-built hall;
under the base of each one he had fixed wheels of gold,   375
so that of their own accord they could enter the gods' assembly
and then return again to his house—a wonder to look upon.
They were nearly finished, but he had not yet added their craftily
worked ear-handles, and he was fitting these, and hammering in
their rivets. While he was working at this with his cunning skill,   380
the goddess silver-footed Thetis came and stood nearby, and
Charis* of the shining headdress saw her and came forward,
lovely Charis whom the far-famed bow-legged god had married;
she gripped her hand firmly in hers, and spoke, addressing her:
'Thetis of the long robe, what can bring you to our house? You are   385
respected and a friend, but before this you have not come often.
Come in with me, that I may put gifts of hospitality before you.'
    So the bright goddess spoke and led her inside, and
seated her on a fine, intricately worked throne with
rivets of silver, and there was a footstool under her feet.   390
Charis called to Hephaestus the renowned smith and spoke to him:
'Hephaestus, come in here! Thetis has need of you.'
    Then the far-famed bow-legged god answered her: 'Well!
I have an awe-inspiring and venerable goddess in my house:

it was Thetis who saved me when I was in agony after   395
my long fall, caused by my mother's will, bitch that she is—
she wished to hide me because I was lame, and I would have suffered
agonies in my heart had not Eurynome, daughter of Ocean
that flows into itself, and Thetis welcomed me to their bosom.
Nine years I spent with them, shaping much cunning
      bronze-work—   400
brooches and curved pins, earrings and necklaces—in their
hollow cave; and around it the streams of Ocean flowed
without ceasing, roaring with foam. No one knew of this,
not any one of the gods nor any one of mortal men,
except that Thetis and Euryonome knew, they who saved me.*   405
And now you have come to my house; so there is a great need on me
to do my best to pay back lovely-haired Thetis for rescuing me.
Charis, offer her good things, fit for a guest; set them in front of her
now, until I have stowed away my bellows and all my tools.'
  So he spoke, and stood up from the anvil-block, a monster
      puffing   410
and limping, though his slender legs moved nimbly beneath him.
He shifted the bellows away from the fire, and collected
all the tools with which he worked into a silver chest;
with a sponge he wiped his face on both sides, and both
his hands, and also his powerful neck and hairy chest, and   415
put on a tunic, and took up a stout staff, and came to the door,
limping. Women servants moved nimbly to support their lord;
these were made of gold, and resembled living young women.
They have in them wits and understanding, and also a voice and
strength, for they have learnt their skills from the immortal gods.   420
These bustled about, supporting their lord, who moved unsteadily
near to where Thetis was, and sat down on a shining throne;
he gripped her hand firmly in his and spoke, calling her by name;
'Thetis of the long robe, what can bring you to our house? You are
respected and a friend, but before this you have not come often.   425
Tell me what is in your mind; my heart urges me to accomplish it—
if, that is, I can accomplish it and such a thing is possible.'
  Then Thetis answered him, weeping tears:
'Hephaestus, is there any goddess of all those on Olympus
who has had to endure in her heart as many bitter sorrows   430
as those that Cronus' son Zeus has given me, above all others?
Choosing me from all the other sea-dwellers he made me subject

to a man, Peleus, Aeacus' son, and I had to endure a man's bed,*
though it was greatly against my will; he now lies in his halls,
worn out with cruel old age, but I have other sorrows—   435
he gave me a son for me to bear and raise, one supreme
among other heroes; he shot up tall like a sapling,
and I nursed him like a young tree in a hill-orchard,
and I sent him away in his curved ships to Ilium,
to fight against the Trojans; but I shall never again   440
welcome him back home to the house of Peleus.
I know that while he is alive and looks on the sun's light
he is deeply troubled, and yet my going to him will bring no help.
And the girl whom the sons of the Achaeans chose as his prize—
lord Agamemnon took her back, out of his hands, and   445
in grief for her his heart wasted away. Then the Trojans
penned the Achaeans by their ships, preventing them from
breaking out, and the elders of the Argives entreated him,
naming the many splendid gifts that they were offering,
but he refused to keep destruction from them at that time;   450
but he did put his own armour on Patroclus, and sent him out
to the fight, and gave him a great force to go with him.
All day long they fought around the Scaean gates, and
indeed they would have sacked the city on that day, if Apollo
had not killed Menoetius' stalwart son after he had caused   455
great ruin among the front-fighters, and given the glory to Hector.
It is for this reason that I come to entreat you at your knees,
in the hope that you will agree to give my short-lived son a
shield and a helmet, and fine greaves fitted with ankle-pieces,
and a corslet; his loyal companion, beaten down by the Trojans,
          has lost   460
the armour he had, and Achilles lies on the ground, his heart full of grief.'
    Then the far-famed bow-legged god answered her:
'Do not despair, and do not let these things trouble your heart.
I wish I could hide him far away from death's gloomy lament,
at the time when his terrible due destiny comes to him,   465
as easily as I shall equip him with fine armour, such as
all men will wonder at in time to come, when they see it.'
    So he spoke, and left her there, and went to fetch his bellows,
and turned them on to his fire, and told them to set to work;
and the bellows, twenty in all, began to blow on his crucibles,   470
giving out well-moderated blasts from all directions, to

help Hephaestus as he hurried to this place and to that,
according as he wished and as the work went on. Into
the fire he threw bronze that does not wear away, and tin
and precious gold, and silver; then he positioned a   475
great anvil on its anvil-block, and in one hand took up
a powerful hammer, and in the other took up some tongs.

First of all he made a huge, heavy shield,* decorating it
intricately all over, and round its edge fixed a triple rim,
bright and gleaming, and hanging from it a silver sword-belt.   480
There were five rings on the shield itself, and on them,
with skilful craft, he created many cunning works of art.

On it he fashioned the earth and the high sky and the sea,
the sun that does not tire, and the waxing moon, and
all the constellations that are a crown for the high sky—   485
the Pleiades and the Hyades and mighty Orion, and
the Bear that men also call the Wain, which turns
always in the same place and keeps careful watch on Orion,
and alone has no share in the baths of Ocean.*

On it he fashioned two cities of mortal men, fine ones.   490
In one there were weddings and feasts, and people
were escorting brides from their chambers through the city
with bright-shining torches, and the loud marriage-song rose up.
Young men were whirling in the dance, and accompanying them
flutes and lutes kept up their sound, and the women   495
stood and marvelled at it, each one by her own porch.
In the meeting-place a crowd of citizens had formed;
a dispute had arisen there, and two men were quarrelling
over the blood-money of a man who had been killed.*
One claimed he had paid it in full, appealing to the people,   500
while the other said he had received nothing; both were anxious
to go to an arbitrator for judgement. The people took sides,
shouting support for both; heralds were holding them back,
while the elders sat on polished stones in a sacred circle,
holding in their hands the loud-voiced heralds' staffs.   505
The disputants rushed up to these men, and they gave their judgements
in turn; two talents of gold lay before them, to be given to
the judge who should deliver to them the straightest verdict.

Around the other city two armies of men were encamped,
glittering in their armour. Two counsels found favour among
    them,   510

either to sack the city utterly, or to divide with the inhabitants
all the wealth that the beautiful city held within it.
But the defenders were not ready to yield, and were secretly
arming for an ambush; and on the wall stood their dear wives
and children, ready to defend it, and with them men in the grip   515
of old age. The rest marched out; Ares and Pallas Athena led them—
both were made of gold, and clothed in garments of gold,
handsome and huge in their armour, and, as befits gods, standing
clearly out; but the people below them were much smaller.
When the men came to a place where there was space for an
          ambush,
                                                                                      520
in a riverbed where there was a watering-place for all kinds of beasts,
there they settled down, armed in their flashing bronze.
Two scouts from the people were posted some way off, on the alert
for when they should catch sight of sheep and crook-horned cattle;
soon enough they appeared, and two herdsmen with them,   525
amusing themselves on their pipes, for they did not suspect a trap.
When those in hiding saw the beasts they ran out, and
quickly rounded up the herds of cattle and the fine flocks
of white sheep, and killed the herdsmen with them.
When the besiegers, sitting in their meeting-place, heard a loud   530
clamour coming from the cattle, they instantly mounted behind
their high-stepping horses and went in pursuit, and quickly
          found them.
Both sides formed up and began a battle along the riverbanks,
each hurling their bronze-tipped spears at the other side.
Strife was among them, and Confusion, and the lethal Death-
          Spectre,
                                                                                      535
holding one freshly wounded man, still alive, and another unwounded,
and dragging another who was dead by his feet through the mêlée;
and the garment over her shoulders was red with the blood of men.
These figures grappled and fought like living mortals,
and each dragged away the dead belonging to the other's side.   540
     On it he set a wide field of rich ploughland, three times
turned over after lying fallow, and on it many ploughmen
were wheeling their teams, driving them up and down;
whenever they reached the field's headland and turned round,
a man would come up to them and put into their hands a cup   545
of honey-sweet wine, and they would turn back along the furrows,
eager to reach the next headland in the deep-soiled field.

Behind them the field grew dark, just as a ploughed field looks,
though it was made of gold; it was indeed a great marvel of art.
  On it he set a king's estate, where hired labourers were   550
reaping with sharp sickles in their hands; some sheaves were
falling to the ground, one after the other, along the reapers' swaths,
while sheaf-binders were tying up others with ropes.
Three sheaf-binders stood over the work, and behind them
boys picked up the sheaves and carried them in their arms,   555
constantly handing them to the binders; and the king stood silently
among them next to the swath, staff in hand, gladdened in his heart.
Some way off heralds were preparing a feast under an oak tree,
busying themselves with a great ox they had sacrificed, and women
were mixing plentiful white barley for the labourers' supper.   560
  On it he set a vineyard, beautifully made of gold, heavily
laden with grapes; the grape-clusters along it were black,
and the vines throughout were propped on silver poles.
Round it he made a ditch in blue enamel, and outside this
he worked a fence of tin; there was a single track to the vineyard, 565
by which pickers would go to gather in the vintage.
Unmarried girls and youths, with lightness in their hearts,
were carrying away the honey-sweet fruit in woven baskets,
and in their midst a boy played beguilingly on a clear-
voiced lyre, and sang the Linus-song* to its accompaniment,   570
in a beautiful, light voice; and they kept time with him,
singing and shouting, and followed him on dancing feet.
  On it he made a herd of cattle with upright horns;
the cows were fashioned from gold and tin, and
were hurrying from the farmyard's dung to pasture   575
beside a murmuring river, next to a waving reedbed.
Herdsmen made of gold were going along with the cattle,
four of them, and nine swift-footed dogs went with them;
two terrible lions had fallen on the first of the cattle
and were seizing a bellowing bull, that roared loudly as it   580
was dragged away, and the dogs and young men pursued it.
But the lions had torn open the hide of the huge ox and were
gulping down its entrails and black blood, and in vain
did the herdsmen urge the swift dogs, driving them on;
but they hung back from the lions, afraid to bite them,   585
and stood close by, barking and keeping out of their way.
  On it the far-famed bow-legged god made a pasture

in a beautiful valley, a great pasture of white sheep,
with farmyards, and roofed shelters, and sheepfolds.
    On it the far-famed bow-legged god worked a dancing-place,   590
just like the one which Daedalus had fashioned in time past
in spacious Cnossos for Ariadne of the beautiful hair.* On it
young men and girls who would earn marriage-gifts of
oxen were dancing, holding each other at the wrist.
The girls wore light linen clothes, while the boys were dressed   595
in well-woven tunics, gleaming faintly with a sheen of oil;
the girls had beautiful garlands, and the boys had
daggers of gold, hanging from silver sword-belts.
At one time they would dance in a circle on skilful feet,
very lightly, as when a potter sits at the wheel that   600
fits his hands and tries it to see if it will run, and at
another they would run up in lines towards each other.
A great crowd was standing around the lovely dance,
watching with delight, [and among them a divine singer
sang and played the lyre]* and in their company whirled   605
two tumblers, taking the lead in the song and dance.
    On it he set the mighty power of the river Ocean, running
round the outermost rim of the cunningly worked shield.
    When he had finished making the huge, heavy shield, he forged
for him a corslet, shining brighter than the gleam of fire, and   610
fashioned for him a strong helmet, fitting close to his temples,
a fine helmet, intricately worked, and on it he set a golden crest;
and he fashioned for Achilles greaves of pliant tin.
    When the far-famed bow-legged god had finished all the armour,
he lifted it up and laid it before the mother of Achilles;   615
and she gathered up the gleaming arms from Hephaestus and
like a hawk came swooping down from snow-clad Olympus.

BOOK NINETEEN

Now saffron-robed Dawn rose up from Ocean's waters,
to bring light to immortals and to mortals, and Thetis
came to the ships, carrying the gifts from the god.
She found her dear son lying with his arms about Patroclus,
weeping loudly; and round him many of his companions were   5
lamenting. Thetis, bright among goddesses, stood beside him in
their midst, and gripped his hand firmly in hers and spoke to him:
'My child, grieved though we are, we should let this man lie,
since it was from the start by the gods' will that he was
beaten down; but take now this glorious, splendid armour   10
from Hephaestus, such as no man has ever worn on his shoulders.'

   So the goddess spoke, and laid the armour in front of
Achilles; and it rang out loud in all its intricately worked glory.
Trembling seized all the Myrmidons, and no one dared look
directly at it, and they drew back in fear. But the more Achilles   15
looked at it the more bitterness came over him, and the eyes
in him flashed out fearfully below their lids, like a flame; and
he was glad as he held the splendid gifts of the god in his hands.
But when he had had his heart's fill of gazing at the intricate work,
he straightaway addressed his mother with winged words: 20
'Mother, this god's gift of armour is indeed such as we would
suppose immortals to have made, and not the work of mortal men.
So now I shall arm myself in it; but I am terribly afraid
that while we delay flies will settle on the wounds of
Menoetius' stalwart son, slashed in him by the bronze, and   25
will breed worms in them, and defile his body, now that
the life has gone from him; and all his flesh will rot.'

   Then the goddess Thetis of the silver feet answered him:
'My child, do not let this be a concern in your heart;
I shall set myself to keep those cruel tribes from him,   30
the flies that eat away at men who have been killed in battle.
Even if he were to lie for the whole of a circling year,
his flesh will remain undecayed, or even firmer than now.
But now you must summon the Achaean heroes to assembly,
and renounce your anger at Agamemnon, shepherd of the people,   35
and at once arm for war and clothe yourself in courage.'

So she spoke, and filled him with a fury that was full of daring,
and through Patroclus' nostrils she dripped ambrosia
and red nectar, so that his flesh should remain undecayed.*

Then glorious Achilles made his way along the seashore,   40
yelling fearfully, and roused the heroes of the Achaeans.
And men who before used to stay in the ships' gathering-place,
those who were steersmen and looked after the steering-oars,
and were stewards in the ships and used to distribute the food,
even they now went to the assembly-place, because Achilles   45
had appeared, after long absence from the painful fighting.
The two attendants of Ares came up limping—Diomedes,
Tydeus' son, steadfast in war, and glorious Odysseus,
both leaning on spears, since their wounds still pained them;
and they came and sat down in the front of the assembly.   50
Last of all to come was Agamemnon, lord of men,
carrying the wound that Coön, son of Antenor, had dealt him
with his bronze-tipped spear in the fierce crush of battle.
When all the Achaeans were gathered together,
swift-footed Achilles stood up and addressed them: 55

'Son of Atreus, was it really a good thing for both of us,
for you and me, to rage grieved in heart at each other
in life-devouring strife, all for the sake of a girl?
If only Artemis had killed her with an arrow by the ships*
on the day that I chose her after I had sacked Lyrnessus,*   60
then so many Achaeans would not have bitten the vast earth,
crushed by their enemies' hands, while I stayed away in my anger.
Only Hector and the Trojans profited from this; the Achaeans,
I think, will long remember the strife between you and me.
Still, that is past and done; we must let it go, grieved though we are,   65
and must keep the spirit in our breast subdued by necessity.
Here and now I abandon my anger; there is no need for me
to rage so unrelentingly. Come then, quickly stir up
the Achaeans with their flowing hair to fight, so that I can
go to meet the Trojans face to face and make trial of them,   70
to see if they are still minded to camp out by our ships. I think
that any of them who manage to escape my spear out of the
savage conflict will be glad enough to rest their knees.'

So he spoke, and the well-greaved Achaeans were glad
that great-spirited Peleus' son had abandoned his anger.   75
Then Agamemnon, lord of men, spoke among them from

the place where he had been sitting, not standing in their midst:
'My friends, Danaan heroes, attendants of Ares, it is
a good thing to listen to a man on his feet, and it is not right
to interrupt him—for that is hard, even for a skilled speaker; 80
how can anyone listen, or speak, when men are making a great
uproar? Even a clear-voiced orator can be thrown off balance.
It is to Peleus' son that I shall declare myself—but each one
of you other Argives should take notice, and mark my words.
Many times have the Achaeans spoken to me about this matter, 85
and they have reproached me; yet it is not I who was to blame,
but Zeus and my destiny and the Fury who walks in darkness,
who drove a cruel delusion into my mind at the assembly,
on the day that I took away Achilles' prize with my own hand.
What could I do? It is a god who brings all things to fulfilment: 90
she is Zeus' eldest daughter Delusion, an accursed thing* that
deludes and drives astray the minds of all; her feet are tender,
and she does not touch the ground, but passes over men's heads,
bringing harm to mankind—and she has shackled others before me.
Indeed, even Zeus was once driven mad by Delusion, he who 95
men say is supreme among gods and men: even he
was beguiled by Hera's womanly deceitfulness,
on the day that Alcmene was due to give birth to mighty
Heracles in Thebes, that city crowned with strong walls.
Zeus, full of boasting, spoke in the presence of all the gods: 100
"Listen to me, all you gods and all you goddesses,
and I will say what the heart in my breast is telling me:
today Eileithyuia, she who attends painful birth, will bring
into the light a man who, born of a line that shares in my
blood, will rule over all those who live round about him." 105
Then the lady Hera, with guile in her heart, addressed him:
"You will be proved a liar, and you will not bring your words to
fulfilment. Come now, Olympian, swear a strong oath to me
that the man who on this day will fall between a woman's feet,
and who is born of those men who are of your blood's line, 110
will surely rule over all those who live round about him."
So she spoke, and Zeus did not perceive her deceit,
but swore a great oath, and so was mightily deluded.
Hera left the peak of Olympus, and swooping down
quickly came to Achaean Argos, where she well knew lived 115
the noble wife of Sthenelus, who was Perseus' son.

She was pregnant with her son, and the seventh month had begun,
and Hera brought him into the light before his due month;
but she delayed Alcmene's childbirth, and held back Eileithyuia.
Then she brought the news in person to Cronus' son Zeus, saying: 120
"Father Zeus of the bright thunderbolt, I will put a word in your
mind: today a noble man is born, who will rule over the Argives—
Eurystheus, son of Sthenelus who was Perseus' son, of your
line; so it is no shameful thing for him to rule over the Argives."
So she spoke, and sharp grief pierced Zeus to his heart's depths; 125
at once, full of anger in his heart, he seized Delusion
by her head of sleek hair, and swore a mighty oath that
she, Delusion, who drives madness into everyone, would
never again come to Olympus and the starry high sky.
So he spoke, and whirling her round in his hand hurled her 130
out of the starry high sky, and she quickly reached the works of men;
but Zeus would always groan at her, whenever he saw his dear son
performing a shameful task in the labours set him by Eurystheus.
So it is with me.* While great Hector of the glittering helmet
was slaughtering Argives by the ships' sterns, I could not forget 135
Delusion, who when this all began drove madness into my mind.
Still, since I was deluded, and Zeus took away my wits, I am
now willing to make amends, and to pay a boundless ransom.
So come, rouse yourself for the battle, and rouse the rest of
    the people;
as for the gifts, I am ready here to offer you everything that
    glorious 140
Odysseus promised you yesterday when he came to your huts.
Or if you wish, wait, even though you hanker after Ares' battle,
and my attendants will take the gifts from my ship and bring them
to you, so that you can see how I will satisfy your desire.'
    Then in answer Achilles of the swift feet addressed him: 145
'Most glorious son of Atreus, Agamemnon, lord of men; as for
the gifts, you may wish to offer them, as is right and proper, or to
keep them; it is your choice. But now, let us call up our battle-lust,
immediately, since this is no time to stay here, talking to no purpose,
or to delay; there is still great work that must be done, 150
so that men may once again see Achilles in the front-fighters,
slaying companies of the Trojans with his bronze-tipped spear.
Let every man of you be mindful of this as he faces his opponent.'
    Then in answer Odysseus of many schemes addressed him:

'Godlike Achilles, great chieftain though you are, do not urge   155
the sons of the Achaeans on to Ilium to fight with the Trojans
when they are hungry; this battle will not last a short time,
when once the companies of men engage with the enemy
and a god has breathed fury into both sides.
No, give orders for the Achaeans to take food and wine   160
beside the swift ships, for that is their fury and courage.
No man will be able to fight hand to hand all day long
until the setting of the sun if he has not taken food;
even if in his heart he is full of rage to fight, heaviness
creeps into his limbs unawares, and thirst and hunger   165
catch up with him, and his knees give way as he moves.
But the man who has taken his fill of wine and food
will do battle all day long against his enemies;
the heart within him is full of daring, and his limbs
will not tire until everyone has withdrawn from the battle.   170
So come, disperse the people, and give orders for supper
to be prepared; and as for the gifts, let Agamemnon, lord of men,
bring them into the midst of the assembly, so that all the Achaeans
can see them with their own eyes; and your heart may be softened.
And let him stand up among the Argives and swear an oath   175
that he has never gone up to the girl's bed or lain with her,
as is the usual way, lord, between men and women;*
and for you too, let the heart within you be ready to forgive.
Let Agamemnon make a rich feast in his huts and seek reconciliation
with you, so that you will not fall short of your due in any way.   180
Son of Atreus, in future you will act more properly towards others
as well; no one can be justly angry with a king if he makes amends
to a man when he has been the first to commit an outrage.'
    Then in turn Agamemnon, lord of men, addressed him:
'Son of Laertes, I am glad to hear your speech; everything   185
that you said in your full account was according to due measure.
I am indeed ready to swear an oath—my heart tells me so—
and I will not swear falsely before a god. Let Achilles
wait here for a while, even though he hankers after Ares' battle,
and let all the rest wait together, until the gifts come from my hut   190
and until we make a solemn truce and pledge friendship.
To you, Odysseus, I give this order and instruction:
choose the best young men out of all the Achaeans
to bring the gifts from my ship, all that yesterday we promised

to give to Achilles, and let them bring the women too.   195
And in the broad camp of the Achaeans let Talthybius
quickly prepare a boar for me, to sacrifice to Zeus and the Sun.'
     Then in answer swift-footed Achilles addressed him:
'Most glorious son of Atreus, Agamemnon, lord of men,
there will be another time when you should attend to this,   200
whenever there is some lull in the fighting, and
when the fury in my breast is not so strong;
but now there are men out there lying disfigured, whom
Hector, Priam's son, beat down when Zeus gave him the glory—
and you two are urging us to eat! For my part, I would order   205
the sons of the Achaeans to enter the conflict now, though
hungry and unfed, and then, at the setting of the sun,
to make a great meal, when we have avenged this insult.
Until then, my desire is that nothing should pass my throat,
neither food nor drink, because my companion is dead,   210
and he is lying there in my hut, disfigured by the sharp spear,
with his feet towards the door,* and around him our companions
mourn. I have no interest in my heart in food and drink, but
only in slaughter and blood and the anguished groans of men.'
     Then in answer Odysseus of many schemes addressed him: 215
'Achilles, son of Peleus, by far the greatest of the Achaeans,
you are stronger than I am, and not a little better than me
with the spear, but I might surpass you by a long way
in judgement, since I am older than you and know more;
so let your heart submit in patience and listen to my words.   220
Men very quickly have their fill of fighting; the bronze
scatters the straw of fighting in abundance on the ground
and yet the harvest is scantiest when Zeus, who is the
dispenser of war to mankind, has tilted his scales.*
The Achaeans cannot mourn a dead man by starving;   225
day after day men fall in great numbers, one after another,
so when could a man ever gain some respite from his toil?
No, we have to bury all those who have been killed,
hardening our hearts, and weeping only enough for one day.
All those who have survived the hateful conflict must   230
turn their minds to food and drink, so that we can fight
all the better against our enemies, on and on without ceasing,
clothing our bodies in tireless bronze. So let none of the people
hang back, waiting for some other summons to action;

this is the call, now, and it will be the worse for anyone who is   235
left behind by the Argives' ships. Let us all march out together,
and stir up bitter Ares against the Trojans, breakers of horses.'
     So he spoke, and took to go with him glorious Nestor's sons,
and Meges, son of Phyleus, and Thoas and Meriones,
and Lycomedes, the son of Creontes, and Melanippus; and   240
they made their way to the hut of Atreus' son Agamemnon.
No sooner was the word spoken than the deed was done:
they brought out of the hut the seven tripods he had promised
to Achilles, and twenty gleaming cauldrons, and twelve horses;
they quickly led out the women, skilled in fine handiwork,   245
seven of them, and the eighth was Briseïs of the lovely cheeks.
Then Odysseus weighed out fully ten talents of gold and led the
way back, and with him the Achaean young men carried the gifts.
These they placed in the middle of the assembly-place; Agamemnon
stood up, and beside the shepherd of the people stood Talthybius,   250
a man whose voice was like a god's, his hands holding a boar.
With his hand the son of Atreus drew out the knife
that always hung beside his sword's great scabbard and
began the offering by cutting hairs from the boar's head,
and prayed, lifting up his hands to Zeus; and all the Argives   255
sat in proper silence in their places, listening to their king.
Looking up to the broad high sky, he spoke in prayer:
'Let Zeus, the highest and best, be my witness first, and
after him Earth and Sun and the Furies, who below the earth
exact repayment from men who have broken their oaths—   260
that I have never laid hand on the girl, Briseus' daughter,
either because I desired her in bed, or for any other reason,
but she has lived in my huts all this time, untouched.
If anything I have sworn is false, may the gods send me all
the sufferings they give to those whose false oaths offend them.'   265
     So he spoke, and cut the boar's throat with the pitiless bronze.
Talthybius swung the body round and flung it into the great
expanse of the grey salt sea, to be food for fishes;* and then
Achilles stood up and spoke among the Argives, lovers of war:
'Father Zeus, how utterly you drive men out of their minds!   270
Never would the son of Atreus have stirred the heart in my
breast to its depths, nor in his stubbornness have taken
the girl away against my will, had not Zeus somehow wished
that death should come to great numbers of the Achaeans.

Now go and make your meal, that we may soon join in Ares' war.' 275
    So he spoke, and quickly broke up the assembly.
So all the rest scattered, each man to his own ship, but the
great-hearted Myrmidons busied themselves with the gifts,
and carried them away to the ship of godlike Achilles;
they set the gifts down in his huts, and settled the women there, 280
and excellent attendants drove the horses to join his herd.
    When Briseus' daughter, who resembled golden Aphrodite,
saw Patroclus lying there, disfigured by the sharp bronze,
she threw herself on him and let out a shrill lament, and tore
her breast and soft neck and beautiful face with her hands; 285
then she, a woman like the goddesses, spoke through tears:
'Patroclus, chief delight of my heart, how wretched I am!
When I went from this hut you were still living, but
now, marshal of the people, I come back to find you
dead; how one evil always follows another for me! 290
I saw the man to whom my father and revered mother
gave me disfigured with the sharp bronze in front of my city,
and my three brothers, born to the same mother as I was,
all of them very dear to me, meeting their day of death.
Even so, when swift Achilles killed my husband and sacked 295
the city of godlike Mynes, you would not let me weep,
but declared that you would make me godlike Achilles'
lawful wedded wife, and would take me in your ships to Phthia,
and would hold a marriage feast among the Myrmidons;*
so now I mourn you inconsolably; you were always kind to me.' 300
    So she spoke, weeping, and the women lamented with her,
outwardly for Patroclus, but each for her own sorrows.
The elders of the Achaeans gathered around Achilles and
begged him to eat; but he refused them with a groan:
'I beg you, my dear companions, if any will listen to me, 305
do not order me to satisfy my dear heart yet with food
or drink, because bitter grief has come upon me; I am resolved
to endure, and will stay here until the setting of the sun.'
    So he spoke, and sent the other kings away; but Atreus'
two sons and glorious Odysseus stayed behind, and Nestor 310
and Idomeneus, and Phoenix the old horseman, trying to
comfort him in his incessant grief; but he would not be comforted
in his heart until he had gone into the bloody jaws of war.
Remembering Patroclus, he fetched up a deep sigh, and said:

'There was a time when you too, ill-fated man, dearest of my   315
companions, would yourself set out a pleasant meal in this hut,
quickly and deftly, when the Achaeans were in haste to
wage tear-laden war against the horse-breaking Trojans;
but now you lie there, disfigured, and my heart wants no part
of food and drink, though they are here in the hut, because of   320
my longing for you. I could not suffer anything worse than this,
not even if I were to hear of the death of my father,
who now, I suppose, is shedding soft tears in Phthia
for the loss of his dear son, while I make war on the Trojans
in a foreign land, for the sake of Helen, that calamitous woman;   325
nor if it were my dear son, being raised for me in Skyros—
if indeed godlike Neoptolemus is still alive somewhere.*
Up to this time the heart in my breast had hoped that
I alone would perish far from Argos, rearer of horses,
here in Troy, and that you, Patroclus, would return to   330
Phthia, and then you could fetch the boy from Skyros
for me in your swift ship and show him everything:
my possessions, maidservants, and great high-roofed house.
Peleus, I think, must already be dead and gone,
or he is somehow clinging to a miserable life in   335
wretched old age, all the time expecting to hear
the cruel news about me, that I have been killed.'
    So he spoke, weeping, and the elders mourned with him,
each one calling to mind what he had left behind in his halls.
As they lamented, Cronus' son saw and took pity on them,   340
and at once addressed Athena with winged words:
'My child, I see you have completely deserted your man;
have you no longer any concern in your heart for Achilles?
He is sitting in front of the ships with their tall sterns,
weeping for his dear companion; all the others have gone   345
to seek their supper, but he is fasting, and does not eat.
Go now, and distil nectar and delectable ambrosia
into his breast, so that hunger does not come upon him.'
    So he spoke, and roused Athena, who was already eager to go,
and she swooped down from the high sky through the clear air,   350
in the likeness of a long-winged, shrill-voiced falcon. While
the Achaeans were arming themselves throughout the camp
she distilled nectar and delectable ambrosia into his breast,*
so that aching hunger should not weaken his knees, and

then returned to her mighty father's strongly built house.   355
The Achaeans began to pour forth, from among their swift ships;
as when snowflakes flutter down thick and fast from Zeus' sky,
frozen, and driven by blasts of the North Wind whose birth
is in the upper air, so then their brightly glittering helmets
and bossed shields and strongly plated corslets and   360
ash spears streamed thick and fast from the ships.
Their gleam reached the high sky, and all around the earth
smiled at the flashing bronze, and the noise rose up under
the feet of men. In their midst glorious Achilles began to arm;
his teeth ground noisily together, and his eyes blazed   365
like the flashing of fire, and unbearable grieving entered
his heart. Full of rage at the men of Troy, he put on the gifts
of the god, which Hephaestus by his craft had made for him:
first he fastened the greaves around his legs,
fine ones, fitted with silver ankle-clasps, and   370
next he put the corslet on around his chest.
Over his shoulders he threw the silver-riveted sword,
made of bronze, and after that lifted up the great, massive
shield, whose far-reaching gleam was like the moon's.
As when the gleam of a burning fire appears to sailors   375
on the open sea, blazing in a lonely sheepfold, high on
some mountain, while they are being driven helplessly
by storms over the fish-rich sea, far from those they love;
so the gleam from Achilles' splendid, intricately worked
shield rose up into the clear sky. He lifted the strong helmet   380
and set it on his head, and the horsehair-crested helmet
shone out like a star, and the golden plumes that Hephaestus
had fastened thickly about the crest were set waving.
Then glorious Achilles tested himself in his armour,
to see if it fitted him and if his bright limbs moved freely;   385
it became like wings to him, and it lifted up the shepherd of
the people. Then from its case he took out his father's spear,
heavy, thick, and massive; no other man of the Achaeans
could lift it, but only Achilles had the skill to lift it—
the Pelian ash spear that Cheiron had given his dear father,   390
cut from a peak of Pelion, to be the death of heroes.
Automedon and Alcimus busied themselves with yoking
the horses, setting the fine yoke-strap on them and fitting
the bits in their jaws, and pulling the reins behind them

on to the well-jointed chariot. Automedon picked up a bright   395
whip that fitted his hand and leapt up behind the horses,
and behind him Achilles mounted, in full armour,
shining brightly in his weaponry like Hyperion the Sun,
and he called to his father's horses with a terrible cry:
'Xanthus and Balius, far-famed children of Podarge!*   400
This time take more care to bring your charioteer back to
the Danaans' soldiery when we have had enough of fighting,
and do not leave him there dead, as you did Patroclus.'

Then from under the yoke the glancing-footed horse Xanthus
spoke to him; it had bent its head down, and all its mane   405
was drooping to the ground from the yoke-pad beside the yoke,
and the goddess Hera of the white arms had given it speech:
'We shall surely bring you back safe this time, huge Achilles;
but the day of your death is near at hand, and it is not we who
will be its cause, but a great god and your powerful destiny.*   410
It was not through our sloth or carelessness that the Trojans
stripped the armour from the shoulders of Patroclus, but it was
the best of the gods, he whom lovely-haired Leto bore, who
killed him among the front-fighters and gave the glory to Hector.
We two could run with the speed of the West Wind,   415
which men say is the fastest of all things; but it is your fate
to be beaten down by the might of a god and of a man.'

When it had spoken in this way the Furies silenced its voice;
and swift-footed Achilles, deeply angered, addressed it:
'Xanthus, why do you prophesy my death? There is no need.   420
I know very well myself that it is my destiny to die here,
far from my dear father and mother; but for all that I shall not
hold back until I have driven the Trojans to eat their fill of war.'

He spoke, and with a yell to the leaders drove out his single-hoofed
    horses.

BOOK TWENTY

So the Achaeans armed themselves by their curved ships,
around you, son of Peleus, who could never have your fill of battle;
and on their side the Trojans armed, on the plain's rising ground.
Meanwhile, from the peak of many-valleyed Olympus,
Zeus ordered Themis* to call the gods to an assembly; and she   5
ranged back and forth and ordered them to come to Zeus' house.
Not one of the rivers stayed away, except Ocean,
nor any of the nymphs who haunt beautiful groves and
springs of rivers and grassy water-meadows, but they all
came to the house of Zeus who gathers the clouds,   10
and took their seats in the polished stone porticoes that
Hephaestus had built for father Zeus with his cunning skill.*
    So they assembled in Zeus' house; nor did the earthshaker
neglect the goddess's summons, but rose from the sea to join
the rest, and sat in their midst, and questioned Zeus' purpose: 15
'Wielder of the bright thunderbolt, why do you call the gods again
to an assembly? Are you anxious about the Trojans and Achaeans,
because war and fighting are very close to blazing out between them?'
    Then Zeus who gathers the clouds answered and addressed him:
'Earthshaker, you know the purpose in my breast, why I have   20
gathered you here; I am concerned for them, dying as they are.
As for me, I shall remain here, seated in a valley of Olympus,
from where I can gladden my heart with watching; but you others
may go and mingle with the Trojans and Achaeans, and
may bring help to either side, wherever you have a mind, since   25
if Achilles fights the Trojans without your help they will not
be able to resist Peleus' swift-footed son, even for a short time;
even before this they would shake with fear when they saw him,
and now that he is terribly angry in his heart for his companion,
I am afraid that he will overstep his destiny and storm the wall.' 30
    So the son of Cronus spoke, and stirred up relentless warfare.
The gods made their way to the fighting, divided in their purposes:
Hera made for the gathering of the ships with Pallas Athena
and with Poseidon the earth-encircler, and Hermes the swift
runner, celebrated for his wise understanding; and Hephaestus   35
too went with them, exulting in his strength, and limping,

though his slender legs moved nimbly beneath him. But to
the Trojan side went Ares of the glittering helmet, and with him
was Apollo of the unshorn hair, and Artemis, shooter of arrows,
and Leto and Xanthus and Aphrodite who loves to smile.   40

For as long as the gods kept themselves apart from the mortals
the Achaeans were mightily triumphant, because Achilles
had appeared after long absence from the painful fighting;
a fearful trembling stole over the limbs of every Trojan, and
they were afraid when they saw Peleus' swift-footed son,   45
the equal of Ares, doom of mortals, shining brightly in his armour.
But when the Olympians came down and joined the mass of men,
then mighty Strife who drives the people on rose up, and Athena
roared, now standing outside the wall, beside the hollowed ditch,
and now shouting loudly down the deep-thundering seashore;
            and   50
on the other side Ares, looking like a black storm-cloud, roared,
urging the Trojans on with his piercing cries, now from the city's
        heights,
and now running along Simoeis' banks, over the hill Callicolone.*

So the blessed gods drove both sides on to crash together,
and caused wearisome strife to break out among themselves.   55
High above, the father of gods and men thundered
terribly, and below Poseidon caused the boundless earth
and the steep crags on the mountains to tremble; on Ida
of the many springs all its foothills and peaks began to shake,
and the Trojans' city and the Achaeans' ships trembled too.   60
In the depths, Aïdoneus,* lord of the dead below, was struck
with horror, and leapt yelling from his throne, terrified that
Poseidon the earthshaker would split apart the earth above him,
and that his dank and dreadful dwellings, which even
the gods abhor, would be laid bare to mortals and immortals;   65
so huge was the crash that rose up when the gods clashed
in strife. Face to face against lord Poseidon, Phoebus
Apollo took his stand, his winged arrows in his hand, and
opposite Enyalius stood the goddess grey-eyed Athena;
against Hera stood Artemis of the golden distaff, goddess of the   70
hunting-cry and arrow-shower, sister of him who shoots from afar.
Against Leto stood mighty Hermes the swift runner, and
opposite Hephaestus stood the great deep-eddying river
whom the gods call Xanthus, but men call Scamander.*

    So they opposed each other, god against god; but Achilles   75
was longing above everything to enter the mass of men and face
Hector, Priam's son—it was with his blood more than others'
that his heart impelled him to glut Ares the shield-bearing warrior.
But Apollo who drives the soldiery on made straight for Aeneas
and roused him to face Peleus' son, filling him with daring fury;   80
he made his voice sound like that of Lycaon, Priam's son,
and in this likeness Apollo, the son of Zeus, addressed him:
'Aeneas, counsellor of the Trojans, where now are those boasts
that you used to make to the Trojans' kings over your wine,
promising to match your strength against Peleus' son Achilles?'   85
    Then in answer Aeneas addressed him:
'Son of Priam, why are you telling me to do this, to face
Peleus' arrogant son in combat, when I have no desire for it?
This will not be the first time that I stand up against swift-footed
Achilles; once before this he drove me with his spear in flight   90
from Ida, at the time when he descended upon our cattle and
sacked Lyrnessus and Pedasus;* but Zeus stirred up fury
in me, and made my knees nimble and came to my rescue—
otherwise I would have been beaten down under Achilles' hands,
and Athena's, who went before him, bringing success, and told him 95
to slaughter the Leleges and Trojans with his bronze-tipped spear.
So it is not possible for a man to fight Achilles in single combat,
since there is always one of the gods beside him, to ward off ruin;
moreover, his spear always flies straight, and does not give up
until it has passed through a man's flesh. But if some god were to   100
stretch war's outcome equally between us, he would not easily
overcome me, not even if he claims to be made entirely of bronze.'
    Then in turn lord Apollo, son of Zeus, addressed him:
'Come now, hero, pray to the immortal gods yourself!
They say that your birth was divine—from Aphrodite,   105
daughter of Zeus, while Achilles is the son of a lesser deity:
one is Zeus' daughter, and the other a child of the ancient of the sea.
Come, then, and make straight for him with the untiring bronze,
and do not let him turn you aside with bitter words or threats.'
    So he spoke, and breathed great fury into the shepherd of the
        people,   110
and went on through the front-fighters, helmeted in gleaming bronze.
But Anchises' son did not go unnoticed by white-armed Hera
as he strode through the mass of men to meet the son of Peleus;

she brought all the gods together and spoke among them:
'Poseidon and Athena, it is you two who must deliberate   115
in your minds how these things will come to pass:
here is Aeneas, helmeted in gleaming bronze, going out
to meet the son of Peleus, and Apollo has sent him.
Come, let it be our charge to turn him straight back,
or let one of us go out and stand next to Achilles, and   120
bestow great power on him; and let him not lack courage,
so that he may know that it is the best of the immortals
who love him, and that those who in the past kept war and
conflict away from the Trojans now have no power at all.
We all came down from Olympus to take part in this battle   125
so that Achilles should not suffer harm at the Trojans' hands,
today—as for the future, he must suffer whatever Fate spun
for him with her thread at his birth, when his mother bore him.*
If Achilles does not hear this by means of the gods' utterance,
he will be afraid when some god comes to match strength with him 130
in battle; and gods are hard to face when they appear undisguised.'

   Then Poseidon, shaker of the earth, answered her:
'Hera, do not be angry beyond reason; there is no need.
For my part, I have no wish to drive the gods together in strife,
us against the rest, since we are much stronger than they are.   135
No, let us now leave this well-trodden field and take our seats
on some high watching-place, and leave the war to men.
But if Ares or Phoebus Apollo sets hostilities going again,
or if they hold Achilles back and keep him from the fight,
they will have a fighting quarrel on their hands with us too;   140
and then I think that they will very quickly break off the battle
and go back to Olympus, to the company of the other gods,
beaten down by the overwhelming force of our hands.'

   So the god of the dark-blue hair spoke, and led them away to
the heaped-up stronghold of Heracles, descended from a god,   145
the high wall built for him by the Trojans and Pallas Athena,
so that he might escape the sea-monster and be safe
whenever it pursued him from the seashore to the plain.*
On this Poseidon and the other gods took their seats, and
covered their shoulders with an impenetrable cloud; and   150
the gods on the other side sat on the brows of Callicolone,
gathered around you, lord Phoebus, and Ares, sacker of cities.

   So they sat on their different sides, devising their schemes,

but both parties shrank from starting the grim fighting,
though Zeus who sits on high had instructed them to do so.   155
    The whole plain was filled with men and horses, and blazed
with bronze, and the earth rang to the beat of men's feet
as they charged at one another. Two men, by far the best,
met in the ground between the two sides, raging to fight—
Aeneas, the son of Anchises, and glorious Achilles.   160
Aeneas was the first to stride forward, full of threats,
his strong helmet nodding; in front of his chest he held
his shield of battle, and he shook a bronze-tipped spear.
On the other side Peleus' son ran to meet him, like a lion
bent on slaughter that a whole village's resolute men have   165
gathered together to kill; at first it pays them no attention and
continues on its way, but when some war-swift young man
hits it with his spear it crouches, jaws gaping, and foam
gathers around its teeth, and the brave spirit in its heart
groans, and with its tail it lashes its ribs and flanks on   170
both sides, and drives itself on to fight; staring-eyed,
its fury carries it straight at the men, hoping either to kill
one of them or to die itself in the forefront of the conflict.
In just this way his fury and noble spirit drove Achilles on
to come face to face with great-hearted Aeneas.   175
When they had advanced to within close range of each other,
swift-footed glorious Achilles was the first to speak:
'Aeneas, why have you come out so far in front of the mass
to take your stand? Does your heart direct you to fight
with me because you hope to rule over the horse-breaking   180
Trojans, Priam's realm? But even if you kill me, Priam
will not for that reason put this prize in your hands;
he still has other sons, and his mind is strong, and not infirm.
Or have the Trojans cut out an estate for you, better than all others—
fine orchards and ploughland, for you to cultivate   185
if you kill me? I reckon you will find that hard to do, for
I think I have once before put you to flight with my spear;
do you not remember when I found you alone with your cattle
and chased you away, to run in swift-footed haste down
Ida's mountain slopes, fleeing without a backward glance?   190
From there you got away to Lyrnessus, but I made an expedition
against it and sacked it, with the help of Athena and father Zeus,
and led its women away as booty, robbing them of their day

of freedom.* Zeus and the other gods protected you then,
but I do not think they will protect you this time, as you   195
imagine in your heart. So I advise you to go back into
the mass of men, and not to stand up against me, in case
some calamity befalls you; even a fool understands after the event.'
    Then in turn Aeneas answered him and said:
'Son of Peleus, do not think you can frighten me with words,   200
as if I were a child; I myself also know well how to
taunt and to fling unseemly abuse at another man.
We know of each other's ancestry, and each other's parents,
for we have heard of their fame through mortal men's words;
but you have never yet set eyes on my parents, nor I on yours.   205
They say that you are the offspring of blameless Peleus,
and your mother is the sea-goddess Thetis of the lovely hair;
but for my part, I can boast that I am the son born to
great-hearted Anchises, and that my mother is Aphrodite.
Of these parents, one couple will today weep for their   210
dear son, because I do not think it is with childish words
such as these that we shall settle this affair and leave the battle.
But perhaps you wish to learn of my ancestry, to
know it well; many men know about my family already.
In the beginning, Zeus the cloud-gatherer fathered Dardanus,   215
and founded Dardania—for sacred Ilium, city of
mortal men, had not yet been built on the plain, and
people lived on the foothills of Ida of the many springs.
Dardanus in his turn fathered a son, King Erichthonius,
who became the richest of all mortal men; he had   220
three thousand mares of his own grazing in meadows on
marshland, delighting in their tender young foals; and while
they were at pasture the North Wind was seized by desire for
them, and lay with them in the likeness of a dark-maned horse,
and they conceived and gave birth to twelve foals.   225
Now whenever these gambolled over the grain-giving earth
they would run on the very tops of corn-ears and not break them,
and whenever they skipped over the sea's broad back
they would run on the very wave-crests of the grey salt sea.
Erichthonius fathered Tros, born to be king over the Trojans,   230
and after this there were born to Tros three blameless sons,
Ilus and Assaracus and godlike Ganymedes, who
as you know was the most beautiful of mortal men, and

who, because of his beauty, was stolen away by the gods
to be the cupbearer of Zeus and to live among the immortals.   235
Ilus in his turn fathered a son, blameless Laomedon,
and Laomedon was the father of Tithonus and Priam
and Lampus and Clytius and Hicetaon, a shoot of Ares.
Assaracus had a son, Capys, and his son was Anchises;
Anchises is my father, and Priam's son is glorious Hector.   240
This, then, is the ancestry and bloodline that I boast is mine;*
but as for bravery, it is Zeus who increases or diminishes it,
according as he wishes, for he is the mightiest of all.
So come, let us no longer bandy words in this way like children,
standing as we do in the middle ground of harsh war;   245
we can both fling insults at the other in such numbers
that not even a hundred-benched ship could bear their weight.
Man's tongue is a pliant thing, and in it there are many words of
different kinds, and the bounds of his speech spread far and wide;
any words you utter you are likely to hear coming back to you.   250
What compulsion makes us quarrel and wrangle face to face,
squabbling and bickering with each other like women who
become angry because of some heart-devouring dispute and
go out into the middle of the street and argue with each other,
with true and untrue words—for anger also makes them lie?   255
I am on fire for this trial of courage, and you will not deflect me
from it with words—not before we have fought with the bronze,
face to face. So come, let us taste each other's bronze-tipped spears.'

    So he spoke, and hurled his massive spear at the other's terrible,
awe-inspiring shield, and the shield rang aloud under the spear's
        point.   260
Peleus' son held the shield away from him in his brawny hand;
he was terrified, because he thought that the far-shadowing spear
of great-hearted Aeneas would pass through it with ease,
fool that he was, who did not understand in his heart and mind
that the splendid gifts of the gods are not lightly   265
beaten down by mortal men, nor will easily yield to them.
And so this time the massive spear of war-minded Aeneas
did not break through the shield, for the god's gift stopped it.
He drove it through two layers, but there were three more,
for the crook-footed god had bonded five layers on to it,   270
two of bronze, two of tin on the shield's inner side,
and one of gold, which was where the ash spear stopped.

Then Achilles in turn hurled his far-shadowing spear,
and hit the perfectly balanced shield of Aeneas on the
outside of its rim, where the bronze ran thinnest, and　　275
thinnest too was the oxhide on top; the Pelian ash spear
tore clean through it, and the shield gave a loud crack.
Aeneas crouched low, and held his shield away from him,
in fear, and the eager spear split both circles of his body-protecting
shield and flew over his back and fixed itself in the ground.　　280
Aeneas, now that he had avoided the long spear, stood there,
terrified because the spear had stuck fast so near to him,
and a huge wave of grief flooded down over his eyes.
Then Achilles drew his sharp sword and sprang at him raging,
giving a terrifying yell; but Aeneas picked up a rock in his　　285
hand—a mighty feat—which not even two men such as mortals
now are could lift, but he easily raised it on his own.
He would have hit Achilles with this rock as he charged, either on
the helmet or the shield that had already saved him from miserable
death, and then Peleus' son would have come close and robbed him
of his life with the sword, had not Poseidon the earthshaker been　　291
quick to see it, and at once spoken out to the immortal gods:
'This cannot be! Grief comes over me for great-hearted Aeneas,
who will quickly go down to Hades' house, beaten down by
Peleus' son, because he listened to the words of Apollo the far-　　295
shooter, the fool—Apollo will not save him from miserable death.
Why does this innocent man* now suffer such pointless agonies
for the sake of others' troubles, when he has always
given pleasing gifts to the gods who live in the broad high sky?
Come, let us lead him ourselves out of the way of death;　　300
even the son of Cronus may become angry if Achilles
kills Aeneas, because it is his destiny to escape, so that
the race of Dardanus shall not perish without issue and
unremembered—Dardanus, whom Cronus' son loved
above all the children borne to him by mortal women,　　305
though now the son of Cronus hates the race of Priam.*
And so mighty Aeneas will rule over the Trojans, he and his
children's children, those who are born in time to come.'
Then the lady goddess ox-eyed Hera answered him:
'Earthshaker, you must decide in your own mind　　310
about Aeneas, whether to save him, or allow him to be
beaten down by Peleus' son Achilles, fine man though he is.

We two have sworn many oaths among the immortal gods,
I and Pallas Athena, that we shall never keep the day of ruin
away from the Trojans, not even when the whole of   315
Troy is ablaze, burning in the ravaging fire, and the
warlike sons of the Achaeans have put it to the torch.'

When Poseidon the earthshaker heard her words
he made his way through the battle and the spears' turmoil,
and came to where Aeneas and renowned Achilles were.   320
Then straightaway he poured a mist over the eyes of
Peleus' son Achilles, and pulled the spear with its sharp
bronze point from the shield of great-hearted Aeneas;
this he laid before the feet of Achilles, and lifting
Aeneas up swept him away, high above the ground.   325
Over many ranks of heroes and over ranks of horses
Aeneas vaulted, sped on by the hand of the god,
and came down at the edge of the violent battlefield,
where the Caucones were arming themselves for war.
Poseidon the earthshaker came very close to him   330
and addressed him, speaking with winged words:
'Aeneas, which of the gods is telling you to fight so recklessly,
hand to hand with the high-hearted son of Peleus,
who is both stronger than you and dearer to the immortals?
Stop; and if ever you are thrown in his path, fall back   335
so that you do not reach the house of Hades before your time;
but when Achilles has met his death and his doom, then
you may take courage and fight among the foremost,
for no other man of the Achaeans is meant to kill you.'

So he spoke, and left him there, when he had explained all this.   340
Quickly he scattered the divinely sent mist from
Achilles' sight, who at once saw clearly with his eyes;
deeply disquieted, he addressed his great-hearted spirit:
'Oh, this is indeed a great marvel that I see before my eyes!
Here is my spear lying on the ground, but I cannot see   345
the man against whom I threw it in my rage to kill him.
It seems that Aeneas was after all loved by the gods,
even though I thought his boasting was vain and empty.
Well, to hell with him; this time he was glad to escape death,
and he will not have the stomach to make trial of me again.   350
Come! I will give instructions to the war-loving Danaans,
and go to face the other Trojans, and put them to the test.'

So he spoke, and sprang into the ranks, and urged on each man:
'Glorious Achaeans, do not any longer stand back from the Trojans,
but let each go forward, man against man, raging to do battle.   355
It is hard for me, powerful as I am, to go in pursuit of
so many men and to engage all of them in battle; not even
Ares, who is an immortal god, nor Athena would have the
endurance to go and face the jaws of such a great conflict.
But whatever my hands and feet and strength can achieve,   360
that I will do, and I shall not give way, not even a little, but
will press on right through their ranks, and I do not think
any Trojan will be glad when he comes within range of my spear.'

So he spoke, urging them on; and illustrious Hector shouted
encouragement to the Trojans, promising to go out and face
    Achilles: 365
'High-hearted Trojans, do not be afraid of Peleus' son;
I too could fight with words, even against the immortals, though
with the spear it would be harder, since they are much stronger.
Nor will Achilles fulfil all that his many words promise;
some things he accomplishes, some he cuts off half-done.   370
I shall go out and face him, even if his hands are like fire—
indeed, even if his hands are like fire, and his fury like gleaming iron.'

So he spoke, urging them on, and the Trojans raised their spears
at the enemy; both sides' fury crashed together, and the battle-cry
rose up. Then Phoebus Apollo stood near Hector and said: 375
'Hector, do not on any account go forward to challenge Achilles,
but wait for him in the mass of men and the battle's roar; otherwise he
may hit you with a spear or wound you from close by with his sword.'

So he spoke, and Hector once again entered the mass of men,
alarmed when he heard the sound of a god's voice.   380
But Achilles, his heart clothed in courage, sprang at the Trojans
with a frightening yell, and the first he felled was Iphition,
the fine son of Otrynteus, commander of a great force,
whom a Naiad nymph* bore to Otrynteus, sacker of cities,
below snow-clad Tmolus, in the rich land of Hyde. As he came   385
straight at him, raging, glorious Achilles hit him with a spear
on the middle of his head, and it was completely split in two;
he fell with a thud, and glorious Achilles boasted over him:
'Lie there, son of Otrynteus, most outrageous of men!
Your death is here, though your birth was by the lake   390
of Gygaea,* where your father's estate is, next to

Hyllus, rich in fish, and the swirling waters of Hermus.'
   So he spoke, boasting, and darkness covered Iphition's eyes.
The Achaeans' horses cut him to pieces with their wheel-tyres
in the battle forefront, and over him Achilles stabbed Demoleon,   395
son of Antenor and a fine man at fending off the battle,
in the temple, right through his helmet's bronze cheek-pieces;
the bronze helmet could not stop the spear-point, which
flew right through and shattered the bone, and his brain
inside was all turned to pulp; so he was beaten down, raging.   400
Next, when Hippodamas had leapt quickly down from his chariot
and was fleeing before him, Achilles pierced him in the back
with his spear; he gasped out his life, bellowing like a bull
when it is dragged by young men around the shrine of the
Heliconian,* while the earthshaker delights in them.   405
Just so Hippodamas bellowed as his noble life left his bones.
Then Achilles went after godlike Polydorus, Priam's son,
with his spear. His father had always forbidden him to fight,
because he was the youngest by birth among his sons, and
dearest to him; and he surpassed everyone in speed of foot.   410
This time he was showing off his prowess in childish display,
storming through the front-fighters, until he lost his dear life.
Glorious swift-footed Achilles hit him with a spear in the middle
of his back as he rushed past, in the place where his belt's
golden buckles were fastened, and the halves of his corslet met.   415
The spear's point went right through and came out by his navel,
and he fell on to his knees with a scream, and a dark cloud
covered him, and he sank down, clutching his guts in his hands.
   When Hector saw his brother Polydorus clutching his
guts in his hands and sinking down to the ground, a mist   420
flooded over his eyes; he could bear no longer to go
back and forth at a distance, but made straight to face Achilles,
shaking his sharp spear and looking like flame. As soon as
Achilles saw him he sprang up, and spoke exultingly:
'Now here at hand is the man who has vexed my heart most of all,   425
the one who killed my honoured companion; now we shall
cower no longer away from each other along the battle-lines of war.'
   So he spoke, and looking darkly at brilliant Hector addressed him:
'Come closer, so you will sooner be caught in the snares of death.'
   Then Hector of the glittering helmet addressed him fearlessly: 430
'Son of Peleus, do not think you can frighten me with words

as if I was a child; I myself also know well how to
taunt and to fling unseemly abuse at another man.
I know that you are great, and that I am much inferior; but
the outcome of all this lies on the knees of the gods, whether   435
I, though a lesser man, will rob you of your life with a cast of my
spear; my weapon too has been proved sharp enough in the past.'
    So he spoke, and poised his spear and let it fly; but Athena,
with the lightest of breaths, turned it aside from
splendid Achilles, and it flew back to glorious Hector   440
and fell there, in front of his feet. Then Achilles,
in a rage to kill Hector, sprang on him full of frenzy,
with a frightening yell; but Apollo snatched him away
with great ease, as a god can, wrapped in a dense mist.
Three times swift-footed glorious Achilles charged at him with   445
his bronze-tipped spear, and three times he struck the thick mist;
but when for the fourth time he rushed at him like some divine being,
he gave a terrible shout and addressed him in winged words:
'You dog, once again you have escaped death, though disaster
came close to you; this time Phoebus Apollo has saved you,   450
the god you doubtless pray to when you enter the thudding of spears.
When I meet you again I shall surely put an end to your life,
if I can find some god somewhere who will help me as well.
But now I shall go after the rest, and hope to overtake them.'
    So he spoke, and speared Dryops in the middle of his neck;   455
he fell in front of Achilles' feet, who left him there, and threw
a spear at Demuchus, Philetor's son, a valiant and mighty man,
and halted him with a spear-strike to the knee. Achilles then
slashed at him with his great sword and took away his life.
Next he leapt at Laogonus and Dardanus, two sons of Bias,   460
and forced them both out of their chariot, one with a cast of his
spear, and the other with a sword-blow at close quarters.
Then Tros, Alastor's son—he had come up to grasp his knees,
hoping that Achilles would take him prisoner and let him go alive,
sparing him death out of pity because he was of a similar age—   465
fool that he was, and did not know that he would not persuade him,
for this was a man with no softness in his heart, nor any gentleness,
but full of rage. As in anxious entreaty Tros tried to touch Achilles'
knees with his hands, he struck him in the liver with his sword,
and the liver slid out of his body, and the dark blood from it   470
filled his lap; he lost hold of his life and darkness covered his eyes.

Achilles next closed with Mulius, and stabbed him in the ear
with his spear, and the bronze tip passed clean through,
and came out of the other ear. Next he struck Echeclus,
Agenor's son, on the middle of his head with his hilted sword,　475
and the whole sword grew warm with his blood, and purple death
and his cruel destiny came down and fastened on his eyes.
Next he hit Deucalion where the sinews join on to the elbow,
and pierced his arm there with his bronze-tipped spear.
Deucalion stood waiting for him, his arm drooping heavily,　480
staring at death before his face; Achilles struck at his neck with
his sword, and sent head and helmet flying together; the marrow
burst out of his backbone, and he lay sprawled on the ground.
Then he set off in search of the blameless son of Peirous,
Rhigmus, who had come from rich-soiled Thrace, and hit him　485
in the midriff with his spear, and the bronze stuck in his lung,
and he tumbled from his chariot. As Rhigmus' attendant Areïthous
turned his horses round Achilles struck him in the back with his spear
and thrust him from the chariot; and the horses were panic-stricken.

　　Just as awesome fire rages through the deep valleys of a　490
parched mountain, and the deep woods keep burning,
and the driving wind sets the flames rolling everywhere,
so Achilles stormed everywhere with his spear like some divine being,
pursuing and killing, and the black earth ran with blood.
As when a man yokes together broad-browed bulls, intending　495
to crush white barley on a well-built threshing floor, and
it is quickly shelled under the feet of the loud-bellowing bulls,
so under great-hearted Achilles' chariot the single-hoofed horses
trampled down dead men and shields alike. The axle beneath
and the rails running round the platform were splashed all over　500
with blood that was thrown up in showers by the horses' hoofs
and by the wheel-tyres. And he, Peleus' son, kept pressing on
to win glory, spattering his unconquerable hands with gore.

BOOK TWENTY-ONE

B UT when they reached the crossing of the clear-flowing river,*
swirling Xanthus, whose father was immortal Zeus, there
    Achilles
cut the Trojan forces into two. Some he pursued across the plain
towards the city, where the Achaeans had fled in confusion
on the day before, when illustrious Hector was full of rage,   5
and here the Trojans streamed away in panic, and Hera spread
a dense mist in front to hamper them. The rest were
penned in against the deep-flowing, silver-swirling river,
and they fell into it with a great noise, and the deep waters roared,
and the banks on both sides threw back the loud echo; yelling,   10
they swam this way and that, whirled about by the eddies.
As when locusts rise fluttering and flee towards a river,
driven by a blast of untiring fire that has suddenly leapt up
in a blaze, and then huddle together in the water,*
so at Achilles' onslaught the stream of deep-swirling Xanthus   15
was filled with a confused clamour of horses and men.
   Achilles, sprung from Zeus, left his spear there on the bank,
leaning against a tamarisk bush, and jumped into the river like a
divine being, with only his sword, intent on terrible deeds, and began
to strike, whirling this way and that; and shameful groans arose   20
from men slashed by his sword, and the water grew red with blood.
As when fish flee the onslaught of a monstrous dolphin, and
cowering in fear crowd into the secret places of a harbour of
good anchorage, and the dolphin gobbles up all those it can catch,
so the Trojans huddled beneath the overhangs along the terrible   25
river's waters. When Achilles had tired his arms with slaughter
he chose twelve young men who were still alive from the river
to be payment for the death of Patroclus, son of Menoetius.
These he drove, stunned like fawns, on to the land and
tied their hands behind them with the well-cut leather belts   30
that they wore around their closely woven tunics, and handed
them over to his companions to take back to the hollow ships.*
Then he sprang back, raging to continue the fighting.
   There he fell in with a son of Priam, descendant of Dardanus,
as he was escaping from the river—Lycaon, whom once before in a 35

night raid he had captured in his father's orchard and brought back,
struggling; Lycaon had been cutting the young branches of a
wild fig tree with the sharp bronze to make into chariot-rails,
and glorious Achilles came on him as an unexpected calamity.
At that time Achilles carried him off in his ships and sold him   40
into well-built Lemnos, and Euneus, Jason's son, bought him.
From there his guest-friend Eëtion of Imbros ransomed him
for a great price and sent him away to bright Arisbe, but he
escaped secretly from there and came to his father's house.
For eleven days after he returned from Lemnos he gladdened   45
his heart among his friends; but on the twelfth day a god
thrust him once again into the hands of Achilles, who would
now send him unwillingly on a journey to the house of Hades.
When swift-footed glorious Achilles caught sight of him
unarmed, without helmet or shield, with no spear in his hand,   50
because he had thrown them all to the ground—for he was weary
and sweating as he climbed from the river, and fatigue sapped his
knees' strength—he was angry and spoke to his great-hearted spirit:
'Well now, here is indeed a great wonder I see before my eyes!
It seems that all the great-hearted Trojans I have killed   55
will rise once again from the murky darkness below,
seeing how this man has escaped the pitiless day, after he was
sold into lovely Lemnos. Not even the grey sea's expanse
could hold him back, though it restrains many against their will.
But now he will taste the point of my spear, so that I can see   60
and know for sure in my mind if he will return in the same way
even from there, or if the earth that gives life to all will
hold him down, as it holds down even the strong man.'
    So he pondered and paused; and Lycaon, bewildered, drew close,
desperate to grasp him by the knees, for he had a great desire   65
to escape miserable death and its black spectre.
Glorious Achilles lifted up his long spear, raging to stab him, but
Lycaon ducked under it and ran up stooping to grasp his knees,
and the spear flew over his back and stuck in the ground,
longing to glut itself on human flesh. With one hand   70
Lycaon held on to Achilles' knees, entreating him, and with
the other gripped the sharpened spear and would not let it go.
Then he spoke, addressing Achilles with winged words:
'Achilles, I entreat you! Show me respect and have pity on me.
Zeus-nurtured man, I come to you as a suppliant, worthy of respect;

you were the first man with whom I ate Demeter's grain on the day   76
that you captured me in our well-ordered orchard and
carried me far away from father and friends and sold me into
lovely Lemnos. I earned you the worth of a hundred oxen,
but then I was ransomed for three times as much;   80
and this is the twelfth day since I came back to Ilium,
after much hardship, and my malignant destiny has placed me
again in your hands. I suppose I must be hated by father Zeus,
who has delivered me up to you a second time. It was a short life
I was born to by my mother Laothoë, daughter of old Altes,   85
ruler over the Leleges whose delight is warfare, who
has his home in steep Pedasus beside the river Satnioeis.*
Priam took his daughter as wife, though he had many others,
and she bore two sons, and now you will have butchered us
both: one you beat down in the front rank of foot-fighters,   90
godlike Polydorus, felling him with your sharp spear,* and
now here you will be my destruction too, for I do not think
I will escape your hands, since some god has brought us together.
But I tell you another thing, and you should store it in your mind:
do not kill me, because I am not from the same womb as Hector,   95
the one who slew your gentle and mighty companion.'

So the illustrious son of Priam addressed him, entreating
him with his words; but he received an implacable reply:
'Fool, do not make speeches to me or talk of ransom.
In the time before Patroclus met the day of his destiny   100
I was in some way prepared in my heart to spare the men
of Troy, and I took many alive and sent them over the sea;
but now there is no man who can escape death, once a god
thrusts him into my hands in front of Ilium—not one man
of all the Trojans, and above all the sons of Priam.   105
So, my friend, you too must die; why lament like this?
Even Patroclus is dead, who was a far better man than you.
Can you not see what kind of a man I am, how handsome and great?
I am the son of a well-born man, and the mother who bore me was
a goddess, and yet over me too hangs death and my harsh destiny.   110
There will be a dawn or an afternoon or the middle of a day
when some man will take the life from me too in Ares' war,
with a cast of his spear or an arrow sped from the bowstring.'

So he spoke, and Lycaon's knees and dear heart were loosened;
he let go of the spear and crouched there, spreading both arms   115

wide. Achilles drew his sharp sword and struck him on
the neck next to his collarbone, and the two-edged sword
sank right in, and Lycaon fell forward on to the earth and lay there
sprawled, and his dark blood flowed out and wetted the ground.
Achilles seized him by the foot and flung him into the river   120
to be carried away, and boasting over him spoke winged words:
'Lie there now among the fish, who will lick away the blood
from your wound without a thought for you; nor will your mother
lay you on a bier and lament over you, but instead swirling
Scamander will carry you into the wide gulf of the salt sea,   125
and fish will dart up through the waves' dark rippling
surface and will feed on the white fat of Lycaon.
Die, all of you, until we reach the citadel of sacred Ilium,
you fleeing and I dealing out slaughter in pursuit.
Not even this clear-flowing, silver-swirling river will help you,   130
this river to whom you have for many years sacrificed bulls
in plenty, and hurled single-hoofed horses alive into its eddies.
No—die, every one of you, a miserable death, until you have
paid the price for Patroclus' death and for the slaughter of the
Achaeans you killed beside the swift ships while I stayed away.'   135
   So he spoke, and the river grew very angry in his heart, and
pondered in his mind how he might put an end to glorious
Achilles' battle-work, and keep destruction away from the Trojans.
Meanwhile the son of Peleus, holding up his far-shadowing spear,
sprang at Asteropaeus, the son of Pelegon, raging to kill him.   140
Pelegon was the son of broad-flowing Axius and Periboea,*
who was the eldest of the daughters of Acessamenus,
and the deep-swirling river Axius lay with her. It was at
Pelegon's son that Achilles sprang as he stood in the river
facing him, holding two spears; Xanthus had put fury   145
in his heart, angry at the slaughter of the young fighters
Achilles had cut down in his waters, showing them no pity.
When they had advanced to within close range of each other
swift-footed glorious Achilles was the first to speak:
'Who are you, and where are you from, that you dare to face me?   150
Unhappy are the parents whose sons oppose my fury!'
   Then in turn the illustrious son of Pelegon addressed him:
'Great-spirited son of Peleus, why do you ask about my ancestry?
I come from Paeonia of the rich soil, far from this place,
and I command the men of Paeonia with their long spears,   155

and this is now the eleventh day since I came to Ilium.
My birth-line goes back to Axius the broad-flowing,
Axius who pours forth the loveliest waters over the earth;
he fathered Pelegon, famed with the spear, whom they say
was my father. Now, illustrious Achilles, let us fight!'   160
   So he spoke, full of threats, and glorious Achilles raised
the Pelian ash spear. The hero Asteropaeus was ambidextrous,
and threw spears from both his hands at the same time;
with one spear he hit Achilles' shield, but it did not break
through, since the gold, the gift of a god, kept it out.   165
With the other he hit Achilles on the right forearm,
grazing it, and a dark cloud of blood spurted out, but
the spear passed beyond him and stuck fast in the ground,
longing to taste flesh. Throwing second, in a rage to kill him,
Achilles let fly his straight-flying ash spear at Asteropaeus,   170
but he missed his mark, and the ash spear hit the high
riverbank and stuck there in the bank up to its mid-point.
Then Peleus' son drew his sharp sword from beside his thigh
and leapt raging at Asteropaeus, who was trying in vain to wrench
Achilles' ash spear from the bank with his brawny hand;   175
three times in his rage to pull it out he made it quiver, and
three times he gave up the struggle. The fourth time he tried to
bend and break the ash spear of Aeacus' grandson, but too soon
Achilles closed with him and robbed him of his life with the sword,
hitting him in the belly next to the navel, and all his guts   180
spilled out on to the ground and he breathed out his life,
and darkness covered his eyes. Achilles jumped on to his chest
and stripped him of his armour, and spoke boastfully over him:
'Lie there, and learn how hard it is, though born from a river,
to pit yourself against the descendants of Cronus' mighty son.*   185
You said you were descended from a broad-flowing river,
but I can claim a blood-line running from great Zeus:
the man who fathered me rules over the numerous Myrmidons,
Peleus, the son of Aeacus; and Aeacus was a son of Zeus.
Zeus is more powerful than rivers that flow into the sea, and   190
therefore the lineage of Zeus is more powerful than a river's.
And here is a great river flowing beside you, who might
help you; but no one can fight with Zeus, the son of Cronus.
Not even lord Achelous can match himself against him,
nor even the immensely strong deep-flowing Ocean,*   195

from whom every river and the sea in its entirety
and all springs and deep wells draw their flow.
Even he is in fear of the lightning-bolt of great Zeus and
his terrible thunder, when it crashes from the high sky.'
  So he spoke, and wrenched the bronze-tipped spear from the
      bank,   200
and left Asteropaeus there, after robbing him of his dear life,
lying where he was on the sands; and the dark water soaked
into him and eels and fishes busied themselves about him,
gnawing at his kidneys and tearing the fat around them.
Then Achilles set off after the horsehair-crested Paeonians,   205
who had been thrown into turmoil along the swirling river
when they saw their champion beaten down in the harsh
conflict by the hands of Peleus' son and the might of his sword.
He now killed Thersilochus and Mydon and Astypylus,
and Mnesus and Thrasius and Aenius and Ophelestes;   210
and swift Achilles would have slain even more Paeonians
had not the deep-swirling river grown angry and addressed him,
speaking from a deep whirlpool in the likeness of a man:
'Achilles, your strength and the violence of your deeds
are beyond all men; the gods are always protecting you.   215
If the son of Cronus has granted it to you to kill all the Trojans,
at least drive them out of me on to the plain and do your worst there;
you can see that my lovely streams are crammed full of dead men,
and there is no way that I can pour my waters into the bright sea,
clogged as I am with dead men, while you continue your brutal
      killing.   220
Come now, let me be! Astonishment grips me, captain of the people.'
  Then swift-footed Achilles addressed him in answer:
'Very well, Scamander, nurtured by Zeus, it will be as you say—
but I shall not give up slaughtering the arrogant Trojans until
I have penned them inside their city, and have tested Hector,   225
matching our strength; either he will beat me down, or I him.'
  So he spoke, and hurled himself at the Trojans like some divine being.
Then the deep-swirling river addressed Apollo:
'God of the silver bow, this is hard! You have not respected
the plans of Cronus' son, he who repeatedly instructed you to   230
stand by the Trojans and to defend them until the evening comes
and the sun goes down at last, shadowing the rich-soiled ploughland.'
  So he spoke, and Achilles, famed with the spear, leapt from the bank

into the middle of the river, who rushed at him in a seething mass,
boiling up all its waters to a crest, and stirring the many dead men   235
killed by Achilles who were lying in him in great numbers;
roaring like a bull he flung them out on to the dry land, but
keeping those who were alive safe along his lovely waters,
hiding them in the vast depths of his swirling stream.
The wave reared up terribly, seething around Achilles,   240
and its watery mass fell on his shield and smashed him back;
he could not find a firm stance for his feet, and he seized a tall,
well-grown elm tree in his hands; but it came away from its roots
and tore the whole bank down with it, and blocked the fine stream
with its thick-growing branches, and as it fell made a barrier   245
right across it. Achilles heaved himself out of the swirling
river and dashed away, flying over the plain on swift feet,
terrified. The great god did not pause, but rose up menacingly
to a dark crest, seeking to put an end to the battle-work of
glorious Achilles and to keep destruction from the Trojans.   250
Peleus' son sprang back from him as far as a spear-cast,
swooping away like the black eagle, the hunting bird, that is
both the strongest and the swiftest of winged creatures;
in this likeness he bounded on, and on his chest the bronze
armour clattered terribly. So he fled, crouching under the river's   255
onslaught, but Xanthus with a mighty roar flowed on in pursuit.
As when a man, a digger of channels, guides a stream's flow
from a spring of dark water through plants in his garden, and,
mattock in hand, clears obstructions away from the channel;
as the water flows onwards it sweeps all the pebbles out of   260
its way, and with a gurgling sound glides quickly down
the land's gentle slope, too fast even for the man digging.
Just so the wave of the river kept catching up with Achilles,
swift though he was, for gods are stronger than men.
As often as swift-footed glorious Achilles strove to make a   265
stand and match his strength with the river, hoping to find if
all the immortal gods who inhabit the high sky were pursuing him,
so often the great wave of the Zeus-fed river would crash
on to his shoulders from above. Anguished in spirit, he kept
trying to leap clear of it, but the river rushed violently beneath him,   270
weakening his knees and sucking the dirt from under his feet.
The son of Peleus looked up to the wide high sky and groaned:
'Father Zeus, to think that none of the gods has promised to save me

from the river, pitiful as I am! After this, I could face any ordeal.
But none of the dwellers in the high sky is as much to blame   275
as my own mother, who beguiled me with lying words,
saying that I would die under the walls of the armoured
Trojans, struck down by the swift arrows of Apollo.*
How I wish that Hector, the best man bred here, had killed me;
a champion would have been the slayer, and a champion the slain.   280
But the truth is that I am fated to die a wretched death,
trapped in a great river like a boy, some swineherd, who is
swept away by a torrent as he tries to cross it in winter.'

So he spoke, and at once Poseidon and Athena came
and stood close to him in the likeness of men, and   285
taking him by the hand spoke encouraging words to him.
The first of them to speak was Poseidon, shaker of the earth:
'Son of Peleus, you must not be greatly alarmed or fearful,
seeing that two gods like us are here to support you, I and
Pallas Athena—and we have come with Zeus' consent.   290
Be sure that it is not your destiny to be beaten down by a river;
this one will soon give up, and you will see it for yourself.
Now I will give you some shrewd advice, and perhaps you will listen:
do not rest your hands from equally balanced warfare until
you have penned all the Trojan people who escape you inside   295
the splendid walls of Ilium. Then, when you have robbed
Hector of his life, go back to the ships; this glory we grant you.'

So they spoke, and went away to join the immortals, and Achilles,
greatly cheered by the gods' advice, made his way to the plain.
It was entirely flooded by the overflowing mass of water, and   300
much fine weaponry and the bodies of young fighters slain in
battle were floating there. Achilles' high-stepping, nimble knees
carried him straight upstream against the current, and the broad-flowing
river could not stop him, for Athena had thrust great strength into him.
Even so Scamander would not abate his fury, but became   305
yet more angry at the son of Peleus, and reared his waters
high to a crest, and called out in a shout to Simoeis:
'Dear brother, let us together hold back this man's strength,
or he will very soon sack the great city of lord Priam, and
the Trojans will not be able to withstand the heat of battle.   310
Come quickly, help me, and fill up your channels with
water from your springs, and stir all your streams into spate.
Raise a huge wave and stir up a great crashing of tree-trunks

and rocks, so that we can restrain this wild man,
who now stands supreme and rages like the gods.   315
I tell you, neither his violence will help him nor his beauty,
nor that splendid armour, which will lie somewhere deep
in my waters, covered in slime. I shall wrap him in sand
and heap up a huge pile of shingle over him, and the
Achaeans will not know where to find his bones in order   320
to assemble them, so deep will be the silt I shall hide him in.
That will be his tomb, and there will be no need to raise a
grave-mound when the Achaeans perform his funeral rites.'

So he spoke, and rearing up in a seething mass rushed at Achilles
in a roaring tumult of foam and blood and dead men.   325
The dark wave of the river fed by Zeus rose high, looming
over the son of Peleus, and was about to overwhelm him;
but Hera gave a great shout, terrified on his behalf
that the great deep-swirling river would sweep him away.
Straightaway she addressed Hephaestus, her dear son: 330
'Up with you, my crook-footed son! You are the one who
we thought could be a fit opponent for swirling Xanthus.
Come quickly now and help me: make a great flame flash out,
and I will go and rouse a violent storm from the salt sea,
blown by the West Wind and the clearing South Wind;   335
it will bring with it a destructive blast that will consume
the Trojans' armour and their dead men. Burn the trees
along Xanthus' banks, and fill him with fire; let him not
on any account turn you back with beguiling words or threats,
and do not cease from your fury until such time as I shout out   340
to you—only then must you hold back your tireless fire.'

So she spoke, and Hephaestus made ready awesome fire.
First of all the fire burnt on the plain, searing the many
dead men who lay there in great numbers, killed by Achilles.
The whole plain was scorched, and the bright water was checked. 345
As when in autumn the North Wind quickly dries up a
newly watered orchard, and the man who tills it is glad,
so the whole plain was scorched dry, and the dead men
were consumed. Then Hephaestus turned his dazzling flame on
the river, and the elms and willows and tamarisks burned,   350
and the clover and rushes and galingale that grew in
abundance around the lovely waters of the river burned too.
All along its eddies the eels and fishes were afflicted,

leaping like acrobats this way and that in the lovely waters,
tormented by the blast of much-scheming Hephaestus.   355
The mighty river himself was on fire, and addressed him by name:
'Hephaestus, no one of the gods can stand up against you,
and I cannot fight you when you blaze with fire like this. Leave off
this strife, and let glorious Achilles drive the Trojans at once from
their city. What is this quarrel to me? Why should I take sides?'   360

So he spoke, burnt by the fire, and his lovely waters were boiling.
As a cauldron is heated by a great fire made of dry wood
that crackles beneath it, and as it seethes inside renders down
the fat of a richly fed hog which bubbles up all around,
so the river's lovely streams blazed in the fire, and his water boiled.   365
He stopped still and had no desire to flow onward; the blast
of mighty Hephaestus of many schemes tormented him.
Pouring out entreaties he spoke to Hera with winged words:
'Hera, why has your son attacked my streams, making me suffer
above others? It is not I who am to blame as much as   370
all the other gods who are helping the Trojans. Very well,
I am ready to stop, if this is what you command—only let
Achilles give up as well. And I will swear an oath in addition,
that I shall never keep the day of destruction from the Trojans,
not even when the whole of Troy is ablaze, burning in the ravaging   375
fire, when the warlike sons of the Achaeans have put it to the torch.'

When the goddess Hera of the white arms heard this
she straightaway addressed her dear son Hephaestus:
'Hephaestus, my far-famed son, restrain yourself! It is not right
to batter an immortal god like this for the sake of mortals.'   380

So she spoke, and Hephaestus quenched his awesome fire,
and the wave rolled back along the river's lovely streams.

When the fury of Xanthus had been beaten down both fighters
stopped, because Hera held them back, angry though she was;
but then a painful, weighty conflict descended on the other gods,   385
and the spirit in their hearts was blown in contrary directions.
They collided with a great crash, and the broad earth groaned,
and the great high sky sounded its trumpet; Zeus heard it
as he sat on Olympus, and laughed with delight in his
dear heart when he saw the gods clashing in strife.   390
No longer did they stand apart from each other: Ares the
shield-piercer began the fighting, and charged at Athena
with his bronze-tipped spear, and spoke insultingly to her:

'Dog-fly, what is this wild daring? Why are you once again
driving the gods against each other, urged on by your great spirit?   395
Do you not recall when you provoked Tydeus' son Diomedes
to wound me, and you yourself took up a spear, for all to see,
and thrust it straight at me and tore my handsome flesh?*
I think that you will now pay me back for what you did then.'

  So bloodthirsty Ares spoke, and lunged with a stab   400
of his long spear at the terrible, tassel-decorated aegis
that not even the thunderbolt of Zeus can overcome.
Athena fell back and picked up a rock in her brawny hand,
a black boulder that was lying on the plain, jagged and huge,
which men of former times had put there to be a field-boundary;   405
with this she struck impetuous Ares in the neck, and loosened his limbs.
Ares fell, with a clatter of armour about him, covering seven
acres, and fouling his hair in the dust; Pallas Athena laughed,
and boasting over him addressed him with winged words:
'Fool, why do you match your strength against mine?   410
Have you not yet learned how much better than you I claim to be?
This way you will pay the full price to your mother's Furies;*
she is angry, and plans mischief against you because you have
abandoned the Achaeans and offer help to the arrogant Trojans.'

  So she spoke, and turned her shining eyes away from him,   415
and Aphrodite, daughter of Zeus, took his hand and led him
away, groaning deeply; he had scarcely recovered his breath.
When the goddess Hera of the white arms saw Aphrodite
she immediately spoke to Athena with winged words:
'Daughter of Zeus the aegis-wearer, Atrytone,* this will not do!   420
Here is that dog-fly again, leading Ares, doom of mortals,
through the mêlée out of the deadly battle. Quick, after her!'

  So she spoke, and Athena sped off in pursuit, glad in her heart,
and closing with Aphrodite hit her on the breast with her brawny
hand; and then and there her knees and her dear heart gave way.   425
So both Ares and Aphrodite lay on the earth that feeds many;
Athena boasted over them and addressed them with winged words:
'Let this be the treatment of all those who help the Trojans
whenever they fight against the armoured Achaeans, and
let them be as daring and unflinching as Aphrodite was   430
when she came to the help of Ares and faced my fury,
and then we would long ago have finished with
this war, and would have sacked the well-built citadel of Ilium.'

So she spoke, and the goddess Hera of the white arms smiled.
But the lord who shakes the earth addressed Apollo: 435
'Phoebus, why do we two keep our distance? It is not right when
the others have begun hostilities, and will be even more shameful if
we return to Zeus' bronze-floored house on Olympus without a fight.
You go first; you are younger by birth, and it would not be
proper for me to start, since I am older and wiser than you.   440
Fool, what a thoughtless heart you have! Do you not
remember the many hardships we endured around Ilium,
we two alone of the gods, when we were sent by Zeus
and served arrogant Laomedon for a year for a fixed
wage, and he gave us our orders and told us what to do?   445
It was my task to build a wall round the city for the Trojans,
a broad, splendid wall, so that the city should be impregnable,
while you, Phoebus, were herdsman to shambling, crook-horned
cattle in the glens of wooded Ida with its many valleys.
But when the joyful seasons brought round the due time for   450
payment, then the appalling Laomedon violently refused us
the whole of our wage and sent us away with menaces,
even threatening to tie our hands and feet together and
to send us off to be sold in some far-distant islands;
he also declared he would lop our ears off with the bronze.   455
So we returned home with resentment in our hearts,
deprived of the payment he had promised but did not fulfil.*
And now it is his people you show favour to, and make no
effort to ensure with us that the overbearing Trojans perish utterly
and wretchedly, along with their children and honoured wives.'   460
    Then in reply the lord Apollo the far-shooter addressed him:
'Shaker of the earth, you would not say I was possessed of a
a sound mind if I were to fight with you for the sake of mortals—
wretched creatures, who like leaves at one time flourish in a
blaze of glory, feeding on the fruits of the tilled earth, and   465
at another wither spiritlessly away. No, let us leave the battle
immediately, and let the mortals fight on by themselves.'
    So he spoke, and turned away, because he felt awe at the
thought of exchanging blows with his father's brother.
But his sister Artemis, haunter of the wild, queen of beasts,   470
reproved him bitterly and spoke to him in words of censure:
'So, shooter from afar, you are running away, handing the victory
entirely to Poseidon, giving him a chance to boast—for nothing.

You fool, what is the point of carrying that futile, useless bow?
Let me not hear you boasting again in the halls of our father,   475
as you have done before among the immortal gods, that you
would match your strength with Poseidon's, face to face.'
    So she spoke, and Apollo the far-shooter gave her no answer;
but Hera, honoured wife of Zeus, was angry with her and
rebuked the shooter of arrows in words of censure: 480
'Reckless bitch, how can you now have the daring to stand up
against me? It will be hard for you to oppose my fury, even
though you carry a bow and Zeus has made you a lioness against
women, and has allowed you to kill those whom you choose.*
I tell you, you would do better to slaughter wild beasts and   485
deer on the mountains than to fight with those who are stronger.
But if you are minded to learn about war, so be it; you will soon
find out how much stronger I am, when you oppose my fury.'
    So she spoke, and with her left hand seized both Artemis' wrists,
and with her right hand pulled the bow and quiver from her
    shoulder,   490
and began to beat her about the ears with her own weapons, smiling
as the other twisted and turned; and the swift arrows fell from the quiver.
Then the goddess Artemis fled cowering and weeping, like a pigeon
that flies from a hawk's pursuit into the hollow of a rock, a
deep cleft, because it was not its destiny to be caught; just so   495
Artemis fled weeping, leaving her bow and arrows where they were.
Then Hermes the guide, slayer of Argus, addressed Leto:
'Leto, there is no way I can fight with you; it is a painful thing
to exchange blows with the consorts of Zeus the cloud-gatherer.
No, you may quite freely boast among the immortal gods   500
that you overcame me by your own strength and might.'
    So he spoke; and Leto gathered up the curved bow and its arrows
that had fallen out here and there in the whirling dust, and
when she had picked up her daughter's weapons she withdrew.
Meanwhile the maiden goddess had arrived at the bronze-floored   505
house of Zeus on Olympus, and sat weeping on her father's lap,
and her immortal robe shivered about her. Her father, Cronus' son,
took her to him, and laughing gently began to question her:
'My dear child, which of the Uranian gods has done this to you
so thoughtlessly, as if you had committed some public mischief?'   510
    Then in answer the fair-crowned leader of the noisy chase said:
'It was your wife who thrashed me, father, white-armed Hera;

because of her, strife and quarrelling have now gripped the immortals.'

So they spoke, one to another, in this way; and meanwhile
Phoebus Apollo had made his way into sacred Ilium—   515
he was concerned for the wall of the well-built city, fearing
that the Achaeans would sack it on that day, before its due time.
But the other gods who live for ever went off to Olympus,
some of them angry, and some mightily triumphant, and
sat down beside the father, god of the dark cloud, while Achilles   520
continued to slaughter the Trojans and their single-hoofed horses;
as when smoke rises from a city that has been fired and reaches
up to the wide high sky, for the gods have unleashed their anger
against it and have sent toil to all and unleashed grief on many,
just so Achilles let loose toil and grief upon the Trojans.   525

Now the old man Priam was standing on the sacred tower,
and he saw towering Achilles, and how the Trojans were
fleeing in confused panic before him, and there was no courage
in them. With a cry he made his way down from the tower
and roused the splendid gate-guards along the wall: 530
'Set your hands to the gates and keep them open, until the
people in their panic flight reach the city. Look, there is Achilles
close behind, driving them on, and I think disaster is near.
When they are safe inside the wall and can catch their breath,
then shut the close-fitting doors again in their places;   535
I am afraid that murderous man may leap inside our wall.'

So he spoke, and they knocked back the crossbars and opened
the gates; thrown wide open they offered safety. Then Apollo
sprang out to meet the Trojans, meaning to keep ruin from them,
and they made straight in flight for the city and the high wall,   540
covered in dust from the plain, their throats rough from thirst;
but Achilles pursued them relentlessly with his spear, and all the time
violent madness had hold of his heart, and he raged to win glory.

Then the Achaeans would have taken Troy of the high gates
had not Phoebus Apollo roused glorious Agenor into action,   545
the worthy, blameless, and mighty son of Antenor.
Into his heart he thrust daring, and he himself stood
beside him, leaning against an oak tree and hidden in a
thick mist, to keep the heavy spectres of death from him.
When Agenor saw Achilles, sacker of cities, he stood   550
motionless, and as he waited his heart was in great turmoil;
deeply troubled, he spoke to his great-hearted spirit:

'How hard this is! If I flee before mighty Achilles to
where the rest have been driven in panic-stricken tumult,
he will still overtake me and cut my defenceless throat;   555
but if I leave these others to be driven in confusion by
Achilles, son of Peleus, and if my feet take me by another way
in flight from the wall to the plain of Ilium, and bring me
to the spurs of Ida where I can hide in its undergrowth—
then in the evening I could wash myself in the river   560
and dry the sweat from my body and get back to Ilium.
But why does my dear heart speak with me in this way?
I am afraid Achilles will see me leaving the city for the plain
and will come after me on his swift feet and overtake me.
Then I shall no longer be able to escape death and its spectres,   565
for he is surpassingly mighty, far beyond all mankind.
But what if I were to go out to face him in front of the city?
It must be that his flesh too can be wounded by the sharp bronze,
and there is but one life in him, and men say that he is
mortal, even though Cronus' son Zeus is giving him the glory.'   570
     So he spoke, and gathering himself waited for Achilles, his
brave heart within him urging him to enter the battle and fight.
Just as a leopard emerges from her lair in a deep wood
to confront the man who is hunting her, and has no fear or
terror in her heart when she hears the baying of his hounds,   575
and though the huntsman might get in first with a stab or a thrown
weapon, she will not slacken her courage, even if skewered
by a spear, until she either closes with him or is beaten down;
just so splendid Agenor, the son of noble Antenor,
had no thought of flight before he put Achilles to the test,   580
but held his perfectly balanced shield steadily before him,
and aimed his spear at him, shouting in a loud voice:
'Illustrious Achilles, doubtless you hoped in your mind to
sack the city of the proud Trojans on this day. You are
a fool! There is yet much anguish to be suffered over it.   585
There are many of us, men of courage, inside the city,
we who keep Ilium safe before the eyes of our dear wives
and children. As for you, you will meet your death here,
however terrifying and daring a fighter you may be.'
     So he spoke, and let fly the sharp spear from his heavy hand.   590
He did not miss Achilles, but hit him on the leg below his knee,
and on his shin the greave of newly forged tin clattered

terribly, and the bronze-tipped spear sprang back after it
struck, and did not pierce him, for the god's gift protected him.
Then in turn the son of Peleus leapt at godlike Agenor,   595
but this time Apollo did not allow him to win glory;
he snatched Agenor away and covered him in a thick mist,
and sent him to make his way quietly from the fighting.
Then the god who shoots from afar separated Achilles from
the people by a trick: he likened himself in every way to Agenor,   600
and stood before Achilles' feet, who rushed to pursue him
and chased him over the wheat-bearing plain, working him
towards the river, deep-swirling Scamander; but Apollo kept
running a little way in front of him, beguiling him with his
trickery, for Achilles always hoped to catch him as he ran.   605
Meanwhile the other Trojans were fleeing in a panic-stricken rout,
and gladly reached the city, and filled it with their crowding.
They had not the courage to wait any longer for each other
outside the city and to find out which of them had escaped
and which were dead in the fighting, but streamed in haste   610
into the city, as their feet and knees were able to save them.

BOOK TWENTY-TWO

So the Trojans ran into the city like terrified fawns, and there
dried the sweat from their bodies and drank to slake their thirst,
leaning against the fine battlements; and the Achaeans
drew closer to the wall, shields held in front of their shoulders.
But Hector's deadly destiny shackled him, making him wait   5
where he was, in front of Ilium and the Scaean gates.
Then Phoebus Apollo addressed the son of Peleus:
'Son of Peleus, why are you pursuing me on swift feet,
you a mortal and I an immortal god? You have not even
recognized me as a god, such is your ceaseless raging.   10
You shirk your battle-work with the Trojans you have put to flight,
and now they huddle in the city while you have strayed out here.
But you will not kill me, for you know I am not the one fated to die.'*
    Then swift-footed Achilles, deeply angered, addressed him:
'You have thwarted me, far-shooter, most deadly of gods,   15
by turning me away from the wall; if you had not, many men
would have clamped their teeth on the earth before reaching Ilium.
Now you have robbed me of great glory by easily saving
these men, because you have no fear of future retribution—
but I would make you pay for this, if only I had the power.'   20
    So he spoke, and made for the city with fearless spirit,
speeding along like some prize-winning horse that races
with its chariot, galloping effortlessly over the plain;
so swiftly did Achilles stir his knees and legs into movement.
    The old man Priam was the first to catch sight of him,   25
shining brightly like a star as he sped over the plain—
the star that rises in autumn, and its rays shine out
blazing among all the other stars in the depths of night,
and men give it the name of Orion's dog;
it is indeed the brightest star, but it is a sign of suffering, 30
and brings with it much fever for wretched mortals.*
Just so the bronze on Achilles' chest blazed as he ran.
The old man let out a groan, and raising his hands high
beat his head, and called out with a great cry, appealing
to his dear son; but Hector had already taken his stand   35
in front of the gates, raging relentlessly to fight with Achilles.

The old man stretched out his hands to him and spoke piteously:
'Hector my dear son, do not, I beg you, wait for this man,
alone, without any others; you will soon meet your death,
beaten down by Peleus's son, for he is far stronger than you,　　　40
and merciless. How I wish he was loved by the gods as much
as he is by me! Then he would soon lie out there, eaten by
dogs and vultures, and bitter grief would leave my heart—
this man who has bereaved me of so many fine sons,
both killing them and selling them to far-distant islands.　　　45
And indeed there are now two of my sons that I cannot see
among the Trojans crowded into the city, Lycaon and Polydorus,*
who were borne to me by Laothoë, a princess among women.
If they are somewhere in the enemy's camp, alive, I can surely
ransom them with bronze and gold, for there is much within;　　　50
the aged Altes, a far-famed man, gave his daughter a huge dowry.
But if they are now dead and in the halls of Hades, then it is
an agony for their parents' hearts, for me and for their mother,
though for the rest of the people the pain will last a shorter time,
as long as you too do not die, beaten down by Achilles.　　　55
Come back inside the wall, my son, and protect
the men and the women of Troy; do not present great glory
to Peleus' son by letting your own dear life be cut short.
Have pity on me, too, while I still have understanding,
unhappy and ill-fated man, whom the father, Cronus' son,　　　60
will destroy at the threshold of old age, in a cruel fate; I will be
forced to witness appalling sights—my sons slaughtered,
my daughters raped, their bedchambers ravaged, little children
flung to the ground in the cruel fighting, and my sons' wives
dragged away by the Achaeans' murderous hands.　　　65
And I myself will be the last to go; my own dogs, gone wild,
will tear me apart at the entrance to my house, after some man
has taken the breath from my limbs with a stab or a spear-cast—
the very dogs I reared in my halls to be by my table and guard
my doors will drink my blood as they lie about my porch,　　　70
driven mad in their hearts. A young man is a seemly sight
when he lies slain on the battlefield, torn by the sharp bronze;
whatever his appearance, everything about him is beautiful,
even in death. But when an old man is killed and his dogs
defile his grey head and grey beard and genitals, it is　　　75
surely the most pitiable thing that can befall wretched mortals.'

So the old man spoke, and seizing his grey hairs in his hands
pulled them from his head; but he could not move Hector's heart.
Then in turn his mother began to lament, weeping tears, unloosing
the fold of her dress and with the other hand holding her breast;   80
weeping tears, she addressed Hector with winged words:
'Hector my child, have respect for this, and show me pity,
if ever I held my breast to your lips to make you forget your cares.
Think on this, dear child, and save us from this deadly man, but
from inside the wall; do not go out and oppose him one against one. 85
Cruel man! If he kills you I shall never mourn you on a
funeral bier, dear child of our line, neither I who bore you
nor your richly dowered wife, but far away from us
swift dogs will devour you beside the ships of the Argives.'
So the two of them wept and addressed many prayers to   90
their dear son, but they could not persuade Hector's heart,
and he waited there for monstrous Achilles to come near him.
As when a snake in the mountains waits for a man by its lair,
a snake that has swallowed lethal poisons, and is full of bitter
anger, and glares terrifyingly at him as it writhes over its lair,   95
so Hector, unquenchable fury in him, would not give ground,
and leant his shining shield against the projecting tower.
Deeply troubled, he spoke to his great-spirited heart:
'What shall I do? If I go back through the gates in the wall
Polydamas will be the first to heap reproaches on me,   100
because he urged me at the start of this last deadly night,
when glorious Achilles rose up, to lead the Trojans into the city.*
I would not listen to him—but it would have been much better.
But now, since I have ruined the people by my recklessness,
I feel shame before the Trojan men and the Trojan women with their 105
trailing robes, in case some man of low rank may say of me:
"Hector trusted in his own might and so ruined his people."
That is what they will say; and then it would be far better
to go and meet Achilles face to face and either kill him and return,
or die at his hands, full of glory, in front of the city.   110
And yet, suppose I lay down my bossed shield and
strong helmet and lean my spear against the wall, and
go out by myself to meet blameless Achilles, and
promise to give back Helen and her possessions with her,
every single thing that Alexander brought to Troy in his   115
hollow ships—which was the beginning of this quarrel—

for the sons of Atreus to take away, and we could also share
with the Achaeans everything else that this city keeps hidden?
Then I could make the Trojan elders swear a solemn oath
not to conceal anything but to divide everything in two,   120
all the treasure that the splendid city holds within itself;
but why does my dear heart speak with me in this way?
I am afraid that if I go out and meet him he will have no pity
and will show me no respect but will kill me there and then
defenceless, like a woman, since I will have taken off my armour.   125
There is surely no way that I can flirt with him
"from a rock or an oak tree"* like a girl with a young man,
in the way that girls and young men flirt together.
No, it must be better to join battle with him as soon as possible,
and then we shall see to which of us the Olympian grants glory.'   130
    So he waited, pondering, and Achilles came up close to him,
looking like Enyalius, the fighter with the glittering helmet,
and brandishing the terrible Pelian ash spear above his right
shoulder; and about him his bronze armour shone like
the brightness of blazing fire or of the sun at its rising.   135
When Hector saw him he was gripped by trembling; he could
no longer hold his ground, but left the gates and fled in fear.
Peleus' son sprang after him, trusting to his swift feet;
like a hawk in the mountains, the swiftest of winged creatures,
that swoops with ease in pursuit of a timid dove, but she   140
flies away from under it, and from close behind it darts at her
again and again, screaming shrilly, its heart urging it on to kill—
so Achilles flew raging straight for Hector, and he ran terrified
along under the Trojans' wall, driving his knees into swift action.
So they raced ever onwards, past the lookout place and the wind-   145
blown fig tree, along the wagon track, away from under the wall,
and came to the clear-flowing springs where two fountains
gush up from eddying Scamander. One of these flows
with warm water, and all around it there is steam
rising, as if it were smoke going up from a blazing fire;   150
and the other sends out a stream in summer like hail
or freezing snow or water that has formed into ice.
Beside these, close by, there are fine wide washing-pools
built of stone, where the Trojans' wives and their lovely
daughters used to wash their shining clothes in former times,   155
in the days of peace before the sons of the Achaeans came.

Past this place they ran, Hector fleeing and Achilles pursuing;
the one fleeing was a fine man, but the swift pursuer was
far better. It was not for a sacrificial beast or a bull's hide that
they competed, such as are the prizes for men in foot-races,   160
but they ran for the life of Hector, breaker of horses.
As when single-hoofed prizewinning horses effortlessly round
the turning-point, in a race in honour of a man who has died,
where the prize is great, either a tripod or a woman,
so these two ran circling three times round the city of Priam   165
on their swift feet. And all the gods were watching them, and
the first to speak among them was the father of gods and men:
'This is a wretched thing! Before my eyes I see a man I love
being pursued around the wall; my heart grieves for
Hector, who has burnt the thigh-bones of many oxen in my   170
honour on the peaks of many-valleyed Ida, and at other times
on the city's heights;* and now here is glorious Achilles
pursuing him on swift feet around the city of Priam.
Come now, gods, share your counsel with me and advise me:
should we save him from death or should we beat him down,   175
noble man though he is, at the hands of Peleus' son Achilles?'

  Then in answer the goddess grey-eyed Athena addressed him:
'Father, god of the bright thunderbolt and the dark cloud—what have
you said! This is a mortal man, whose own fate was fixed long ago;
is it really your desire to release him from death's gloomy lament?   180
Go, do it; but all we other gods will not approve it.'

  Then in answer Zeus who gathers the clouds addressed her:
'Be comforted, my dear child, Tritogeneia;* I do not speak
with serious intent; and towards you I am minded to be gentle.
Go where your mind leads you, and hold back no longer.'   185

  So he spoke, and encouraged Athena, who was already eager to act,
and she went swooping down from the peaks of Olympus.

  Meanwhile swift Achilles drove on unremittingly at Hector.
As when on the mountains a hound starts a deer's fawn
from its covert and hunts it through glens and clearings,   190
and even if the fawn deceives it by cowering under a bush
the hound noses it out and keeps running until it finds it,
so Hector could not shake off Peleus' swift-footed son.
As many times as he gathered himself to dash under
cover of the well-built bastions by the Dardanian gates,   195
in the hope that those above might protect him with missiles,

so many times Achilles would get in front and, flying along
between him and the city, would turn him towards the plain.
As in a dream a man cannot catch another who runs from him—
the quarry cannot escape, nor can the pursuer catch him—   200
so Achilles could not run Hector down nor Hector escape Achilles.
How then could Hector have escaped the spectres of death,
if Apollo had not come to meet him for one last time and
stood close and stirred up fury in him and made his knees swift?
Glorious Achilles signed with his head to his people, telling them   205
not to hurl bitter weapons at Hector, in case someone
felled him and so won the glory, and he came second.
But when they had reached the fountains for the fourth time,
then indeed the father held up his golden scales and placed
in them two spectres of death that brings long misery,   210
one for Achilles and another for Hector, breaker of horses.
Taking the bar by the centre he held it up, and Hector's fated day
sank down; his way lay to Hades, and Phoebus Apollo left him.*
Then the goddess grey-eyed Athena came up to the son of Peleus
and standing nearby addressed him with winged words: 215
'Illustrious Achilles, dear to Zeus, now I can hope that we two
will carry off great glory to the ships for the Achaeans,
when we slay Hector, insatiable for battle though he is.
It is no longer possible for him to escape from us to safety,
not even if Apollo who shoots from afar were to submit to every   220
indignity and grovel before father Zeus who wears the aegis.
Now, stand here and catch your breath, and I will go and
persuade Hector to fight with you, matching strength to strength.'

So Athena spoke, and he followed her orders, glad at heart,
and stood there, leaning on his bronze-pointed ash spear.   225
She left him there, and caught up with glorious Hector,
likening herself in form and unwearying voice to Deïphobus.
She stood close to him and addressed him with winged words:
'Brother, I can see that swift Achilles is tormenting you sorely,
pursuing you round the city of Priam on his flying feet.   230
Come, let us make a stand here, and defend ourselves together.'

Then in turn great Hector of the glittering helmet addressed him:
'Deïphobus, you were always by far the dearest to me of my
brothers, all those who are the sons of Hecuba and Priam;
and now I think I shall value you all the more, because   235
when you caught sight of me you had the courage to come out

beyond the wall for my sake, while all the rest stayed inside.'

Then in answer the goddess grey-eyed Athena addressed him:
'Dear brother, our father and revered mother and my companions
around me clasped my knees and begged me at length, one after   240
another, to stay behind, so greatly do they all tremble at Achilles;
but the heart within me was worn down by painful anxiety for you.
So now let us go straight for him, raging, and let there be
no sparing of spears, and we shall then know if Achilles will
kill us both and carry off our bloodstained armour as spoils   245
to the hollow ships, or if he will be beaten down by your spear.'

So he spoke; and Athena by her trickery led Hector on.
When they had advanced to within close range of each other
the first to speak was great Hector of the glittering helmet:
'No longer, son of Peleus, shall I run from you, as before I fled   250
three times around Priam's great city, and I did not have the
courage to wait for your attack. Now my heart tells me to
take my stand against you; and I shall be killed, or else kill you.
So, come on! Let us offer each other our gods; they are the best
witnesses and overseers of agreements, and will be such for us: 255
I shall commit no shameful outrage on you, if Zeus grants me
the endurance to win and I take your life from you; when
I have stripped you of your fine armour, Achilles, I shall
give you back, dead, to the Achaeans. You must do the same.'

Then swift-footed Achilles looked at him darkly and said: 260
'Hector, accursed man, do not speak to me of agreements!
There are no binding oaths between lions and men,
and wolves and lambs are never of the same mind, but
all their lives harbour hostile thoughts against each other;
so friendship between you and me is not possible, and   265
there will be no oaths between us, until one or the other
dies and gluts Ares, the shield-bearing warrior, with his blood.
Summon up all the valour you can; now more than ever
you must show yourself a spearman and a daring fighter.
There is no longer any escape; Pallas Athena will quickly beat   270
you down with my spear, and now you will pay me in full for all
the sufferings of my companions you killed in your spear-frenzy.'

So he spoke, and poised his long-shadowing spear and threw it;
but illustrious Hector was looking ahead and avoided it;
he saw it and crouched, and the bronze-tipped spear flew over him   275
and stuck in the earth. But Pallas Athena caught it up and

returned it to Achilles, unseen by Hector, shepherd of the people.
Then Hector addressed the blameless son of Peleus:
'You missed! It seems after all, godlike Achilles, that
you do not yet know from Zeus when I shall die, though you   280
thought you did; you are a glib man, cunning with words,
saying that fear would make me forget my courage and fury.
But you will not fix your spear in my back as I run from you;
no, drive it straight through my chest as I come raging at you,
if a god gives you the chance. Now in your turn try to avoid my   285
bronze-tipped spear. May you catch it fully in your flesh;
then the war would be easier for the Trojans to bear,
if you were dead, since you are their greatest affliction.'

So he spoke, and poised his long-shadowing spear and threw it,
and did not miss but hit the middle of Peleus' son's shield;   290
but the spear rebounded far from the shield, and Hector was angry
that his swift weapon had flown uselessly from his hand, and
he stood there downcast, since he had no other ash spear.
He called out with a great shout to Deïphobus of the white shield,
and demanded a long spear from him; but he was nowhere near.   295
Then Hector knew the truth in his heart, and spoke:
'This is the end; the gods are surely calling me to my death.
I was certain that the hero Deïphobus was near at hand,
but he is inside the wall, and Athena has deceived me.
Now indeed a miserable death is close, no longer far off,   300
and there is no escape. So, after all, this is what Zeus and his son
who shoots from afar have long wanted, they who before this
were glad to protect me. Now my destiny has overtaken me.
Let me at least not die without a struggle and without glory,
but only after doing some great deed for future men to hear.'   305

So he spoke, and drew out the sharp sword that hung,
huge and massive, down at his side, and gathering himself
swooped like an eagle that flies high in the sky and
stoops down to the plain through murky clouds,
meaning to seize a tender lamb or a cowering hare.   310
So Hector swooped down, brandishing his sharp sword.
And Achilles charged too, his heart filled with wild fury,
holding his fine, intricately worked shield in front of his chest
to cover himself; and his shining helmet with its four plates
nodded above, and the fine golden plumes that Hephaestus   315
had fastened thickly about the crest were set waving.

Like the star that moves among others in the darkness of night,
Hesperus, the loveliest star that is set in the high sky,
so light flashed from the tip of the sharp spear that Achilles
brandished in his right hand, with deadly thoughts for glorious   320
Hector, as he eyed his fine flesh for the least-protected place.
Now most of Hector's flesh was covered by the fine bronze armour
that he had stripped from mighty Patroclus when he killed him,*
but the place where the collarbones hold the shoulders from the
neck was visible—the gullet, where death comes quickest—and   325
at this, as Hector charged at him, glorious Achilles drove his spear,
and the point passed clean through his soft neck. But the ash spear,
heavy with its bronze, did not shear through his windpipe,
and he could still address words to Achilles by way of answer.
He toppled over in the dust, and glorious Achilles boasted over him: 330
'Hector, doubtless you thought when you stripped Patroclus that
you would be safe, and you did not heed me, for I was far away.
You fool—he who was left far behind by the hollow ships was a
much better man than Patroclus, and would avenge him. I am he,
and now I have loosened your knees; dogs and vultures will   335
tear you shamefully, but the Achaeans will bury him with due rites.'

Then Hector, with little life now left in him, addressed Achilles:
'I beg you, by your life and your knees and by your parents' name,
do not let the dogs of the Achaeans devour me by their ships!
Take for yourself bronze and gold as much as you want,   340
gifts that my father and my revered mother will give you,
and return my body to its home, so that in death the Trojans
and their wives may grant me the due rite of fire.'

Swift-footed Achilles looked at him darkly and addressed him:
'Dog—do not entreat me by my knees or my parents' name!   345
I wish there was a way that my heart's fury could give me leave
to carve and eat your raw flesh, to pay for your terrible deeds,
as surely as there is no one who can keep the dogs from your head,
not even if your people bring a ransom here and weigh it out,
ten or twenty times your offer, and if they promise more besides,   350
nor even if Dardanus' descendant Priam orders them to hand over
your weight in gold—not even then will your revered mother,
the one who bore you, lay you on a bier and lament over you;
no, the dogs and vultures will share you out and devour you utterly.'

Then, dying, Hector of the glittering helmet spoke to him: 355
'I know you well as I look at you, and I was never going

to persuade you. Truly, you have an iron heart in your breast.
But think on this; it may be that my death will provoke the gods'
anger against you, on the day that Paris and Phoebus Apollo
slay you, fine man though you are, beside the Scaean gates.'*   360

    As he said this the end of death enveloped him, and his shade
winged its way from his limbs and went down to Hades,
lamenting its doom and leaving behind its manliness and youth.
Glorious Achilles addressed him, even now he was dead:
'Die now: as for my death-spectre, I will accept it whenever   365
Zeus and the other immortal gods are minded to bring it on.'

    So he spoke, and wrenched his bronze-tipped spear from the dead man
and laid it aside, and then stripped the armour from his shoulders,
all bloodstained; and other sons of the Achaeans ran up and stood
around him, gazing in wonder at the stature and amazing beauty   370
of Hector; not one of the bystanders failed to wound him, and
this is what they would say, each man looking at his neighbour:
'Look at this! Hector is certainly a softer man to deal with
now than when he set our ships ablaze with burning fire.'

    So they spoke, standing around Hector and stabbing him.   375
When glorious swift-footed Achilles had stripped the dead man
he stood in the midst of the Achaeans and spoke winged words:
'My friends, leaders and rulers of the Argives,
since the gods have granted me to beat this man down,
who caused more suffering to us than all the rest together,   380
come, let us make a circuit round the city under arms and test
the Trojans, to see if we can discover what their intentions are:
will they abandon their citadel now that this man has fallen, or
are they determined to stay inside, even though Hector is dead?
But why does my dear heart speak to me in this way?   385
There is a dead man lying by the ships, unlamented and unburied—
Patroclus, whom I shall never forget, so long as I am in
the world of the living and my knees have power to move.
And though in Hades the dead may forget the dead, yet
even there I shall always remember my dear companion.   390
Come now, young men of the Achaeans, let us go to
the hollow ships, carrying this man, and strike up a victory song.
We have won great glory: we have killed glorious Hector, who
the Trojans would pray to throughout their city as if he were a god.'

    So he spoke, and devised shameful treatment for glorious
        Hector: 395

at the back of the feet he made holes by the tendons, from heel
to ankle, and threaded straps of oxhide through them, and tied
them to his chariot, leaving the head to drag behind.
Then he lifted the famous armour into his chariot and mounted,
and whipped his horses to make them go, and they flew willingly on.   400
As Hector was dragged along a cloud of dust arose, and his
dark hair streamed out on both sides, and his head that before was
so handsome was tumbled in the dust, for now Zeus had handed
him over to his enemies to treat shamefully, in his own fatherland.

     And so Hector's head was completely fouled in the dust. When   405
she saw her son his mother began to tear her hair, and flung her
bright headdress far from her and raised a loud, mourning wail.
And his dear father cried piteously too, and all about them
through the city the people gave way to wailing and lamenting.
It was as if the whole of jutting Ilium was now smouldering   410
with fire all the way from its top to its bottom.
Only with difficulty did the people hold back the aged man
in his raging desire to go out beyond the Dardanian gates;
he rolled round in the dung and implored all of them,
calling on them and addressing each man by his name: 415
'Hold back, my friends! Though you care for me, give me
leave to go from the city to the ships of the Achaeans,
alone, to entreat this man, this violent doer of monstrous deeds,
to see if he will have respect for my age and take pity on
my years. He too has a father of the same age as I am—   420
Peleus, who gave him life and raised him to be an affliction
to the Trojans; but to me beyond all others has he brought pain,
for he has killed so many sons of mine in the prime of their life.
Yet despite my misery I do not mourn for them all as much as
I do for one, bitter grief for whom will carry me off to Hades—   425
Hector. How I wish that he had died in my arms, for then
we could have had our fill of weeping and mourning,
his mother who bore him, ill-fated woman, and I myself.'
     So he spoke, weeping, and the citizens joined their groans to his.
And among the Trojan women Hecuba began the unbroken dirge: 430
'My child, how wretched I am! Why should I live in cruel
suffering now that you are dead—you who were night and
day my boast throughout the town, and a source of strength
to the Trojan men and women all over the city, and they
greeted you like a god. You were indeed a great glory for them   435

while you lived, but now death and your destiny have overtaken you.'

So she spoke, weeping. Now Hector's wife had not yet learnt
what had happened, for no trustworthy messenger had come
to tell her that her husband had stayed outside the gates.
She was at her loom in the tall house's innermost part, weaving   440
a red double cloak, and working a pattern of flowers into it.
She called out through the house to her lovely-haired servants
to set a great tripod over the fire, so that Hector might have
a warm bath when he returned from the fighting—poor
innocent that she was, and did not know that grey-eyed Athena   445
had beaten him down at Achilles' hands, far away from baths.*
She heard the wailing and lamentation coming from the tower,
and her limbs shook and she dropped the shuttle to the ground.
Immediately she called out to her lovely-haired maids:
'Come here, two of you, and follow me; I want to see what has   450
happened. I heard the voice of my husband's respected mother,
and the heart in my breast leapt into my mouth, and my knees
locked together; some disaster must be near for Priam's children.
May my words be as if unsaid! But I am terribly afraid
that glorious Achilles may have cut off my bold Hector   455
from the city on his own and pursued him towards the plain,
and indeed has put an end to that dangerous valour that has always
possessed him; for he would never hang back in the mass of men,
but would always run far ahead, yielding to no one in his fury.'

So she spoke, and rushed through the hall like a maenad,*   460
her heart beating wildly; and her women servants went with her.
When she reached the tower and the massed gathering of men
she stood on the wall, looking all about her, and saw him
being dragged along in front of the city, swift horses
hauling him heedlessly towards the Achaeans' hollow ships.   465
Black night came down and enveloped her eyes, and
she fell backwards and gasped out her life-breath,
flinging far from her head her shining headdress with its
headband, its kerchief, and its plaited binding, and the
headscarf that golden Aphrodite had given her on the day   470
that Hector of the glittering helmet had brought her from
Eëtion's house, after giving him countless bride-gifts.
Her husband's sisters and his brothers' wives crowded round her,
holding her up in their midst, distraught to the point of death.
When she regained her breath and the spirit was gathered into   475

her breast, sobbing deeply she spoke among the Trojan women:
'Hector, how wretched I am! So we were born with the same fate,
both of us: you in Troy in the house of Priam, and I in Thebe
under wooded Placus, in the house of Eëtion, who raised me
from a baby—unhappily fated father of a child who was   480
born to a cruel destiny; how I wish he had never given me life!
Now you are going to the house of Hades, deep in the depths
of the earth, and you are leaving me in hateful mourning,
a widow in your halls; and our son, whom you and I, ill-fated
parents, gave life to is still but an infant. But you are dead,   485
Hector, and will bring no delight to him, nor he to you:
even if he escapes tear-laden war with the Achaeans
struggle and hardship will always be his, because
other men will fix their boundary-stones on his land.
The day that orphans a child parts him utterly from his fellows: 490
his head for ever bowed down, and his cheeks wet with tears,
he approaches his father's companions full of need,
tugging at the cloak of one man and the tunic of another;
some take pity, and one man briefly offers him a cup,
enough to wet his lips but not to moisten his palate.   495
Then a boy with both parents living shoves him away from
the feast, beating him with his fists and shouting abuse at him:
"Get out of here! Your father does not share in our feast!"
Then the boy goes back in tears to his widowed mother—
Astyanax, who in former times, sitting on his father's knees,   500
would eat only marrow and the rich fat of sheep, and
when he had finished his playing and sleep took him
he would sleep in his bed in the arms of his nurse, on
soft bedding, his heart filled with contentment.*
But now he has lost his beloved father he will suffer terribly—   505
Astyanax, 'Lord of the City', as the Trojans have called him—
because you alone used to defend their gates and long walls.
And now beside the curved ships, far from your parents,
squirming worms will eat you as you lie naked when the
dogs have had their fill; yet there are clothes lying ready   510
for you in your halls, delicate and beautiful, woven by
women's hands. I shall burn them all in a blazing fire;
they will be no use to you, because you will never lie in them,
but they will be your glory in the sight of Trojan men and women.'

So she spoke, weeping, and her women lamented with her.   515

BOOK TWENTY-THREE

So the Trojans lamented throughout the city; meanwhile
the Achaeans returned to their ships and the Hellespont,
and most of them dispersed, each man to his own ship,
but Achilles would not allow the Myrmidons to disperse,
and he addressed his warfare-loving companions: 5
'Swift-horsed Myrmidons, my trusty companions, let us not
unyoke our single-hoofed horses yet from the chariots,
but let us drive our horses and chariots close to Patroclus
and mourn him, for that is the privilege of the dead.
And when we have had our hearts' fill of cruel lamentation   10
we shall all set our horses loose and make our supper here.'

So he spoke, and they mourned loudly together, and Achilles led them;
three times they drove their fine-maned horses round the dead man,
lamenting; and among them Thetis stirred up the desire to weep.
The sands were wet with the men's tears, and their gear was wet   15
with tears, such was the man they had lost, a deviser of panic rout.
Among them the son of Peleus began the unbroken lament,
laying his man-slaying hands on his companion's chest:
'Hail and farewell, Patroclus, even in the halls of Hades!
All that I promised you before this I am now fulfilling: 20
I have dragged Hector here, to give him, raw, to the dogs to eat,
and I shall cut the throats of twelve noble sons of the Trojans
in front of your pyre; so great is my anger at your death.'*

So he spoke, and devised shameful treatment for glorious Hector,
laying him sprawled on his face in the dust beside the bier of   25
Menoetius' son. Then each man of the Myrmidons put off his
gleaming bronze armour and untied his loud-neighing horses, and
they sat down beside the ship of Aeacus' swift-footed grandson
in their thousands, and he gave them a funeral feast to satisfy
their hearts: many sleek oxen slumped to the ground, slaughtered   30
with the iron knife, and many sheep too and bleating goats,
and many white-tusked hogs, rich with fat, were
stretched out over Hephaestus' fire to be singed; and
all around the dead man the blood flowed in cupfuls.

Now the Achaean kings were taking the swift-footed lord, Peleus'   35
son, to the hut of glorious Agamemnon, having persuaded him

with difficulty, for he was still angry at heart for his companion.
When their journey brought them to Agamemnon's hut
they straightaway gave orders to the clear-voiced heralds
to set a great tripod over the fire, hoping to persuade   40
the son of Peleus to wash the bloody gore from himself;
but he stubbornly refused, and moreover swore an oath:
'By Zeus, who is the highest and best of the gods, I will not!
It is not lawful to let water come near my head until I have
set Patroclus on his pyre and heaped up a grave-mound and   45
shorn my hair,* since as long as I remain among the living
grief such as this will never come to my heart again.
Still, let us agree for the moment to eat, hateful though that is;
and in the morning, Agamemnon, lord of men, rouse the people
to gather wood and make ready everything that is proper for a   50
dead man to have when he goes to the murky darkness below,
so that unwearying fire may quickly burn this man away
from our sight, and that the people may turn again to their work.'
   So he spoke, and they listened intently and did as he said.
They hurried to prepare their supper, and then feasted in separate   55
companies, and no one's heart lacked a fair share in the meal.
When they had put from themselves the desire for food and drink
all the rest went to prepare for sleep, each man to his own hut,
but the son of Peleus lay down on the shore of the loud-roaring
sea, groaning deeply, surrounded by his many Myrmidons,   60
in an open place where the waves broke on to the seashore.
When sleep took hold of him, sweet slumber pouring over him
and relieving the cares of his heart—for his glorious limbs
were weary with chasing Hector towards windswept Ilium—
there came to him the shade of unhappy Patroclus,   65
exactly resembling him in his stature and lovely eyes and
voice, and his body was clad in the same clothes as before.
He stood over Achilles' head and addressed him in these words:*
'You sleep, Achilles, and you have forgotten me; when I
lived you did not neglect me, but you do now that I am dead.   70
Bury me as quickly as you can, and let me pass Hades' gates;
the shades there, images of the dead, are keeping me out,
and will not yet allow me to cross the river and join them, and
I wander aimlessly by the house of Hades of the wide gates.*
Give me your hand, I beg you; I will not come again   75
from Hades, once you have granted me the due rite of fire.

Never again in life shall we two sit apart from our companions
and make our plans together, for over me gapes the hateful
death-spectre which was appointed me right from my birth.
And for you too, godlike Achilles, your destiny is fixed,   80
to meet your death below the walls of the noble Trojans.
And I say another thing to you, a request, if you will agree:
do not lay my bones in a different place from yours, Achilles,
but together, just as we were brought up in your house,
after Menoetius had brought me as a child from Opous   85
to your house because of a calamitous slaying of a man,
on the day that I killed the son of Amphidamas in childish folly,
not with intent, but being angry over a game of knucklebones;*
and then the horseman Peleus welcomed me into his house
and raised me with kindness and named me your attendant.   90
So may one and the same vessel hide the bones of us both,*
the golden, two-handled jar that your revered mother gave you.'

    Then in answer swift-footed Achilles addressed him:
'Dear brother, why have you come here to me, and why
do you give me all these instructions? I will surely fulfil   95
everything that you tell me to do, and will do as you say.
But come, stand closer to me, and for this brief moment at least
let us embrace and enjoy our fill of cruel lamentation.'

    So he spoke, and held his arms out to Patroclus, but he
could not grasp him, and like smoke the shade slipped   100
squeaking away below the earth. Achilles jumped up, amazed,
and beat his hands together and his words were full of sorrow:
'So it is true after all: there is a shade and image of the dead
in the house of Hades, but there is no real substance to it;
all this night a shade of unhappy Patroclus has been   105
standing over me, wailing and lamenting, and giving me
exact instructions; and it looked marvellously like him.'

    So he spoke, and aroused in them all the desire to weep;
and they were still mourning over the piteous dead man when
Dawn with her rosy fingers appeared. Then lord Agamemnon   110
gave orders for mules and men to go from all the huts
to fetch wood; and in charge of them was a noble man,
Meriones, who was the attendant of courteous Idomeneus.
So they went off, holding in their hands wood-cutting axes
and well-twisted ropes, and the mules walked in front of them.   115
Uphill and downhill they went, along and aslant the hills,

and when they came to the spurs of Ida with its many springs
they at once busied themselves with felling high-leaved oaks
with their sharp-bladed bronze, and the trees crashed noisily
as they fell. The Achaeans then split the trunks and tied them   120
behind the mules, and their hoofs cut furrows in the ground
as they passed through the dense thickets, eager to reach the plain.
All the woodcutters too were carrying logs, for these were
the orders of Meriones, attendant of courteous Idomeneus.
They threw these down in a row on the shore, where Achilles   125
had planned a great grave-mound for Patroclus and for himself.

When they had piled up vast quantities of wood everywhere
they sat down and waited all together. At once Achilles
ordered the Myrmidons, lovers of warfare, to put on their
bronze armour and every man to yoke the horses to his   130
chariot, and they arose and clothed themselves in armour and
mounted their chariots, fighting-men and charioteers alike,
men in chariots in front and a cloud of foot-soldiers following,
numberless; and in their midst his companions carried Patroclus,
covering all his body with their hair that they had cut off and   135
heaped on him. Behind them glorious Achilles held Patroclus' head,
grieving, for he was sending his blameless companion to Hades.

When they came to the place that Achilles had described to them
they laid Patroclus down, and quickly raised an ample pile of wood.
Then swift-footed glorious Achilles had one more thought: 140
he stood some way from the pyre and cut off a lock of his fair hair
that he had been growing long to offer to the river Spercheius;
deeply moved, he looked out over the wine-faced sea and spoke:
'Spercheius, my father prayed to you in vain, when he
promised that when I returned home to my dear native land   145
I would cut off my hair for you and offer you a holy hecatomb,
sacrificing fifty uncastrated rams there and then into the
springs where you have your precinct and smoking altar.
So the aged man prayed, but you have not fulfilled his intent.
So now, since it seems I am not to return to my dear native land,   150
may I give this lock to the hero Patroclus to take with him instead.'*

So he spoke, and placed the lock in the hands of his dear
companion, and roused in all of them the desire to weep.
And indeed the sun's light would have set on their lamentation
had not Achilles quickly stood by Agamemnon and spoken to him: 155
'Son of Atreus, you are the man whose words the Achaean people

follow above all; men may indeed have their fill of mourning,
but disperse them for now from the fire and tell them to prepare
their meal. We, who are closest to the dead man, will occupy
ourselves with all this; but let the leaders stay with us.'   160

When Agamemnon, lord of men, heard Achilles' words
he at once dispersed the people to their well-balanced ships,
but the mourners stayed where they were and heaped up the wood
and built a pyre of a hundred feet each way, and on top of
the pyre, grieving in their hearts, they laid the dead man.   165
In front of the pyre they flayed many strong sheep and shambling,
crook-horned cattle, and prepared them, and from all of them
great-spirited Achilles took the fat and covered the dead man
from his head to his feet, and piled the flayed bodies around him.
On the pyre he laid two-handled jars of honey and oil,   170
leaning them against the bier. Then, with loud groans,
he hurriedly flung four strong-necked horses on to the pyre.
Lord Patroclus had kept nine dogs by his table, and Achilles
cut the throats of two of these and threw them on to the pyre,
and with the bronze slew twelve noble sons of the great-spirited   175
Trojans, for that had been the cruel plan he had in his heart.*
Then he let loose the iron fury of fire to feed on the pyre.
With a lamenting cry he called out the name of his dear companion:
'Hail and farewell, Patroclus, even in the halls of Hades!
Everything that I promised before this I now fulfil for you: 180
here are twelve noble sons of the great-spirited Trojans, all of
whom the fire will consume with you. As for Hector, Priam's son,
I shall not give him to the fire, but to the dogs to tear apart.'

So he spoke, threatening; but the dogs never busied themselves
around Hector, since Aphrodite, daughter of Zeus, kept them away   185
day and night, and anointed him with deathless oil of roses so that
Achilles should not tear the skin from him as he dragged him along.
And Phoebus Apollo brought a dark cloud down from
the high sky to the plain and covered all the place where
the dead man lay, so that the sun's fury should not too soon   190
shrivel the flesh that lay all around his sinews and limbs.*

But the pyre of the dead Patroclus would not catch fire.
Then swift-footed glorious Achilles had one more thought:
standing some way from the pyre he prayed to the two winds,
the North and West, and promised them splendid offerings;   195
pouring liberal libations from a golden cup he begged them

to come, so that the wood might quickly be kindled and
the corpses make haste to blaze in the fire. At once Iris heard
his prayer and set off to carry the news to the winds.
They were together in the house of the stormy West Wind,   200
enjoying a feast; Iris came running and stood there on the
stone threshold, and when they saw her before their eyes
they all leapt to their feet and each one invited her in
to join them, but she refused to sit down and said:
'No chair for me; I am on my way back to the streams of Ocean,   205
to the Ethiopians' land,* where they are offering hecatombs to the
immortal gods, so that I too may have a share in the sacred feast.
But Achilles is praying to the North and the roaring West Wind
to come to him, and is promising you splendid offerings,
hoping that you will set ablaze the pyre on which Patroclus   210
is lying, the man for whom all the Achaeans groan aloud.'
    So she spoke, and went away, and they arose with an
astounding noise, driving the clouds headlong before them.
Quickly they reached the open sea and blew on it, making the
waves rear under their shrill blast, and arrived at rich-soiled Troy   215
and fell upon the pyre, and the awesome fire gave a great roar.
All night long they beat the flames of the pyre together,
blowing shrilly; and all night long swift Achilles, holding a
two-handled cup, drew wine off from a golden mixing-bowl
and poured it on to the ground and soaked the earth,   220
calling on the shade of Patroclus, that unhappy man. As a
father mourns, burning the bones of his newly married son
who in dying has brought grief to his unhappy parents,
so Achilles mourned as he burnt his companion's bones,
dragging his steps around the pyre with frequent groans.   225
    At the time when the Morning Star rises to proclaim light over
the earth, and saffron-robed Dawn follows, spreading over the sea,
then the burning pyre began to sink and the flames abated,
and the winds set off to make their way home over the
Thracian sea, making its waters roar and heave into a swell.   230
Then the son of Peleus turned from the pyre to another place
and lay down exhausted, and sweet sleep overtook him;
but Atreus' son and those with him gathered together,
and as they came near the noise and clamour awoke Achilles.
He started up and addressed them with these words: 235
'Son of Atreus and you other chieftains of all the Achaeans,

first you must quench the burning pyre with gleaming wine,
all of it, as far as the fire's fury has reached, and after that
let us gather together the bones of Patroclus, Menoetius' son,
separating them properly; they are easy to recognize, for   240
he was lying in the middle of the pyre, while the others burnt
far from him, horses and men jumbled together at its edges.
Let us place these bones in a golden jar, in a double layer
of fat, until such time as I myself lie hidden in Hades.
As for the grave-mound, I order you not to toil at building it   245
up high, but make it a fair size; and later the Achaeans may
make it broad and tall, those of you who will be left behind
here in your ships with many benches, after I have gone.'*
    So he spoke, and they did as swift-footed Peleus' son said.
First they quenched the burning pyre with gleaming wine,   250
as far as the flames still had hold and the ash had settled deep;
then, weeping, they gathered the bones of their gentle companion
and placed them in a golden jar inside a double layer of fat,
and then wrapped it in a linen cloth and laid it in his hut.
To make his grave-mound they marked a circle round the pyre   255
and set stones on it as a base. Then they quickly heaped earth
over it, and when they had raised the mound they made to go away;
but Achilles held the people back and made them sit in a
wide assembly, and brought prizes from his ships,* cauldrons
and tripods and horses and mules and mighty oxen,   260
and women who wore fine girdles, and grey iron.
    First, for the swift horsemen, he put before them splendid prizes—
a blameless woman, skilled in crafts, and a two-eared tripod
that held twenty-two measures, as a reward for the winner.
For the man coming second he put up a six-year-old mare,   265
unbroken and carrying a mule-foal in her womb.
For the third he put up a cauldron as yet untouched by fire,
a fine one, holding four measures and still bright as new.
To the fourth he offered two talents of gold, and for the fifth
he put up a jar with two handles that was untouched by fire.   270
He stood straight up and spoke to the Argives in these words:
'Son of Atreus and you other well-greaved Achaeans,
these are the prizes that wait for the horsemen in this contest.
If we Achaeans were now competing in honour of some other man
then I myself would win first prize and carry it off to my tent,   275
for you know how far my horses surpass others in excellence,

because they are immortal, and Poseidon gave them to
my father Peleus, who then handed them on to me.*
But I and my single-hoofed horses will stay where we are,
such is the splendid fame of the charioteer they have lost—   280
a kindly man, who would often pour smooth olive oil over
their manes after he had washed them down in bright water.
So they both mourn for him as they stand there, and their manes
are drooping to the ground as they stand with grieving hearts.
So bestir yourselves throughout the camp, all you Achaeans   285
who are confident in your horses and your close-jointed chariots.'

So the son of Peleus spoke, and the charioteers quickly assembled.
The very first to rise to his feet was Eumelus, lord of men,
the dear son of Admetus, a man supreme in horsemanship.
After him there rose the son of Tydeus, mighty Diomedes,   290
and he led under his yoke the horses of Tros that he had taken
from Aeneas some time before, though Apollo saved their master.*
Next after him there rose Atreus' son, fair-haired Menelaus,
sprung from Zeus, and he led his swift horses under the yoke,
Agamemnon's mare Aethe and his own horse Podargus.   295
Echepolus, son of Anchises, had given Aethe to Agamemnon
as payment to avoid going with him to windswept Ilium, so that
he could stay at home and live at ease; Zeus had given him great
wealth, and he lived in Sicyon of the wide dancing-places, and it was
this mare, impatient for the race, that Menelaus led under the yoke.   300
The fourth to harness his fine-maned horses was Antilochus,
the splendid son of high-hearted lord Nestor, who was the son of
Neleus, and the swift-footed horses that drew his chariot were
bred in Pylos. His father stood near him and with generous
intention gave him advice—though Antilochus was shrewd enough: 305
'Antilochus, even though you are still young, Zeus and Poseidon
show you favour and have taught you all the many arts of
charioteering, and so there is no great need to instruct you;
you know well how to wheel round the turning-post, but your horses
are the slowest runners, and so I fear it will turn out badly for you.   310
These others' horses are swifter than yours, but their drivers
are no more skilled than you at planning what to do.
So come, my dear son, fill your heart full of cunning,
so that negligence does not cause you to lose the prize.
It is by cunning, not by brute force, that the woodcutter excels,   315
it is by cunning that the helmsman steers his swift ship

on the wine-faced sea when it is tossed by the winds, and
it is by cunning that one charioteer can outwit another.
Another man, even if he trusts in his horses and his chariot,
may in his carelessness take a wildly circling line, so that   320
his horses wander over the course and he cannot control them;
but he who though driving an inferior team has useful skill
always keeps the post in sight and turns close to it, and knows
how to strain his horses to the limit with the oxhide reins,
keeping his team out of danger and watching the man in front.   325
Now I will tell you of a sure sign, which you are bound to see:
there is a stump of dry wood, standing a fathom above the ground,
of oak or pine; it never rots away in the rain, and two white
stones are set against it, one on either side, where the course
bends back and there is smooth ground to drive on both sides.   330
It is either a memorial to some mortal man, long since dead, or
it served as the race's turning-point in the time of former men;
and now swift-footed Achilles has made it the halfway mark.
As you drive your chariot and horses hold closely to this,
and lean a little way yourself to the left in your well-woven   335
chariot-body, whipping on and calling out to your
right-hand horse, giving it free rein with your hands;
let your left-hand horse run very close to the turning-post,
so that the nave on your well-made wheel seems to graze
its edge—but take care not to touch the stone, or you may   340
damage the horses or shatter the chariot entirely, which
would be a joy to all the rest and a reproach to you yourself.
So, my dear son, be prudent and stay on your guard;
if at the turning-point you come up and overtake the
rest there will be no one who can catch or pass you,   345
not even if he comes from behind driving glorious Arion,
Adrestus' swift horse, who was descended from the gods,
or the horses of Laomedon, who are the finest bred here.'
    So Nestor, son of Neleus, spoke, and sat down again in his place
when he had told his son how to handle each part of the race.   350
    The fifth man to harness his fine-maned horses was Meriones;
and then they all mounted their chariots and cast lots.
Achilles shook the lots, and out jumped the lot of Antilochus*
Nestor's son; and after him lord Eumelus drew his starting-place,
and after him Menelaus, son of Atreus, famed with the spear,   355
drew his starting-place, and after him Meriones, and the last

to draw was Tydeus' son Diomedes, by far the best of them.
They stood in line abreast, and Achilles pointed out the turning-
post, far away on the level plain; he had stationed an umpire
beside it, godlike Phoenix, the attendant of his father,   360
to watch the running and to bring back a true account of it.

So they all at the same time lifted their whips over the horses
and flicked them with the reins, and shouted commands to
make them run, and the horses quickly galloped over the plain,
leaving the ships far behind; under their chests the dust   365
rose and hung in the air like a cloud or a whirlwind, and
their manes streamed behind them, blown by the wind's gusts.
The chariots at one time bent low to the earth that nurtures many
and at another bounded high in the air; their drivers stood
in their chariots, and each man's heart was beating hard   370
in his desire for victory, and each man was calling out to
his horses, as they flew across the plain in clouds of dust.

When the swift horses were finishing the last part of the course
and turning back towards the grey sea, then as the horses ran
at full stretch each man's prowess became clear; soon the swift   375
mares of Pheres' grandson Eumelus broke into the lead, and
keeping pace with them came the stallions of Diomedes,
the horses of Tros. They were not far behind, but very close,
seeming always on the point of mounting Eumelus' chariot and
blowing with their warm breath on his back and broad shoulders,   380
for they were holding their heads right over him as they flew along.
And indeed Diomedes would have driven past him or made the
race a dead-heat, had not Phoebus Apollo been enraged with
Tydeus' son and struck the shining whip from his hands.
Tears of rage flowed from Diomedes' eyes; he could see   385
Eumelus' mares drawing further and further ahead, while
his own horses were thwarted, since they ran without the whip.
But Apollo's cheating of Tydeus' son did not escape Athena's
notice, and she quickly chased after the shepherd of the people
and gave him back his whip and filled his horses with fury.   390
Then she strode angrily after Admetus' son Eumelus and—
as a goddess can—smashed his chariot's yoke, and the mares
ran off the track and the pole dropped to the ground.
Eumelus himself was tossed out of the chariot beside the wheel;
the skin was torn from his elbows and mouth and nose,   395
and his forehead above his brows was bruised, and his eyes

filled with tears, and his hearty voice was choked.
Tydeus' son pulled his single-hoofed horses sideways and,
holding them straight, got well clear of the others, for Athena
had filled them with fury and had put glory into himself.   400
Next after him came Atreus' son, fair-haired Menelaus,
and then Antilochus, who called out to his father's horses:
'Press on, the pair of you; now for an all-out effort!
I am not urging you to compete with those there, the horses
of Tydeus' war-minded son, on whom Athena has   405
just now bestowed speed and has put glory into Diomedes.
Faster now, try to catch the horses of Atreus' son! Do not fall
behind, and do not let Aethe, who is only a mare, pour scorn
over the pair of you. Why are you lagging, my champions?
I tell you this plainly, and it will surely be fulfilled: 410
you will get no more care from Nestor, shepherd of
the people, but he will kill you at once with the sharp bronze
if your slipshod ways mean that we win a lesser prize.
So off you go after them, run as fast as you can!
My part will be to fashion and devise some stratagem   415
to slip past them in a narrow place; I shall not miss the chance.'

So he spoke, and they, trembling at their lord's loud rebuke,
ran faster for a while. Soon afterwards Antilochus, steadfast in
battle, saw a place where the track became narrow and hollowed;
there was a gully in the ground where water had collected in winter   420
and broken part of the track, scooping out all the ground, and
along this Menelaus drove, making it hard for chariot wheels to run
side by side. Antilochus pulled his single-hoofed horses sideways
off the track and held them straight, pursuing him a little to one
side. Atreus' son was alarmed, and shouted to Antilochus: 425
'Antilochus, you are driving like a madman! Keep your horses back!
The track is narrow, but it will soon get wider, and you can pass;
do not risk crashing into my chariot and wrecking us both.'

So he spoke, but Antilochus drove even harder, urging his
horses on with the whip, and it was as if he had not heard.   430
As far as the length of a discus-cast that a fit man throws,
swinging from the shoulder as he tries the strength of his youth,
so far they ran on together; but then the mares of Atreus' son
fell back, and he himself was glad to give up driving them,
for fear that the single-hoofed horses should crash together on   435
the track and overturn the well-woven chariot-bodies, and that they

themselves should tumble in the dust in their haste for victory.
Then fair-haired Menelaus shouted abusively to Antilochus:
'Antilochus, there is no mortal more destructive than you;
to hell with you! We Achaeans were wrong to think you had any   440
sense; but you won't win a prize without a challenge on oath.'*

So he spoke, and called out to his horses, saying:
'Come on now, do not hold back! Do not stand there grieving
in your hearts! Their hoofs and knees will become tired
before yours do, because they are both well past their youth.'   445

So he spoke, and they, trembling at their lord's loud rebuke,
ran on faster, and quickly closed on Antilochus' team.

Now the Argives were sitting in assembly and watching
the horses as they flew over the plain, raising clouds of dust.
The first to catch sight of them was Idomeneus, captain of the   450
Cretans, sitting as he was outside the assembly on a high place;
and when he heard a man shouting to his team, though far away
he knew who it was, and he recognized the horse in front,
which was marked by being chestnut overall except that
it had white blaze on its forehead, circular like the moon.   455
He stood straight up and spoke to the Argives in these words:
'My friends, leaders and rulers of the Argives, is it
only I who can see the horses, or can you too? It seems
to me that the horses in front of the others are not the same,
and a different charioteer is coming into sight. The mares that   460
up to now were winning must have been impeded out there
on the plain; I saw them rounding the turning-post first but
I cannot now make them out, though my eyes are scanning
everywhere on the Trojan plain as I look out for them.
Perhaps the reins dropped from the driver's hands, and he failed   465
to hold his course round the post, and came to grief on the turn.
I think he would then have fallen out and smashed his chariot,
and his mares would have swerved, their hearts gripped by fury.
Come, stand up and look for yourselves; I cannot
make him out clearly, but I think the man in front is   470
Aetolian by birth, one who rules among the Argives—it is
the son of Tydeus the horse-breaker, mighty Diomedes.'

Then swift Ajax, son of Oïleus, rebuked him with shameful words:
'Idomeneus, why are you always ranting on like this? Those
high-stepping mares are still far off, flying over the wide plain.   475
You are by no means the youngest among the Argives,

nor are the eyes in your head the sharpest-sighted,
yet you are always flinging words about when there is no need
for this kind of crass talk; there are others here better than you.
Those in front are still the same mares as led before, Eumelus'   480
horses, and he is standing in the chariot, holding their reins.'
    At this the captain of Cretans spoke angrily in reply:
'Ajax, you dolt, you are a master of abuse, but in all else you are
inferior to the Argives, because you have a stubborn disposition.
Come, let us two make a wager—a tripod or a cauldron—   485
as to which horses are leading, and let us appoint Atreus' son
Agamemnon as referee; you will find out who it is when you pay.'
    So he spoke; and swift Ajax, the son of Oïleus, leapt angrily
to his feet, ready to answer him with bitter words; and
indeed the quarrel between them would have gone further   490
had not Achilles himself stood up and spoken to them:
'No more flinging harsh and bitter words at each other,
Ajax and Idomeneus; it is not the proper thing to do.
Indeed, you would both be angry with anyone else who did this.
No, take your seats in the assembly and watch out for   495
the horses; they will soon be here, straining after victory,
and then each one among you all will know which of the
Argives' teams is coming in first and which is second.'
    So he spoke; and now Tydeus' son was driving very near them,
repeatedly swinging his whip from the shoulder, and his horses   500
were stepping high as they skimmed swiftly over the plain.
Showers of dust fell continually on their charioteer,
and the chariot, covered all over with gold and tin,
ran on behind the swift-footed horses; and there was
scarcely a wheel-mark left behind them by the tyres   505
in the powdery dust as the two horses flew eagerly on.
Diomedes drew up in the midst of the assembly, and abundant
sweat dripped to the ground from his horses' necks and chests.
He himself leapt to the ground from his shining chariot and
propped his whip against its yoke, and mighty Sthenelus without   510
waiting rushed up to receive the prize; he gave the woman
to his high-hearted companions to lead away and the two-eared
tripod for them to carry off. Then he unyoked the horses.
    After him Antilochus, Neleus' grandson, drove up his horses,
having outstripped Menelaus not by speed but by trickery.   515
Even so Menelaus held his swift horses close behind him;

as wide as is the gap between wheel and horse as it
strains hard to pull its lord in his chariot over a plain, and
the hairs at the tip of its tail keep touching the wheel's tyre,
and there is no great space between them as the wheel keeps   520
running close to the horse on its career over the wide plain—
by such a distance did Menelaus trail blameless Antilochus.
Though at first he was left behind by the length of a discus-cast,
he had caught up very quickly, because the strong fury of
Aethe, Agamemnon's fine-maned mare, was always increasing,   525
and if both had had to run still further he would have passed
Antilochus and there would have been no dispute at the end.
Next came Meriones, the valiant attendant of Idomeneus,
lagging behind splendid Menelaus by a spear-cast;
his fine-maned horses were the slowest in the race, and   530
he himself was the weakest at driving in a chariot-race.
Last of them all came Eumelus, son of Admetus, dragging
his fine chariot himself and driving his horses in front.
When glorious swift-footed Achilles saw him he felt pity,
and standing among the Argives he spoke in winged words: 535
'The last man to drive up his single-hoofed horses is the best!
Come, let us give him a prize, for that is the proper thing to do—
the second prize, for Tydeus' son must carry off the first.'
    So he spoke, and they all approved of his proposal; and
he would have given Eumelus the mare, since the Achaeans had   540
agreed, if Antilochus, great-hearted Nestor's son, had not
stood up and answered Peleus' son Achilles with an objection:
'Achilles, I shall be very angry with you if you carry out what
you have said; you are minded to rob me of my prize because
Eumelus' chariot and swift horses were wrecked, just as   545
he was, fine man though he is. He should have prayed to the
immortals, and then he would not have lagged and come in last.
If you feel pity for him and he is dear to your heart,
there is in your hut much gold and bronze and many sheep,
and you also have maidservants and single-hoofed horses;   550
choose from these and give him an even greater prize later,
or do it here and now, and the Achaeans will applaud you.
But as for the mare, I will not give her up; anyone who feels
inclined may test me by fighting for her with his fists.'
    So he spoke, and swift-footed glorious Achilles smiled,   555
pleased with Antilochus, who was his dear companion,

and in answer addressed him with winged words:
'Antilochus, if you are telling me to give some further prize
from my hut's store to Eumelus, I will certainly do this:
I will give him the corslet that I took from Asteropaeus,*   560
made of bronze, and there is a layer of shining tin
worked around it; and it will be worth a great deal to him.'

    So he spoke, and ordered his dear companion Automedon
to bring it from his hut, and he went and brought it for him,
and laid it in the hands of Eumelus, who received it with delight.   565

    Then Menelaus stood up among them grieving in his heart,
unrelenting in his anger at Antilochus; a herald put the
staff in his hand and ordered the Argives to be silent, and
then the man who was like a god addressed him: 'Antilochus,
you used to be a man of good sense; but see what you have done!   570
By fouling my horses and driving yours ahead—though they
are far inferior—you have brought shame on my manhood.
Come now, you leaders and rulers of the Argives,
judge impartially between us both, without favour to either,
so that no man of the bronze-shirted Achaeans can say,   575
"Menelaus forced a win over Antilochus by lying, and
went off with the mare; his horses were far inferior, but
he himself was his superior in manhood and in strength."
Or rather, I myself will propose a solution, and I think
no Danaan will find fault with me, for the case will be just.   580
Come, Zeus-nurtured Antilochus, and as is right and proper
stand in front of your horses and chariot; hold the pliant
whip with which you drove just now in your hands, and
touching your horses swear by the holder and shaker of the
earth that you did not mean to impede my chariot by cheating.'   585

    Then in turn Antilochus, a man of good judgement, answered him:
'One moment! I am a long way younger than you, lord
Menelaus, and you are an older and a better man than me.
You know how a young man's rash acts come about;
his mind may be quicker but his judgement is a flimsy thing.   590
So let your heart bear with me; I will freely give you
the mare that I won, and if you were to ask for anything
better from my house I would willingly give it to you
here and now rather than fall out of favour with you,
Zeus-nurtured man, and become a wrongdoer in the gods' sight.'   595

    So the son of great-spirited Nestor spoke, and led the mare

up to Menelaus and handed her over to him; and Menelaus'
heart was softened, as when the dew falls on ears of corn in
the season when the ploughland is bristling with a growing crop.
So, Menelaus, the heart in your breast was softened,   600
and you addressed Antilochus, speaking with winged words:
'Antilochus, I will now give way and leave off my anger
against you; you were never wild or thoughtless before this,
though this time youthful spirits overcame your judgement;
another time be careful to avoid deceiving your betters.   605
No other man of the Achaeans could easily have won me over,
but you have endured much and struggled hard on my
behalf, you and your noble father and your brother;
and so I will listen to your entreaties, and will give you back
the mare, even though she is mine, so that these men also   610
may know that my heart is never arrogant or unbending.'

So he spoke, and gave the mare to Antilochus' companion Noëmon
to lead away, and took for himself the brightly shining cauldron.
Meriones took away the two talents of gold, since he had
come in fourth. The fifth prize, the jar with two handles, was   615
left over, and Achilles carried it through the assembly of the
Achaeans and presented it to Nestor; standing next to him he said:
'Here now, aged man, this is for you, a keepsake to remind you
of the burial of Patroclus, for you will not see the man again
among the Argives; I give you this prize without a contest,   620
since you will certainly not fight with fists again, nor wrestle,
nor will you ever enter for a spear-contest or a running race,
because now burdensome old age presses hard upon you.'

So he spoke, and laid the jar in Nestor's hands, and he was
delighted to receive it, and addressed Achilles in winged words: 625
'All that you have said, my son, is according to due measure:
no longer are my limbs steady, my friend, nor my feet, nor
do my arms swing easily from both my shoulders.
I wish I was in my prime again and my strength was as sound
as when the Epeians made a burial for lord Amarynceus   630
at Buprasium, and his sons held games in honour of the king.
Then there was no man who was my equal, not of the Epeians
nor of the Pylians themselves nor of the great-spirited Aetolians.
In the boxing I overcame Clytomedes, the son of Enops, and
in the wrestling Ancaeus of Pleuron, who stood up against me.   635
In the foot-race I overtook Iphiclus, fine man though he was,

and in the spear-cast I threw further than Phyles and Polydorus.
It was only in the chariot-race that Actor's two sons beat me;
they got in front by force of numbers, begrudging me the victory
because the greatest prizes were reserved for this contest.   640
These men were twins; one of them held steadfastly to the reins,
and while he held them the other urged the team on with the whip.
Well, that is what I was once; it is now the turn of younger men
to take part in such things, while I must give in to wretched
old age—but then I was someone of distinction among heroes.*   645
Go now and honour your companion with funeral games;
I accept this gift with pleasure, and my heart is glad because
you always remember me as a friend, and you do not forget
the honour that is my rightful due among the Achaeans.
May the gods reward you bountifully for this act of yours.'   650

So he spoke; and Peleus' son went back through the great gathering of
Achaeans when he had heard the son of Neleus' generous praise.
Next he set up the prizes for the painful business of a boxing match:
he brought into the assembly and tethered there a hard-working mule,
a female six years old and unbroken, the kind that is hardest to
        control;   655
and for the man who would lose he presented a two-handled cup.
He stood straight up and spoke to the Argives in these words:
'Son of Atreus and you other well-greaved Achaeans,
to compete for these prizes we summon the two men who are best
at putting up their fists and landing blows. The man to whom   660
Apollo grants endurance, and is judged so by all the Achaeans,
may take this hard-working mule and go back with her to his tent,
while the one who loses will take this cup with two handles.'

So he spoke, and at once there rose to his feet a valiant and
mighty man, skilled at boxing, Epeius, the son of Panopeus,   665
who laid his hand on the hard-working mule and spoke:
'Let the man approach who will carry off the two-handled cup;
as for the mule, I say that no man of the Achaeans will
beat me at boxing and take it away, since I say I am the greatest.
You say, and well you may, that I am a poorer soldier than the rest;   670
but there is no way that a man can be expert in everything.
I tell you this plainly, and it will surely be fulfilled:
I shall split his skin with a straight blow and smash his bones
to pieces; let those who care for him wait here all together,
to carry him away when my hands have broken him.'   675

So he spoke, and they all remained silent and still.
The only man to rise was Euryalus, a man like the gods,
the son of lord Mecisteus, whose father was Talaus; this
Mecisteus had long ago come to Thebes when Oedipus fell,
for his funeral games, and there overcame all the Cadmeians.*   680
The spear-famed son of Tydeus acted as Euryalus' second, and
rallied him with his words, since he greatly wished him to win.
First he laid his loincloth by him on the ground, and then gave
him the well-cut thongs made from the hide of a field-ox.*
So the two boxers put on their loincloths and strode into   685
the midst of the assembly, and putting up their powerful hands
they fell upon each other, and began to trade heavy blows.
A dreadful cracking of jawbones ensued, and sweat flowed from
all their limbs; then glorious Epeius advanced, and as Euryalus
looked for an opening he caught him on his cheek; there his   690
bright limbs failed him, and he could no longer stand upright.
As when the sea is roughened by the North Wind and a fish arches up
from weed-strewn shallows and then disappears again in the dark water,
so Euryalus arched at the blow; but great-spirited Epeius put his arms
around him and set him upright, and his companions stood
                    round him   695
and led him through the assembly, his feet dragging behind him,
spitting gouts of blood and drooping his head to one side.
They took him and sat him down in their midst, still stupefied,
and themselves went up and collected the two-handled cup.
        Then Peleus' son quickly set up the prizes for the third
                    contest,   700
which were for a pain-laden wrestling match, and displayed them
to the Danaans: for the winner a great tripod, made to stand over
a fire, that the Achaeans valued among themselves at twelve oxen,
and for the man defeated he brought into their midst a woman
who was skilled in many crafts, and they valued her at four oxen.   705
He stood straight up and spoke to the Argives with these words:
'Stand up, any two who wish to try themselves in this contest!'
So he spoke, and there stood up huge Ajax, Telamon's son,
and then much-scheming wily Odysseus rose to his feet.
They both put on their loincloths and strode into the midst   710
of the assembly, and grasped each other's arms with their
powerful hands, like crossing rafters that a renowned carpenter
has fitted in the roof of a high house to keep off the wind's violence.

Their backs creaked under the force of their sturdy arms'
unremitting grip, and the sweat ran off them in streams,   715
and weal after weal, red with blood, kept starting up
along their sides and shoulders, while all the time they
struggled to win the prize of the well-made tripod. But
neither could Odysseus trip Ajax and throw him to the ground
nor could Ajax Odysseus, since his mighty strength held firm.   720
But when the well-greaved Achaeans began to grow restive,
then huge Ajax, son of Telamon, addressed Odysseus:
'Son of Laertes, sprung from Zeus, Odysseus of many schemes,
either lift me or I will lift you; all the rest can be left to Zeus.'
    So he spoke, and lifted Odysseus, who did not forget his usual
        guile   725
but caught and struck the back of Ajax's knee and loosened his limbs,
and threw him on to his back; Odysseus dropped on to
his chest, and the people were astonished as they watched.
Then in turn much-enduring glorious Odysseus tried to lift Ajax;
he moved him a little way off the ground, but could not raise him,   730
and so hooked his knee round the other's, and they fell to the
ground side by side, and were both begrimed in the dust.
Then they would have leapt up and begun to wrestle a third time
had not Achilles himself risen to his feet and stopped them:
'No more struggling—do not wear yourselves out with your
        efforts;   735
both of you have won; share the prizes equally and go,*
so that other Achaeans can take part in the contests.'
    So he spoke, and they listened carefully and did as he said,
and when they had wiped off the dust they put on their tunics.
    Then Peleus' son quickly put up other prizes for speed of foot: 740
a finely worked silver mixing-bowl that held six measures,
and in beauty was by far the best in the whole world,
for the Sidonians who are skilled in many crafts had fashioned it,
and men of Phoenicia had ferried it across the misty sea
and had put in to harbour and given it as a gift to Thoas.   745
Euneus, who was Jason's son, had given it to the hero
Patroclus as a ransom for Lycaon, the son of Priam; and now
Achilles presented it as a prize in honour of his companion,
to the man who should prove to be fastest in the swift foot-race.*
For the man who came second he offered a great ox, rich with fat,   750
and for the last runner he offered a half-talent of gold.

He stood straight up and spoke to the Achaeans in these words:
'Stand forward, any who wish to test themselves in this contest!'
So he spoke, and at once there stood up swift Ajax Oïleus' son,
and also Odysseus of many schemes, and after him Nestor's son 755
Antilochus, who always beat the young men in the foot-race.
They stood in line abreast, and Achilles pointed out the turning-
post, and right from the starting-line they ran at full stretch; soon
Oïleus' son took the lead, and after him came glorious Odysseus,
running very close, as close as the weaving-rod of a fine-girdled 760
woman is to her breast as she deftly draws it tight with her hands,
pulling the spool along the warp, and holding it close to her
breast; so close was Odysseus as he ran behind Ajax, his feet
pounding in his tracks before the dust could settle into them;
and as glorious Odysseus kept up his swift running his breath 765
kept drifting about Ajax's head. All the Achaeans cheered on
his desire for victory, and applauded his mighty efforts.
When they were completing the last part of the course
Odysseus quickly prayed in his heart to grey-eyed Athena:
'Hear me, goddess; be good to me and come to help my running!' 770
So he spoke in prayer, and Pallas Athena heard him
and made his limbs light, both his legs and his arms. But
when they were on the point of dashing up for the prize
Ajax slipped as he ran—for Athena had caused him to stumble—
in the place where dung was spread from the slaughter
  of the loud- 775
bellowing oxen that swift-footed Achilles had killed for Patroclus.
His mouth and nostrils were crammed full with ox-dung, and
much-enduring glorious Odysseus carried off the mixing-bowl,
because he had come in first. Illustrious Ajax took the ox,
and stood there, holding in his hands a horn of the field-ox 780
and spitting out dung, and spoke out among the Argives:
'That was unfair! It was the goddess who tripped me! She has
before this stood by Odysseus like a mother and helped him.'
  So he spoke, and they all laughed happily at his distress.
Then Antilochus carried off the last prize with a smile, 785
and spoke among the Argives with these words:
'My friends, you all know what I am going to say to you—
that even now the gods honour men who are older born.
Ajax is a little older than I am, but Odysseus here
is from an earlier generation and from men of past times; 790

men say he is on the verge of old age, but it is hard for the
Achaeans to compete with him on foot, except for Achilles.'
   So he spoke, flattering the swift-footed son of Peleus,
and Achilles answered him, addressing him in these words:
'Antilochus, your words of praise will not go for nothing;   795
here, I give you a half-talent of gold, in addition to your prize.'
   So he spoke, and put it in his hands, and Antilochus was glad
to receive it. Then Peleus' son took a far-shadowing spear
and laid it down in the gathering, and also a shield and helmet—
the arms of Sarpedon, that Patroclus had taken from him.*   800
He stood straight up and spoke to the Achaeans in these words:
'To compete for these arms we order two men, the best,
to put on their armour and take up the flesh-splitting bronze
and to test each other in front of the gathered soldiery.
Whichever of them first makes a hit on the other's handsome flesh 805
and gets through to his innards past armour and black blood,
to him I shall give this sword here with its silver rivets,
a fine sword from Thrace, which I took from Asteropaeus;*
as for the armour, let both take and hold it in common,
and we shall put before them a splendid feast in the huts.'   810
   So he spoke, and huge Ajax, the son of Telamon, rose up,
and the son of Tydeus, mighty Diomedes, also stood up.
When they had armed themselves on either side of the soldiery
they both advanced into the middle ground, raging to fight
and glaring terribly; and amazement gripped all the Achaeans.   815
When they had advanced to within close range of each other,
three times they charged and three times lunged from close quarters.
Then Ajax stabbed at Diomedes' perfectly balanced shield, but
did not pierce his flesh, because the corslet behind it saved him.
Then Tydeus' son all the time kept threatening to strike at   820
Ajax's neck over his great shield with the bright spear's point,
so much so that the Achaeans feared greatly for Ajax
and called on them to stop fighting and take equal prizes.
And so Achilles gave the great sword to the hero Tydeus' son, and
handed it to him with its scabbard and belt of skilfully cut leather. 825
   Next the son of Peleus laid before them a mass of iron, formed in
the melting-furnace, that the mighty Eëtion used to throw;
but swift-footed glorious Achilles had killed him, and had
brought this lump in his ships, together with his other treasures.*
He stood straight up and spoke to the Achaeans in these words: 830

'Stand up, anyone who wishes to try for this prize too;
even if the rich lands of the man who wins it are very remote
its usefulness will last him for five circling years, and
none of his shepherds or ploughmen will be forced to
go to the city for want of iron, but it will be there for them.'*   835
     So he spoke, and Polypoetes, steadfast in war, rose to his feet,
and also mighty Leonteus, a man like the gods,
and also Ajax, son of Telamon, and glorious Epeius.
They stood in a line, and glorious Epeius picked up the weight
and whirling round threw it, but the Achaeans all laughed at him.   840
The second to take his turn and throw was Leonteus, a shoot
of Ares, and the third to let fly from his powerful hand was
huge Ajax, son of Telamon, and he passed all the others' marks.
But when Polypoetes, steadfast in war, lifted up the weight
he hurled it as far as an oxherd flings a throwing-stick, and   845
it flies whirling through his cattle in the fields; so far did
Polypoetes hurl it beyond all the competitors, and everyone
shouted, and the mighty man's companions stood up and
carried their king's prize off to their hollow ships.
     Then for the archers Achilles put up a prize of dark iron.   850
He set up a row of ten double axes and ten single axes,
and fixed the mast of a blue-prowed ship far off
in the sand, and tied a timid dove to it by the foot
with a thin cord, and ordered them to shoot at it:
'Let the man who succeeds in hitting the timid dove   855
take the double axes as his prize and carry them home;
and if he hits the cord but misses the bird he will take
away the single axes, since he is less of a marksman.'
     So he spoke, and there rose to his feet mighty lord Teucer,
and after him Meriones, the valiant attendant of Idomeneus.   860
They took two lots and shook them in a bronze helmet,
and Teucer's lot won first place; straightaway he let fly
an arrow with great force, but did not promise to sacrifice
a splendid hecatomb of firstborn lambs to the archer lord.
Because Apollo grudged him this success he missed the bird   865
and hit the cord by which it was tied at its foot, and
the bitter arrow sliced the cord clean away; the bird
at once soared up to the high sky, and the cord hung down
towards the earth, and the Achaeans shouted in approval.
But Meriones rushed up and tore the bow from Teucer's   870

hand—he had been holding an arrow while the other aimed—
and straightaway promised to sacrifice a splendid hecatomb
of firstborn lambs to Apollo who shoots from afar.
He could see the timid dove high up under the clouds,
and as it circled in flight he hit it in the breast under   875
its wing, and the arrow passed clean through and fell back
and stuck in the earth before Meriones' feet; but the bird
was caught on the mast of the blue-prowed ship, its neck
hanging limp and its fast-beating feathers drooping.
Quickly the breath flew from its limbs, and it fell all the way
          down   880
from the mast; and the people were astonished as they watched.
Meriones took as his prize all ten double-axes and
Teucer carried off the single-axes to his hollow ships.

Next the son of Peleus brought a far-shadowing spear and a cauldron
untouched by fire, embossed with flowers and worth an ox, and   885
set them down before the assembly. Up rose the javelin-throwers,
and up rose the son of Atreus, wide-ruling Agamemnon,
and up rose Meriones, the valiant attendant of Idomeneus.
But swift-footed glorious Achilles spoke among them:
'Son of Atreus, we know how far you outstrip all others,   890
and how much you are the best in the strength of your throw;
so take this prize and go back to your hollow ships, and
let us give the spear to the hero Meriones, if you too
wish it in your heart, for it is I who urge you to do this.'

So he spoke, and Agamemnon, lord of men, did not dissent;   895
the hero gave the bronze-tipped spear to Meriones, but to
his herald Talthybius he presented his own magnificent prize.

BOOK TWENTY-FOUR

So the assembly broke up and the people dispersed, each
company to its swift ships, and all their thoughts were of food
and the pleasure of sweet sleep; but Achilles wept ceaselessly
as he remembered his dear companion, and sleep that subdues
all took no hold of him. He tossed and turned, thinking with   5
longing of Patroclus, of his manhood and his valiant strength, of
all that he had accomplished with him and the trials he had endured,
of wars of men undergone and the arduous crossing of seas.
As he called all this to mind he let fall huge tears,
lying at one time on his side and at another on his back,   10
and then again on his face; then he would rise to his feet and
wander distraught by the shore of the salt sea, and would never
fail to see the Dawn as she appeared over the sea and its shores.
Then he would harness the swift horses to his chariot
and lash Hector to it, to be dragged along behind it;   15
three times he would haul him round the burial-mound of
Menoetius' dead son, and then he would rest in his hut and leave
Hector sprawled face-down in the dust. But Apollo protected
his flesh from shameful disfigurement, feeling pity for the man,
even in death, and covered him all over with his golden aegis,   20
so that Achilles would not tear his flesh as he dragged him along.

So Achilles in his rage kept trying to disfigure glorious Hector;
but when the blessed gods saw this they took pity on him, and
continually urged the keen-eyed slayer of Argus to steal him away.
All the other gods were pleased with this plan, but it would never   25
find favour with Hera or Poseidon or the grey-eyed maiden,
who stuck to the hatred they had felt from the beginning for
sacred Ilium and Priam and his people, because of Alexander's
deluded folly: he had insulted the goddesses when they came to
his sheepfold, choosing the one who rewarded him with fatal lust.*   30
But when the twelfth dawn after Hector's death appeared
then Phoebus Apollo spoke out among the immortals:
'You are unbending, you gods, and cruel! Did Hector never burn
the thigh-bones of cattle and flawless goats as offerings to you?
And yet now you could not bring yourselves to rescue him, even   35
in death, for his wife and for his mother and his son to see,

and for his father Priam and his people to burn him in
the fire and carry out the funeral rites that are his due.
No, you gods, you prefer to stand by deadly Achilles, even
though his wits are not in their rightful place and the mind   40
in his breast is not easily bent. He has a cruel nature, like a
lion that gives in to its great strength and proud heart when it
wants to feed, and attacks the sheep-flocks of mortal men.
Just so Achilles has killed pity, and there is no respect in him,
respect that both greatly harms and also benefits men.   45
Any man, I suppose, is likely to have lost someone even dearer
to him than this, a brother born of the same mother, or even a son,
but in the end he gives up his weeping and lamentation,
because the Fates have placed in men a heart that endures; but
this Achilles first robs glorious Hector of his life and then ties him   50
behind his chariot and drags him round the burial-mound of his
dear companion. Yet he should know that there is nothing fine
or good about this; let him beware of our anger, great man
though he is, because in his fury he is outraging mute earth.'

Then in anger Hera of the white arms addressed him: 55
'Lord of the silver bow, your words would be reasonable if
all of you mean to give equal honour to Achilles and to Hector.
But Hector is a mortal, and sucked at a woman's breast,
while Achilles was born of a goddess, one whom I myself
raised and nurtured,* and I gave her as wife to a mortal,   60
Peleus, who was dearest of all men to the immortals' hearts.
All of you gods were at the wedding, and you, Apollo, feasted
among them, lyre in hand—you ever-devious friend of the wicked.'

Then in answer Zeus who gathers the clouds addressed her:
'Hera, do not take your anger with the gods to excess;   65
the honour given to these men will not be the same. Even so,
Hector was always the dearest to the gods of mortals in Ilium—
certainly to me, for he never failed to offer me pleasing gifts.
Never has my altar lacked a fair share of the feast, of drink-
offerings and the savour of burnt flesh, which is our privilege.   70
But as for stealing bold Hector away, let us say no more of it—
this is not possible without Achilles' knowing, and his mother
is all the time by his side, in the day and in the night.
No, let some god go and summon Thetis to my side, and I
will give her carefully considered advice, how Achilles may   75
receive gifts from the hands of Priam and so ransom Hector.'

So he spoke, and storm-footed Iris rose to take the message,
and dived into the dark expanse of the sea between Samothrace
and rocky Imbros;* and the waters groaned as she entered them.
She dropped to the depths of the sea like a lead weight,   80
mounted on horn from an ox that is kept in the field,
which as it sinks brings death to ravenous fishes.
She found Thetis in a hollow cavern, and around her the other
sea-goddeses were seated, gathered together, while she in their
midst was weeping over the fate of her blameless son, who was to   85
die, taken from her, in rich-soiled Troy, far from his native land.
Standing next to Thetis swift-footed Iris addressed her:
'Up with you, Thetis! Zeus whose plans are immortal summons you.'
Then in answer the goddess Thetis of the silver feet said:
'Why does that great god send me orders? I feel shame at   90
joining the gods, for the grief I have in my heart is never-ending.
Still, I will go, and his words will not be in vain, whatever he says.'
   So she, bright among goddesses, spoke, and took up her
deep-blue veil—there is no darker garment than this—
and set off on her way, and wind-footed swift Iris went first   95
and guided her; and the waves of the sea opened around them.
They came out on the seashore and sprang up to the high sky,
and found Zeus the wide-thunderer, and around him all the other
blessed gods who live for ever were sitting gathered together.
Athena gave up her place and Thetis sat next to father Zeus,   100
and Hera put a beautiful golden cup in her hand and spoke
words of welcome; and Thetis drank and handed back the cup.
Then the father of gods and men began to speak among them:
'So you have come to Olympus, goddess Thetis, despite your sorrow;
you have grief in your heart that you cannot forget—I too know this,   105
but even so I will tell you why I have summoned you here.
For nine days a quarrel has arisen among the immortals
concerning Achilles, sacker of cities, and the body of Hector.
They want the keen-sighted slayer of Argus to steal it away;
but I will tell you of the glory that I intend to grant Achilles,   110
and so keep your respect and friendship in time to come.
Go quickly now to the camp and give your son my orders:
tell him that the gods are displeased with him, and that I above
all the immortals am angry because in his frenzied heart
he keeps Hector by his curved ships and has not released him;   115
and in this way he may come to fear me, and ransom Hector.

Then I shall send Iris to great-hearted Priam, telling him to
go to the ships of the Achaeans and ransom his dear son,
taking with him gifts for Achilles such as will gladden his heart.'
   So he spoke, and the goddess silver-footed Thetis did not
      disobey him,   120
and she went swooping down from the peaks of Olympus
and came to the hut of her son. She found him there, weeping
without respite, and around him his dear companions were
bustling about their tasks and preparing their early meal;
they had sacrificed a great fleecy sheep for themselves in the hut.   125
His revered mother sat down very close to Achilles, and
stroked him with her hand and spoke to him, saying:
'My child, how long will you eat your heart out with
grieving and lamentation, giving no thought to food or to
bed? It is indeed a good thing to lie with a woman,   130
since your life will not be long and I shall lose you, and
already death and your harsh destiny stand beside you.
Come now, listen to me; I come to you as Zeus' messenger.
He says that the gods are displeased with you, and that he above
all the immortals is angry because in your frenzied heart you   135
keep Hector beside your curved ships and have not released him.
So come, let him go, and accept a ransom in return for the body.'
   Then in answer swift-footed Achilles addressed her:
'Let it be so; may he who brings the ransom also take away the body,
if indeed the Olympian himself commands me with all his heart.'   140
   So mother and son spoke to each other in the gathering-place
of the ships, exchanging many winged words.
Then the son of Cronus roused Iris to go to sacred Ilium:
'Go now, swift Iris; leave the seat of Olympus and go to
Ilium and announce to great-hearted Priam that he must go to   145
the ships of the Achaeans and ransom his dear son, taking
with him gifts for Achilles such as will gladden his heart;
but he must be alone, and no other Trojan must go with him.
Let some older man, a herald, follow him, to guide
the mules and the well-wheeled wagon, and to bring back   150
to the city the dead man whom glorious Achilles has killed.
And let him have no concern or fear about death in his heart,
since I shall provide him with a worthy guide, the Argus-slayer,
who will lead him on his way until he reaches Achilles.
When Hermes has conducted him into his hut Achilles   155

will not kill him, and will keep all the others away from him;
he is neither witless nor heedless, nor is he wicked, but will
treat a man who is his suppliant with kindness, and spare him.'
    So he spoke, and storm-footed Iris rose to take the message.
She arrived at Priam's house and found there crying and wailing: 160
in the courtyard his sons were sitting around their father,
soaking their clothes with tears, and the old man was in
their midst, tightly wrapped in his cloak, and his head and
neck were covered with the quantities of dung that he had
gathered up in his hands as he grovelled on the ground.*   165
In the house his daughters and wives of his sons were weeping,
remembering the many noble men who were lying dead,
those who had lost their lives at the hands of the Argives.
The messenger of Zeus stood beside Priam and addressed him,
speaking in a low voice; but even so trembling seized his limbs: 170
'Do not despair in your heart, Priam of Dardanus' line, nor be afraid;
it is not to foretell calamity that I come to this place, but with
good intentions towards you. I am indeed the messenger of
Zeus, who though he is far off cares greatly and pities you.
The Olympian commands you to ransom glorious Hector,   175
taking with you gifts for Achilles such as will gladden his heart;
but you must be alone, and no other Trojan must go with you.
Let there be some older man, a herald, to follow you, to guide
the mules and the well-wheeled wagon, and to bring back
to the city the dead man whom glorious Achilles has killed.   180
Do not have any concern or fear about death in your heart,
since a worthy guide will accompany you, the slayer of Argus,
who will lead you on your way until you reach Achilles.
When Hermes has conducted you into his hut Achilles
will not kill you, and will keep all the others away from you;   185
he is neither witless nor heedless, nor is he wicked, but will
treat a man who is his suppliant with kindness, and spare him.'
    So swift-footed Iris spoke, and departed from him;
and Priam ordered his sons to make ready a well-wheeled
wagon, drawn by mules, and to fasten a wicker basket on top.   190
He himself went down into a sweet-smelling, high-roofed
chamber, built of cedarwood and containing many precious things;
then he called to his wife Hecuba and addressed her:
'Dear wife, an Olympian messenger has come to me from Zeus,
telling me to go to the Achaeans' ships and ransom my dear son,   195

and to take with me gifts for Achilles, such as may gladden his heart.
Come, tell me, how does this seem to you in your heart?
As for me, the fervour in my heart urges me strongly to go
down there to their ships, into the wide camp of the Achaeans.'

So he spoke, and his wife shrieked and answered him: 200
'You are mad! Where has that good sense gone that you were
famous for among foreigners and among the people you rule?
How can you want to go alone to the ships of the Achaeans,
into the sight of the man who has slaughtered so many of
your noble sons? Your heart must be made of iron.   205
If he sets eyes on you and makes you his captive, that
treacherous eater of raw flesh will show you neither pity
nor the smallest respect. No, let us instead sit here in our halls,
far from him, and lament; this was how his harsh destiny once
spun the thread for Hector at his birth, at the time I bore him,   210
that he should glut swift-footed dogs far from his parents,
by a violent man's side; how I wish I could fasten my teeth
deep into his liver and devour it—and then there would be
vengeance done for my son! He was no coward when Achilles
killed him, but was standing firm to defend the Trojan men and   215
their deep-bosomed women, thinking neither of flight nor shelter.'

Then in his turn the old man, godlike Priam, addressed her:
'Do not try to hold me back; I am determined to go. And do not
be a bird of ill-omen in our halls, for you will not persuade me.
If it were someone else, a mortal, who was ordering me,   220
one of our prophets or diviners from sacrifice or priests,
we would say the message was false and would take no notice;
but as it is I have heard the goddess' voice myself and seen her
face to face, and I shall go, and her words will not be empty. If it
is my fate to die beside the ships of the bronze-shirted Achaeans,   225
that is what I want. Let Achilles kill me quickly as I hold my son
in my arms, after I have put from myself the desire for weeping.'

So he spoke, and opened the handsome lids of the coffers,
and lifted out of them twelve robes of great beauty, and
twelve simple cloaks and as many blankets, and as many   230
white mantles, and as many tunics to go with them.
He weighed and brought out a total of ten talents of gold,
and lifted out two gleaming tripods and four cauldrons,
and lifted out a cup of great beauty which men of Thrace had
given him when he went on an embassy, a great treasure; but the   235

old man did not spare even this in his halls, for he wished fervently
in his heart to ransom his dear son. Next he drove all the Trojans
out of his portico, rebuking them with words of abuse:
'Get out, you worthless things, bringers of shame! Have you no
lamentation at home, that you come here to cause me misery?   240
Do you think it nothing that Zeus, Cronus' son, has given me the pain
of losing the best of my sons? You will learn soon enough for
yourselves, when you prove to be easier for the Achaeans to
slaughter now that Hector is dead. But as for me, may it happen
that I go down to the house of Hades before I see my city   245
plundered and laid waste before my very eyes.'

So he spoke, and chased the men away with his staff, and they
retreated before the old man's outburst. Then he shouted to his
sons, rebuking them: to Helenus and Paris and glorious Agathon,
to Pammon and Antiphonus and Polites, master of the war-cry,   250
to Deïphobus and Hippothous and to splendid Dius, nine
in all that the old man shouted his harsh orders to:
'Go quickly, you wretched children, bringers of disgrace, who
should all have been killed by the swift ships instead of Hector!
Oh what a miserable destiny is mine! I fathered the best sons   255
in broad Troy, but now I cannot say that any of them is left:
Mestor who was like a god, and Troïlus the charioteer,
and Hector, who was a god among men, and seemed
to be the son not of a mortal man but of a god. But Ares has
killed them, and all those who are left bring disgrace on me—   260
tellers of lies, dance-experts, masters of fancy footwork,
robbers in your own country of other people's lambs and kids!
Go, make ready a wagon for me as quickly as you can, and
load all these things on to it, so that we can be on our way.'

So he spoke, and they were terrified at their father's
    loud rebuke,   265
and brought out a wagon with fine wheels, drawn by mules,
a splendid one, newly built, and they lashed a basket on top of it;
from its peg they lifted down a mule-yoke made of boxwood,
complete with its boss and well fitted with guide-rings, and
with it they brought out a yoke-strap nine cubits long.   270
The yoke they fitted carefully on to the well-polished shaft
at its front end, and put the ring over its peg and wound
the strap three times over each side of the boss; then they
lashed this repeatedly round the shaft and tucked in its end.

From the store-chamber they brought out the boundless ransom   275
for Hector's body and piled it on the well-polished wagon, which
they then yoked to strong-hoofed mules that worked in harness,
which the Mysians had once presented to Priam as a splendid gift.
Then to Priam's chariot they yoked some horses which the old man
kept for himself and reared at their well-polished manger.   280

    So these two had their teams yoked in the lofty palace,
the herald and Priam, with many thoughts in their minds;
and Hecuba came and stood next to them, troubled at heart,
holding in her right hand mind-cheering wine in a golden
cup, for them to make a drink-offering before they went.   285
Standing in front of the chariot she spoke to them in these words:
'Here, make a drink-offering to father Zeus, and pray that you will
return home in safety from among your enemies; it is your heart
that is driving you to approach their ships, and I do not wish it.
So come, pray to Cronus' son, the lord of the dark clouds,   290
he who has his seat on Ida and from there watches all Troy,
and ask for a bird-omen—the swift messenger, which of all
birds is the dearest to him and whose strength is the greatest—
to appear on the right hand, so that you see it with your own eyes
and trust in it as you go to the ships of the swift-horsed Danaans.   295
But if Zeus the wide-thunderer refuses to send you his messenger
then I would certainly not urge you to go to the ships
of the Argives, however strongly you desire to do so.'

    Then in answer godlike Priam addressed her:
'Wife, I will certainly not disregard this advice of yours; it is   300
a good thing to raise hands to Zeus, to see if he will have pity.'

    So the old man spoke, and ordered his housekeeper servant
to pour clean water over his hands, and she stood
beside him holding a jug and a basin in her hands.
When he had washed he took the cup that his wife offered   305
and stood in the middle of the courtyard and poured out
some wine, looking up to the high sky, and spoke these words:
'Father Zeus, greatest and most glorious, ruling from Mount Ida,*
grant that I may find friendship and pity in Achilles' hut.
Send me a bird-omen—your swift messenger, which of all   310
birds is the dearest to you and whose strength is the greatest—
to appear on the right hand, so that I see it with my own eyes
and trust in it as I go to the ships of the swift-horsed Danaans.'

    So he spoke in prayer, and Zeus the counsellor heard him,

and at once sent an eagle, the most prophetic of winged creatures,   315
the dark hunter, the one that men call the dusky eagle.
As wide as is the door of a high-roofed chamber that has been
built for a rich man, a door that fits tightly when it is shut,
so wide did its wings extend on both sides; and it appeared to them
on the right hand, sweeping over the city. And they rejoiced   320
when they saw it, and the heart in all of them was gladdened.

Then the old man made haste and mounted his chariot and
drove it through the outer gate, out of the echoing portico.
In front of him the mules drew the four-wheeled wagon
which keen-minded Idaeus was driving; behind came the   325
horses that the old man was urging swiftly through the city*
as he wielded his whip, and all his family kept up with him,
full of lamentation, just as though he was going to his death.
When they had gone down through the city and reached the plain,
his sons and sons-in-law turned back towards Ilium;   330
but Priam and Idaeus did not escape the notice of Zeus
as they emerged on to the plain, and when he saw the old man
he felt pity for him and quickly spoke to Hermes, his dear son:
'Hermes, it is your special pleasure to be men's companion,
and you always listen to those to whom you are partial;   335
go now and escort Priam to the hollow ships of the Achaeans
in such a way that no one of the Danaans sees or is aware
of him until you have reached the hut of Peleus' son.'

So he spoke, and the guide, the slayer of Argus, did not disobey him.
Immediately he bound under his feet his beautiful sandals,   340
golden and deathless, that carried him over the watery sea
and the boundless earth with the speed of the wind; then
he picked up the wand with which he charms the eyes of
those he chooses, and rouses others from their sleep.
Holding this in his hands the mighty slayer of Argus flew down   345
and quickly arrived at Troy and the Hellespont, and set off
on his way in the likeness of a young prince, one whose beard
is beginning to show, which is the most charming time of youth.

Now when the two men had driven past the great burial-mound
of Ilus they pulled up the mules and horses for them to drink   350
in the river, since now darkness had come over the earth.
Then, when Hermes was close at hand, the herald looked up
and saw him, and spoke to Priam with these words:
'Priam of Dardanus' line, take care! There is something here that

calls for care. I see a man, and I think we shall soon be cut to pieces!   355
Quick, let us make our escape in the chariot—or let us catch him
by the knees and beg for mercy; he may take pity on us.'

So he spoke, and the old man's mind was confused, and he was terribly
afraid, and the hairs on his bent limbs stood up, and he stood there
in bewilderment; but the swift runner came and stood by him,   360
and taking the old man's hand questioned and addressed him:
'Father, where are you driving these horses and mules
through the deathless night, while other mortals are asleep?
Are you not afraid of the Achaeans who breathe fury,
your ruthless enemies, who are camped close by you?   365
If any of these were to see you bringing all these precious things
through the swift black night, what could you think of doing?
You are not a young man yourself, and this man attending you
is too old to defend you against any man who picks a fight.
But I shall do you no harm, and I will protect you from anyone   370
who may attack you; you have the look of my own father.'

Then in answer the old man, godlike Priam, addressed him:
'Everything that you say, dear child, is close to the truth.
It seems that some god is still stretching his hand over me,
in that he has sent such a traveller to fall in with me, a bearer of   375
good fortune; your stature and beauty are to be wondered at,
and you are shrewd in mind—your parents are indeed blessed.'

Then in turn the guide, the slayer of Argus, addressed him:
'Old man, all that you have said is according to due measure.
But come, tell me this, and give me an exact account: 380
are you sending all these splendid treasures away somewhere,
to men in some foreign land, where they can wait for you
in safety, or are you all now abandoning sacred Ilium in
terror because a man is dead, the best among you, your
son, who was never found wanting in battle with the Achaeans?'   385

Then in answer the old man, godlike Priam, addressed him:
'Who are you, lord, and who are your parents, you who
speak so unerringly about the fate of my unlucky son?'

Then in turn the guide, the slayer of Argus, addressed him:
'You are testing me, old man, asking me about glorious Hector: 390
many times I have seen him before my eyes in the battle where
men win glory, especially when he was killing the Argives he had
driven against their ships, butchering them with the sharp bronze.
We stood in amazement, not moving, because Achilles

would not let us fight, being full of bitterness at Atreus' son.   395
I am his attendant, and one well-made ship brought us here.
I am one of the Myrmidons, and my father is Polyctor,
who is a wealthy man, and an aged man like you; he has
six other sons, and I am the seventh. I cast lots with the
other sons, and it fell to me to accompany Achilles here. Now   400
I am on my way from the ships to the plain, because at dawn
the darting-eyed Achaeans will set the battle going around the city;
sitting idle makes them chafe, and the kings of the Achaeans
cannot hold them back, impatient as they are for battle.'

Then in answer the old man, godlike Priam, addressed him: 405
'If you really are an attendant of Peleus' son Achilles,
then come, tell me the whole truth—is my son
still lying beside the ships, or has Achilles by now
chopped him up and thrown him limb by limb to his dogs?'

Then in turn the guide, the slayer of Argus, addressed him: 410
'Aged man, the dogs and vultures have not devoured him
and he is still there, lying in Achilles' hut beside his ship,
just as he was; and this is the twelfth day that he has been
lying there, and his flesh has not decayed, and he has not
been eaten by the worms that feed on men killed in war.   415
To be sure, whenever the bright dawn appears Achilles drags him
ruthlessly round the burial-mound of his dear companion,
but he causes him no shameful injury; if you went up to him
you would be amazed how he lies as fresh as dew, and the blood is
washed away, and there is no defilement. The wounds where he was   420
stabbed are all closed up, even though many men drove the bronze
into him. It seems that the blessed gods care for your son,
even in death, since he was dear to their hearts.'

So he spoke, and the old man was gladdened and answered:
'My child, it is indeed a good thing to give the immortals   425
their proper offerings. Never did my son—if ever I had one—
forget in his halls the gods who dwell on Olympus. And so
they have repaid the favour, if only after his destined death.
But come, accept this handsome cup from me and
protect me and be my escort—together with the gods—   430
and help me to come to the hut of the son of Peleus.'

Then in turn the guide, the slayer of Argus, addressed him:
'You are testing me, aged man, a younger man than you, telling
me to accept your gift without Achilles' knowledge. You will not

persuade me; I am afraid of him, and would feel shame in my heart   435
at robbing him, in case something bad comes my way in future.
Still, I am ready to be your escort, even as far as famous Argos,
accompanying you in a swift ship or on foot, as is right;
no one will attack you out of contempt for your guide.'

So the swift runner spoke, and leapt into the chariot behind the   440
horses and quickly took the whip and reins into his hands,
and breathed great fury into the horses and the mules.
When they reached the ditch and the wall protecting the ships,
the sentries had just begun to busy themselves with their meal;
and the guide, the slayer of Argus, poured sleep over them all   445
and at once thrust back the bars and opened the gates, and
conducted Priam inside with the wagonload of splendid gifts.
When they arrived at the hut of the son of Peleus,
the tall hut that the Myrmidons had built for their king—
they had felled pine trunks and then covered it with a roof   450
of rough thatch that they had gathered in the meadows, and
after that had built for their king a large courtyard, surrounded
with close-set stakes, and it had a door with one bar
made of pine; it took three of the other Achaeans to ram the
great locking-bar shut and three to pull it back to open it,   455
but Achilles could ram it shut, even on his own—there
Hermes the swift runner opened the gate for the old man
and brought in the splendid gifts for Priam's swift-footed son,
and then got down to the ground from the chariot and spoke:
'Aged man, it is indeed an immortal god who has come to you;   460
I am Hermes, and my father sent me to be your escort.
But now I must go back again, and will not appear before
the eyes of Achilles; it would attract blame if an immortal
god was entertained face to face by mortals in this way. But
as for you, you must go in and grasp the knees of Peleus' son   465
and entreat him in the name of his father and his lovely-haired
mother and his child, in the hope that you will move his heart.'

So Hermes spoke, and went back to high Olympus,
and Priam leapt to the ground from the chariot and
left Idaeus where he was, to wait and look after the   470
horses and the mules. The old man went straight into
the dwelling where Achilles, dear to Zeus, usually sat, and he
found him; his companions were sitting some way apart, and
only two, the hero Automedon and Alcimus, a shoot of Ares,

were busy attending him. He had just finished eating and 　　475
drinking at his meal, and the table still stood beside him.
Great Priam entered, undetected by the two men, and stood
close to Achilles and took his knees in his arms and kissed the
terrible man-slaughtering hands that had killed so many of his sons.
As when delusion* takes tight hold of someone who has killed a 　　480
man in his own country, and he comes to another people, to the
house of a rich man, and amazement seizes the onlookers,
so Achilles was amazed when he saw godlike Priam; and
the others too were amazed, and looked at one another.
Priam spoke to Achilles, entreating him with these words: 　　485
'Achilles, man like the gods, think now of your own father,
a man of my years, on the grim threshold of old age;
it may be that his neighbours round about are vexing him,
and there is no one to protect him from damage and
destruction, but when he hears that you are still living he 　　490
rejoices in his heart, and day after day he hopes to
see his dear son returning home from Troy. As for me,
I am most ill-fated of all men, for I fathered the finest sons
in broad Troy, and yet cannot say that any one of them is left.
Fifty I had when the sons of the Achaeans came; 　　495
nineteen of them were born to me from one womb,
and other women bore the rest to me in my halls.
Impetuous Ares loosed the knees of most of them; but
the one left to me, who protected the city and its citizens—
you killed him not long ago as he was defending his country. 　　500
He was Hector; and for his sake I now come to the ships of the
Achaeans, to redeem him from you, bringing a boundless ransom.
Come, Achilles, respect the gods, and have pity on me,
remembering your own father; yet I am more worthy of your pity,
for I have endured to do what no other mortal on earth has done: 　　505
to raise to my mouth the hand of the man who killed my son.'
　　So he spoke, and aroused in Achilles a desire to weep for his father.
Taking hold of the old man's hand he gently pushed him away;*
they both remembered their own, Priam crouched at Achilles'
feet and weeping without ceasing for man-slaying Hector, 　　510
while Achilles wept for his own father, and then again for
Patroclus; and their groaning went up, spreading through the hut.
Now when glorious Achilles had had his fill of lamentation
and the desire for it had gone from his mind and his limbs,

he rose at once from his seat and with his hand raised the old man,   515
because he felt pity for his grey head and his grey beard,
and addressed him, speaking with winged words:
'Ah, poor man, you have endured much misery in your heart!
How could you bring yourself to come alone to the Achaeans'
ships, into the sight of a man who has killed so many fine sons   520
of yours? Surely your heart must be made of iron.
But come, sit here on this chair, and let us leave our pain
to lie at rest in our hearts, grieved though we are.
There is nothing to be gained from chill lamentation; that is
how the gods have woven the threads for wretched mortals,   525
to live with grief, while they themselves are without sorrow.
There are two jars standing on Zeus' threshold, full of the
gifts that he dispenses, one of bad things and the other of good.
When Zeus who delights in the thunder gives a man a mixture,
he meets at one time with ill fortune and at another with good, but   530
when he gives only from the store of bad things he makes a man
despised; cruel hunger drives him over the bright earth, and
he wanders up and down honoured by neither gods nor mortals.*
So it was that the gods also gave Peleus splendid gifts
from the time of his birth: he stood out above all men in   535
prosperity and in wealth, and ruled over the Myrmidons, and
though he was a mortal the gods gave him a goddess for wife.
But even to him the gods brought misery, in that he had
no offspring of princely sons born to him in his halls, but
fathered only one, and him doomed to an early death; I cannot   540
care for him as he grows old because I sit here idly in Troy,
far from my native land, bringing sorrow to you and your children.
And we hear tell that you too, aged man, were once prosperous:
all that is bounded out to sea by Lesbos, seat of Macar, and
up-country by Phrygia, and by the vast Hellespont—in all   545
these lands, they say, you were supreme in wealth and in sons.*
And yet the dwellers in the high sky have now brought this affliction
on you—constant battles and killings of men round about your city.
You must endure, and not mourn unceasingly in your heart;
there is nothing to be gained by grieving for your son, since you will   550
not bring him back to life; you will sooner suffer another sorrow.'
     Then the old man, godlike Priam, answered him:
'Zeus-nurtured man, do not make me sit down as long as
Hector is lying uncared-for in your huts, but release him to me

at once, so that I can see him with my eyes; then you may accept   555
the huge ransom that we bring you. May you have pleasure in it
and so return to your native land, because you have
allowed me to live and to gaze on the light of the sun.'

Then swift-footed Achilles looked at him darkly and said:
'Do not provoke me too far, aged man. I myself am minded to   560
release Hector to you, for a messenger came to me from Zeus—
my mother who bore me, daughter of the ancient of the sea.
Furthermore, Priam, you do not deceive me: I know that one of
the gods has conducted you to the swift ships of the Achaeans.
No mortal would dare to come here into the camp, not even one   565
in the prime of youth; he would not be able to pass the sentries
unnoticed, nor could he easily push back the bars of our gates.
So do not rouse the pain in my heart any further, aged man,
in case I break the ordinances of Zeus and forget to spare you,
even you, while you are a suppliant here in my hut.'   570

So he spoke, and the old man was afraid and did as he said.
Then the son of Peleus leapt out through the door like a lion,
not alone, but there were his two attendants with him,
the hero Automedon and Alcimus, the two whom Achilles
valued most of all his companions after the dead Patroclus.   575
These now freed the horses and mules from under their yokes
and led in the herald, the old man's summoner, and
sat him down on a chair; and from the well-polished wagon
they took the boundless ransom for the body of Hector.
They laid apart two cloaks and a skilfully woven tunic for   580
Achilles to wrap him in when he gave him to be carried home.
Then Achilles called his maidservants and told them to take Hector
aside so that Priam should not see his son, and to wash and anoint him,
for he was afraid that in the grief of his heart Priam would not restrain
his anger when he saw his son, and that his own heart would be   585
disturbed so that he killed Priam, and broke the ordinances of Zeus.
When the maidservants had washed and anointed Hector with
olive oil they wrapped him in the fine cloak and the tunic, and
Achilles himself lifted him up and laid him on a bier, and his
companions hoisted him on to the well-polished wagon.   590
Then Achilles cried out and called on his dear companion by name:
'Do not bear me rancour, Patroclus, if you come to hear, even in
the house of Hades, that I have released glorious Hector to his
dear father because he has brought me a not-unfitting ransom.

I shall in time hand over to you the share in this that is your due.'   595
    So glorious Achilles spoke, and went back into his hut, and sat
again on the intricately worked chair from which he had risen,
which was set against the opposite wall. Then he spoke to Priam:
'There, aged man, your son is released to you, as you asked,
and is lying on a bier. As soon as dawn appears you will see him,   600
and may take him away; but now let us turn our thoughts to eating.
You must know that even lovely-haired Niobe thought of food*
after her twelve children had been killed in her halls—
six daughters she had, and six sons in the prime of youth.
Apollo killed the sons with arrows from his silver bow, being   605
angry with Niobe, and Artemis the shooter of arrows slew the girls,
because Niobe had compared herself with Leto of the lovely cheeks,
saying that Leto had borne only two while she had borne many;
and so the gods, though they were only two, killed all Niobe's children.
For nine days they lay in their gore, and there was no one to   610
bury them, for the son of Cronus had turned the people to stone;
but on the tenth day the gods who dwell in the high sky buried them.
Then it was that Niobe, worn out with weeping, remembered food;
and now today, somewhere among the rocks on some lonely mountain,
on Sipylus, where men say that the goddess nymphs who leap   615
in the dance about Achelous* have their resting-places, there,
though now a stone, she broods on the sorrows sent her by the gods.
Come then, aged and glorious man, let us two turn our minds to
food, and afterwards you may mourn your dear son, when you have
taken him back to Ilium; and he will surely bring forth many
        tears.'   620
    So swift-footed Achilles spoke, then leapt up and slaughtered a
white sheep, and his companions flayed and prepared it expertly,
and chopped the meat skilfully and threaded it on to skewers,
and cooked it with great care and then drew it off.
Automedon fetched bread and set it out on the table   625
in fine baskets; but Achilles apportioned the meat.
They reached out for the good things lying ready before them, and
when they had put from themselves the desire for food and drink
then Priam of Dardanus' line looked in amazement at Achilles,
seeing how huge and handsome he was, for he seemed like the
        gods;   630
and Achilles too was amazed at Priam of the line of Dardanus,
seeing his noble appearance and hearing him speak.

When they had taken their pleasure from looking at each other
the first to speak was godlike Priam, who said:
'Quick now, Zeus-nurtured man, give me a place to lie, so that   635
we may take the pleasure of being lulled by sweet sleep;
my eyes beneath my eyebrows have not closed
since the time my son lost his life at your hands, and
all this time I have groaned and brooded on my thousands of
sorrows, rolling in the dung in the stalls of my courtyard.*   640
Now at last I have tasted bread and poured gleaming wine
down my throat; but before this time I could eat nothing.'

   So he spoke, and Achilles told his companions and maidservants
to lay out a bed underneath the colonnade and to throw
fine red rugs on top of it and to spread coverlets over them,   645
and to set out fleecy woollen cloaks to be a covering over all.
The maids went out of the hall with torches in their hands
and quickly set about laying beds for the two of them.
Then in a bantering tone* swift-footed Achilles addressed Priam:
'Lie outside there, aged man, in case any of the Achaean   650
counsellors comes this way, one of those who from time to time
sit here and make plans with me, as is the proper custom.
If one of these were to see you through the swift black night
he would at once report it to Agamemnon, shepherd of the people,
and then there would be a delay in releasing the body.   655
So come, tell me and give me an exact account of how many
days you are minded to conduct glorious Hector's funeral rites,
so that I myself can cease for that time and also restrain the people.'

   Then the old man, godlike Priam, answered him:
'If you really wish me to give glorious Hector a proper burial,   660
then it would be a kindness to me if you do what I shall ask.
You know how we are penned close in the city, and it is a long way
to fetch wood from the mountain, and the Trojans are terrified;
give us leave to lament over Hector in our halls for nine days,
and on the tenth we will bury him and the people will feast,   665
and on the eleventh day we will build a burial-mound over him
and on the twelfth we will fight again, if fight we must.'

   Then in answer swift-footed glorious Achilles addressed him:
'Very well, aged Priam; it will all be as you ask it:
I shall hold back the fighting for the time that you tell me.'   670
   So he spoke, and took the old man by the wrist of his
right hand so that he should have no fear in his heart.

And so those two, the herald and Priam, lay down to rest there
in the forecourt of the building, with many thoughts in their minds;
but Achilles slept in the inmost part of his well-built hut,   675
and beside him lay Briseus' daughter of the lovely cheeks.

   Now all other beings, gods and horse-marshalling men,
slept the whole night long, overcome by soft sleep,
but sleep did not take hold of Hermes the swift runner as he
pondered in his heart how he should escort Priam the king   680
away from the ships unnoticed by the devoted gate-guards;
he stood over Priam's head* and spoke to him in these words:
'Aged man, you have no thought of danger, sleeping soundly like this
among men who are your enemies, since Achilles has spared you.
Now you have paid a great price to redeem your dear son,   685
but in return for your life your sons who are left at home would
give a ransom of three or four times as much, if Agamemnon,
son of Atreus, and all the Achaeans found out you were here.'

   So he spoke, and the old man was afraid and roused the herald.
Hermes yoked the horses and mules for them, and himself   690
drove them swiftly through the camp, and no one saw them.
But when they came to the crossing of the clear-flowing river,
swirling Xanthus, who was fathered by immortal Zeus,
Hermes immediately went away to high Olympus, and Dawn
in her saffron robes was spread over the whole earth; and   695
Priam and the herald drove the horses with groans and lamentation
towards the city, while the mules brought the dead man. No one
from among men or women with their lovely girdles saw them
except Cassandra, she who resembled golden Aphrodite;
she had gone up on to Pergamus and recognized her dear father   700
as he stood in the chariot, and the herald, the town-crier, with him.
And she saw him too, Hector, lying on a bier in the mule-wagon,
and shrieked aloud and her shout went through all the city:
'Men and women of Troy, if ever you were glad to see Hector
returning from the battle when he was alive—for he was a
          great joy   705
to the city and all its people—come and gaze on him now.'

   So she spoke, and soon there was no man or woman left in
the city, for unendurable sorrow had come upon them all.
They met Priam near the gate as he brought back the body, and
first to them were Hector's wife and his revered mother, tearing
          their   710

hair for him and throwing themselves at the well-wheeled wagon and
touching his head; and the mass of people stood weeping round them.
And indeed, as they shed their tears before the gates, they would have
mourned Hector the whole day long until the setting of the sun,
had not the old man spoken to the people from his chariot: 715
'Give way there, let the mules pass through! After that you may
have your fill of weeping, when I have taken him to his home.'
    So he spoke, and they stood aside and let the wagon pass.
When they had brought Hector into his famous house they
laid him on a fretted bed and caused bards to sit beside him   720
to begin the lament; and these sang a song of mourning
while the women moaned in answer to their lamentation.
Among the women white-armed Andromache began her dirge,
holding the head of man-slaying Hector in her hands:
'Husband, you are dead, gone from life too young, leaving me a   725
widow in our halls! Our son, whom you and I, ill-fated parents,
gave life to, is still but an infant, and I do not think he will
reach manhood. Before that happens this city will be sacked
from top to bottom, because you, its guardian, are dead, you who
always protected it and kept its devoted wives and little children   730
safe; but they will very soon be carried off in hollow ships, and
I among them, and you, my child, will either accompany me
to a place where you will work at tasks that bring shame on
you, labouring for a pitiless master, or else some Achaean
will seize and hurl you from the walls* to a cruel death,   735
angry because Hector may have killed his brother or his
father or even his son, for great numbers of Achaeans
have fastened their teeth on the vast earth at Hector's hands;
your father was never gentle in the savage warfare, and
that is why the people lament him throughout the city.   740
Hector, you have brought cursed wailing and grief to your
parents, but for me especially there will be left cruel anguish;
you did not hold out your arms to me from our bed as you died,
or speak a memorable word to me, something that I could
remember through the nights and days as I weep tears for you.'   745
    So she spoke, weeping, and the women answered her with their moans.
Then in turn Hecuba began her unbroken lament among them:
'Hector, by far the dearest to my heart of all my sons!
I know for certain that you were dear to the gods in life, and now
it is clear that they care for you even in your fated death.   750

All the other sons of mine whom swift-footed Achilles captured
he would sell for ransom over the resounding sea, to Samos
or to Imbros or to Lemnos that is surrounded in mist; but
when he had taken away your life with the sharp-bladed bronze
he dragged you many times round the tomb of his companion   755
Patroclus, whom you killed—yet he did not bring him back to life.
But now I see you lying dewy-fresh and unsullied in your
halls, like someone whom Apollo, lord of the silver bow,
has gone after and put to death with his kindly shafts.'
    So she spoke, weeping, and aroused ceaseless lamentation.   760
Then after her Helen was the third to begin her lament:
'Hector, by far the dearest to me of my husband's brothers!
My husband is indeed Alexander who looks like the gods,
who brought me to Troy—and I wish I had died before
that happened! But this is now the twentieth year* since   765
I came from Sparta and deserted my father's country,
and I have never yet heard an unkind or reproachful word
from you. If someone else spoke harshly to me in the halls,
one of your brothers or sisters or a brother's fine-robed wife, or
your mother—your father is always as gentle as if he was my own—   770
you would always calm and restrain them with your words,
by your tenderness of spirit and your gentle speech.
And so, grieved at heart, I weep for you and for myself, luckless
as I am; there is no one left in broad Troy who could show
me such kindness or friendship, but everyone shudders at me.'   775
    So she spoke, weeping, and the vast crowd echoed her groans.
Then the old man Priam spoke out among the people, saying:
'Bring wood into the city, men of Troy, and do not be afraid
in your hearts of any crafty ambush laid by the Argives;
Achilles promised when he sent me from the black ships   780
that he would do us no injury until the twelfth dawn comes.'
    So he spoke, and they harnessed oxen and mules to the yokes
of carts and straightaway gathered in front of the city.
For nine days they kept bringing in wood in vast quantities,
and when the tenth dawn that brings light to mortals appeared   785
then at last, pouring forth tears, they carried out daring Hector
and laid the dead man on a lofty pyre and set fire to it.
    Then, when early-born Dawn with her rosy fingers appeared
the people all collected around the pyre of famous Hector,
and when they had assembled and were gathered together   790

first they quenched the burning pyre with gleaming wine,
all of it as far as the fire's fury still had hold, and then
his brothers and companions collected his white bones,
lamenting, and huge tears kept flowing down their cheeks.
When they had assembled the bones they placed them in a   795
golden coffin, covering them with soft red robes; this they
quickly laid in a hollow grave, and over it they spread a
layer of great stones, closely set together. Then they swiftly
heaped up an earthen burial-mound, and set lookouts all around it,
in case the well-greaved Achaeans should attack before the due time.   800
When they had heaped up the mound they went back to the city
and duly assembled and took part in a magnificent feast
in the house of Priam, the king nurtured by Zeus.

So they conducted the funeral rites for Hector, breaker of horses.

EXPLANATORY NOTES

BOOK ONE

The poet invokes the Muse and sets out the subject-matter of his poem (1–7). The narrative begins with the arrival of Chryses, a priest of Apollo, to the Achaean camp: he has come to offer ransom in return for his daughter, who was captured by the Achaeans on an earlier campaign; Agamemnon refuses to release the girl, who is now his slave, and threatens her father; Apollo, angered at the treatment of his priest, inflicts a plague on the Achaeans (8–52). Encouraged by Achilles, the prophet Calchas reveals the cause of the plague; Agamemnon agrees to release Chryses' daughter—but only if the Achaeans compensate him for his loss (53–120). Achilles protests, and Agamemnon demands to be given Achilles' own slave Briseïs; in anger, Achilles declares he will no longer fight for the Achaeans (121–87). Agamemnon reacts with contempt, and Achilles comes close to killing him; the goddess Athena restrains him (188–303). The Achaeans make sacrifice to Apollo, and two heralds collect Briseïs from Achilles' tent (304–50). Achilles complains to his mother, the marine goddess Thetis, who hears him from the depths of the sea, and comes to shore: she tries to console him, and promises to entreat Zeus on his behalf (351–430). Odysseus delivers Chryseïs to her father, and the Achaeans pray and sacrifice to Apollo (431–87). Thetis entreats Zeus, who promises that he will make the Achaeans lose for as long as Achilles refuses to fight (488–535). Hera, who supports the Achaeans, discovers this with some displeasure; tension mounts on Olympus, until Hephaestus manages to calm down Hera; at dusk, Apollo and the Muses make music for the gods, and the Olympians feast together, until Zeus and Hera withdraw to their marital bed (536–611).

1 *anger*: the original text starts with a rare Greek word, *mēnis*. This word describes the vengeful anger typical of the gods: at 1.75, for example, it is used of Apollo's anger, which results in the plague. Achilles' *mēnis* is equally destructive: it will cause heavy Achaean losses.

3 *Hades*: the Underworld; also used of the god of the Underworld; cf. 15.187–93.

7 *Atreus' son*: Agamemnon, leader of the Achaeans.

9 *The son of Zeus and Leto*: Apollo.

14 *the woollen bands of Apollo who shoots from afar*: fillets (perhaps of wool, though the original text is unclear) are tied around Chryses' staff: they are part of his ritual attire.

38 *Cilla . . . Tenedos*: Cilla was probably on the west coast of the Troad; Tenedos is an island flanking the west coast of the Troad.

39 *Smintheus*: the meaning of this cult name of Apollo was debated also in antiquity: perhaps 'lord of mice', a term possibly related to Apollo's power to inflict (and protect from) contagious disease.

40 *fat-wrapped thigh-bones*: see note to 1.447–68.

65 *hecatomb*: a sacrifice of 100 oxen or, more generally, a large sacrifice.

96 *the shooter from afar*: Apollo.

147 *the far-worker*: Apollo.

155 *Phthia*: in north-east Greece, see Map 1; land of Achilles and his father Peleus.

201 *winged words*: an arresting Homeric expression. Readers have wondered about its exact meaning: the medieval commentator Eustathius thought of words flying straight to the listener, like birds. More recently, scholars have suggested that the expression may evoke feathered arrows. It always introduces direct speech.

202 *aegis-wearing Zeus*: the aegis was a protective garment or weapon associated especially with Zeus and his daughter Athena; there was some uncertainty, also in antiquity, about its precise nature, perhaps 'cloak made of goat-skin'. For a detailed description, cf. 5.738–42.

248 *Pylians*: the people of Pylos in the south-west Peloponnese, see Map 1. Nestor was their ruler.

263–4 *Peirithous . . . Polyphemus*: the Lapiths from Thessaly, famous in myth and art for fighting against the Centaurs.

265 *Theseus son of Aegeus, who resembled the immortals*: Aegeus was a mythical king of Athens, his son Theseus was the most famous Attic hero. Some scholars suspect that this line is an Athenian addition to the *Iliad*.

307 *the son of Menoetius*: Patroclus, Achilles' closest friend.

314–15 *When they had purified themselves . . . into the sea*: the Achaeans wash themselves and then throw the dirty water into the sea, which was thought to have purifying powers.

337 *sprung from Zeus*: Patroclus is not Zeus' son; this epithet is used of many heroes, and corresponds to Zeus' standard description as 'father of gods and men'.

366 *Thebe, the sacred city of Eëtion*: see note to 6.397.

403–4 *Briareus . . . Aegaeon*: a monster. There are three other passages in the *Iliad* where the poet draws a distinction between human and divine names: 2.813–14, 14.291, and 20.74.

407 *take hold of his knees*: cf. note to 1.500–1.

423 *Ocean . . . Ethiopians*: a river that was thought to surround the earth. Ethiopians were a people thought to live at the edges of the world, in the far East and the far West, 'most distant' of people (*Odyssey* 1.22–4). Xenophanes, in the sixth century BC, described them as 'snub-nosed and black'.

447–68 *Quickly . . . meal*: a full description of a ritual sacrifice. The sacrificers
threw barley-groats at the animals, so as to make them lift their heads, and
'willingly' expose their necks to the cut. Then they slaughtered and skinned
the cattle. Finally they wrapped the thigh-bones in fat and, together with
small pieces from all parts of the animal, burnt them as an offering to the
gods. The rest of the animal was roasted for human consumption.

473 *paean*: a hymn in honour of Apollo.

489 *sprung from Zeus*: see note to 1.337.

500–1 *Sitting . . . chin*: the gestures of a formal supplication.

538 *the ancient of the sea*: Nereus; on his daughters, cf. 18.35–64.

561 *You are possessed!*: this expression translates the Greek *daimonie*, a word used
to address somebody who acts in an unaccountable way, as if possessed by a
daimōn, a divine power.

593 *Lemnos*: island in the north-east Aegean, the main cult centre of Hephaestus
in the Greek world.

594 *Sintian men*: probably a reference to the pre-Greek population of Lemnos.

600 *shuffling*: bustling about the place, and probably limping too, as the ancient
commentators thought; see note to 18.395–405.

BOOK TWO

Zeus sends a deceptive dream to Agamemnon (1–34). Thinking that he is
about to conquer Troy, Agamemnon reveals his dream to the council of elders, and then plans a deception of the Achaeans, in order to test their resolve
(35–83). He tells the troops that, according to a dream he has just had, they will
never conquer Troy: at this, the Achaeans immediately scatter in disarray, eager to sail home (84–154). Hera and Athena discuss the situation, and
Athena enlists the help of Odysseus, who calls the troops to order (155–210).
Thersites—a disorderly and ugly soldier—speaks up against Agamemnon
(211–42). Odysseus rebukes and beats him, provoking general merriment
(243–77); he then addresses Agamemnon and insists that the Achaeans should
stay and fight (278–332). Nestor also speaks to Agamemnon, who accepts his
advice (333–93). The Achaeans then make sacrifice and Agamemnon prays
that he may conquer Troy on the following day; Zeus accepts the offerings
but does not grant Agamemnon's wish; Nestor sets out a plan of action; and
the Achaeans prepare for battle (394–483). The poet enlists the help of the
Muses, then launches into the Catalogue of Ships (484–760); and names the
best Achaean horses (761–85). He then turns his attention to the Trojan army
(786–815), offering a Catalogue of the Trojans and their Allies (816–77).

20 *It stood above his head*: the position always taken by dream figures.

103 *the guide, slayer of Argus*: obscure epithets of Hermes. Some ancient readers thought that the second epithet meant 'slayer of Argus'. According to
one myth, Zeus fell in love with a girl called Io and, in an attempt to hide

his new love from Hera, turned Io into a caw. Hera realized this and set Argus, a dog/monster with eyes all over his body, to watch over the cow. Zeus asked Hermes to help him solve the problem.

105–8 *Pelops . . . Argos*: Pelops is the father of Atreus and Thyestes, and the ancestral king of Argos. We know from later sources that Thyestes usurped the throne, and was punished by Atreus, who killed his children, cooked them, and served them up to their father. There is no overt reference to these events in the *Iliad*.

145 *Icaria*: a small island off the coast of Asia Minor. The stretch of sea between Icaria and Samos is especially rough.

157 *Atrytone*: a traditional epithet of Athena whose meaning was debated also in antiquity; perhaps 'unwearied'.

287 *Argos*: in Homer the name can connote the city of Argos in the north-east Peloponnese, or the whole Peloponnese, or the land of the Argives more generally (i.e. what we would call Greece).

304 *Aulis*: in Boeotia, see Map 1. The Achaean contingent gathered there before sailing to Troy.

336 *Gerenian*: standard epithet of Nestor, of obscure meaning.

461 *the streams of Caÿster*: near Ephesus, on the coast of Asia Minor. Similes do not usually refer to specific places: this is an exception, and prompted ancient and modern readers to wonder whether the poet Homer came from this area.

465 *Scamander*: one of the two rivers near Troy, cf. note to 5.773–4.

493 *So I shall relate the ships' captains and the number of their ships*: for the places listed in the Catalogue of Ships, see Map 1, except for Crete, Rhodes, and Cos on Map 2. The poet starts in Aulis, which is where the Achaean contingent gathered before sailing to Troy, then moves in a spiral west, north, east, and south (494–580). A second spiral starts in Lacedaemon and moves west and north (581–614). A third spiral starts in Elis, and again moves west and then north to include Ithaca and Calydon (615–44). In a fourth spiral, the poet mentions Crete, then moves east and north, including Rhodes and Cos (645–80). The Catalogue concludes in northern Greece, starting in Phthia, then moving north and west to Dodona, and then back east to Pelion (681–759).

505 *Lower Thebes*: see note to 4.406.

540 *a shoot of Ares*: the expression simply means 'a warrior', contrast Ascalaphus and Ialmenus at 512, who really are sons of Ares.

625 *Dulichium*: the location, and even existence, of this island is much debated.

642 *and fair-haired Meleager was dead*: Phoenix tells the story of Meleager's anger at 9.529–99 (see note to that passage); his death is mentioned only here.

718–25 *their captain was the skilled archer Philoctetes . . . beside their ships*: the Achaeans eventually sent a delegation to Lemnos to retrieve Philoctetes. Sophocles staged a version of that episode in his tragedy *Philoctetes*.

743 *Centaurs*: the Greek text simply says 'the Beasts', but clearly refers to the Centaurs.

755 *the waters of Styx, dreadful river of oaths*: the Styx is the main river of the underworld, cf. note to 8.362–9. According to 15.37–1, the gods swear their 'greatest and most terrible oath' by the river Styx.

782–3 *as when . . . Typhoeus' bed*: cf. Hesiod, *Theogony* 820–68, where Zeus strikes down Typhoeus with his thunderbolt. The location of the 'land of the Arimi' was debated also in antiquity, and was identified with several volcanic or lightning-blasted areas. The phrasing in Homer may suggest awareness of several different stories about this land.

793 *the burial-mound of ancient Aesyetes*: the only mention of this landmark in the poem.

811–14 *There is . . . Myrine*: another landmark mentioned only here. For the poet's ability to distinguish between human and divine names, see note to 1.403–4.

815 *There now the Trojans and their allies marshalled themselves*: for the Catalogue of the Trojans, see Map 2. The poet starts in Troy then spirals outwards, first north-east, then south again (816–43). He then resumes in Thrace and moves west to Paeonia (844–57). From Mysia, further south, he moves east to Phrygia (858–63); then, when listing the Maeonians, the poet moves from west to east (864–6); finally, starting from Miletus, he moves south-east to Lycia (867–77).

BOOK THREE

The armies line up, ready for battle: Paris steps forward, but quickly withdraws when he sees that Menelaus is ready to fight against him (1–37). Hector rebukes him bitterly (38–57), and Paris declares himself willing to face his rival (58–75). The two sides agree that the winner will take Helen and her possessions (76–120). Meanwhile, Helen is busy weaving a robe depicting the Trojan war, when Iris—disguised as Priam's daughter Laodice—calls her out to witness the events on the battlefield (121–45). The old men of Troy comment on Helen's beauty as she approaches the city walls, and yet declare themselves ready to hand her over to the Achaeans; Priam addresses her kindly, and asks her to identify the main Achaean warriors on the battlefield (146–244). The two sides swear an oath, and make sacrifice before the duel (245–323). Paris and Menelaus start fighting and Menelaus quickly gains the upper hand, when Aphrodite wraps Paris in mist, removes him from the battlefield, and deposits him in his own bedroom (324–82). Then, disguised as an old woman, she tells Helen to go and join him there; Helen recognizes the goddess from her lovely neck and breasts and vents all her anger and frustration; ultimately, however, she must comply (383–420). Back in the bedroom, Helen addresses Paris with contempt, and he expresses his overwhelming desire for her; finally they make love (421–47). On the battlefield Agamemnon declares Menelaus the winner,

and demands the return of Helen and her possessions, as well as compensation
for war damages (448–61).

5 *the streams of Ocean*: see note to 1.423.

6 *Pygmy men*: the Pygmies and their battle with the cranes are mentioned
only here in Homer, but are popular in later poetry and art.

16 *Alexander*: more frequent than the alternative name Paris. Homer never
explains why this character has two names. 'Paris' does not seem to be Greek
in origin, and 'Alexander' may be a memory of Alakšandu, prince of Wilusa,
mentioned in a Hittite treaty of the early thirteenth century BCE.

21 *dear to Ares*: often of Menelaus, not because he is especially bellicose, but
perhaps because he is implicated in the causes of the Trojan War.

56–7 *you would be | wearing a stone garment*: i.e. you would have been killed
by stoning.

145 *the Scaean gates*: the main gates facing the battlefield. The Trojans often
observe the battlefield from a tower near or above the gates.

186 *Otreus . . . Mygdon*: otherwise unknown.

187 *Sangarius*: in Asia Minor, discharging into the Black Sea.

189 *Amazons*: described in the *Iliad* as warlike women who posed a threat to
the populations east, north, and south of Troy. In the *Aethiopis*, an early
sequel to the *Iliad* (now largely lost), the Amazons join forces with the
Trojans, and Achilles kills their queen Penthesilea.

205–6 *Glorious Odysseus has been here before . . . concerning you*: see note to
11.139–40.

250 *son of Laomedon*: on Priam's father, see note to 21.441–57, and cf. the
family tree included in the note to 20.215–41.

276 *ruling from Mount Ida*: Zeus is invoked here as a local deity. In the *Iliad* he
often observes the Trojan War from Mount Ida, south-east of Troy.

278–9 *and you two . . . false oaths*: the ancient scholar Aristarchus took this as a
reference to Hades and Persephone (cf. 9.456–7); alternatively, it may be a
reference to the Furies (cf. 19.259–60).

444–5 *the island | Cranaë*: the location of this island was debated in antiquity;
the name probably just means 'rocky island'.

BOOK FOUR

The gods hold an assembly; Zeus maliciously suggests that they could end the
war after the botched duel between Paris and Menelaus; Hera and Athena are
outraged, and the latter swoops down to the battlefield like a shooting star: she
ensures that hostilities resume by giving some ill advice to Pandarus, a Trojan
ally (1–103). Inspired by her, Pandarus breaks the truce by shooting an arrow
against Menelaus: Athena deflects it, like a mother brushing away a fly from her

sleeping baby, and Menelaus receives only a superficial wound (104–222). The
war resumes and Agamemnon reviews the Achaean contingents, distributing
praise and blame (223–49); he is delighted with Idomeneus, leader of the Cretans
(250–71); then expresses his approval for the two leaders called Ajax (272–91);
he has a positive exchange with Nestor (292–325); then rebukes Menestheus and
Odysseus, because their men are idle (326–63); and finally criticizes Diomedes,
comparing him unfavourably to his father (364–421). After Agamemnon's review
the Achaeans advance in silence, like waves, listening out for the orders of their
leaders; the Trojans, by contrast, loudly call out to each other in their different
languages, like bleating sheep (422–45). The battle breaks out, and the poet lists
the first individual encounters and deaths (446–544).

8 *Hera of Argos and Athena of Alalcomenae*: there was a famous cult of Hera
   at Argos; the worship of Athena at Alalcomenae in Boeotia is less well
   attested.

91 *the waters of Aesepus*: cf. 2.824–7.

101 *Lycian-born Apollo*: only here and at 119; the epithet, perhaps a neologism,
    may express Pandarus' own perceptions, since he is himself a Lycian from
    the Troad.

128 *who gathers the spoils*: this is a possible translation of *ageleiē*, though the
    meaning of the epithet is far from transparent.

142 *a woman of Maeonia or Caria*: we have no specific knowledge about
    Maeonian or Carian craft, though elaborate western Asiatic ivory objects
    have been found in Mycenaean graves and, occasionally, in early Iron Age
    ones too.

173 *Argive Helen*: i.e. 'Greek', not 'from the city of Argos'. She is never called
    'Helen of Troy' in the *Iliad*.

194 *Asclepius*: described as an ordinary mortal in Homer. From the sixth cen-
    tury onwards Asclepius became the patron god of important healing cults,
    most famously at Epidaurus.

319 *Ereuthalion*: Nestor recalls his duel with Ereuthalion also at 7.136–56.

365–7 *the son of Tydeus . . . Capaneus*: both Diomedes and Sthenelus are
    Epigoni, i.e. sons of those who fought in the disastrous expedition of the
    Seven against Thebes. The *Iliad* often alludes to the war between the
    two sons of Oedipus, Eteocles and Polyneices, over the rule of Thebes.
    Polyneices led the expedition of the seven against Thebes, besieged the
    city, and failed to conquer it. The two brothers killed each other in front
    of one of the seven city gates.

378 *a campaign against Thebes' sacred walls*: the campaign of the Seven against
    Thebes is remembered in the *Iliad* as a great but disastrous war fought in
    the previous generation.

385 *Cadmeians*: the people of Thebes, named after Cadmus, the mythical
    founder of the city.

394–5 *Maeon . . . steadfast in war*: mentioned only here.

406 *since we actually captured the city of seven-gated Thebes*: in the Catalogue of Ships there is only a reference to Lower Thebes (2.505), presumably because the citadel was razed by the Epigoni.

508 *Pergamus*: the acropolis, or highest part of Troy.

515 *Tritogeneia*: a traditional epithet of Athena, of obscure meaning.

BOOK FIVE

Encouraged by Athena, Diomedes begins his onslaught, and immediately dominates the battlefield like a river in flood (1–94). Although Pandarus wounds him with an arrow, Athena grants him extraordinary strength, and his onslaught continues (95–165). Aeneas seeks out Pandarus, and together they plan how to stop Diomedes (166–239). As the two approach him, Diomedes steps forward to meet them (240–73). In the confrontation that follows Pandarus dies, and Diomedes smashes Aeneas' hip with a stone; Aphrodite intervenes to rescue her son Aeneas, and Diomedes wounds her too (274–362). Ares takes Aphrodite back to Olympus, and her mother Dione consoles her; Athena and Hera, by contrast, make fun of her with Zeus, and he finally tells Aphrodite to concern herself with love, not war (363–430). Diomedes tries to attack Apollo, who tells him to step back; the god then fashions an image of Aeneas, over which the two sides fight while he rescues the actual hero; Apollo finally tells Ares to put an end to Diomedes' rampage; and Aeneas, now healed, returns to the battlefield (431–518). The Trojans slowly gain ground, until Athena and Hera determine to stop Ares: they enter the battlefield with Zeus' permission, and Athena leaps on to Diomedes' chariot, making it creak under her weight (519–845). At the instigation of the goddess Diomedes wounds Ares, who screams as loud as nine- or ten-thousand men and withdraws to Olympus; Zeus expresses his contempt for Ares, and yet ensures that he is healed; Hera and Athena return to Olympus, having accomplished their mission (846–909).

5 *the star*: Sirius, see note to 22.27–31.

84–6 *As for the son of Tydeus . . . with the Achaeans*: the front ranks are intertwined and Diomedes cuts his own course.

105 *the lord son of Zeus*: Apollo.

222 *the horses of Tros*: when Zeus abducted the beautiful boy Ganymedes he gave some divine horses to King Tros, the boy's father, by way of compensation, see below on 5.268–70.

268–9 *Anchises . . . Laomedon's knowledge*: the divine breed of horses was handed down from king to king: Tros, Laomedon, and finally Priam. Anchises belongs to a different branch of the family (see note to 20.215–41) and thus has no right to the horses, which are evidently a royal prerogative. This is one of several passages where the line of Anchises and Aeneas is subordinated to that of Priam and Hector, see especially 13.460–1 and 20.179–83.

330 *Cypris*: Aphrodite.

333 *Enyo*: goddess of war, cf. Ares' epithet Enyalius.

373 *Uranian*: descendants of Uranus, Zeus' grandfather.

385–91 *when Otus . . . wearing him down*: there is no other reference to this episode, though another myth about the two brothers is mentioned at *Odyssey* 11.305–20. There we learn that their father was Poseidon, that they were giants (9 fathoms tall at age nine), and that they challenged the Olympians.

392 *the mighty son of Amphitryon*: Heracles.

395 *Monstrous Hades suffered too with the rest*: Heracles' wounding of Hades at Pylos is attested only here, and provoked much debate in antiquity.

401 *Paeëon*: a god of healing mentioned only here and at *Odyssey* 4.232, and later identified with Apollo.

408 *such a man has no homecoming . . . conflict*: in fact Diomedes did return, though some late sources claim that he was not welcomed home and immediately left for Italy, because by then his wife had settled with another man. This myth seems to spell out the consequences of offending Aphrodite, as Diomedes does in the *Iliad*.

446 *in the holy shrine on Pergamus . . . stood*: i.e. in Troy, cf. note to 4.508.

447 *Leto and Artemis*: Apollo's mother and his twin sister are not normally associated with healing, but on this occasion seem to act on Apollo's behalf.

500 *Demeter*: one of the very few references to this goddess in the *Iliad*.

543 *Pherae*: one of the seven Messenian cities promised by Agamemnon to Achilles at 9.151, probably on the site of modern Kalamata.

640 *the mares of Laomedon*: see note to 5.268–70. Heracles saved Laomedon's daughter from a sea-monster and was promised some of these semi-divine horses in return. When Laomedon cheated him of them, he proceeded to sack Troy.

750 *the Seasons*: see note to 8.394.

773–4 *When they came . . . unite their waters*: the battlefield consists of a triangle formed by the two rivers and the walls of Troy; the Simoeis and the Scamander unite before reaching the sea. The actual geography of the area does not fit Homer's description, and may never have done: ancient geographers also struggled to reconcile this and other passages in the *Iliad* with the landscape of the Troad.

789–90 *Dardanian | gates*: the ancient scholar Aristarchus thought this was a different name for the Scaean gates, but it is possible that it refers to another entrance to the city.

804 *as an envoy to Thebes*: cf. 4.380–4.

902–4 *As when fig-juice thickens white milk . . . stirs it*: fig-juice was used for curdling milk. This is a good image for the coagulation of human blood, though here it describes the swiftness of Ares' divine recovery.

BOOK SIX

As soon as the gods leave the battlefield the Achaeans gain ground and break through the lines (1–71). Helenus addresses Hector and Aeneas, telling them to line up the army; he then adds that Hector should return to Troy and tell the women to entreat Athena; the Trojans make a stand and Hector departs (72–118). Glaucus and Diomedes drive forward between the lines, ready to fight each other; Diomedes asks Glaucus whether he is human or divine (119–43), and Glaucus gives a full account of his genealogy (144–211). Diomedes remembers an old bond of hospitality that links him to Glaucus and proposes an exchange of gifts (212–36). Hector enters the city and is surrounded by women asking after their dear ones; he then meets his own mother, Hecuba, who tries, and fails, to delay him with an offer of wine (237–85). Hecuba and the other women then go to the temple of Athena, promise a sacrifice, and ask for help—but the goddess rejects their entreaties (286–311). Hector looks for Paris and, when he finds him handling weapons in his own bedroom, tells him to return immediately to the battlefield; Helen invites Hector to sit down while Paris gets ready (312–68). Hector declines her invitation and leaves, hoping to see his wife Andromache: he does not find her at home, but eventually meets her at the Scaean gates. After an anguished exchange, he takes leave from her and their baby son, and she returns home, mourning for her husband as if he were already dead (369–502). Paris catches up with Hector and, after a brief exchange, the two brothers head out (503–29).

22 *the river nymph . . . Bucolion*: we know nothing else about this nymph.

35 *steep Pedasus*: in the south Troad, the city was founded by the Leleges (21.86–7) and destroyed by Achilles (20.92).

56–7 *Can it be . . . in your own home?*: an allusion to the rape of Helen.

130 *mighty Lycurgus*: king of the Edonians, a prominent figure in Greek myth, though mentioned only here in Homeric epic.

133 *Nysa*: birthplace of Dionysus. Its exact location was debated also in antiquity, though it was generally thought to be somewhere in the east.

130–40 *Not even . . . immortal gods*: one of the rare mentions of Dionysus in Homeric epic.

152 *Ephyre*: ancient readers speculated that this was another name for Corinth, but that is far from clear.

153–4 *Sisyphus . . . son of Aeolus*: the story of how Sisyphus tried to cheat death is not told in Homer, but is certainly old; this passage implies that he tried to gain some sort of unfair advantage. Later sources tell several different

tales of how Sisyphus tried to escape death. Eventually, the gods punished
him for his tricks by making him push a huge rock up a hill, and then letting the rock roll back again every time Sisyphus was close to completing
his task.

155 *Bellerophon*: most famous for his hubristic attempt to reach heaven on
his winged horse Pegasus, a gift of Poseidon (his divine father). There
is no explicit reference to the story here, except a vague mention of
Bellerophon's divine ancestry (6.191), and a cryptic statement that the
gods punished him towards the end of his life (6.200).

157 *Proetus*: only here in Homer, though other sources mention him as a king
of Argos or Tiryns. According to the Hesiodic *Catalogue of Women*, his
daughters suffered from sexual incontinence; here it is a characteristic of
his wife.

184 *Solymi*: Herodotus 1.173 describes them as an indigenous population of
Lycia.

186 *Amazons*: see note to 3.189.

201 *Aleian plain*: the name of the plain puns on *alato*, 'he wandered', suggest-
ing that this is a place of wretched wanderings; the location is left unspeci-
fied, though Herodotus 6.95 mentions a place called Aleion in Cilicia, east
of Lycia.

216 *Oeneus*: Diomedes' grandfather.

395 *Eëtion*: king of Cilician Thebes.

396–7 *Thebe | under Placus*: ancient readers located Cilician Thebes opposite
the island of Lesbos.

402–3 *Scamandrius . . . Ilium*: the boy is named Scamandrius after the river
flowing near Troy, and Astyanax (lit. 'keeper of the city'), because his
father keeps Troy safe.

435–7 *three times . . . stalwart son*: there is no other mention of these attacks in
the *Iliad*; some ancient readers accused Andromache of lying.

457 *Messeïs or Hypereia*: probably generic names for springs, 'Middle Spring'
and 'Upper Spring' respectively.

BOOK SEVEN

Hector and Paris enter the battlefield; Athena swoops down to help the
Achaeans but Apollo intercepts her: they decide to stop the war for the day
(1–42). Perceiving the intention of the gods, Helenus tells Hector to challenge
an Achaean warrior; Athena and Apollo observe events perched like vultures
on an oak tree (43–91). Menelaus accepts Hector's challenge, but Agamemnon
tells him not to fight against a better man; Nestor rebukes the other Achaeans
for their reluctance to fight against Hector and nine warriors eventually volunteer for the duel; Ajax is selected by lot, much to everyone's relief (92–205).
Hector and Ajax fight hard until the heralds interrupt them at nightfall; at that

point they exchange gifts as tokens of friendship (206–312). Nestor proposes a truce for burying the dead, and outlines a plan for building a wall and trench around the Achaean camp; the Trojans tell Paris that he should hand Helen back to Menelaus, but he refuses to do so; he only concedes that he would be willing to return her possessions and offer more in addition (313–64). A herald conveys Paris' offer to the Achaeans, who reject it outright; the two sides then agree on a truce (365–411). After burying their dead, the Achaeans build a wall—which annoys Poseidon; ships from Lemnos bring wine to the Achaeans in exchange for hides, cattle, and slaves; Zeus thunders ominously while the Achaeans try, and fail, to enjoy their feast (412–82).

9 *Arne*: in Boeotia.

22 *by the oak tree*: near the Scaean gates, cf. 6.237.

86 *a grave-mound . . . beside the broad Hellespont*: a large mound was visible on the shore near Troy in Homer's time.

127 *questioning me in his house*: Nestor and Odysseus went to Phthia to recruit Achilles, cf. 11.769–90.

133–5 *when men fought . . . Iardanus*: a reference to the conflict between Pylians and Arcadians; the location of Pheia was much debated also in antiquity.

136 *Ereuthalion*: Nestor remembers his famous duel with Ereuthalion also at 4.319.

137–41 *Areïthous . . . with an iron club*: little is known about Areïthous; his weapon is unusual, and may have featured in stories about brigands.

166 *Enyalius*: cf. note to 5.333.

202 *you who rule from Ida*: see note to 3.276.

221 *Hyle*: perhaps Hyle in Boeotia, mentioned at 2.499–500.

334–5 *take a man's bones . . . to our native land*: these two lines are generally considered a late addition, because the custom of bringing back bones or ashes is unparalleled in Homer.

338 *a high-towered wall*: references to the Achaean wall have been much discussed by ancient, and indeed modern, readers: Thucydides 1.11.1 insists that the Achaeans must have built their wall at the beginning of the war; Aristotle, fr. 162 Rose, considers the wall a 'creation of the poet' (see also note to 12.1–33).

346 *next to Priam's gates*: i.e. outside Priam's palace, on the acropolis.

348 *Trojans and Dardanians*: two different ways of referring to the Trojans.

427 *Great Priam forbade them to cry out*: presumably because excessive displays of grief would weaken morale.

452–3 *the wall which Phoebus . . . Laomedon*: see 21.441–57 (and note to it), where Poseidon claims that he alone built the wall, while Apollo looked after Laomedon's cattle.

468–9 *Euneus . . . whom Hypsipyle had borne to Jason*: a rare reference to the voyage of the Argonauts, which took place a generation before the Trojan War. The Argonauts stopped at Lemnos on their journey, and were warmly welcomed by the Lemnian women, who had been abandoned by their husbands. Jason slept with King Thoas' daughter, Hypsipyle, who subsequently gave birth to Euneus.

BOOK EIGHT

Zeus threatens the gods, and warns them not to interfere with the war; he then leaves Olympus for Mount Ida and, from there, observes the fighting (1–52). The two sides are evenly matched until midday, when Zeus starts favouring the Trojans; Diomedes comes to the rescue of Nestor, and together they drive forward to face Hector; Zeus, however, arrests their progress with a thunderbolt, and Hector advances (53–197). Hera is angry, but fails to persuade Poseidon to help the Achaeans; Agamemnon rallies the troops; the Achaeans pray to Zeus, and are granted temporary respite (198–252). Diomedes leads the counter-attack; Teucer hides behind the shield of his half-brother Ajax, and kills several men with his arrows; Hector finally hits him with a stone (253–334). The Achaeans are forced to withdraw behind the ditch; Hera and Athena plan to come to their rescue, but Zeus sees them from Mount Ida and sends Iris to stop them (335–437). Zeus announces that the Trojans will keep winning until the death of Patroclus (438–83). At nightfall, the Achaeans finally experience some relief from the fighting, whereas Hector feels frustrated: he tells the troops to light fires on the plain and camp out, ready to resume the fighting at dawn (484–565).

13–16 *murky Tartarus...above the earth*: ancient and modern commentators have worried about the apparent lack of symmetry here. Under the earth there is Hades and, below that, Tartarus (presented, also in Hesiod's *Theogony*, as a nether place where insubordinate gods and monsters are imprisoned). Tartarus is as far from earth as is the 'high sky', i.e. (probably) the sky above Olympus.

19 *rope of gold from the high sky*: the details of this scenario have intrigued and puzzled readers. In antiquity the passage gave rise to a debate about the location of Olympus, which here seems to be suspended somewhere in the upper sky. Elsewhere in the *Iliad*, however, it is clearly conceived as a mountain.

69 *golden scales*: see note to 22.209–13.

108 *I captured them from Aeneas*: cf. 5.259–73 and 318–24.

203–4 *Helice . . . Aegae*: Poseidon had a cult at Helice, in the northern Peloponnese, and was thought to have a submarine palace at Aegae—various conjectures have been put forward concerning the precise location of Aegae, but it seems to have denoted no more than a mythical place, somewhere deep down in the Aegean Sea.

230 *loud boasts that you made on Lemnos*: the Achaeans stopped at Lemnos on their way to Troy; Philoctetes stayed behind, because he was bitten by a snake (cf. 2.716–25).

304 *Aesyme*: the location of this city is unknown.

349 *Gorgo*: a female monster whose gaze turned people into stone.

362–9 *He has not the smallest memory . . . Styx*: an allusion to the labours of Heracles, which Hera inflicted on him. Only one labour is specifically mentioned: the stealing of Cerberus, a many-headed dog that guarded the gates of the underworld (Erebus), beyond the river Styx. With Athena's help Heracles managed to conquer death, cross the Styx, steal Cerberus, and return from Hades. Now Athena suggests that she only helped Heracles because Zeus has told her to do so: this admission seems designed to increase Hera's resentment against Zeus, and create a stronger bond between the two goddesses.

394 *the Seasons*: daughters of Zeus and Themis in Hesiod's *Theogony* 901–2.

479 *where Iapetus and Cronus sit*: Tartarus (see note to 8.13–15). Iapetus is the father of Prometheus, and an insubordinate Titan; Cronus was defeated by his son Zeus and confined to Tartarus.

548 and 550–2 *[and they sacrificed . . . for the immortals]*: the pseudo–Platonic dialogue *Alcibiades 2*, 149d, quotes these four lines, which, however, do not appear in our manuscripts of the *Iliad*. They seem to be an addition to the poem that circulated already in antiquity.

BOOK NINE

Agamemnon, in tears, tells the Achaeans that they will never win and might as well sail home; Diomedes is indignant; Nestor outlines security measures for the night (1–88). Agamemnon entertains the leaders of the Achaeans in his tent, and Nestor mentions the wrongful seizure of Briseïs (89–114). Agamemnon acknowledges his mistake, and declares himself ready to give her back to Achilles, together with many other presents; Nestor makes plans for an embassy to Achilles (115–81). Odysseus, Ajax, and Phoenix, together with two heralds, leave for Achilles' tent, and are kindly received (182–204). Odysseus speaks first (205–306); Achilles—in a stunning speech—rejects all his entreaties (307–429). All remain silent, amazed at the force of his words; then Phoenix addresses Achilles again, as his mentor, and warns him through the example of Meleager (430–605). Achilles does not relent, but asks Phoenix to remain with him for the night, in case he should decide to return to Phthia with him in the morning (606–19). Achilles signals to Patroclus that he should start preparing Phoenix's bed, hoping that the others might take the hint and leave; Ajax briskly addresses Odysseus, telling him they must accept that the embassy has failed, and then condemns Achilles' behaviour; Achilles agrees with Ajax, but is too incensed with Agamemnon to reconsider his position (620–68). The embassy returns to the camp, and Odysseus reports on their failed mission; amid general despair, Diomedes delivers a resolute speech (669–713).

34 *You have already insulted my courage in front of the Danaans*: cf. 4.370–400.

142 *Orestes*: the only mention of Orestes in the *Iliad*. The poet assumes that his audience know about him, and offers no elaborate introduction. The *Odyssey* describes the fate of Agamemnon (murdered on his return home and avenged by Orestes, his son). In light of that, the suggestion that Achilles might enjoy life like Orestes will have sounded ominous.

145 *Chrysothemis and Laodice and Iphianassa*: there is no mention here of Electra or Iphigenia (prominent daughters of Agamemnon in later texts). Iphianassa may be Iphigenia, but in that case there is no reference here to her sacrifice in Aulis at the beginning of the Trojan expedition (an event which features prominently in tragedy).

146 *without bride-gifts*: see note to 11.243.

150–2 *Cardamyle . . . vines*: all the towns mentioned are located near the Messenian Gulf, between Lacedaemon and Pylos, see Map 1.

182 *they*: in Greek, the word for 'they' is dual rather than plural, i.e. it indicates that there are only two ambassadors, rather than the three designated by Nestor: Phoenix, Odysseus, and Ajax. The duals recur at 183, 185, 192, 196, 197, and 198 (with one plural at 186, and consistently plurals after 198): this is puzzling. Several explanations have been put forward: some scholars have argued that the duals are a survival from an earlier version of the story, where there were only two ambassadors; alternatively they may indicate that Odysseus and Ajax are the ambassadors proper, accompanied by Phoenix and the messengers, or that Phoenix has gone ahead on his own.

184 *Aeacus' grandson*: Achilles. Aeacus was the first king of the Myrmidons, and father of Peleus.

188 *when he sacked Eëtion's city*: cf. 6.414–28.

327 *for the sake of their wives*: i.e. for the sake of Menelaus' wife, Helen, but including Briseïs as a reason for fighting (cf. 9.335–43).

355 *there once he waited for me alone*: there is no other reference to this episode, but it clearly anticipates the final confrontation between Achilles and Hector at 22.5–366.

381–2 *Orchomenus . . . Egypt*: Orchomenus was one of the most powerful cities in the Mycenaean age; Egyptian Thebes and more generally Egypt are remembered for their wealth in Homeric epic.

405 *Pytho*: an older name for Delphi, this is one of the very few Homeric references to the oracle.

411 *two spectres carrying me towards the end of death*: at 1.352 and in several other passages Achilles claims he was destined to be short-lived. Here, he maintains that he can still choose between fame and a long life.

457 *Zeus of the world below*: i.e. Hades.

458–61 *[I planned . . . the Achaeans]*: these lines do not feature in the manuscripts of the *Iliad*; they are quoted by Plutarch at *Moralia* 26 (and in part at *Moralia* 72b and in the *Life of Coriolanus* 32). Plutarch claims that the Alexandrian scholar Aristarchus 'removed' them from the *Iliad*. It seems unlikely, however, that even the influential Aristarchus could have had such a pervasive effect on the manuscript tradition; it seems likelier that the lines are an intelligent ancient expansion: Phoenix shows that he can sympathize with Achilles' challenges to authority, while urging him to listen to his elders.

484 *Dolopians*: mentioned only here in Homer.

529–99 *The Curetes and Aetolians . . . for nothing*: the saga of Meleager took place before the Trojan War (cf. 2.638–42: the sons of Oeneus are now all dead). Phoenix adapts a story about the past in order to make it suitable as an example to Achilles. According to this and other versions, Meleager's father Oeneus offended Artemis, who punished him and his people by setting against them a wild boar; Meleager killed the Caledonian boar, as a result of which a dispute between Curetes and Aetolians arose over its spoils; Meleager killed his maternal uncle(s) in the course of that dispute, and his mother cursed him for that. In most versions she did so by throwing a firebrand that represented his life into the fire—as the firebrand burned, Meleager's strength ebbed away. In Phoenix's version, however, Meleager takes to his bed out of anger at his mother—while his companions and relatives urge him to return to the fighting, offering him gifts. Meleager's wife Cleopatra, in particular, begs him to fight. He rejects all entreaties, but in the end must take up arms to defend his house, even without gifts. It is unclear when and how the folk-tale elements (a mother cursing her son, the firebrand, the boar) became part of a heroic saga (the war of the Curetes and Aetolians); it is also unclear to what extent Phoenix modifies the story so as to create parallels with Achilles' situation. It seems likely that the theme of Meleager's anger, and the role of Cleopatra (who resembles Patroclus in name and function) are specific to this version.

607 *an honour*: i.e. the recompense mentioned by Odysseus.

632–6 *a man will accept compensation . . . amends*: Ajax refers to the practice according to which a murderer offered compensation to the family of his victim.

668 *Skyros*: Aegean island, east of Euboea.

BOOK TEN

Sleepless Agamemnon goes to see Nestor and meets Menelaus on the way. After several meetings and messages, the Achaean leaders converge near the trench, and discuss the situation (1–179). Nestor calls for a volunteer to go and spy on the Trojans, and Diomedes declares himself willing to go, provided that somebody accompany him (180–226). Many volunteer, and Diomedes chooses Odysseus, the most suitable companion for this kind of expedition: the two set off, and Athena sends a favourable omen (227–98). Meanwhile, in the Trojan

camp Hector is looking for somebody to go and spy on the Achaeans; Dolon
volunteers, because Hector promises that he will give him Achilles' horses:
as Dolon moves towards the Achaean camp Diomedes and Odysseus notice
him, hide among the corpses, then cut him off from the Trojan camp, capture
him, and interrogate him (299–389). Dolon, hoping to save his life, reveals that
Rhesus, leader of the Thracians, has just arrived in a gold-and-silver chariot
pulled by a team of magnificent white horses; after they have gained all the information they need Diomedes and Odysseus kill Dolon (390–464). They then
reach the Thracian camp: Diomedes kills Rhesus and twelve other Thracians
in their sleep, and Odysseus makes off with the horses; the two warriors then
withdraw, following Athena's advice (465–514). Apollo alerts Rhesus' cousin,
who wakes up the other Trojans; Diomedes and Odysseus make it safely back
to camp (515–79).

Since antiquity, Homeric scholars have considered book 10 a late addition to
the *Iliad*.

261–5 *a helmet of leather . . . a felt cap*: the boar's-tusk helmet fell out of use
after the fifteenth-century BCE. It is remarkable that the poet describes, in
accurate detail, a Bronze Age helmet: perhaps he inherited the description
from an age-old tradition of poetry, though there is nothing particularly
ancient in the language of these verses. It seems more likely that he had
seen a depiction of it, or was familiar with an actual surviving specimen.

266–71 *Autolycus had once stolen this . . . Odysseus*: the poet gives a full history of this remarkable helmet, following its whereabouts from Eeon in
Boeotia, to Cythera (between Crete and Laconia), to Crete (Meriones'
homeland). Autolycus was the maternal grandfather of Odysseus.

284 *Atrytone*: see note to 2.157.

286 *when he went as an envoy from the Achaeans*: Agamemnon mentioned the
same events to Diomedes at 4.382–98.

315 *Dolon*: this character features only in book 10; his name translates as
'Sneaky'.

415 *the grave-mound of godlike Ilus*: Ilus was the son of Laomedon and grandfather of Priam (see note to 20.215–41). His grave-mound is repeatedly
mentioned as a prominent landmark on the Trojan plain.

428–31 *Carians . . . Maeonian horse-marshals*: for Carians, Paeonians, Mysians,
Phrygians, and Maeonians, see Map 2. The Leleges come from the southern
Troad; the Caucones can only be placed generally in Asia Minor; the Pelasgi
cannot be located at all: they are a mythical autochthonous people.

434–5 *the Thracians . . . Eioneus' son*: for the Thracians, see Map 2. Rhesus
seems to be a genuine Thracian name. The ancient commentaries (scholia
A and bT *ad* 435) preserve two further stories about Rhesus, which were
either inspired by *Iliad* 10, or were known and adapted by the composer
of this book. According to one version, Rhesus arrived late at Troy, and

fought so valiantly that Hera sent Diomedes and Odysseus to kill him. According to another story, an oracle revealed that Rhesus and his horses would become invincible if they drank from the river Scamander; however, Diomedes and Odysseus killed Rhesus on the night he arrived at Troy, before he had a chance to drink.

497 *had that night stood over his head*: see note to 2.20.

BOOK ELEVEN

Zeus sends Strife to the Achaean camp; Agamemnon arms himself, and leads the Achaeans to battle; Hector advances with the Trojans (1–66). The Achaeans initially break through the Trojan lines, and Zeus warns Hector to keep away from Agamemnon (67–217). The poet invokes the Muse, and offers a catalogue of Agamemnon's brutal killings; his last victim, Coön, wounds him, and Agamemnon must finally withdraw (218–83). On seeing this, Hector immediately goes on the attack (284–309); Odysseus and Diomedes oppose him; Diomedes hits Hector's helmet without wounding him, and Paris hits Diomedes in the foot with one of his arrows (310–400). Odysseus continues to fight on his own, but he too is wounded eventually; at this point, Menelaus and Ajax come to his rescue: Menelaus takes Odysseus back to safety, while Ajax kills several Trojans before retreating himself (401–595). Achilles observes the wounded leaders as they return to the ships, and sends Patroclus to make enquiries (596–617). Patroclus bursts into Nestor's tent while the old man is drinking from his famous cup: Nestor explains the situation to him, talks about his own past exploits, and tells Patroclus that he should persuade Achilles to return to the fighting, or—failing that—that he should don Achilles' armour and lead the Myrmidons out to battle himself (618–803). On his way back to Achilles' hut Patroclus meets another injured warrior, Eurypylus, and tends his wound (804–48).

62 *the death-bringing star that appears rising out of the clouds*: Sirius, see note to 22.27–31.

139–40: *Menelaus . . . on an embassy with godlike Odysseus*: the embassy is also mentioned at 3.205–24. Here, the poet reveals that Paris bribed Antimachus (124), in order to ensure that Helen would not be returned.

166 *the burial-mound of old Ilus*: see note to 10.415.

167 *the wild fig tree*: also mentioned at 6.433 and 22.145. It marks the most vulnerable part of the walls.

170 *the Scaean gates and the oak tree*: see note to 7.22.

243 *though he had given much*: Homeric marriages typically involved both a bride-price and a dowry; the bride usually moved in with the husband, although there were exceptions to this custom: in this case, Iphidamas first moved to Thrace, then married a local girl and stayed there.

385 *You archer*: clearly meant as an insult; the bow is repeatedly disparaged in the *Iliad* as a treacherous and ineffectual weapon.

543 *[for Zeus . . . better man]*: this line does not feature in the manuscripts; it is cited with slight variations by Aristotle, *Rhetoric* 1387a35, Plutarch, *Moralia* 24c, and pseudo-Plutarch, *Life of Homer* 2.132. It must have been an addition designed to explain why Hector did not confront Ajax.

625 *Tenedos when Achilles sacked it*: cf. 9.328–9, where Achilles boasts about his raids on the towns near Troy.

632 *a very beautiful cup*: several actual vessels have been compared to Nestor's cup: for example, a gold cup found in a grave in Mycenae features two bird-shaped handles. More interesting, however, is a modest clay cup found in Ischia, and dated to the Geometric period (750–700 BCE): it bears an inscription in hexameter verse, which probably starts with the statement: 'I am Nestor's cup ...' There is no physical resemblance between the modest clay cup and Nestor's gold vessel, but the inscription may be an early, playful reference to it. The inscription is one of the earliest surviving examples of Greek writing, and informs arguments about the possible date of composition of the *Iliad*; see Introduction.

635 *two feet*: possibly extensions of the handles, but the exact design of the cup is unclear. The Greek text may not refer to 'feet', but to a double or false bottom.

670 *I wish I was as young and healthy . . .* : Nestor describes in detail his earlier exploits, in order to set an example: Achilles, or at least Patroclus, should think about the common good, and lead the eager Myrmidons back to war. The events are clearly set out: first, Nestor and the Pylians engaged in a cattle raid, and he killed Itymoneus. The booty was driven down to Pylos, and Nestor's father took the greatest share. The Epeians retaliated by attacking Thryoessa, a Pylian city. When news of this reached Pylos, Nestor led the eager Pylians to war, against the will of his own father (who was worried for him); the Pylians camped by the river Alphaeus, near Thryoessa, and on the next day defeated the Epeians; Nestor killed Mulius, and would have killed the Moliones too, except that their father Poseidon protected them. The Moliones, we know from other sources, were eventually killed by Heracles. There are also other, more explicit references to Heracles in Nestor's account: these help to set Nestor's story in the distant past, since Heracles belonged to an earlier generation of heroes.

671 *Eleians*: only here, apparently used as a synonym for Epeians.

673 *Elis*: in the north-western Peloponnese, see Map 1.

701 *Augeias*: his son Phyleus is mentioned at 2.627–30, where he is said to have left Elis because he was angry with his father.

722 *There is a river called Minyeïos*: mentioned only here, location unknown.

723 *Arene*: mentioned in the Catalogue of Ships immediately after Pylos (2.591); its exact location is unknown.

750–2 *the two Moliones . . . a dense mist*: the Moliones are identified by both their divine and their human father; this is not uncommon, cf. e.g. Heracles, who is described as the son of Amphitryon and of Zeus.

756–8 *Buprasium . . . Alesium*: mentioned also in the Catalogue of Ships, in the Epeian entry (2.615–17).

832 *Cheiron, most just of the Centaurs*: several archaic Greek texts describe Cheiron as Achilles' mentor. Centaurs are generally hubristic; Cheiron is an exception.

BOOK TWELVE

The battle reaches the Achaean wall which—the poet reveals—is destined to collapse soon (1–33). For now, however, the Achaeans retreat behind it, and the Trojan horses baulk before the ditch; Polydamas suggests to Hector that they leave the horses behind and continue their attack on foot, and Hector agrees (34–87). Asius alone remains on his chariot and—because the main gate to the camp is still open—charges ahead; Leonteus and Polypoetes defend the gate, and frustrate his attack (88–174). The poet declares that it would be impossible to describe the attack on the wall in all its details (175–94). Hector is about to charge forward when a portent spreads panic among the Trojans: Polydamas offers a cautious interpretation, and Hector declares that he recognizes the authority of only one omen—fighting for one's country (195–250). The battle intensifies: Ajax, son of Telamon, and Locrian Ajax are in charge of the defence; Sarpedon addresses Glaucus in a famous speech, in which he presents the prospect of death as a reason for fighting in the first line of battle (251–328). The Achaeans rally; Glaucus is wounded; Sarpedon tears down a piece of the battlement with his bare hands, and Ajax and Teucer restrain his attack (329–441); Hector smashes the gate with a huge boulder, and bursts into the camp; some Trojans follow him, while others scale the wall (442–71).

20–1 *Rhesus . . . Simoeis*: an impressive list that attracted the attention of ancient and modern commentators alike. The Rhesus, Heptaporus, Caresus, and Rhodius are not securely identified; the Granicus and Aesepus flow east of the Troad, the Scamander and Simoeis are the two rivers flowing near Troy.

5–33 *They had built this . . . before*: an intriguing revelation. Aristotle, fr. 162 Rose, took it to be an attempt on the poet's part to explain why no traces of the wall were visible in his own time, cf. note to 7.338.

96–7 *Asius . . . Selleïs*: cf. 2.838–9.

113–17 *he would not escape death's evil spectres . . . son of Deucalion*: this passage foreshadows 13.383–93.

BOOK THIRTEEN

Zeus and Poseidon observe the Trojan plain from opposite mountain-tops: as soon as Zeus turns his gaze away Poseidon takes advantage of his distraction, leaves for his underwater palace, arms himself, and intervenes in the

fighting (1–58). The Achaeans immediately take courage (59–154). Meriones
breaks his spear and returns to the Achaean camp (155–68). The Achaeans
press forward, but the Trojans kill Amphimachus, Poseidon's grandson
(169–205). Spurred on by the grieving god, Idomeneus arms himself and
meets Meriones, who was looking for a replacement spear: rather defensively,
they talk about their own valour, then join the fighting on the left (206–329).
The wills of Zeus and Poseidon are pitted against each other, and the battle
intensifies (330–60). Idomeneus kills Othryoneus and Asius; Antilochus slays
Asius' charioteer; Deïphobus kills Hypsenor; Idomeneus slays Alcathous—
and mocks the Trojans (361–454). Aeneas—who has been skulking behind
the battle-lines because he thinks that Priam neglects him—joins forces with
Deïphobus: they force Idomeneus to withdraw, and Deïphobus kills Ares' son
Ascalaphus, though Ares does not notice this (455–525). Deïphobus then takes
Ascalaphus' helmet, but Meriones wounds him in the hand so he has to let
go of it (526–39). The Achaeans keep their advantage in a sequence of intense
fighting (540–672). Hector, who is engaged in the centre, comes under increasing pressure from Achaean missiles: Polydamas advises him to consult with the
other Trojan leaders, and Paris tells Hector that many of the Trojans fighting
on the left are now dead or injured (673–787). Hector rallies the troops; the
Achaeans, led by Ajax, resist (788–837).

4–6 *horse-breeding Thracians . . . the Abii, most upright of men*: for the
    Thracians and the Mysians, see Map 2. The other two populations have
    speaking names: 'Hippemolgi' literally means 'mare-milkers', and the
    'Abii' are 'men without violence'; the poet draws attention to the etymolo-
    gies of these names.

12 *on the topmost peak of wooded Samothrace*: island to the north-west of Troy.

21 *Aegae*: cf. note to 8.203–4.

32 *There is a wide cavern at the bottom of the deep sea*: this is not a reference
   to an actual submarine cave, but a display of the poet's divine knowledge
   even of the depths of the sea, cf. 24.77–86.

172 *Pedaeon*: unidentified.

207 *Amphimachus*: Amphimachus' father, one of the two Moliones, is
    Poseidon's son, cf. note to 11.750–1.

217–18 *in all Pleuron and in | steep Calydon*: in western Greece, see Calydon
    on Map 1.

257–8 *since I shattered the one I was carrying before . . . arrogant Deïphobus*: cf.
    11.159–66.

299 *with him goes his dear son Panic*: personified Panic is described as Ares' son
    also in Hesiod's *Theogony* 934.

301–2 *and these two leave Thrace . . . the Ephyri or the great-hearted Phlegyans*:
    Ares was traditionally thought to come from Thrace; the Ephyri and the
    Phlegyans probably lived in Thessaly, in northern Greece.

345 *the two mighty sons of Cronus*: Zeus and Poseidon.

363–9 *Othryoneus from Cabesus . . . he was fighting*: Otryoneus is an obscure character, and the location of Cabesus was debated also in antiquity.

427–9 *Alcathous, the dear son of Aesyetes . . . Hippodameia*: a prominent and well-connected Trojan warrior. Aesyetes' tomb was a landmark on the Trojan plain (cf. note to 2.793); Hippodameia, daughter of Anchises and hence sister of Aeneas (cf. 13.462–7), is mentioned only here in the *Iliad*, though features prominently in other Greek texts.

450–4 *In the beginning Zeus fathered Minos . . . the other Trojans*: Idomeneus explains in what sense he is 'Zeus' offspring' (449). Minos was a mythical king of Knossos.

518 *Enyalius' son*: cf. note to 5.333.

546–7 *the vein . . . until it reaches the neck*: presumably the spinal marrow.

588–90 *as when on a great threshing-floor . . . the winnower's swing*: the winnower tosses the beans and lentils against the wind with a flat wooden shovel, in order to separate them from their husks. As they fall, the pulses bounce on the threshing-floor.

643 *king Pylaemenes*: cf. 5.576–89.

656 *Paphlagonians*: from northern Asia Minor, see Map 2.

669 *the Achaeans' heavy war-fine*: this is the only explicit mention of a fine for those who refused to join the Trojan expedition, though cf. 23.296–7.

696 *because he had killed a man*: the episode is mentioned also at 15.333–6.

778 *ever since you roused your companions to fight by the ships*: at 13.149–54.

781 *Deïphobus and the mighty lord Helenus*: cf. 13.526–39 and 593–600.

793 *Ascanië*: i.e. the area around lake Ascanië, near the sea of Marmara, see Map 2.

BOOK FOURTEEN

Nestor, who was tending the wounded Machaon in his hut, hears the din of battle, goes out to investigate, and meets with the wounded Diomedes, Odysseus, and Agamemnon (1–63). They realize that the ships are in danger, and Agamemnon suggests that they should drag them out to sea and moor them with anchors (64–81). Odysseus and Diomedes think this is a very bad idea (82–132). Poseidon encourages Agamemnon with a speech and the whole army with a mighty shout (133–52). Hera, who does not want Zeus to notice Poseidon's intervention, prepares to seduce him: she tricks Aphrodite into lending her a love-charm, and bribes Sleep to accompany her to Mount Ida (153–291). As soon as Zeus sees her he is overcome with passion, and the two make love shrouded in a golden, dewy cloud (292–351). Sleep tells Poseidon that Zeus has fallen asleep, and the god immediately rouses the Achaeans, who redistribute armour so that the strongest are also the best equipped (352–401).

Hector aims his spear at Ajax, who answers by knocking him out with a stone: the Trojans manage to rescue their leader, and take him to the river Xanthus (402–39). In Hector's absence the Achaeans gain the upper hand; Peneleos thrusts his spear through Ilioneus' eye-socket then cuts off and brandishes his head aloft; this spectacle terrifies the Trojans (440–507). The poet invokes the Muse, and offers a brief catalogue of killings (508–22).

30–6 *Their ships had been drawn up . . . along the coastline's wide bay*: because the beach could not hold all the ships, they were drawn up in rows along the entire curved coastline, and were hence arranged 'like a theatre', as the ancient scholar Aristarchus put it.

115–20 *Portheus had three blameless sons . . . the will of Zeus and the other gods*: this seems to be an allusion to a violent Aetolian saga, which Diomedes does not here want to describe in detail. It seems that Tydeus did not just wander away and settle in Argos, but went into exile after killing one of his uncles, cf. the Hesiodic *Catalogue of Women*, fr. 10d.50 ff.

171 *anointed her clothing*: the original text is obscure, but seems to refer to the Mycaenean practice of anointing clothes with perfumed oils.

201–10 *Oceanus, first father of the gods . . . respect for ever*: a reference to an unusual myth of origins, in which the sea-gods Oceanus and Tethys are the primeval parents of the universe. Hera alleges a quarrel between them, and also remembers a time of cosmic upheaval, when Zeus imprisoned his father Cronus: she thus presents herself as a cosmic peacemaker, whereas in fact she is planning to deceive Zeus and destabilize his rule.

214–15 *and untied from her breasts . . . were crafted*: probably a band passing over one shoulder and under the opposite arm, and then back over the shoulder and across to the other arm, forming an X at the cleavage.

226–30 *Pieria and lovely Emathia . . . godlike Thoas*: Hera first reaches Pieria, at the foothills of Mount Olympus, then continues north along the Macedonian coast to Mount Athos, and crosses the sea to Lemnos. From there, she continues north-east to Imbros, then south down the coast of the Troad to Lecton, and finally travels across the mainland to Ida. Her itinerary may seem erratic, but in fact makes perfect sense: she avoids open water, just as real-life sailors did.

249–62 *a task you set me once before . . . you are telling me to do something impossible*: for Heracles' sack of Troy, see note to 5.640. Zeus gives more detail about what happened to Heracles when he left Troy at 15.24–8 (on which see note). For Hera's hostility towards Heracles, cf. notes to 8.362–9 and 19.95–134.

269 *[Pasitheë . . . your days]*: this verse is a late addition clumsily modelled on line 276.

271 *the inviolable water of Styx*: river of the underworld, cf. note to 8.362–9.

278–9 *all the gods | who are under Tartarus, and are called Titans*: see note to 8.13–15.

281–5 *they left the cities of Lemnos and Imbros . . . shook under their feet*: for this itinerary, cf. note to 14.226–30.

291 *the gods call 'chalcis' and men call the hawk-owl*: for other instances where Homer distinguishes between divine and human speech, see note to 1.403–4. This seems to be an allusion to a girl called Chalcis, who was transformed into an owl.

315–28 *Never before has desire for a goddess or for a woman so . . . seized me*: a list of Zeus' most famous love affairs. Ancient and modern readers have worried that this list might offend, rather than attract, Hera. It also draws attention to the fact that the ensuring union, unlike the others he lists, fails to result in the conception of a child.

512 *Mysians*: the people living east of Troy, see Map 2.

BOOK FIFTEEN

Zeus wakes up, realizes what has happened, and threatens Hera (1–33). She cleverly swears that Poseidon acted of his own accord when he decided to help the Achaeans (34–46). Zeus sends Hera back to Olympus and asks her to summon Iris and Apollo to Ida: she returns to Olympus at the speed of thought, addresses the gods—with a frown hardly disguised by a smile—and reveals that Ascalaphus, Ares' son, is dead (47–112). This creates havoc: Ares wants to avenge his son, but Athena manages to restrain him (113–41); Iris and Apollo go to see Zeus on Mount Ida: he dispatches Iris to Poseidon, and she persuades him to withdraw (142–219); then he sends Apollo to revive Hector, and his renewed strength causes alarm among the Achaeans (220–80). On Thoas' advice most of the Achaean troops retreat, while the best warriors try to slow down the Trojan advance (281–342); Hector urges on the Trojans, and Apollo kicks down the Achaean wall like a boy destroying a sandcastle (343–66). The fighting rages near the ships; Patroclus hears it and leaves Eurypylus' hut in order to try and persuade Achilles to fight (367–404). The battle has now reached the ships, and the fighting intensifies (405–673). Ajax leaps from ship to ship, attacking the enemy with a long pike; Hector gets hold of Protesilaus' ship and calls to the Trojans to bring him fire; Ajax keeps killing the Trojans as they try to bring torches to Hector (674–746).

18–24 *Or do you not remember . . . there was little life in them*: the punishment of Hera is presented as a case of domestic violence. And yet it also has cosmic significance: it recalls other myths where the sky-god establishes his superiority over the earth-goddess, e.g. Zeus' confrontation with Gaia and her son Typhoeus in Hesiod's *Theogony*.

24–8 *Even so . . . well-populated island*: Sleep already alluded to this episode at 14.249–62 (on which see note). Quite what happened to Heracles in Cos is unclear.

37 *downwards*: the Styx was thought to drip down from a cliff, cf. Hesiod, *Theogony* 786.

64–7 *He will then send his companion . . . glorious Sarpedon*: a clear prediction of what will happen in book 16.

87 *but accepted a cup from Themis*: personified 'Right' is the goddess who presides over divine assemblies, and traditionally protects Zeus' power. Her role here suggests that order will soon be restored among the gods.

110–12 *I believe, suffering has been laid up for Ares . . . his own*: cf. 13.518–25.

187–93 *We are three brothers . . . the earth and high Olympus were left common to all three*: this division of the cosmos is paralleled in Babylonian mythology.

204 *the Furies always side with the firstborn*: the Furies were in charge of punishing breaches of respect in the family.

225 *even the gods who live with Cronus below the earth*: see note to 8.13–15.

229 *take the tasselled aegis*: unusually, Zeus gives the aegis to Apollo, cf. note to 1.202.

334 *Phylace*: in Thessaly.

335 *because he had killed a man*: see note to 13.696.

388–9 *with the long jointed pikes . . . for fighting at sea*: these pikes were made of sections glued together and held with pins, cf. 13.677–8. A Theran fresco depicts Bronze Age ships with pikes in their bows.

390–4 *Now Patroclus . . . black pains*: cf. 11.837–48.

531 *Ephyre*: it seems that three different cities are called Ephyre in the *Iliad*, cf. note to 6.152. This one must be located in Elis, in the north-west Peloponnese, see Map 1.

548 *Percote*: see Map 2.

668 *And Athena drove an amazing cloud of mist from their eyes*: ancient and modern critics have rightly pointed out that this is the first time we hear of a mist enveloping the Achaeans. Yet there is no reason to believe that the poet ought to have mentioned the mist before: human vision is always limited, cf. 5.127–8, where Athena lifts a mist from Diomedes' eyes so that he can suddenly tell apart gods from men. Now all Achaeans, whether in the first line of battle or at the rear, can suddenly see the danger they face.

676 *half-decks*: images of ships from the Geometric period (*c*.900–700 BCE) show that they had two half-decks, one at the prow and one at the stern.

679–84 *As a man well skilled in horsemanship . . . while the horses fly along*: the simile describes a rider bringing four horses from the stables or pastures into the city; the horses are harnessed together, and he rides each in turn, changing mounts as they gallop (either to show off, or to avoid overtiring a single horse). Just like the rider, Ajax leaps from the half-deck of one ship to that of the next.

705–6 *which had brought Protesilaus . . . native land*: Protesilaus' death is remembered also at 2.698–701. He was the first Achaean to disembark at Troy, the first to be killed, and now his ship is the first to come under attack. His ship is in fact the only one that gets burnt: cf. 16.122–4 and 294.

BOOK SIXTEEN

Patroclus begs Achilles to intervene in the fighting, and Achilles agrees to let him lead the Myrmidons instead (1–100). The Trojans burn Protesilaus' ship; Patroclus dons Achilles' armour and prepares for battle (101–54). Achilles exhorts the Myrmidons, and a catalogue of their leaders follows (155–209). Back in his tent Achilles prays for Patroclus' success and safety—but Zeus grants only his first request (210–56). Unnerved by Patroclus' sudden appearance the Trojans withdraw behind the ditch, suffering heavy losses (256–418). Sarpedon, Zeus' son, makes a stand, and Zeus considers saving his life; Hera objects, and Zeus limits himself to honouring Sarpedon with a shower of blood (419–61). Sarpedon kills Patroclus' trace-horse, and Patroclus kills him; Glaucus prays to Apollo for strength, but does not manage to protect Sarpedon's body (462–547). A fierce battle breaks out around it, and he is stripped; Zeus then sends Apollo, Sleep, and Death to carry off the body so that Sarpedon may be buried in Lycia (548–683). Patroclus pursues the Trojans all the way to the city walls, where Apollo issues a warning (684–711). Patroclus kills Hector's charioteer with a stone (712–76); the Achaeans strip him, and Apollo hits Patroclus on the back with the flat of his hand, stunning him; Euphorbus wounds him in the back, and Hector finally stabs him in the belly (777–842). Before dying, Patroclus tells Hector that Achilles will avenge his death (843–67).

100 *so that we alone could tear down the sacred headdress of Troy*: the walls of Troy are compared to a woman's headdress, which is torn off as she is dragged into captivity.

142–4 *the Pelian ash spear, which Cheiron . . . Pelion*: the centaur Cheiron lived on Mount Pelion. Several seventh-century vase paintings depict him with Achilles.

149–54 *Xanthus and Balius . . . Pedasus . . . immortal horses*: Achilles' horses reflect his status as the son of a goddess. They are immortal, and have prophetic powers (cf. 19.404–17); Poseidon gave them to Peleus as a wedding gift. The trace-horse Pedasus (taken after the sack of Andromache's city, cf. note to 6.397) is mortal but exceptionally fast, just like Achilles himself.

168 *There were fifty swift ships*: the Catalogue of the Myrmidons (168–97) is configured as an addition and expansion of the Myrmidons' entry in the Catalogue of Ships (2.681–94). The Myrmidon contingent is guided by five leaders, each of whom is in charge of ten ships. Menesthius, Eudorus, and Peisander are mentioned only here: their biographical details suggest that they are similar but inferior to Achilles.

229 *sulphur*: a holy substance in ancient Greek culture, often used to fumigate and purify.

233–5 *Lord Zeus, god of Dodona, Pelasgian . . . whose feet are unwashed*: Achilles invokes Zeus as the god presiding over the ancient oracle at Dodona, in north-western Greece. The Pelasgians were a prehistoric tribe, considered indigenous. The strange habits of the Selli, the local priests, may reflect local religious taboos.

286 *beside the stern of the ship of great-spirited Protesilaus*: see note to 15.705.

287–8 *and he hit Pyraechmes . . . from the broad-flowing Axius*: for the Paeonians, cf. 2.848–50. For the location of the river Axius, see Map 2.

380 *The immortal swift horses that the gods had given to Peleus*: on Achilles' horses, see note to 16.149–54.

437 *the rich land of Lycia*: see Map 2.

459 *began to rain a shower of bloody raindrops upon the earth*: an unusual portent, foreshadowing Sarpedon's imminent death. Rain in southern Europe sometimes does deposit red sand from the Sahara.

510–12 *for he was hurt . . . at the high wall*: Teucer wounded Glaucus at 12.387–91.

558 *was the first to leap on to the Achaean wall*: Sarpedon was not actually the first to enter the Achaean camp. Ancient and modern readers have been worried by the apparent inconsistency introduced by this line.

571–6 *glorious Epeigeus . . . to fight against the Trojans*: the episode is mentioned only here, and the location of Boudeion is unclear. Unusually, the poet here presents Peleus and Thetis as still living together.

614–15 *[Aeneas' spear . . . powerful hand]*: these lines are a medieval addition, which arose from a mistake in copying.

838–42 *he doubtless said to you . . . your witless wits*: this is not true. Achilles actually recommended caution, and warned Patroclus against Apollo, cf. 16.83–96.

BOOK SEVENTEEN

Menelaus kills Euphorbus and Apollo incites Hector; Menelaus retreats, calling on Ajax for help (1–122). Ajax successfully protects Patroclus' corpse; Glaucus meanwhile rebukes Hector, who decides to don Achilles' armour (123–97). Zeus reflects that Hector is about to die and decides to grant him temporary strength (198–236). Menelaus again calls for help; Zeus shrouds Patroclus' body and those fighting over it in a mist, and Ajax continues to defend it well (237–318). Apollo rebukes Aeneas, while Ajax remains in control: the fighting over Patroclus' body intensifies (319–425). Achilles' horses mourn the death of Patroclus, and Zeus pities them (426–55). Energized by Zeus, the horses start moving again; Automedon protects them on foot, and Hector fails to capture them (456–542). Athena swoops down to the battlefield like a rainbow; encouraged by her presence, Menelaus kills Podes (543–81). Apollo exhorts Hector, and Zeus thunders his support for him; the Achaeans flee towards the ships (582–625). Ajax begs Zeus to disperse the mist and sends Menelaus to find Antilochus: the latter should then run to Achilles and convey the bad news to him; Antilochus himself is stunned to hear that Patroclus is dead and that Hector has taken Achilles' armour (626–99). Together with Meriones, Menelaus finally manages to drag Patroclus' body off the battlefield, while Ajax, son of Telamon, and Locrian Ajax hold off the Trojans; the poet illustrates the intense struggle with five similes (700–61).

24–6 *Yet the mighty Hyperenor . . . insulted me*: Menelaus killed Hyperenor, brother of Euphorbus, at 14.516–19.

73 *Mentes, leader of the Cicones*: features only here.

75–8 *you are now running after what you cannot reach . . . to an immortal mother*: on Achilles' horses, see note to 16.149–54.

150–1 *now you have abandoned Sarpedon . . . their prey and prize*: cf. 16.656–65.

162–3 *we could bring Sarpedon himself into Ilium*: Glaucus is unaware that the gods have carried Sarpedon's body to Lycia, cf. 16.666–83.

195–6 *which the gods . . . had given to his father*: the gods attended the marriage of Peleus and Thetis (cf. 24.62), and brought gifts (cf. 18.84–5).

269 *the son of Cronus poured a thick mist*: the gods repeatedly spread or dispel mist, but only here do we get a full account of the mist's onset, continuation (366–77), and dispersal (643–50).

288 *Hippothous, the illustrious son of Lethus the Pelasgian*: on the Pelasgian allies of Troy, cf. 2.840–3.

366–77 *and you could not have said . . . the mist and the fighting*: cf. note to 17.269.

389–93 *As when a man gives the hide of a great ox . . . is stretched right through*: a detailed description of leather tanning.

426 *But the horses of Aeacus' grandson*: on Achilles' horses, see note to 16.149–54.

644–50 *for they themselves . . . the battle was all made plain*: cf. note to 17.269.

BOOK EIGHTEEN

Achilles fears that Patroclus may be dead, and Antilochus confirms this (1–21). He cries out, grief-stricken, and covers his head in ash; Thetis laments Achilles' own fate together with her sea-nymph sisters in their underwater palace, and then goes up to visit him, followed by them (22–77). Achilles summarizes the events of the past days and declares his intention to avenge Patroclus and kill Hector (78–92). Thetis warns him that he will die soon after, then tells him not to return to battle until she has given him new armour (93–147). Meanwhile, the Achaeans and the Trojans are still fighting over Patroclus' body; Hera sends Iris to summon Achilles to the fighting: he hesitates because he has no armour, but Athena throws her aegis around him, and the Trojans retreat in terror as soon as they see him and hear his war-cry; twelve Trojans die on the spot, entangled in their own weapons, while the Achaeans bring back Patroclus' body (148–238). Hera forces the sun to set early; the Trojans hold an assembly, and Polydamas recommends a retreat; Hector angrily rejects his good advice and declares himself ready to fight Achilles; in his tent Achilles mourns Patroclus and thinks about his own death (239–355). On Olympus Zeus congratulates Hera on Achilles' return and teases her; she replies that it is only right she should try and get her way (356–67). Thetis reaches the home of Hephaestus and his wife Charis, who give her a warm welcome: Hephaestus remembers that Thetis rescued him in the past, and readily agrees to make new armour for her son (368–467). He fashions an amazing shield, corslet, helmet, and greaves (468–617).

9–11 *my mother once foretold to me . . . Trojan hands*: this is the only time this particular prophecy is mentioned, though at 17.408–11 we are told that Achilles often heard about Zeus' plans from Thetis.

13–14 *I told him . . . against Hector's*: at 16.86–96.

117–19 *Not even the mighty Heracles . . . beat him down*: in the *Iliad* Heracles is the hero who comes closest to immortality, cf. note to 8.362–9. Other ancient texts depict him as a god.

122–4 *let me force some Trojan woman . . . her tender cheeks*: the *Iliad* ends precisely with the women's funeral laments for Hector.

290–2 *these fine treasures have been spent . . . lovely Maeonia*: Hector is worried about the cost of paying for the allies; for the location of Phrygia and Maeonia, see Map 2.

336–7 *I shall cut the throats of twelve | noble sons of the Trojans*: Achilles will carry out his savage plan at 21.27–32 and 23.175–6.

382 *Charis*: personified 'Grace'; in the *Odyssey* Hephaestus is married to Aphrodite herself.

395–405 *it was Thetis who . . . saved me*: this story features only here, and emphasizes Thetis' role as a motherly goddess. At 1.590–4 Hephaestus claims that Zeus hurled him from Olympus when he tried to help Hera— and that he became lame as a result. In this passage the suggestion is that Hephaestus was lame from birth, and that Hera cast him off in disgust. Mythical variations on a theme (in this case: Hephaestus' fall and lameness) were common in ancient Greece.

432–3 *he made me subject . . . and I had to endure a man's bed*: the *Iliad* never explains why Zeus married Thetis off to a mortal but, according to other ancient sources Zeus himself wanted to marry Thetis, until a prophecy revealed that her son would be stronger than her partner; on hearing that, Zeus married her off to Peleus; see especially [Aeschylus], *Prometheus Bound* 907–27; Pindar, *Isthmian Ode* 8.26–48. This myth also left its mark on the pictorial record: some early vase paintings represent Thetis as she takes on different shapes in an attempt to resist the approaches of her mortal husband.

478   *First of all he made a huge, heavy shield*: the exact layout of Achilles' shield has been much debated. The shield is round and seems to have four concentric, decorated bands. One possible reconstruction, based on the description at lines 478–608, is this: the centre is taken up by the earth, sea, sun, moon, and stars; the innermost band is divided between a representation of the city at peace and one of the city at war; the next band depicts the four seasons, starting with ploughing in spring, then reaping, the vintage, and finally cattle and sheep rearing; the third band is decorated with dancers; the river Ocean flows in a circle around the rim. Some Cretan bronze shields and Phoenician silver bowls dated to the late eighth century BCE closely resemble Achilles' shield: they too feature concentric bands decorated with different scenes (war, hunting, processions, wild and domestic animals, etc.). Homer's description, however, emphasizes movement, sound, and the passing of time: it turns images into stories. It also adds a cosmic dimension: the shield as a whole is a powerful representation of the world, and of human life in it.

486–9   *the Pleiades and the Hyades . . . in the baths of Ocean*: these are among the most prominent constellations. The Pleiades and Hyades are star clusters near Orion; Orion is the most prominent constellation in the southern sky during winter; the Bear is the most prominent constellation in the northern sky and, for viewers in the northern hemisphere, never dips below the horizon (or, as Homer puts it, 'has no share in the baths of Ocean').

499   *the blood-money of a man who had been killed*: see note to 9.632–5.

569   *the Linus-song*: Linus was a famous mythical singer.

591–2   *just like the one which Daedalus . . . beautiful hair*: this is the only reference to a dance-floor built by Daedalus, a mythical craftsman. He was more generally credited with building the Labyrinth for Ariadne's father, Minos, who kept the Minotaur in it.

604–5   *[and among them a divine singer | sang and played the lyre]*: this seems to be a late addition, taken from *Odyssey* 4.18–19, and designed to provide the dancers with some music.

BOOK NINETEEN

Thetis brings the new armour to Achilles and finds him mourning for Patroclus (1–39). Achilles admires Hephaestus' work, then calls an assembly and declares that he is ready to let go of his anger and fight again (40–73). For his part, Agamemnon admits that he must have been the victim of Delusion when he antagonized Achilles, then tells of Delusion's power over Zeus himself, and finally declares himself ready to make amends (74–144). Achilles insists that he does not care about Agamemnon's gifts and wants to enter battle immediately; Odysseus points out that the men have not eaten, that Agamemnon's gifts need to be displayed, and that Agamemnon must swear that he has not touched Briseïs (145–83). Despite Achilles' impatience, Agamemnon follows Odysseus' instructions (184–275). On returning to Achilles' tent Briseïs laments the death of Patroclus, and claims that he had promised her she would marry Achilles after the war; all the women mourn in response—ostensibly for Patroclus, but actually for their own reasons; Achilles, meanwhile, refuses to eat (276–308). The leaders gather in his tent to console him while the soldiers have a meal; Athena fortifies Achilles with ambrosia and nectar, he dons his armour, and the Achaeans prepare for battle (309–403). Achilles rebukes his horses, and Xanthus responds by prophesying his master's death; Achilles declares himself ready to die, and drives forward (404–24).

38–9 *and through Patroclus' nostrils . . . remain undecayed*: see note to 19.353.

59 *If only Artemis had killed her with an arrow by the ships*: Artemis was generally held responsible for the death of women.

60 *Lyrnessus*: in the Troad; the fall of this city is described at 2.690–3.

91 *she is Zeus' eldest daughter, Delusion, an accursed thing*: delusion, or *atē*, is invoked by speakers when they try to excuse themselves for behaviour that is so bad that it actually has no explanation, cf. English: 'I do not know what got into me.' Even though Agamemnon talks of Delusion as a powerful goddess, from a judicial point of view he remains accountable—and indeed offers compensation for his actions.

95–134 *Indeed, even Zeus was once driven mad by Delusion . . . So it is with me*: as in many other stories, an ill that was once experienced by the gods is then banned from Olympus and inflicted on human beings alone. The particular story of how Hera manipulated the birth-dates of Heracles and Eurystheus may not have involved Delusion in other versions, but here Agamemnon is drawing a rather exalted parallel between himself and the supreme god.

177 *as is the usual way, lord, between men and women*: this line features only in some manuscripts, and may have been added by analogy with 9.276. Alternatively, it might have been left out from some manuscripts for reasons of modesty.

212 *with his feet towards the door*: the traditional position in which bodies were laid out before burial.

221–4 *Men very quickly have their fill . . . tilted his scales*: the precise meaning of this metaphor was much debated also in antiquity. Odysseus seems to compare the cut straw to the bodies of dead soldiers on the battlefield; the scanty harvest helps him make the point that there may be many casualties with little gain—particularly as the soldiers are now hungry, and the last thing they need is scanty food.

267–8 *Talthybius swung the body round and flung it . . . to be food for fishes*: it seems that animals sacrificed in an oath-taking were thought to be polluted and could not be eaten.

297–9 *but declared that you would make me . . . a marriage feast among the Myrmidons*: this detail features only here; through her lament, Briseïs is publicly raising the possibility of marriage with Achilles.

326–7 *nor if it were my dear son . . . still alive somewhere*: Achilles fathered Neoptolemus on the island of Skyros. Later texts explore in detail the circumstances of his stay there, but the *Iliad* does not go into detail.

353 *she distilled nectar and delectable ambrosia into his breast*: nectar and ambrosia are food of the gods; at 19.38–9 they are used to preserve Patroclus' body.

400 *Xanthus and Balius, far-famed children of Podarge*: on Achilles' horses, see note to 16.149–54.

410 *a great god and your powerful destiny*: Apollo will kill Achilles—or rather Paris will shoot him with an arrow, with Apollo's help. See further notes to 21.276–8 and 22.359–60.

BOOK TWENTY

Zeus summons all the gods to an assembly and invites them to take part in the war: they march out and line up for battle (1–74). Apollo, in the guise of Lycaon, rebukes Aeneas and urges him to challenge Achilles: Aeneas is reluctant to do so, particularly because in an earlier confrontation he shamefully ran away from Achilles; Apollo points out that Aeneas' mother—the goddess Aphrodite—is much more powerful than Achilles' own divine mother Thetis (75–109). Stung in his pride, Aeneas challenges Achilles; Hera expresses her alarm, and Poseidon suggests that they monitor the situation from a distance; the gods withdraw: those supporting the Achaeans observe events from a stronghold originally built for Heracles, while the Trojan faction occupies a nearby hill (110–55). Achilles taunts Aeneas by saying that Priam prefers his own children to him, and by reminding him of their past encounter; Aeneas makes great boasts about his ancestry (156–258). The duel begins: each warrior casts his spear in vain, then Achilles draws his sword and Aeneas picks up a huge stone—at this point Poseidon reflects that Aeneas is not destined to die at Troy, and rescues him (259–339). Achilles exhorts the Achaeans, and Hector marshals the Trojans; Apollo warns Hector not to face Achilles in single combat; Achilles kills many Trojans, including Hector's own brother Polydorus (340–418). Enraged, Hector charges forward, but Athena intervenes and Apollo drives him away to safety; Achilles meanwhile resumes his slaughter of the Trojans, who withdraw in disarray (419–503).

5 *Themis*: see note to 15.87.

7–12 *Not one of the rivers stayed away . . . cunning skill*: the presence of the river-gods and the nymphs prepares for the role Scamander plays in the ensuing battle of the gods.

53 *Callicolone*: this hill near the Trojan plain is mentioned only here and at 20.151.

61 *Aïdoneus*: another name for Hades.

67–74 *Face to face against lord Poseidon . . . Scamander*: the following gods line up on the Achaean side: Poseidon, Athena, Hermes, and Hephaestus; they are met, on the Trojan side, by Apollo, Enyalius (i.e. Ares), Leto, and the river Scamander. Aphrodite may have taken Zeus' warning to heart (cf. 5.426–30), and does not line up now—though she will later try to assist Ares, and will consequently suffer at the hands of Athena (21.416–33).

90–3 *once before this he drove me with his spear . . . Lyrnessus and Pedasus*: on the sack of Lyrnessus, see 2.690–3; Pedasus is another city in the Troad. This confrontation between Aeneas and Achilles featured in the *Cypria*, an early epic poem now largely lost, and is also remembered by Achilles at 20.188–94 (on which see note).

127–8 *he must suffer whatever Fate spun . . . when his mother bore him*: the image of the spinning Fates was widespread in antiquity, indeed one name for them was 'the Spinners'.

145–8 *the heaped-up stronghold of Heracles . . . from the seashore to the plain*: when Laomedon failed to pay Poseidon for building the walls of Troy, Poseidon inflicted a sea-monster on the Trojans. Heracles offered to defeat the monster for them—and Laomedon failed to pay him for that (cf. notes to 5.640 and 21.441–57). Heracles' stronghold is mentioned only here.

188–94 *do you not remember when I found you . . . freedom*: cf. note on 20.90–3. One of the women Achilles captured after the fall of Lyrnessus was Briseïs.

215–41 *In the beginning, Zeus . . . the ancestry and bloodline that I boast is mine*: Aeneas' mother, Aphrodite, easily trumps Thetis (cf. 20.105–7). For this reason, Aeneas now sets out his ancestry on his father's side: his boasts, however, only confirm Achilles' observation that Aeneas will not inherit the throne (cf. 20.179–83). On the horses of Tros, see also notes to 5.222 and 5.268–70. This is the family tree of the Trojan royal family:

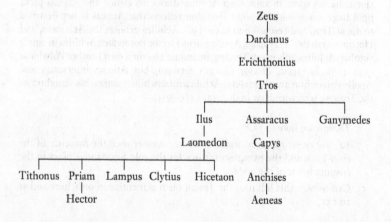

297 *this innocent man*: this is a reference to Laomedon's outrageous behaviour (cf. note to 21.441–57). Aeneas is not a descendant of Laomedon, and therefore should not suffer for what he did.

302–6 *because it is his destiny to escape . . . the race of Priam*: this is the only reference to Aeneas' survival in the *Iliad*, and it has caused much debate. It is unclear how early Greek audiences understood these lines, and who they took Aeneas' descendants to be (an aristocratic family living in the Troad is a plausible suggestion); Roman and later readers of the *Iliad* understood these lines to allude to the events told in the *Aeneid*.

384 *Naiad nymph*: a minor goddess living near or in water; from the Greek verb *naiō* = 'flow'.

385–91 *Tmolus . . . Gygaea*: see Map 2.

404–5 *the shrine of the | Heliconian*: 'the Heliconian' is Poseidon.

BOOK TWENTY-ONE

Achilles pursues the Trojans right into the waters of the river Scamander (1–33). He kills Lycaon, a son of Priam whom he had previously captured and sold into slavery (34–135). Achilles' behaviour enrages the river Scamander, especially after he kills Asteropaeus, a grandson of the river Axius (136–204). The river issues a warning, then pursues Achilles over the plain; Poseidon and Athena intervene to reassure Achilles (205–97). Scamander enlists the help of the river Simoeis, and comes close to overwhelming Achilles (298–329). Following Hera's request, Hephaestus burns the plain and parches the river; Scamander begs for mercy, and promises never to help the Trojans again (330–82). Ares attacks Athena, who knocks him out with a stone (383–414). Aphrodite comes to Ares' rescue, and Athena—encouraged by Hera—hits her on her breasts, knocking her out too (415–33). Poseidon tells Apollo that they too ought to fight each other, but Apollo insists there is no point fighting over mortals (434–67). Artemis taunts Apollo; Hera gets angry with her and boxes her ears (468–88). Hermes sees this and thinks that he had rather not fight against Leto, another powerful consort of Zeus; Artemis complains to Zeus about Hera (489–513). All the gods return to Olympus—except for Apollo, who heads for Troy; Priam makes arrangements for the Trojans to find refuge inside the city gates (514–43). Inspired by Apollo, Agenor makes a stand: he fights briefly against Achilles, until the god rescues him and takes on his appearance: Achilles runs after the disguised Apollo, while the Trojans find safety inside the gates (544–611).

1 *the crossing of the clear-flowing river*: the exact location of the ford in relation to other landmarks on the Trojan plain was much debated in antiquity, and remains unclear today.

12–14 *As when locusts rise . . . then huddle together in the water*: the simile describes the ancient practice of driving locusts out of the fields with fire.

27–32 *he chose twelve young men . . . to take back to the hollow ships*: cf. 18.336–7 (with note).

85–7 *daughter of old Altes . . . in steep Pedasus beside the river Satnioeis*: the Leleges were a people of the Troad; Achilles sacked Pedasus, cf. note to 20.90–3. Laothoë and her father Altes, ruler of Pedasus, are mentioned again at 22.46–51.

90–1 *one you beat down in the front rank . . . with your sharp spear*: for Polydorus' death, cf. 20.407–18.

141 *Pelegon was the son of broad-flowing Axius and Periboea*: the river Axius flows through Macedonia, see Map 2. Pelegon was mentioned before, but here the poet draws attention to his river-ancestry.

185 *against the descendants of Cronus' mighty son*: Achilles, rather than referring to his mother Thetis, stresses his father's descent from Zeus.

194–5 *Not even lord Achelous . . . the immensely strong deep-flowing Ocean*: Achelous is the longest river in Greece and was always considered important, indeed the name 'Achelous' was sometimes used as a synonym for 'water'. On Oceanus, see note to 1.423.

276–8 *as my own mother . . . struck down by the swift arrows of Apollo*: references to Achilles' imminent death become increasingly more specific in the last books of the *Iliad*: at 18.96 Thetis reveals that Achilles will die soon after Hector; at 19.404–17 the horse Xanthus predicts that Achilles will be killed by a god and a man (cf. note to 19.410), and now Achilles remembers Thetis' claims that he will be struck down by an arrow. Moments before dying, Hector gives an even fuller account: Achilles will die in front of the Scaean gates, killed by Paris and Apollo, see note to 22.359–60. The lost cyclic poem *Aethiopis* told the story of how an arrow, shot by Paris with Apollo's aid, killed Achilles.

396–8 *Do you not recall when you . . . tore my handsome flesh?*: cf. 5.855–61.

412 *This way you will pay the full price to your mother's Furies*: Ares' mother is Hera, and she supports the Achaeans. On the Furies, see note to 15.204.

420 *Atrytone*: see note to 2.157.

441–57 *Fool . . . he had promised but did not fulfil*: Poseidon taunts Apollo by remembering a specific episode, when Laomedon, king of Troy, refused to pay Poseidon and Apollo for their services (they had built the Trojan wall and tended his cattle, cf. note to 7.452–3). Quite why the two gods were in service to the king is unclear: ancient commentators claim that they had been punished by Zeus for an act of insubordination, or that they were testing Laomedon. The story continued with the gods' revenge: Apollo inflicted a plague, and Poseidon sent a sea-monster against the Trojans (cf. note to 20.145–8). Poseidon now makes the point that Apollo foolishly supports the Trojans, despite Laomedon's offences.

483–4 *Zeus has made you a lioness . . . kill those whom you choose*: cf. note to 19.59.

BOOK TWENTY-TWO

Hector remains outside the walls, and Apollo taunts Achilles (1–24). Priam and
Hecuba beg their son to retreat inside the city, but Hector feels too ashamed to
do so (25–130). As Achilles draws near, Hector briefly considers talking to him,
then turns and flees; the two men run three times around the city walls, as the
gods look on; Zeus wonders whether he should save Hector, and Athena objects
to that (131–87). When Achilles and Hector reach the springs for the fourth
time Zeus holds up the scales of fate and Hector's side sinks: at this, Apollo
instantly abandons him and Athena joins Achilles (188–223). The goddess persuades Hector to make a stand by taking on the appearance of his favourite
brother Deïphobus (224–46). Hector tries to strike a deal with Achilles before
fighting: the winner should return the corpse of the loser; Achilles violently
objects to this, then casts his spear and misses (247–88). Hector manages to
hit Achilles' shield, but his spear rebounds—and he realizes that Athena has
tricked him (289–305). Again he begs Achilles to spare his body after death, and
is refused; Achilles wounds him in the neck and, before dying, Hector predicts
Achilles' own death (306–66). The Achaeans draw near and stab Hector's corpse;
Achilles drags it behind his chariot (367–404). Priam and Hecuba lament the
death of their son (405–36). Andromache, who was weaving at home and making
arrangements for Hector to have a warm bath, hears the commotion outside,
rushes to the wall, and faints; she then laments Hector's death (437–515).

8–13 *Son of Peleus . . . fated to die*: Apollo's contemptuous speech alludes to
    Achilles' imminent death, and exposes the futility of his actions. 'Swift-
    footed' Achilles cannot catch up with a god, let alone kill him—in fact, it
    is Achilles who will soon die at the hands of Apollo, see notes to 21.276–8
    and 22.359–60.

27–31 *the star that rises in autumn . . . for wretched mortals*: Sirius, the brightest fixed
    star. It first becomes visible in the eastern horizon before dawn in mid-July,
    and the Greeks associated it with the intense heat of the summer months.

47 *Lycaon and Polydorus*: Achilles killed Lycaon at 21.34–135, and Polydorus
    at 20.407–18.

101–2 *because he urged me at the start . . . to lead the Trojans into the city*: cf. the
    debate between Polydamas and Hector at 18.243–313.

127 *"from a rock or an oak-tree"*: this expression seems to have been proverbial;
    its exact meaning is unclear.

170–2 *who has burnt the thigh-bones . . . on the city's heights*: Hector regularly
    sacrificed to Zeus, both on the mountain-tops of Ida and in the city of
    Troy. As a result, Zeus feels some obligation towards him.

183 *Tritogeneia*: see note to 4.515.

209–13 *the father held up his golden scales . . . and Phoebus Apollo left him*: the
    scales of Zeus are mentioned also at other crucial moments in the narrative,
    cf. esp. 8.68–74. Here they mark the moment when Hector's fate is sealed.

323 *that he had stripped from mighty Patroclus when he killed him*: cf. 17.125–97.

359–60 *on the day that Paris and Phoebus Apollo . . . beside the Scaean gates*: moments before dying, Hector describes Achilles' death with prophetic clarity. This is the most specific prediction of it in the whole *Iliad*, cf. note to 21.276–8.

437–46 *Now Hector's wife had not yet learnt . . . far away from baths*: at 6.490–3 Hector told Andromache to return home, see to the weaving, and supervise her servants. This is precisely what she is doing now.

460 *a maenad*: a frenzied female devotee of the god Dionysus.

490–504 *The day that orphans a child . . . filled with contentment*: affecting as this image of Astyanax's future is, what will actually happen to him is far worse; see note to 24.734–5.

BOOK TWENTY-THREE

Achilles and the Myrmidons lament over Patroclus (1–34). Achilles refuses to wash and eat; Patroclus' shade appears to him in a dream to demand a proper burial (35–107). At dawn the Achaeans make preparations for the funeral (108–60). After sacrificing sheep, cattle, horses, dogs, and twelve Trojan captives, Achilles lights the pyre and, because it fails to burn, prays to the winds for help; Iris summons them (161–225). After a night of lamentation Achilles finally falls asleep, but is woken up by the arrival of the Achaean leaders: he gives final instructions for the burial, and then brings out prizes for the funeral games (226–61). The contestants for the chariot-race get ready (262–361). The race is tense (362–447); the spectators Idomeneus and Locrian Ajax argue about who is in the lead (448–98). Prizes are awarded, after some disagreements are settled (499–650). Epeius beats Euryalus in the boxing contest (651–99). Ajax and Odysseus compete in wrestling: after a while Achilles interrupts the match, declaring it a draw (700–39). In the foot-race Locrian Ajax is in the lead, until Athena makes him slip on a pile of dung and grants victory to Odysseus; Antilochus comes last, but doubles his prize by flattering Achilles (740–96). Ajax, son of Telamon, and Diomedes compete in the armed duel: fearing for their lives, the Achaeans stop the contest (797–825). Polypoetes wins the throwing contest (826–49). Achilles offers two prizes for archery: for the man who hits a dove tied to a mast, and for the man who hits the string; Teucer forgets to pray to Apollo and hits the string, then Meriones shoots the dove as it flies away (850–83). Achilles awards first prize to Agamemnon for spear-throwing, without bothering to have a contest between him and Meriones (884–97).

23–4 *and I shall cut the throats . . . my anger at your death*: cf. 18.336–7 (with note).

46 *shorn my hair*: cutting one's hair in mourning was common practice in ancient Greece.

68 *He stood over Achilles' head . . . these words*: cf. note to 2.20.

71–4 *Bury me as quickly as you can . . . Hades of the wide gates*: here Patroclus implies that only after burial will he be able to join the shades of the dead; other Homeric passages, however, do not conform to this view.

85–8 *after Menoetius had brought me . . . angry over a game of knucklebones*: exile for homicide is common in the *Iliad*; the details of Patroclus' crime are mentioned only here.

91 *So may one and the same vessel hide the bones of us both*: later in the book Patroclus' ashes are stored in Achilles' hut, until he too has died, cf. 243–4 and 252–4.

140–51 *one more thought . . . to take with him instead*: there are other examples of young men offering their hair to their local river, usually in thanksgiving for their nurture; the practice features, for example, in Pausanias, *Description of Greece* 1.37.3 and 8.41.3. Here Achilles' gesture expresses the thought that he will soon die himself.

175–6 *with the bronze slew twelve noble sons . . . the cruel plan he had in his heart*: see note to 18.336–7.

184–91 *but the dogs never busied themselves . . . his sinews and limbs*: similarly, Thetis intervened to preserve Patroclus' body; see note to 19.353.

206 *the Ethiopians' land*: see note to 1.423.

245–8 *As for the grave-mound . . . after I have gone*: Achilles indicates that Achaeans should build a broader and higher mound when he dies too.

259 *prizes from his ships*: the funeral games are meant to honour Patroclus (cf. 23.646), and the prizes function as mementoes of his death (cf. 23.618–20 and 748). They are also material tokens of Achilles' greatest exploits. Several other funeral games are mentioned in Homer, cf. 23.630–1 and 678–80, as well as 22.162–6 (a simile) and *Odyssey* 24.85–92 (the games in honour of Achilles).

276–8 *for you know how far my horses surpass . . . who then handed them on to me*: on Achilles' horses, see notes to 16.149–54 and 17.195–6.

291–2 *and he led under his yoke the horses of Tros . . . Apollo saved their master*: on the horses of Tros, see notes to 5.222 and 5.268–70. Diomedes gains possession of them at 5.319–27.

353 *Achilles shook the lots, and out jumped the lot of Antilochus*: Achilles draws lots in order to establish the placing of contestants in the race. The contestant driving nearest to the post is best placed to win. For the practice of shaking lots out of a helmet, cf. 7.175–83.

441 *but you won't win a prize without a challenge on oath*: cf. 23.581–5, where Menelaus challenges Antilochus to swear that he has not used trickery to defeat him.

560 *I will give him the corslet that I took from Asteropaeus*: cf. 21.182–3.

630–45 *as when the Epeians made a burial for lord Amarynceus . . . among heroes*: cf. 11.699–702 where we are told that Neleus sent a four-horse chariot to compete at another contest in Elis.

679–80 *Mecisteus had long ago come to Thebes . . . all the Cadmeians*: in this Homeric version Oedipus dies at Thebes. The story that he died in Athens seems to be an Athenian myth.

684 *well-cut thongs made from the hide of a field-ox*: ancient Greek boxers bound their hands in leather thongs.

736 *share the prizes equally and go*: also ancient readers were at a loss as to how the prizes could be divided equally.

741–9 *a finely worked silver mixing-bowl . . . fastest in the swift foot-race*: as often, the poet draws attention to an object not by describing it in detail, but by telling its story. This particular bowl is linked to the capture and release of Lycaon, and functions as a reminder of his death at the hands of Achilles, cf. 21.34–135.

800 *the arms of Sarpedon, that Patroclus had taken from him*: again the prizes function as reminders of exploits described earlier in the poem, cf. 16.663–5.

808 *which I took from Asteropaeus*: cf. 23.560 (with note).

827–9 *that the mighty Eëtion used to throw . . . together with his other treasures*: another echo of Achilles' past exploits; for his killing of Eëtion, Andromache's father, see especially 6.413–28.

833–5 *its usefulness will last . . . it will be there for them*: the idea is that the iron will be used to make tools for the farmers, and that no other iron will be needed for five years. Modern scholars have worried that an isolated farm might not have had a forge, but it seems unlikely that Achilles would have worried about such practicalities: his speech is a display of largesse.

BOOK TWENTY-FOUR

Achilles cannot sleep; at dawn he drags Hector's corpse three times round the tomb of Patroclus, then leaves it there face-down in the dust (1–21). The gods take pity on Hector and debate whether Hermes should steal his body; after twelve days Zeus decides to send Thetis as a messenger to Achilles: obediently, she tells her son that he must release Hector's corpse (22–137). Zeus then sends Iris as a messenger to Priam; she finds the king in deepest grief (138–87). Following her orders, Priam tells his sons to prepare a wagon so that he may carry ransom to Achilles; Hecuba is alarmed by this plan, but Zeus sends a good omen (188–321). Hermes meets Priam on his way to Achilles' hut and escorts him there (322–467). When Priam appears, Achilles has just finished eating: the old man clasps his knees, kisses his hands in supplication, and Achilles pushes him gently away—they both weep (468–512). Achilles then raises Priam, recognizing in the old man an image of his own father (513–51). Priam asks for the immediate release of Hector's body; Achilles warns him not to provoke him, then makes arrangements for the body to be returned, apologizing to Patroclus (552–95). Achilles quotes to Priam the story of Niobe, and invites him to eat: after their meal the two men gaze at each other in wonder, then

Priam asks for a place to sleep and Achilles goes to bed with Briseïs (596–676). Hermes wakes up Priam and escorts him out of the Achaean camp; Cassandra sees him returning with Hector's body and spreads the news; Andromache and Hecuba come to meet him (677–717). Professional singers begin the lament for Hector, followed by Andromache, Hecuba, and Helen (718–75). The Trojans collect wood for nine days, and on the tenth they set light to the pyre; finally they hold a funeral feast for Hector (776–804).

29–30 *he had insulted the goddesses . . . fatal lust*: the only explicit reference to the judgement of Paris in the *Iliad*.

59–60 *one whom I myself | raised and nurtured*: this detail is mentioned only here, and seems designed to explain why Hera should intervene in favour of Thetis (of whom she was so suspicious at the beginning of the poem). Hera's upbringing of Thetis features in later texts (e.g. Apollonius, *Argonautica* 4.790–8). In a fragment from the early epic *Cypria*, Thetis refuses marriage with Zeus as a favour to Hera.

78–9 *between Samothrace | and rocky Imbros*: the poet displays his knowledge even of the depths of the sea, cf. note to 13.32.

163–5 *and his head . . . as he grovelled on the ground*: cf. 22.414.

308 *ruling from Mount Ida*: cf. note to 3.276.

324–6 *the four-wheeled wagon . . . swiftly through the city*: Idaeus drives a four-wheel wagon drawn by mules; Priam drives a light, two-wheel chariot drawn by horses.

480 *delusion*: cf. note to 19.91.

508 *Taking hold of the old man's hand he gently pushed him away*: Achilles' initial reaction is to push Priam aside, i.e. reject his supplication.

527–33 *There are two jars standing on Zeus' threshold . . . mortals*: these famous lines express the idea that mortals can either experience a mixture of good and evil, or undiluted evil; there are several references to these lines in later Greek literature.

544–6 *all that is bounded out to sea . . . supreme in wealth and in sons*: Achilles defines the southern (Lesbos), eastern (Phrygia), northern and western (Hellespont) boundaries of Priam's kingdom. In Homer, 'the Hellespont' is used of the sea west and north of Troy, not just the Dardanelles. *Macar*: the legendary founder and king of Lesbos.

602 *You must know that even lovely-haired Niobe thought of food*: the poet selects only the most relevant aspects of the story of Niobe, and seems to have adapted it quite radically so as to turn it into a close parallel for Priam's situation. The main point of the story is to invite Priam to eat, even in his bereavement: Achilles himself refused to eat after the death of Patroclus (cf. 19.205–14 and 314–55). He is now imparting a lesson he has only just learned.

616　*Achelous*: here the word refers to the water flowing from the rock identified as Niobe, i.e. her tears. On Achelous as a synonym for water, cf. note to 21.194–5.

640　*rolling in the dung in the stalls of my courtyard*: cf. 22.414 and 24.162–5. Similarly, Achilles reacted to Patroclus' death with an act of self-defilement: 18.22–7.

649　*in a bantering tone*: it was normal practice to offer guests a bed under the portico. In this case, it is hard to see how Priam could escape the notice of night-visitors when sleeping there: the bantering draws attention to this. Achilles knows that his guest must leave by night (and this is what Priam actually does); his speech thus hints at the reasons for Priam's imminent departure, while still making a hospitable gesture.

682　*he stood over Priam's head*: see note to 2.20.

734–5　*or else some Achaean | will seize and hurl you from the walls*: Astyanax will indeed die in this manner. The lost cyclic poems *Iliupersis* and *Little Iliad* described in detail how Astyanax was hurled from the city walls; the episode was also the subject of an early seventh-century vase painting; for a later account, cf. Euripides, *Trojan Women* 721–5 and 1134–5.

765　*this is now the twentieth year*: twenty is a standard figure in Homer, here it means 'a long time', 'more than ten years'. The events narrated in the *Iliad* take place in the tenth year of the Trojan War; Helen's reckoning seems to take account of some episodes that happened between her abduction and the beginning of the war itself. Odysseus returns home in the twentieth year since he left, according to the *Odyssey*: that chronology is not strictly compatible with this one.

INDEX OF PERSONAL NAMES

IN this translation Greek names are generally Latinized (e.g. Achilles) and the Latin forms are sometimes Anglicized (e.g. Priam rather than Priamus); since practice in the treatment of Greek names in English is not fixed, a degree of flexibility allows familiar forms to be used in preference to a strictly consistent, but more artificial system.

The index aims to provide full guidance to readers, but does not list every mention of each character. References below are to the book and line number in the translation.

Abantes, a people of Euboea 2.536–44, 4.464

Abarbareë, a river-nymph 6.22

Abas, a Trojan 5.148

Abii, a distant people 13.6

Ablerus, a Trojan 6.32

Acamas (1), a Trojan 2.823, 11.60, 12.100, 14.476–89, 16.342

Acamas (2), a captain of the Thracians 2.844, 5.462, 6.8

Acessamenus, a Thracian 21.142

Achaeans, a general name for all those fighting against the Trojans and their allies 1.2, 5, and *passim. See also* Argives and Danaans

ACHILLES, son of Peleus and Thetis, grandson of Aeacus, leader of the Myrmidons 1.1, 7, 2.4, 220, 239, 241, 377, 685, 688, 769, 875, 4.412, 5.788, 6.99, 414, 423, 7.113, 228, 8.224, 9.106, 164, 166, 10.107, 404, 11.8, 104, 112, 625, 652–4, 656, 664, 762, 806, 831, 12.10, 13.324, 348, 14.50, 139, 366, 15.64, 68, 77, 402, 16.709, 837, 854, 860, 17.78, 121, 186, 195, 402, 504, 654, 691, 701, 18.305–9, 19.295, 20.26, 42, 125–31, 139, 21.550, 22.92, 113, 446, 455; rouses the Achaeans 19.4–53; and Aeneas 20.160–350; quarrels with Agamemnon and refuses to fight 1.121–91, 223–44, 292–305, 489–92; and Agamemnon's heralds 1.329–44; still refuses to fight after Agamemnon sends him an embassy 9.186–668; is reconciled with Agamemnon 19.55–281, 304–8; and Agenor 21.583–605; and Apollo 21.596–605, 22.7–24; has new armour forged for him 18.478–615; arms himself 19.364–98; and Asteropaeus 21.139–204; and Athena 1.194–220; begins to take an interest in the fighting 11.599–615; returns to the fighting 20.75–8; and Hector 20.423–54, 22.131–404; outrages Hector's body 23.21–6, 182–3, 24.15–18, 50–2; agrees to ransom Hector's body to Priam 24.471–676; and his horses 19.399–424; and Iris 18.167–201; and Lycaon 21.34–128; arms the Myrmidons 16.155–209; Nestor remembers him 11.772–803; allows Patroclus to fight in his place 16.2–129; mourns Patroclus 18.2–35, 343–54, 19.309–58, 23.8–23; and Patroclus' ghost 23.59–107; conducts funeral rites for Patroclus 23.4–257; holds funeral games for Patroclus 23.259–897; proposes solution to plague 1.54–91; and Thetis 1.348–427, 18.69–137, 19.6–36, 24.121–43; shows himself to the Trojans 18.203–47; kills Trojans and encourages the Achaeans 20.351–503; kills Trojans 21.1–210, 520–33; 21.139–204; and Xanthus/Scamander 21.212–328; 605, 22.7–24; prays to Zeus 16.220–56

Acrisius, father of Danaë 14.319

Actaeë, a sea-nymph 18.41

Actor (1), father of Menoetius 11.785, 16.14

Actor (2), son of Azeus 2.513

Actor (3), supposed father of the Moliones, Cteatus and Eurytus 2.621, 11.750, 13.186, 23.638

Actor (4), father of Echeclus 16.189

Adamas, a Trojan 12.140, 13.560–75, 759, 771

Admetus, father of Eumelus 2.713, 23.289, 391, 532

Adrestus (1), king of Sicyon 2.572, 5.412, 14.121, 23.347

Adrestus (2), a captain of the men of Adresteia 2.280

Adrestus (3), a Trojan 6.37–65

Adrestus (4), another Trojan 16.694

Aeacus, grandfather of Achilles 2.860, 874, and *passim*

Aegaeon, a monster, also called Briareus by the gods 1.404

Aegeus, father of Theseus 2.265

Aegialeia, wife of Diomedes 5.412–15

AENEAS, son of Aphrodite and Anchises 2.820–1, 5.247–8, 534, 11.58, 12.98–9, 14.425, 15.332; fights Achaeans 5.541–60, 564, 572–3, 17.344; and Achilles 20.160–291, 344–50; and Aphareus 13.541–4; and Aphrodite 5.312–17, 343–6, 377–8; and Apollo 5.432–3, 445–53, 512–18, 17.323–33, 20.79–113; and Ares 5.467–8; and Deïphobus 13.459–67; and Diomedes 5.297–311; and Glaucus 16.536; and Hector 17.334–41, 484–93, 512–13, 533, 754–9; and Helenus 6.75–7; his horses 5.263–73, 323–7, 8.108, 23.292; and Idomeneus 13.468–505; and Meriones 16.608–25; and Pandarus 5.166–78, 217–38; and Poseidon 20.292–340

Aenius, a Paeonian 21.210

Aeolus, father of Sisyphus 6.154

Aepytus, an Arcadian of former times 2.604

Aesepus, a Trojan 6.21–8

Aesyetes (1), a Trojan prince of former times 2.793

Aesyetes (2), father of Alcathous 13.427

Aesymnus, an Achaean 11.303

Aethe, a mare of Agamemnon's 23.295, 408, 525

Aethices, a people of Thessaly 2.744

Aethon, one of Hector's horses 8.185

Aethre, maid to Helen 3.144

Aetolians, a people of W. Greece 2.638–43, 4.527, 5.843, 9.529–99, 13.218, 15.282, 23.471, 633

Agacles, father of Epeigeus 16.571

Agamede, daughter of Augeias, wife of Mulius (1) 11.740

AGAMEMNON, son of Atreus, brother of Menelaus, king of Argos and Mycenae, leader of the Trojan expedition 1.24, 90, 94, 411, 442, 2.221, 402, 477–83, 576, 3.81–3, 118, 178, 5.38, 537, 6.33, 7.57, 162, 313–15, 470, 8.78, 9.672–5, 11.661, 13.112, 14.29, 380, 16.26, 58, 273, 17.249, 18.111, 257, 19.35, 51, 172, 23.36, 110, 155, 296, 486, 887, 24.654, 687: orders the Achaeans to stay and fight 2.441–44; reviews the Achaean troops 4.223–400; urges the Achaeans to action 8.218–44; quarrels with Achilles 1.130–87, 319–25; promises gifts for Achilles 9.120–61; is reconciled with Achilles 19.55–281; and the two Ajaxes 4.272–91; arms himself 11.15–46; quarrels with Calchas 1.102–20; admits his delusion 9.114–19, 19.76–144; and Diomedes 4.368–400, 10.233–9; and the Dream 2.6–75; identified by Helen 3.178–80; and Idaeus 7.405–11; and Idomeneus 4.257–71; and Menelaus 10.42–71; names Menelaus victor 3.455–60; and the wounded Menelaus 4.148–97; rebukes Menelaus 5.53–65; and Nestor 1.285–91, 2.369–93, 4.313–25, 10.3–127, 14.41–81; and Odysseus 4.336–63, 14.103–8, 19.184–97; and Poseidon 14.139–46; recommends retreat 2.100–41, 9.9–28; and Teucer 8.278–91; fights and kills Trojans 11.91–180, 231–83; prays to Zeus 2.411–18, 3.267–94, 19.252–65

Agapenor, a captain of the Arcadians 2.610

Agasthenes, an Elean 2.624

Agastrophus, a Trojan 11.338

Agathon, a son of Priam 24.249

Agauë, a sea-nymph 18.42

Agelaus (1), a Trojan 8.257

Agelaus (2), an Achaean 11.302

Agenor, son of Antenor 4.467–9, 11.59, 12.93, 13.490, 598–600, 14.425, 15.340, 16.535, 20.475, 21.545–600

Aglaea, mother of Nireus 2.672

Agrius, an ancestor of Diomedes 14.117

Aïdoneus, another name for Hades 5.190, 20.61

Ajax, son of Oïleus, captain of the Locrians 2.527, 13.66–75, 201–5, 701–18, 14.442–8, 520–2, 16.330–4, 17.256–7, 23.473–93, 754–83. Often referred to, together with the son of Telamon, as 'the pair called Ajax'

AJAX, son of Telamon, from Salamis 1.138, 145, 2.406, 528, 557, 768, 4.273, 285, 5.519, 7.164, 321, 8.79, 224, 330, 9.169, 223, 10.53, 110, 228, 11.7, 526, 542, 12.342, 349, 13.46, 76–80, 197–202, 321, 709, 14.511, 15.249, 16.358–9, 555, 17.102, 229, 531, 668, 732, 752, 18.157–64, 23.838, 842; and Acamas 6.5–11; defends the Achaean ships 15.674–88, 727–46, 16.101–22; defends the Achaean tower 12.365–405; encourages the Achaeans 12.265–77, 15.501–13; and Amphius 5.610–26; arms himself and fights Hector 7.206–312; and Diomedes 23.811–23; and Hector 7.183–99, 13.190–3, 809–32, 14.402–20, 15.415–18; identified by Helen 3.229; and Menelaus 11.464–71, 17.115–39, 237–45, 626–55, 715–21; and Odysseus 9.622–42, 23.708–39; and Polydamas 14.459–74; and Simoeisius 4.473–89; and Teucer 8.267–72, 15.436–77; surrounded by Trojans 11.544–95; kills Trojans 11.485–97, 17.278–85, 293–315, 356–61

Alastor (1), a captain of the Pylians 4.295, 8.333, 13.422

Alastor (2), a Lycian 5.677

Alastor (3), father of Tros (2) 20.463

Alcandrus, a Lycian 5.678

Alcathous, a Trojan 12.93, 13.427–96

Alcestis, wife of Admetus, mother of Eumelus 2.714–15

Alcimedon, a captain of the Myrmidons 16.197, 17.467–506, also called Alcimus 19.392, 24.474, 574

Alcimus, follower of Achilles 19.392

Alcmaon, an Achaean 12.394–6

Alcmene, loved by Zeus, mother of Heracles 14.323

Alcyone, another name for Cleopatra

Alegenor, father of Promachus, 14.503

ALEXANDER, another name for Paris

Aloeus, father of Otus and Ephialtes 5.386

Altes, king of the Leleges 21.86

Althaea, mother of Meleager 9.555

Amarynceus, an Epeian 23.360

Amatheia, a sea-nymph 18.48

Amazons, a tribe of warlike women 3.189, 6.186

Amisodarus, a Lycian, father of Atymnius and Maris 16.328–9

Amopaon, a Trojan 8.276

Amphiclus, a Trojan 16.313

Amphidamas, a man of Cythera 10.268

Amphimachus (1), a captain of the Epeians 2.620, 13.185

Amphimachus (2), a captain of the Carians 2.870–5

Amphinome, a sea-nymph 18.44

Amphion, a captain of the Epeians 13.692

Amphithoë, a sea-nymph 18.42

Amphitryon, human father of Heracles 5.392

Amphius (1), a captain of the men of Adresteia 2.830

Amphius (2), a man of Paesus 5.612–22

Amphoterus, a Trojan 16.415

Amyntor, father of Phoenix 9.448, 10.266

Ancaeus (1), a former opponent of Nestor 23.365

Ancaeus (2), father of Agapenor, 2.609

Anchialus, an Achaean 5.609

Anchises, a Trojan prince, father of Aeneas 2.819–21, 5.248, 268–72

Andraemon, a captain of the Aetolians 2.638

ANDROMACHE, wife of Hector, daughter of Eëtion, mother of Astyanax 8.187, 17.208; and Hector 6.371–502; learns of Hector's death, laments for him 22.437–514, 24.723–45

Anteia, wife of Proetus 6.160–5

Antenor, a Trojan elder 2.822, 3.148, 203, 262, 312, 5.69, 6.299, 7.347–57

11.262, 12.99, 14.463, 473, 15.517, 20.396, 21.546, 579

Anthemion, father of Simoeisius 4.474

ANTILOCHUS, son of Nestor 6.32, 13.93, 479, 14.513, 16.317–20, 17.653–5; and Achilles 18.2–34; and Aeneas 5.565–75; and Adamas 13.560–5; and Asius' charioteer 13.396–401; in the chariot-race 21.301, 353, 402–41, 514–27, 541–611; and Echepolus 4.457–62; fights Trojans 13.550–9; in the foot-race 23.756, 785–98; and Hector 15.583–91; and Hypsenor 13.418–20; and Melanippus 15.572–82; and Menelaus 15.568–71, 17.685–704; and Mydon 5.580–9; and Nestor 23.306–50

Antimachus, father of Peisander and Hippolochus 11.123–5

Antiphates, a Trojan 12.191

Antiphonus, a son of Priam 24.250

Antiphus (1), a captain of the men of Cos 2.678

Antiphus (2), a son of Priam 4.489, 11.101–19

Antiphus (3), a captain of the Maeonians 2.864

Aphareus, an Achaean 9.83

APHRODITE, goddess of love, daughter of Zeus and Dione 3.54, 64, 5.131–2, 759, 820–1, 9.389, 19.282, 20.105, 24.699; and Aeneas 2.820, 5.312–18, 20.209; and Ares 5.355–63; and Athena and Hera 5.422–5, 21.416–26; and Diomedes 5.330–51, 458, 883; and Dione 5.370–417; and other gods 20.40; and Hector's corpse 23.185–91; and Helen 3.383–425; and Hera 14.188–224; and Iris 5.352–69; and Paris 3.374–82; 4.10–12; 5.247–8, 312–17; and Zeus 5.427–30

Apisaon (1), a Paeonian 17.348

Apisaon (2), a Trojan 11.578, 582

APOLLO, god of prophecy, music, and disease, son of Zeus and Leto, brother of Artemis 1.14, 21, 72, 315, 373, 438, 603, 2.371, 766, 827, 4.101, 5.509, 760, 7.81, 272, 452, 8.311, 9.405, 560, 15.441, 521, 16.94, 844, 17.118,

18.454, 20.138, 21.515–17, 538–9, 22.220, 359, 24.605–6; deceives the Achaeans 21.599–605, 22.7–20; carries the aegis 15.307–27; and Aeneas 17.322–34, 20.79–85, 103–8, 23.292; rescues Aeneas 5.344–6, 445–50; and Agenor 21.545–9, 596–8; and Ares 5.454–9; and Athena 7.20–42; prayed to by Chryses 1.35–42, 450–7; and Diomedes 5.433–42, 23.383–8; destroys the Achaean ditch 15.355–66; prayed to by Glaucus 16.513–29; fights with gods and goddesses 20.67–8; rebukes the other gods 24.32–54; and Hector 16.715–26, 17.71–81, 582–90, 20.375–8, 22.203–4, 213; rescues Hector 11.363–4, 20.443–51; preserves Hector's body 23.188–91, 24.18–21, 758–9; and Patroclus 16.700–11, 788–804; sends plague on the Achaeans 1.43–53; and Poseidon 21.435–78; and Teucer 23.863–5; encourages the Trojans 4.507–14, 10.515–18; plans to destroy the Achaean wall 12.17–34; watches mortals fighting 7.58–61; and Xanthus/Scamander 21.228–32; and Zeus 16.666–81; ordered by Zeus to rouse Hector 15.55–62, 220–62

Apseudes, a sea-nymph 18.46

Arcadians, a people of central Greece 2.603–11, 7.134

Arcesilaus, a captain of the Boeotians 2.495, 15.329

Archelochus, a Trojan 2.823, 12.100, 14.464–8

Archeptolemus, a Trojan 8.128, 312–15

Areïlycus, a Trojan 16.308

Areïthous (1), Boeotian club-wielder 7.10, 137, 146

Areïthous (2), a Thracian 20.487

ARES, god of war, son of Zeus and Hera 2.110, 512–15, 3.128, 4.439, 5.289, 563, 699, 757, 762, 824, 7.146, 208–10, 241, 9.82, 13.298–300, 444, 16.543, 613, 17.210, 18.516, 20.38, 51, 152, 22.267, 24.260, 498; and Aphrodite 5.355–63; and Apollo 5.454–9; his son Ascalaphus

is killed 13.518–25, 15.110–20; and
  Athena 5.30–6, 15.127–42, 21.391–
  414; fights Diomedes and complains
  to Zeus 5.827–906; imprisoned by
  giants 5.385–91; encourages the
  Trojans 5.462–70, 507–13, 702–4;
  leads the Trojans 5.592–4
Aretaon, a Trojan 6.31
Aretus, a Trojan 17.494–519
Argeas, father of Polymelus 16.417
Argives, a general name for all those
  fighting against the Trojans and their
  allies 1.79, 119, and passim
Ariadne, daughter of Minos 18.592
Arion, Adrestus' racehorse 23.347
Arisbas, father of Leiocritus 17.345
ARTEMIS, goddess, daughter
  of Zeus and Leto, sister of
  Apollo: and Aeneas 5. 447–8; and
  Andromache's mother 6.428; rebukes
  Apollo 21.471–7; and Briseïs 19.59;
  fights with gods 20.39, 71; thrashed
  by Hera 21.480–96; and Niobe's
  daughters 24.606; and Laodameia
  6.205; and Oeneus 9.533–42; and
  Polymele 16.183; and Strophius 5.51–3
Asaeus, an Achaean 11.301
Ascalaphus, a son of Ares, captain of the
  Minyans 2.512, 9.82, 13.478, 518–27,
  15.111
Ascanius, a Trojan ally 2.862, 13.792
Asclepius, healer, father of Machaon and
  Podaleirius 2.731, 4.194, 204, 11.518,
  614, 14.2
Asius (1), from Percote 2.837, 12.95–7,
  110–36, 162–72, 13.384–93, 760, 771
Asius (2), a brother of Hecuba 16.717
Assaracus, son of Tros (1) 20.232
Asteropaeus, a captain of the
  Paeonians 12.102, 17.217, 351–2,
  21.140–204
Astyalus, a Trojan 6.29
Astyanax, son of Hector and Andromache,
  also called Scamandrius 6.400–2,
  466–81, 22.500–14
Astynous (1), a Trojan 5.144
Astynous (2), another Trojan 15.455
Astyoche, mother of Ascalaphus and
  Ialmenus 2.513
Astyocheia, mother of Tlepolemus 2.658

Astypylus, a Paeonian 21.209
ATHENA, goddess, daughter of
  Zeus 1.400, 2.279, 547, 3.439, 4.8,
  390, 439, 541, 5.61, 256, 290, 405, 510,
  908, 6.88, 293, 300, 7.154, 8.287, 9.254,
  390, 10.516, 11.45, 714, 721, 729, 758,
  13.128, 14.178, 15.71, 613, 17.398,
  18.217–18, 311, 516, 20.33, 95–6,
  115, 146, 192, 21.284, 22.270, 23.774,
  24.100; helps the Achaeans 15.668–73,
  17.544–52; encourages the Achaeans
  with the aegis 2.446–52; and
  Achilles 1.194–222, 18.204–14,
  20.438–40, 21.214–23, 276–7, 304;
  and Aphrodite 21.423–33; and
  Apollo 7.17–43; and Ares 5.29–36,
  765–6, 853–6, 15.123–42, 21.392–415;
  and Diomedes 5.1–8, 115–32, 793–
  863; prayed to by Diomedes 10.283–
  95; fights with the other gods 20.48,
  69; and Hector 21.238–47, 22.299,
  445–6; and Hera 2.156–65, 4.20–3,
  5.713–47, 8.351–91, 426–31, 20.314,
  21.419–22; interferes in the chariot
  race 23.388–400; and Iris 8.413–24;
  and Menelaus 17.553–70; and
  Odysseus 2.166–81, 11.437–8;
  prayed to by Odysseus 10.277–82,
  461–4, 23.769–72; prayed to by
  Theano 6.305–11; persuades the
  Trojans to break the truce 4.64–104;
  watches mortals 7.58–61; and
  Zeus 5.420–5, 8.30–40, 444–60,
  19.341–51, 21.177–87
Athenians, the people of Athens 2.551,
  558, 4.328, 13.195, 689, 15.337
Atreus, father of Agamemnon and
  Menelaus 1.7, 11, and passim
Atrytone, a title of Athena 2.157, 5.115,
  714, 10.284, 21.420
Atymnius (1), a Trojan 16.317
Atymnius (2), father of Mydon 5.581
Augeias, king of Elis 11.701, 739
Autolycus, grandfather of
  Odysseus 10.266
Automedon, Patroclus' charioteer 9.209,
  16.145–52, 219, 472–4, 684, 864–6,
  17.429–31, 452, 459–83, 498–539,
  19.392–6, 23.563–5, 24.474–5, 574–5,
  625–6

Autonous (1), an Achaean 11.301

Autonous (2), a Trojan 16.694

Autophonus, father of Polyphontes 4.395

Axylus, a man from Arisbe 6.12–19

Azeus, father of Actor (2) 2.513

Balius, one of Achilles' horses 16.149, 19.400

Bathycles, a Myrmidon 16.594

Bellerophon, grandfather of Glaucus 6.155–96

Bias (1), a captain of the Pylians 4.296

Bias (2), a captain of the Athenians 13.691

Bias (3), father of Dardanus (2) and Laogonus (2) 20.460

Bienor, a Trojan 11.92

Boeotians, a people of Greece 2.494, 510, 526, 5.710, 13.685, 700, 14.477, 15.330, 17.597

Borus (1), father of Phaestus 5.43

Borus (2), husband of Polydore 16.177

Briareus, a monster, the gods' name for Aegaeon 1.403

Briseïs, daughter of Briseus 1.184, 323, 346, 2.689, 9.107, 19.246, 261, 282–301, 24.676

Briseus, father of Briseïs 1.392, 9.132, 274

Bucolion, father of Aesepus and Pedasus 6.23–5

Cadmeians, the people of Thebes 4.385–98, 5.804–8, 10.288, 23.680

Caeneus, a Lapith 1.264

Calaesius, Axylus' charioteer 6.18

Calchas, Achaean seer 1.69–101, 105–20, 2.300, 322–33, 13.45, 70

Caletor (1), a Trojan 15.419–21

Caletor (2), father of Aphareus 13.541

Callianassa, a sea-nymph 18.46

Callianeira, a sea-nymph 18.44

Capaneus, father of Sthenelus 2.564

Capys, father of Anchises 20.239

Carians, a people of Asia Minor 2.867, 4.142, 10.428

Cassandra, daughter of Priam 13.366, 24.699–706

Castianeira, mother of Gorgythion 8.305

Castor, brother of Helen 3.237

Caucones, a people of Asia Minor 10.429, 20.329

Ceas, father of Troezenus 2.847

Cebriones, a bastard son of Priam, Hector's charioteer 8.318–19, 11.521–31, 12.91–2, 13.790, 16.727–8, 738–81

Centaurs, wild creatures 1.268, 2.743

Cephallenians, people from the coast of W. Greece and the islands facing it 2.631, 4.330

Chalcodon, father of Elphenor 2.541

Charis, wife of Hephaestus 18.382–92

Charops, a Trojan 11.427

Charopus, father of Nireus 2.672

Cheiron, a Centaur, Achilles' tutor 4.219, 11.832, 16.143, 19.390

Chersidamas, a Trojan 11.423

Chimaera, a monster 6.179, 16.329

Chromis, a captain of the Mysians 2.858

Chromius (1), a captain of the Pylians 4.290

Chromius (2), a Lycian 5.677

Chromius (3), a son of Priam 5.160

Chromius (4), a Trojan 8.275

Chromius (5), another Trojan 17.218, 494

Chryseïs, daughter of Chryses 1.112, 143, 182, 310, 369, 439

Chryses, priest of Apollo, father of Chryseïs 1.11–42, 370, 442, 450–6

Chrysothemis, daughter of Agamemnon 9.145, 287

Ciconians, a people of Thrace 2.846

Cilicians, the people of Eëtion 6.397, 415

Cinyras, a lord of Cyprus 11.19–23

Cisses, father of Theano 11.224–6

Cleitus, a Trojan 15.445–53

Cleobulus, a Trojan 16.330

Cleopatra, wife of Meleager, also called Alcyone 9.556–65, 590–5

Clonius, a captain of the Boeotians 2.495, 15.340

Clymene (1), maid to Helen 3.144

Clymene (2), a sea-nymph 18.47

Clytemnestra, wife of Agamemnon 1.113

Clytius (1), a Trojan elder 3.147, 20.238

Clytius (2), father of Dolops 11.302

Clytomedes, a former opponent of Nestor 23.634

Coeranus (1), a Lycian 5.677

Coeranus (2), Meriones' charioteer
 17.610–19
Confusion, a goddess 18.535
Coön, a son of Antenor 11.248–63
Copreus, herald and father of Periphetes
 15.639
Coronus, father of Leonteus 2.746
Courage, a goddess 5.740
Creion, father of Lycomedes 9.84
Crethon, an Achaean 5.541–60
Croesmus, a Trojan 15.523
Cronus, deposed father of Zeus 1.398,
 405, and passim
Cteatus, father of Amphimachus
 2.620–1
Curetes, a people of Aetolia 9.529–51, 589
Cymodoce, a sea-nymph 18.39
Cymothoë, a sea-nymph 18.41
Cypris, a title of Aphrodite 5.330, 422,
 458, 760, 883

Daedalus, a Cretan craftsman 18.592
Daetor, a Trojan 8.275
Damastor, father of Tlepomenus (2)
 16.416
Damasus, a Trojan ally 12.183
Danaans, a general name for all those
 who fought against the Trojans and
 their allies 1.42, 56, and passim
Danaë, mother of Perseus 14.319
Dardanians, descendants of Dardanus,
 Trojans led by Aeneas 2.819, 3.456,
 22.194, 413, and passim
Dardanus (1), a former king of
 Troy 2.701, 3.303, 5.789, 20.215–19
Dardanus (2), a Trojan 20.460
Dares, a Trojan 5.9, 27
Dawn, a goddess 1.477, 2.48, 6.175, 8.1,
 9.707, 11.1, 19.1, 23.109, 227, 24.12,
 695, 788
Death, a god 14.231, 16.454, 672, 682
Deïcoön, a Trojan 5.534
Deïochus, an Achaean 15.341
Deïopetes, a Trojan 11.420
Deïphobus, a son of Priam 12.94,
 13.156–66, 258, 402–16, 446–68, 490,
 516–39, 758, 770, 781, 22.227–46,
 294–9, 24.251
Deïpylus, a companion of Sthenelus 5.325
Deïpyrus, an Achaean 9.83, 13.478

Deisenor, a Trojan 17.217
Delusion, a goddess 9.504–5, 511, 19.88,
 91, 126, 128
Demeter, goddess of grain 5.500,
 14.326, 21.76
Democoön, a bastard son of Priam 4.499
Demolion, a Trojan 20.395
Demuchus, a Trojan 20.457
Deucalion (1), father of Idomeneus, a
 former king of Crete 13.451
Deucalion (2), a Trojan 20.478–83
Dexamene, a sea-nymph 18.44
Diocles, father of Crethon and
 Orsilochus 5.542–9
Diomede, Achilles' concubine 9.665
DIOMEDES, son of Tydeus, king of
 Argos 2.563, 5.1, 225, 232, 376, 413,
 519, 782, 881, 6.306, 7.163, 8.115,
 194, 11.373–4, 660, 16.25, 74, 21.396,
 23.472; advises against accepting
 Priam's proposal 7.399–404; and
 Aeneas 5.302–10, 432–5; and
 Agamemnon 4.365–421, 9.31–49,
 696–711, 10.234–47, 14.109–32; and
 Ajax son of Telamon 23.812–25;
 and Aphrodite 5.330–51; and
 Apollo 5.436–44, 23.383–4; and
 Ares 5.846–68; and Athena 5.793–839,
 10.509–11, 23.388–90; prays to
 Athena 5.114–32, 10.283–95;
 and Axylus 6.12–19; in the
 chariot-race 23.290–2, 377–90;
 and Glaucus 6.119–236; and
 Hector 5.596–606, 8.160–71, 532–8,
 11.345–67; and Nestor 8.134–56,
 9.53–60, 10.150–79, 219–26; and
 Odysseus 8.91–6, 10.248–98, 340–579,
 11.312–19; and Pandarus 5.277–96;
 and Paris 11.375–400; and
 Sthenelus 4.410–18, 5.242–74, 319–30;
 kills Trojans 5.134–65, 11.320–35
Dione, a goddess, mother of Aphrodite
 5.370–4, 381–417
Dionysus, a god, son of Zeus and Semele
 6.132–7, 14.325
Diores, a captain of the Epeians 2.622,
 4.517–25
Dius, a son of Priam 24.251
Dolon, a Trojan 10.314–457, 478, 570
Dolopians, a people of Phthia 9.484

Dolopion, priest of Scamander in
    Troy 5.77
Dolops (1), an Achaean 11.302
Dolops (2), a Trojan 15.525–38
Doris, a sea-nymph 18.45
Doryclus, a bastard son of Priam 11.489
Doto, a sea-nymph 18.43
Draceus, a captain of the Epeians 13.692
Dresus, a Trojan 6.20
Dryas (1), a Lapith 1.263
Dryas (2), father of Lycurgus (1) 6.130
Dryops, a Trojan 20.455
Dymas, father of Hecuba 16.718
Dynamene, a sea-nymph 18.43

Echecles, a Myrmidon 16.189
Echeclus (1), a Trojan killed by
    Patroclus 16.694
Echeclus (2) a Trojan killed by
    Achilles 20.474
Echemmon, a son of Priam 5.160
Echepolus (1), a Trojan 4.458
Echepolus (2), king of Sicyon 23.299
Echius (1), father of Mecisteus 8.333
Echius (2), an Achaean 15.339
Echius (3), a Lycian 16.416
Eëriboea, stepmother of Otus and
    Ephialtes 5.389
Eëtion (1), king of Thebe, father of
    Andromache 1.366, 6.395–6, 416,
    8.187, 9.188, 16.153, 17.575, 22.472,
    479, 23.827
Eëtion (2), a guest-friend of Priam's
    family 21.413
Eileithyiae, goddesses of childbirth,
    daughters of Hera 11.270, 16.187
Eïoneus, an Achaean 7.11
Elasus, a Trojan 16.696
Elatus, a Trojan 6.33
Eleians, the people of Elis 11.671–86
Elephenor, a captain of the
    Abantes 2.540, 4.463
Eneti, a people of Paphlagonia 2.852
Enienes, a people of Dodona 2.749
Eniopeus, Hector's charioteer 8.120
Ennomus (1), a bird-seer, captain of the
    Mysians 2.858, 17.218
Ennomus (2), a Trojan 11.422
Enops (1), father of Satnius 14.443–5
Enops (2), father of Thestor 16.402

Enops (3), father of Clytomedes 23.634
Enyalius, another name for Ares 2.651,
    7.166, 8.264, 17.259, 18.309, 20.69,
    22.132
Enyeus, king of Skyros 9.668
Enyo, goddess of war 5.333, 592
Epaltes, a Lycian 16.415
Epeians, a people of the W.
    Peloponnese 2.619, 4.537, 11.688–
    761, 13.686, 691, 15.519, 23.630, 632
Epeigeus, a Myrmidon 16.570–80
Epeius, a boxer 23.665–75, 679–97,
    838–40
Ephialtes, a giant 5.383
Ephyri, a northern people 13.302
Epistrophus (1), a captain of the
    Phocians 2.517
Epistrophus (2), a man of
    Lyrnessus 2.692
Epistrophus (3), a captain of the
    Halizones 2.856
Erechtheus, former king of Athens 2.547
Ereuthalion, an Arcadian 4.319, 7.136, 149
Erichthonius, a former king of
    Troy 20.219
Eriopis, wife of Oïleus 13.697
Erylaus, a Trojan 16.411
Erymas (1), a Trojan killed by
    Idomeneus 16.345
Erymas (2), a Trojan killed by
    Patroclus 16.415
Eteocles, a Theban, son of
    Oedipus 4.386
Ethiopians, a distant people 1.428, 23.206
Euaemon, father of Eurypylus (1) 2.736
Euchenor, an Achaean 13.663–72
Eudorus, a captain of the Myrmidons,
    son of Hermes 16.179–86
Euenus (1), father of Mynes and
    Epistrophus 2.693
Euenus (2), father of Marpessa 9.557
Euippus, a Lycian 16.417
Eumedes, father of Dolon 10.315
Eumelus, a captain of the Thessalians
    from Pherae 2.714, 764, 23.288, 354,
    379, 386, 480, 559, 565
Euneus, king of Lemnos 7.468–71,
    23.746
Euphemus, a captain of the Ciconians
    2.846

Euphetes, from Ephyre by the river Selleïs 15.532

Euphorbus, a Trojan 16.808–15, 17.11–60, 81

Europa, *see* Phoenix (2)

Euryalus, a captain of the men of the Argolid 2.565, 6.20, 23.677–99

Eurybates (1), Agamemnon's herald 1.320, 9.170

Eurybates (2), Odysseus' herald 2.184

Eurymedon (1), an attendant of Agamemnon 4.228

Eurymedon (2), an attendant of Nestor 8.114, 11.60

Eurynome, daughter of Ocean 18.398–9, 405

Eurypylus (1), a captain of the Ormenian Thessalians 2.736, 5.76–83, 6.36, 7.167, 8.265, 11.575–93, 809–48

Eurypylus (2), king of Cos 2.677

Eurystheus, former king of Mycenae 8.363, 15.640, 19.123, 133

Eurytus (1), from Oechalia 2.596, 730

Eurytus (2), one of the two Moliones 2.621

Eussorus, father of Acamas (2) 6.8

Exadius, a Lapith 1.264

Furies, vengeful Underworld goddesses 9.454, 571, 15.204, 19.87, 259, 418, 21.412

Galateia, a sea-nymph 18.49

Ganymedes, a son of Tros 5.266, 20.232

Gerenian, a title of Nestor 2.336, 433, 601, and *passim*

Glauce, a sea-nymph 18.39

Glaucus (1), Lycian, cousin of Sarpedon 2.876–7, 6.119–236, 7.13, 12.102–4, 309–32, 387–93, 14.426, 16.492–547, 593–601, 17.140–82, 216

Glaucus (2), father of Bellerophon 6.154–5

Gorgon, a monster 5.741, 8.349, 11.36

Gorgythion, a son of Priam 8.303–8

Gouneus, captain of the men of Dodona 2.478

Graces, goddesses 5.338, 14.269, 17.51

Gyrtias, father of Hyrtius 14.512

Hades, god of the Underworld, brother of Zeus and Poseidon; also the Underworld itself 1.3, 3.32 and *passim*

Haemon, a captain of the Pylians 4.296

Halië, a sea-nymph 18.40

Halius, a Lycian 5.678

Halizones, a people on the Black Sea 2.856, 5.38

Harmon, father of a Trojan smith 5.40

Harpalion, a Trojan ally 13.643–59

Hebe, a goddess, cup-bearer to the gods 4.2, 5.722, 905

Hecamede, a maidservant of Nestor 11.624–41

HECTOR, son of Priam and Hecuba, leader of the Trojans, husband of Andromache 1.242, 2.816, 3.116, 4.505, 5.211, 467, 699, 7.158, 8.88, 110, 377, 9.304, 10.49, 104, 200, 356, 388, 406, 562, 11.327, 820, 12.10, 290, 13.1, 54, 129, 316, 720, 14.44, 364–75, 15.42, 583, 671, 714, 16.77, 552, 17.107, 291, 428, 449, 503, 638, 754, 18.14, 103, 150, 19.63, 21.5, 22.5, 23.64, 24.57–8, 390; fights and kills Achaeans 5.606–9, 690–1, 704–10, 7.1–16, 8.337–49, 11.57–73, 299–309, 497–8, 531–43, 12.39–57, 13.183–205, 15.328–31, 515–17, 604–9, 17.83–9, 107; and Achilles 9.351–6, 651–5, 18.114–16, 335, 20.76–7, 419–54, 21.225, 279–80, 296, 22.131–405, 24.115–16; Achilles outrages his body 23.21–6, 182–3, 24.15–18, 50–2; and Aeneas 17.334–41, 483–90; and Ajax 7.169, 216–305, 13.809–32, 14.402–40, 15.9–12, 415–41, 16.114–16, 16.358–63; and Andromache 6.369–94, 22.437–514; her lament for him 24.724–46; and Apollo 7.38–42, 15.221, 239–62, 326–7, 16.712–25, 17.72–81, 582–91, 18.456, 19.414, 20.375–80, 24.32–8; Apollo revives him 15.269–92; addresses both armies 3.76–94, 7.54–91; holds an assembly 8.489–541, 10.299–312, 414–16; and Automedon 17.525–9; recognized by Cassandra 24.707–14; and Cebriones 11.521–30; finds a new

charioteer 8.124–9, 36–19; and
Coeranus 17.616–19; and Diomedes
5.601–3, 8.117–24, 148–56,
11.345–66; and Dolon 10.318–31,
391–9; prepares for the duel
of champions 3.314, 324–5;
and Epeigeus 16.577–80; his
funeral rites 24.786–804; and
Glaucus 16.536–47, 17.141–82;
addresses his heart 22.92–130; and
Hecuba 6.251–85, 22.81–91, 431–6;
her lament for him 24.748–60; and
Helen 6.342–68; her lament for
him 24.762–76; and Helenus 6.75–
101, 7.46–53; his horses 8.184–97;
and Idomeneus 17.605–9; and
Iris 2.802–7, 11.197–209; and
Melanippus 15.545–59; and
Menelaus 7.105–19; and Odysseus
9.237–43; and Paris 3.38–75,
6.313–41, 515–29, 13.765–88; and
Patroclus 16.382, 730–2, 755–64,
818–63, 18.154–65, 175–7; takes
Patroclus' armour 17.122–98,
693, 18.21, 82–5, 131–3; and
Periphetes 15.637–52; and Polydamas
12.60–82, 210–50, 13.725–53,
18.284–313; and Priam 22.35–78,
425–8, 24.254–9; Priam seeks to
ransom his body 24.175, 471–674;
seizes Protesilaus' ship 15.704–25;
and Sarpedon 5.471–93, 684–99; and
Schedius 17.304–11; nearly sets fire
to the Achaean ships 8.217–19, 235;
and Teucer 8.301–2, 310–34,
15.458–65; encourages the
Trojans 5.494–7, 590–1, 6.102–15,
8.172–83, 11.210–17, 284–98, 14.388,
15.346–55, 484–500, 506–8, 17.210–32,
20.364–72; leads the Trojans 12.88–
107, 438–71, 13.40–2, 123, 136–56,
674–89, 15.306–11, 688–94; abandons
the Trojans 16.367–71; looks for the
Trojan heroes 13.758–64, 802–8; goes
back into Troy 6.116–18, 237–50;
mourned by the Trojans 24.707–14;
and Zeus 8.473–6, 12.173–4, 255,
437, 13.347, 15.59–68, 292–3,
610–11, 694–5, 16.648–58, 799,
17.198–208, 566, 19.204, 24.67–71,

76; Zeus withdraws him from the
fighting 11.163–4
HELEN, wife of Menelaus, abducted
by Paris 2.161, 177, 356, 3.70, 282,
458, 4.19, 174, 6.292, 7.350, 401,
9.140, 339, 11.125, 19.325, 22.114;
and Aphrodite 3.383–426; and
Hector 6.323–64; her lament for
Hector 24.761–76; and Iris 3.121–45;
and Paris 3.427–47; points out the
Achaean heroes 3.154–244
Helenus (1), a son of Priam, the Trojan
bird-seer 6.76–101, 7.44–54, 12.94,
13.576–600, 758, 770, 781, 24.249
Helenus (2), an Achaean 5.707
Helicaon, son of Antenor, husband of
Laodice 3.123
Hellenes, a people of Thessaly 2.530, 684
HEPHAESTUS, god of metalworking,
son of Hera 2.101–2, 426, 5.10,
23–4, 8.195, 9.468, 14.166–8,
239–40, 338–9, 15.214, 309–10,
18.191, 19.10–11, 368, 382–3, 20.12,
35–7, 22.316–17, 23.33; makes
armour for Achilles 18.406–613;
supports Hera 1.571–600, 607–8;
and Hera 21.330–42, 377–82; and
Scamander 20.73–4, 21.343–76
HERA, goddess, wife and sister of
Zeus, daughter of Cronus 1.55–6, 400,
2.14–15, 5.418, 832, 892–4, 908, 7.411,
9.254, 11.271, 13.826, 15.130, 214,
18.119, 168, 19.407, 20.33, 70, 21.6, 434;
encourages the Achaeans 5.778–92;
and Agamemnon 8.218, 11.45–6;
and Aphrodite 14.188–221; and
Apollo 15.143–8, 24.55–63; and
Athena 2.156–65, 5.711–19,
8.350–80, 426–31, 21.418–22;
sends Athena to Achilles 1.195,
208; and her chariot 5.720–32,
748–52, 767–77, 8.381–96, 432–7; and
Hephaestus 1.571–96, 21.328–41,
377–82; and Heracles 5.392–4; and
Iris 15.144–8; and Poseidon
8.198–211, 20.112–43, 309–17; and
Sleep 14.231–79; makes the sun
set 18.239–42; addresses Themis
and the other gods 15.79–112;
and Thetis 24.101–2; and

Xanthus 21.368–76; and Zeus
1.519–22, 536–69, 611, 4.5–67,
5.753–6, 8.407–8, 447–84, 15.5–77,
16.432–57, 18.356–67, 19.97, 106–24,
24.64–76; plans the seduction of
Zeus 14.153–351

Heracles, a hero, son of Amphitryon/
Zeus and Alcmene 2.653, 658, 666,
5.392–404, 628, 638–42, 648, 8.363–9,
11.690, 14.250–6, 266, 324, 15.25–30,
640, 18.177, 19.99, 20.145

HERMES, god, son of Zeus 2.104,
5.390, 14.490–1, 15.214, 16.181–6,
20.34–5, 21.497–501, 24.24, 109;
escorts Priam 24.333–468, 679–94

Hicetaon, a Trojan elder 3.147, 20.238

Hippasus, father of Charops and
Socus 11.427, 450

Hippocoön, counsellor of the Thracians
10.518

Hippodamas, a Trojan 20.401

Hippodameia (1), mother of Peirithous
2.742

Hippodameia (2), daughter of Anchises,
wife of Alcathous 13.429–32

Hippodamus, a Trojan 11.335

Hippolochus (1), father of Glaucus (1)
6.119, 144, 197, 206–10

Hippolochus (2), a Trojan 11.122–47

Hippomolgi, a distant people 13.5

Hipponous, an Achaean 11.303

Hippothous (1), a captain of the
Pelagians 2.840, 842, 17.217,
288–303, 313, 318

Hippothous (2), a son of Priam 24.251

Hippotion, a Trojan 14.514

Hypeirochus (1), a Trojan 11.335

Hypeirochus (2), father of
Itymoneus 2.673

Hypeiron, a Trojan 5.144

Hyperenor, a Trojan 14.516, 17.24–8

Hypsenor (1), a Trojan 5.76

Hypsenor (2), an Achaean 13.411

Hypsipyle, mother of Euneus 7.469

Hyrtacus, father of Asius (1) 2.837 passim

Hyrtius, a Trojan ally 14.511

Iaera, a sea-nymph 18.42

Ialmenus, a son of Ares, captain of the
Minyans 2.512, 9.82

Iamenus, a Trojan ally 12.139, 193

Ianassa, a sea-nymph 18.47

Ianeira, a sea-nymph 18.47

Iapetus, a Titan 8.479

Iasus, a captain of the Athenians 15.337

Idaeus (1), Priam's herald 3.248–58,
7.276–86, 372–417, 24.325, 352–7,
470–1, 673–4, 689–91

Idaeus (2), a Trojan 5.11–24, 27–8

Idas, father of Cleopatra 9.558–60

IDOMENEUS, captain of the Cretans,
son of Deucalion 1.145, 2.405,
645, 6.436, 7.165, 8.78, 263, 10.53,
112, 11.501, 12.117, 15.301, 17.258,
19.311, 23.113; and Achilles 23.491–8;
and Aeneas 13.469–505; and
Agamemnon 4.252–71; and Ajax,
son of Oïleus 23.473–87; and
Alcathous 13.424–45; and Asius
13.384–93; and Deïphobus 13.402–4,
446–57; and Erymas 16.345–50;
and Hector 17.605–16; identified
by Helen 3.230–3; acts as lookout
in the chariot-race 23.450–72;
and Meriones 13.240–329,
17.621–5; and Nestor 11.510–16;
and Oenomaus 13.506–8; and
Othryoneus 13.361–82; and
Phaestus 5.43–7; and Poseidon
13.210–39; retreats 13.510–15; fights
Trojans 13.330–2

Ilioneus, a Trojan 14.489–505

Ilus, a former king of Troy 10.415,
11.166, 372, 20.232

Imbrasus, father of Peirous 4.520

Imbrius, a son-in-law of Priam
13.171–81, 197, 201, 203–5

Ionians, a Greek people 13.605

Iphianassa, a daughter of
Agamemnon 9.145, 287

Iphiclus, a former opponent of Nestor
23.636

Iphidamas, a son of Antenor raised in
Thrace 11.221–47

Iphinous, an Achaean 7.14

Iphis, Patroclus' concubine 9.667

Iphition, a Lydian 20.382

Iphitus (1), father of Schedius and
Epistrophus (1) 2.518

Iphitus (2), father of Acheptolemus 8.128

Iphius, a Trojan 16.417
IRIS, goddess, messenger of the gods
5.353, 15.55; and Achilles 18.166–201;
and Hector 11.195–210; and Helen
3.121–38; and Hera 5.365–9, 15.144–8;
and Hera and Athena 8.409–25; and
Poseidon 15.168–217; and Priam
24.159–88; and Thetis 24.77–99;
and the Trojans 2.786–807; and the
winds 23.198–211; and Zeus
8.398–408, 11.185–94, 15.150–67,
24.117–19, 143–58
Isandrus, son of Bellerophon 6.197, 203
Isus, a bastard son of Priam 11.101–7
Ithaemenes, father of Sthenelaus 16.586
Itymoneus, an Eleian 11.672
Ixion, human father of Peirithous 14.317

Jason, the Argonaut 7.468, 21.41 passim

Laerces, father of Alcimedon 16.197
Laertes, father of Odysseus 2.173, 3.200
and passim
Lampus (1), a Trojan elder 3.147
Lampus (2), one of Hector's horses
8.185
Laodamas, a Trojan 15.516
Laodameia, daughter of
Bellerophontes 6.197, 205
Laodice (1), a daughter of Priam 3.124,
6.252
Laodice (2), daughter of Agamemnon
9.145, 287
Laodocus, a Trojan 4.87
Laogonus (1), a Trojan 16.604
Laogonus (2), another Trojan 20.460
Laomedon, Priam's father and former
king of Troy 3.250, 5.640, 649, 6.23,
7.453, 20.236–7, 21.444, 451–5
Laothoë, daughter of Alters, mother of
Lycaon (1) 21.85, 22.48.
Lapiths, a people of Thessaly 12.128,
141–53, 181
Leiocritus, an Achaean 17.344
Leïtus, a captain of the Boeotians 2.494,
6.35, 13.91, 17.601–5
Leleges, a people of Asia Minor 10.429,
20.96, 21.86
Leonteus, a captain of the Lapiths
2.745, 12.130, 188, 23.837, 841

Lethus, lord of Larissa 2.843
Leto, a goddess, mother of Apollo and
Artemis 1.9, 36, 5.447, 14.327,
19.413, 20.40, 72, 21.497–8, 502–4,
24.607–8
Leucus, a companion of Odysseus
4.491–4
Licymnius, uncle of Heracles 2.663
Limnoreia, a sea-nymph 18.41
Locrians, a people of N. Greece 2.527,
13.712–22
Lycaon (1), a son of Priam 3.333, 20.81,
21.34–127
Lycaon (2), father of Pandarus 2.826,
4.89, 93, 5.193, 198
Lycians, a people of Asia Minor 2.876,
4.197, 207, and passim
Lycomedes, an Achaean 9.83, 12.366,
17.345–9, 19.240
Lycon, a Trojan 16.335–41
Lycophontes, a Trojan 8.275
Lycophron, an Achaean 15.430–5
Lycurgus (1), persecutor of Dionysus
6.130–40
Lycurgus (2), killer of Areïthoüs 7.142–9
Lysandrus, a Trojan 11.491

Macar, king of Lesbos 24.544
Machaon, a healer, son of Asclepius
2.372, 4.193, 200, 11.506–7, 517–18,
598, 613, 651, 833–5, 14.3–7
Maemalus, father of Peisander (3) 16.194
Maeon, a captain of the Thebans 4.394,
398
Maeonians, a people of Asia
Minor 2.864, 10.431
Maera, a sea-nymph 18.48
Magnetes, the men of Magnesia 2.756
Maris, a Trojan 16.319
Marpessa, wife of Idas 9.557
Mastor, father of Lycophron 15.430
Mecisteus (1), an Achaean 8.333,
13.421–3
Mecisteus (2), another Achaean 15.339,
23.678–80
Medesicaste, daughter of Priam, wife of
Imbrius 13.173
Medon (1), a captain of the Phthians
from Methone 2.727, 13.693,
15.332–6

Medon (2), a Trojan 17.216

Meges, captain of the men of Dulichium 2.627, 5.69, 13.692, 15.302, 519–45, 19.239

Melanippus (1), a Trojan 8.276

Melanippus (2), another Trojan 16.295

Melanippus (3), a man from Percote 15.547–56, 576–83

Melanippus (4), an Achaean 19.240

Melanthius, a Trojan 6.36

Melas, an ancestor of Diomedes 14.117

Meleager, former leader of the Aetolians 2.642, 9.543–99

Melite, a sea-nymph 18.42

MENELAUS, son of Atreus, brother of Agamemnon, husband of Helen, king of Lacedaemon 1.159, 2.408, 587, 3.52, 232, 253, 5.552, 715, 7.373, 392, 470, 8.261, 10.230, 11.125, 139, 487, 17.587, 626; addresses the Achaeans 7.94–103, 17.246–55; addresses both armies 3.96–110; and Adrestus 6.37–53; and Aeneas 5.561–9; and Agamemnon 4.150–97, 6.53–62, 7.104–21, 10.32–72, 240; and Ajax 11.463–71, 17.113–39, 237–45, 651–78, 702–16; Antenor's recollection of him 3.206–15; and Antilochus 5.569–75, 15.568–71, 17.679–93, 23.425–41, 515–27, 566–613; arms himself 10.25–31; and Athena 17.554–66; and Automedon 17.507–15; takes part in the chariot-race 23.293–300, 355–6, 401, 422–47, 515–27; and Dolops 15.540–3; and Euphorbus 17.11–60, 80; and Helenus 13.581–95; and Machaon 4.204–40; and Meriones 17.717–46; and Nestor 10.114–18; and Pandarus 4.94–103, 115, 127–47; and Paris 3.21–37, 69, 90–1, 136, 153–5, 284–5, 307, 339, 349–82, 403, 431–6, 439, 452, 457; protects Patroclus' body 17.1–8, 79; and Peisander 13.601–42; and Podes 17.578–81; and Pylaemenes 5.578–9; and

Scamandrius 5.49–58; and Thoas 16.311–12; and Zeus 4.7–19

Menesthes, an Achaean 5.609

Menestheus, captain of the Athenians 2.552, 4.327, 12.331–50, 13.195, 690, 15.326

Menesthius (1), an Achaean 7.9

Menesthius (2), a captain of the Myrmidons 16.173–8

Menoetius, father of Patroclus 11.765, 771, 785, 16.14, 664, 18.325, 23.85 and passim

Menon, a Trojan ally 12.193

Mentes, captain of the Cicones 17.73

Mentor, father of Imbrius 13.171

Meriones, a captain of the Cretans 2.651, 4.254, 5.59–68, 7.166, 8.264, 9.83, 10.59, 196–7, 229, 260, 270, 13.93, 159–68, and passim, 14.514, 15.302, 16.342–4, 603–32, 17.259 and passim, 19.239, 23.113 and passim

Mermerus, a Mysian 14.513

Merops, a seer from Percote 2.831–4, 11.329–32

Mesthles, captain of the Maeonians 2.864, 17.216

Mestor, a son of Priam 24.257

Minos, former king of Crete 13.450–1, 14.322

Mnesus, a Paeonian 21.210

Molion, a Trojan 11.322

Moliones, the twin sons of Actor/Poseidon 11.709, 750

Morys, a Trojan ally 13.792–4, 14.514

Mulius (1), an Epeian 11.739

Mulius (2), a Trojan 16.696

Mulius (3), another Trojan 20.472

Muses, goddesses of song 1.1, 604, 2.484, 594, 598, 761, 11.218, 14.508, 16.112

Mydon (1), a Trojan 5.580–8

Mydon (2), a Paeonian 21.209

Mygdon, captain of the Phrygians 3.816

Mynes, king of Lyrnessus 2.692, 19.296

Myrine, a dancer after whom a hill is named 2.814

Myrmidons, Achilles' people, from Phthia in Thessaly 1.180, 328, and passim

Mysians, a people of Asia Minor 2.858, 10.430, 13.5, 14.512, 24.278

Nastes, a captain of the Carians 2.867–71
Naubolus, father of Iphitus 2.518
Neleus, father of Nestor 11.682–3, 696–706, 717–19, and *passim*
Nemertes, a sea-nymph 18.46
Neoptolemus, son of Achilles 19.327
Nereus, father of Thetis 18.38, 49, 52, 20.107
Nesaeë, a sea-nymph 18.40
NESTOR, king of Pylos, son of Neleus, father of Antilochus and Thrasymedes 2.20–1, 405, 555, 601, 7.181, 11.501, 579, 611, 618, 840, 17.382, 19.311, 23.411; addresses the Achaeans 1.246–76, 2.77–83, 336–59, 6.66–72, 7.123–61, 170–4, 325–43, 9.60–8, 165–73, 10.203–17, 532–9, 15.658–67; and Achilles 1.277–80; 23.617–50; and Agamemnon 1.275–86, 2.360–74, 433–41, 4.312–25, 9.69–79, 94–115, 162–4, 10.18–20, 54–8, 73–130, 14.39–81; and Antilochus 23.304–50; his cup 11.632–7; and Diomedes 8.100–11, 116–18, 137–58, 9.52–9, 10.150–76; and Idomeneus 11.510–20; and Machaon 14.1–8; and Odysseus 9.180, 10.137–47, 219–26, 543–63; and Patroclus 11.647–803; encourages the Pylians 4.293–309; resists the Trojans 8.80–96; wonders what to do 14.9–24; prays to Zeus 15.370–8
Night, a goddess 14.259–61
Niobe, who challenged Leto 24.602–17
Nireus, captain of the men of Syme 2.671–5
Noëmon (1), a Lycian 5.678
Noëmon (2), an Achaean 23.611
Nomion, father of Amphimachus and Nastes 2.871

Ocean, river(-god) surrounding the earth 1.423, 3.5, 5.6, 7.422, 8.485, 14.201, 246, 302, 311, 16.151, 18.240, 398, 402, 489, 607, 19.1, 20.7, 21.195, 23.205

Ochesius, father of Periphas 5.843
Odius (1), captain of the Halizones 2.856, 5.38
Odius (2), an Achaean herald 9.170
ODYSSEUS, king of Ithaca, son of Laertes 1.138, 2.407, 631, 3.268, 314, 5.519, 7.168, 8.222, 10.109, 231, 11.5, 140, 661, 767, 806, 14.28, 380, 16.26, 19.48, 141, 247–8, 310, 23.709; addresses the Achaeans 2.298–35; and Achilles 19.154–72, 215–37; leads an embassy to Achilles 9.169, 180, 192, 223–429, 657; and Agamemnon 2.278–97, 4.329–63, 9.673–92, 14.82–108, 19.172–88, 192–5; and Ajax 9.624–36, 11.485–6, 23.709–39; and Antenor 3.203–24; arms himself for the night attack 10.260–73; and Athena 2.169–82; prays to Athena 10.277–82, 460–4, 19.770–2; returns Chryseïs to her father 1.311, 431–47; and Democoön 4.499–504; and Diomedes 8.92–8, 10.243–53, 340–64, 476–502, 513, 527–31, 564–79, 11.312–19, 346, 396–7; and Dolon 10.382–445; addresses his heart 11.401–11; identified by Helen 3.191–202; fights and kills Lycians 5.669–79; and Menelaus 11.487–8; and Nestor 10.138–49, 544–63; runs in foot-race 23.755–93; and Socus 11.428–58; and Thersites 2.220, 244–77; surrounded by Trojans 11.459–84; fights and kills Trojans 4.494–8, 6.30–1, 11.321–8, 335, 412–27
Oedipus, king of Thebes 23.679
Oeneus, father of Meleager 2.641, 9.534–41
Oenomaus (1), an Achaean 5.706
Oenomaus (2), a Trojan ally 12.140, 13.506
Oenops, father of Helenus (1) 5.707
Oïleus (1), father of the Locrian Ajax 2.257, 727, and *passim*
Oïleus (2), a Trojan 11.93
Onetor, father of Laogonus (1) 16.604
Opheleistes (1), a Trojan 8.274

Opheleistes (2), a Paeonian 21.210

Opheltius (1), a Trojan 6.20

Opheltius (2), an Achaean 11.302

Opites, an Achaean 11.301

Oreithyia, a sea-nymph 18.48

Oresbius, a Boeotian 5.707

Orestes (1), an Achaean 5.705

Orestes (2), son of Agamemnon 9.142, 284

Orestes (3), a Trojan 12.139, 193

Ormenus (1), a Trojan 8.274

Ornemus (2), father of Amyntor 9.448

Ornemus (3), a Trojan 12.187

Orsilochus (1), an Achaean 5.541–60

Orsilochus (2), a Trojan 8.274

Orthaeus, a Trojan ally 13.791

Ortilochus, father of Diocles 5.546–7

Orus, an Achaean 11.303

Othryoneus, a man of Cabesus 13.363–82

Otreus, captain of the Phrygians 3.186

Otrynteus, father of Iphition 20.383–5

Otus (1), a giant 5.385

Otus (2), a man of Cyllene 15.518

Paeëon, god of healing 5.401, 899–90, 904

Paeonians, a people of north-eastern
    Greece 2.848, 10.428, 16.287, 291,
    21.105, 205, 211

Pallas, a title of Athena 1.200, 400, and
    passim

Palmys, a Trojan ally 13.792

Pammon, a son of Priam 24.250

Pandarus, captain of the people from
    Zeleia 2.827, 4.88–126, 5.95, 168–
    216, 229–38, 246, 276–96

Pandion, an attendant of Teucer 12.372

Pandocus, a Trojan 11.490

Panic, a god 4.440, 5.739, 9.2, 11.37,
    13.299, 15.119

Panope, a sea-nymph 18.45

Panopeus, father of Epeius 23.665

Panthous, a Trojan elder 3.146, 17.40

Paphlagonians, a people on the Black
    Sea 2.851, 5.577, 13.656, 661

PARIS, son of Priam and Hecuba,
    abductor of Helen, also known as
    Alexander 3.16, 27, and *passim*, 87,
    136, 281, 288, 390, 403, 450, 4.96,
    5.62, 6.280, 313, 356, 7.2, 374, 388,
    400, 8.82, 11.124, 505–7, 12.93,
    13.490, 15.341–2, 22.115, 359, 24.28,

249, 763; kills Achaeans
    7.2–10; arms himself 3.325–38;
    and Antenor 7.355–64; and
    Diomedes 11.369–95; and
    Euchenor 13.660–72; and
    Eurypylus 11.581–4; and
    Hector 3.38–75, 6.321–41, 503–28,
    13.766–88; and Helen 3.425–48; and
    Menelaus 3.16–37, 340–80

Pasitheë, one of the Graces

PATROCLUS, son of Menoetius,
    Achilles' companion 1.337, 345,
    8.476, 15.65, 17.113, 120, 159, 18.28,
    179, 451, 19.403, 412, 21.28, 100,
    107, 134, 22.323, 619, 747, 776,
    800, 24.575, 756; encourages the
    Achaeans 16.268–74; the Achaeans
    recover his body 18.233–8; and
    Achilles 11.602–17, 17.401–11,
    18.81–93, 102, 24.591–5; in Achilles'
    hut 9.190, 195, 201–20, 620–1,
    658–9, 666–8, 16.2–101, 125–9;
    Achilles laments for him 18.315–55,
    19.4–6, 22.386–90, 23.8–23, 108–9,
    24.3–13, 512; appears in a dream
    to Achilles 23.65–107; Achilles
    holds funeral rites for him 23.45–6,
    127–257; Ajax and the Achaeans
    protect his body 17.137–9, 240–1,
    286, 354–5, 543–4, 18.195; and
    the Ajaxes 16.554–61; Antilochus
    reports his death 17.689–93,
    18.20–1; and Apollo 16.700–11,
    784–806; arms himself 16.130–44;
    and Automedon 16.145–54, 219–20;
    Briseïs laments for him 19.283–
    302; and Cebriones 16.738–76;
    and Erylaus 16.411–14; and
    Euphorbus 16.806–17; and
    Eurypylus 11.806–48, 15.390–405;
    and Hector 16.724–32, 818–62,
    17.125–7, 182, 187, 229, 18.151–4;
    Menelaus protects his body 17.2–17,
    79–81, 253–5, 563–74, 706; Menelaus
    abandons his body 17.665–72;
    and Nestor 11.644–805; and
    Pronous 16.399–401; and
    Pyraechmes 16.297–92; and
    Sarpedon 16.434, 460, 466–502
    543, 647; and Sthenelaus 16.586–7;

Thestor 16.401–10; Thetis preserves his body 19.38–9; and Thrasymelus 14.463–5; fights and kills Trojans 16.415–18, 581–5, 684–97; drives the Trojans from the ships 16.257–305, 372–98
Pedaeus, a Trojan 5.69
Pedasus (1), a Trojan 6.21–8
Pedasus (2), one of Achilles' horses 16.152, 17.426–58
Peirithous, former king of the Lapiths 1.263, 2.741–2, 12.129, 182, 14.318
Peiroüs (1), a captain of the Thracians 2.844, 4.520–32
Peiroüs (2), father of Rhigmus 20.484
Peisander (1), a Trojan 11.122–47
Peisander (2), another Trojan 13.601–42
Peisander (3), a captain of the Myrmidons 16.193
Peisenor, father of Cleitus 15.445
Pelagon (1), a captain of the Pylians 4.295, 5.695
Pelagon (2) a Lycian 5.695
Pelasgian, a title of Zeus 16.233
Pelasgians, an autochthonous people 2.840
Pelegon, son of the river Axius, father of Asteropaeus 21.140–1, 159–60
Peleus, father of Achilles 1.1, 146, and passim; 7.125–31
Pelops, grandfather of Agamemnon and Menelaus 2.104
Peneleos, a captain of the Boeotians 2.494, 13.92, 14.487–505, 16.335–41, 17.597–600
Peraebi, men of Dodona 2.749
Pergasus, father of Deïcoön 5.535
Periboea, mother of Pelagon 21.141
Perieres, father of Borus 16.177
Perimedes, father of Schedius 15.515
Perimus, a Trojan 16.695
Periphas (1), an Aetolian 5.842, 847
Periphas (2), a Trojan herald 17.323
Periphetes (1), a Trojan 14.515
Periphetes (2), an Achaean 15.638–51
Persephone, goddess of the Underworld 9.457, 570
Perseus, a mortal son of Zeus 14.320
Phaenops (1), father of Xanthus and Thoön 5.152

Phaenops (2), a guest-friend of Hector 17.581–90
Phaestus, a Maeonian 5.43
Phalces, a Trojan ally(?) 13.791, 14.513
Phausius, father of Apisaon (1) 11.578
Phegeus, a Trojan 5.11, 15, 19
Pheidas, a captain of the Athenians 13.691
Pheidippus, a captain of the men of Cos 2.678
Phereclus, a Trojan shipbuilder 5.59–68
Pheres, father of Admetus 2.376
Pherousa, a sea-nymph 18.43
Philetor, father of Demuchus 20.457
Philoctetes, original captain of the Thessalians from Methone 2.718–25
Phlegyans, a northern people 13.302
Phocians, a people of central Greece 2.517, 525, 15.516, 17.307
Phoebus, a title of Apollo 1.43, 64, and passim
Phoenix (1), Achilles' tutor 9.168 and passim, 16.196, 17.555–61, 19.311, 23.360
Phoenix (2), father of Europa 14.321
Phorbas (1), father of Diomede 9.665
Phorbas (2), father of Ilioneus 14.490
Phorcys, a captain of the Phrygians 2.862, 17.218, 312–18
Phradmon, father of Agelaus (1) 8.257
Phrontis, wife of Panthous 17.40
Phrygians, a people of Asia Minor 2.862, 3.185, 10.431
Phthians, a people of N. Greece 13.686, 693, 699
Phylacus, a Trojan 6.35
Phylas, father of Polymele 16.181
Phyles, father of Meges, former opponent of Nestor 2.628, 23.367
Pidytes, a Trojan 6.30
Pittheus, father of Aethre 3.144
Pleas, goddesses 9.502, 507
Podaleirius, a healer, captain of the Thessalians from Tricce 2.732, 11.833–6
Podarces, captain of the Thessalians from Phylace 2.704–9, 13.693
Podarge, mother of Achilles' horses 16.150
Podargus (1), one of Hector's horses 8.185

Podargus (2), one of Menelaus' horses 23.295

Podes, son of Ëetion, friend of Hector's 17.575–81, 589–90

Polites, a son of Priam 2.791, 13.533, 15.339, 24.250

Polyaemon, father of Amopaon 8.276

Polybus, a Trojan 11.59

Polyctor, named as his father by the disguised Hermes 24.398

Polydamas, a Trojan captain 11.57, 12.60–80 and *passim*, 13.725–53, 756, 790, 14.425, 449–74, 15.339, 446, 454, 518, 522, 16.535, 17.599, 18.249–83, 22.100

Polydeuces, brother of Helen and Castor 3.237

Polydore, daughter of Peleus, mother of Menesthius 20.175–8

Polydorus (1), a son of Priam 20.407–18, 21.348, 22.47

Polydorus (2), a former opponent of Nestor 23.637

Polyeidus (1), a Trojan 5.148

Polyeidus (2), an Achaean 13.663

Polymele, mother of Eudorus 16.179–90

Polymelus, a Trojan 16.417

Polyneices, a Theban, son of Oedipus 4.377

Polyphemus, a Lapith 1.264

Polyphetes, a Trojan ally 13.791

Polypoetes, a captain of the Lapiths 2.740, 6.29, 12.129, 182–7, 23.836, 844–9

Polyxeinus, a captain of the Epeians 2.623

Portheus, an ancestor of Diomedes 14.115

POSEIDON, god of the sea, brother of Zeus 1.400, 2.479, 11.728, 13.434, 15.8, 51, 20.34, 21.472, 23.277, 306, 24.26; encourages the Achaeans 13.351–60, 14.362–90; and Achilles 21.284–98; and Aeneas 20.291–308, 318–42; and the two Ajaxes 13.45–65; and Antilochus 13.554–5, 563; and Apollo 12.17–34; causes an earthquake 20.57–66; fights other gods 20.67–8; and Hera 8.200–11,

15.41–6, 20.115–49, 309–17; and Idomeneus 13.206–39; and Iris 15.158–85, 200–19; rises from the sea and goes to the Achaean camp 13.10–45; and Sleep 14.355–60; and Zeus 7.445–63, 15.57–8, 186–98

PRIAM, king of Troy, husband of Hecuba, father of Hector 1.19, 255, 2.37, 160, 176, 304, 332, 373, 788, 803, 4.18, 28, 31, 35, 47, 165, 173, 290, 5.536, 614, 6.283, 449, 451, 7.296, 346, 8.552, 9.136, 278, 12.11, 15, 13.14, 460, 16.448, 17.161, 18.288, 20.181, 237, 306; 21.309, 22.165, 173, 230, 251, 351, 453, 478, 24.28; and Achilles 24.469–676; and Cassandra 13.365–9, 376; father of Hector 2.817, 5.704, 7.47, 8.377, 9.651, 11.197, 200, 15.239, 244, 18.154, 20.240, 22.37–78, 24.37, 76, 789–804; watches Hector and Achilles 22.25–36; prepares to ransom Hector 24.189–99, 228–47, 265–82, 322–9; conducts Hector's funeral rites 24.696–804; and Hecuba 24.200–27, 283–321; observes the Achaean warriors with Helen 3.141, 161–202; and Hermes 24.331–468, 677–94; and Iris 24.160–88; father of Lycaon 21.34, 88, 97, 23.747; and Melanippus 15.551; and Medesicaste 13.173–6; his palace 2.414, 6.242–50, 317; his sons 2.791, 4.499, 5.159, 463–70, 6.512, 7.44, 8.303, 11.102–4, 12.94, 16.738, 20.81, 21.105, 22.234, 24.248–64; advises the Trojans 7.366–78, 386, 427, 21.526–36; makes a truce 3.105, 117, 249–313; and Zeus 24.117–19, 145–58

Proetus, king of Tiryns 6.157–70

Promachus, a Boeotian 14.476, 482, 503

Pronous, a Trojan 16.399

Protesilaus, former captain of the Thessalians from Phylace 2.698, 706–7, 13.681, 15.705–6, 16.286

Prothoënor, a captain of the Boeotians 2.495, 14.450–2, 472

Prothoön, a Trojan 14.515

Prothous, a captain of the Magnesians 2.756

Protiaon, father of Astynous (2) 15.455

Proto, a sea-nymph 18.43

Prytanis, a Lycian 5.678

Ptolemaeus, father of Eurymedon (1) 4.228

Pygmy men 3.6–7

Pylaemenes, captain of the Paphlagonians 2.851, 5.576

Pylaeus, captain of the Pelasgians 2.840

Pylartes (1), a Trojan 11.491

Pylartes (2), another Trojan 16.696

Pylon, a Trojan 12.187

Pyraechmes, a Paeonian 16.287

Pyrasus, a Trojan 11.491

Pyris, a Trojan 16.416

Rhadamanthys, a former king of Crete 14.322

Rhea, a goddess, wife of Cronus 14.203

Rhene, mother of Oïleus 2.728

Rhesus, captain of the Thracians 10.435–97

Rhigmus, a Thracian 20.485

Rhodians, the people of Rhodes 2.654

Rout, a goddess 9.2, 5.740

SARPEDON, son of Zeus, captain of the Lycians 2.876, 6.199, 12.101, 14.426, 15.67, 16.522, 533, 541, 549–53, 559, 17.150, 162, 23.800; Apollo conveys his body to Lycia 16.667–83; his body is fought over 16.639–65; and Glaucus 12.309–27; and Hector 5.471–93; and Patroclus 16.419–30, 462–507; and Tlepolemus 5.629–67, 682–98; attacks the Achaean wall 12.292–308, 392–9; Zeus debates whether to let him die 16.431–57

Satnius, a Trojan 14.443–8

Scamander, also called Xanthus, a river(-god) on the Trojan plain 20.74, 21.212–21 and passim

Scamandrius (1), a Trojan 5.50

Scamandrius (2), son of Hector and Andromache, also called Astyanax 6.402

Schedius, a captain of the Phocians 2.517, 15.515, 17.306–11

Seasons, goddesses 5.750, 8.394, 433

Selagus, father of Amphius (2) 5.612

Selepus, father of Euenus 2.693

Selli, priests of Zeus 16.235

Semele, loved by Zeus 14.323–5

Sidonians, a people of Phoenicia 6.290, 23.743

Simoeisius, a Trojan 4.474, 477–88

Sintians, a people of Lemnos 1.594

Sisyphus, grandfather of Bellerophontes 6.153–4

Sleep, a god 14.231–76, 354–60, 16.454, 672, 682

Smintheus, a title of Apollo 1.39

Socus, a Trojan 11.427–49, 456

Solymi, a people of Asia Minor 6.148, 204

Speio, a sea-nymph 18.40

Spercheius, a river(-god), 16.174, 176

Sphelus, father of Iasus 15.338

Stentor, an Achaean 5.785

Sthenelaus, a Trojan 15.586

Sthenelus (1), a captain of the men of the Argolid 2.564, 4.367, 5.108, 111, 241, 835, 8.113, 9.48, 23.511

Sthenelus (2), father of Eurystheus 19.116, 123

Stichius, a captain of the Athenians 13.195, 691, 15.329

Strife, a goddess, 4.440, 5.518, 740, 11.3–14, 73, 18.535, 20.48

Strophius, father of Scamandrios (1) 5.50

Talaemenes, father of Mesthles and Antiphus 2.865

Talaus, father of Mecisteus (1) 2.566

Talthybius, Agamemnon's herald 1.320, 3.117, 4.192–3, 7.276, 19.196, 250, 267, 23.897

Telamon, father of Ajax from Salamis 2.578, 768, and passim; 8.283–4

Telemachus, son of Odysseus 2.260, 4.354

Tenthredon, father of Prothous 2.756

Terror, a god 4.440, 11.37, 15.119

Tethys, a goddess, wife of Ocean 14.201

Teucer, bastard son of Telamon 6.31, 8.266–334, 12.336 and passim, 13.91, 170, 182–4, 14.515, 15.437, 442–70, 478–83, 16.511, 23.859–69, 883

Teutamus, father of Lethus 2.843

Teuthras, an Achaean 5.705

Thaleia, a sea-nymph 18.39

Thalpius, a captain of the Epeians 2.620

Thalysius, father of Echepolus (1) 4.458

Thamyris, a Thracian singer 2.595

Theano, Trojan priestess of Athena, wife of Antenor 6.298–310

Thebaeus, father of Eniopeus 8.120

Themis, a goddess 15.87–91, 93, 20.5

Thersilochus, a Paeonian 17.216, 21.209

Thersites, an Achaean 2.212–76

Theseus, king of Athens 1.265

Thessalus, a son of Heracles 2.679

Thestor, a Trojan 16.401–10

THETIS, goddess, mother of Achilles, wife of Peleus, daughter of Nereus 1.538, 555, 4.512, 6.136, 8.370, 9.410, 16.34, 574, 16.332, 20.207, 23.14, 24.74; and Achilles 1.351–427, 16.222–4, 18.71–138, 19.2–39, 24.122–42; and Hephaestus 18.146–8, 369–407, 422–61, 615–17; and Iris 24.83–96; and Nereus' daughters 18.51–65, 139–44; and Zeus 1.495–527, 15.76–7, 599, 24.98–120

Thoas (1), captain of the Aetolians 2.638, 4.527, 529, 534, 7.168, 13.92, 216, 222, 228, 15.281–99, 19.239

Thoas (2), king of Lemnos 14.230, 23.745

Thoas (3), a Trojan 16.311–12

Thoë, a sea-nymph 18.40

Thoön (1), a Trojan 5.152

Thoön (2), another Trojan 11.422

Thoön (3), another Trojan 12.140, 13.545–9

Thoötes, an Achaean herald 12.342–3, 351–63

Thracians, a people of N. Greece 2.844, 4.519, 533, 537, 5.462, 617, 10.434–525, 13.4, 14.227, 23.234

Thrasius, a Paeonian 21.210

Thrasymedes, son of Nestor 9.81, 10.255–9, 14.10, 16.321, 17.378, 705

Thrasymelus, a Lycian 16.463

Thyestes, brother of Atreus 2.106–7

Thymbraeus, a Trojan 11.320, 322

Thymoetes, a Trojan elder 3.146

Titans, ancient gods 14.279

Tithonus, son of Laomedon, husband of the Dawn 11.1, 20.237

Tlepolemus (1), son of Heracles, captain of the Rhodians 2.653, 657–9, 661–70, 5.628–46, 648, 655–61, 669

Tlepolemus (2), a Trojan 16.416

Trechus, an Aetolian 5.706

Troezenus, father of Euphemus 2.847

Troïlus, a son of Priam 24.257

Trojans, the people of Troy 1.152, 160, and passim

Tros (1), the founder of Troy 5.222, 266, 8.106, 20.230–1

Tros (2), a Trojan 20.463–71

Tychius, a leatherworker 7.220

Tydeus, father of Diomedes 2.406, 4.370–400, 5.126, 800–13, 6.222, 10.285–90, 14.114, 119–25

Typhoeus, a monster 2.782–3

Ucalegon, a Trojan elder 3.148

Uranus, an elder god, father of Cronus 5.898 and passim

Xanthus (1), a river (-god) on the Trojan plain, also called Scamander 6.4, 8.561, 14.434, 20.40, 74, 21.2 and passim, 24.693

Xanthus (2), a Trojan 5.152

Xanthus (3), one of Hector's horses 8.185

Xanthus (4), one of Achilles' horses 16.149, 19.400–17, 420

ZEUS, son of Cronus and Rhea, father of the gods, husband and brother of Hera 1.9, 21, 63, 175, 202, 353, 419, 502, 511, 609, 2.116, 412, and passim; and Aphrodite 5.427–30; and Apollo 15.143–56, 220–36, 16.666–76; and Ares 5.889–98; and Athena 1.399, 4.69–73, 5.421–5, 8.30–40, 365, 444, 457–9; and Delusion (Atē) 19.91–5, 126–33; father of the gods 1.423–5, 494–5, 570–83, 4.1, 8.2–27, 438–43, 14.203–4, 256–8, 15.135–7, 20.153–5, 21.388–90, 443–4; and Hera 1.399, 519–22, 539–67, 609–11, 4.5–19, 24–68, 5.762–6, 8.444–84, 14.293–352, 15.4–78, 16.439–58, 18.356–67, 19.97–124, 24.64–6; influences human action 6.234, 357, 8.236, 9.18, 23–5, 11.163, 544, 13.1–9, 794, 14.69–73,

522, 15.461–5, 488–93, 567, 594–5, 694, 724–5, 16.385, 656, 688–91, 799, 17.176–8, 198–208, 401, 627, 630–2, 18.431, 19.87, 224, 24.527–33; and Iris 2.786, 8.397–408, 11.182–210, 15.146–68, 24.117–19, 143–58; his plans 1.5, 128, 2.38, 8.470–7, 12.235–40, 13.347–50, 15.59–77, 232–5, 596–602, 16.249–52, 644–58, 17.201–8, 443–55, 21.230–2, 24.110–19; and Poseidon 1.399, 7.446–63, 13.351–5, 15.185–99, 211, 20.19–30;

is prayed and sacrificed to 3.104, 350, 5.174, 6.259, 475, 8.242, 250, 526, 9.172, 11.727, 736, 773; and Sarpedon 6.198, 16.431–48, 459–61, 522, 567–8, 667–75; send signs and omens 2.2–15, 308–30, 353, 4.381, 8.76, 133, 170–1, 247–50, 9.236–7, 11.53–4, 12.252–5, 15.377, 16.459–60, 567–8, 17.593–6, 20.56, 24.315–21; and Thetis 1.498–530, 8.370–2, 15.76–7; watches the conflict 8.41–52, 11.80–3, 16.644, 20.22–4

American Literature

British and Irish Literature

Children's Literature

Classics and Ancient Literature

Colonial Literature

Eastern Literature

European Literature

Gothic Literature

History

Medieval Literature

Oxford English Drama

Poetry

Philosophy

Politics

Religion

The Oxford Shakespeare

A complete list of Oxford World's Classics, including Authors in Context, Oxford English Drama, and the Oxford Shakespeare, is available in the UK from the Marketing Services Department, Oxford University Press, Great Clarendon Street, Oxford OX2 6DP, or visit the website at www.oup.com/uk/worldsclassics.

In the USA, visit www.oup.com/us/owc for a complete title list.

Oxford World's Classics are available from all good bookshops. In case of difficulty, customers in the UK should contact Oxford University Press Bookshop, 116 High Street, Oxford OX1 4BR.

Classical Literary Criticism

The First Philosophers: The Presocratics
  and the Sophists

Greek Lyric Poetry

Myths from Mesopotamia

APOLLODORUS   The Library of Greek Mythology

APOLLONIUS OF RHODES   Jason and the Golden Fleece

APULEIUS   The Golden Ass

ARISTOPHANES   Birds and Other Plays

ARISTOTLE   The Nicomachean Ethics
                       Physics
                       Politics

BOETHIUS   The Consolation of Philosophy

CAESAR   The Civil War
                       The Gallic War

CATULLUS   The Poems of Catullus

CICERO   Defence Speeches
                       The Nature of the Gods
                       On Obligations
                       Political Speeches
                       The Republic and The Laws

EURIPIDES   Bacchae and Other Plays
                       Heracles and Other Plays
                       Medea and Other Plays
                       Orestes and Other Plays
                       The Trojan Women and Other Plays

HERODOTUS   The Histories

HOMER   The Iliad
                       The Odyssey

A SELECTION OF   OXFORD WORLD'S CLASSICS

HORACE	The Complete Odes and Epodes
JUVENAL	The Satires
LIVY	The Dawn of the Roman Empire
	Hannibal's War
	The Rise of Rome
MARCUS AURELIUS	The Meditations
OVID	The Love Poems
	Metamorphoses
PETRONIUS	The Satyricon
PLATO	Defence of Socrates, Euthyphro, and Crito
	Gorgias
	Meno and Other Dialogues
	Phaedo
	Republic
	Selected Myths
	Symposium
PLAUTUS	Four Comedies
PLUTARCH	Greek Lives
	Roman Lives
	Selected Essays and Dialogues
PROPERTIUS	The Poems
SOPHOCLES	Antigone, Oedipus the King, and Electra
STATIUS	Thebaid
SUETONIUS	Lives of the Caesars
TACITUS	Agricola and Germany
	The Histories
VIRGIL	The Aeneid
	The Eclogues and Georgics
XENOPHON	The Expedition of Cyrus

A SELECTION OF   **OXFORD WORLD'S CLASSICS**

THOMAS AQUINAS	**Selected Philosophical Writings**
FRANCIS BACON	**The Essays**
WALTER BAGEHOT	**The English Constitution**
GEORGE BERKELEY	**Principles of Human Knowledge** and **Three Dialogues**
EDMUND BURKE	**A Philosophical Enquiry into the Origin of Our Ideas of the Sublime and Beautiful** **Reflections on the Revolution in France**
CONFUCIUS	**The Analects**
DESCARTES	**A Discourse on the Method**
ÉMILE DURKHEIM	**The Elementary Forms of Religious Life**
FRIEDRICH ENGELS	**The Condition of the Working Class in England**
JAMES GEORGE FRAZER	**The Golden Bough**
SIGMUND FREUD	**The Interpretation of Dreams**
THOMAS HOBBES	**Human Nature** and **De Corpore Politico** **Leviathan**
DAVID HUME	**Selected Essays**
NICCOLÒ MACHIAVELLI	**The Prince**
THOMAS MALTHUS	**An Essay on the Principle of Population**
KARL MARX	**Capital** **The Communist Manifesto**
J. S. MILL	**On Liberty and Other Essays** **Principles of Political Economy** and **Chapters on Socialism**
FRIEDRICH NIETZSCHE	**Beyond Good and Evil** **The Birth of Tragedy** **On the Genealogy of Morals** **Thus Spoke Zarathustra** **Twilight of the Idols**

A SELECTION OF OXFORD WORLD'S CLASSICS

Bhagavad Gita

The Bible Authorized King James Version
    With Apocrypha

Dhammapada

Dharmasūtras

The Koran

The Pañcatantra

The Sauptikaparvan (from the
    Mahabharata)

The Tale of Sinuhe and Other Ancient
    Egyptian Poems

The Qur'an

Upaniṣads

ANSELM OF CANTERBURY   The Major Works

THOMAS AQUINAS   Selected Philosophical Writings

AUGUSTINE   The Confessions
    On Christian Teaching

BEDE   The Ecclesiastical History

HEMACANDRA   The Lives of the Jain Elders

KĀLIDĀSA   The Recognition of Śakuntalā

MANJHAN   Madhumalati

ŚĀNTIDEVA   The Bodhicaryāvatāra

A SELECTION OF   OXFORD WORLD'S CLASSICS

The Anglo-Saxon World

Beowulf

Lancelot of the Lake

The Paston Letters

Sir Gawain and the Green Knight

Tales of the Elders of Ireland

York Mystery Plays

GEOFFREY CHAUCER   The Canterbury Tales
Troilus and Criseyde

HENRY OF HUNTINGDON   The History of the English People
1000–1154

JOCELIN OF BRAKELOND   Chronicle of the Abbey of Bury
St Edmunds

GUILLAUME DE LORRIS   The Romance of the Rose
and JEAN DE MEUN

WILLIAM LANGLAND   Piers Plowman

SIR THOMAS MALORY   Le Morte Darthur